Broken Muses of Manderley Academy

A reverse harem bully romance

Steffanie Holmes

A NOTE ON DARK CONTENT

I wouldn't say that the Manderley Academy series is particularly dark by romance reader standards. Reading should be fun, so I want to make sure you don't get any surprises, and that's why I'm writing this wee note. If you're cool with anything and you don't want spoilers, then skip this note and dive in.

Keep reading if you like a bit of warning about what to expect in your romance novels.

- There is some bullying in the first book of Manderley Academy, but our heroine holds her own. No heroes in this series threaten or are involved in physical or sexual assault of the heroine.

- In *Spirited*, Faye fights off a sexual assault attempt, which may be triggering to some readers.

- You'll definitely stumble over a few dead bodies and some vengeful ghosts.

- Faye and her three muses – Titus, Dories, and – Ivan have a consensual sexual relationship which sometimes involves all of them together. This series also contains MM – meaning two of Faye's men are also involved with each other. This is a reverse harem series, which means that our heroine does not choose one partner at the end of the story – she gets her happily ever after with them all.

If that's not your jam, that's totally cool. I suggest you pick up my Nevermore Bookshop Mysteries series – all of the mystery without the trauma and violence.

Enjoy, you beautiful depraved human, you :) Steff

Join the Newsletter for Updates

Grab a free copy of *Cabinet of Curiosities* – a Steffanie Holmes compendium of short stories and bonus scenes – when you sign up for updates with the Steffanie Holmes newsletter.

www.steffanieholmes.com/newsletter

Every week in my newsletter I talk about the true-life hauntings, strange happenings, crumbling ruins, and creepy facts that inspire my stories. You'll also get newsletter-exclusive bonus scenes and updates. I love to talk to my readers, so come join us for some spooky fun :)

VOLUME ONE
GHOSTED

*To Niccolò, Johann, Wolfgang, and Franz –
the original Bad Boys of Baroque.*

FAYE

Beep beep. Beep beep.

The machine echoed in my ears like a drumbeat sounding my doom. The sound of everything I'd worked for scattered to ash.

The sound of my mother slipping away from me.

I leaned back in the hard plastic hospital chair, rubbing my burning eyes. I had no idea what day it was or how long I'd been sitting there. A cramp shot up my leg – a dull ache that had nothing on the searing pain in my heart. I stretched out my leg, gasping as the cramp arced down the muscle.

It's like they deliberately make hospital rooms as uncomfortable as possible. Because watching someone you love waste away doesn't suck enough.

My foot brushed the violin case on the floor. Before I knew it, I held my instrument in my hands. The chin rest perfectly fitting my body and the familiar weight of the neck against my fingers gave me comfort. It felt as natural as breathing to run the bow across the strings, to play the familiar trembling notes of Bloch's *Nigun*.

The Swiss composer wrote this piece in the memory of his mother, and it's based on Jewish improvised chants. The idea is that by losing yourself in music, you become closer to God. Right now, I felt like strangling the big bastard in the sky for what he'd done to my mom, but I wasn't playing for him.

Nigun was one of my mother's favorite pieces – I learned it to play for her fortieth birthday. She'd hosted her party in her chic warehouse office in the East Village. All her investors and the executive team watched me in awe while she glowed with pride.

Beep beep. Beep beep.

Now, I played it beside her hospital bed, to an audience of one.

The doctors say she might be able to hear music inside her coma. This might be my only shot at speaking to her, at drawing her back.

Mournful notes rang out as my bow danced over the strings. The grey hospital room came to life in that moment, the sterile edges washed away under a wave of lament. I fancied I saw the shadows of others who had sat in this same chair to cry over their loved ones. I conjured their pain and made it my own.

Music *was* magic.

I needed a little magic right now.

As I played, a cloying scent reached my nostrils. Fake floral – like the bowls of potpourri my grandmother used to leave around her house. Old English roses and hyacinths drenched in sticky toffee and covered in mothballs. The scent tugged at a forgotten memory, a ghost of the past.

My pinkie finger slipped on the string, causing a dull note. I winced, forcing myself to ignore the smell, and kept playing. It happened sometimes when I was lost in the music – the melody conjured images, smells, or feelings from deep in my subconscious. They felt real until I set down the bow, and then I'd realize how stupid that was. *Obviously*, I didn't conjure scented memories with music.

It's just the smell of the hospital disinfectant or something. Don't get distract—

No, it's not. Deja vu tugged at me, bringing with it an ugly foreboding. *I've smelled that* exact *scent before.*

I reached the end of the piece and lowered the bow. A familiar ache settled along my arm – pain was another thing I never felt until after I stopped playing. I once smashed my foot while climbing on stage. I played Beethoven's entire *Violin Sonata No. 9* standing on a broken toe, and I didn't even notice.

Someone clapped.

What the fuck?

I jumped out of my skin.

My eyes flew to my mother, but she lay in the bed, immobile. The machine beep-beeped behind her. I whirled around.

"*Brava.*" A woman stood in the corner of the room. I hadn't noticed her come in. Her Eastern European accent seemed so out-of-place in this ordinary hospital in the shittiest part of NYC. That wasn't the only thing about her that was odd – an old-fashioned floor-length gown in black lace and linen clung to her ample figure, and she clutched a large carpet bag with gold clasps. The fake floral smell rolled off her in waves. "You are still talented."

I set down the violin, angry she'd intruded. "This is a private room." The one indulgence I'd made in this entire shitshow, so I could grieve and hope and rage in private. And soon even that would be gone unless I came up with more cash.

"I am aware. I wish to speak to you, Faye de Winter."

How does this strange woman know my name? Her presence tugged at me, the deja vu growing stronger. That smell and her voice were so familiar. Even that black dress sparked some hint of memory, but I couldn't think where I'd have occasion to speak with such a woman. She looked like she'd got lost on the way to a Twilight fan convention.

Beep beep. Beep beep.

Tension sang in the air between us. I didn't want her here, infecting my mom's space with her scent. But I had to know why she knew my name and why'd she'd sought me out. I sighed. "Yeah?"

"Perhaps you do not recognize me. I am Madame Usher."

That name pierced my heart like an arrow.

Of course. The perfume. How could I forget the way it made me choke during music classes, or how it clung to my father when he came home from his private lessons?

I hadn't seen Madame Usher of Manderley Academy since my mother pulled me from her classes when I was nine years old. Alongside her husband on piano, she had been an accomplished violinist in her day but now ran an elite conservatory in the mountains offering expert tutelage for only the most exceptional musicians. She used to come to the city to teach a handful of super-rich students – children and adults, including me and my dad. But ever since Dad's disappearance, her name had been poison in our house, never uttered.

"I see that you remember now. It has been, what, nine years?"

"Ten." I would turn twenty this year.

"You were just a tiny wisp of a thing back then, but you mastered your Bach. The only person I heard play the Chaconne from *Partita No. 2* better was Donovan."

"Don't talk to me about him," I hissed.

"I see you've inherited your mother's bitterness."

"Get the fuck out." I jabbed my finger at the door.

"Excuse me?"

"You don't come into *my* mother's hospital room and accuse her of being bitter. I'd be upset too if I found out the husband who I supported through an expensive music education was fucking his teacher."

"Such foul language." Instead of retreating, Madame Usher stepped into the room and closed the door behind her. "You should know that I loved him with a passion I only ever reserved for music. My husband was a convenience – for the sake of our international career, it made sense to marry Victor. But when Donovan and I played, it was as though we made love through our instruments."

I balled my hands into fists, resisting the childish urge to jam my hands over my ears. "Read my lips – I. Don't. Want. To. Hear. This."

The smile on Madame Usher's lips boiled my blood. "He planned to leave your mother, and I to leave Victor. We were to run away together. But then he disappeared, and I have never known such pain before or since."

"Get out," I growled, stepping toward the call button. "Or I'll have you removed by security."

Bitch.

Madame Usher continued as though I'd never spoken. "After your mother removed you from my classes, I kept my eye on you, Faye. You might think of me as a guardian angel, hovering in the background, waiting for Donovan's talent to blossom within you. Your father always believed you would one day surpass him, but I admit, I had my doubts. I do not accept just anyone into my tutelage, and you were never serious about your studies, always running about with Dorien."

Dorien Valencourt. I closed my eyes, remembering the little boy who'd been my only friend growing up. Dorien took piano lessons from Victor Usher, but we always paired up for ensembles and recitals. Dorien was rich in a way my family could never hope to be – we practically lived in poverty to fund Dad's career and my tuition – but I was too young to understand the gulf between us or why the other rich kids shunned me so openly. I just knew Dorien's slate-grey eyes gleamed with joy whenever I showed up in class. We'd been the twin terrors of Madame Usher's junior city school. The day Dorien placed his pet iguana in the baby grand and it jumped out just as Victor Usher sat down—

No. I couldn't think about Dorien now, not on top of everything else. That pain still cut too deep.

"Dorien was never serious either, and he's done well for himself," I shot back.

"Ah. So you have followed his career?"

Even if I'd never wanted to hear his name again (which I definitely didn't), I couldn't help but see Dorien everywhere. Every week there was a new article gushing over Broken Muse, the ensemble Dorien formed with two of his friends. The music press delighted in following the trio –who they'd dubbed the Bad Boys of Baroque – as they tore up the European scene with their antics. They were my age, but their flamboyant playing style, modernized Baroque costumes and strings of exotic lovers were giving the stuffy Classical world a playboy makeover. Early last year they stopped touring and dropped off the face of the earth – no one knew where they were, which only added to their mystique. But I wasn't going to give Madame Usher the satisfaction of revealing I knew any of that. So I ignored her question. "Tell me what you want, and leave."

"I've come into the city to speak with music teachers and private schools. For months I've despaired at finding a student to fill our last open place. Your school's music teacher put your name forward, and although I initially dismissed it because of the usual dross she tries to send me, the memory of your father's talent encouraged me to seek you out. I've had a devil of a time tracking you down, but eventually, the trail led me here. I'm delighted it did. There is no need for you to audition – I've heard enough to offer you a place at Manderley if you want it."

If I wanted it? The fuck was she kidding? It didn't matter that I hated her guts. Of course I wanted it. Saliva pooled on my tongue, as if the very thought of stepping inside that hallowed mansion made me hungry.

Beep beep.

The machines pulled me back to reality. Mom's mysterious sickness. The mountains of medical bills. The two jobs I'd been working in an attempt to pay them off. I shook my head. "I can't."

"Faye, an offer like this is not extended lightly, and it will not be offered again."

Don't use my first name. We're not, nor will we ever be, close. I gestured to the prone figure on the bed. "She needs me."

"You do not understand." Madame Usher moved to the end of the bed, standing over my mother and looking down at her with pursed lips. "I am not merely offering you a place at Manderley, but a chance at a future. I expect every musician who graduates to go on to a stunning international career. You cannot do that tethered to a hospital bed. We have the means to help you."

"Help me how?"

"Your tuition will be paid by my late husband's endowment fund. I shall provide your room and board, and an allowance for clothing and necessities. Most importantly, I will pay your mother's medical debts and move her to a more advanced facility closer to the school, so you can visit her on weekends. In exchange, you will extend your services to the school."

"My... services?"

"You will cook meals, keep the house and rooms clean, make sure the instruments are stored correctly, that sort of thing."

"What did your last maid die of?" I muttered.

Madame Usher's mouth tugged at the corner. "A broken neck."

I sucked in a breath. *Is she serious?*

Madame Usher nodded to my phone on the nightstand. "I will not dredge up that unfortunate incident by speaking of it aloud. Look it up if you still have your penchant for morbidity."

She referred to the fact I'd been a strange kid. I was obsessed with horror books and ghost stories. Still was. My favorite thing to do on a Friday night was curling up in bed with Mom and a stack of junk food to watch a spooky film. I knew all the tropes by heart, but I never got tired of hiding under the covers from ghosts and monsters.

I picked up the phone and tapped a line into the search bar. A few moments later, the headline popped up: "MAID DEAD AT ELITE MUSIC ACADEMY." The maid had been found crumpled at the bottom of the stairs – a nasty fall. A terrible accident. The journalist took a kind of morbid delight in describing the trauma to her skull, suggesting the angle of her body meant that she'd been pushed. Police investigated, but they eventually ruled her death an accident, although the journalist enjoyed speculating otherwise.

Knowing Madame Usher, she probably folded the towels wrong.

Madame Usher frowned at my phone. "As you may be able to guess, it becomes difficult to find new help when the press has made every attempt to suggest your maid died of foul play. Hence, I was inspired to seek you out. We can help each other."

A charity case.

I sank into the chair. The plastic creaked as it sagged under my weight. I was never supposed to be a charity case. After Dad disappeared, taking all our hopes of living off his music career with him, Mom swore that we de Winter women would make our own way in the world. She was sick of working sixty-hour shifts as a taxi driver to support a man's dream. She went back to school for business, and built a successful PR firm from the ground-up. After years living on the skin of our asses, we had money. We moved into a gorgeous East Village townhouse. Mom paid for the best violin tutor money could buy who wasn't Madame Usher. I went to a fancy prep school where I was ignored because I wasn't 'old money,' but the students were all little shits, so I didn't give a fuck. We took vacations in exotic places like Vietnam and Istanbul. We weren't mega-rich, but we were comfortable. We didn't need anyone or anything but ourselves.

Except, as it turned out, we also needed health insurance.

Mom's illness crept up on us without warning. One moment she was taking her team on a spa vacation in Hawaii to celebrate her best year ever, complaining the resort food gave her stomach cramps, the next she was lying unresponsive in the back of an ambulance. I called our insurance company to pay the bills and discovered Mom had forgotten to pay her premium, so they had canceled our coverage.

What started as bouts of nausea and cramping turned into a host of strange gastrointestinal problems, and then her kidneys started failing. She'd been deteriorating over the last two years, in and out of the hospital, while they did tests and tried medications and dialysis, but nothing worked. Every new treatment, every flight to a different state to try some new diagnostic machine, stretched our dwindling savings. I sold the townhouse. I graduated high school (barely), moved her to this cheap-ass chop-shop hospital, and took two jobs to try and keep up. Then, a week ago, she slipped into a coma, and the doctors still had no idea what was wrong with her.

What medical dramas on TV don't tell you is how fucking expensive it is to keep someone on life-support. If I didn't come up with some way to pay the bills soon, I'd have no choice but to shut her off.

My mom was my whole life. I wasn't saying goodbye. Not yet.

I'll do whatever it takes to keep her alive.

If that means bowing and scrubbing for this witch, just call me Cinder-fucking-rella.

I leaned over the bed, pressing my lips to Mom's forehead. How odd it was to see her this still. Mom was always bouncing off the walls, a ball of boundless energy. "I won't slow down – you slow down, you die," she admonished me once after she'd nearly walked out of the house with her underwear on her head because she was so excited about a client's TV appearance. "The only time I'll lie still is if you put me in a coma." Fate is a fucking cruel mistress.

Beep beep, the machines admonished me for my betrayal.

I straightened up and picked up my violin case, hugging it to my chest. All through Mom's illness, even as I sold off our possessions, she forbade me to sell my violin. She had it custom-made by an artisan luthier as my thirteenth birthday present, and it was the most precious thing I owned.

So I'd kept it, even though I'd all but given up hope of a career in music. The money Mom set aside for college had been eaten by her medical bills in the first three months. This was a second chance for both of us – for her and for me.

My father walked out and left us with *nothing*. If I took Madame Usher's deal, then at least something good came of his *trahison des clercs*.

The smile that crossed Madame Usher's face was chillier than the winter I'd just survived in my shitty, non-heated apartment. "Your father would be so proud. Faye de Winter, welcome to Manderley Academy."

FAYE

Well, fuck.

A week passed since I accepted Madame Usher's offer. During that time I walked out of my hotel receptionist's job and worked my last shift at the dive bar. I packed Mom's things and filled in the paperwork to have her transferred to a first-class suite at a private hospital an hour's drive from Manderley.

I balanced my laptop on my knees as I leaned against the bare wall of my apartment – refreshing the school's website a million times, poring over the images of the opulent Victorian bedrooms, grand rehearsal spaces, and sprawling gardens.

But *nothing* prepared me for seeing Manderley Academy up close for the first time.

I shouldn't start there. I should start with the limo.

The motherfucking *limo* they sent to pick me up.

Madame Usher told me to wait on the curb with my bags at 7AM sharp. She had no idea women my age shouldn't chill out alone on street corners in my neighborhood. Or maybe she did. I wouldn't put anything past that witch.

I fingered the knife in my pocket as I peered both ways down the street. *Please, get here soon.*

A gang of guys with huge shoulders and mean expressions loitered on the corner opposite, eyeing up the white girl with the violin case and all her possessions in a duffel bag nervously jumping from foot to foot. The skin on my neck started to prickle. I stared the guys down with my best 'don't fuck with me' glare – a look I'd perfected long before our move to Bushwick. That look was all that stood between me and certain destruction at my old prep school.

One of the guys jumped off the curb and made his way toward me, his swagger all business, his smirk unmistakable. *Fucktrumpets. This is just what I need.*

My mind whipped through my options and was just choosing an optimum escape route when a black limo tore around the corner. The guy leaped back as the tires bumped over the curb. The side mirror scraped along the side of a parked car, and the insane vehicle jerked to a stop in front of my building.

"What the fuck?" the guy across the street cried out as he fell on his ass in the ditch. His friends guffawed, all four of them staring at the tinted windows like they were sure some famous rapper was about to emerge.

I agreed with the guy's sentiment. *Who the fuck drives a limo into Bushwick? This dick is blocking the street, so the car Madame Usher sent won't be able to park—*

The driver's door swung open. A stout old man with white hair and a neatly-pressed waistcoat hopped out and slid open the passenger door. "Can I take your bags, ma'am?" he asked me.

I hugged my violin case to my chest and shook my head before I realized he was here for *me*.

"Um... yeah. Sure." I handed him my bag, and he whisked it away. I settled into a plush leather seat, rested my violin case against my legs, and surveyed the minibar. Tiny bottles of hooch crowded the shelves beneath the touchscreen. There were even snacks. My stomach rumbled with desperation – feeding myself hadn't been a priority lately. While most kids my age were dealing with the Freshman Fifteen, I'd lost at least sixteen pounds since Mom got sick – not that it had made much dent in my ample *derriere*. I usually ate a plate of fries or nachos at the bar, but that would be my only meal for the day. I grabbed a candy bar and bit into it, letting the gooey caramel pool on my tongue.

I could get used to this.

"Did you want to say goodbye to your friends?" the driver asked as he slid into his seat, indicating the guys on the corner.

I wound down the window and flashed the one who'd approached me my middle finger. "They know I'll miss them."

Not.

The driver stomped on the gas. We flew off. *Goodbye, Bushwick.* I didn't even look back. I was happy to forget this part of my life.

The driver pressed a button on the dash, and his friendly voice boomed over the intercom. "My name is Harrison. Madame wanted to be here herself, but she has a lot to do now that classes are in session, so I have the honor of escorting you to Manderley. I'm the driver, groundskeeper and general dogsbody for the estate."

I finished my candy bar and picked up a bag of potato chips. Leaning over, I rapped on the glass divider. "Roll this down."

"I'm not supposed to—"

"It's a long drive, and I'm not having a conversation through the intercom like I'm the Duchess of York. We're the hired help, Harrison – we gotta stick together."

Harrison flashed me a toothy grin as he pressed another button and the glass rolled down.

"That's better. So, Harrison..." I leaned over through the window and offered him a potato chip. He looked like he was going to say no, but then his eyes twinkled and he reached into the bag. "How long have you worked at Manderley?"

"Forty-three years I've worked for the Usher family." Harrison puffed out his chest with pride. "Just like my Pappy before me. I grew up at the house, running around in the forest with Victor Usher. We were boyhood friends before he became master of the house, but he was always good to me. He said I'd have a job with the family for as long as I wanted it."

I couldn't imagine living and working at the same house, year in and year out, for your entire life. I was like my mother, whose Mexican blood bubbled to life when she traveled. Music was supposed to be my ticket to seeing the world. Now, it would be the noose around my neck. And Madame Usher was my executioner. "What about Madame Usher?"

"I still remember when he first brought her to the house," Harrison tapped the wheel as he sped through a set of lights, completely oblivious to the drivers honking on either side of us. "Back then, Manderley was just the family home, although it was always filled with music. Victor Senior was quite the fiddler, and Mary taught her son the piano. Victor met Gizella while touring Europe – she was first violin for the Hungarian National Philharmonic when he premiered his *Nocturne*, and it was love at first sight. They eloped to Spain, and he brought her home – his new bride, but she was anything but blushing. She walked through the door like she owned the place, and before long she ruled the house with an iron fist. They'd been married less than a year when she convinced Victor to shuffle his parents off to a retirement home and open the music school."

"She sounds like your favorite person."

"Pardon me, Miss. I shouldn't speak ill of the Madame. She allowed me to stay on after Victor died last year. These old houses aren't much common anymore – I'd be hard-pressed to find a new groundskeeper's job. I'd probably end up raking grass at the big golf course." The horrified look on Harrison's face told me exactly what he thought of such a career change.

"Did you know the maid who was killed?"

"I did, I did. Clare... such a sweet girl." Harrison's fingers tightened on the wheel. "I was the one who... on the staircase... I was mending a broken pane in the library when I heard the scream. I've never seen anything so horrible in all my years. Her neck all twisted, her eyes wide, and her mouth was open like she was still screaming."

"I read in the paper the police decided it was an accident."

"Accident my foot." Harrison's jaw clenched. He looked like he wanted to say more. "She was pushed."

He sounded so certain that a cold chill ran down my spine. *Blast the fucktrumpets – what have I walked into?* "Tell me what happened."

"Clare was carrying on with one of the male students – a real charmer, using his wealth and good looks to take advantage of her sweet nature. She told me with stars in her eyes that he planned to take her to Europe on his next tour, and ask her to marry him under the Eiffel Tower, all sorts of girlish fancies – but he never intended any of it. He had women on speed dial all across the world, but Clare couldn't see it. It boiled my blood, it did – in my day we learned how to treat a lady right."

"I can tell you're a gentleman of the highest order." I smiled, and Harrison beamed and puffed out his chest. I noticed a wedding ring on his finger, dirt smeared between the delicate filigree. The smile fell from his face as he continued his story.

"One night, I found Clare in the pantry, sobbing. She wouldn't tell me what was wrong, only that she'd had a fight with her fella. Two days later, she was dead. And *he* was there, fawning over her body, crying that she'd fallen."

"You think he pushed her?"

Harrison nodded. "I *know* he pushed her. That bastard's still there, swanning about like he's God's gift to music. Mark my words, Miss Faye, you watch yourself around those students, especially the young men. They've all got sticks shoved so far up their asses you could wave 'em about like lollipops."

I laughed at the image, but Harrison's words unnerved me. If he was right, and a murderer was still at the school...

Don't be ridiculous. This is real life, not a horror film. The police would have questioned this guy. If they let him go, there must be a good reason.

We drove out of the city and into the mountains. Tall trees loomed over the road, and I made Harrison open the sunroof so I could stick my head out and bask in the fresh air. My hair whipped around my face, and for a moment I forgot that I was penniless and alone. For a moment, I was free.

Then the weight of my mother's illness and my agreement with Madame Usher slammed down on my shoulders. I slid back into the limo and yanked the sunroof shut.

We passed through a few small towns and a larger city, where Harrison pointed out the gleaming hospital building on the hill. "Your mother's already settled in her new room. She has a lovely view over the river. I've seen to all the details."

On the other side of the city, we turned into a winding wooded road that curled up the mountains, zigzagging through dense forest and over bubbling streams. I was just thinking about rolling back the sunroof again when the road ended at a set of wrought-iron gates nearly entirely obscured with vines. Beyond them, a small brick gatehouse peeked from between the trees.

Harrison rolled down the window and the crisp mountain air rushed in, washing over me – a primal exhalation that reminded me of being on stage with the audience's collective breath releasing as the music pulled them under.

"Welcome to Manderley." Harrison pushed a button on the dashboard, and the gates swung open. A narrow driveway snaked through the woods. Branches scraped the side of the limo as we inched our way forward, and it was impossible to see anything through the thick trees and towering cones of vicious-looking thistles. Here and there I saw the edges of stone walls – these gardens had once been well-kept, but now the mountains had crept down upon them unawares – nature reclaiming what was hers.

I remembered all the famous musicians, composers, and conductors listed in the brochure who supposedly visit Manderley every year. I couldn't match up the glittering black-tie galas in the pictures with this overgrown, neglected driveway.

Just when I thought the road couldn't get any narrower, it widened out into a circular drive, surrounding a dried-up fountain – Cupid peered out at me from behind his lyre atop a weed-choked plinth. Beyond it, I got my first glimpse of Manderley Academy.

The place is insane.

If you were looking to cast a creepy house for a gothic horror film, you'd come to Manderley. The gabled roof chewed at the bitter sky with serrated teeth. Twin turrets jutted from the corners, and walls of grey stone stood like the battlements of a castle, immovable against the progress of time. A wide porch wrapped around the front – a later addition, by the looks of it – held up by elaborately-carved wooden poles and wreathed with delicate iron railings. Dormer windows along the roof loomed over me, catching the sun on the glass – gleaming eyes watching. Judging.

The driveway fanned out in both directions, leading off to stone and wooden outbuildings scattered deeper in the trees. I recognized what might've once been a stable. At any moment I expected to see a horse and cart roll by or to hear someone yelling to bring out the plague victims.

The only nod to modernity was the row of cars parked in a small clearing under the trees. A Porsche, a Jaguar F-type, a little pink Corvette, some kind of enormous blinged-out pickup truck ... all of them freshly buffed and polished, despite the danger of tree sap looming directly above them.

"Thanks," I said to Harrison as he pulled my duffel from the trunk and handed it to me.

"A pleasure, Miss de Winter. If you'll forgive me, normally I'd come inside with you, but I need to collect the wood before those clouds roll in. I believe I'll be seeing you later when you begin your work." Harrison doffed his hat at me and set off toward the outbuildings, whistling a merry tune.

He seems nice enough. A little odd, but you'd have to be to live in the middle of nowhere waiting on rich, snooty musicians who park their fancy sports cars under trees. I bet they weren't the ones cleaning them.

I shifted my violin case to my other hand so I could grip the iron balustrade as I ascended the steps. Up close I could see that the house was as shabby as the grounds. Shingles were missing from the roof, and weeds choked the drain pipes and snaked up the crumbling stone walls. It was weird how Manderley was so prestigious, only accepting a handful of students every year, and yet the place had been allowed to deteriorate into such a state. It was a far cry from the polish of the brochure. I inspected the rotting wood of the steps as I climbed. *These don't look structurally sound—*

FUCK.

The plank cracked under my boot. My violin case went flying as I dropped straight through the porch. I pitched forward, throwing out my hand to catch myself before I face-planted into the door.

How I managed to look graceful on stage when I was such a klutz in real life was one of life's great mysteries, like the fact there existed people who enjoyed black jelly beans.

I winced as I looked down at my leg buried in the porch nearly up to my upper thigh. My foot dangled free in the darkness below, and for a brief moment I imagined all the rats and critters that might be down there, and a shudder ran through me. A stinging bite along my calf told me I'd scraped off a ton of skin on the jagged edges of the rotting wood.

Dickweasels. So much for a great first impression.

I struggled to free my leg, but I didn't quite have the upper body strength to push myself up. I glanced behind me, hoping Harrison was still around, but he'd driven the limo off somewhere. I threw my head back, ready to yell for help.

A long velvet rope dangled down the side of the door, extending up into the heavens. I wriggled and bopped and scraped and eventually managed to wrap my fingers around the knot on the end. I gave it a sharp tug, half expecting it to bring the roof caving in on top of me. Instead, a deep gong sounded from within the house.

The door flung open. On the threshold stood the most beautiful girl I'd ever seen.

Honey-blonde hair cascaded over her shoulders in tight, silken ringlets. It must take her hours every morning to get her hair to behave like that, framing her Californian good looks – tanned skin, eyes like the Pacific Ocean, a nose that was just made for looking down on the plebs. Soft, bow-shaped lips curled back into a smile that was anything but friendly.

"Hi." I waved sheepishly from my hole. "My name is Faye de Winter. I'm a new student here, and I seem to be having a disagreement with the porch. Could you give me a hand or get Harrison or something—"

"You can't come in here."

Her voice dripped like honey off a spoon, sweet and summery. She sounded like she was singing as she spoke. But beneath all that saccharine sweetness was a stinger that would cause serious damage if I crossed her. Apparently, just my existence was enough to bring out this girl's claws.

I shrugged, as if it were no big deal, as if I got stuck in porches every day. "I told you, I'm a student here, so—"

"See this?" She stepped backwards, gesturing to the grand stone arch, polished wood paneling and antique sideboard in the hall behind her. "All *this* is for the students who can actually *afford* tuition. You may be sitting in on our classes, but you're not one of us. You're a *servant*. Use the servant's entrance."

"But—"

She slammed the door in my face.

FAYE

Bitch.
Twatface.
Cockpoodle.

I glared at the door, screaming my most imaginative insults inside my head.

Guess I'm on my own. Fine. Whatever. I'd been on my own for a long time. De Winter women looked after ourselves. I worked two jobs, graduated high school with a 3.8 GPA *and* aced my Sibelius piece for violin exams, all while managing my mother's money and dealing with her useless board of directors and being by her bedside every chance I got. I'd done all that, so I could pull myself out of this fucking porch.

I grabbed the velvet rope again. The dong sounded inside the house, but I figured no one was coming. I leaned back against the rope, sitting as much as I could on the porch and bracing my other leg against the door as I hauled myself up.

Dooooooong.

The gong continued to ring as hand-over-hand I hauled myself out. Sweat dripped down my face. Finally, my leg flew free, and I bounced onto the porch in one piece.

Mostly in one piece. A jagged cut opened down the side of my jeans, enough so I could see the long scrape and dribble of blood. I rubbed off the dirt and spiderwebs as much as I could, but there was nothing I could do about my ruined outfit until I got inside.

Guess I'd better find the servant's entrance.

I picked up my violin case and hobbled around the side of the house, my leg stinging. The blood boiled beneath my skin. That blonde girl didn't even give me a second to explain myself. She could see I needed help, and she'd slammed the door in my face. Now I had to go inside and serve her food and clean up after her.

I guess I have to get used to being talked to like that.

As I hobbled and fumed, I passed under a window partially obscured by creeping ivy. The pane was open a crack. I stopped in my tracks, arrested by the music flowing from inside.

The lightest flutter on the keys made the piece sound effortless, but I recognized it immediately as Liszt, *La Campanella*. Liszt is one of the hardest composers to play since the rotten bastard loved to create knotty compositions that seemed to defy the laws of physics. If you made even a couple of mistakes, the whole thing sounded like complete shit, so it was gutsy to add a piece like that to your repertoire.

This musician wasn't just playing Liszt, they created *magic* with Liszt. The skips and runs carried with them a wild passion that evoked the master's unconventional style, but with a playfulness that was completely unique.

I couldn't help myself. I set down my violin and stepped onto the raised garden bed, craning my neck to peer through the window. The music drew me up short, grabbing my heart in my chest. I needed to see who could play like that.

I squinted into the darkened room, my breath catching in my throat as I struggled to make out the shapes of furniture and people. A girl sat at the piano, her delicate features bent toward the keys, her eyes heavy-lidded as she *felt* her way through the piece. A waterfall of white-blonde hair – perfectly straight and shimmering like threads of silver – cascaded down her back. In the shadows, I could just make out the folded legs of the tutor, sitting in rapt contemplation.

The pianist was a tiny wisp of a thing, everything about her light and effortless, her eyes closed, her features serene. How did a girl like *that* channel the kind of raw emotion that made tears prick at the corners of my eyes—

"Ms. de Winter," a sharp voice broke my reverie. "What do you think you're doing?"

FAYE

I jumped at the voice, slamming my head into the stone lintel. Red welts danced in front of my eyes.

At least I'm not thinking about the pain in my leg anymore.

Rubbing my head, I turned to face Madame Usher. She stood on the path in another of her sweeping lace gowns – this one black and purple – her hands on her hips and an expression of utter disgust on her painted face.

Great. Because this day couldn't get any worse.

"Skulking around the grounds and peering in windows like a cat burglar," she tsked. "This is not the conduct of a Manderley student. Under my tutelage, you represent not just me but all the graduates of our fine school. I will not tolerate this kind of antisocial behavior. Do you understand?"

"I was trying to find the entrance, and I—"

"A simple, 'Yes, Madame Usher' will suffice." She hit me with that smile again, the one that promised pain if I didn't obey.

I bit back a hundred wicked retorts. "Yes, Madame Usher."

The words tasted like sandpaper. I hated having to bow and scrape for this woman – the bitch who'd seduced Dad with all her promises, leaving Mom broken and me without a father.

"Good. Follow me."

I jumped down from the garden wall, sending a jab of pain through my skull. I must've hit the lintel harder than I thought. As I bent to pick up my violin case, Madame Usher's mouth pinched like she was sucking a lemon.

"We enforce a strict dress code. I realize you've been living 'in the hood', but your hobo-chic style will not be tolerated here."

What's she talking about— Oh, right. I glanced down at my torn and filthy jeans, which now boasted a few dead leaves and dewy patches from the overgrown garden. "I fell through a rotting board on the porch. I was hoping to change before I saw you—"

"When I want you to talk, Ms. de Winter, I will make a request."

Okay, fine. It's going to be like that.

Her demeanor made no sense to me. In the hospital, she claimed to still love my father. She was impressed by my playing. She even used the word 'delighted.' But now she seemed almost annoyed that I was here.

For a slight woman, Madame Usher walked fast, with purpose. I had to jog to keep up, which only made my leg and head hurt more. She led me along a wide path and through a small iron gate into a kitchen garden overgrown with weeds. A narrow wooden door broke the monotony of the brick wall. Madame removed a set of keys on a metal loop and selected one, turning the ancient lock until it clicked.

How was she planning to let me in if the door was locked?

The door opened onto a short hallway, cloaked in shadows. A single fluorescent bulb swung from the ceiling, barely penetrating the corners.

She showed me into the first room – a narrow pantry stacked with supplies. A whiteboard on the wall detailed shopping lists and menus in delicate, looped handwriting. The floor had this gritty feeling, like someone had upset a salt shaker but never bothered to clean it up.

The cupboard opposite held cleaning supplies. Another led to a laundry with an ancient washing machine and drying racks suspended from the ceiling. I half expected there to be a hand-cranked wringer and a stone for grinding flour.

The final door led into a low-ceilinged kitchen. One entire wall was taken up with an old-fashioned wooden stove with cast-iron pots and pans suspended from a rig that wouldn't look out of place in a sex dungeon. Dark mahogany cupboards lined both sides, with wooden tops scuffed and marked with age. A narrow window above the sink looked out across the back garden and outbuildings, over a bubbling stream and down the mountain valley beyond.

This place is unreal. I've stepped back in time.

"Harrison will cut the firewood. The woods around the house are part of our estate, and we also manage the forest on this side of the mountains – thinning the trees is an important part of management, but that's Harrison's concern. It's up to you to monitor the household wood supply and let him know when you're running low. The oven is wood burning, and there are three fireplaces on this floor, plus one in every bedroom. During winter you'll need to light the fires in the morning and bring up the wood to the bedrooms. I provide a weekly budget for food and cleaning supplies. All of this is detailed here." She opened a drawer and showed me a leather-bound ledger, the corners stained with flour-dusted fingertips.

In the center of the room, a farmhouse table with bench seats groaned under the weight of at least ten boxes. Flies buzzed lazily around the pile, and I noticed some weird red stains on the corner of the cardboard leaking onto the table.

"This is the last grocery order. It's a few weeks old now. We've been ordering catering from the village since Clare…" Madame Usher left the sentence hanging. "It is not sufficient. You'll need to clean this up and make a new order for what we're missing. The details are in the ledger."

I stared at the pile, appalled. "You just left all this food here to rot?"

She sniffed. "I've been a little preoccupied with preparations for the school year – and the police snooping around the house, asking unsavory questions about Clare's accident. The other students don't even know how to boil an egg. They have more lofty concerns. Here are your keys."

An loop of keys sat on the kitchen table, identical to the ones Madame Usher held. I picked them up, surprised by the weight of them. Lots of locked rooms in this house. Lots of secrets.

Dread settled in my stomach as Madame Usher led me out of the kitchen and down a narrow hallway to emerge from a small door under a grand staircase. *The* staircase where Clare had fallen to her death.

I stood in the entrance hall I'd seen earlier. Thick velvet drapes hung from the front windows, allowing only a sliver of dull light through the gaps. Patterns leaped at me from the floral carpet and the gilded moldings to the painted decorations on the heavy wooden furniture and the faded Victorian wallpaper. From this angle, I got a good look at the portraits crowding the walls. Previous teachers, students, and patrons of the school, judging by the number of fancy wigs and instruments.

Faint snatches of music echoed through the lofty room, snatching at the lifeless details of the house, threatening to bring the patterns to life.

I noticed an empty square on the wall at the foot of the staircase. The wallpaper stood out in vibrant colors – women clothed in sheer shifts surrounding a basket floating in blue-tinged water – showed that a painting had been recently removed.

"What happened here?" I pointed to the empty square. "Did someone take up a career in the evil jazz and have to be excommunicated?"

"That portrait has been sent for repairs." Madame Usher started across the entrance hall, her skirts sweeping behind her. "Do not trouble yourself with it. Follow me."

She led me down a wide hallway lined with even more antiques and gilded portraits. My feet sank into a heavy rug. Here, the Liszt grew louder, the sound muddied by another voice – a haunting violin melody from behind a different closed door that rose and fell through the piano, playing a completely different song. The two compositions meshed together into something dissonant and vaguely threatening.

"We have three practice rooms on the ground floor. These must be shared between all students." Madame flung open a wide door to reveal an azure-blue parlor. Velvet chairs lined the walls, facing inwards to scattered music stands and a second grand piano – a Bösendorfer, by the look of it. *Wow, they only make like, a few hundred of those a year. Madame Usher must be hella loaded.* "This is the Blue Room. The others – the Yellow and the Red Rooms in the turret – are currently occupied. You may book slots on the sign-in sheets located on the noticeboard in the hall."

"Wow." I'd seen the pictures in the brochure, but being here in person, surrounded by all the heavy furniture and gilded finery... all I could think of was how long it was going to take to dust.

"We have lessons and guest lectures in the morning, from 8 until 11 in the Red Room or the Ballroom. At 11AM we break for lunch. In the afternoon, you will have your private lessons with Master Radcliffe. When you are not in lessons, you will be practicing in groups or alone, completing your assignments, or attending to your household duties. We offer regular opportunities for students to perform in the community and abroad, and we also give several recitals, galas, and showcases throughout the year. Many of the top conductors, patrons, and industry professionals will be in attendance, so it is important you participate and that you continue to meet our high standards. At the end of the year, Master Radcliffe and I will choose one student to accept the Manderley Prize. That student will be awarded \$200,000 and is practically guaranteed an international career. It is unlikely you will be in the running for this, given your sub-standard education after you left my tutelage. But nevertheless, I believe in equal opportunities, and I'd love nothing more than to award this to Donovan's child."

"Gee, thanks." *Because the only thing worthwhile about me is the fact I'm his daughter.*

She continued without acknowledging my reaction. "These rooms must be kept immaculate. If the housework is not kept up to our standards, you will not be allowed to continue here as a student. I will show you the bedrooms."

I nodded, the ball of dread inside me spinning faster. The study program she just described would be intense on its own, and I'd have to keep this huge house with all these antiques clean and cook on top of it? It sounded impossible.

Obviously it's impossible. She's made it that way on purpose.

As soon as the thought occurred to me, I knew it was true. I had no idea why, but Madame Usher *wanted* me to fail. But then why was I here? She didn't have to invite me to her rich school or pay for Mom's care. She could have just ignored my teacher's recommendation, pretended she never knew I was still playing the violin. So what was her deal?

I didn't understand, but I was determined to find out.

I expected us to return to the entrance hall to ascend to the second story. Instead, Madame Usher led me down a narrow corridor, past two wide mahogany doors opening into a grand ballroom with yet *another* grand piano, to a narrow flight of plain wooden steps.

The servants' stairs.

We ascended to emerge at the end of another long, wide hall. On each door was a gilded plate displaying each student's name and instrument.

TITUS THIBODEAUX, CELLO, I read as we walked past. Thibodeaux? I wondered if Titus was any relation to Amos and Delphine Thibodeaux, the famous New Orleans Classical duet who injected their jazz heritage into their performances.

AROHA RAWHIRI, PIANO... Someone inside practiced a dissonant Russian piece. HEATHER DANVERS, VIOLIN... IVAN AND ELENA NICO-LESCU, VIOLIN AND PIANO... I wondered why they shared a room. Were they married? Interesting – students usually entered a conservatory like Manderley straight out of high school, or even before they were eighteen. How could they get married so young?

"...expect these ensuites to be tidied and the sheets changed every week. Other than that, the students are responsible for their own rooms. There are guest suites on this floor for parents or visiting musicians, and you'll need to dust—"

Madame Usher's voice receded into the background. The door on the far end of the hall hung open. I stepped in front of it, and curiosity drew my gaze inside.

Sprawled across an enormous canopy bed hung with blue curtains was the most beautiful guy I'd ever seen. He was my age, but the look in his slate-grey eyes was older and dripping with sin, like he'd seen some shit and was responsible for most of it. Soft lips set into a cruel slash as haunted eyes flickered over my body.

Familiar haunted eyes.

Eyes I'd recognize anywhere.

It can't be.

I willed myself to turn away, but my gaze drew down his naked chest, across the ink that curved around his pecs, down impossibly sculpted arms to his hands, where treble clef tattoos danced across long fingers.

It was none other than Dorien fucking Valencourt.

My childhood friend, the boy who'd torn my heart out and stomped it so hard that I'd never open it for anyone else, shot me a wily smile as his fingers stroked the most enormous cock I'd ever seen.

Faye

Dorien Valencourt.

This is impossible. Of all the gin joints in all the world, how can he be here? There's no way.

Sound the fucktrumpets, I'm doomed.

My throat dried. I tried to tear my eyes away, but they'd fixed on that cock like I was radar and it was a German U-boat – a rigid vessel plundering the oceans...

Ahem.

Dorien slid his perfect body off the bed. He didn't bother to throw a towel over himself or pull on a shirt or anything, because the universe was not that fucking kind to me. As he strode toward the door, my mind flicked between past and present.

Dorien's shit-eating grin as he smeared peanut butter into another student's clarinet. Dorien embracing me with joy when we found out we would be in the same advanced class. Dorien's cold eyes stripping my soul bare as he told me we weren't friends anymore—

Me with my eyes ringed in red, sitting in that uncomfortable plastic chair in Mom's hospital room, staring in rapt attention at my computer screen as it played a montage of Dorien's concert footage from his last tour with Broken Muse. My body responding with fire and flame as those same inked fingers danced over the keys.

The other two musicians playing with Dorien were hot as sin, too, but that just made things worse. An African American cellist shredded his bow across the strings, his beaded cornrows swinging around his head as he contorted the music to his will. He turned his head toward the camera, and the instant my eyes met his midnight orbs I felt a sizzle run down my spine – a magnet pulling me into the screen, into a twisted world where a guy like that would notice a girl like me. Then the camera flicked to the violinist – a white-haired beauty with eyes of pure ice, whose long fingers curled around the strings with such exquisite grace an unshed tear squeezed from my eye. And I thought I'd already cried all the tears I had in me...

As the memories flooded me, recognition flashed in Dorien's eyes. His stride faltered for just a moment, but he regained himself, wiping over his expression with a hardness that sent a shiver down my spine.

"Stay out of my private room, trash." Dorien's voice was like music on my body, strumming me in all the right places even as he insulted me.

The door slammed in my face, the sound ricocheting through the house like a gunshot. From Aroha's room, I heard a bow screech across the strings and someone curse.

Dorien, what's happened to you?

The old Dorien, my childhood best friend, was a total ham. He was always playing practical jokes and trying to make me laugh when I got too serious. He loved to make people laugh, to make them adore him.

I saw nothing of that bright, fun little dude in those stony eyes. All the fun had been sucked out of Dorien's soul. Sure, he was fucking gorgeous beyond belief, but what good were brooding good looks and playboy ways if you were shriveled up inside?

His soul may be shriveled, but his dick—

I had to bite my lip to stop myself salivating. What was wrong with me? Get a grip, *Faye. You're here so your mother can get the best medical care, and that's it. You're definitely 100% not here to chase after a guy who already rejected you once.*

If Madame Usher noticed Dorien's nakedness, she seemed unperturbed. She continued my tour past a row of guest suites, bathrooms, another tiny practice room, a small gallery/storage room filled with instruments donated to the school, and a library in a double-height room filled with dusty old books and scores no one had ever read. I nodded and listened with half an ear, my mind occupied with Dorien.

What changed him?

Why is he here?

Dorien didn't need Manderley. He already had an international career. Having the prestigious program on his resume might look good, but so would touring internationally as a soloist or with the other two Broken Muse hotties, and he couldn't do both at once. That dead, haunted look in his eyes – he didn't want to be here. So why was he?

I bet it's his parents. Even when Dorien was being a complete shit, he loved the music, and he wanted so badly to do well. His parents pushed him hard – his mother always sat in the back of the class, her eyes burning holes in his back as she memorized his every movement to criticize later. They were both super odd – I went to their house once for Dorien's birthday, and his father made us play in this room that had no furniture and only a box of wooden blocks – but Mom said that was just how old money people were. They seemed to like me, though, although it was primarily my father's fame that interested them. I always wondered if they were the reason Dorien broke up our friendship, but I didn't want to make excuses for his dickweasel behavior—

With a start, I realized Madame Usher had stopped in her tracks. I skidded on the heavy carpet in an attempt to halt my momentum before I slammed into her. I succeeded, but it threw me off-balance. My flailing hand caught a vase, toppling it off the edge of its stand. I lunched and caught it before it smashed on the floor.

"Watch yourself." Madame Usher gestured to a heavy wooden door at the end of the hall with a NO STUDENTS sign engraved on it. "I live in the east wing of the house. No student is to enter my private rooms unless invited. Disobeying this rule will result in an *immediate* expulsion. Do not take this lightly, as I have dismissed students before."

I nodded.

"Master Radcliffe lives in the stable house toward the rear of the grounds. He joins us for meals unless he is traveling. You've met Harrison already – he lives in the gatehouse you saw when you came in. If you need to know where to find anything, he's the best person to ask. I'll be too busy with the school to be concerned with small details. This is the first year I'll be running our program without Victor, and it must run flawlessly. Any questions?"

A million, but none I wanted to ask her. "Where's my room?"

"You will be on the third floor. Follow me."

Up another flight of stairs, so steep and narrow I had to hug my violin case to my chest in order to fit. We emerged on a small landing, the walls of clapboard sloping inward at such a steep angle I had to stoop as I climbed up. Madame Usher pulled a string and a single, bare bulb lit the space.

We were obviously in the attic of the house. Facing me were three doors. I assumed that when the building was used as a stately home, servants lived in these rooms. It seemed fitting then that I'd be given one. Madame Usher found another key on her ring and shoved it into the lock of the middle door.

"We had these rooms remodeled three years ago when we employed Clare. The room on your left is your bathroom – this outside door is blocked off, so the only access is through your room. The other door must remain locked at all times," she said. "We use it for storage, and it contains many old tools and other odds and ends. It becomes a health and safety issue if students are wandering inside, so I've not given you a key for it."

She swung open the middle door to reveal a surprisingly large space. The walls sloped toward the center of the room, and a dormer window cast cool light across the grey shag rug and comfortable – if worn – furniture. A white brass bed made with cream sheets faced the window. A stack of blankets rested on a carved wooden chest. The stone chimney rose through one corner of the room, so at least I would stay warm when the downstairs fire was lit.

Sticking me in the attic was obviously another part of Madame's plot to humiliate me, but she'd have to do better. The room was actually pretty cool – it had more personality than the ritzy suites downstairs. I set my violin case beside the chair at the window. "Thank you."

I hovered there, waiting for her to leave. When she didn't, I upturned my duffel bag on the bed and picked through the clothes I'd hastily shoved inside, pulling out my two concert dresses to hang on the rack beside the window, and a spare set of jeans to change into.

"What are you doing?" she demanded.

"Unpacking."

"No time for that." She glanced at her watch. "It is past ten. We dine promptly at eleven. You need to get back to the kitchen."

Faye

An hour of frantic chopping and sautéing later, I had prepared a passable lunch with what I found still usable in the fridge and pantry – herb-encrusted lamb medallions, a warm chorizo and sweet potato salad, and some stale bread that I'd sliced into croutons and grilled with a little garlic and served with a caramelized onion preserve I'd found on the shelves. Mom may not have been a virtuoso dickhead like my father, but I learned a lot from her – namely, how to rock the fuck out of a bare kitchen.

Bringing the heavy plates of food into the dining room was another matter entirely. It was another chance for my natural coordination to shine. As I rounded the corner of the staircase, one of the croutons slid off the plate and landed preserve-side down on the hallway rug.

Great. That's going to leave a stain. Remember to pick it up later.

Talking and laughing echoed off the high ceilings as I entered the room and got a first look at my fellow students.

Dorien Valencourt sat at the right-hand side of Madame Usher, where he held court over the table. He must've just said something hilarious, because the honey-haired girl who left me stuck in the porch tossed her hair over her shoulder and laughed. Her laugh sounded like water trickling down a waterfall.

The white-haired waif I'd seen at the piano sat beside a boy who... wait a second.

It was the violinist from Dorien's videos, I was *sure* of it. He and the girl looked practically identical – the same perfectly-straight silver hair, arresting eyes and sharp cheekbones. While she had the appearance of a pixie, he was a dark elf, the kind that lured you off the path into a magic circle where he'd make wild love to you and then cut your head off and suck out the blood. He placed his hand over his sister's, his icy gaze sweeping me with that a menace that made it clear he was as dangerous as he was beautiful.

Twins. That explained their identical last name, but not why they shared a room. Wouldn't they want their own space?

Across the table from the twins was a girl with curves like mine (maybe we could be friends...) – her skin a deep, rich brown, and her eyes sparkling with mischief. She wasn't African American, but I couldn't place her features. She wore a tight leather skirt and a black tank top that showed off swirling black tattoos across her shoulders and only barely covered her tits, as well as an attitude that told the world to fuck right off. She bent her head to speak with a guy I immediately recognized as the third Muse from Dorien's video. He could only be Titus Thibodeaux. In the dim candlelight, he *was* the spitting image of his father Amos, except that Titus' smoky eyes – the edges tinged with midnight – shared none of the maestro's warmth. He looked like he'd spent the day at back-to-back funerals with a quick stop in between for a root canal.

Madame Usher sat at the head of the table, and a white-haired man with soft grey eyes and a slightly-hooked nose faced her on the other end. Master Radcliffe, I guessed. A rare musician who had mastered three instruments, the brochures made a big deal about his presence on Manderley's staff. He was the only person who smiled at me as I approached the table.

Dorien Valencourt stood as I slunk forward, my knee stinging from where the porch bit me. He wore clothes this time, thank fuck, although his skintight black jeans and fitted red shirt with Baroque embroidery on the collar and cuffs did nothing to disguise that hot-as-sin body beneath. A hand reached out to me, those treble clef tattoos dancing over his fingers, and I imagined what it would feel like to have those hands dance across my naked skin—

I stiffened, my hands trembling. *Is he coming to speak to me? Is he going to lead me to my seat like a gentleman and—*

Dorien's eyes trailed across my body, searching my rumpled t-shirt and torn jeans for something he didn't find. He turned away with a snort of disgust and grabbed a decanter of red wine from the sideboard, pouring the dark liquid into crystal glasses.

Madame Usher nodded to me. I set the platters in the middle of the table, then stepped back awkwardly, not sure what to do. Did I sit at the table, or did she have a closet somewhere where Harrison and I shared a bowl of gruel?

"Join your fellow musicians," Madame Usher commanded me.

No closet for me. Counting that as a victory, I pulled out the only empty chair – next to the one Dorien had vacated. Six heads whipped around. Six pairs of eyes stared me down.

"Students, this is Faye de Winter. She will be joining us for the master class on violin, as well as taking over duties from dear departed Clare."

"There's only supposed to be six students," Titus broke in, his deep voice rumbling over my bones. Cornrows tumbled over his shoulders as he grabbed for the meat, narrowly missing dragging his hair in the food. "Master Radcliffe never takes more than six students, and Victor isn't here any longer to teach piano, so—"

"The Master has accepted Faye as a favor to me, as we're in need of domestic help. Her father is *the* Donovan de Winter, my greatest love." Madame's eyes glazed over, and for a moment she was lost in some memory of my father. Funny, so was I, although I doubt we saw the memories in the same way.

"He *was* my father," I corrected her. "Now he's taking a dirt nap."

Across the table, the brown-skinned girl snorted. Madame Usher gave no indication she heard me. "If Faye has even an ounce of his talent, then she will be a serious contender for the Manderley Prize."

This was the opposite of what she told me, but it was obvious from the six hostile glares around the table that Madame wanted me to be hated.

Dorien handed out glasses to everyone except the male twin – he of the sapphire eyes. It was weird to be drinking alcohol at lunchtime, on what was technically a school day, when I bet most of us were still under twenty-one, but I'd been at prep school long enough to know there were different rules for the rich and snooty. When Dorien came to my glass, he'd finished the decanter, so he had to open another bottle. He fiddled with some aerator device on the lid, then filled my glass to the rim – double the amount of alcohol than he'd given the others.

"Why didn't you save yourself the effort and hand me the bottle?" My voice dripped with sarcasm as I tried not to spill on the pristine white tablecloth.

"I bet that's how they drink wine in the *Bronx*." Dorien let the word drip from his tongue, the plosive slapping me across the face. Interesting. How did he know where I'd been living? When I knew him, we lived in the East Village.

If Dorien knows about Mom's illness and our fall from grace... could the floor just swallow me now?

My fingers curled into fists. I could flatten Dorien's perfect nose. It would even things out between us if he had a ruined face to match my ruined life, but that was probably exactly what Madame Usher wanted – the perfect excuse to get rid of me.

Not to mention the fact that messing up a face that perfect was a cardinal sin.

Remember, you're not here for yourself.

It took a buttload of self-control to uncurl my fist and hold my glass like I was grateful for it. As long as I toed the line, Mom got the best medical care money could buy. Maybe these fancy new specialists could figure out what the cut-rate chop-shop Dr. Frankensteins at the last hospital could not, and bring her back to me.

Now that I knew Madame Usher set me up to fail, I was more determined to stay, to win, and to find out exactly what her story was. Why was she so determined to have me here if she also wanted me to fail? Why offer to help my mom when she tried to steal her husband? And why *now*?

My scraped leg stung, and I knew I'd trailed cobwebs across the rug. Under their scrutiny, I felt myself coming apart. They all wore designer clothes and smiles of cut glass. Ivan ran his hands through a feathered haircut that probably cost more than a month's rent at our Bronx apartment. The brown-skinned girl, who I guessed was Aroha (was that Hawaiian? I didn't think I could ask) wore several large rings on her fingers, the diamonds twinkling beneath the flickering candles.

Dorien's eyes flicked over me, stripping away my clothing with his mind, the way his music laid my soul bare. I shuffled in my seat beside him, completely naked. He smirked – a mean expression. He didn't like what he saw.

An awkward silence settled over the table as everyone sipped their wine and stared at the food as if it might sprout tentacles and devour them all. Madame Usher frowned at my wine glass until I took the hint and sipped. It tasted foul, like rotten apples soaked in feet. I hoped she didn't expect me to drink the whole thing.

Finally, Master Radcliffe leaned forward and picked up the platter of lamb. "This looks delicious." His voice had a melodious tenor to it, as though he was still within a song. He scraped three medallions onto his plate, along with a generous helping of salad. That seemed to be an unspoken cue for everyone else to dive in. I waited until all the students had food on their plates before leaning in to serve myself. They hadn't left me any lamb (greedy bastards) so I loaded up with salad and bread. I'd need it to soak up the wine, which was already making me feel ill and, judging by Madame Usher's furious glances, I was expected to finish.

"So, Faye, please tell us about yourself," said the Master in his pleasant tone. "Who have you been studying under?"

I was about to say, "Ms. Finch for History and Mr. Sacks for Mathematics," when I clicked that he was referring to my music teachers.

Eyes bored into me. "Emma Garrison," I muttered into my plate. My tongue stuck to the roof of my mouth, and there was this strange harshness in the back of my throat.

Across the table, snickers were muffled with napkins.

"Emma Garrison? I can't say I've heard of her. Is she with the Berlin school?"

I shook my head. *Is he deliberately baiting me, or does he not know?* "She's... independent."

"What Faye means is that she's been under the tutelage of *amateurs*," Madame Usher offered up. "This Ms. Garrison is her high school music teacher – and their music program is far from distinguished. Such a waste of rare and exquisite talent. You'll have your work cut out for you, Maestro."

Across the table, Aroha choked back a snort. She tried to cover up the sound by crunching on some bread, but my skin bristled.

What did I expect? These rich assholes had been studying under accomplished masters since they were still in diapers, while I had to give up my expensive lessons *twice* so we could survive. The gaps in my knowledge put me behind them before we'd even began.

"I remember your father well," Master Radcliffe continued. "We met on several occasions at symphony events in the city. I saw him perform Sibelius with the London Philharmonic, and it was one of the most sublime performances I've ever encountered. The world was not ready to lose him."

I nodded. What else was there to say? I hadn't been ready to lose him, either. Too bad I had no say in the matter. One minute, Dad was yelling at Mom that she didn't appreciate his need for artistic space after she'd worked twenty-two hours straight to cover his flights to Venice and couldn't understand why he'd been home all day and hadn't cooked dinner. The next, he'd disappeared without a trace.

A memory surfaced that I hadn't thought of in a long time, that I'd shoved into that little black box in my head of things too painful to think about. A much younger, much skinnier Madame Usher standing in our doorway, her lips wet with crimson lipstick and her faux floral scent bowling through our house like Hurricane Bitchface. My mother facing her with a rigid back and hardened eyes. The pair of them sitting opposite each other at the kitchen table, untouched cups of coffee and an unopened white envelope between them. Nine-year-old me sitting on the stairs and straining to listen, but they spoke so low and in such harsh voices... when Madame Usher left, she carried the envelope and wore a satisfied smirk that didn't reach her eyes, and Mom stopped crying. She didn't shed a single tear for Dad after that.

I did the crying for us both, and a fat lot of good my overactive tear ducts did, sobbing over a man who I now knew was nothing but a rotten cheater.

I still didn't know what they'd said that day, or what was in that envelope.

"—Victor's most accomplished pupil," Madame Usher was still gushing about my father. "Donovan was to be the shining star of Manderley Academy, but the fates had other ideas."

I wished the Master would change the subject before me and my steak knife took a trip to stabby town. Instead, he reached for a second helping of salad. "You aspire to a career in music?"

"I don't know." That was the honest answer.

"If you don't know, then why are you here?" Madame Usher snapped.

More giggles from across the table. Only the waifish girl – Elena – looked uncomfortable.

"I'm here because you were in desperate need of my culinary skills." I popped a piece of chorizo in my mouth. As if she didn't know – I couldn't go off on a world tour while my mother still lay in a hospital bed.

The conversation moved on to discussing an upcoming recital the students were giving at a museum in New York City. An animated debate broke out over which showpieces they should perform. I longed to join in, but I'd never heard them play, and I got the vibe my opinion wasn't welcome.

Beside me, Dorien dominated the conversation. As he teased Ivan about his fingering technique, I caught a hint of the mischievous boy I'd grown up with. Being this close to all three Muses made my body light up and my stomach twist in ways I didn't understand. I averted my gaze across the table, but Titus's dark eyes bore into mine with unsettling intensity, as if he saw nothing wrong with cutting me open to study my entrails. I decided staring at my food was the best option. Between glances up from my salad, I noticed the honey-blonde (Heather?) hanging on Dorien's every word, nodding in agreement to whatever he said.

Yes, Dorien. Of course, Dorien. Polish your cock for you, Dorien—

"Oops." Dorien knocked my fork off the edge of the table. "Let me get that for you."

It's fine, I wanted to say, not wanting him any closer. But my mouth didn't work. Too much hot in this room.

As Dorien bent over to reach under the table, his head drew close to my thigh. His breath tickled the bare skin behind my knee, where my jeans had torn. I sucked in a breath. Fire shot through my limbs.

Dorien hesitated, his body stiffening. A lock of dark hair fell forward, brushing my thigh. He whipped his head around to glare up at me, his lips dangerously close to... to... places a guy that hot had never been close to before. My body reacted instantly, all the fire inside me converging between my legs. I clamped my thighs together, but it was too late. A faint gasp escaped my lips... a gasp Dorien Valencourt heard.

Dorien's lips curled back into a smirk. He knew exactly what he was doing, hovering over me like that. What a Dickweasel.

"You like this?" He arched a perfect eyebrow. My tank top had ridden up, and his lips blew hot air against my already-burning skin. I could almost imagine him as the Dorien I used to know. *Almost.* If not for that coldness in his eyes.

"I'd like my fork back," I managed to choke out.

Dorien sat up, leaving me flushed. He dropped the fork onto my plate and leaned toward me. Carpet fluff rolled off into my food, but I didn't care. I hated the sizzle that swept through my veins as his breath tickled my ear.

"You don't belong here, Sprite," he whispered. "And we're going to make sure you know it."

DORIEN

F*uck.*
  Faye de Winter.
  Double fuck.

My mind spun, and I struggled to push out any coherent thought other than the mountain of trouble I'd brought down on my own head. When Madame Usher informed me the Master wished to offer a place to Faye de Winter, I told myself it didn't matter. I stopped caring about Faye a long time ago. I'd be able to do what I had to do to keep my place at Manderley.

I lied to Madame.

I lied to myself.

Next to me, Faye hunched over her plate, her skin deliciously close. She stared at her salad like it held the mysteries of the universe. The wine stained her lips with a hint of red, like the blush of an intense kiss.

My skin crawled with her scent. Lavender and orange blossom – a distinctive perfume. The scent of my childhood. Of another time, when I'd been happy, free, not trapped in a nightmare of my own making.

I'd steeled myself for seeing Faye again, but the minute she appeared in my doorway it all went to shit. I pulled that stunt in the bedroom to throw her off, to show her right from our first meeting that she was *nothing* to me, but that was a lie, too. I'd known it as soon as I slammed the door and my dick sprang to life in my hands.

Then she waltzed into the dining room with that defiance blazing in her eyes, her clothes all torn and filthy and exuding 'don't fuck with me' from every pore. She wore her half-Mexican heritage with pride – that tumble of black curls down her back and that slightly broad nose turned up, like *she* was too good for *us*, instead of the other way around.

My Faye. My Sprite.

The sooner she was gone from Manderley, the better.

Heather let her gaze fall to Faye's glass, then turned to glare at me, the question obvious on her face. I kicked her foot under the table. Heather could fuck right off if she expected me to explain myself to her. My little fork stunt wasn't part of the plan, but it worked. Too well. I gritted my teeth as I remembered Faye's tiny gasp, a chink in that armor she wore, a hint that the fire scalding my skin was also burning her up inside.

I intended to disarm Faye, to wipe that defiance off her face, but her scent... it sent my head spinning, in a good way what was so fucking bad. My dick was hard again.

For a moment, I fancied I saw a pale face in the corner of the room, hiding in the folds of the curtain. But I blinked, and realised it was just the light falling in a certain way.

Get control, Dorien. Don't let her disarm you. This isn't about you.

I tried to focus on the discussion, anything to take my mind off Faye. I noticed Titus had that sparkle he got in his eyes when someone new walked into his life. He always wanted everyone in the room to love him, and they usually did. I hope his desire to be needed wouldn't fuck up our plan.

Master Radcliffe had turned his attention to Elena and the piece for the upcoming recital. While Elena discussed the merits of the different song choices in her breathless voice, I caught her brother's gaze. Ivan sat ramrod straight, and the venom in his eyes could have poisoned us all.

Of all of us, Ivan had the most to lose to Faye, and that was saying something. I'd seen that look in his eyes before. Once on our last tour, we'd been delayed at the airport in France for sixteen hours, and the airline could only get us to Canada in time for our show if Elena took a later flight. Ivan let *certain facts be known* with his typical Romanian sledgehammer personality, and ten minutes later all four of us had seats in first class.

I cut in with my opinion, trying to insert myself between Elena and Radcliffe, to lead the conversation somewhere that made Ivan less stabby. I kicked Heather again, and she finally took the hint and stopped glaring at Faye long enough to contribute.

I jabbed the lamb on my plate, chewing hard. It looked amazing, but all I could taste was cardboard. Cardboard flavored with lavender and orange-blossom. Unable to help myself, I reached across the table for the pepper and snuck a look at Faye. She sipped her wine again, her hair curtaining her face – a wall of protection against the world, against me.

I hated myself for what I was about to do, but I hated *her* more.

Ten years ago, I told Faye de Winter I never wanted to see her again. Now, she tore through my life like a fucking hurricane. If I didn't strike first, she'd destroy everything. That scent already dragged me under. Those fire-rimmed eyes would burn down everything I'd worked for. She'd ruin me.

I had to ruin her first.

FAYE

You don't belong here, Faye. And we're going to make sure you know it.

Dorien's chilling words haunted me all afternoon as my nausea grew worse, mingling with Harrison's warnings and visions of the last maid sprawled at the bottom of the stairs. My stomach churned as I stacked the dishwasher, and I kept looking over my shoulder, expecting to see Dorien or one of the other students sneaking up behind me, brandishing a knife.

By the time I finished in the kitchen, the house sang with faint, stolen notes of perfection as the students practiced. I hiked back to my room to change into a pair of black dress pants and grab my violin. During the day, the attic had heated to an unbearable temperature – a combo of pre-Victorian construction and heat rising through the house. I cracked the window and went to the bathroom to splash cold water on my face, but it did nothing to stop my churning stomach or the flush of sickly heat pooling in my cheeks – heat that had nothing to do with the warm attic and everything to do with those three unnervingly beautiful guys who already seemed to hate me for no reason.

I was heading back downstairs to find a spare practice space when Master Radcliffe stepped out of the music library.

"Faye, I wondered if you might accompany me to the ballroom," he said. "I'd like to hear you play, so we can get a sense of where you are. It's not often I teach students with your... unorthodox training."

He meant my *lack* of training, but he was polite enough not to say it. So far, the Master was the only person in this freak show haunted house who treated me like a human being. But I still found him intimidating – he'd been a superstar a decade ago, but he'd given it all up abruptly to teach at Manderley. There were rumors of a mental breakdown because of the pressure of his career, and of a scandal hushed up, but his warm brown eyes peering at me from behind bifocal glasses betrayed only kindness, and I needed some of that right now.

"Sure. I'd love to play for you."

Master Radcliffe held out his arm and I looped my hand in his, indulging in the old-fashioned and chivalrous way he accompanied me down the main staircase. Already, Manderley seemed like a house stuck in time.

He shoved open the doors of the ballroom. I stepped inside, my stomach lurching as my gaze drew up to the crystal chandeliers dangling from the impossibly high ceiling.

"This room is nearly double-height." Master Radcliffe drew back the velvet curtains, casting a square of grey light across the piano. Outside the towering windows, the forest encroached, trees reaching sinewy fingers toward the windows. "I often imagine the bright parties and balls held in this room, the ladies in their muslin dresses dancing, the dynasties forged and the scandals whispered between gossips. This is my favorite room in the house. As you will soon discover, the acoustics are superb."

He sat down at the piano bench, crossing his legs and folding his hands on his lap. "Please, indulge me with some of your favorites from your repertoire. It will allow me to see your strengths and weaknesses. If you wish me to accompany you, you have only to ask." He tapped out the first bar of Bach's *St Matthew Passion*. "I still have a little fire in my fingers yet."

I rested my violin against my chin and started to tune. Nerves tingled along my spine, and my stomach lurched. For perhaps the first time, I crashed headlong into what it meant to be in a school like this. I knew I would be behind the other students, but I was so focused on Madame Usher's money funding Mom's care that I hadn't considered how it would feel to play for a *maestro*, to see disappointment etched onto his features.

While I tuned, Master Radcliffe kept up a running commentary about my father. "...most exquisite fingering I'd ever seen. He'd have gone on to be one of the greatest virtuosos of our time, if only he'd—oh dear." He winced as I made a bum note. "Do you need more time, perhaps?"

I need you to stop comparing me to that bastard. But instead, I smiled. "It's fine. It's nice to hear from someone who knew my father."

Nice like a hole in the head.

"He came to my summer school in its inaugural year," Master Radcliffe said. "He would have won a full-ride scholarship had he not been so distracted by... social pursuits. He allowed other students to pull ahead of him. I hope you will not make the same mistake."

"I don't intend to." To shut him up, I launched into Brahms' *Violin Sonata No. 3*.

I loved this melancholy piece and usually played it well, but the weight of my father's legacy dragged my arm. I knew as soon as I hit the first arpeggio that I was sluggish. My fingers stiffened on the strings. I closed my eyes so I couldn't see Master Radcliffe's mouth turn down with disappointment.

Halfway through my fumbling attempt at Vivaldi's *Winter*, the door creaked open. All six students slipped in to stand along the wall. Titus was a towering mountain in the corner of the room, his dark energy sucking the last dregs of life from my performance and pummeling them against his bulk. The twins' expressions were featureless, two porcelain dolls sitting on a shelf, silently judging me. Dorien's eyes bore into mine, his smile wide and dark and triumphant.

It was a smile that said, *I'm going to eat you for breakfast.*

My stomach twisted as humiliation burned on my cheeks. *They can't be here. They can't see me play like this.* I'd seen Dorien's dick in all its glory, yet *I* was the one stripped naked.

As I turned my back to the students, my stomach gurgled in protest. Hot bile rose in my throat. I swallowed, but the sensation only grew stronger.

Maybe it wasn't nerves twisting my stomach. Maybe I was going to throw up.

My fingers wobbled on the strings as I shuddered against the rising bile. A wave of nausea crashed into me, turning me about until I lost what little focus I had left. I fumbled my way through the final movement, not daring to take my bow lest I puke all over Master Radcliffe's shoes.

When I lowered my arms, my hands trembled. I knew I'd played badly. If I wanted to prove to Dorien and his posse that I deserved my place here, I'd fucked that right up.

"You have promise, but your technique lacks precision." Master Radcliffe stood up. He took my hand, turning my fingers over and curling them around in an awkward position. I leaned on him more than I should have as another wave of nausea hit me. "That is what comes from having a second-rate education. It may be too late to repair the damage. We will have to work very closely together to transform your technique."

Behind me, Titus snorted. Master Radcliffe looked over his shoulder, for the first time noticing our audience. "Shouldn't you be rehearsing your Elgar, Titus?" he remarked.

With a flash of his obsidian eyes, the midnight edges disappearing in the shadows of the ballroom, Titus stood. "Sorry, Master. We were curious about the new girl."

Dorien stood too. "We won't disturb you any longer."

Interesting. Dorien may strut about like he owned this place, but he respected Master Radcliffe enough to listen to him. I stored that information for later. Any potential advantage I had over Dorien Valencourt was going to prove useful.

Not as useful as a bathroom. I grabbed my protesting stomach as the bile reached the back of my throat.

"May I be excused?" I managed to choke out. Master Radcliffe nodded. I tossed my violin on the settee and sprinted shakily from the room.

"She hasn't even bothered to pack away her instrument," I heard Heather whisper as I jerked open the door. "Trailer trash like her have no respect for their art."

Luckily, the ground-floor bathroom was right across the hall. I slammed the door behind me and hurled into an old-fashioned toilet.

As I wiped my eyes and spat repeatedly into the sink, my thoughts spun faster than my stomach. *Why do I feel so sick?* I'd been fine on the drive, and I'd never had any kind of stage-fright. Nerves, yes, but nothing that would make me physically sick. I'd only started feeling strange after lunch, and it couldn't have been anything I ate because I cooked it all—

The wine.

I thought it tasted gross, but chalked it up to knowing nothing about expensive wine. I remembered something else – Dorien's eyes gleaming as he opened a new bottle. Just for me.

He put something in the wine.

Fucking dickweasel.

And I'd drained the whole glass like a fool, thinking they were testing me. I leaned my cheek against the cool mirror, not caring that I left a smudge I'd have to clean up later.

When I emerged from the bathroom, Heather and Titus waited in the hall. Heather smirked as I walked past. "I'd be sick too if I played that badly. Such a waste of a place at the academy. The garbage disposal plays better than you, that's why we call you trash."

I stalked past her without responding. Titus' immovable bulk towered over me as I headed straight to the noticeboard to see if any of the practice rooms were free. None were. In fact, the rooms had been booked for the rest of the week. Hastily, I scribbled my name in the two remaining gaps in next week's list. I knew I needed all the practice I could get.

I collected my violin from the ballroom and clambered back to the attic. By clambered, I mean I crawled on my hands and knees while doubled over in agony. My phone was still sitting on the bed amongst my strewn belongings. There was a text from the hospital saying Mom had arrived safely. I was too wired to finish unpacking. I dragged a chair under the window, turning it so I could face outside at the sloping, overgrown back garden and stream surrounded by wilderness, the tops of the mountains hidden in the mist.

I placed the violin against my chin and drew the bow across the strings, wishing I could use it to saw off Dorien's stupid gorgeous neck.

I pushed through the pain in my stomach as I launched into a fast piece, building a tremolo with my wrist on the upper part of the bow, then moving to the middle until the bow began to bounce. The harder I pressed, the more the bow bounced, and the faster I could play. My head bobbed as I kept time, the screaming notes echoing the pain gasping at my belly.

This is how I should have played for Master Radcliffe. If Dorien Valencourt hadn't sabotaged me.

As I played, my eyes flicked to the window. The woods, branches reaching toward the house like outstretched hands, waited to grab me and welcome me. It was the kind of woods that appeared in a children's picture book – like the illustrations in an old copy of *Grimm's Fairy Tales* my father gave me – filled with scary monsters and yellow eyes that watched you.

I shook off the melancholy thoughts. *I think the scary monsters are inside the house—*

Wait, who's that?

A figure stalked across the lawn, heading for the trees. A lighter flickered, and a curl of smoke circled a head of straight black hair. I recognized stylized tattoos on her bare shoulders. *Aroha.*

I wonder where she's going?

I itched to go after her, if for no other reason than to bum a cigarette. Behind me, my alarm buzzed.

Fuck. *Have two hours gone by already?* I grabbed my things and headed down to the kitchen. No time for cigarettes when you had rich cockpoodles to serve.

Ivan

"What do you think of the new girl?" I slouched into Dorien's room and tapped the door shut with my foot. Titus was already there, kicking off the wall so he could spin the desk chair around in fast circles. *He's far too large a person to be so energetic all the time.*

Dorien looked up from where he was draped across his bed, his eyes flashing. "You're late."

"Elena's lesson ran over." Dorien didn't ask why I was sitting in on my sister's private class, or why I couldn't leave her there alone. He didn't have to, and I appreciated that. Dorien may be a *măgar*, but he kept my secrets like they were his own. I threw myself on the end of the bed, picking at a loose thread on the embroidered border. "What's the verdict on Miss de Winter?"

"Terrible violinist, but eminently fuckable." Titus scooted the chair over to the window and lifted the sash as high as it could go. He leaned outside and lit up a joint. Smoke curled around his lips as he held it out to me.

I shook my head. I needed that weed to get Faye de Winter out of my head. My body crawled with the awful sensation of being watched by invisible eyes, and I longed for something to take the edge off. But Elena hated drugs and she'd smell it on me. "I agree."

"I wouldn't put my dick in that. You don't know where it's been." Dorien scooted to the corner of the bed and leaned toward the window, grabbing the joint from Titus and taking a deep drag.

I didn't like the look in Dorien's eyes. He'd had the same look the night he handed me those plane tickets in Prague – the night he fucked our lives forever. It was the same murderous rage that burned bright as the police took him away for questioning after Clare's fall.

Watching Faye's face as she struggled through the Vivaldi should have brought me satisfaction. It was going to be too easy to break her, to go on with our lives. But all I felt was a dull ache in my gut. It was an ache borne of failure – in her eyes shone the defiance that coursed through my veins back in Prague, an echo of the man I might have been. Now I'd sold my soul to the devil to save my sister, and made both of us slaves. Not even the music was doing it for me these days. I made myself numb because numb was the only way to get through this, to reconcile the things I had to do.

Nothing made me feel anything except Elena's smile. I'd do anything to see that smile.

"You've met her before, right?" Titus took the joint from Dorien and curled his fat lips around it, swiping a cornrow out of his face. "You used to have lessons with her."

"Back when my parents were crass enough to let me hang around with plebs, yeah." Dorien leaned back on the bed and folded his arms behind his head. "She was mediocre then, too."

The way he said it, we all knew the truth. Faye de Winter was anything but mediocre. That was why she had to go.

"We're going to have to perform with her in ensembles." Titus was talking himself into action. He needed to believe the lie – and he'd tell himself these fairy tales until they became facts in his mind. "She's going to drag down the reputation of the entire school, if Madame Usher bringing her here hasn't achieved that already."

"It won't come to that." Dorien's eyes fixed on the ceiling. He made a good show of pretending he didn't care, but that haunted look in his eyes gave him away – it was the same look he got when he sat down at the piano, when the music took him over, and it was the reason women flocked to him more than us. Faye de Winter had got under Dorien's skin, and that in itself was interesting. "We need to get rid of her."

I shook his head. 'Why bother? She'll eliminate herself with her masterful grasp of Vivaldi."

Titus laughed. Dorien did not.

"It's her first day. It's probably nerves." Dorien waved a dusty glass bottle in front of my face. "And the syrup of ipecac I put in her wine."

"The what?"

"It's this stuff the Victorians used to use if someone was poisoned to induce vomiting. Clare found all these strange old bottles in the chest in her room. I kept this one – thought it might come in handy one day."

Titus clapped Dorien on the back as he passed the joint back to me. "You're such a shit. No wonder she ran away so fast."

"That's fucking hilarious." *Dorien is dangerous. Right now he's on your side, but never forget he could do that to Elena if you cross him.*

"It was Heather's idea, and we've got a ton more where that came from. We'll make sure Faye leaves Manderley by the end of the semester. Nothing will come back to us." Dorien sat up again, grabbing the joint from Titus and hanging it from his lips. "This is our territory. We're invincible."

Invincible. I used to believe that. The three of us playing sold-out shows in London, Vienna, Berlin, the press dubbing us The Bad Boys of Baroque and unwittingly showering us in a mountain of beautiful women, the promise of bigger and brighter things to come. I'd sure felt invincible then, but then Dorien and I fucked it all up, and now we were all prisoners.

"Here's what Heather and I decided. No one is to talk to her. Don't acknowledge her. Don't insult her. Just act like she isn't there."

"Wait, why is Heather in on this?" I glared at Dorien.

He looked away. "Drop it, Nicolescu. She's got a stake in this, too. She'll keep your precious hands clean for Elena. As far as you're concerned, Faye's ghosted. We'll take care of the rest."

Dorien's wrath was one thing. Dorien making plans with Heather and not sharing with us? A shiver ran down my spine.

Faye de Winter better watch out, Dorien had her in his sights – he planned to enjoy toying with her, and the Prince of Darkness liked to break his toys.

FAYE

After another excruciating meal with the students, during which they all acted like I didn't exist, I slumped back to my room. My stomach and throat still burned from whatever Dorien put in my wine, and I barely picked at my food. As soon as I could excuse myself, I loaded the dishwasher and escaped to my room.

The stuffy air in the attic clung to my clothes. I pushed open the window to let a fresh breeze circulate. Voices and laughter rushed up to greet me. I peered down to see the students gathered around a table at the edge of the garden. Heather looked up and saw me. Her nose turned up as though I gave off a bad smell. Sighing, I stepped away from the window, flung my clothes on a chair and collapsed on the bed in my panties, letting the breeze brush my clammy skin.

The stomach cramps had mostly subsided, replaced by a dull ache. Whatever Dorien had slipped me in the wine, it seemed like I'd be better in the morning. But if they were spiking my wine on the first day, what fresh horror would wait for me tomorrow?

I pulled my phone from my purse and I was halfway through a text to Mom when I remembered, she wouldn't answer because she was in a coma. My beautiful, vibrant mother who'd brought grown men to their knees in the boardroom and on the dance floor had been felled by some mysterious illness, and I had no one left to talk to. It didn't seem as though I was going to make any friends at this school.

Instead, I rang the hospital and checked in with the nurse on duty. She'd been settled in okay – Madame Usher had been as good as her word and moved Mom to their best room. There was no change to her condition.

I scrolled through my contacts list, looking for someone to call. I had a few friends I'd hung out with in high school, mostly fellow music students, but I'd ghosted them when Mom got sick. Amelia moved to Boston to study architecture, and John was backpacking across Europe. I'd seen their pictures on Facebook, but we didn't really talk anymore. I had my excuse, but I was still a shit friend. I hadn't been there for them at all since school finished, and I couldn't call them now when I needed them.

Fuck it. I tossed my phone on the bed in disgust. I was Marguerite de Winter's daughter. I could handle a few rich dickweasels.

I rolled over and picked up the battered paperback I'd shoved in my bag for the drive. It was this reverse harem romance set in a creepy gothic school called Miskatonic Prep. The main character, Hazel, is bullied by three rich kings of the school, but she holds her own and there's something about her that's not 100% normal—

Creak.

I jerked my head up at the noise. "Hello?"

Creak, creak, creaaaaak.

That sounds like footsteps.

I flung a t-shirt over my bare breasts and went to the door. I opened it gingerly, expecting to see someone on the landing. The square of light from my open door illuminated the narrow space. No one was there.

I must've imagined it.

I pushed the door shut and went back to bed. As soon as I sank into the sheets, the creaking started again. I paused, listening. *It's just the house settling, nothing to worry about—*

Creak, creak, creeeeak.

Nope, that's footsteps.

Definitely footsteps.

On this *floor.*

I slid out of bed, silently this time, grabbing the lamp off the bedside table and yanking the cord from the wall. The creaking continued as I crossed the room and leaned against the door, raising the lamp above my head as my fingers closed around the handle.

Creak. Crea—

"Fuck off," I yelled as I flung open the door and leaped into the gloom.

The creaking stopped.

My breath froze.

The landing was completely empty.

I swung in a circle, then leaned out to check the staircase. No one there, either. My blood rushed in my ears as my fingers tightened around the lamp. "Dorien, if that's you, I'll be reporting this as harassment. I don't care how rich your daddy is."

Silence answered me. I stood until my sweaty fingers could no longer grip the lamp, trying to figure out what the fuck was going on.

Back in my room, I slammed the lamp down and poked my head out the window. Down below, the students gathered around a wrought-iron table, passing a bottle of something around. I recognized all of them – the twins, Heather, Aroha, Titus... and Dorien.

How had he got back outside so quickly?

As if sensing my silent accusation, Dorien looked up. When his eyes met mine, he flashed me a smile that was all teeth and menace. He raked a hand through his hair – the moonlight painted his dark locks with shades of russet and crimson. A rush of heat coursed through my body, and I hated myself for it.

I couldn't be attracted to Dorien Valencourt, or any of the Muses, especially when they turned their ire toward me.

With a roar of frustration, I slammed the window shut and yanked the curtain across. A wave of exhaustion washed over me. I'd only been at Manderley one day and already I wanted to leave. I slouched over to the bed and wriggled under the covers.

But even though my body ached with weariness, I couldn't sleep. My skin crawled with the sensation of being watched. I flicked the light on, scanning the empty room, then flicked it off. But the feeling didn't go away.

And then, just as my eyelids fluttered shut, I heard it again.

The creak of footsteps against the floorboards. Slower now, more deliberate and careful. Only this time, I could tell that they weren't coming from outside my door.

They echoed along the wall opposite my bed.

The footsteps were coming from the locked storage room.

FAYE

Briiing.

I rubbed my eyes, trying to drag my brain from a disturbing dream. *What time is it? Am I late for my shift?*

As my eyes adjusted to the gloom, I stared at my sparse surroundings with confusion. *Did our apartment get robbed? Crap, is Mom okay? Is she...*

Then I remembered. Mom was in her new hospital, getting the best care money could buy. And I was in the attic room at Manderley Academy, about to start my morning duties like a maid of yore. It wasn't even light outside, and I had to be downstairs to make breakfast and clean the rooms before the day's lessons began.

I hadn't heard Dorien or whoever he sent to hide in the storage room again, probably because I buried my face in the pillow and refused to acknowledge their childish stunt. But I'd lain awake for hours, my senses on alert for the next evil trick. The old house creaked and groaned around me – each stirring a fresh wave of nerves, and every gust of wind rattled a windowpane with ill portent.

Now, in the warm light of the morning, I wasn't afraid. I was *pissed as hell.*

I pulled on the plain black dress Madame Usher had given me as a maid's uniform. The wool scratched my skin. *She's laying on this servitude thing a bit thick.* The dress was just another of her subtle digs at my status, marking me out as different from the other students, who all wore designer clothing and owned those expensive cars parked outside.

The zipper stuck. I grabbed it and jumped up and down, tugging until it pulled free. The dress was a little tight across my tits, but otherwise, it wasn't a bad fit. It was pretty unflattering – making me look broad and boxy instead of accentuating the hourglass shape of my hips – but I wasn't at Manderley to be admired. I was here to play music and get my mom the care she needed.

Speaking of which... I picked up my phone for the hundredth time and checked to see that I hadn't missed a message from the hospital saying she'd woken up. Nope, the universe wasn't that kind to me.

Dress on, all I needed was some foundation and a swipe of mascara and I was ready to face the Muses. I shoved open the door to the bathroom.

And screamed.

Scrawled across my mirror in blood-red were the words, LEAVE MANDERLEY.

Titus

Faye's scream echoed through the mansion. I stared up at the canopy of my bed, red fabric covered in gold stars, and imagined I had the superpower of seeing through solid objects. I peeled away the fabric and ceiling and floorboards in my mind and pictured those feisty eyes wide with terror, her wild hair streaming down her back as she slammed the bathroom door.

My cock stirred, and I wrapped my fingers around it. I closed my eyes. I imagined she was screaming my name.

Faye de Winter.

Everything about her intrigued me. And I haven't been intrigued in a long time. Manderley bored me to death – the crusty old furniture, the dull compositions, the endless hours of practicing the same pieces over and over again. I longed to be back on the road – a new city every night, a new girl in my bed, the applause of the audience washing over me, drowning my veins in pulsing, exhilarating *life*.

Instead, I was trapped here, miles from anything interesting. The only thing to entertain me was Dorien's vendetta against the new girl. When Faye walked into the dining room carrying those trays, I saw something in her eyes I recognized – a wild animal trapped behind bars. She was so much more than her bedraggled clothes and mediocre performance let on. She was more than the ghost from Dorien's past, and if he took his head out of his ass for a second, he'd be able to see it, too.

Not that I wanted him to see it. I wanted Faye for myself.

My hand moved faster, and my cock jerked. Upstairs, someone stomped across the attic floorboards. I pictured Faye as I'd seen her last night while I hovered in her doorway, the key tucked in my hand, waiting for Heather to finish in her bathroom. Moonlight streaked across the bed from the open window, making a pale face appear on her clothes rack. I started, then realised it was just an optical illusion, the same way the moonlight danced shadows across Faye's serene features. Raven hair fanned out across her pillow, falling like ripples of a silken river over the duvet. Looking down at her stirred something inside me – a mixture of fascination, desire, and repulsion at myself. My parents always warned me Dorien was a bad influence, and now here I was, sneaking into a girl's room and watching her sleep like a stalker creep.

I thought about shaking the ankle that peeked out from beneath the sheets. I wanted Faye to wake up, to see us in her room, to scream and rage and wake up the whole house. At least it would shake the cobwebs out of this place.

I wanted her to throw herself at me, to feel her warm skin against mine as her fists pummeled me or her lips devoured me. Either option worked for me, although my cock much preferred the latter.

Instead, I had turned and followed Heather outside. We locked Faye's door behind us and returned to our rooms.

And now I was wanking while Faye freaked out over the message we left in her locked room.

I'm a fucking horrible person.

My breath came out in quick gasps as I pumped harder. *Fuck, fuck, fuck. This is sick. It's disgusting. But it's as close as I'll ever get to Faye de Winter.*

I was forbidden to speak to her. Dorien's orders. That dude had been there for me more times than I could count. I didn't like to play by the rules, but this was one that I had to obey.

My body dropped back to reality. My cock softened in my hand as the vision of Faye faded from my mind, replaced by something equally beguiling but even more dangerous.

The secret hidden under my bed. The reason I couldn't get close to Faye de Winter. The shame that would eat me alive even as my soul petrified in this house.

The addiction I couldn't shake.

FAYE

What the fuck?

I swiped my finger through the wet letters and brought it to my nose. My stomach churned afresh. My mind flicked to Harrison's drawn face as he told me the last maid at Manderley had been murdered.

I scrunched up my face. *I don't want to do this.*

I sniffed.

Odd.

I'd seen enough horror films to expect the metallic tang of blood but instead, I smelled lipstick. In fact... I opened my eyes and rubbed the red between my fingers. Yep, that was definitely lipstick. The color looked suspiciously similar to the one Heather wore yesterday.

A juvenile prank. Just Dorien's style.

Dickweasels.

What concerned me most wasn't the stupid message, but the fact that one of the students snuck into my room *while I was asleep*. They couldn't have climbed in the window, which only left the door.

The door I'd most definitely locked.

I crossed the room in three strides and checked – still locked. I yanked the door open and inspected the mechanism. Nothing broken.

Which means... they have a key.

That probably meant they also have a key to the storage room next door. That would explain the creaking sounds last night. One of them must've hidden in there and waited until I went to sleep, then snuck in to write the message.

Dorien.

But no – I realized with a start that Dorien couldn't have done it if he was hiding in the storage room. I saw him with the other students hanging out around that table, and there was no way he could have made it from there up the stairs to the storage room without me hearing him – the stairs creaked more than an Edgar Allan Poe poem.

My heart leaped in my chest as I crossed to the window and drew back the curtain. Sure enough, there was the table, with an ashtray and an empty bottle of Scotch. They might've snuck up while I was asleep to do the mirror, but that didn't explain the footsteps. I couldn't see how anyone around that table could have been making the footsteps in the storage room.

Unless...

It must've been Aroha. She hadn't been with the group at the table, I remembered.

Great. So they were all in on it with the Muses. Dorien's hatred of me was personal, and I didn't understand it. He was the one who broke *my* heart. But whatever. We at least had a history. The others... they didn't even know me. Aroha didn't look like rich-bitch Heather. Something about her clothes and the tattoos and the way she carried herself told me she didn't give a fuck what anyone thought of her or Dorien's petty problem with me. So why was she sneaking around in the storage closet and writing messages on my mirror?

I turned from the window, squaring my shoulders.

I grabbed my violin case and thundered downstairs, not caring that I sounded like a herd of elephants charging through the silent house. I stood in front of the door to Madame Usher's private chambers.

They have a key to my room. I don't feel safe. Even as the resident charity case, that's unacceptable.

"Madame Usher?" I knocked. "I need to report something. Some of the students broke into my room last night and wrote things on my walls."

Scuffling sounded inside the room. I pressed my ear to the wood as a faint voice hissed something. There were a couple of dull thuds, then footsteps padded toward me.

The door flung open. Madame Usher blocked the door, her eyes blazing. "What did I tell you?"

"Yes, but—"

"I don't care if the house is burning down around us or a flying saucer lands on the roof, you *do not* disturb me. This would be grounds for expulsion, but on account of our arrangement, I will give you a second chance." She glared at me. "Don't do it again."

"Wait. I—"

The door slammed in my face.

"Morning, trash. Sleep well?"

I whirled around. Dorien leaned against his doorframe, wearing only a pair of boxers and a smirk that would raise the Titanic from the bottom of the ocean. The saliva dried on my tongue as I glimpsed the tattoos dancing across his naked skin. *Don't give him the satisfaction of looking. That's exactly what he wants—*

Yeah, turns out I have no self-control. My eyes swept over the hard lines of his torso. Dorien was sin itself – his unearthly angelic beauty hid the bitter pride and desolate state of his soul. I paused at the Gothic lettering spelling out a Latin phrase across his chest. *In Cauda Venenum.*

So different from the boy I'd known, and yet exactly how I'd pictured him. Dorien was always destined to be a rebel. Being the Bad Boy of Baroque was written in his future from the very first time he put red paint on Madame Usher's chair.

Why do the bad boys have to grow up so damn fine?

"No ghosts visit you in the night?" Dorien lifted one perfect eyebrow.

"Fuck you." I stormed past him. His scent hit me – the dark heart of cinnamon and frankincense, dappled with sweet violets. Pure lust shot with innocence. I longed to drown in that scent, to allow it to pull me under even as it warned me that I could lose myself in its depths. "And stay out of my room."

Dorien's cruel laughter followed me down the stairs.

Over a breakfast of granola, Greek yogurt, and frozen berries (if the students thought they were getting bacon from me every morning, they had another thing coming) Madame Usher informed us that Dimitri Solokov – the producer of the Moscow Philharmonic Orchestra – would dine at Manderley on Friday.

"Following your private lessons, gather in the ballroom this afternoon. You will each perform your best concerto for Master Radcliffe, who will choose one student to perform for Master Solokov."

My heart pounded. I'd only been at Manderley one night, and already Madame Usher dangled an incredible opportunity in front of me. To have Dimitri Solokov rapt by a solo performance... that was a fucking big deal. Even when Mom was rich enough to send me to the prep-school and my private lessons, I could never even hope for that kind of connection.

The other students continued shoveling food into their mouths as if Solokov's presence was no big deal, as if bombshells like this dropped every week. Maybe they did.

I've walked into a whole other world.

Madame Usher rose, indicating breakfast was over. I rose, too, circling the table to collect the plates. As the students filed out of the dining room on the way to composition class, Titus drew up beside me, his broad shoulders blocking the door so I had to slow my step to avoid crashing into him. Damn, that boy was *fine* – that buzzed haircut with the cornrows down the middle, tied away from his face so they flowed down his back, the body of a freight train if locomotives modeled Calvin Klein, and those eyes of fire and brimstone. If Dorien was the Lord of Hell, then Titus was Demon-at-Arms. Too bad he'd already decided which side he fell on. He leaned in close to whisper in my ear, "Don't even bother showing up today. Fingering like yours is only good for strangling cats."

I didn't dignify Titus with an answer, but I shot him a look that I hope articulated how little I cared what he thought. His words only made me more determined to succeed.

His lips curled back into a smile. It wasn't warm exactly – the same fire in his eyes flickered across his face. "You drool in your sleep. It's adorable."

The words slammed into me. I stopped in my tracks, my body rigid. Behind me, Heather swore as she crashed into me. She shoved me aside without a word and stomped away. My head spun.

Titus was in my room. He watched me while I was asleep. Now he's smiling at me like that's not creepy at all.

He could have done *anything*. Fear rippled through me – a fear born of uncertainty, of knowing I was at the bottom of the food chain and these guys could do anything they liked to me without consequences. Clearly, they planned to do just that.

An image flashed in my mind – a maid in the same scratchy wool dress I now wore, crumpled at the bottom of the stairs, her neck bent at an impossible angle. Titus opened his mouth to say something else, but I shoved my way past him and fled toward the kitchen.

As I rounded the corner, my chest heaving, I glanced back over my shoulder and noticed Dorien glaring at Titus, who shrugged and pushed past his friend on his way to the practice rooms. *Weird. What's that about?*

In the kitchen, I dumped the crockery into the dishwasher without rinsing it. I had no time to collect myself, to reel from what I'd just learned. I splashed cold water on my face and rushed to the Red Room in the turret for composition. Master Radcliffe had already started the class. No one acknowledged me as I took my seat at the end of a semi-circle surrounding the piano.

For the next three hours, I forgot all about the shitty students and the note on my mirror and the scratchy dress and even Mom's illness. Music could do that to me – it was my escape from reality. Composition wasn't my strongest area, but the way Master Radcliffe explained and demonstrated the concepts held me rapt. When he played through a short piece he'd composed in the moment, tears sprung in my eyes. If I could be even *half* as good as him, I'd be a world-renowned *Maestra*.

I had to leave the class early to prepare lunch. It sucked dragging my ass from the chair and leaving the others to soak up the final minutes of Master Radcliffe's wisdom.

Yesterday, I'd hurriedly scheduled a food delivery. When I entered the kitchen, the table groaned under the weight of the bags. Harrison moved through the space, making the low kitchen seem smaller somehow as he shifted the meat and frozen vegetables into the chest freezer in the pantry.

"Thank you for helping." He'd just saved me a ton of time, and I know he was busy repairing the hole I made in the porch.

"'Tis my pleasure." Harrison dusted off his hands on his filthy overalls. "It's nice to have a break from the weeding. How are you finding the school?"

"It's... different." I flopped a salmon fillet onto the chopping block, wishing I was slapping the wet fish across Dorien's smug mouth or Ivan's icicle stare or Titus' glorious cheekbones.

"Those students are giving you trouble." It wasn't a question.

I nodded. "It's nothing I can't handle. They've got a key to my room. Do you have a spare lock to replace it?"

Harrison's face clouded over. "You need to tell Madame Usher."

"I did. She didn't want to hear it, so I guess I'm on my own."

"I'm making a trip into town tomorrow." Harrison dropped a stack of salmon fillets into the freezer. "I'll bring you back a new lock. Victor never tolerated their bad behavior, but the Madame lets them get away with..."

Murder, he was about to say. And a thought niggled at me – that the students weren't the only ones who wanted me gone from Manderley. If Madame Usher wanted me to leave without getting her hands dirty...

I thought of Titus standing over me in the darkness while I slept, and those footsteps pacing back and forth across the room. A horrible thought hit me – he admitted to being in my room, but Titus couldn't have possibly made those footsteps. *He'd been outside with the others. I saw him...*

The thought left an unsettled feeling in my gut. "Harrison, tell me straight – am I in danger here?"

"You be careful, especially of that Dorien Valencourt. He's her pet." Harrison looked like he wanted to say more. Instead, he slammed the lid of the freezer down and scurried away, like he couldn't bear to be in the big house a moment longer than necessary.

I dressed a shoulder of pork, covered it in foil, and whacked it in the oven to slow cook for dinner while I tossed vegetables in truffle oil and grilled the salmon steaks. When I carried lunch into the dining room, Dorien was on his feet again, pouring the wine. He started with the Master and worked his way around the table. I needed to cross his path to set down the platters.

"Excuse me," I mumbled under my breath. I balanced four plates in my hands. They were much heavier than his wine bottle.

Dorien pretended he didn't hear me, shifting his body so I ended up doing an awkward dance to get around him. As I stepped toward the master, Dorien stuck out his foot. I tripped, splattering juicy steaks and salad across the pristine tablecloth.

"Ew." Heather leaped back, clawing at her head. "She got tomato in my hair."

"Ms. de Winter," Madame Usher boomed. "Clean this up at once."

"But—"

"Not another word." Madame Usher stood up and held out her plate. "Salvage what you can. We will take our lunch in the drawing-room while you deal with the mess you made."

Fuming in silence, I scooped meat and salad back onto the platters, handing one to her and the other to Elena. I tried to meet the Romanian girl's eyes, but she kept her chin held high. She might not actively participate in whatever the Muses had planned for me, but she certainly went along with it.

By the time I'd scrubbed at the tomato stains on the rug and put the tablecloth on to soak, they'd polished off the food. They hadn't left a single piece for me. I grabbed an apple from the kitchen. While the others spread out across the practice spaces, I got a mop and bucket out of the storage cupboard and cleaned the bathrooms on both floors, then moved on to scrubbing the marble tiles of the Red Room until they shone. I dusted down all the antiques so the place would be perfect for Andrei Solokov's visit.

My chores done, I returned to my room and practiced for two hours. I chose Bartok's *Violin Concerto No.2* for my audition piece – I'd been wrapping my head around the fiery, conflicted music for the last year. When Bartok composed the concerto in the lead-up to the First World War, he was being attacked in his native Hungary for his anti-Fascist views, and the concerto reflects his frenzied state of mind. It perfectly matched my mood after learning about Titus' invasion of my privacy, and the fact that his confession didn't explain all the noises I heard. By the end of my practice, the notes hummed in my veins. I knew I played the piece with heart, with fire, and I'd give all three Muses a run for their money.

Back down in the kitchen, I roasted some vegetables and made *rotkohl* – red cabbage, cloves, bacon, and apples. A recipe handed down from my German grandmother on my father's side. We never saw her after my dad disappeared – I didn't know if it was too painful for Mom or if she suspected Grandma knew something she hadn't revealed. It was no big loss – the best thing about Grandma had been her cabbage. The bitter woman died a few years ago. We didn't go to the funeral.

Tension crackled in the air as I served dinner, with less joking between the students than normal. *Of course, tonight they weren't friends, but rivals.* No one spoke to me, but Ivan kept sneaking glances at me between bites – those intense icicle eyes sweeping over my face. His expression never changed – I had no idea what he was thinking, and it both terrified and angered me. The skin on my neck prickled with nerves, and I kept looking over my shoulder, certain there was some horror about to be visited upon me from behind.

Dinner finished in record time. I hurried to stack the dishwasher while the others went upstairs to change clothes and tune their instruments. By the time I arrived in the Blue Room – the largest of the practice spaces – sweaty and still wearing my wool dress, six perfectly groomed students lounged on all the available chairs, carefully avoiding acknowledging me.

I stood awkwardly beside the sideboard, trying to avoid looking anywhere near the guys. Madame Usher poked her head in. "The Master and I won't be a moment. Faye, pour us all a glass of port. It calms the nerves."

I went to the liquor cabinet and found the port decanter and eight glasses. I splashed a generous slug of the dark liquid into each glass and arranged them on a silver tray. The door opened, and Master Radcliffe walked in. As I held the tray out to him, Dorien slid his foot across the rug and kicked my ankle. I went down hard, the tray flying from my hands and splattering sticky port all over Master Radcliffe.

FAYE

The Master frowned at the red stain dripping down the front of his silk shirt. "I must change clothes."

He flounced from the room, leaving me alone with my six enemies. Heather no longer bothered to hide her laughter behind her hand. Aroha let out a booming roar that got Titus going, and soon Dorien was chortling, too. Elena and Ivan stared at the floor, apparently unmoved by it all.

Dorien pointed to the port stain on the floor. "Clean that up," he commanded.

I made the only possible response to such a request. I flipped him off.

"You're the servant. Do your duty. If that's not gone by the time Madame Usher returns, you'll pay."

"*You* clean it up," I shot back. "You're the one who tripped me. Do you think it's fun to pick on people, Dorien? You're like a spoiled only child throwing his toys out of the sandbox because he doesn't want to share."

Dorien's eyes flashed at me. "You don't know what you're talking about."

I snorted. "I know exactly what I'm talking about. Are you so afraid that I'll beat you? Why are you even *here*, anyway? International career not going so well?"

Something inside Dorien snapped. I knew I'd got to him; I just didn't know how or why. I clenched my hands into fists, ready to drive the knife deeper, desperate to hurt Dorien the way his insults hurt me, when Madame Usher entered the room. Her eyes immediately fell on the stain on the floor. "Miss de Winter, can you not perform one task without spillage?"

"Dorien tripped me deliberately—"

"You are accusing Dorien Valencourt to cover up your incompetence." Madame Usher flashed me with her cold smile. "Dorien has thousands of adoring fans waiting for him on the other side of Manderley's walls. He has no need to resort to petty pranks. You will clean that immediately. And then you will go to your room and think about whether you really want to be here."

"But the audition—"

"You will not be auditioning."

Her words hit me like a punch in the gut. It was one thing to be ordered around like a servant. I could handle that if it meant Mom was safe. But to be deprived of this opportunity because of Dorien's assholery? I gulped back the venom that danced on my tongue.

Madame Usher took a seat on the velvet chaise under the window, spreading her skirts around her. "Hop to it, girl. There's carpet cleaner under the dresser. You better not be here when Master Radcliffe returns."

"Yes, Madame."

I loathe you. I hate you.

Mocking eyes burned into me as I knelt down and located the spray. On my hands and knees, I scrubbed at the stain. Above my head, Dorien and Heather held court, clinking their glasses together as they gloated over my humiliation.

"Too bad you can't whip insolent slaves anymore," Dorien mused, and there was a wicked edge to his voice that made something warm and wanton slither down my spine and pool between my legs. I hated him so much in that moment, but not as much as I hated myself for wanting him.

"Trash like her is probably gagging for it," Heather giggled. My ears rang with rage. "What a waste of perfectly decent port."

"It's not a waste. There's a fine view from over here," Titus' murmur reached my ears.

His friends laughed. My cheeks burned with humiliation. I stood, smoothing the front of my dress, now creased and covered with fluff from the rug, and tucked the cloth into my pocket just as Master Radcliffe entered again, his shirt swapped out for a new one. He sat behind the piano and indicated for Dorien to begin. I hovered by the door, my violin clasped at my chest, hoping Madame had changed her mind and—

"Get out," she rasped. "For your insolence, you will be confined to the school grounds this weekend. Allowing the use of Harrison for driving is a privilege, not a right."

"But I have to visit my mother—"

"You should have thought of that before you made a mess of my home. Don't make me regret bringing you here, Miss de Winter."

The door slammed shut behind me, echoing down the hall.

I slumped against the door, my body vibrating as the first fluttering notes of Dorien's concerto reverberated through the door. Even when I was part of the most elite music academy in the country, I was still shut out.

I can't see my mother, and it's all his *fault.*

It would be bearable if Dorien was a shit musician, but when his fingers touched the keys he created magic. He didn't just play Beethoven, he made love to

Beethoven. He fucked Beethoven slow and steady from behind. Dorien made Elena's performance from the other day seem like a novice.

I tore myself from the door, determined not to give him the satisfaction of listening any longer. Brilliant musician or not, Dorien was intent on seeing me fail, and he'd convinced all the other students to help him. Something Madame Usher said nagged at me. *He has no need for petty pranks.*

She was right – Dorien had already made a name for himself in the Classical world. He had fame and fortune and groupies galore. He didn't need Manderley or the prize. And yet, he was going to great lengths to drive me away.

Dorien Valencourt saw me as a threat.

That knowledge bolstered me. I curled my fingers into fists. Dorien may have meant something to me once, but now he was just another hurdle in my way. I'd survived my mother's mysterious disease – dealing with the Bad Boys of Baroque was nothing compared to that. Not only would I keep my place at the Academy and ensure Mom had the best medical care, but I would finish the year with the Manderley Prize, and I'd rub it in their self-righteous, chiseled, gorgeous faces.

FAYE

It turns out, Dorien's efforts to sabotage me were in vain. Master Radcliffe chose Elena to play for the visiting conductor, with Ivan accompanying her on the violin. They practiced all day in the Red Room while I worked on my composition in the smaller Yellow Room. Listening to the twins through the walls was like a lesson in concert performance. Elena had that kind of rare talent that would leave audiences broken and haunted, glued to their seats after the house lights came up, unsure if they'd yet returned to the real world.

And Ivan... he was a masterful violinist, but it was clear to me that he hung back, allowing his sister to shine. Odd, because I'd seen him play with Dorien and Titus in the videos – he was as fast and furious as either of them. Ivan could hold his own and command a stage. Yet, when he played with Elena, he became background noise.

After a while, I set down my violin and picked up my duster to clean the bookshelf beside the window, watching grey clouds move across the mountains and the trees bend in the approaching gale while I listened through the wall. I couldn't imagine Ivan being anyone's background noise – not with those intense blue eyes and those cheekbones that could cut glass. And yet... he seemed happy to let his sister take the limelight. Another mystery of Manderley, one I was unlikely to solve while everyone ignored me.

The storm grew more intense. Rain rolled down off the mountains and pooled in low spots on the lawn, creating muddy puddles that reflected dark clouds the exact color of Dorien's eyes. Harrison had to cancel his trip into town – he couldn't drive on those roads – which meant I wouldn't get my new lock until next week.

Dimitri Solokov arrived during the peak of the storm – rain sleeting sideways into the windows, thumping a steady rhythm that kept me company while I worked.

The gong echoed through the house, signaling someone had arrived. When I emerged from the practice room, Madame Usher was greeting the producer in the hall, draping his sodden coat over the antique stand. She snapped her fingers at me and pointed to the Blue Room. I knew what she wanted – drinks must be poured.

"Faye is a charity case," she explained to Master Solokov as I held out the tray of drinks. "Out of the goodness of my heart, I've accepted her into Manderley's program in exchange for her service. I shan't think I'll do it again. Her father was Donovan de Winter—"

Solokov's face lit up at the mention of my father's name.

"—alas, she does not share his talent. On a good day, she can strangle Vivaldi out of her violin, but I wouldn't expect more than that from her."

I bit back a retort. *It doesn't matter how she treats me and what she says about me. I'm still here in her school, learning from Master Radcliffe. She's still paying for medical care for a woman whose husband she tried to steal. I still have as much of a chance as anyone else of winning the Manderley Prize.*

I left them to talk as I returned to the kitchen, where I'd laid out an assortment of hors d'oeuvres for Solokov's visit. Tonight, I'd gone all out into my mother's Mexican heritage, serving up esquites, crispy deep-fried chimichangas with salsa roja, and cinnamon churros with a dark chocolate dipping sauce. Hearty, warming food for staving off the cold. I reached down to grab the trays and noticed something.

Someone had taken three of the chimichangas from the tray.

I smirked. If someone thought stealing a few nibbles would scare me away, they had another thing coming. I rearranged the food so the gaps weren't noticeable and took the trays out to the Blue Room, arranging them on a table in the corner.

I half expected Madame Usher to ban me from the room, but she seemed to have forgotten about me as soon as Master Solokov arrived. Harrison had lit the fire, and it blazed with welcoming heat. I settled myself on the chesterfield by the fire, letting the warmth soak into my limbs.

The others filed in as they finished their practice and groomed themselves. Heather's curls caught the light, bouncing beneath the chandelier. Elena looked like an elf with her silver waterfall of hair streaming down her back. Aroha wore a floor-length dress printed with bold swirling designs that matched her tattoos. The three Muses filed in last, and I stifled a gasp.

They wore the black ruffled shirts and tight pants from their European tour. On anyone else, those outfits would be ridiculous costumes, but the three of them were unholy gods. Dorien's dark hair flopped over his eyes and curled around his collar, every inch the dark prince. Titus had to duck under the lower arms of the chandelier to avoid hitting his head. As he did, the cornrows trailing down his back fanned out, and the beads at the ends clicked together. That guy was just so big, it was hard to picture him playing a beautiful instrument with precision, and yet he could shred that cello like no one else. Ivan stood in contrast to them both, with his silver hair matching the threads of glittering embroidery on his cuffs and collar, and his Eastern European features hard and focused.

Dorien and Ivan took up places across the room, near Madame Usher, but Titus slumped down beside me on the low couch. His leg brushed mine, and sparks shot up my leg. My mind might've been disgusted at the idea of him sneaking into my room and watching me sleep, but my body had no such qualms.

When we were all gathered, Elena and Ivan took their places and performed their piece. As the music flowed through me, the warmth of Titus' leg penetrated my skin until I could feel it in my bones, and his scent danced across my nostrils – red musk and myrrh, cut with fragrant roses – its intensity conjured by the music and by the electric attraction I felt to him.

Something is seriously wrong with me. I've spent far too many hours cooped up in Mom's hospital room with only elderly doctors for company. A week at Manderley with the Bad Boys of Baroque and I've turned into a mess of hormones.

I tried to focus on Elena's fingers and Ivan's solemn notes, but Titus' presence loomed large beside me. Every breath he took and every subtle movement of his body translated through that square of skin where we touched until I was a mess of want and frustration.

I refused to look at him, instead focusing on the grim features of our Russian visitor. Solokov's expression gave nothing away, but when Elena lifted her hands from the piano he rushed at her, collecting her fingers in his, and kissed the knuckles of her hand.

"You will go far. You should already be in Europe, not wasting away in this stuffy school."

In her seat, Madame Usher bristled and looked to Ivan as if to demand his support. Ivan slunk back into the shadows by the door. It was Master Radcliffe who came forward to stand beside Elena. He threw his arm around her shoulders.

"Elena is my star pupil," he said, and there was a hint of challenge in his voice. "Like a delicate flower, she must be allowed to bloom at the right time. Too early and she will wilt, her beauty fading."

Madame Usher rose from her seat, and everyone started talking at once, surrounding Solokov and offering him drinks, food, a place to sit. Titus turned his body to me. He didn't say anything, but there was a confidence in his broad shoulders that told me I didn't want to be near him. I shot up and darted around the group to the door. To where Ivan lurked like a vampire in the night.

I leaned my back against the wall beside him, my fingers brushing the paper, feeling a crack where the wall met the wainscoting. A faint draft tickled my fingers. "Your sister is so talented."

Ivan glanced up at me. This close, his eyes became shards of sapphire – facets of twinkling beauty catching the light. So clear they drew me in until I lost myself in their depths, toppling into a lake of frozen emotion.

He turned away, his lip jutting out – a deliberate and conscious movement to avoid answering me. Ivan fixed his gaze on his sister in the center of the room, surrounded by the adoration of teachers and students, while he stood here, forgotten. Across the room, Dorien swept his head up and caught Ivan's gaze, and an unspoken conversation flickered between them.

I slipped out of the room. I knew I wasn't wanted. Madame Usher wouldn't let me speak with Solokov, and the others were intent on ignoring me, so what was the point? I clicked the door shut behind me—

Down the hall, a door slammed. The sharp *BANG* of wood cracking against the frame echoed through the walls, trembling the vases on their plinths.

I whirled around, my heart leaping into my chest. "Who's there? Harrison?"

No one answered.

I stalked down the hall, glancing into the rooms on either side of me, searching the shadows for an answer. The door to the Yellow Room was shut – the only one in the hall, and I knew I left it open earlier – the heavy wood held back by a brass stopper.

It's okay. It was just a gust of wind blowing the door shut. Someone must have opened a window. Which was ridiculous, because of the raging storm outside, but the Yellow Room was at the back of the house, where the eaves hung lower, and it could get quite stuffy.

My fingers closed around the handle. My breath came out in short gasps. *It's nothing. It's just this creepy old house capturing your imagination.* But I couldn't stop the niggling, tight sensation in my chest, the scratching on the back of my neck that signaled someone watching me.

Willing my heart to return to normal, I pushed the door open and stepped inside. The windows were all closed, and there was no breeze in the room. *Of course, the storm could have rattled the frame so much the window slid down.* I gulped back the lump in my throat as I crossed the room. The skin along my arms prickled, overwhelming me with a sense that I wasn't alone in the room. I scanned all around, but I couldn't see anyone, and there was nowhere for someone to hide unless they crawled into the piano.

My fingers shook as I drew back the curtains. All the windows were tightly latched. Not a breeze or draft touched my bare arms.

So how had the door slammed shut? *Everyone's inside the Blue Room.* It couldn't have been any of them.

Except for Harrison... I cupped my hands against the glass, but I could barely even see the gatehouse lights through the downpour. I picked up the house phone from its cradle beside the window seat, my hand trembling, and dialed his extension.

"Gidday," Harrison's gruff voice answered.

The words rushed out. "Hi, Harrison, it's me. You weren't just down at the house, were you? Specifically, in the Yellow Room?"

"Not me. I didn't want to be a bother while Madame entertained her guest, so I knocked off early." I could hear a TV blaring in the background. "Why do you ask?"

"The door slammed, but there's no one here, and no windows open. And—" I paused. I couldn't explain the weird feeling in my gut without sounding insane.

"Always strange noises in that house." A crunching sound as Harrison opened a packet of something. "Knocking in the walls. Footsteps where there should be no footsteps. Cold spots. Clare complained about food missing from the kitchen."

I remembered the three missing chimichangas, and a fresh wave of unease rocked through my body. "You might've mentioned this before."

Harrison munched on his dinner for a moment. "But it can all be explained, can't it? Rats stealin' the food, drafts between the walls, old houses creaking and settling, rotten rich kids pulling pranks."

"Yeah. You're right. Thanks, Harrison." I hung up the phone and turned back to the door.

I wanted so badly to believe he was right – there was a logical explanation for what happened. Of course, if this was a horror movie, Harrison would be the killer for sure – the harmless old groundskeeper with a sordid past and thirst for blood.

But I knew Harrison couldn't have been here. He picked up the phone in the gatehouse only a couple of minutes after the door slammed. Even a fit person couldn't have made it back down the driveway in time, and not in this storm. Besides, the windows were all latched from the inside. There was no way out of the room unless someone crawled up the chimney like Santa Claus.

My eye caught the bookshelf beside the window.

I froze.

I *knew* when I dusted that shelf earlier today it had been perfectly in order. Now, several books had been pulled out and scattered across the floor.

I gathered up the books and shoved them back onto the shelf. A sliver of ice crawled up my spine as my fingers curled around a battered leather volume.

Grimm's Fairy Tales.

Odd, it looked *exactly* like a book I had when I was a child. My father got it for me as a gift when he returned from a tour of Germany. He used to read a chapter to me every night before I went to sleep. When he was on tour, he'd call me as often as he could from the other side of the world, and we'd read the stories together over the phone. He did the best voices – I broke into giggles at his rumbling monsters and cackling witches. When he disappeared, I threw the book into the trash.

Lightning cracked outside the window, and the raw energy of the storm sizzled in my veins as I held that book in my hands, memories I didn't want to recall flooding my mind.

I flipped open the cover.

My heart flew to my throat.

The book clattered from my hands, the frontispiece falling open on the floor.

There, written in looping script across the corner of the page, was the message:

MY DARLING FAYE,
MAY ALL YOUR DREAMS COME TRUE
LOVE DAD

DORIEN

After Elena's performance, Madame Usher dismissed us so she and Radcliffe could talk shop with Solokov. In the hall, Heather threw her arm in mine. "You should have been the one playing for him," she said. "You know you're the most talented pianist here – especially when I accompany you. Madame only chose Elena because she's exactly *his* type."

"Mmmm." My gaze fell to the stairs, where Ivan and Elena walked hand in hand, their heads bowed in hushed conversation. Heather had so many reasons to be jealous of Elena – who was a hundred times the musician Heather could ever hope to be – but Radcliffe's attention was not one of them. Ivan's hand on Elena's shoulder trembled with rage as he led her to their room, the door slamming behind her. I thought about following Ivan, trying to calm the rage that had already threatened to unleash itself tonight, but I was in no state to be a good friend. Besides, he had Elena, and that was all that mattered. For now.

Faye slipped out after the performance. Madame flashed me a satisfied smile that felt like something slimy crawling up my spine, and I knew that old witch had something planned, something she hadn't told me. I didn't like not knowing shit, especially when Madame Usher was involved.

But I couldn't just warn Faye, not without risking everything. I couldn't speak to her, and she despised me, which was exactly what Madame Usher wanted. I needed to *think*. I needed to know why he hadn't fucking messaged me in two weeks. I needed the silence to stop so I could figure out my next move on this fucked-up chessboard with enemies on all sides—

"Dorien," Heather's shrill voice pierced my thoughts. "You're not listening to me."

"Not one bit," I growled.

She leaned against me, rubbing her cheek against my shoulder and staring up at me with heavy-lidded eyes. I'd seen the look on hundreds of girls – in the front row of concert halls in Milan, in the lineups of Amsterdam whorehouses, in Clare's deep brown irises. "Come up to my room, and I'll find ways of taking your mind off Elena. I stole a bottle of port from Madame's stash. We could drink it together and—"

"No." I kicked open the door to the kitchen, and rushed through to the back door and out into the night.

Rain droplets splattered my face and clothes, but I didn't give a fuck. I needed air. Inside the house, I felt like I was choking on the lies and the shit and Faye's goddamn intoxicating scent.

I walked to the back of the garden, following the overgrown path toward the gazebo. The storm had eased off, though a bitter wind still tore at my exposed flesh and the rain splashed into puddles between the gnarled tree roots. My fingers fumbled in my pocket. I tugged out my phone and tapped the screen, cupping my hand against it to protect it from the rain. No messages.

Don't panic. He said he'd text when he could. Just because you haven't heard from him doesn't mean he's in trouble.

I scrolled back to his last text, my eyes flicking over the words even though I knew them by heart.

Father Aaron took my shoes today.

Six words. Six measly fucking words. I scuffed the ground, my sock squelching where the water had soaked through. The wind whipped my hair across my face, flogging the strands against my skin – a self-flagellation that didn't feel nearly perverse enough. Even though it was still technically summer, the mountains could be unforgiving.

Over the roar of the rain, I caught the wafting notes of a violin. I glanced back at the house, but no one should be playing now. We had a strict curfew – no music after 10PM. It was almost midnight, and Solokov would be sleeping over in one of the guest rooms. No one would dare risk Madame's wrath.

Someone clearly didn't give a fuck about Madame's rules, and I had a feeling I knew exactly who that would be.

I followed the mournful notes down the path to the gazebo. I didn't recognize the melody, but I didn't have to for it to fill my chest and wrap around my heart. The melody had an ethereal quality to it, as though the music came from another place entirely – every note an invitation to fall through a hole and end up in some strange and forgotten fae realm.

A shadowed figure stood under the ruined structure, and I knew even before they came into focus who it would be. No other musician could make me step outside myself the way she could.

Faye turned in a slow circle, her eyes closed as she drew the bow over the strings. I'd heard flashes of the piece she played through the walls when she practiced, but here with the rawness of nature raging around her, she wove magic into the very air. Her fingers flew with ease over the arpeggios, and her bow made light work of the spiccato. The music lifted through the storm, bringing hope and light and beauty to this place of darkness. Her damp hair clung to the curve of her back, and I almost expected wings to sprout from between her shoulders or a sprite to peek out from behind her ear.

I drew forward, mesmerized, not noticing where I stood until my foot caught on a loose stone, kicking it into the side of the gazebo.

Faye's eyes flew open. The bow squeaked on the strings. The music stopped, and the spell that drew me to her broke. She glared at me and jabbed her bow toward the house.

"Go away."

"It's a free garden." I stepped closer. The moonlight played off her raven hair. She must have come outside when it was still raining heavily, because she had mud splattered up her legs and her dress was soaked through, the fabric clinging to her skin, revealing every curve of that fucking gorgeous body.

"You talking to me now?"

I let a slow smirk play across my lips. Even with that defiant flame in her eyes, she still couldn't resist rising to my challenge. "You're playing out in the rain when there's a perfectly good bed inside. Consider me intrigued."

"I don't have to explain myself to you, Dorien." Faye shook her head, and a sadness flickered in her eyes that reminded me so much of his desperation that I had to look away to catch my breath. When I turned back to her, that sadness had disappeared. "Why are you doing this? We haven't seen each other for ten years. I stayed away from you, just like you wanted. It's not my fault we ended up at the same school. So why are you so determined to make me leave? You of all people should know I don't fucking bend to anyone's will."

I never wanted you to stay away.

The thought tasted bitter. Or maybe that was just the decade of resentment that bubbled inside me. Because Faye was lying – she didn't bend to anyone's will, except mine. I told her to leave me, and she left me. And I hated her for it, but not as much as I hated myself.

That decision was supposed to hurt for only a moment. I was supposed to lock up my heart so I could forget Faye, so I would never again feel the sting as her heart broke in front of me, as tears drowned out the fire in her eyes. I told myself it had worked for ten years, as I wandered the earth a ghost of a person, an empty box without a key. But now the decision that cost me my only true friend threatened to destroy someone else I loved, and Faye had stormed back into my life and blown the box to smithereens.

Fourteen days and no text. He has to know I'd be going fucking crazy.

I closed the space between us in three strides. Faye yelped in surprise as my fingers circled her wrist, pulling her close so our bodies pressed together, chest to chest. Her heart danced a wild rhythm through the thin fabric of her sodden dress, matching the violence of my own. Red lips parted, and the urge... the urge overwhelmed me... to slip my tongue between them, to tease out the sorcery inside, to drink and drink of her until I burst with her magic.

But those six words ran around and around in my head, blurring together until they lost all meaning. Until I knew only one thing – that I had someone else to protect, someone who needed me more than I'd convinced myself I needed Faye.

Hurting her should come naturally to you. After all, you did it once before.

"Little hint." My fingers tightened around Faye's arm. She whimpered, but it wasn't a sound of fear. I strained through my desire, searching for a threat. "If you want to survive the next year, you should walk out the gates now and never come back. If you stay, I'll destroy you. That is my solemn promise."

My body buzzed with the urge to flip Faye over, to lift up that sexy skirt of hers, bend her over the railing, and enter her. How many times over the years had I wondered how she'd feel, the girl I let go – how hot and slick and inviting, how she'd push back against my cock and throw back her head and howl at the moon like the wild woman she was. I growled, low in my throat, and the sound was meant to scare her, but it sent a tremble of desire through her body that echoed in my own. Could she feel my cock hard against her thigh?

Fuck. Fuck. I'm in deep shit.

"Why are you trying to frighten me?" Faye whispered, glaring back at me with defiance, with triumph, as a prickle of unease jolted across my shoulders. The air around us shifted, disturbed by some foriegn presence. I wanted to look behind me, but I didn't dare break our gaze. "I'll never be afraid of you. I've seen real horrors, Dorien. I've lived through pain you could only imagine, and trying to keep me from my mother is not going to break me. To me, you're nothing but a scared little boy."

"You think you know me?" I growled. "You think you have a monopoly on pain? You're about to find out just how little you know. That boy you remember died a long time ago, and the man he grew into is callous and dangerous. I'll stop at nothing to get what I want, and what I want is for you to *leave*."

Faye smirked. "Funny. I could have sworn you were after something else when you grabbed me."

I threw her arm from me, sending her reeling across the gazebo. She yelped in surprise, but I couldn't hear it. I had to shut myself off to everything she was, everything she could be. I struggled to control my breathing as I rasped my parting words. "This is your last warning. Poor little Sprite. You're trapped in the spider's web, and you don't even know it. Leave Manderley forever, or you'll be the next ghost to haunt these walls."

FAYE

Still shaking from my encounter with Dorien on top of missing my visit with Mom and finding my father's book, I slammed the attic door and flopped down on the bed, kicking off my shoes. Going outside was a mistake, that was obvious. I'd spent a good hour being pummeled by the rain as I stomped around in the garden bed under the window, looking for signs someone had been there. But the only footprints were my own.

I should have gone to bed then, but as I tiptoed through the hall in my damp clothes with the fairy tale book under my arm, I could still hear the others in the Blue Room – Elena's tinkling laugh and Titus' booming voice regaling the group with stories from the last Broken Muse tour. I hadn't thought. I didn't even pause to change my clothes. I dumped the book beside my bed, grabbed my violin, and rushed out into the biting wind.

I just needed to *play*. Somewhere away from *them*. Maybe the wind would carry the notes to my mother. As soon as I struck the bow to the strings, I felt better. I closed my eyes and transported myself far from Manderley, to a different time and place, when Mom and I were happy and the future looked bright.

Dorien just *had* to find me and ruin it.

I shook myself, like a dog drying himself after rolling in a puddle, and threw myself down on my bed. I wished I could shake off the trembling in my fingers that had nothing to do with the cold. Heat pooled in my chest and other places I didn't want to think about.

When Dorien held me, his lips dangerously close, his stiff cock pressing against my thigh, how close had I come to leaning in to kiss him, to taste the cruel words flowing from his lips like honey?

"Cockpoodles," I muttered into my pillow. *This whole night is completely fucked up.*

I flipped myself over, turning on the lamp and pulling the book across the bed to rest on my knees. I pinched the familiar pages between my fingers, staring at those words scrawled across the frontispiece until they ceased to make sense. It *was* my father's book. *My book.* The grief from losing him came in waves of rage and despair, each powerful and uncontrollable. I'd tossed it away during one of the rages. So how had it ended up at Manderley?

And why did someone *want* me to find it?

FAYE

On Saturday a week after Solokov's visit, Madame Usher announced over lunch that he'd been so impressed he invited Elena to perform in Moscow over the winter break. I tried to smile, but it came out as a grimace. Across the table, I noticed Dorien's eyes were stormy even as he joined the applause.

Elena's pale skin glowed with joy, and the faintest smile tugged at the corner of her mouth. She turned to Master Radcliffe. "What about Ivan?"

"This will be a solo opportunity, Elena," Master Radcliffe replied in his friendly voice. "Don't be concerned. I'll accompany you to Moscow to ensure you're settled and see your early performances."

The smile slipped from her lips. Ivan reached across and squeezed her hand. Elena shook her head. "I can't go without Ivan. I *won't*."

Tension crackled across the table, although I couldn't understand why. My gaze fell on Ivan's face – his eyes shards of sharpened stone, ready to cut the Master down.

"You're going, and that's the final word on the matter." Madame Usher glared at the twins. "You need to grow up sometime. *Both* of you."

Nothing more was said about Moscow, or anything else. Lunch finished in stony silence, Ivan piercing each person at the table with an icy glare. As I stacked the dishwasher and wrapped up the rest of the roast beef to make into sandwiches, Harrison walked into the kitchen carrying an armload of wood.

"I brought up fresh supplies. The forecast is for another storm to hit this week. Will we be visiting your mother this afternoon?"

"Hell yes." I slammed the fridge door and wiped my hands on my apron. "I can leave right now. I'll just need to run upstairs and grab my violin."

"Good. I'll meet you around the front in the limo. If you see Dorien, tell him I'm waiting."

"Dorien's going to be with us?"

Harrison's face darkened. "I don't like it, either, but his family lives near the hospital and it makes sense for us all to drive together."

I sighed. Obviously, saving the environment and all that. "I know why I don't like him, but what's your beef?"

"He was the one dating Clare when she had her accident."

My hand flew to my mouth. *Dorien?* I knew what Harrison suspected, could hear the accusation dripping from his words. I'd seen the cruelty in Dorien's eyes directed at me, but I couldn't believe the Dorien I knew would kill a girl.

But did I know him still? Dorien had more secrets than a heart-shaped box. Plus, he had tormented me since the moment I arrived, and once upon a time he cared about me. If this Clare crossed him, what would he do to her?

I slunk out of the kitchen and headed for the stairs. As I ascended, my gaze fell to that empty square on the wall where the portrait used to be. It hadn't come back from the cleaners yet. I wondered why Madame Usher, usually such a stickler for everything in its proper place, hadn't gone postal with them yet about its late return. *Maybe she reserves all her ire for her staff.*

I reached the first story landing and turned toward Dorien's room. He was already leaning against his door wearing a black t-shirt that clung tight across his shoulders over black jeans and combat boots. A leather jacket slung over his shoulder crackled as he moved. Curls of dark hair flopped over his eyes as he frowned down at his phone, running his fingers over the edge of his stubbled jaw. So effortlessly sexy – too bad he was such a fucktrumpet.

When he heard me coming, Dorien shoved the phone in his pocket, as if he were hiding some kind of national secret.

"Harrison's just bringing the car around front, so meet him there." I jabbed a finger at the staircase.

Dorien didn't acknowledge me. Fuck, I hated this ghosting thing, especially after what happened in the gazebo. I spun on my heel and stalked up the narrow attic stairs to my room.

I grabbed my purse and violin case and took the stairs back down two at a time, too on edge to care if I slipped and broke my neck. I missed Mom so much. If she'd been awake and coherent, she'd have advice on how to handle Manderley and Broken Muse. I could just imagine her with a cappuccino in her hands, sloshing hot coffee everywhere as she gesticulated wildly, regaling me with a tale of how she won over some difficult executives with her wit and acumen.

When I slid into the limo, Dorien was already inside, staring at his phone screen with a foul expression. I sat near the front, beside the bar, and rapped on the glass. Just because Dorien wouldn't talk to me the whole trip didn't mean that I had to endure his silence.

"Hey Harrison, you ever use the sound system on this thing?"

Harrison flicked on the radio knob, and a loud burst of static blasted through the speakers. "No reception until we get closer to town."

"No problem." I pushed the button on my phone to sync the Bluetooth, then hit my finger on the perfect playlist – the upbeat pop songs Mom loved to play while she cooked or pottered around the house.

Lady Gaga's voice blasted out the stereo. I sat back and sang along at the top of my lungs. I kept one eye on Dorien, who didn't lift his eyes from his phone.

Ten minutes down the road and three pop songs later, a vein was throbbing in Dorien's head. I flipped through my music list, choosing song after song I knew would drive him crazy. I put on 'Achy Breaky Heart' and Harrison belted out the words, his voice a wonderful rumbling tenor.

I kept up a stream of 80s hits – my mom's favorite music – and was having so much fun I barely noticed the drive go by. Harrison turned down a narrow country road. A high stone fence ran alongside the ditch, barbed wire curling around the top. Dorien stared out the window, still as a statue. The mood in the car turned frosty, and not even Prince's greatest hits could thaw it out.

Harrison pulled up outside a high iron gate – the only break in the stone wall for miles. Through the narrow bars I could just make out a crumbling driveway curving off into the trees, and a giant pile of garbage stacked beside the gate. Signs along the wall read KEEP OUT and NO TRESPASSING. A gabled roof peeked through the tops of the trees, like some kind of medieval fortress. "What are we doing here?" I asked. *This is a weird place to be running errands.*

Dorien had already flung open the rear door and clambered out. "Thanks." He nodded to Harrison. "I'll see you back here at 4PM."

Harrison nodded, tearing away from the gate so fast the back wheels spun out. I pressed my face against the back window, watching the gates swing open to admit Dorien. His black-clad body faded into the distance as we sped away.

"What was that?" I slid back across the leather seat and grabbed a bottle of apple juice from the bar.

"That's the Valencourt estate." Harrison gripped the wheel so hard his knuckles turned white. "I don't like to stick around. It gives me the heebie-jeebies."

"An accurate description." I studied the high stone wall and barbed wire as we careened around the first corner. I visited Dorien's home in New York City that one time, and it had been the usual decadent mansion of the elite. I'd pictured their country estate as rolling lawns and stables, not... whatever this was. "It looks more like a prison."

"Mmmmm. Dorien's parents haven't been seen in public for ten years. There are all sorts of strange rumors about the place."

I waited for Harrison to elaborate, but he didn't. We drove into the city, and Harrison dropped me outside the hospital. It took me a bit to get my bearings and find the correct ward, but finally, I stood outside a room with a DE WINTER nameplate on the door.

"Hey, Mom. How're things?" I slid into the chair beside her bed. No hard plastic here. The room was a bit like a 4-star hotel room if you squinted hard and ignored the hospital bed and the beeping machinery keeping my mother alive. "I'm sorry I couldn't come last week. I missed you."

I touched her hand, steeling myself against the warmth in her fingers. I always expected her to feel cold, lifeless, because of the way she looked. But that warmth gave me hope, and that hope kept me glued to her, paying the mounting hospital costs week after week.

Seven weeks she'd been in a coma. Her prognosis was slim because her kidneys were failing, and they didn't even know what was wrong with her. But I couldn't bear the thought of my vibrant, boisterous, forgetful mother gone from the world. And so I hung on, long after I should, but I couldn't quench the flame of hope that burned inside me.

"Are you Mrs. Usher?"

I whirled around at the voice. A youngish doctor stood in the doorway, her mouth set in a line born of late nights and grim results. I burst out laughing.

"I haven't been cast out from a gothic horror story, so nope, not me."

"Sorry." She glanced at the tablet in her hand, a strand of lank strawberry-blonde hair falling out of her bun and dangling over her face. "I have an Usher on file as admitting her, along with a man named Harrison. No one else has visited her since she arrived. I'm Doctor Henrietta Nelson, and I'm assuming you're the daughter, Faye?"

"That's me."

"I was going to call Mrs. Usher at the end of my shift, but since you're here now, I can tell you. We've had some test results back that have shed light on what happened. It appears your mother was poisoned."

FAYE

"Poisoned?"

Dr. Nelson nodded. "At this time, we can't assume it was deliberate – that's for the police to decide."

"The police? Are you saying it's..." I couldn't force the word *murder* from my lips. That word didn't belong in any sentence associated with my mother.

"There are two ways poison can cause damage in the body. One is by taking a large dose all at once. The other is when a patient ingests a small amount of a poison over a long period – each individual dose isn't enough to do any harm, and in some cases isn't even detectable on tests, but over time it builds up in the body until one day..." she looked down at my mother with concern.

"You think that's what happened here?"

She nodded. "We call it chronic poisoning – it was a common way poisoners administered arsenic during the 19th century, but we don't see it often in a modern hospital as people will usually go to their doctor with symptoms before it reaches this stage. This isn't arsenic, though – it's not something we've ever seen before, which is why your mother's doctors couldn't help her before now. I'll know more once our lab identifies the poison, which they're working on now as their top priority. The most likely culprit is some kind of unregulated supplement or non-traditional medicine. Was your mother eating or drinking anything outside of her usual diet, something those around her weren't partaking of?"

I squeezed my eyes shut, trying to remember. "She used to have these special herbal teas. Her assistant would order them in bulk and make one for her each morning. Mom said they helped her memory and cognitive skills, but they tasted so bitter and gross I never wanted to drink them."

"Would you have access to any of these teas? If they're the source, it would help us identify the poison."

"I doubt it." The teas had probably been thrown out when the office was cleared out by the liquidators. "But I can check."

Poisoned.

Dr. Nelson must've seen the horror on my face, for she stepped into the room and placed her hand over mine. Her stoic features crumpled into something like a smile. "I know this is hard to hear, but it might be good news. If we can find the source of the poison, there may be a way to create an antidote. Some of your mother's internal systems have been damaged, but the coma has halted the breakdown of her organs. I don't want to get your hopes up until we know what we're dealing with, but there is still hope to cling to here – more hope than most."

I nodded. My fingers closed around my mother's, squeezing as hard as I dared. "Okay. Thank you."

"Don't thank me yet." She stepped back, rearranging her face back into her practical mask. "I'll do everything I can for her. But Faye, you need to speak with the police and find out anything you can about this tea. If that's the source of the poison, it needs to be pulled off the market immediately. We deal with a number of cases of health complications from people taking herbal remedies made with dangerous ingredients. Wellness is big business, but so many of those products are untested. If we could save other lives..."

My other hand curled into a fist. "Don't worry – I'm not letting them get away with this."

Dr. Nelson left, and I pulled out my violin. I usually played *Nigun* for my mother, but today, I was too on edge from the news to do that piece justice. Instead, I launched into Paganini's Caprice No. 5, filling the room with brashness and light and fury as my thoughts whirled around me.

Poisoned.

My head spun. It didn't make sense. It was something out of a bad murder mystery. Dr. Nelson seemed to believe it might be the fault of an unscrupulous herbal tea company, but there was another option. One I didn't like to consider, but had to.

Someone could have laced my mother's tea with poison. My first thought was her assistant, Natalie, who made the tea and who had long coveted a larger role in the company, but it could have been anyone with access to the storage room where the tea was kept.

But why would someone want to poison my mother?

~

The police came by later that day, and I gave them my statement and a list of names of people I remembered working at Mom's company, as well as a description of the tea and its packaging. They took another statement from Dr. Nelson, then left me alone to play for Mom again.

Next thing I knew, Harrison rang to say he was downstairs. I packed away my violin and kissed her warm cheek. In the hallway, Dr. Nelson strode past, clipboard in hand. "Thank you," I called out to her. "This is the first time in two years we've had anything like an answer."

"I'll call you if we learn anything else." She patted my shoulder. "You play beautifully, by the way. Next time you visit, do you think you'd be interested in playing for some of our other patients? There's not much to cheer them up around here – I think they'd love to hear beautiful music."

"I'd love to."

Outside, Harrison had parked in a pick-up zone right outside the doors. I slid into the backseat and gave a start as Dorien's features came into view, emerging from the darkest corner of the limo. Seeing that smirk twisting across his lips and knowing my mother lay upstairs with poison in her veins tore me up inside. I couldn't deal with any of his shit today.

"I finished with my chores early," Harrison explained. "I even picked up a new lock for your room, which I'll install as soon as we get back. I decided to swing out and pick Dorien up first, to give you a little more time with your mother."

I nodded, a lump forming in my throat. I wanted to thank Harrison, but if I opened my mouth, I'd burst into tears, and I refused to cry in front of Dorien.

"Would you like your music on again?" Harrison asked as we pulled out of the parking lot.

"No thanks." I sunk back into my seat, my mind still reeling from Dr. Nelson's news and the statement I'd just given to the police.

Across from me, Dorien's eyes flicked to mine, their deviant depths plunging into me, trying to draw out my secrets. "What's got your tongue?"

I ignored him.

Dorien leaned forward, clasping his hands together and resting his elbows on his open knees, giving me this tantalizing glimpse of his toned thighs, of the buttons on his crotch tugging at their seams. Those eyes swept over me, and for a moment I was back in the practice room at Madame Usher's New York City school, with Dorien grinning wickedly at me from behind the piano.

Back when things were simple.

I shook my head. He wasn't getting his hands on this secret. He already knew too much about me, had too tight a grip on my heart. But Dorien never took no for an answer. His eyes tugged at mine. In their fathomless depths stirred all sorts of depraved and deviant things, all the rumors and stories of his exploits, all the promise of what I might feel in his expert hands. I could forget myself in Dorien's eyes, and I had to be careful because right now that thought was way too tempting.

"You're upset." His words burned my skin like fire. It wasn't a question. "Is it your mom?"

"You don't care."

"Faye…" The way his mouth lifted up at the edges as he spoke my name, and how his eyes revealed the deviant thoughts he kept for his own amusement… *fuck.* I'd tell him all my darkest secrets if that look was really for me.

"I'll tell you about my mom if you tell me why your house is surrounded in barbed wire," I shot back.

Just like that, his eyes turned to stone. Dorien leaned back, folding his arms over his chest, walling himself up in a private prison. And although I was grateful for the space from him, part of me longed for him to break through what bound him and tell me what he was hiding, so that I could break too, and share the pain I carried by myself for so long.

But it was not to be. We drove the entire way back to Manderley in stony silence, regarding each other with wariness from opposite ends of the limo while Harrison's warning played over in my head.

Who are you, Dorien Valencourt? What do you have to hide?

FAYE

My days at Manderley faded into each other – one lonely hour after the next. The students continued to ignore me. At mealtimes they'd talk around me, filling the room with news of their upcoming recitals and visits with friends. Most nights one of them would shuffle around in the storage room to keep me awake. I bet they took turns – they always emerged for breakfast so well rested, whereas I looked like a crack panda 24/7.

That didn't bother me so much. At least, I told myself it didn't bother me.

My new humiliation was ensemble work, where everyone had to go off in groups to work on concertos. The twins were inseparable, and Ivan's sapphire shards made it clear he'd stab me if I got close to his sister. Aroha and Titus had a definite flirtatious thing going – a jealous seethe ached in my belly at the idea of being stuck in that sandwich – and Heather seemed permanently attached to Dorien's hip. I left the room whenever they played together. I told myself it was because it was such a shame to see Dorien's talent dragged down by Heather, the succubus who sucked the life out of every piece of music she played. But really it was the jealousy again.

Which was fucking ridiculous, because it wasn't like any of the Muses wanted to pluck my strings. But it was more that I wanted them to see me as an equal, as someone worthy to share their spotlight. It was like being picked last for teams in gym class, only a hundred times worse because unlike gym, I was actually *fucking good*.

At the violin, maybe not the sex. I'd only done *that* once before. Not that I wanted to get vertical with any of the guys. I had no desire to have Ivan's cold eyes locked on mine, or feel Titus' enormous hands on the small of my back, or feel Dorien's cock...

Nope. *Not at all.*

It was a moot point since none of them would talk to me. The only people who so much as uttered a word in my direction were Master Radcliffe, during our lessons, and Madame Usher, to snap at me for some perceived infraction.

Still, I had the music. I filled my head with Master Radcliffe's knowledge. The hours I got to spend alone with my violin lifted my spirit. But what surprised me was how much I'd started to enjoy composition. For the last two years I'd done nothing but work dead-end jobs, try to get my schoolwork done, and sleep in that cursed plastic chair while Mom underwent tests. Being able to learn something for the sheer pleasure of it lit a flame inside me I thought had been extinguished forever.

One evening after returning from another visit to my mother (no change, no results from the lab yet), I was in the kitchen, planning menus for the following week and chopping and roasting a bunch of vegetables I could use over the next few days. I figured out that if I took each Monday as a prep-night, I'd be able to get most of the food cooked, giving me more time during the week to practice.

While I stood at the stove, caramelizing onions, I noticed a figure dart from the porch toward the trees. *Aroha*. Without thinking, I switched off the stove, flung my hoodie over my shoulders, and headed after her.

I cut through the walled garden and emerged on the overgrown path leading down through the trees. Moonlight glinted off Aroha's leather jacket as she picked her way around the ruined gazebo and continued deeper into the forest. I followed, wondering if I was making a huge mistake. *This is how girls in horror films get stabbed or exsanguinated or eaten alive...*

The path emerged into a small clearing. It might once have been beautiful – a ring of trees surrounding a domed glasshouse. But neglect had wreathed the structure in weeds, had broken several glass panes, and had given the plants inside a life of their own. They overgrew their pots with such vivacity they tangled together into an impenetrable mess that spilled out through every available crack and cranny, trailing vines and delicate floral tendrils across the forest floor. Aroha sat on an upturned terracotta pot, wreathed in the shade of some strange plant with weird, elongated leaves. A cigarette dangled from her lips.

"Piss off, trash," she muttered when she saw me, but the words had no venom.

I shifted my weight from foot to foot. Aroha had spoken to me, of her own accord. Sure, it might have been to insult me, but it showed one thing – Aroha didn't conform to the rules Dorien had put in place. Foolish hope surged in my chest, the kind of hope borne of loneliness and desperation.

I lifted an eyebrow. "Can I bum a smoke?"

Aroha shrugged. I took that as an invitation. I grabbed another pot and upturned it, plonking down on the damp surface beside her. I picked up the cigarette box gingerly, expecting her to snatch it from my hands. She stared at the box as if she was debating it, then shrugged again. I tipped a cigarette from the packet and brought it to my lips. I didn't really smoke – I tried it a few times at my shitty school in an attempt to fit in. It turns out smoking doesn't make dorky music geeks cool unless you looked like Dorien Valencourt. Who would have guessed? Sometimes I shared one with the other staff after a late shift at the bar – Creepy Cory couldn't be around cigarette smoke because of his asthma, so it gave me a break from his lewd comments about my body.

Silence stretched between us.

"You come out here a lot?" I asked.

"If you'd said you wanted to talk, I wouldn't have given you a ciggie," Aroha snapped without looking at me.

My turn to shrug. "Fine."

I took a long drag of the cigarette, letting the smoke fill my lungs. A calmness swept over my body. This almost felt normal.

"I come out here because sometimes I can't stand it in that house," Aroha said, tapping her diamond ring against the terracotta. "All that fancy furniture. All those dead eyes staring at you from the walls. It feels like a time capsule or a dead person's house after they've passed on. I like being out here where things are living, reclaiming the edges of the estate. It reminds me of home."

"Where's home?" I asked, daring to continue the conversation. Loneliness ached inside me. I didn't realize how much I'd missed just interacting with another person, just how much I longed for my mother's boisterous laugh. Aroha reminded me of her in some ways.

"New Zealand. My parents run a church. We used to live right on the edge of a mountain range called the Waitakeres. I spent my childhood climbing trees, shooting rabbits, catching eels in the creek. Then Dad decided to become a preacher and we moved to the city, and then they shipped me off here." She sounded bitter about it, but that might have been her reluctance to talk to me.

Ah, her accent made perfect sense now. "Do you miss New Zealand? It must've been interesting to grow up there."

She shrugged. "It's normal, I guess. There aren't exactly wild hobbits running around everywhere like most Americans assume. My family is Maori – the indigenous people of Aotearoa, New Zealand. We used to live on our marae – that's like a meeting house for our community. I was practically raised by my aunts and cousins. There was always music and laughter and games. My parents gave up a lot when they moved to the city, and the city didn't always accept them in return. It's the Pākehā world."

"Pākehā?"

"White people." She elbowed me in the arm. "They sent me to a Catholic boarding school, all prim and proper and white as fuck. There were no traditional instruments, so I learned violin instead."

"But you love the music." Aroha adored atonal pieces, which she played with a loose aggression.

"Of course. But more than that, I love being a brown girl in a fucking white musician's world." She grinned. "Just you wait, trash. As soon as I get out of here, I'm gonna use this upstanding Classical education to bring my musical heritage into the spotlight. I've got plans, so don't you fuck them up for me by letting on that I tolerate your presence."

"How would that mess up your plans?"

"We're not supposed to talk to you. Dorien's orders. Usually, I don't give a fuck what anyone says, and you seem harmless, but the Broken Muse boys seem particularly keen to get you out of here, and they're a direct line to Madame Usher. I need her to like me or I won't graduate." A darkness passed over Aroha's eyes, but it was gone in a moment.

I leaned forward, dangling my cigarette between my fingers, my heart thumping. She knew something. "You think if you don't do what Dorien asks, he'll influence Madame Usher?" *Would he really mess with someone's entire career like that?*

Aroha shrugged. "Have you met Dorien? Dude is hot as sin, but he's got crazy serial killer eyes."

"Were you here when Clare... fell down the stairs?" I remembered just in time that I shouldn't reveal Harrison's suspicions to anyone, least of all a fellow student.

"Yup." She shuddered at the memory. I reached behind me, curious about the strange plant poking out from a crack in the glass. "All of us were in the house except the twins, who were at a recital. Clare was a bit cray-cray, sooooo obsessed with Dorien, but he— don't touch that!"

Aroha slapped my hand. Hard. The sting arced across my palm. I rubbed at the spot. "What was that for?"

"That's monkshood. It's highly poisonous. If you get the sap on your skin, it's bad news."

"How do you know?"

Aroha gestured to the greenhouse. "Duh. This whole place is a poison garden."

"A... what?"

"It's a Victorian curiosity. Apparently, one of the Usher ancestors fancied himself a botanist. He collected all these different poison plants from all over the world and grew them inside the greenhouse. He did lots of experiments and made some important scientific discoveries. Madame Usher warned us all not to go inside – apparently, some of the plants are so toxic you only have to brush past them to fall over and die. Look."

She pointed to a rotting wood panel above the shuttered door. I peered at it, unsure of what she was referring to, when carved letters came into view. A phrase in Latin: *In cauda venenum.*

The same phrase tattooed across Dorien's chest.

My mouth dried. "Do you know what it means?"

She snorted. "Right. Like I have time to study Latin."

Fuck. *Fuck.*

My mind whirred with impossible thoughts. Like why Dorien would have the same tattoo as a poison garden, and how I happened to find that out right after I learned my mother was poisoned. A vision of a crumpled body at the bottom of the stairs flashed in my mind again.

No, it's impossible.

Aroha must've seen something in my face because her expression softened.

"Look, Dorien's not *actually* a serial killer. He's just a cocky shit. A fucking gorgeous one, but a shit all the same."

I grinned. "The word is dickweasel."

Aroha tossed her head back and laughed. "You're all right, trash. Come bum a smoke from me any time."

"But you won't speak to me inside the house?"

"Hell no. I'm not incurring their wrath. It's not just Dorien you've gotta watch out for – Titus and Ivan are no angels. Little word of advice, trash. Everyone at Manderley is running from something. The Muses make it their business to discover what that something is, and then they'll use it to twist you to their will. Hold your secrets close. Don't let them into your head, or they'll tear your heart out while it's still beating. That's what they did to Clare." She stood up, grinding her cigarette butt into the dirt with the heel of her boot. "We should head back."

As we walked back along the path, my eyes scanned Manderley's facade. From this angle, the house appeared even larger and more foreboding – straight out of a Bram Stoker novel, especially given the number of sexy Romanians wandering its halls. I felt a tiny glimmer of peace when my eyes landed on the window of my room. It had been my little square of sanctuary since Harrison changed the lock. I'd left the light on because the bulb at the top of the steps blew. I could just make out the outline of the edge of my clothing rack and—

I gasped.

There in the window, staring down at us through the glass, was the outline of a face.

FAYE

"Shit." I surged forward, crashing into Aroha. She wobbled in her high boots, throwing her arm out against a tree trunk to stop herself from falling over. "What the fuck, trash?"

"Do you see it?" I jabbed a finger at the attic window.

"See what?"

"That face in my bedroom. It was looking right at us—" The face had gone.

"I don't see anything— hey, where are you going?"

I took off at a run toward the house, my heart pounding in my chest. *Oh, no you don't.*

There was only one staircase up to the attic. If I could get there fast enough, I'd be able to see who came down. I threw open the kitchen door. It slammed shut behind me as I barreled through the kitchen, taking the shortcut through the servants' corridor to the main entrance hall. As I took the stairs two at a time, Heather's tinkling laugh floated up from the Blue Room, and the unmistakable flutter of notes that could have only been Elena. So it wasn't either of them – no way would they have been fast enough to get to those rooms without me seeing or hearing them.

I reached the second landing and glanced around. None of the bedrooms were open, and no one stood around in the hall. *Maybe they're still up there, trying to hide.* I jangled the keyring in my pocket. They weren't getting away this time.

"I know you're up there," I called, trying to keep my voice steady as I took the steps two at a time. On the top landing, I paused, my ears prickling. All was silent.

Too silent.

My heart plummeted in my chest as I realized there was no light shining through the crack under my door. I shoved my key into the brand new lock and slowly, cautiously, pushed it open.

The light in my room had been turned off.

100 STEFFANIE HOLMES

The light in my room had been turned off.

FAYE

S_hit._

I flicked the light on, stepping boldly into the room even though my heart hammered against my chest. "All right, you can come out now."

My eyes swept over my furniture. Had I left the books like that? Was my underwear drawer supposed to be half-open? What about that dent in the bed? Everything felt tainted, befouled, because I _knew_ someone had been in here.

How did they get in? How could they have a key to my new lock?

I looked into every dark corner and in every conceivable hiding place, my ears pricked for the sound of someone fleeing back down the stairs. But there was nothing. The room was empty.

Of course, they wouldn't hide in here. They must be in the storage room. They know I don't have a key.

I held up my phone's flashlight to the storage room's large keyhole and tried to peer inside, but it was so dark all I could see was the pale silhouette of the moon through the window behind slacks of boxes and old furniture. If they were still inside, they weren't moving.

"I know you're in there." I hit the door with my fists. "Show yourself."

The fear tightening my chest turned to anger. _This is ridiculous. They're not in here. They must have slipped down while I was in my room. They're probably great at sneaking for all the nights they climb up here without me catching them. In fact, this is an old house – there's probably a secret passage or something. There's always a secret passage in the movies._

I turned on my heel and stormed downstairs. I stormed toward Dorien's door, but his voice floated up from the Blue Room below. _It can't be him, then. But I know who it has to be._

I grabbed the handle of Titus' room and turned, expecting it to be locked. The door flung open, and I stumbled through it, my foot catching on the edge of the rug and sending me spinning. My knee cracked against a metal bed-frame, and my hands skimmed something large and warm as I struggled for balance.

Sheets rustled. "What the fuck?" Titus' face appeared over the side of the bed as I rolled over, my knee throbbing.

"Don't you 'what the fuck' me." I got to my feet with as much dignity as I could muster and leaned over the bed, hands on hips, legs wide, making myself bigger the way a cat fluffed up their fur before they went into battle with a pitbull. "You were in my room just now. And you sneak into the storage room at night. I *heard* you—"

I'd intended to threaten Titus with the police, with anything I could to get him to stop breaking into my room and stomping around in the storage room. Now that I was in here, and he stared up at me with tangled eyelashes and a pillow crease across his cheekbone, his sheet slipping down over his gloriously tattooed torso, the words dried on my throat.

Titus rubbed his eyes. He certainly *seemed* like he'd been asleep. But I hadn't imagined the face or the light going off in my room. And he admitted to being there once before.

Before I could find the words, Titus' hand shot out, circling my wrist. He rose up from between the sheets, revealing tattoos of snakes twining over his dark skin and abs that belonged on a bodybuilder. How did a dude get that toned playing cello? My fingers itched to touch Titus' skin, to drag my nails over those snakes, to watch them dance as he rolled on top of me and...

Titus leaned so close his breath kissed my lips. The air between us sizzled with tension. I didn't know what would happen next, what I *wanted* to happen next.

"I didn't go near your room." Mmmmm, his New Orleans accent came out thicker when he was tired.

"Yes, you did," I managed to choke out. "I was outside and I saw a face at the window. I was outside and I saw the light in my room, and when I got back it was turned off."

"Not me." Titus grabbed the chain around his neck and dangled it in front of my face. *A key.* The exact type of key that opened the old lock on my bedroom door. "This doesn't work no more. I haven't been upstairs since that first night, when I watched you drool on your pillow."

"Where did you get that?" I lunged for the key, but Titus held it beyond my reach.

"Clare gave Dorien a copy so he could sneak up in the night. I could hear the bed creaking from down here. Friendly warning – Dorien's got a real thing about shagging the help. Must be something about this tight black dress." Titus rubbed his finger down the inside of my arm, and even through the thick wool fabric it sent a fire through my body.

I knew I was rapidly losing control of the situation and myself, but the anger and violation still surged in my veins. *I must have that key.* It was a symbol of claiming back my space. I lunged again, taking Titus by surprise. As I reached for the key, my chest brushed his, sending a jolt through me like I'd stuck my nipple in an electrical socket. Titus felt it too, because his eyes narrowed, the lashes tangling together.

Titus didn't flinch away. Instead, he leaned in closer, his fingers dancing up my arm as I scrambled for the key. My breath came out in ragged gasps as I fought against my desire. His face hung inches from mine, so close his musk and myrrh swirled around me, and the notes of rose conjured a memory that seared my skin with pain. Roses sent to my mother's hospital room by her board members, back when she thought she'd be cured in a week, back before the coma and the poisoning and—

"You should stay away from me," Titus hissed. His deep voice reverberated through my entire body, bringing me back to myself, to the present moment, to the scant inch of air that was all that protected me from the most delicious mistake of my life.

"Or what?" I tried to issue it as a challenge, but the words came out husky, thick with desire.

"Or—" He chose to finish the thought with his eyes, the fire within them promising darkness and depravity and beautiful obsession. Tension crackled between us, a lightning storm flickering between our eyes. Why, *why* did I let Titus do this to me?

Titus' fingers walked over my wrist, trailing along the veins pulsing against my skin. The touch was featherlight, but it left a trail of fire against my skin that melted my insides into a wobbly mess. My breath hitched, and I dared myself to lean a little closer, a little... to feel the air shift as his lips brushed mine—

"Bro, you wouldn't believe—what the *fuck?*"

Dorien. His voice shattered the spell. I wrenched my arm from Titus' grip and turned to the doorway. Dorien stood in the hall, a storm in his grey eyes, tension tightening his shoulders to rock. Titus stared bug-eyed at his friend, his mouth moving but no sound emerging, while I staggered toward the door, shoving my way past Dorien.

Shame burned in my cheek as the fire in my veins cooled to ice. *What the fuck just happened? What am I doing? That guy openly admits to tormenting me, and I was about to... I wanted to...*

Sound the fucktrumpets, I want to shag my bullies.

TITUS

"What was that about?" Dorien demanded.

"She thinks I was in her room." I lifted my knees so Dorien didn't have to see the tent in the bedsheets. My veins throbbed with fire from Faye's presence. "You didn't go up there? Apparently, she was outside with Aroha and someone turned the light off in her bedroom."

"What's she doing outside with Aroha? Our no talking to the trash rule still applies." Dorien glared at me.

I shrugged. "You know Aroha likes to flaunt our rules."

"She's not the only one."

"So you weren't up there?"

Dorien shook his head. "No way to get in with that new lock Harrison installed."

I sank down on my bed, Faye's scent spinning me out. When she burst in, her hair wild around her face and that defiant look in her eyes, I was *so fucking close...*

The only thing that stopped me was Dorien. He was in the room, a ghost between us, before he appeared at the doorway.

"And the storage room? She seemed to think someone has been up there at night, moving around."

"Usher would never give up the key to that place, not even if it meant getting her out of here forever. Sprite probably heard rats or something. Why do you care?"

Sprite. Hearing that childhood nickname fly from his lips made my stomach twist up with envy. It could have just as easily been me who had a history with Faye, if my parents had sent me to a different New York school. I looked away so I wouldn't fall apart under Dorien's gaze. "I don't care. I just think it's a waste of energy to terrorize her. She's a shit musician and can't keep up with Madame's rules. She'll eliminate herself."

"What energy? The only thing you have to do is not talk to her, but apparently, that's too difficult. Heather and I are taking care of the rest." The petulant tone in Dorien's voice reminded me of the first time we met at a music camp in Colorado in our teens, and he complained to the staff because he didn't want to share a room with me. It was touch and go for a while as to whether we'd end up friends or bitter enemies, but Dorien had a magnetism that drew you in, and I was a kid desperate for anyone's approval. By the time that camp finished we were like an old married couple. The kind of married couple where Dorien was the alpha and I went along with everything he said.

"You made me go into her room with Heather. While she was asleep." A cold shudder ran through my body. I didn't like the way that made me feel – like a creepy stalker. That was why I told Faye, even though I disguised it as another part of her torture. She deserved to know the truth.

"It's fine. I won't ask you to do it again. From now on, consider yourself out of the loop."

I shook my head. "Don't be like that. I don't want to be out. I just..."

"*What?*" Dorien barked. He sounded pissed as fuck, but I knew what lurked beneath that annoyance was fear. I'd never seen Dorien afraid before, not the way he'd been since we returned to Manderley.

He's not the only one.

I rolled over, shoving my feet out of the bed and standing in front of him, bringing half the blankets with me. "I need to go to the woodshed."

"We're not done here."

"We're done." I dropped to my knees and reached under the bed, dragging a case out into the light.

Dorien stiffened when he saw what I was holding. "You shouldn't keep that in here. If *she* finds out—"

"What's the worst she can do to me?"

Dorien smirked at that. He picked up a black t-shirt from my bureau and tossed it at my chest. "True. But be careful, you're not the only one she has by the balls. I'm not sure I can protect you."

I straightened up, my eyes meeting his, and an unspoken message passed between us. People heard Dorien in concert and read about what he got up to in the tabloids and thought they knew him. They saw the bad boy, the deviant, the one making a mockery of serious classical music. But I saw something different – the only person who had my back even when I fucked up again and again. The guy who never told me I wasn't good enough. The friend who never put a price on his loyalty. "Thanks."

I pulled on the shirt and some jeans, and slipped down the stairs, wincing as I stepped on a loose board and a loud *CREAK* echoed in the dim house. Downstairs, I padded through the servant's hallway and across the kitchen. Faye's scent clung to every surface, hidden behind the wafting Mexican spices she used liberally in her cooking.

That scent did things to my head. I couldn't fucking *think*.

The case slapped against my leg as I stepped out into the frigid mountain air and hurried across the grass. Over the lawn, down the path, around the back of the woodshed to the locked door. I lied to Faye – Heather had the key to her old room. The one around my neck unlocked my secrets.

I unlocked the door and kicked it open, shuffling the heavy case inside and locking it behind me. I shone my phone's flashlight around until I found what I was looking for – the small generator I set up out here to give me light and power. I flicked it on, and the low rumble sent a shiver of anticipation through me.

I unlatched the case. It swung open. My secret stared back at me, beautiful and deadly.

Images and sensations swirled in my mind – Faye's face drawing toward me, those sexy lips parted ever so slightly, the feel of her skin shuddering beneath my touch – as I reached inside and drew it out.

DORIEN

Sunlight streamed through the high windows of the twelfth-floor studio, casting golden ripples across the cascade of Faye's hair. She faced away from me, out at the toy city far below, the violin against her neck as she slashed the strings with the bow in her signature overwrought style. Today she played a haunting Bach piece that grabbed my heart and squeezed, so tight. Or maybe that was the reality of what I was about to do.

Faye finished the movement with a low, trembling note, stepping back and bowing to her imaginary audience. I clapped, the noise like gunshots in the vast, empty space.

"Dorien." Faye whirled around. The grin on her face wavered when she saw my face. "What's the matter?"

"I came to say goodbye."

"What do you mean?" Her hair bounced on her shoulders. "You just got here. Class starts in fifteen minutes—"

"I mean, this is the last time we'll see each other. Mom's transferred me to another music school."

"No, that sucks." But her face brightened. "I know! I'll ask Mom to transfer me too. I can't stand Madame Usher, anyway. She doesn't seem to like me much. I think she only puts up with me because of Dad—"

I shook my head. She didn't get it.

Harden your heart.

"I don't want you to transfer. I'm leaving *because* of you. I don't want to see you again."

Faye's face froze in shock. "What is this? What do you mean? We're going to perform the Beethoven together and—"

"I don't want anything to do with you, Sprite."

Tears welled in the corners of her eyes. "Don't use that name when you're being horrible. Is this about me coming to your house last week? I'm sorry I pushed you into inviting me, but we had fun, didn't we? Dorien, please, explain this to me."

Please, please don't make this even harder.

"There's nothing to explain. I don't like you, Faye. I pretended to like you because my parents wanted me to get closer to your father. But it's not worth it anymore." I narrowed my eyes and conjured up the dark desires and seething hatred that burned inside me, and I threw them up between us like a Greek warrior raising his shield.

At the time I didn't entirely understand my action, but I did now. She had to see me as a bad person, as this selfish, self-centered asshole who wasn't worth her time. I had to give her all the ammo she needed to forget me.

It was the only way she'd be safe.

"Dorien, I..." Her words trailed off as the tears spilled over her eyes and rolled down her cheeks. Faye never cried, not even when Madame Usher yelled at her or her father went away on tour and forgot to call. I commanded my feet to move, to go to her so I could throw my arms around her and take her pain away. But I couldn't. Because I was the root of that pain, the cause of those tears.

"I don't understand." Faye slid onto an overstuffed ottoman, her violin falling across her lap. "I thought your parents liked me. At your house they said—"

"They were being polite. And so was I." I turned on my heel. If I had to look at her any longer, I'd lose my shit.

"Dorien, wait!" The crack in her voice sent a shudder through my body. I didn't turn around.

Every inch of my body wailed in protest, but I walked away.

Out the door.

Into the elevator.

Across the parking lot.

Away from her.

It wasn't so hard to pretend to be an asshole. Maybe I wasn't pretending. After all, I learned from the best.

My mother waited in the back of the car, her brown robe pulled high around her neck. As soon as I slid into the seat, she indicated for the driver to take us home.

Mom patted my leg. "It's not too late to change your mind, Dorien. She is a good match; Father Aaron says so."

I nodded. I couldn't speak, or I'd scream.

"Not to worry." She had that fake brightness in her voice, the tone she always took when Father Aaron wanted us to do something she didn't agree with. The tone had no power – she never contradicted him. "We've already found you someone even better, from a less volatile family. You'll meet her at your new school. Her name is Heather Danvers."

My phone beeped, startling me out of my dream. I rubbed my eyes, trying to smudge away that image of my mother's hopeful face and Faye's cheeks streaked with tears. As I scrambled for the phone, my eyes fell on the portrait Clare made me. *No. I don't want to think of her now.*

I turned the portrait away and grabbed my phone, my heart thumping as I saw it was a text from him.

Hey I hope I dont wake you but things are bad here Aaron hit mom hes angry all the time and he talks about this thing called ascension I wish you would come back.

That was the longest text he'd ever sent. It must've taken him a long time to write all the words. My parents never allowed him proper schooling, so he was slow to read and write.

My chest twisted with cold, ugly hate. How could they not see what they were doing to him? How could they believe that this life was better? My mother blamed me. "You turned out the way you did because we gave you everything on a silver platter. You have no discipline. You're corrupted by the world of material wealth. I'll not make the same mistakes twice."

No, I turned out the way I did because you never loved me unless it had conditions attached. Because I was never fucking good enough so I stopped trying. Because you keep calling me 'a mistake.'

They hadn't even let me see him when I visited the other week. Father Aaron ushered me into the room that had once been our breakfast nook, now emptied of all furniture except for a circle of lumpy pillows on the floor. Anger radiated off him in waves. He didn't want me there in my fancy clothes and expensive cologne, reminding the others about the temptations of the world outside.

More than anything, I wanted to escape this cage I'd made for myself the day I dropped Faye as a friend, but I was trapped. Madame Usher's words echoed in my ears. *A new student will be arriving soon. I need you to destroy her. Do as I say, or I'll cut you off. How long will you last when the world finds out the truth about your family?*

She thought that was all I cared about. *She doesn't know the half of it.*

Of course, Madame remembered Faye and I used to be friends. That was why she chose me – if anyone could burrow inside Faye's heart and rot her from the inside, it would be me. That was what I did – I turned everything I touched into ashes and dust.

I lay awake, imagining Faye in her bed above me, wearing those sexy as fuck Snoopy pajamas that clung to her curves, fuming because I'd interrupted whatever was going on with her and Titus. And even though the thought of them touching made my body burn with jealousy, I didn't care – Titus was a good dude, almost good enough for her. He wouldn't fuck her over... unless I commanded it.

But I did wish...

I imagined creeping upstairs, rolling in bed beside Faye, my fingers tangling in her hair as I trailed a path of kisses along her neck, across her collarbone, my lips closing over her nipple until she writhed and begged for more. Mmmmm. To hear Faye de Winter beg for me...

But I remained still, paralyzed even as my dick jerked with anticipation, turning over the situation in my mind, looking for a loophole, a solution.

There was none.

I couldn't help him without the Manderley Prize. And I couldn't get the prize unless Faye left Manderley. Unless I broke her. And my time was running out.

FAYE

W*hose face was it?*

I bent over my laptop in my corner of the library. I was supposed to be working on an essay on Sibelius, but I couldn't focus. My fingers kept tracing the skin on my arm where Titus had touched me. My lips tingled with the memory of that sizzling tension drawing us together.

Stop it. Stop thinking about it.

Don't picture Titus naked under the sheets. Don't consider that he *couldn't* have been the one up in my room. He wouldn't have risked running down the stairs naked, which meant that in the time I'd made it to the second floor, he ran downstairs, and climbed into bed without being out of breath or smelling of sweat...

I just didn't believe it.

So who else could have done it? Harrison had gone down to the gatehouse, and Master Radcliffe's lights had been on in the stable house when I walked back to the house. So neither of them were inside. Madame Usher could barely fit up that staircase – no way would she have been dextrous enough to get back down so quickly, so it wasn't her, either. Aroha had been with me, and Elena, Dorien, and Heather had been in the Blue Room.

The only one I couldn't account for was Ivan. I'd assumed he was in the Blue Room because he never left Elena's side, but someone had to have been in my room... because the only other possibility was that a ghost did it, and that was ridiculous.

Ivan was the only one who could have done it. And I was sick to death of taking the Muses' shit. It was time to fight back.

~

It took me a couple of days to figure out how to get back at Ivan. He and Elena went everywhere together, and despite the fact she never said a word to me and looked like a stony-faced bitch, I didn't want to involve her. This wasn't her battle.

Then, one night over dinner, Madame Usher announced an upcoming visit from the conductor of the Berlin Philharmonic. He was in America recruiting students for a week-long intensive residency and requested a performance from each of us, so we'd be hosting him for a full-blown recital of our most polished work. Something my mother said flitted through my mind.

She'd been trying to land a contract with a celebrity actor who was launching a line of merchandise, but another PR company was angling for the deal. The guy who ran this company was famous for not disclosing sponsored content on social media – he built a couple of successful celebrity brands off the back of his "authentic" influencer marketing, while my mom did everything above board, which meant her campaigns had less reach. He badmouthed her all over the city, and I kept asking her why she didn't fight back. She'd smiled. "Don't you worry about me. I'm keeping my hands clean while he digs his own grave."

Sure enough, two weeks later, an investigative article in the New York Times exposed this guy's shady practices, and the FTC swooped in. No one wanted to touch him. De Winter PR got the celebrity deal.

Mom was clever. She knew that people who refuse to play by the rules eventually got caught out in their own lies. She'd given me all the tools I needed to show the Muses that they couldn't fuck with Faye de Winter.

FAYE

While the students sat through one of Madame Usher's history of music lectures, I had to clean the bathrooms, change the sheets, and vacuum any visible floor space in their bedrooms. Usually, I tried to hurry through it as quickly as possible, but today I hesitated at the door of Elena and Ivan's room.

Let him dig his own grave.

I whipped through the bathroom, cleaning as I went. It was Elena's domain – her cosmetics decorated the counter, and a pyramid of her dirty laundry wedged the door permanently open. More clothes and shoes obscured her bed – it was a miracle she slept at night without accidentally poking a Louboutin heel through her eye.

Ivan's things were much neater – his bed made with military precision, a small pile of dirty clothes placed in the hamper, a stack of music books arranged on his desk. That made it obvious where I needed to search. I pulled out drawer after drawer in his armoire, hunting for the skeletons I knew had to exist. I didn't find anything other than perfectly folded shirts and rolled socks. Marie Kondo would be so proud—

Hello, what's this?

At the back of his sock drawer, my fingers grazed a baggie. I pulled it out and held it up on the light, watching white crystals cascade through the plastic.

Jackpot.

I knew enough about drugs to know I was looking at a *serious* quantity of cocaine.

Apart from the occasional joint, I'd never even seen drugs up close before. But I *had* seen the effects at Mom's business events. Guys completely whacked out, chasing women who didn't want to be chased. Women believing they were invincible because they had money and a shield of drug haze. In our last apartment, I got to see another side – addicts on street corners, shop windows punched in. Once, a guy chased me four blocks while loudly declaring his desire to slit me open and eat my intestines.

This baggie of white gold was exactly what I'd been looking for – it was the shovel that Ivan would use to dig his grave. I just wasn't expecting quite such a large shovel.

This wasn't a personal stash – it was enough for a Robert Downey Jr. yoga retreat or a Hannaford Prep study party. And people who dealt drugs tended to be dangerous, or have dangerous friends.

But then I thought of how I struggled to sleep, of how I looked over my shoulder every time I walked into a room and had to check under my bed in case one of the guys was hiding there. I thought of my eroded sense of safety, of peace, and I squared my jaw. *This is the right thing—*

"What are you doing?"

I jumped at the voice, hitting my elbow on the open drawer. My hand flew behind my back, shoving the coke into the waistband of my skirt. I glared at Ivan, who leaned against the doorframe and looked me over with eyes of ice and sapphire. That impenetrable stare that would make any girl long to be the one to crack open his frosted heart.

I straightened up, trying to paint my face into a picture of innocence. "What does it look like? I'm dusting, like a good maid."

"You usually dust in underwear drawers?"

Heat burned in my cheeks. Ivan folded his arms, and something tugged at the edge of his mouth. On anyone else, I might have mistaken it for a smile, but Ivan Nicolescu didn't smile. He was a glacier – hard and cold, and if you dug beneath the surface, there was just more ice.

That was just the thing. I couldn't see Ivan as an addict or a dealer, but then... Manderley was a house of secrets. I couldn't back down now that I'd uncovered his.

"Fair's fair. You were in my room." I straightened up, trying to move my body without letting the bag slip out from my shirt.

He didn't deny it. Instead, he took a step toward me, his long legs stretching over a pile of his sister's junk. My heart hammered. "You believe this makes us even?"

Even his voice sounded glacial – slow and primal, that Romanian accent edged with ice. It vibrated through my body even as I took a step away from him. As Ivan picked his way closer, I noticed the way he moved – a tightness in his limbs, a tension in his step. He battled to maintain control.

We circled each other like two animals ready to pounce, but what would happen if one of us made the move – bloodbath or fuckfest? Both were equally likely outcomes, but only one made my body tingle with anticipation.

Ivan stepped toward the bed, and I circled around the wall until I had a clear run for the door. As I backed into the hall Ivan spoke again. "Faye?"

My name on his lips was fucking *poetry*. I raised an eyebrow.

Ivan's features didn't waver, but something flickered in his eyes – a hint of emotion, a clue that he wasn't entirely made of ice. "Be careful."

I opened my mouth to ask him what he meant, but he'd slammed the door in my face.

Faye

The day of the conductor's visit arrived. I'd stayed up past midnight the night before, preparing the evening meal so that I would only be heating things up the next day. I polished the silver setting until it shone. When I'd finally crawled into bed, I longed for sleep, but the Muses had decided to step up their torture. Instead of the creaking footsteps in my room, the faintest sound of violin music scratched the air.

It had to be a recording – it was too quiet to be someone playing in the storage room, and no one would dare play downstairs this late at night for fear of Madame Usher's wrath. *This is their assault on me because they know I was snooping in Ivan's room. They probably know I've got the coke. They're trying to keep me awake so I play badly tomorrow. Well, bet they didn't know that after my father left the only way Mom could get me to sleep was to put on recordings of his concerts. I love falling asleep with music playing. So there.*

Only, it turns out, I wasn't a kid anymore, and violin music can be fucking annoying when you add it to a stuffy attic, performance nerves, and the plot to destroy a Muse. I tossed and turned all night, fighting for every snatch of sleep I wrestled from the disturbed darkness. When the alarm went off at 5:30, I threw it across the room.

I dragged myself downstairs, made grilled cheese for myself, set out granola and yogurt for the royal dickweasels, and loped back to the attic.

Back in my room, I began my daily inspection of the cupboards and corners for an intruder. I shoved aside the bed, bureau, and locked chest to stomp on the floorboards. Then, I pressed on every wood panel and clawed at every crack in the room, searching for a secret passage. I hated that I was letting the students get to me even after I had the lock changed, but knowing they could come into my room any time they wanted and touch my stuff had me permanently on edge. Every creak and groan of the old house had me sitting upright in bed, heart in my throat.

I didn't believe in ghosts, but I honestly *wished* I was being haunted. It would be easier to deal with.

I crawled out from under the bed, satisfied that no one was spying on me today. Moving to my clothing rack, I pulled my concert dress from its dry-cleaning bag and hung it over my chair. Mom brought me this dress for my audition for Juilliard last year, back before she got seriously sick, when both our futures looked bright. Bonus, it had a little secret pocket in the seam of the skirt – perfect for a cocaine stash.

I stripped off my scratchy black dress and stepped into the shower, lathering up and rinsing as quickly as I could, my heart in my throat. Usually, I liked to take my time, letting the heat of the water melt away any performance nerves, but I couldn't rid myself of the itchy sensation of someone watching me. The Muses had stripped away that simple pleasure, too.

I wrapped a towel around myself and padded back into my room. Nerves crawled between my shoulders. *I fucking hate this.* I tipped my chin defiantly. If one of the guys was watching, let them have a fucking show.

At the thought of their eyes on me, warmth flared between my legs. My body betrayed me, aching for something that didn't exist. *They're trying to destroy me, and all I can think about is how much I want them. Any of them. All of them. I'm sick. I need help.*

Fuck you, Dorien, Titus, Ivan. You're going down.

I dropped the towel to the floor.

In the storage room next door, something banged. I jumped ten feet in the air, my heart in my mouth.

It's just the pipes clanging. They always do that after you've had a shower. Calm down. There's no one here.

My fingers trembled as I unhooked the clasps and pulled the slinky material over my head. Crimson satin pooled over my legs, clinging to my hips and flaring out into a fishtail skirt that accentuated my hourglass shape. A panel of red lace between the sweetheart neckline tied in a halter round my neck, leaving my shoulders bare. I did a little twirl and smirked at my reflection.

I might not be a skinny rake like Heather, but I could still look *damn fine*.

I stuffed the cocaine into the secret pocket, picked up my violin case, and descended the staircase as the other students gathered in the entrance hall. Even though it was just 10AM, Heather and Elena clutched glasses of Champagne - Elena's pixieish beauty only enhanced by her sky-blue dress, while Heather looked like she was auditioning for season 1 of *My Big Fat Baroque Wedding* with an enormous, puffy-sleeved monstrosity. The Broken Muse boys could pull off pseudo-Baroque frippery because of their superhuman good looks, but Heather didn't have the same blessings.

As I descended the staircase, my leg rubbing against the cocaine with every step, three pairs of eyes followed my every move. The grey storm, the dark blaze, the sapphire shard – their collective gaze turned me about and did strange things to my insides. I didn't understand how this sexual tension had risen up between us in the midst of the power struggle we had going on. But for today I was determined I wouldn't let the Muses see how they affected me. Tonight was my turn to fight back.

Madame Usher swept in, her black skirts trailing behind her. "You all look fantastic. If you haven't already, please go to the music room and tune your instruments."

"I tuned earlier, and so did Titus and Ivan," Heather said in that annoying trill of hers. "It's always good to be prepared and treat your instrument well."

Gag me.

I followed Aroha into the music room, setting down my violin case next to Ivan's. While she shut the door behind us and pulled the lock across, I flicked the latches on Ivan's case and shoved the bag of cocaine inside. I stood up just as she turned to me, a vicious smile playing across her lips.

It was a symptom of the Muses' bullying that my mind immediately jumped on the idea that she was going to do something to me.

"Why did you lock the door?" I tried to keep my voice even as I wiped my sweating palms on my dress.

"Chill out, trash. I just didn't want to share with the others." Aroha set down her violin case and withdrew something from the inside pocket. A tiny bag of white powder. "Want some? I always take it before a performance. Helps with the nerves."

Cocaine.

Blood rushed to my ears. After I'd spent the last twenty-four hours with Ivan's stash in my possession, I was being offered *more* drugs? *Is this some kind of test?*

When I'd reeled from the shock, I shook my head. I was held to a different standard than the others. If I was caught with illegal drugs in my system, it would give Madame Usher the excuse she needed to get rid of me.

Aroha smirked. "Suit yourself." She knelt down beside the coffee table and tapped out a line. My fingers shook as I unlocked my case and removed my instrument. *Don't think about what she's doing. It's not your concern. It doesn't matter.*

But it *did* matter. It mattered so much that my hands shook as I tried to tune. And I couldn't figure out why. Aroha wasn't really my friend. Why did I care what she did?

Is it because I know she didn't come from the kind of wealth the others enjoyed? That Ivan was a drug dealer taking advantage of her nerves to get her addicted to a habit that could cost her career?

Yep. That probably had something to do with it.

When she'd finished, Aroha wiped her nose and stood up. "That's better. Now I can face them."

"Was that from Ivan?" I tried to keep my voice casual.

"Ivan?" Aroha's giggle had a slightly manic quality to it. "Fuck no. That straight-edged posh pimp won't even let a sip of alcohol touch his precious lips, let alone evil drugs."

My stomach lurched. Had I made a big mistake? But no, the coke was in Ivan's drawer. It had to be his. Besides, it was too late to fix it now.

Let him dig his own grave.

We finished tuning and left our instruments ready on opposite corners of the room. I followed Aroha as she joined the others in the entrance hall. Dorien passed us on his way to the bathroom, and she grinned and sashayed her hips at him. Her behavior puzzled me – Aroha was a strong, sassy woman who never had any trouble speaking her mind or talking to the others – why did she need drugs to get her through an informal performance?

Dorien arrived back in the entrance hall just as Harrison pulled up in the limo. Madame Usher threw open the doors. "Hans," she threw out her arms as a lanky man picked his way up the steps. They did that air kissing thing people in music always did, the sloppy sound of saliva hitting flesh.

"Allow me to introduce this year's students." She swept him into the hall, taking his coat and tossing it to me. I hung it over the hook that was right behind her.

"Ah, Dorien Valencourt needs no introduction." Dorien leaned forward to do the air-kissing thing with the conductor, who had shoulder-length grey hair swept back into a ponytail, and a hooked nose straight out of my fairy tale book. "And I see Titus and Ivan have joined you. It has been too long since you played for us in Berlin."

"Agreed. Broken Muse would love to return to Germany."

Boris tsked. "Last time we hosted you, you threw a TV into a swimming pool and caused the police to be called to your hotel."

"Three times," Titus piped up, a wicked grin spreading across his face.

Dorien glared at him.

Hans nodded. "Ja, three times. My orchestra cannot afford another scandal, or we'll lose funding."

Dorien made the sign of the cross. "I swear on the Almighty the three of us are on our very best behavior."

"I'll believe it when I see it. And Elena Nicolescu." Hans clasped her hand, his eyes drinking her in. "You're still as enchanting as ever."

"Thank you." Her waifish voice soared with pleasure.

Madame shoved Aroha forward. "This is Aroha Rawhiri, from New Zealand. And this is Heather Danvers, of the New Jersey Danvers."

"And who is this crimson beauty in the corner?" Hans' eyes swept over me like he was the Big Bad Wolf and I'd just showed up at the door with a red hood and a basket of blackberry tarts.

Seven pairs of eyes flew to me, most of them flaring with annoyance.

"That's... Faye." Madame Usher answered stiffly. "She was a student of my New York school before moving to the public school system. I'm afraid her technique won't ever recover."

I love the way she says 'public school' like it's a disease.

"Faye *de Winter*," Aroha piped up from the back. I glared at her, and she gave me a sly wave.

At the mention of my last name, Hans' eyes widened with interest. "As in, Donovan de Winter?"

"He was my father," I said through gritted teeth.

"Astounding. That man had a *spiccato* technique that has never been replicated. The entire Classical world was devastated when he disappeared. I had no idea he had a *protégé*. You must share with me all you know of his whereabouts."

Yes, if I had information about my missing cockpoodle of a father, I'd totally be willing to reveal it to a complete stranger with an obnoxious ponytail.

Hans clasped his hands together. I could practically see him salivating. "Madame Usher, you never told me I was to expect such a star-studded lineup."

"Save your praise until after the recital." She led Hans into the Blue Room, the rest of us shuffling behind.

As Hans settled himself into the chair by the window, usually reserved for Master Radcliffe, I poured him a glass of Champagne. As I handed it to him, my gaze caught my music stand near the window.

My violin wasn't there.

Panic seized me.

There was Ivan's violin exactly where I left it, the case still locked tight. On the other side of the room, by the piano, was Aroha's piece. Heather's violin and Titus' cello sat together in the corner. But my instrument was nowhere to be seen. "Where's my violin?"

"Shhhh." Heather glared at me, obviously forgetting about the no-talking-to-Faye rule. "Don't make us look bad."

I snorted. "Sure, wouldn't want to put your *neck ruffs* to shame, Marie Antoinette. I left my violin set up by the window, but it's missing."

Madame's eyes flashed. "You're accusing another student of taking your violin?"

"No." My cheeks burned with heat. *This can't be happening.* "I'm just saying that it's gone—"

"I certainly didn't move your violin. None of my other students would have moved your violin. The only conclusion is that you forgot your instrument after I *specifically* said to have everything prepared for Mr. Brandt's visit."

Behind me, Heather stifled a giggle.

"Go." Madame Usher snapped, waving her hand at the door. "Bring your instrument. We will have words tomorrow."

I tore from the room, my heart in a panic. I knew I didn't leave my violin in my room – not fifteen minutes ago, I tuned it while Aroha snorted coke. The only way it could have moved was if someone *took* it.

Aroha? Possible. She left the room after me, but I looked back at her and I would've seen it in her. Or Dorien? He'd gone back to the bathroom—

Of course. I shoved open the door of the men's bathroom. Sure enough, there was my violin on top of the sink.

Smashed to a thousand pieces.

The aftermath of Paik's *One for Violin Solo.*

My worst fucking nightmare.

Splinters of wood decorated the marble tiles, unrecognizable as once belonging to a beautiful instrument. Strings curled into springs that bounced in the air, mocking me.

No.

Please, no.

Tears pricked in the corners of my eyes. That violin was a gift from my mother for my sixteenth birthday. It came from an artisan luthier in upstate New York and was a work of art in its own right.

It was *mine.*

How *dare* they ruin this for me?

Panic shot through me. They were all expecting me back, Hans eager to hear the daughter of Donovan de Winter strut her stuff. I still had to witness Ivan's downfall. I had to get back in that room now and deal with this later. If I couldn't use my instrument, *any* violin would do.

I raced through the foyer, taking the stairs two at a time. When I reached my bedroom, I grabbed the thick ring of keys from my bed and jogged back down to the first floor. At the end of the hall, just before Madame Usher's private chambers, was a small storage room housing a variety of instruments gifted to the school over the years.

I stepped inside and flicked on the light, illuminating immaculate rows of glass cases and racks of instruments standing silent and sentinel. My fingers traced a rack of violins, passing over a Sanctus Seraphin with the distinctive reddish varnish before picking up a beautiful, simple instrument that could have only come from the workshop of Carl Becker, the greatest luthier of the 20th century.

As soon as my fingers touched the neck, I knew this was the instrument I had to play. A tingle of fire ran down my hand – the same sensation I got when I touched Titus or stared into Ivan's eyes or traded barbs with Dorien: giddiness tinged with fear. I grabbed the instrument and the bow and flicked off the lights.

As I shoved the key in the lock and turned back toward the staircase, I noticed that the door to Madame Usher's private quarters was open a crack. I jolted.

She never leaves this open. Never.

Unable to stop myself, I crept forward, my chest prickling. I shoved the door open a crack, and peered inside.

The door opened into a receiving room, empty of furniture, with heavy drapes blocking the light from the windows. The fire looked as though it hadn't been lit for some years, and the floor was caked with dust save for a path of footsteps leading through to an inner door. Beyond that, I could just make out the shapes of furniture in a sitting room beyond.

My ears caught something else. The faintest snatches of a familiar melody. The same mournful song that I heard late at night – the mysterious music that seemed to flow from the walls of my room, that was familiar to me even though I couldn't place it.

It was coming from *inside* Madame Usher's chambers.

I knew it wasn't noise traveling from the ballroom downstairs because I could *also* hear the pounding of keys as Dorien and Heather performed their concerto.

I stepped forward, drawn by that music, by my desperate need to get to the bottom of who was haunting me, and *how*. I knew now it had to be Madame Usher, but why would she leave the recording running in here when she knew I'd be downstairs?

As soon as my foot fell inside the room, I realized my mistake. My heel made a loud clack on the marble. The violin stopped. I looked down and realized my print stood out amongst the jumble of others at the threshold. Madame Usher didn't wear heels.

Shit. *Shit.*

I reached down and smudged the print with my hand, but that only made *more* obvious. It was too late to do anything. I backed out and shut the door behind me.

Heather and Dorien were finishing when I entered the room. Dorien's eyes flicked to mine, and he raised an eyebrow at the violin in my hands. Hans stood and clapped, his eyes shining.

"Beautiful and enchanting. Dorien, you were adequate, as usual." But he said it with a twinkle in his eye, because obviously Dorien was the superior of the two. "I'd like to hear from the Nicolescu twins next."

Dorien slid out from behind the piano and inclined his head to Elena. Ivan picked up his violin case and opened the latch. As he took out his violin, the bag slid out onto the rug at Hans' feet.

Ivan's eyes bugged out when he saw it. It took everything I had not to burst out laughing to see stoic, buttoned-up Ivan Nicolescu look so completely shocked.

But this was no laughing matter.

The entire room fell silent as Hans bent down and picked up the bag, holding it up to the light and inspecting it as if hoping the substance inside might magically transform into table salt.

"Well, Ivan," he said mildly. A vein throbbed on his temple. "What do you have to say about this?"

Ivan said nothing. He masked his face with ice, even as his shoulders sagged. Dorien and Titus rose to stand behind him – silently throwing their towel in with their friend's crimes.

Hans dumped the bag into Madame Usher's claws. "This is your mess to deal with. I won't say a word about what I saw here today, but you must know I cannot host any of the Broken Muses for our residency."

"What?" Titus' deep voice rose at least two octaves. Dorien looked like he was ready to cut someone. Ivan stared at a spot on the wall behind Boris' head. I recognized the vacancy in his eyes – it was the same way I felt when the doctors talked about my mother's chances of recovery. I left my body and floated somewhere behind my shoulders, watching the scene unfold before me with cool detachment. It was a survival mechanism – if I didn't detach and become Faye the floating ghost-girl, I'd go postal, and hospitals tended to frown on displays of Keith Moon-esque destruction.

That was what Ivan had done – he'd floated away so he could deal. Knowing I had something in common with him made my stomach church with a sensation I didn't like – sympathy.

Nope. Not gonna feel that shit. This is my revenge, and I'm going to enjoy it. I deserve *to enjoy it.*

Madame Usher glared at the three boys. "Ivan, leave. Now. The rest of you, either you go with Ivan or *sit down*. I don't want to hear another word about this."

Dorien stepped forward. "But it's not—"

"I said, *not another word*." The two of them glared at each other, a battle of wills playing out on an invisible chessboard stretched between them. Dorien might have been a raging storm trapped in the body of the Prince of Darkness, but Madame Usher was like some ancient fucking demon goddess. She held dominion over storms. Hell, she could castrate the Devil himself with that glare.

Dorien backed away, lowering his eyes. Ivan swirled on his heel and left the room, the door clicking shut behind him. Elena didn't move a muscle, but a single tear rolled down her cheek.

It was that tear more than anything that shattered my triumph. In getting back at Ivan, I'd cost all three of the Muses their chance of the residency, and ruined Elena and Ivan's performance.

Then I remembered my beautiful violin smashed to pieces, and I shoved down that rotten feeling of regret. I *basked* in Hans' tight face and Dorien and Titus exchanging worried looks while Elena played through a solo piece – her notes all the more heart-wrenching because of the silent tears cascading down her cheeks.

"*Brava*, Elena, you were fantastic." Hans rose to kiss her damp cheeks when she was done. "Who is next?"

"I see Miss de Winter has returned, so perhaps— What are you doing?" As Madame Usher turned to me, she shrieked. "That's not your violin."

"*Someone* destroyed mine." I glared at Dorien as I held the Becker in front of me, like a shield. "I took this from the instrument room to play for tonight, until I can get a replacement—"

"That's not yours!"

For the second time that night, the room fell deadly silent. Madame Usher strode forward and tore the instrument from my hands. Beneath her caked-on makeup, her face had gone as white as a sheet.

Any other night I might have been able to calm myself enough to find a way out of this, but between my terrible sleep and Ivan's revenge and seeing my instrument bashed to fucking pieces, something had broken inside me. I leaned right in Madame's face and screamed, "What am I supposed to do, then? My violin is gone, and I need to *play*."

Madame Usher tapped her foot. "I'm disappointed. This isn't the behavior of a professional musician. Master Brandt, please don't accept Faye's attitude as a representation of our students. You will not perform. Dorien, you will go next – perform one of your solo pieces."

I headed for the door, but Madame grabbed my arm, her nails digging into my skin.

"You stay," she hissed. "For your insolence, you will suffer through his perfection."

Bitch.

I froze, my body riveted in the spot by Dorien. He played *A Graveside Story*, his most famous composition, the piece that made his career with Broken Muse. It was everything he was – dark and seductive, dragging you under a fierce and choppy ocean and holding you until the water closed your throat and you couldn't breathe for the beauty of it. For he was perfection. Every note was a blade slicing through my skin, baring my soul for him to devour with those slate eyes.

Why couldn't he have been my friend? I hadn't had a real friend since he dropped me. Except for my mom. She'd attended every one of my recitals, even skipping out on important meetings to be front row center. She went out to the store for snacks when I was in the middle of my Juilliard audition prep. She curled my hair and gossiped about boys and celebrities like we were BFFs instead of mother and daughter. And above all, she showed me by example what a woman had to do to succeed, for in business as in life she was fierce and unapologetic and impossibly kind.

Now she was in a coma.

And poison put her there.

Now I cried for real – fat, silent tears rolling down my cheeks like Elena's had moments before, smearing my perfect makeup. I didn't dare wipe them away and draw attention to myself.

Dorien finished and stood to take his bow. He returned to the piano to accompany Heather for some Vivaldi. He was faultless, of course, but her notes were flat and lifeless – or perhaps that was because I heard them through a lens of my own silent screams. After Heather, Aroha wowed with a performance of Turkish composer Fazil Say's sultry *Cleopatra*. Her cheeks glowed with pleasure as Hans praised her treatment of the unique piece. Looking at her, it was hard to believe she needed drugs to step into her power.

Madame Usher clapped her hands and signaled for us to leave. Numb, I followed her from the room, peeling off into the men's bathroom to collect the broken pieces of my violin. When I emerged clutching the remains of my instrument in my trembling hands, Dorien and Heather were just leaving the ballroom. Heather looped her arm in his and leaned into him as they passed me.

Dorien's eyes fell on the pieces in my hands. He stopped in his tracks, wrenching Heather's arm. She yelped in surprise, then she tried to pretend it was intentional.

"Dorien, you are *vicious*," she purred, gazing up at him with adoration. "I thought you were going to hide her instrument. This was so much better."

"I didn't destroy it," Dorien's voice coursed through my body. "I hid it in the bathroom. That's all."

What a fucktrumpet filled with shit. We were all together in the ballroom. Who else could have destroyed it? Harrison? The manor ghost?

"I didn't do this." Dorien looked up at me. A different sort of storm flashed in his eyes, dragging me back out to sea, to a recital when we were eight years old where he missed a note and his mother yelled at him in front of everyone. "Faye, I *swear*. I knew how much this violin meant to you."

He did. He *did* know. He'd been there – the three of us having a fancy birthday dinner at Denny's (all we could afford after my tuition and Dad's career) when Mom presented me with the box.

He knows exactly how to cut me to make me bleed.

I shook my head. If I opened my mouth to speak, I'd scream. Heather broke down into a fit of laughter, her singsong voice peeling along the vaulted hallway. "Oh, the poor little charity girl. Are you going to cry, Faye? Are you going to blubber like a baby? Look at you, all dressed up like you think you're one of us. Your fat rolls are spilling out of that dress. You're disgusting."

I'd been called fat and ugly my whole life. The words rolled off my skin, unable to penetrate because I didn't care what people thought of me. But tonight I held the remnants of my violin in my hands, and I stood in front of a boy who'd once been my friend, and I *broke*.

I slammed my fist into Heather's face. My knuckles connected with a *CRACK*. Heather cried and reeled back. Blood slattered along the wall and across the front of her designer dress. Triumph surged through me as I drew back my fist and felt the bruise blooming across my knuckles. Heather dropped to her knees, clutching her face, as more blood spurted betwee her fingers.

"You broke my nose, you *bitch*."

"Sprite—" Dorien stepped forward, but I jerked away, spinning on my heel and fleeing to the not-safety of my attic room, Heather's screams chasing me the whole way.

IVAN

I slammed the door so hard the entire wall rattled. A cascade of Elena's lipsticks toppled from the overstuffed shelf and skittered across the floor. My whole body trembled. Fuck. *Fuck*.

I knew I should have gotten rid of that coke. I *knew* it. But I kept it because… because I was a *bou* of the first order.

Across the room, Elena curled up on her bed, like a dragon queen guarding her gaudy treasures. My own eyes peered back at me from behind her long, tangled lashes, wide and frightened.

"What's going to happen to us now?" she asked in a small voice.

I shook my head. I had no idea. Neither of us stuck around after the recital to find out what Madame Usher had in store for us. That Sword of Damocles would dangle over us for a bit longer.

Would she wash her hands of us? Send us back to Romania? Cold dread washed over me as the options lined themselves up in front of me, each bleaker than the last. Would she hush it up and add more to our sentence?

Elena's lip trembled. I knew she was thinking the same things – what would this mistake cost us, for we both knew everything we did came with a price. I crossed the room in three strides and dropped beside her, sweeping her into my arms. Cosmetic tubes and handbags jabbed into my spine as I lay beside her. Elena rested her head on my chest, her fingers tracing the filigree patterns on my shirt. She waited for me to speak, to announce my grand plan. I was the older by two minutes – all our lives Elena had looked to me to be the responsible one, to find a way out of any mess.

But I could see no way out – only darkness, only the gilded bars of our cage closing in on us. We were in too deep.

"Ivan, open up." Dorien hammered his fists against the door.

"Dorien, what the fuck—" I jerked upright just as he rammed the door with his shoulder, tearing the lock from its screws. The door banged open and Dorien barged past, moving to the window to pull the curtains shut. He turned to Elena, his voice a maelstrom of barely-restrained rage.

"Get out."

"Don't talk to her like that." I threw myself in front of my sister, hands balled into fists. "This is her life, too."

Dorien's face softened, just a fraction. "Ease off, mate. You know I love Elena like my own sister, but we need to talk. *Alone.* Aroha's in the bathroom helping Heather plaster up her nose. They might want company."

Elena wiped her eyes and rolled off the bed. She leaned in and kissed my cheek. "We'll be fine. We'll find a way."

I wasn't so sure about that, but I kissed her back.

Titus stepped out of the way to allow her past. "Don't snort anything I wouldn't snort, Little Sis." They all called her that, and it usually warmed me, but not today. Elena swatted him in the arm, and then she was gone, hair flying behind her.

I loved that my friends cared for her like she was their own. They were the only real family we'd ever had.

Titus had to turn sideways to move his shoulders through the doorway. He locked the door and leaned against the frame, while Dorien paced across the floor. I shoved my hands in my pockets so I wouldn't do anything stupid.

"What happened to Heather's face?" I asked.

Titus laughed. "Faye punched her. It was glorious."

Dorien whirled to face me. "I need to know, did you smash Faye's violin?"

His words only made Titus laugh harder. "That's the most important thing here? Not that brick of coke in Ivan's violin case? What the fuck, man?"

Dorien glared at Titus. "That's not a brick, and we'll get to the drugs. First, Faye's violin."

"*You* did that." I glared at him.

"I didn't. I took it after she left the room with Aroha, sure. I hid it in the guys' bathroom. But I didn't smash it. That's *fucked*."

Agreed. I recalled Faye's face as she'd returned to the room, her chin held high but quivering, her voice rasping as she told Madame her violin had been destroyed. She hadn't panicked – she'd gone to collect another instrument. She was stronger than any of us would have been under those circumstances. A swell of admiration rose in my chest. I spent all my life being strong for other people – for our mother, for Elena, for Dorien and Titus. I saw something of myself in her. Maybe that was why I felt...

No. Feelings are pointless here.

But I knew what Faye had done, stealing that cocaine and planting it in my violin case – and that wasn't like me at all. Her wrath was pure Dorien. That explained why the two of them raged against each other. When they finally broke down and fucked, it would tear a hole in the universe. I knew she'd choose him over me – women always did. *I just wished…*

But wishing wouldn't shove the coke back into the violin case. Faye had royally fucked me, and I couldn't even blame her.

Dorien kicked the dresser, splintering the wood. "Answer me, you fuckhead."

Titus and I exchanged a glance. This wasn't the Dorien we knew – those frantic eyes, that clenched jaw. I couldn't tell if he was going to break down or punch someone. I'd never seen him like this before. Even when he'd handed Elena and I those fake passports in Prague, he'd been calm. Determined. When Clare had been found dead, he'd held on to himself. But this…

Ever since Faye came to Manderley, Dorien had been pulled deeper into his madness. But how deep did that go?

Titus shook his head. "Why are you questioning us, man? We were all in the ballroom. No one left until Madame Usher sent Faye to find her instrument."

"If someone else in this house is out to get Faye, I want to know about it. There are too many fucking secrets around here."

"You can say that again." Titus stared at his shoes.

"Heather? I wouldn't put it past her to do it, but she would have owned it. Aroha was high as a kite again, or…" Dorien almost smiled. "Did Faye destroy her own instrument in the hopes of somehow framing me? She could have done it when she found the violin in the bathroom. I hadn't considered that before – how amusing."

"Dorien." Titus didn't yell. With that deep voice of his, he didn't need to. Just by opening his mouth he could cut through Dorien's bullshit.

"I know, I know. *Fuck.*" Dorien dragged his fingers through his hair. He swirled to meet me, collecting himself, pushing down whatever it was that agitated him so much. "You. Coke? I can't believe this shit. You won't even take a sip of wine."

"It wasn't mine," I mumbled.

Big fucking mistake.

Dorien grabbed my collar and threw me against the wall. My back slammed into the stone, my bones cracking from the force. His face, inches from mine, twisted as he struggled to control the demon that threatened to overwhelm him. "I am *this* close to putting your head through a wall. It was in your violin case. What the fuck is going on?"

I screwed up my face. In all the years we'd known each other, all the world tours and trashed hotel rooms and stupid fights and dark shit, we made a pact to be truthful with each other at all costs. I had no secrets from these two. *Until now.* I had to take this secret to my grave – I was going down, and I wouldn't drag them or Faye or Elena with me.

"It belongs to Aroha. I was keeping it so she wouldn't… so she'd sober up. I hid it in my drawer, but I'm pretty sure Faye found it and slipped it into my violin case."

"Faye wouldn't do that," Dorien growled, his fingers tightening around my collar.

"Oh, yeah? She wouldn't try to get us back for bullying her?" I choked out.

"Heather's ruined nose suggests otherwise. Maybe Faye thinks Ivan was the one in her room the other night," Titus said from the door. "She had this logic all worked out when she thought it was me, but it didn't make sense because I didn't do it. Dorien, let him down. You're not helping."

Dorien's eyes flashed, but he let go of my collar. I sank to the floor, pulling my knees up to my chest, sucking in deep breaths to try and get my racing heart under control. Titus crossed to my bed, dropping a bag of weed on the coverlet and rolling a joint.

"You've both got to chill out." He held out a joint to me. I shook my head.

"Don't do that in here. Elena—"

"—is the least of your problems, bro." Dorien accepted the joint, pulling a lighter from his pocket. He didn't even bother to move to the window, just letting the smoke curl around his face. Titus rolled another, and soon the two of them were puffing away, tendrils of smoke curling around their faces. The tension in the room dropped.

"We can't blame Faye for standing up for herself." Titus leaned against the wall, puckering his lips as he exhaled. "But we've got to do damage control. She'll be gunning for one of us next, probably Dorien, after he destroyed her—"

"I didn't do it," Dorien growled.

Titus shrugged. "Why do you care? You wanted to hurt her. Looks like mission accomplished. So why aren't we celebrating?"

Dorien's expression twisted, and I felt a familiar, jealous stab in my gut. Dorien thought he had it so hard, but he was the kind of guy who would always land on his feet, always find a solution, always get the girl. If he could pull his head out of his ass he'd see how he felt about Faye, and then they'd have loud kinky sex I'd be able to hear all the way from jail.

Faye and Dorien were written in the stars. And that left me down below with the weeds and monsters.

Dorien snorted. "We're not celebrating, because Ivan is about to go to jail. Or get kicked back to Romania, which is worse."

"Right. Fuck. What do we do?"

No one answered him. We all knew what had to happen next. There was one person at Manderley who had the power to make this go away, but she would demand a price. There was always a price. She'd already taken her pound of flesh from each of us. What else did I have to give?

DORIEN

Titus and I waited with Ivan all night. I spooned him in Elena's bed while Titus twisted his bulk to fit on Ivan's bed, the way we used to sleep in the early days of Broken Muse when we could only afford cheap twin rooms. Not that I slept – dark thoughts kept my eyes open, fixed on the door of Ivan's room, on a tiny shaft of light from the curtains that almost looked like a face leering back at me—

Madame Usher didn't come for Ivan. The police didn't bang down the door. But that didn't mean he was safe.

No one was safe at Manderley.

The next morning at breakfast, Madame Usher gushed over my performance. "Hans was so taken with your mastery and presence, Dorien." She ruffled my hair like I was a favored son. "I believe he will get over his reluctance to deal with an ex-Muse and invite to you the summer residency in Berlin."

Those words should have given me a thrill. Berlin was one of my favorite cities – to return there to perform and learn from a world-class orchestra would be a big deal for my career. Not to mention bringing me a step closer to what I'd come to Manderley to do. But the triumph felt hollow, meaningless.

I earned it off the back of Faye's misery.

Because even if I hadn't ruined her violin, everyone believed I did. I knew the truth that hid in Madame's words. *This is your reward for ruining her.*

But who had done it? And why didn't they come forward to claim their reward?

Faye pushed through the dining room door, but Madame Usher swept in her path. "You're not welcome today. The Master has not forgiven you for taking his violin."

That was a lie. Master Radcliffe hadn't been the one to react when Faye showed up with that Becker – but Madame Usher had. She *screamed* at Faye – in all the years I'd known her, I'd never, ever seen her lose it like that.

What was it about that violin? I had to know. We needed something, anything we could use against Madame Usher.

Faye's eyes leaped with fire as she stared down her foe. She looked like she was about to argue. Instead, she shoved a tray of scrambled eggs and bacon into Madame's hands, turned on her heel and stormed away.

After breakfast was composition. Madame Usher smiled at Ivan as he slunk into the room – a smile that said she would keep his secret along with all the others she hoarded like a mouse stockpiling cheese, but her silence would come at a price to be paid in the future. I shuddered to think of what the price might be.

Faye didn't show up for composition class, either. I couldn't focus with her gone. When I paired up with Heather to tackle her composition, my fingers were all over the place. Finally, she put her instrument down and glared at me, touching the dressing on her nose with annoyance. "If you're not going to take this seriously, I'll partner with Titus instead."

"Fine." I slid my fingers off the keys. "Be my guest."

"Don't be silly. You know we're perfect together." Heather raised her bow. "Do it again."

This is stupid. I shouldn't feel bad for Faye. I was getting exactly what I wanted – she'd have to leave soon. She would no longer be in danger, or a threat to my plan. I'd win the Manderley Prize, and everything would be okay.

But I didn't feel okay. I felt like a complete shit.

When we emerged from class, the dining room table was already set with platters of cold sandwiches. Faye was nowhere to be seen. Heather wrinkled her nose as she picked up the bread, but the movement made her flinch with pain. "Canned tuna? What is this shit?"

While the others bickered and gossiped about Faye, I pushed my food around on my plate. *This is stupid. I can't leave things like this. I can't have her believe I destroyed her violin.*

It shouldn't matter, but it did.

I shoved my plate aside and stood up. "I'm not hungry."

Heather searched my face, her eyes widening with annoyance. "Dorien—"

But I was already bounding up the stairs. Before I knew it, I stood on the narrow attic landing, my back stooped and the one dim lightbulb swinging against my cheek. I shuttered myself against the wave of memories – of Clare's excited face in the dark when I came to visit her, of all the things she said in the dim morning hours that I ignored, too lost in my own bullshit—

I knocked on Faye's door.

Nothing. No sound. Not even the string of profanity I deserved. I knocked again, and was just about to call out when the door swung open.

My breath caught in my throat. Faye opened her mouth to speak, but no sound came out. She looked... well, she was fucking gorgeous. But today it was a beauty borne of fragility – of red-rimmed eyes and tousled hair and a pillow crease along her cheek – not the strength that carried her. She clutched a battered old book in her hands. The fire in her eyes had gone out, and her chin quivered when she raised her face to meet me.

Her eyes, her face... it broke me.

"You happy?" she hissed, grabbing the door and slamming it behind her.

I stood in the hall, frozen and mute.

Fuck. *Fuck.*

That haunted look in her eyes. I'd done that. I'd *broken* her.

It was my job. I couldn't defy Madame Usher. Not without putting my entire future – *his* future – at risk.

Unless...

I slumped on the top step, my head in my hands, my mind whirring with possibilities. This blackmail thing could work two ways. There was some reason Madame Usher wanted Faye to leave Manderley. It didn't make any sense, because she didn't have to offer Faye a spot in the first place. But Faye was here, and Madame wanted her gone, but she refused to get her hands dirty. That was where Broken Muse came in – Madame had all three of us over a barrel, and she relished it.

She traded in secrets. But she had secrets of her own. If I could find out why she wanted me to destroy Faye so badly, then I might have a chance to set all of us free of her web.

FAYE

I hate you, Dorien Valencourt.
You're next.

DORIEN

"Wanna jam some Bach?" Titus leaned over my desk, his cornrows falling over his ears. His deep voice echoed across the library.

I slammed my laptop screen shut and glared at my friend. "Can't. I've got to finish that essay on Baroque compositional structures. Go bother Ivan. He looks like he could use a break from perfection."

Titus punched me in the shoulder and slid off the corner of my desk to head for the twins, who sat together in the window seat. A set of old scorebooks lay open between them, ignored. Elena had some bright new idea, for her face was luminous with joy as she talked a mile a minute at Ivan. I knew from that strained look on his face that even patient Ivan was reaching peak Elena overdose. He looked relieved when Titus inserted himself between them.

Satisfied I was alone again, I flipped up my laptop screen, where I'd opened a new file titled "Concerning the Fall of the House of Usher." If anyone found it I could claim it was song inspiration. Underneath I'd written everything I knew, which wasn't much – Madame Usher invited Faye to the school, but she told me it had been Master Radcliffe's decision. He'd never corrected her lie. She blackmailed me into bullying Faye, and into pulling Titus and Ivan into it.

And then, there were these strange happenings – things done to Faye I couldn't explain. The ruined violin. The face at the window. Faye saying something about music playing at night. All things we weren't responsible for.

We weren't the only ones haunting Faye. That knowledge chilled my blood like nothing else.

I added to the list Madame's crazed reaction when Faye brought in that violin from the instrument room. At the time, I assumed Faye had picked up some particularly rare piece, but although it was a Carl Becker, it was on the low end of value for her collection. I'd never heard Madame screech like that – losing grip of her tightly bound control. For whatever reason, that violin was *personal*.

I just didn't know why. The instrument room was locked, and I didn't have a key. This would be easier if I could talk to Faye. But then if I was allowed to talk to her, I wouldn't be in this mess.

One thing was clear – Faye was the center of this. I realized just how little I knew about her life since we stopped being friends. Curious, I switched to the browser and Googled her name. I expected to see the usual news stories about the disappearance of her father, the ones I'd scoured for months after I'd left the music school, desperate to see a glimpse of her in the images, to know she was okay.

Instead, what came up were stories from the last eighteen months. PR LEGEND STRUCK DOWN BY MYSTERY ILLNESS, one headline read. I clicked on it and pulled up the article.

"Marguerite de Winter, the East Village It girl who built a PR empire from the ground up, was struck down this week with a mysterious illness. Her company, De Winter PR, will continue to operate with executive assistant Natalie Baker keeping De Winter advised in her hospital room.

De Winter is familiar in certain classical music circles not as the PR giant but as the wife of famed virtuoso Donovan de Winter, who disappeared without a trace a decade ago. She has no family in America, apart from her daughter Faye, who has declined to comment to media on her mother's condition. Ms. Baker has explained that de Winter's condition is critical, with doctors having no clue as to the origin of her ailment—

I clicked on another link from six months ago: DE WINTER PR DECLARES BANKRUPTCY.

"De Winter PR announced its bankruptcy this week after the CEO's daughter Faye de Winter drained its coffers to pay her mother's medical bills. The firm will cease operations at the end of the week and vacate its trendy East Village office.

Faye declined to comment, but sources within the company explain how this tragedy came to pass. "We understand Faye's position, of course. Marguerite's health must take priority. But we're shocked and saddened that everything Marguerite built has now been torn apart."

How did such a successful businesswoman end up in this position? Of course, Marguerite de Winter couldn't have predicted her illness, but she could have protected her business. Chief Operations Officer Natalie Baker explained, "Marguerite was a force of nature – she tore through life like a hurricane, and that was how she built such a successful business. She kept a big, beautiful vision in her head and relied on those around her to fill in the details. She was a total scatterbrain – constantly forgetting things, leaving her keys behind, dropping important documents at the cafe. I'm not surprised she struggled to remember to pay insurance bills."

According to Baker, De Winter's tragic story should be a warning to all business owners. "It's a powerful message that even those who are successful should take care of the little things. If Marguerite had paid her bills on time, her insurance wouldn't have lapsed and her legacy wouldn't have been dismantled."

Interesting that this Natalie was previously an assistant and was now promoted to COO. My heart pounding, I kept clicking. A short piece on an industry blog from a week before Faye arrived at Manderley noted that Marguerite De Winter had fallen into a coma.

Shit.

I knew Faye was visiting someone at the hospital because Harrison picked her up there, but I had no idea... Faye's mom was on life-support, with *no insurance*. She had no money to her name.

She was alone.

I knew what that felt like.

Shit.

No wonder Faye was so determined to stay at Manderley no matter what I did to her. She needed the prize money just as much as I did. *More.* And that was saying something.

Madame Usher knew that. She dangled the Manderley Prize over Faye's head, making Faye dance like a puppet for her own amusement. Surely, Faye could see Madame would never reward her the prize even though – and it burned in my throat to admit it – she probably deserved it for her composition talents alone.

Madame Usher pulls the strings, and we both dance.

But why?

My mind flashed back to the nightmare I relived every night as I lay down to sleep.

Clare lying at the bottom of the staircase, her neck bent at an impossible angle.

Her words, shouted at me seconds before she fell to her death.

Dorien, listen to me! I have to tell you something about Madame Usher. About the noises in the walls.

I squeezed my eyes shut. I told myself it was an accident. Clare was running after me, trying to get my attention, and she tripped on the stairs and fell. That was what I had to believe. For his sake.

My eyes flew open. *I can't ignore the truth.* Clare's death. Faye's mother's illness. Madame Usher's strange behavior. It all came back to one question – why?

Madame Usher usually handled her own dirty work, but this time she'd entrusted three broken muses. I'd make her regret that decision.

FAYE

After the disastrous recital for Hans and my confrontation with Dorien and Heather, no one in the house spoke to me for a week. Good. I didn't want to speak to them either.

To punish me for punching Heather, Madame docked my pay. It was worth it to see the bitch walking around with a giant plaster over her nose. Every time I looked down at my bruised knuckles, I smiled.

The eyes of the Muses followed me everywhere I went – itching across my shoulders, boring into my soul. Perhaps they suspected I was responsible for putting Ivan's coke in his violin case. Not that he got any kind of punishment for it. I refused to acknowledge them in any way – if they wanted to treat me like a ghost, I'd become one.

I gathered the pieces of my ruined violin. In my room, I laid them out under the window on top of my father's fairy tale book. As the moonlight cast its glow over the shards and splinters, I cried all the tears I'd held inside ever since Mom went into hospital. It was a bloodletting, and afterward, I felt better. I wrapped the remains in a scarf my mother gave me and took them outside. I found a shovel in the woodshed and dug a hole in the dirt behind the gazebo.

I opened my door on Monday morning to find a brand new violin on the landing – a beautiful Venetian instrument in the style of Sanctus Seraphin. I dragged it inside and turned it every which way, hunting for a label that might say who it was from, but there was nothing. My mind flickered to the three Muses, but that was ridiculous. They were the ones who destroyed my violin, so why would they replace it?

I didn't want to accept the gift without knowing who it was from, or why they'd given it. But I wouldn't get far at Manderley without an instrument, and Madame made it clear that the pieces in the school's collection were off-limits to me. So I held the instrument to my chin and played until my fingers bled, until the music had seared determination for revenge into my soul.

I refused to eat in the dining room with the other students. Instead, I'd set the table and retreat to the kitchen. At least there I could cling to the belief that the silence was of my own choosing.

No one acknowledged me or the new instrument when I walked into class on Monday morning. I held my head high as I took my seat in the corner. I channeled my mother. I wouldn't let their scorn get to me.

I held that new violin to my chin, and I played every note flawlessly.

But it wasn't enough to repair what had shifted when I picked up that Becker violin. Even Master Radcliffe seemed at a loss for what to do with me. Although he was cordial in our lessons, a tension tugged between us that had never existed before. After Monday's lesson, I decided to save us both the agony and skip classes to practice my Sibelius and Paganini alone in my room.

Someone got to Harrison, because instead of his usual jovial greeting when he brought the wood in, all I got was silence and a pitying stare. I didn't realize how much I desperately needed his kindness until it had been taken from me.

The Muses did this.

They hate me this much. All because I... what? Existed?

Their ghosting shit was getting insane. My senses worked overtime. I fancied I heard footsteps following me as I moved around the house. Groans and creaks followed me inside the walls. Yet every time I turned around, the hallway would be empty.

Eerie violin music wafted into my room at night, keeping me awake. Hiding under the sheets from a resident ghost was not as fun as the movies made out. Even through my noise-canceling headphones I caught snatches of the same haunting tune, played over and over.

By the end of the week, I was a zombie. I dropped a glass at dinner and Madame Usher screamed that my mother raised me as an animal. I sat at the kitchen table, fighting back tears as I devoured an entire package of Red Vines.

As I stacked the dishwasher, I noticed a figure moving across the back porch. Odd. Titus couldn't have come through the kitchen, because I would have seen him. I cupped my hands over the window and squinted into the gloom. The window to the Yellow Room was pushed all the way up, the curtains flapping in the wind. He must have slipped out there. But what was one of the Muses doing sneaking around in the dark? They usually stomped about like they owned the place. Titus jogged down the path toward the woodshed, looking over his shoulder at the house as if he didn't want anyone to follow him. A large, rectangular case slapped against his leg.

Hmmmm.

He hadn't come back to the house by the time I finished the dishes. Curious now, I peered at the clock above the fridge. Nearly 8PM. I could hear the others laughing and playing music in the Blue Room. Why wasn't Titus hanging out with them?

Come to think of it, I wasn't sure I'd ever seen Titus wandering around the house in the evenings. Was he sneaking out to the woodshed every night? If so, what was he doing out there?

A rising rage seethed inside me. Thanks to those guys, I'd lived through a hellish week. They took pleasure in making me look like I flouted Madame Usher's authority at every step, when really *they* were the ones running circles around her.

Maybe it was time I turned their cruelty back on them. *I bet Madame Usher would be interested to know where Titus goes at night.*

I grabbed my coat from the hook by the kitchen door and pushed it open as silently as I could. The wind was up tonight, howling down the valley and scraping the branches across the walls.

I closed the door as silently as I could and darted through the kitchen garden, pausing at the gate to check no one was coming from the main house. The coast was clear. I unlocked the gate, wincing as the creaking hinges pierced the night. The wind whipped the sound against the house. If Titus knew I was coming after him, it wouldn't be because of that sound.

I slipped through and crept down the path, keeping close to the house. I reached the woodshed with its open bay where Harrison stacked firewood to dry and stored his rusting garden machinery. I couldn't see Titus anywhere.

Behind the woodshed was another outbuilding – I'd never noticed it before, but then I didn't spend much time out here. It was long and low and made of brick, hidden by the overhanging trees. A faint light flickered at the dirt-smeared window.

Gotcha.

I crept over, pausing at the door to press my ear against the wood, struggling to hear.

There was a strange noise, like a... I couldn't explain it. A dull buzz. A flicking sound. Titus grunted. *Ah, he's got a girl in there. Some local woodcutter's daughter? A scandal worthy of a Broken Muse, for sure.*

I smiled to myself. I had him now.

Welcome to your worst nightmare, Titus Thibodeaux.

I shoved the door open and stepped inside.

It took a moment for my eyes to adjust. The buzzing came from a small generator in the corner, belching noxious fumes into a jerry-rigged chimney pointing out a window facing the forest. A pair of lanterns sat on crumbling wooden shelves, their light aimed like twin spotlights at the far wall.

And what they lit up... robbed my lungs of breath.

Titus stood in the lanternlight, legs spread-eagled, flinging his head around in frantic circles so his cornrows flew about like plumage. Headphones covered his ears, and their cord snaked across the floor to a small amplifier and head unit plugged into the generator.

Slung low across his hips, his fingers flying over the strings so fast they were a blur, was a battered Gibson Flying-V electric guitar.

FAYE

I stood, frozen by the sight in front of me, my mind casting back to the hours of video I'd seen of Titus on stage, the ferocity of which he stabbed at the cello, that unwieldy instrument putty in his hands.

His eyes flickered open. He saw me standing there, and he leaped so high in the air he smashed his head into the low ceiling of the shack.

"What the fuck?" Titus tore off his headphones and marched toward me, tearing the headphone cable from the socket. His guitar slapping against his naked chest, and the amp emitted a loud buzz.

I swallowed hard. He looked angry as fuck – angry enough to do something...

Well, fuck him. I had a few things to be angry about myself.

"What's this about, Titus?" I angled my phone toward him, snapping a couple of pictures I could use as security. Because he clearly wanted this a secret, otherwise he wouldn't be hiding out in a shack in the freezing wind. I hoped the bright flashlight would slow him down if he lunged at me.

"None of your business." Titus tore the guitar from around his neck and dropped it into a case covered with band stickers, his eyes never leaving my face. His shoulders trembled with rage, and I realized how stupid it was to walk into this remote shack to face off against this guy.

"Wrong." With more bravado than I felt, I slid my phone into my pocket and patted it with satisfaction. A stack of old tools stood against the wall. I grabbed up a shovel and held it in front of me. "Broken Muse has been trying to ruin my life ever since I arrived at Manderley. After Dorien destroyed my violin, I thought you'd won. But with these photos, I've got something on you."

"What are you going to do?" He narrowed those sinful eyes at me.

"Nothing. For now." I let a slow smile play across my face. "But if you or your friends do anything else to me, these photographs go straight to Madame Usher. And maybe a few of my friends in the music media."

"You wouldn't," he growled.

"Don't presume what I would or wouldn't do."

I whirled around and flounced away before he could think to come after me.

Outside, my bravado broke down, and my legs shook so badly I had to lean against the woodshed to catch my breath. I dropped the shovel in the dirt and dug out my phone, flicking through the photographs again.

I finally had something on the guys. I held my freedom from their bullying in my hands. But all I could think about was the fear flickering in Titus' eyes. He was the most intimidating person I'd ever met, so what could make a guy like that so afraid? And why was he playing guitar in secret in an abandoned shack in the first place?

And why did I *care?* It couldn't have been because of that time in his room, when I *swear* his lips brushed mine, where I'd wanted so badly to fall into him and lose myself.

How fucked up did I have to be to crave my bully when I finally had power over him?

TITUS

"I'm fucked." I buried my head in my hands.

"You're not fucked." Dorien leaned out his window, sucking the last pleasure from a joint. He'd offered me a toke, but I was way too agitated. I didn't need to calm down. I needed…

Fuck. I needed to get those photographs back from Faye. I needed to see her again. I needed her lips on mine, to feel her body succumb beneath me as she gave in to the insane chemistry between us.

But while she had those photos, she might as well have my cock in a vise.

"Sprite won't talk." Dorien closed the window and crossed the room to face me. He looked far too calm considering the situation.

"She's got no reason to stay quiet," I shot back. "She's still upset about me being in her room. You saw what she did to Ivan. I'm next. She's got all the ammo she needs to get me out of the picture."

"I'll talk to her," Dorien growled. "I'll make her see reason."

I didn't like that tone in his voice, the way he said *make her* with a dangerous inflection. I knew all about Dorien's powers of persuasion. I'd seen him work them on hundreds of girls on tour. The idea of Faye being another notch on his bedpost when she meant so much… "No, I should do it. I dug the hole, I should be the one to fill it in again."

"To her, you're just a pervert stalker. Faye and I have history. She trusts me, even though she won't admit it. I'll talk to her."

There was a gleam in his grey eyes that I didn't think even he understood. Dorien wanted Faye, and he wanted to keep me away from her.

And Dorien always got what he wanted.

DORIEN

I set my alarm for 5AM and snuck downstairs before Faye snagged her morning practice room. She'd been practicing early in the day so she could fit her chores in around us without having to see us. I hid in the corner so she wouldn't have the opportunity to shut the door on my face, and waited.

At 5:30AM, Faye unlocked the door with her house key and let herself in, flicking on the lights. For the briefest moment, I thought I saw a white face with a gaping mouth staring at me from the china cabinet, but it was just an illusion formed by reflections on the glass. Faye set up her music stand and was mid-scale when I stepped out from behind the sideboard.

"*Shit.*" She dropped her bow. "Dorien, you twatface."

Real fear darkened her eyes. Fear that I'd hurt her. And why shouldn't she be afraid? I'd done nothing but hurt her, and now I was hiding in the corner. I hated seeing my cruelty reflected back at me.

It made me feel unfamiliar things. Hurt. Regret. Self-loathing.

I held up my hand. "This isn't about you and me. It's about Titus. You can't tell anyone what you saw last night."

Faye narrowed her eyes. For someone afraid, she stood her ground, moving her feet apart in a power stance, making herself bigger. Faye de Winter never backed down. "Why not?"

"Titus hasn't done anything to hurt you. Except for that one time he was in your room with Heather, and he *hated* it. He told me he wouldn't do anything else to you, Sprite. So just pretend you never saw him out there."

"Don't use that nickname. You lost your right to it a long time ago. I can't just pretend I never saw Titus, because it doesn't make any sense. Why is he out in the cold with a guitar? Why is that such a secret?"

I sighed. It wasn't my secret to tell, but Faye wasn't going to drop this. I had to make her understand. "Titus' parents... you know they're quite famous—"

"Amos and Delphine Thibodeaux. I'm not stupid."

"Right. Well, they want him to follow in their footsteps, carry on their legacy. That's been his destiny since the moment he was conceived. But it's not what he wants."

Faye snorted. "Titus wants to give up his Classical career to join Iron Maiden?"

"Yes. Titus has been secretly playing guitar for most of his life. He hid an ax at my house. He used to stay with me whenever his parents were on tour and play in our ballroom. Until that... wasn't an option anymore. He's *good*. He could be fantastic, but his parents refuse to hear of it. If he came out as a heavy metal guitarist, they'd disown him, cut him off."

"Titus is legally an adult. He can do what he wants."

"I've told him that a hundred times, but you don't know Titus like I do. He can't stand the idea of his parents hating him. Their approval and love are everything to him. That's why you have to keep his secret. No one else knows – not Madame Usher, not Heather or Aroha, *no one*. If anyone finds out and the media gets hold of the story, or if the others find out about it, they'll tell his parents, and it's all over for him."

"Why haven't you used it against him? Get him out of the way for a clear shot at the Manderley Prize." Her eyes flashed. "Or is it only me you're hellbent on destroying?"

"Titus has had my back more times than I can count. I'll kick his ass in the competition, but I'm not going to sabotage him. You may not believe this, but I take friendship seriously."

"You're right." She grabbed her bow and held it across her chest like a medieval knight. A memory flashed in my mind – Faye and I collapsing into giggles as we had a swashbuckling sword fight with our bows. "I *don't* believe it. Now get out, I've reserved this room."

"So you won't—"

"*Get out.*"

 FAYE

I can't believe him.

I dragged the bolt across the door and shoved a chair under the lock for good measure. My hands flew to my violin, the agitation and fear in my body desperate for release. I drew the bow across the strings, launching first into Paganini's caprices and then divulging off along an unknown path, following the music where it led.

I wasn't even thinking – this was pure improvisation, conjuring images from my past that meshed with the present. I craved Dorien. I hated him. I wanted to crawl inside his spice and violet scent and live there forever.

Three Broken Muses. All I smelled, all I could feel, were Dorien, Titus, and Ivan. They flowed in my veins, inseparable from their music – the magic that stirred my soul and made me feel things I didn't understand.

With a cry of frustration, I tore the violin from my chin, spinning across the room in a reckless dance. From the corner of the room, a faint scratching sound echoed from the wall, followed by the creak of receding footsteps.

"You're the most useless fucking ghost I've ever met!" I yelled at the wall.

FAYE

That Sunday, I had a spare block of time I'd set aside to visit my mother. But Harrison was conspicuously absent when I went to find him. Tears pricked in my eyes. I knew it wasn't that he'd forgotten. Someone was deliberately keeping me from her.

I called a taxi company to see if I could get someone to pick me up – it would cost every cent of Madame's allowance that I'd saved, but it was worth it. Suddenly I wanted nothing more in the world than to be in Mom's presence, even if she was asleep. But when I called to order a taxi to Manderley, the guy on the end of the phone laughed at me.

"You'll never get anyone to make the trip out there. Even if they were willing to travel that far, they wouldn't do it because that place is haunted."

"That's ridiculous. It's just an old house owned by an eccentric lady."

"Eccentric? Hah. We all know the stories – footsteps in the night, noises in the walls, music playing when no one's sitting at the keys. And that girl died there not two months ago, all mysterious like. Manderley is haunted, you mark my words."

My heart leaped into my throat. Those were the exact same things that were happening to me. But ghosts? *Really?* Manderley was old and creepy, sure, but I was fairly certain its creep-factor was entirely down to the dickweasels who inhabited it.

What about Dorien's face when you confronted him with the violin?

He looked horrified. Completely taken aback. He insisted he only *moved* my violin. Every other awful thing he'd done to me he freely admitted. He reveled in his cruelty – that was part of the torture. He wanted me to know he was out to bring me down. But he refused to admit he destroyed my violin.

And none of the guys admitted to being that face in my window, or breaking into my room to switch off the light. I remembered how I'd checked every corner of my room, how I'd never heard anyone creep down the stairs, how my fancy new lock hadn't been disturbed and I found no trace of a hidden panel. It seemed impossible that anyone could have been there and yet, I *knew* what I saw.

Unless it was a ghost—

Stop it. I shook my head. *You're being ridiculous. Don't let Manderley get to you. There's no such thing as ghosts.*

The urge to throw myself down on my bed and sob into my father's book threatened to overwhelm me, but I squared my shoulders and put on my war face. If I couldn't see Mom, I'd at least make sure my day was productive.

All the practice rooms were taken, but I still had an essay to finish. It wasn't due for months, but it wouldn't hurt to get a head start. Perhaps if I handed it in early I could claw back some of Master Radcliffe's respect. I wasn't ready to give up on the Manderley Prize just yet. I headed toward the library.

Dorien glanced up from a table by the window as I pushed open the door. *Great.* I shot him a 'don't fuck with me' look and pointedly sat down as far from him as possible, pulling books from the shelves with venom. *THUMP THUMP THUMP.* I slammed volume after volume on the table, relishing the loud noise echoing throughout the high-ceilinged room.

I slumped down in a cubby and got to work on the essay, but it was impossible to concentrate with Dorien in the same room being all Dorien-like. I read the same page on Paganini's performance techniques five times before I gave up. I let my hair curtain over my face, and I dared a glance through the strands across the room.

From over his laptop, Dorien's grey eyes peered back at me.

Fuck.

I glared at him and returned my eyes to my books, but the sensation of being watched didn't leave me. Unlike the crawling in my skin that usually beset me at night, this felt different – I welcomed it. I *craved* it. And I couldn't understand why. Of all the Muses, I hated Dorien the most.

He destroyed my violin – the most precious thing I owned.

What I'd done to Ivan was *nothing* on the hell I was going to rain down on Dorien… just as soon as I worked up the nerve.

I dared another look across at the Bad Boy of Baroque. He didn't even try to hide that he was watching me. He leaned back in his chair, a smirk playing across his lips.

Dickweasel.

Those perfect lips parted. "Sprite, I—"

BANG.

I leaped out of my skin. My books clattered across the floor as the door banged against the wall. Heather strode across the room. She still wore the plaster over her nose, and somehow it made her look even more beautiful – like a valkyrie returning from the battlefield.

Heather planted both hands on either side of Dorien's desk. "There you are. I've been looking everywhere for you. We're supposed to practice together."

"I'm not dueting with you." The smirk never left Dorien's face, but when he turned it toward Heather, it took on that cruel quality he'd hitherto reserved only for me.

"Dorien, don't be silly. We have a month of recitals coming up. You know we play perfectly together, inside a concert hall and other places..." she trailed her fingers across his arm.

He shoved her hand away. "Heather, I've tried being nice, but you don't seem to be getting the message. I'm not playing with you anymore. We're over."

"Don't be so stupid." Her voice took on a shrill tone, all the musicality sucked away. "You know I am your destiny, Dorien. You don't screw with destiny."

That's kind of a weird thing to say.

"I screw whoever I choose, and it's not you."

"You'll regret this." Heather's fingers curled into fists at her side. The vintage fur she wore slipped down over her shoulder. "You still think you're so important, Mr. Bad Boy of Baroque. But you've slashed and burned your European career, and if you have any hopes of reaching the top again, you need me – and you know it."

"I've never needed anyone, and that hasn't changed. *If* I decided to bring someone else to the top with me, it wouldn't be five feet of spoiled bitch and weak fingering wrapped in dead animal skins. You're not even interesting enough to string along anymore."

"You'll regret that. Call me when you come to your senses," Heather hissed through gritted teeth. The door slammed behind her.

Interesting.

Nope. I reached for a book that had slid right to the back of the shelf. *Not interesting. So two horrible people decided to be horrible separately. That is no concern of mine. I have an essay to write—*

Dorien slid his chair out, the legs squeaking against the parquet floor. I went back to picking up my scattered books, crawling under my desk on my hands to reach a volume that had slid under the shelf.

"Faye."

I jumped at my name on his lips, the word churning up a storm on my insides. My head hit the underside of my desk, sending my drink bottle flying off the end to bounce off my tailbone. *Fucktrumpets. Ow.*

I dared a peek over my shoulder. There was Dorien, in all his dark and brooding glory, leaning against the stacks with that smirk on his face as he stared at the most unflattering view of my ass I could have possibly presented him.

Dear Manderley ghost, if you really do exist, I'd appreciate you rattling some chains or splashing some ectoplasm around right now, or just opening the floor so I can fall in, please and thank you.

"Go away." I slid out of the desk, my skirt riding high on my thighs. Color blazed in my cheeks, and I hated myself for it. I had no reason to feel embarrassed in front of Dorien, especially not after what he did.

"I want to talk about your mother."

"Maybe I don't want to talk to you."

"Faye…" Dorien threw a glance over his shoulder, his eyes darting around the room. He was nervous, but why would he be? Dorien Valencourt had never been nervous a day in his life. "I don't know if you know this, but we used to have a maid before you. Her name was Clare. She fell down the stairs and broke her neck."

"Harrison thinks you pushed her," I shot back.

I regretted it instantly. Even on his cruelest days, I couldn't believe Dorien capable of such an act. But that was before my violin. I dared a glance into those limitless eyes, and what I saw there grabbed my heart and squeezed. His grey eyes swirled with pain and regret – not the look of a cold-blooded killer, but something much more human and un-Dorien-like.

Dorien sighed. "Of course he does. The police had their suspicions, too. I was an asshole to Clare, no argument. She liked me, and I strung her along. But I couldn't have pushed her. I was already on the staircase ahead of her. I'd just reached the bottom when she fell. Clare was running after me. She wanted to tell me something about Madame Usher."

"I don't care. Go away."

"You should care. Because I think you're in danger. Madame Usher…" Dorien looked away. "She doesn't want you here."

"*You* don't want me here. And so far you and Titus and Ivan are the only ones tormenting me, destroying my—" I choked on the word. I couldn't even talk about my violin around him; it still cut too deep.

This time, Dorien didn't look away. A storm made of torment swelled in his eyes. "I did those things on her orders. I didn't have a choice. And I swear on my brother's life that I never smashed your violin and none of us was the face at your window. You have to believe me—"

I didn't know Dorien had a brother.

"Why should I believe you? You've done everything in your power to make me miserable, and what did I ever do to you except be your friend? Now you want me to talk about my mom – the most horrific experience that's ever happened to me? Why do you think I owe you?"

"You owe me nothing." Dorien stepped toward me, his eyes hardening to stone. "I owe you, Sprite. I owe *everything* to you."

I opened my mouth to ask what the fuck he meant by that, but then Dorien mashed his lips on mine.

The kiss drove all rational thought from my head. Dorien's hot, demanding lips dragged me under, sweeping me up in the storm of his need. All those nights I'd huddled over my computer watching videos of Dorien on stage – those cruel lips pouting as he caressed the piano keys like a lover – touching myself as I imagined what it would be like to have the attention of a guy like that. Now I knew, now I fucking knew – it was *everything*.

Music danced over my skin as Dorien wrapped his fingers around my neck, tugging me closer, his lips devouring mine. The song of our lives played out in a tangle of tongue and lips and sinful touches. A moan escaped my throat that made

Dorien's body shudder. He swallowed my gasp as his fingers tightened on my neck, and a deep growl rumbled in his throat – raw and primal and *so fucking hot*.

The fingers of Dorien's other hand curled in mine, pressing my palm back against the shelves. Books toppled around us as he ground against me, playing my body the way he played piano – hard and relentless and wickedly delicious. I felt like my skin would melt away from the heat searing through my body.

The image of my violin in pieces flickered in my mind, and all the heat drained from my skin. I tore myself away from him.

"Sprite?" The eyebrow cocking, that cruel mouth turning up in a question. Dorien still had no fucking *clue*.

I can't believe I'm kissing him. Sound the fucktrumpets, because this is messed up.

I needed space. I needed to *think*.

"Get off me."

I drew back my foot and slammed my knee between his legs, feeling a satisfying jolt as it connected with its target. Dorien's smirk collapsed into a grimace of pain. He doubled over, crashing into the opposite stack and sending an avalanche of books down on himself as he writhed in agony, gasping for air.

"You break off our friendship without explanation, you act like I've deliberately come here to ruin your fun, you *destroy my violin*, and then you use that nickname you made for me like nothing has changed, and then you *kiss* me? I don't care if you're the Bad Boy of Baroque and every girl wants you. I'm not your plaything."

"I never..." The storm in Dorien's eyes raged against my fire. His chin quivered as he fought against the pain. I wanted to look away, but the magic he conjured in his eyes held me trapped. "Faye, I wasn't trying to...fuck, this hurts...I don't even know what I was doing. But you have to believe I didn't—"

I refused to let him finish. I tore myself away and fled the library.

DORIEN

I watched her flee through a haze of pain, black hair weaving around her, hot ass sashaying through the stacks. I wanted to go after her, but I knew it was pointless. Besides, I couldn't exactly move at the moment.

I leaned back against the shelf and fought for breath. My lunch was in serious danger of being spread across the rug. My balls were on *fire*. I doubted I'd walk right for a week, and I deserved it.

Faye had every right to hate my guts. I'd been horrible.

But now that I'd tasted her, no fucking way was I letting her go.

Faye was right about one thing – she wasn't like other girls. Classical musicians didn't have groupies like rockstars, but when the tabloids named you 'The Bad Boy of Baroque,' it carried with it a certain mystique. I had enough girls falling at my feet in every city that my bed never went cold. I learned tricks from the whores of Amsterdam that were whispered in reverent tones between Maestra in green rooms across the Continent. But no matter who I conquered – how rich or beautiful or talented they were – they all blended together in the end. Willing vessels into which I poured my sorrows, vices in which to numb myself, a parade of nameless pleasures to distract myself from the gaping hole of misery that was my life.

None of them had ever kneed me in the nuts before.

Only one face stood out to me. Only one. Faye – the only person who cared about me enough for me to scar.

Faye wanted me. The desperate way she sucked my lip, that gorgeous growl she made when I brushed my hand over her nipple, the way her body bent toward me, every curve yielding.

Before the ruination of my testicles, that is.

I winced as I rolled on my side and tried to stand. They were still tender.

Faye wants me, and she hates herself for it. I know that fucked-up dance well.

Yet she could bite down on that want and ignore the sparks between us through sheer force of will. If I wanted her, I had to earn her.

Luckily, I knew her well enough to understand exactly how to touch her heart. There were two things Faye loved more than anything in the world – her mother, and music.

As soon as Master Radcliffe entered composition class the next morning, I pounced on him. "Master, I'd like to ask that I work together with Faye on a joint composition. I've heard the piece she's working on, and I believe turning it from a sonata into a duet between piano and violin would give it a depth it's currently lacking."

Master Radcliffe raised an eyebrow in surprise, but he knew better than to question me. "Certainly, Dorien. I think that's a wonderful idea. Faye would benefit from working alongside a musician with more... *traditional* training."

Just then, Faye walked in, her cheeks flushed from rushing through her chores, the black dress clinging to her curves in a delectable way. Her eyes narrowed as I walked over to her, blocking her way to her usual spot in the shadowed corner of the room.

"Out of my way." She held her violin case like a Roman shield and barged at me. My testicles shrunk inside me at the memory of their cruel treatment, but instead of fighting against her, I stepped out of the way. I wasn't fast enough to avoid a violin case in the ribs, but I caught Faye's arm as she stumbled forward.

"Of course." I gestured to the piano. "Do you want to work in here, or in the ballroom?"

She wrenched her arm away. "What are you talking about?"

"Master Radcliffe paired us together to work on a composition."

Faye's already stormy eyes churned into maelstroms. "He didn't."

"He did." I flashed her the smirk that turned most girls to butter. Most girls, but not Faye. "Lucky me."

Master Radcliffe stood from where he was sitting next to Elena and came over. "Ah, Faye. I've told Dorien he should work with you on your composition. Your piece is extremely accomplished, and I believe adding the piano will give it the depth it needs to be truly exceptional."

Faye's face did this twisting thing as she fought against her dueling urges to please Master Radcliffe and strangle me until I turned blue. I knew a little about how she felt – at that moment I wanted to crack up laughing and throw her up against the wall and kiss her at the same time. I opted for neither, instead offering my hand. "Ballroom, then. Shall we?"

Faye shot me a filthy look, lifted her violin, and shoved her way past me and out the door. I grinned as I followed her, watching that gorgeous ass swinging down the hall, while Heather jabbed daggers into my back with her eyes.

BANG. Faye threw open the ballroom door so hard it slammed against the wall, rattling a dresser filled with china plates. She stomped across the room and threw down her violin case on a velvet ottoman. A shaft of diffused light beamed from the window and fell across her face.

"I don't know what your game is," she snapped. "But you can stop right now. That kiss was a mistake. You took advantage of me, caught me off-guard, and I—"

"You, Faye Winter, taken advantage of? My nuts remember things differently."

She smirked, and that satisfied smile was worth all the tenderness in my crotch area.

I dared a smile back. "I still remember how you used to yell and kick and scream when Madame Usher paired you up with other students until she'd cave and let you work with me. You never did anything unless it was *exactly* what you wanted. The way your body curled around mine, you wanted me." I slid onto the piano stool, lifting the lid. "You *still* want me, Sprite."

Using my old nickname for her was a gamble, but it paid off. Faye snorted, but I noticed her chest heave as she took a position in the middle of the floor, facing me. The shaft of light cut across her chest, highlighting the curve of her breasts even through that severe black dress. I wet my lower lip.

"What game are you playing now?" she demanded. "Is this a distraction while Titus and Ivan destroy my room? Are you planning to dump a bucket of pig's blood on my head?"

"No pig's blood. We're going to make beautiful music together." My mouth turned up as I reached out to touch my fingers to her wrist, to feel the pulse of her blood in her veins. "Maybe I'll bend you over this piano and make you scream my name as you come."

Faye jerked her arm away, and a wall of shame hit me. After everything I'd done to hurt her, I didn't blame her for being suspicious.

But that kiss gave me hope. Faye had melted into my body like she was made for me. She wanted this as much as I did. She just had to forgive me first. My balls could attest that forgiveness wouldn't come easy, but I knew what I had to do to earn it.

I had to figure out what Madame Usher wanted from her.

"You make one wrong move, Dorien Valencourt, and I will murder you. I just want to get through this composition without doing that. The last thing I need is to be thrown in jail for homicide."

I settled down. "Then we'll work. Play for me."

Faye closed her eyes and raised the violin to her chin. She sucked in a shuddering breath, and I wondered if she was trying to rid the scent of me from her body, erase me so that I didn't infect her music.

Too late.

She struck the first note. It was the piece she'd been playing in the garden that night, only she'd refined it, drawing out the theme, turning it over itself to create a melody so achingly haunting that it stole my breath.

Her music held me mesmerized, but it was *Faye* that sent me reeling. The way she immersed herself fully in the moment, giving body and heart and soul to the song. That was my Faye, my sprite – she lived for the here and now. Although she played with the grace of a seasoned performer, she eschewed the stoic stillness of traditional posture for passion, her body moving as she played through the sweeping arpeggios that were part of her signature style.

I was back in the drafty classroom of Madame Usher's old school, the two of us giggling as we made a classical arrangement for the Muppets Mahna Mahna song, which we played at a recital to rapturous applause even though Madame Usher frowned at us the whole time.

I remembered Faye as the bright, happy-go-lucky child, the antidote to my dark moods. Father Aaron hadn't walked into our lives and burned everything to the ground yet, but my parents only noticed me when I did something wrong. As soon as I walked through the doors of Madame's studio and Faye's bright eyes lit up to see me, the world seemed happier.

She needed me, and I abandoned her.

Even though I saw her fallen face in my dreams, I'd been too selfish, too mired in my own shit to think about how that must have hurt her. I'd spent the last few weeks rubbing salt in her wound.

She set down her violin, inclining her head. To clap now would be to break the moment.

Instead, I turned to the piano and started to play.

I hadn't prepared anything, but it was as if her composition was perfectly designed for me, for my style. I picked up on the theme of her piece, expanding and deepening it, giving it more emotional punch at just the right moments. I wanted to look, to see her reaction, but I knew that if I broke my focus, I'd lose the magic that wrapped around my fingers.

I gave her this music, this piece of me. With every note, I tried to say words that had never fallen from my tongue before.

I'm sorry. I miss you.

I need you.

I finished with a flourish, my fingers sweeping the air. I dared to look up. Faye stood in place, her fingers clutching the neck of her violin like she was about to break it in two.

I raised an eyebrow. "You like it?"

She nodded.

I patted the stool. "Come sit beside me."

Faye hesitated, a million arguments playing out in her eyes. Her shadow side won, because she walked across the room like she was in a trance and sank onto the cushion beside me.

Where our knees touched, heat flared through my skin, leaping between us. I debated my options.

She'd look amazing bent over the piano, her dark hair spread out across the keys as she writhed in ecstasy—

No. I tried to ignore the throbbing in my cock. In the library, I broke through her defenses. I'd seen her stripped bare, vulnerable. She hated me for it because she believed she'd shown weakness, given ground to me that she couldn't take back. That was what the kneeing was about.

I had to show Faye that her arrival at Manderley had shaken me.

I took a deep breath. My fingers touched the keys. The back of my shoulders itched, as though someone watched me from behind, but I knew the room was empty. Manderley did that to you after awhile, made you imagine all kinds of ghosts. I thought of that pale face I imagined I'd seen – a face that looked far too much like Clare – and had to supress a shudder.

With a single hand, I played a little ditty, the kind of thing we used to invent together all the time when we were kids.

"Do you remember that day you came over to my house?" She nodded. "I didn't tell you, but it was the last time I ever celebrated my birthday. That guy who interrogated you – Father Aaron – he's not my uncle. He's a... he used to be a priest, but he was kicked out of the church for his extremist views, so he formed his own religion. My mother was his first and most loyal convert."

Faye looked surprised. I think of all the things she expected me to say, this wasn't it. "She wore this long robe..." she remembered.

"Yes. All Aaron's disciples wear those robes unless they are in public. They weave and sew the cloth themselves. Aaron believes that humans have become disconnected from nature and the heartbeat of Mother Earth, so his cult is all about returning to that. At first, he spent a lot of time at our house, then he seemed to have an opinion on everything my parents did, then I got back from a residency in London and he'd moved in permanently.

"Aaron only targets the super-rich. When he discovered my musical talents, I became a key part of his plan. He saw a way to get his message out to many wealthy people – through my music. He took over decisions about my career. He uses my parents to control me, and me to control them. And that's where you come in."

Faye looked shocked. "Me?"

"At first, my parents were happy that we were friends. They approved of your father's rising career. They saw you as part of the plan. They actually went to your mother and offered her money if she would promise you'd marry me."

Faye's eyebrows shot up. "She never told me that."

"She probably forgot about it. According to my mother, Marguerite de Winter laughed in their faces and told them where they could shove their money."

"That sounds like her." A smile tugged at the corner of Faye's mouth, but it was quickly snatched away by that melancholy. "I can't believe your parents tried to arrange your marriage. That's barbaric."

"That's Father Aaron's influence. That's why I told you we couldn't be friends anymore. I had to do it, or—" I caught myself in time.

"Or what?" Faye jabbed her fingers into the keys. "Dorien, or what?"

I opened my mouth and shut it again. I couldn't. All these years of silence and indoctrination. I couldn't break the bonds of my cage, not even for Faye, not even when I desperately wanted to.

Instead, I laid my hand over hers, my fingers pressing down on the keys, playing the notes of the Mahna Mahna song. Faye's lips parted in a silent O of surprise and delight. She let her left hand wander down the keys, playing the chords that must have come to her like muscle memory.

"I can't believe you remember this," she whispered.

"I remember you," I whispered.

This time when I kissed her, I took it slow. My lips lingered on hers for a moment, giving her the chance to pull away. I needed her to feel in control, to take this moment.

I needed to protect my balls.

Faye's eyes widened, but she didn't pull away. I could see the decision burning inside her, before a decisive moment where she gave way to her shadow side and collapsed into my arms.

Yes. Yes...

Her pocket vibrated, breaking the spell of lust and fury that locked us together.

"That's my phone."

"Leave it," I growled. My heart ached with a need to have her, to taste all of her.

"I can't. It could be the hospital."

Faye's eyes never left mine as she dragged the phone from her pocket. The call ended. The name DOC NELSON flashed across the screen. Faye punched the button to call back, pressing the phone to her ear so hard I worried she'd embed it into her skull.

"Faye? I'm so glad I caught you." Doctor Nelson's voice sounded far away – something that didn't belong in our moment. "Come quickly. There's been an incident."

FAYE

"Faye, you can talk to me." Dorien's fingers drummed on the wheel of his Porsche as he waited for the lights to turn green.

I didn't say anything. I couldn't. If I opened my mouth now, I'd scream.

My fingers clawed the edge of the leather seat as I stared straight ahead. When the lights changed and Dorien hit the gas, my stomach lurched. I'd spent the last hour tying it up in knots, and the insane speed he drove didn't help.

Not that I was complaining. As much as I hated his guts, Dorien was my savior today. When I remembered in a panic that Harrison was AWOL, Dorien offered to drive me to the hospital. I was in no state to refuse.

He tore out of Manderley's drive and careened around the forest trails like we were on a racetrack. On the freeway he ducked and weaved between cars, reaching the city in record time. I would have voiced my appreciation if I wasn't such a fucking emotional wreck.

Dorien hadn't even pulled to a stop outside the hospital when I was out of the car and running for the doors, my heart clenched, my eyes stinging with unshed tears.

Doctor Nelson met me at the nurse's station. "We've conducted a thorough check of all the equipment – she's fine, nothing was tampered with. I know this is distressing to you, but I want to assure you we take this extremely seriously. We have our hospital security combing through the CCTV footage right now. We'll catch the creep who did it."

I shook my head. "I doubt it. The only people who'd do this wouldn't get their hands dirty. They'd hire someone and make sure it's untraceable."

The doctor looked skeptical. "I think this might just be a random attack. They happen from time to time. People are upset at the healthcare system in this country, and they act out their personal aggressions on strangers."

I shook my head, too enraged to speak. Doctor Nelson must've noticed the smoke coming out my ears because she leaned forward and squeezed my shoulder, leading me down the hall to my mother's room.

As soon as I laid eyes on her, the tears spilled over.

I rushed to Mom's bed and bent over her, crushing her body with the force of my one-sided embrace. The nurses had done a good job of scrubbing her forehead, but the word scrawled across her skin still remained visible.

The handwriting was appalling, but I understood it clear enough.

LEAVE

To do this to a person who couldn't fight back, who was fighting for her life in a hospital bed... my stomach turned. I clamped my hand over my mouth, fighting to keep my lunch.

Doctor Nelson nudged a tissue box toward me. "I can go if you want to be alone—"

"No." I swallowed hard, rallying myself. I lay my head on Mom's chest the way I did as a child, listening to the slow beat of her heart, feeling the rise of her chest – an ocean tide, sweeping me home. Behind me, the machines beeped their constant, steady rhythm.

She's still alive. That's what matters. At least the bastards didn't tamper with her machines.

"You called the police?"

Doctor Nelson nodded. "They're with the security team right now. I've told them you're here. If you're up to it, they'd like to speak to you as well."

"I can do that."

Doctor Nelson shifted on her feet, flipping through pages on her clipboard. "Faye, I don't know if you want to talk about this now, but I prepared it for your visit." She unclipped some papers and handed them to me. "Your mother's lab reports have come back. I've made you copies. It's definitely chronic poisoning from *Aristolochia clematitis* – a plant commonly known as birthwort."

I sat up, taking the papers from her in shaking hands. "What?"

"It was commonly used by the Ancient Egyptians and in the Classical World to ease pain during childbirth. There was this pervasive belief that if a plant looked like a certain part of the anatomy, it would help with ailments of that area. The flowers are shaped like a uterus, hence... birthwort. By the Victorian era, it was a known poison, but the plants were still sometimes cultivated in manor gardens for their beauty. It's not a common plant now, and your doctors didn't spot it in previous tox screens because no one thought to look. I never would have thought of it either, if you hadn't told me about your mother's herbal teas. That gave me the idea to investigate poisonous ingredients in natural medicine. Birthwort is still used in some herbal medicines despite FDA warnings, and this might have been how your mother ended up ingesting such a large amount."

I sank back against the bed, struggling to process this new information. After all these months of hospital visits and my mother begging doctors to take her pain seriously, even as her kidneys shut down, we *finally* had a name for what was killing her.

Naming the enemy was one thing, but could it be fought?

Doctor Nelson anticipated my questions. "The good news is, now that we understand what happened, we believe we can help her."

My heart pattered against my chest. "You can?"

She smiled. "It's involved a lot of digging through old Victorian poison books and some lab experiments, but we think we can halt the poison's progress on her body. Once this treatment is administered, as long as she doesn't ingest any more and we monitor her kidneys for complications, she should be able to live a normal life. We'd like your permission to proceed with treatment."

"What does that mean, exactly?"

"First, we'll administer a small amount of antidote and monitor changes. If that goes well – and we expect it to, as her body would have processed much of the poison in her system by now – we can attempt to wake your mother from her coma."

Those words... those magic words I'd been wanting to hear for weeks rushed at me. My head spun, and I gasped for breath. This was too much. It was amazing. It was the hope I hadn't dared to feel in so long.

"If she's..." I swallowed the lump rising in my throat. "Best case scenario, what will happen when she wakes up?"

"She'll still have organ damage, and she'll likely need dialysis. But many people live full and happy lives with greater damage than she's taken. The wildcard is her brain. There's just no way of knowing what damage has been done by the prolonged coma."

I nodded, not trusting myself to speak.

"If you're okay with it, we'll start the initial tests immediately. If they go well, we can discuss the next steps. I don't want to leave her under any longer than necessary now that I know we can help her. How does that sound?"

I nodded again. "Th—thank you."

The police came shortly after, and I answered their questions and stumbled out of the hospital in a daze. Dorien slouched on the hood of his car, sipping from a cardboard coffee cup.

"The hospital cafeteria food was shit, so I went out for the real deal." He shoved a coffee cup and paper bag filled with doughnuts into my hands. "I remembered you liked these."

I stared down into the bag, hesitating before peeping inside, half expecting some enormous spider to crawl out and go for my face. Instead, a heavenly smell greeted me. Four doughnuts heaped with Oreo cookie crumbs. They looked and smelled just like...

A memory assailed me. I was eight years old. That day at school Rebecca Marshell and her posse of mean girls stole my clothes from the gym changing rooms and pinned them to the noticeboard under a sign that read WHALE NETS. I went straight from school to practice in tears. Dorien ran away as soon as he saw me, and I thought my life couldn't get any worse. But he came back ten minutes later with a bulging bag of peanut-butter Oreo doughnuts from a little shop around the corner called Nothing But the Dough. We hid in a storage room and ate them all, and in minutes he had me laughing. I forgot about those stupid girls. Ever since then, peanut butter Oreo doughnuts had been our go-to whenever something bad happened, whenever we needed cheering up. Until Dorien became the bad thing in my life, and I hadn't touched them since.

Nothing But the Dough was all the way in the East Village, if it even still existed. *Dorien can't have—*

"Go on. Try one."

I pulled a doughnut out of the bag, scattering Oreo crumbs down the side of the car. I bit into it. Chocolate dough and peanut-butter frosting exploded in my mouth. A rush of emotion slammed into me – all the horror of seeing my mother with that word scrawled across her forehead crashed into the memory of the doughnuts and what they meant. For what felt like the first time since my mother's nightmare began, I wasn't entirely alone. *Dorien's here.*

My chest tightened. Fuck, I didn't want to have to do this alone anymore.

I stared up at him with wide eyes. "How did you—"

Dorien flashed me his signature smirk, the one that promised mischief. "I'm rich as fuck, remember? It cost a fortune to get a delivery person to drive them out here on a motorcycle, and I wasn't even sure they'd arrive in time. But it was worth it to see your face."

I wiped frosting off my chin. "To see me covered in peanut butter?"

Dorien stepped close. The doughnut bag was the only thing that stood between us, and suddenly I found it very hard to breathe. "To see you smile, Sprite. You don't know how much I've missed your smile."

The tears I'd been holding back spilled over, rolling down my cheeks and dropping on the bag. I wanted so badly to fall forward into Dorien's arms, to let him hold me, to give myself over to the idea that someone fucking cared about me.

But doubt scratched at the back of my neck. *That's exactly what he wants you to do.*

Getting me to trust him again was all part of his plan. That was why he got the doughnuts and told me that story about his parents being in a cult. Dorien knew how to manipulate a situation for his own gain, and he was playing me like a sonata right now. This was deception with doughnuts.

He guessed that I didn't believe he killed Clare. Now he knew about my mother too, so he could also guess at how much I needed the Manderley Prize. He knew I wouldn't give that up without a fight. Now he was trying to convince me that Madame Usher was behind all this, that he had no choice, but the bullying was over because he kissed me and brought me doughnuts.

But I couldn't believe it. I couldn't be that gullible. *How far will he go to get what he wants?*

LEAVE MANDERLEY was written on my mirror in lipstick, and then someone writes LEAVE on Mom's forehead? Obviously, they were connected. It had nothing to do with Mom – it was a message for *me*.

The ghosting, the stupid messages, the sounds that kept me up at night – it was all juvenile stuff. Trying to convince me it wasn't him... that took some doing. But breaking my violin? Hurting my mother just to affect my performance?

What a sick, horrible thing to do.

Is it him? Is it?

My fingers tightened around the doughnut bag. I pulled one out and slammed it into Dorien's face.

"Ow, what the fuck?" Dorien staggered back, peanut frosting dripping down his cheek. Oreo flakes peppered the front of his shirt. I wanted to burst out laughing, but the rage burned too raw inside me.

Without another word I whirled around and stormed out of the parking lot, dragging my phone from my pocket. No way was I driving back in the same car as him, even if that meant I had to walk all the way back to Manderley.

"Sprite, wait!"

"Go away!" I screamed.

"Sprite... please." Dorien's voice broke, and it took all my self-control not to turn around to him. "At least it wasn't my nuts this time. I'm calling Harrison. He'll come and collect you. Don't run off by yourself. I'll go. Sprite, I'm sorry."

I'm sorry. I never imagined I'd hear those words from the lips of Dorien Valencourt. Too bad they were a fucking joke. I swiped angrily at the tears falling down my cheeks, refusing to turn around until I heard the Porsche's wheels spin as Dorien sped away.

My mouth still tasted of peanut butter frosting – one of the few happy memories of him that he'd destroyed. My jaw set in a hard line.

It's time.

I'd been holding back on retaliation, unsure if I was ready for what I planned to do. I wouldn't be letting Dorien dig his own grave – this plan meant breaking a few laws. It meant doing something I could never turn back from. But it was the only way.

Dorien had seen right into my heart, into the music of my soul, and he'd smothered the notes with his cruelty. If I wanted Dorien Valencourt to pay, I would have to hit him where it hurt.

His wallet.

FAYE

"Thank you, Harrison." My legs wobbled as I climbed into the back of the limo. "I'm sorry you had to come all this way…"

"Any time, my pet. I am just sorry I couldn't have brought you here in the first place." His face shifted uncomfortably. "She gets these ideas in her head, the Madame—"

"I know. Don't worry about it." I knew now how much power Dorien truly had in that house – Madame Usher had given Harrison an order to ignore me, but one call from Dorien and here was my limousine. Everything he told me in the library was a lie. His lips devouring mine, his fingers on the back of my neck, that growl he made as he sucked my lip…

All lies.

"I hope your mom's okay. I hope they get the bastard who did this. Dorien said that something happened."

"*Dorien* happened," I muttered, my hands curling into fists.

"You think Dorien—"

I didn't say anything. I *couldn't*. If I opened my mouth, I'd explode.

Harrison swore, something I'd never before heard him do. "He won't get away with this, love." He jerked the car out of the hospital lot. "You make him pay."

Oh, I planned on it. Sound the fucktrumpets, Dorien Valencourt was going down.

~

"Hey, Cory," I whispered, cupping my hand around the receiver.

"Faye?" Creepy Cory – the mouth-breather who worked across the bar from me sounded surprised and fucking *delighted* to hear from me. Gag. "They told me you weren't coming into work anymore. I was so worried. I even went around to your house to see you, but the place is empty."

Obviously, you creepy stalker. Cory was half the reason I was so glad to leave that place. He was always leaning too close, always asking me out and trying to walk me home, always staring at me like he was wondering what my organs would look like splayed across his bed. "Yeah. I've enrolled in a fancy music school. I won a scholarship."

"That's amazing. Can I come and see you perform?"

"It's not really that kind of a school. The thing is, there's this guy who's being horrible to me." I let my voice simper, giving Cory something to latch onto – the chance to be my hero. "I'm... scared. He's a bully, and he's turned all the other students against me. It would usually be the kind of thing a swift throat punch would handle but..."

"But?" Cory's voice sounded kind of choked-up. I bet he was remembering that time he tried it on with me after closing and I throat punched him. He couldn't talk for a week.

"But... this guy has resources. He's a rich dickweasel, and I need him not to be able to destroy me. I was hoping you'd be able to help."

"You want me to teach this guy a lesson?"

"Something like that. I want him to know that this kitten has claws."

"I can help. Give me ten minutes. You'll have to friend me on Facebook again if you want to see. What's his name?"

"Dorien Valencourt." I hung up the phone, flipped open my laptop and logged into Facebook. I'd blocked Cory months ago because ick, so I went into my settings to unblock him. He popped up instantly with a link. 'Click that.'

I clicked the link. A window popped up, showing a login for a managed fund account. A cursor moved across the screen of its own accord and a line of asterisks appeared as Cory typed in a password.

"Your creep isn't very bright. I broke his password in seconds," Cory messaged. A moment later, a list of accounts and transactions popped up on the screen. The banner across the top of the screen read, "Welcome, Dorien."

I can't believe I'm doing this.

Cody passed control over to me, and I clicked on the first account. Dorien used his money to wield control over not just me but everyone at Manderley. The only way to show him that he couldn't control me was to take that money away.

My finger hovered over the mouse. What I was about to do was hella illegal. I was *stealing* money. A lot of money. Not for myself – I'd chosen the perfect charity to receive Dorien's generous donation. They offered music tuition to underprivileged inner-city children, sending the best and brightest to conservatories all over the world on scholarships. Just the sort of thing Dorien would be behind one hundred percent.

Yes. I'm doing this.

I exhaled sharply as I clicked Dorien's main account, bringing up a list of transactions. My finger hovered over the Make a Transaction button when I noticed something odd.

Huh?

His account held only $224.67.

That can't be right. That's probably his last withdrawal or something. A guy like Dorien spends that much on luxury silk boxers.

I clicked through to his statements, searching for the honey pot. I didn't find it. What I *did* find was a steadily dwindling total. Three years ago, Dorien had over half a million dollars in the fund. Month by month, that money had been withdrawn and never replaced.

Where's all his money?

I rang Cory again. "Does Dorien have any other funds? We must've made a mistake. There's no money in this account."

"Not that I can see. He's got a checking account with his bank, but I already hacked that and it only contains $23. Plus three credit cards, all practically maxed out. The last transaction was yesterday, for a little over $400 to NOTHING BUT THE DOUGH in the East Village. $400 on doughnuts, can you believe it? He must rack up tens of thousands of dollars each month then get Mommy and Daddy to pay them off. Rich bastards, right?"

"Right." Curiouser and curiouser. "Thanks anyway, Cory. Listen, could you keep looking into Dorien? I'd love to know where all the money is going."

"Sure thing. But you're going to have to keep me unblocked on Facebook." Cory sounded like a hopeful puppy. I'd feel sorry for him if not for the fact I remembered what his unwanted hand felt like cupping my tits.

I sighed. "I suppose so. Bye, Cory."

"But wait. Shouldn't we meet up and strategize? Maybe I could take you on a date Friday night—"

I stabbed my finger on the END CALL button and flung the phone on the bed. My skin crawled. *I can't believe I just did that. I tried to steal Dorien's money.*

I can't believe Dorien doesn't have *any money.*

I turned back to the computer. My hand hovered over the mouse. I'd steeled myself for this revenge plan. I'd justified it with the fact that Dorien was a rich bastard sitting on a big stash. His parents owned that enormous estate, after all. They were old money. They'd never run out.

But $225? Maxed-out credit cards? What was going on with Dorien? Could I really take his last penny?

Grinning, I slid my finger over the trackball, typing out the information to send every last cent of Dorien's money to the charity.

Dorien had made it his business to learn my secrets and use them to hurt me. But it turned out the biggest Bad Boy of Baroque hid a secret of his own.

Dorien Valencourt was dirt broke.

FAYE

I turned over this new knowledge in my head for the next few days, unsure of what to do with it. The police called to tell me they had identified a man on the security footage, and were chasing down a number of leads to identify him. The detective in charge was interested in hearing about Doctor Nelson's discovery of the poison and my mother's herbal teas. I gave her the name of my mother's old assistant. If anyone could remember the name of that tea company, it would be Natalie.

Dorien hadn't spoken to me since I got back from the hospital, but his stormy eyes followed my every movement. Unlike with Cory, it didn't make my skin crawl but instead sent sparks of electricity through my veins. I hated myself every time I felt his gaze sweeping my body and I lapsed into a memory of his lips on mine.

I'm supposed to hate him, not want him.

And he's not even the only one I want. There's Titus with the eyes of fire and huge hands. I bet he knows exactly how to use them. And Ivan, who didn't even come undone when he got caught with those drugs. What would it be like to see him lose control...

I'm sick. I should be in that hospital bed beside Mom.

Mom. Fuck, I wished I could talk to her. She'd know exactly what to do. With her successful business and wild personality, Mom had a constant string of powerful men vying for her affections. Once, she even dated a semi-famous rapper for a few months, and his paparazzi followed us to the dry cleaners. She'd know exactly how to handle Dorien and Titus and Ivan.

But she wasn't here. I had to deal with all this on my own.

Despite Dorien's gaze and the looks I was getting from Titus and Ivan, no one else talked to me. Heather glared at me like I'd grown a third head. Tension crackled whenever I walked into a room, and I had this creeping sense of foreboding that soon everything would boil over into a big mess.

When Dorien discovers what I've done...

I couldn't face composition class with the others, so I skipped it and headed to the library to work on my final essay. I'd chosen to write about Paganini – he was this amazing violin virtuoso in the nineteenth century. Paganini had all these stage tricks he liked to play – he'd tamper with his violin strings before a performance so they'd break during the night. By the end of his performance, he'd be playing an entire caprice on one string. Some of his lost compositions were rumored to be so impossible to play that it was said Paganini made a pact with the devil in exchange for his talent. He was the original bad boy of classical music, and so obviously I adored him.

I told you I had a thing for the bad boys.

I shoved my earbuds in my ears and put on my indie rock playlist (a girl can't live on Paganini alone). My phone beeped with a message from Doctor Nelson. She'd been amazing, updating me every day about the progress with Mom's illness, offering to text me instead of calling in case I couldn't handle a phone conversation.

"Hi, Faye. I suspect you'll get a call from the police soon, as I've just got off the phone with them. They have good news and bad news, I'm afraid. The good news is, they caught the guy who assaulted your mother. The bad news is, he's a homeless man who did it for cash. He doesn't have a name or description of the person who hired him."

I'd suspected as much, but seeing it written in black and white made my blood seethe. At first, I assumed someone from the PR world had done it – Mom made a lot of enemies when she clawed her way to the top, and I'd already given the police a long list. But when I'd made the connection between the word LEAVE and the message on my mirror, I knew who did it. I told the police that, too, but they said it would be tough to prove. They didn't want to go after a powerful family like the Valencourts. Cowards.

I tapped my fingernails against the desk.

When I walked around the mezzanine level to collect a volume on Paganini's life, I noticed Dorien hunched over a cubby in the corner, frowning at his laptop. He slammed it shut as I walked past, and he glanced up at me, the slash of his smirk lacked its usual venom.

"What's wrong, Dorien?" I cooed. "Poor baby in trouble again?"

Dorien made a growling noise low in his throat, like a cornered lion preparing to lash out. That growl sank through my body, pooling between my legs, spreading warmth to dark and hidden places inside me.

"What are you smiling about?" he rasped.

I lifted a hand to touch my face. He was right – I *was* smiling. It had been so long since I had something to smile about that I forgot what it felt like.

"Nothing," I said sweetly. "I'm just reading a really funny book."

"*'Translations and Annotation of Choral Repertoire'* is a funny book?" Dorien narrowed his eyes at the title in my hand.

"Oh yes." The heat in my body bubbled through my veins, turning to a giddy mirth that warmed my skin. "It's fucking *hilarious*."

As I walked out of the room, I burst out laughing. And I *know* I imagined it, but I fancied I heard the faintest chuckle in the air, as if somewhere in the house the ghost was laughing, too.

DORIEN

I slammed the door to my room so hard the wall shuddered. Faye's gleeful face as she stood over my computer played over in my mind, imprinted on top of her vicious scowl as she smashed the doughnut into my face.

She did it.

How she did it wasn't important, and the why was obvious. Revenge for the shit I'd put her through since she came to Manderley. She was working her way through all of us – first Ivan, then Titus, now me. She thought I had something to do with her mother's assault.

What rattled my bones more than anything was what this meant.

She knows your secret.

I grabbed my phone off the bed, my fingers flying over the keys to text him, but I deleted all the words before I hit send. What could I say that would make a difference?

Calm down. Don't lose your shit. She doesn't know everything. She knows about the money... or lack thereof. But she can't know where it's gone, or why.

She'll figure it out. And you only have yourself to blame. You mentioned your brother. You poked the bear, and now the bear's not going to rest until she's clawed out your guts.

And this secret... it could cost the life of the one person in the world I cared about more than Faye.

"Fuck. Fuck. Fuck." I grabbed a pillow off my bed. That was the annoying thing about being stuck at this school in the middle of nowhere. There was no one to punch. I could punch Titus, I supposed, but since he was lending me money and he was the size of a freight train, all that would achieve was breaking my knuckles.

Ivan? I could punch him. That would be kind of satisfying – I'd at least get a reaction out of him. But he'd punch me back, and Ivan might be small, but behind that icy facade lurked decades of repressed Romanian fury. I was quite fond of the shape of my nose as it was.

I'd happily punch Master Radcliffe until his face was a bloody pulp, but that would make things worse for Ivan and Elena, and I couldn't do that.

With nowhere to direct my anger, I slammed my fist into the pillow. Feathers flew everywhere, blanketing my room in a soft, yellow snowstorm.

I flung the pillow away in disgust. It hit the photo frame on my bedside table, sending it flying. Glass shattered across the floor.

Faye. I bet she was loving this. Those red lips of hers had tugged back into a genuine smile because she bested me. I imagined those lips slipping around my cock, her tongue flicking over the tip as she took me deep. I moaned at the thought of surrendering to her.

With trembling fingers, I tapped a message into my phone on the Broken Muse private chat. We needed to sort this shit out, once and for all. We were dancing too close to the flames – one of us, or all of us, were going to get burned.

TITUS

I was chilling in the Blue Room, drinking wine and watching reality TV shows on Aroha's laptop, when my phone vibrated.

"Ooooh, I'll have some of that." Aroha wriggled her ass in the chair, shooting me her wicked grin. Her pupils were wide, dilated. *She's on something. Shit.*

We all knew Aroha had a crippling fear of performing, one she hid with cocaine and cigarettes and her fuck-off attitude. But we were just hanging out, no pretense, no performance, so why was she snorting now?

As if we didn't have enough to worry about. I opened my mouth to ask her about it, but then my phone buzzed again.

Across the room, on the sofa he shared with his sister, Ivan was frowning at his screen. That could only mean one thing.

Dorien.

"I have to go." I stood up, untangling Aroha's arm from around my shoulders and handing her back her computer. She flashed me a megawatt grin.

"When the Prince of Darkness calls, his little minions go running." She rolled her eyes.

"I'll watch TV with you, Aroha." Elena slid in beside her, tucking the bottle of wine into her lap. Aroha grabbed the laptop and started scrolling through the selection. I met Elena's eyes and she nodded. She'd seen the haze in Aroha's eyes, too. She wouldn't leave Aroha alone.

In the hallway, Ivan and I exchanged a look. "Faye?" he whispered. I nodded. It had to be. She was the only thing that could twist Dorien up in knots like this.

Faye de Winter.

Her scent followed me everywhere, seeping from the wallpaper, curling from the stuffy furnishings and threadbare carpets, filling my nostrils with the promise of more.

But there could never be more, because Dorien had already stamped his claim. And what Dorien wanted, he got.

Faye was proving a formidable opponent. She'd gone after Ivan and nearly got him kicked out of Manderley. If anyone else had done that, Dorien would tear them to pieces, but he never even considered it. He went to Madame Usher and smoothed things over. Ivan remained at school and we would never speak of the incident again. I hadn't the courage to ask what Dorien bargained to get that, but I know it had to have hurt him. Bad.

Although we were still ghosting Faye, he seemed to have given up on the plot to destroy her. He drove her to the hospital the other day, and then called to have Harrison pick her up. He snapped at me when I asked what happened, and Faye had been avoiding him and glaring at him across the room. I'd never seen him spun out on a girl before – it was weird. A little scary.

And it sucked, because I wanted her. But Dorien had first dibs, as he always did. Broken Muse was supposed to be a democracy, but we all knew that was bull-shit. Dorien called the shots, and Faye was his the moment she walked through the doors of Manderley.

He'll tear her apart like he does everything in his life, like he did with our band. If Faye thinks being hated by Dorien was hell on earth, then she should try having his love.

As we ascended the stairs, Ivan cleared his throat. I turned to him, but he crumpled under my gaze, swallowing down whatever he'd been about to say. We reached Dorien's room in silence. I shoved open his door.

"What happened in here? Faye finally give you the tar and feathering you deserve?"

Feathers flew in all directions, spinning in lazy circles through the air to settle on Dorien's stuff. He lay on the bed with his knees in the air, picking at the down sticking to his trousers. A dusting of duck-down snow clung to his hair, his shirt, even his cheeks. In the corner of the room, the feathers swirled in the air, forming a shape that at first glance looked like a pale face with a wide, black mouth. I blinked, and the unsettling image disappeared. *It's just feathers. My imagination is going wild in this stupid house.*

Beside me, Ivan covered his mouth with his hand, stifling a laugh.

"You're fucking hilarious." Dorien glared at me. A yellow feather stuck to his eyebrow. "Faye knows about my money."

That stopped me short. I slammed the door shut and folded my arms. "How?"

"She hacked my account and cleared out everything that was left, not that there was much. She donated it all to some charity for underprivileged musicians."

I couldn't help it. Laughter burst out of me like fireworks on the Fourth of July.

Dorien glared at me. "Chortle away. She'll be coming for you next, Van Halen."

I shrugged. "Let her. Maybe I *want* her to come after me."

"What does that mean?"

"I want to ask her out."

I hadn't intended to say those words. They'd burst out along with the laughter, and I couldn't stuff them back in. Ivan glanced between us, pressing his back against the wall and moving his feet into a position to run if things got violent.

Dorien tossed back his head. The laughter started deep in his stomach and bubbled out of him like a volcano starting to erupt. He kicked his legs in the air and caught a floating feather in his hand, crushing it between his fingers.

"I can't believe this shit. Good fucking luck, bro. We've spent the semester bullying her. She thinks you snuck into her room while she was sleeping. If you think you can charm her into overlooking that and giving you a chance, you're welcome to try. You don't need my permission – but I recommend packing some groin protection."

"So you don't care if I ask her?"

Dorien shrugged. "I didn't say that. I just said it's pointless."

My fingers curled into fists. "You can't lay claim over her just because you knew her before. You fucked that up, and she's made it pretty clear she can't stand you. Give someone else a chance."

Dorien sat up, his feet slamming on the floor. When his eyes met mine, the storms threatened to blow me over. "She kissed me back in the library. Fuck, she made this delicious moaning sound... you should have heard it, it'll turn your dick stone hard."

"Don't be a *bou*, Dorien," Ivan warned. "She kicked up in the nuts, also."

"That she did," he grinned. "It was hot as fuck."

My fingers tightened, nails digging into my skin.

Dorien spread his arms wide. "Go on, Titus. Lay me out. You know you want to."

"Fuck off." I turned to his bureau and tipped a stack of music books to the floor. *Thump, thump, thump.* They bounced on the rug. That didn't make me feel better, but it did break the hypnotic hold he had over me.

Dorien laughed again, and the sound was hysterical and a little bit terrifying. "You're right, bro. Faye can't stand me. She thinks I hired some bum to break into her mother's hospital room and write on her face. But that doesn't mean there isn't something there. Trust me, one thing I know *for a fact* is that I don't own Faye de Winter. But you know I will tame her. So why are we fighting over this? It's not like the two of us haven't been into the same girl before. Remember Cherie in Paris? We found a way to—"

"Three," Ivan said from the door.

I whirled around. "Excuse me?"

Ivan swallowed. "I said, the three of us had the same girl before. And we want the same girl now."

I lifted an eyebrow. "You too?"

Interesting. I wasn't sure if Ivan had ever liked a girl. I was the one who fell hard for every chick who batted her eyes at me or complimented my playing. Dorien was a force of nature, and he sucked everything and everyone in his path. But Ivan... he had only one love, and that was Elena.

Until now, apparently.

Ivan nodded as he stepped forward. "I don't want us to fight over her."

Dorien flopped back on the bed, sending up a flurry of feathers. "Who's fighting? Here's the thing – as far as us three and our cocks are concerned, it's Faye's choice. One of us, two of us, all three of us, we can give her the option, but it's her call, right?"

"Right..." I said slowly, not sure where he was going with this.

"So there's nothing to argue about. We simply present Faye with a buffet of options – the best Broken Muse has to offer. No sabotage, no playing each other off to win, no jealousy. Faye chooses, and we accept her choice. Fair?"

Ivan and I glanced at each other. On the surface, everything Dorien said was perfectly reasonable. And it wasn't unusual for us. We'd shared girls before. Things got pretty wild on tour, especially when we hit Amsterdam. Or Berlin. *Oh, Berlin... how could I forget the jelly, and the things Fraulein Ana did with giant pickles...*

But this wasn't just some Broken Muse groupie. This was *Faye*. Dorien's Faye. And just because he agreed to this didn't mean he intended to fight fair.

But fair or not fair, I wasn't going to miss my chance.

"Deal." I stepped forward, offering my fist.

"I agree." Ivan placed his fist on mine.

Dorien thrust his fist on top, the treble clef tattoos dancing over his knuckles. "Good. Because we have something bigger to deal with then your overeager cocks. Someone who isn't us is after Faye. Someone is trying to get to her through her mother. And we need to focus all our resources on bringing that person down, even if it means Manderley falls with it."

FAYE

The three boys disappeared into the city for a recital, and Madame Usher ordered me to clean the rooms while they were away. As soon as I opened Dorien's door, I was greeted with a fluffy, downy mess.

Feathers. *What?*

I assumed this was some new way to torture me until I found the source of the down – a pillow torn through the middle. My shoe crunched on something – a broken photo frame lying amongst scattered books and other things. The room looked like a war zone, with duck casualties and Dorien's intoxicating scent laid out like barbed wire ready to trip me up.

As I carefully packed the glass into a trash bag, I slid out the photograph to place it on Dorien's bureau. It was a picture of Dorien – his slate-grey eyes glaring defiantly at the camera, accentuated with dark, smudged eyeliner, arresting any viewer who dared gaze upon him. He wore a black shirt with a ruffled collar and stage makeup that gave him the appearance of a mesmerizing vampire – timeless and breathtakingly beautiful. He had his arm around a smiling girl, pulling her against his chest, his body language possessive.

Beside the photograph, someone had used lace and diamantes to create a collage, with a handwritten note in the center. "Dorien. Thank you for the greatest night of my life. Love, Clare."

Clare.

My finger traced over her face. This was the dead maid. Seeing her face – young and fresh and happy, with a slightly-turned up nose and friendly green eyes and brown hair swept up into a high bun – made her real to me for the first time. She lived in this house, slept in my room, died on the hallway carpet. The loopy hand-writing on the note matched that I'd rubbed off the old whiteboard in the pantry.

And she had been with Dorien. He'd taken her on a date. *The best night of my life.* I squinted harder at the lights in the background. *Are they in New York City—*

Creeeak. Creak.

I whirled around, my heart in my throat. "Who's there?"

No one answered. Obviously they didn't. Because it was just the house settling. But my nerves were already shot. I dropped the photograph onto the bureau and cleaned up the room as quickly as I could, all the while feeling the scratch of invisible eyes on the back of my neck.

Being around Dorien's scent like that... touching his things, stroking my fingers along the raw silk of his comforter... it did things to me. It made me doubt my earlier conviction that he'd been behind Mom's attack. It made me wish for things that could never be.

I needed to let the tension from my body. If I couldn't fuck, then I needed to play.

Luckily, with three students still away at the recital, the practice rooms were empty. I scrawled my name down on the whiteboard for the Yellow Room and slipped inside. I remembered the last time I'd been in here, when I found my father's book, and my shoulders tightened with tension. My fingers buzzed with pent-up energy as I removed my violin from its case and rested it against my chin.

I drew the bow over the strings, and in that first lingering note I transported myself out of my body and into the music. I played through *Nigun* as a warm-up, letting the mournful notes conjure images of my mother that made my chest ache, before launching into Paganini's explosive caprices.

My fingers flew along the strings, and my mind became a mess of color and light and sensation. The caprices aren't so much musical movements as they are exercises in madness – it took every ounce of concentration I possessed to keep my fingers on the strings as I executed the double-stop trills and impossible jumps. No memory could push through the wall of music, not even Dorien's scent.

In some faraway corner of my mind, I became dimly aware of the door creaking open. Elena appeared at the edge of my vision. She hovered in the doorway a moment, casting a glance over her shoulder, before slipping inside and locking the door behind her.

Instantly, the hairs on my neck stood up. My finger slipped on the string. *Why is she here? What fresh torture have the Muses cooked up for me?*

I didn't stop playing, but I tracked Elena as she crossed the room and perched on the end of the velvet chaise under the window. Sunlight peeked through the lace curtains, dappling her golden hair. She watched me, her expression serene. I waited for Elena to speak, or for *something* to happen. But she said nothing, so I kept playing.

I didn't dare close my eyes, the way I usually did when I played for myself. Instead, I focused on the new techniques Master Radcliffe taught me – resting my hand against the body of the violin so I could use my thumb as a pivot to accomplish the stretches. A cramp ran down the side of my index finger, but I ignored it.

As the last notes of the caprice trembled from the strings, Elena rose. Her eyes met mine – that frozen pixie stare that lured men like the Titanic attracted icebergs. I was surprised to see a tear fall down her cheek. She acknowledged me with a nod as she left the room, a trail of exotic perfume wafting after her.

What the fuck was that about?

I nestled my violin back in its case, unable to control my pounding heart. Did Elena come in here to spy on me? Was it the first stage of some new torture the Muses dreamed up? But that tear... it seemed impossible, but I couldn't help but wonder if Elena came to *listen to me play.*

The gong sounded through the house as the Muses arrived home. A commotion in the hallway drew my attention. I clipped the case shut and crept to the door, pulling it open a crack to peer outside. Ivan and Elena stood at the foot of the staircase. Elena's fingers curled around the carved banister, while Ivan tugged on her free wrist, trying to draw her back to face him.

"Where were you?" Ivan managed to spin her, wrapping his arms around her waist, holding her in place against his body. I tightened my grip on the door, debating interfering, but it didn't look like he was trying to dominate her. More... that he was desperate. Afraid. "I could not find you when we left. I was worried. I thought—"

She shook her head, pressing her hands to his back, letting her cheek fall against his shoulder. "I wasn't with him. I wanted to see Faye. I had to make sure she is worthy of you, and I believe she is."

Wait, what?

Ivan frowned. "You can't disappear like that."

"Please, Ivan. Drop it."

"I can't drop it. What he's doing to you... it's wrong. It's all so wrong." Ivan's voice trembled with rage. He let out a string of words in his native Romanian.

Elena replied to him in the same language, her shoulders sagging with defeat. I was just about to close the door again when she switched back to English. "There's nothing we can do. We are prisoners here. But he will help us be free. That is the only reason I let him near me, and that is my promise, Ivan. It will all be worth it."

Ivan spat a reply, his hands curled into fists against his back. I didn't have to understand Romanian to know he threatened violence against someone. But who was the *he* she referred to? Was it Dorien?

I drew back and tapped the door shut with my foot, leaning my ass against it. Why had Elena come to watch me play? Why didn't she want Ivan to know where she was? And what did she mean when she said that they were prisoners?

Was this another secret lurking in the walls of Manderley?

FAYE

"Students, as a special treat, Master Radcliffe and I would like to invite you to attend the gala performance of the New York Philharmonic this weekend as our guests, as well the ball afterward."

My ears perked up. Mom and I used to attend performances all the time. When we were well-off she was a patron of the orchestra, and I danced with her at many a gala ball under glittering chandeliers. Even in a room filled with stuffy rich dickweasels, my mother wasn't afraid to scorch the floorboards and draw the eye of every man in the room. A Wall Street banker once interrupted us mid tango to propose marriage to her.

Going without her would feel... about as shit as everything else I had to do without her, but it would be wonderful to be immersed in the music and remind myself what I was fighting for.

"As punishment for certain misdeeds, Ivan and Dorien will stay behind." Madame raised her nose in the air. "And, of course, Faye is much too busy with her chores to attend."

Ivan shot a glance at Elena, his fork clattering out of his hand. Elena placed her fingers over his. "I can't go without Ivan," she said, eyes meeting Madame's in a showdown of wills. Her wispy voice robbed her of the power in her sapphire gaze, and she quickly gave in, dropping her eyes to her plate.

"Don't be daft. You're a grown woman who can live without your brother for a night. What will happen when you're touring solo?" Ivan was shaking. Madame glared around the table, daring someone to challenge her. "The rest of you, be ready to depart at 10AM sharp Saturday morning. I've already booked hotel rooms in the city."

Not getting to go to the gala didn't bother me nearly as much as an entire weekend alone with Dorien and Ivan. I took an armload of plates into the kitchen, and when I returned to finish clearing the table, I noticed Dorien and Heather whispering together at the other end of the hall. Heather no longer had a plaster on her nose, but it still looked bruised, even through her makeup. She jerked her thumb in my direction, her voice dripping with venom. I stopped in my tracks.

They're talking about me. What the fuck?

Dorien whirled on his heel and strode away. Heather screamed after him, "If you don't have the stomach to finish what we started, I'll do it myself."

"Do that, and I'll ruin you." Dorien didn't yell, but the threat was clear in his voice.

Heather slammed the Red Room door in his face. Dorien stared at it for a few moments, his chest rising and falling, his hands balled into fists. He stalked down the hall toward me; the storm in his eyes could sink a battleship.

Dorien's step wavered as he spotted me, then he narrowed those slate orbs at me and quickened his pace. His boots thudded on the thick rug. He made his intention clear. If I didn't get out of his way, he'd mow me down and feel no remorse for it.

He must've discovered his charitable donation.

A strain. A break. Even a bruising could impact my playing. I couldn't afford to get hurt.

But I also knew I couldn't let Dorien win. If I gave this dickhead an inch, he'd destroy me.

I stepped toward Dorien, squaring my shoulders, making it clear that I wasn't budging.

Dorien kept coming, that beautiful jaw set in grim determination. The space closed between us, bringing a wave of his intoxicating scent that almost knocked me back. But I didn't stop, didn't slow down.

At the last possible second, I slammed my body against the wall and stuck out my foot. Dorien's heavy boot slid beneath it, and he dropped like a log.

"What the fuck?" he groaned as he rolled over to kneel on the rug. He clutched his hand, which had slammed against the dado rail.

"It speaks." I stood over him with arms folded. A smile crept across my face, and I let it linger. I liked this view of him, groveling beneath me with a bewildered expression on his face.

"You... tripped me." Dorien raised his arm. It had sliced down the hook on the wall, opening a small cut along the side of his forearm. "I'm bleeding."

"Don't sound so surprised." A twinge of guilt wriggled in my gut, but I pushed it down. "You intended to hurt me just now, *and* you tripped me twice. You hurt my mother. All's fair in war and prize money."

Dorien pulled himself to his feet, using the arm that wasn't bleeding to flick dark curls of hair from his eyes. "I never touched your mother, and if you thought about it for a moment, you'd realize you know that. Even if you were the best musician in this school, which you're not, Madame Usher will never give you the Manderley Prize."

"Maybe not, but I can stop it going to any member of Broken Muse." I shrugged. "I get it. You hate me. But I'm not going anywhere, so you're wasting your energy tormenting me."

"It's not a waste." Dorien dusted off his trousers. "I enjoy it."

"There are so many *more* enjoyable ways to spend your time."

The words flew out of my mouth before I could stop them. A flush formed on my cheeks, and I resisted the urge to bash my head against the wall until I wiped all memory of Dorien's raised eyebrow and shocked expression from existence.

Dorien pushed past me, leaving a trail of frankincense and violets and a fluttering in my chest in his wake.

Did I imagine it, or did Dorien Valencourt just flash me a *smile*?

FAYE

The weekend rolled around. Heather, Aroha, Elena, and Titus went off in the limo with Madame Usher and Master Radcliffe, which meant it was just Dorien, Ivan, and me for dinner.

While I was chopping vegetables I got a call from the police about Mom's case. They had security footage of the homeless guy standing with someone at an ATM two hours after the incident. They couldn't see the figure's face or even if they were male or female. It couldn't be Dorien, because he'd been with me.

He could have hired someone, or it could have been one of the others, but... I just didn't believe it. And then there was all that stuff Dorien was trying to say in the library, about Madame Usher and... the $400 doughnut delivery didn't lie. Just like I didn't believe Dorien capable of murdering Clare in cold blood, I couldn't see Broken Muse orchestrating this.

But if not them, who?

Feeling villainous, I cooked the hottest, spiciest chili I knew how to make – with my mom's classic *mole* sauce – and piled spoonfuls on top of two heaped mounds of rice. I took their mounds out to the dining room, dumped them on the table, and returned to the kitchen to serve a more reasonable portion to myself.

A few minutes later, a creak sounded by the door. I looked up from my book, a knot of fear twisting in my stomach. But instead of a ghost, two muses leaned against the frame, holding their plates.

"What's this?" Dorien stared at his mountain in unveiled disgust.

"You're talking to me now?" I winked at him from the table.

They crossed the room and slid onto the wooden bench opposite me. Dorien jabbed his chili with a fork. "Only to tell you that this food looks like dog shit. It's inedible. Get me something else."

Ivan was already eating, his eyes flicking between Dorien and I. He made no reaction as the chili hit his mouth. *Is that guy made of stone or something?*

"This is what I cooked," I said. "If you don't want to eat it, you're welcome to make yourself something. Otherwise, eat up."

Dorien picked up his fork, letting chili and guacamole splatter on the table. "It looks like someone already did."

"It's nice." Ivan shoveled in another mouthful. My mouth burned just *watching* him.

"It's not even proper Mexican food. It's an abomination. I've eaten at Aarón Sánchez's restaurant, and he wouldn't deem this fit to feed the peasants who shine his shoes."

"You wouldn't know proper Mexican food if it bit you on the ass, and you're not getting anything else, so eat up." I crunched a corn chip extra loudly. "You could have gone to the fancy gala dinner with the others if you'd begged Madame. You're not in the dog house with her like me and Ivan."

"You know I couldn't."

I choked on my chili. "What do you mean?"

The room sizzled with tension.

"I opened my account to find the last of my money has been donated to a charity." Dorien shoved back his chair. "I don't know how you did it, but that's harsh."

Ivan set down his fork and glared at his friend, but Dorien ignored him. As I watched his face for a reaction, I realized what he meant when we confronted each other in the hallway. He didn't have the money to pay anyone to hurt my mother. I'd have seen it when I was trawling through his funds. Relief washed over me with a force I wasn't prepared for. *Why did I want Dorien to be innocent so badly?*

"I would never do such a thing," I said sweetly. "But *if* I did, I might've been surprised to discover just how little money was there. Seems at odds with the rich asshole image you've created for yourself. I wonder how the press would feel if they knew the Bad Boy of Baroque was really the Bad Boy of Broke?"

Dorien stiffened. Something in his eyes glinted at me. Something like... admiration.

"Well played." Dorien drummed his fingers on the table. "Ivan, you got plans tonight?"

Although he spoke to his friend, his eyes never left my face. Ivan answered with the same intense attention – those sapphire shards cutting slivers from my skin. Once again, I longed to know what Ivan was thinking behind that icy stare.

"We've got this whole house to ourselves," he answered without emotion.

"And I have a key to the liquor cabinet," Dorien grinned. "What do you say, Faye? Titus isn't here, but that doesn't mean we can't have a proper Muse party."

For a moment I didn't register what they were getting at. "You're asking me to hang out with you?"

"C'mon. It's Friday night, and Ivan needs a distraction from worrying about his sister. You should let your hair down, Sprite." Dorien reached across the table, his fingers brushing my cheek as he curled a strand of my hair around his fingers.

For a moment, time stopped. All that existed was the warmth of Dorien's fingers on my cheek, and the slight tug on my hair that made fire plunge through my body to pool between my legs, and Ivan's eyes tugging at me, a flicker on the edges of his ice that promised *something*...

I collected myself, just barely, and slapped his hand away. I slid the bench back, doing my best to ignore the crackle of fire across my skin from where he touched me.

"I've got dishes to do."

"We'll help." Dorien gave a bitter laugh. "After all, servitude might be in my future."

~

Dorien and Ivan carried the plates to the dishwasher while I wiped down the table. When I turned around, they'd both tied frilly embroidered aprons over their dress shirts. Ivan filled the sink with hot water while Dorien tried to flick his ass with the tea towel.

"If you're here to help, you need to actually help." I pointed to the dishwasher. "Finish filling that, and give everything that doesn't fit to Ivan."

"Aye, aye, Kitchen Mussolini. And while we're slaving away, what will you be doing?"

Pinching myself to make sure I'm not hallucinating this madness. "I've got to tidy the spice rack and fold the laundry."

Having them in the kitchen was odd. A memory flashed in my mind – of a different kitchen, and a different boy. Dorien's eyes widening as he took in the tiny confines of our shitty walk-up the first time he came over after music lessons. "Wow," he bounded over to look at the colorful Mexican tiles my mother used to decorate the wall. "This place is *so cool*."

I'd never thought of our little apartment as cool, especially not when I compared it to Dorien's penthouse. I only went there once for his birthday, and it looked more like a Star Trek set than a home – everything glistening so white it hurt my eyes, his mother hovering over us in a floor-length brown robe with this creepy smile on her face, and that guy Dorien called Uncle Aaron grilling me about my father's career while we ate a gross buckwheat birthday cake.

And Ivan... that guy looked like he was made to put on a pedestal to be worshipped in a pagan temple – hella distracting when one was trying to clean the counters. He moved around the kitchen with such quiet grace that I kept stopping to watch him and forgot what I was doing. He followed me into the laundry as I pulled the sheets out of the dryer and silently picked up the corners to help fold them. I worked hospitality jobs for long enough that I was pretty neat and tidy, but his military-straight corners fascinated me.

"I folded a lot of laundry as a boy," he volunteered. "Lots of tourists visit our city because of its medieval buildings. Our mother would do laundry for the hotels for extra money. Elena and I had to go around to collect the dirty sheets, and return the clean linens." That was the most words he ever said to me. Actually, the most words I heard him say to *anyone*.

"When did you come to the States?" I asked.

"We were eight years old. We played a recital in Bucharest. Elena... even then she played like no one else. Master and Madame Usher approached my parents afterward and offered to bring us both to the United States. They would act as our guardians and ensure we had the best education. They named a figure that had my father's eyes bugging out of his head, and my parents agreed right there. They did not ask us what we wanted." His eyes flashed with resentment. "We have been at Manderley now fifteen years."

I knew we were skating around the crux of why he worried about Elena off on her own, but he wouldn't reveal more. The words were out of my mouth before I could stop them. "How can you *stand* it?"

Ivan dropped his eyes to the sheet, which slid through his deft fingers as he folded it with precision. "It is not a matter of choice."

I was puzzling over those words when Dorien poked his head around the corner. "Dishwasher is on. Is it time to play yet?"

"What's the sudden interest in me?" The memory of our kiss scorched through my body. My toes curled into the floor. And then I flashed back to the weeks of ghosting, the rotten pranks, my violin in pieces on the bathroom sink, and I wanted to kick myself.

"Relax, Sprite. We're just hanging out." Dorien's lips curled back into his signature smirk. "Unless you have a standing engagement with the resident ghost."

At the word *ghost*, a flicker of panic crept up my spine. All the things I'd seen and heard and felt at Manderley that I couldn't explain, that were connected to the Bad Boys of Baroque in some way... and here I was agreeing to spend time with them, *alone*.

I could just say no and return to my room and read a book or practice my Paganini.

I *could* say no...

But standing between Ivan and Dorien, with their eyes locked on mine, no was not an option. I thought of my mother in her hospital bed, and her lifelong resolve to take every opportunity and seize the days while she still had them. I shrugged, hoping they couldn't hear my heart pounding against my chest. "Sure."

I followed the Muses down the hall. Dorien ducked into the Blue Room and pulled a bottle of Scotch from the cabinet. Tucking it under his arm, he led the way to the ballroom, shoving the double doors open to reveal the vast space, shrouded in cool, dappled light that peeked through the trees.

Ivan moved to light the silver candlesticks on the sideboard. I noticed someone had moved my violin case from the practice room to under the window, next to Ivan's. Dorien sat down at the piano, his fingers sweeping over the keys as he pulled the stopper and took a swig straight from the bottle. "Play with us."

The way he said it, with the corner of his mouth twisted up, purred through my body. I knew he wasn't just talking about music. I held my hand out for the bottle. When Dorien pressed it into my fingers, his touch lingered on mine, and the pounding in my heart ratcheted up a notch.

I yanked the bottle away and took a deep swig. The alcohol burned the back of my throat and pooled warmth in my belly. The tiniest bit of my nerves slipped away. I slapped the bottle into Ivan's outstretched hand and picked up my bow. "What are we playing?"

"Ladies' choice," Ivan said.

"What about the Broken Muses piece, 'Confessions of an Opium Eater'?" All their pieces had weird titles like that, many referencing old gothic literature. I loved this piece because it was a perfect example of what Classical music could do – it transported you as the listener into a darkened corner of an opium den and sent you on a dizzying high before crashing you through the despair of addiction.

Dorien tapped the opening bar. "It's not written for two violins."

"I might have a few ideas about that." I didn't tell them that the notes haunted my dreams so much that I'd toyed with the composition.

Ivan nodded to Dorien and lifted his violin to his neck. Dorien's part was low, the notes long, the sound reaching me deep in my belly. Ivan's eyes locked on mine as he came in with the melody. He conjured the sweet scent of the drug, the air heady with smoke, the seductive promise of unexplored parts of the mind...

I came in on the third bar, layering my melody over his, adding a melancholy that hinted at the future turmoil of the third movement, where the pleasure of opium has morphed into the pain.

I turned toward Ivan as I played, and as the music took me over my body moved, swaying and dipping with the music. Ivan's gaze followed me, that ice burning my skin like fire. A laugh escaped my throat as the music lifted away my fears, my inhibitions. I felt like I was sinking under opium's spell.

Or perhaps that was the spell cast by the two beautiful, broken muses who played for me, toyed with me, their eyes raking my skin even as their fingers called forth more old and reckless magic.

Ivan moved closer, his eyes never leaving mine as he faced me, bow to bow, our fingers and wrists working in unison – an evenly-matched duel where the winner would take away... what? The tension between us pulled taut, like a cord that would either crush us against each other or snap apart and fling us across the room. We hung there, suspended inside the music, our bows casting magic into the air.

Dorien's fingers slid from the keys, leaving me and Ivan on our own. Violins screeched through the cavernous space as we descended into the dark euphoria of the second movement. I didn't stop playing as Dorien moved behind me, his presence dancing across my skin. I couldn't stop. The music had taken hold of me.

Dorien's hand slid up my thigh.

His touch was pure sin and fire. Ivan's eyes captured me, trapped me between them. Every inch of my skin sizzled with heat.

Fingers touched my hair, trailing through the strands as Dorien pushed it aside. Warm lips grazed my neck as the hand slid further around me. His fingers splayed across my stomach, pressing me back against him, grinding my ass against his jeans until I could feel his hard cock.

Hard for *me*.

Ivan's bow squealed on the strings. My mouth opened as Dorien kissed a trail of fire along my neck.

"Fuck this," Ivan groaned. He tossed his violin onto the chair, not caring that the instrument slid off and bounced on the rug. He closed the space between us, pressing his body against mine, trapping my hands so I could no longer play.

His lips met mine with a longing that knocked my breath away. Ivan clung to me like he was drowning and I was his lifeline. I sank into him, reveling in the joy of being wanted.

Ivan's fingers wrapped around my neck, pulling me closer, crushing my instrument between us. Dorien grabbed the neck, and I released my grip so he could tug it away. Now nothing separated us but the promise hanging in the air.

Dorien's finger slipped under the hem of my t-shirt. I gasped into Ivan's mouth as warm fingers touched the bare skin of my stomach. Ivan made this growling noise that was so fucking delectable.

Dorien tugged at my shirt, dragging his hands over my flesh as he rolled it up. His hands grasped my breasts through my bra, and his teeth dragged over my neck.

Fingers circled my nipples through the sheer fabric of my bra, and I thought my pounding heart would burst from my chest. I'd lost all sense of whose hands were where; all I knew was how amazing I felt.

I had so many questions, but if I asked, we'd have to stop. And I didn't want to stop. Not when their hands were everywhere and their lips and tongues...

"Piano bench," Dorien rasped, his voice tight with need.

Ivan looped his fingers in mine and led me to the bench. He splayed his fingers across my shoulder, pressing me back until I lay down against the floral fabric. The filigree moldings on the ceiling framed Ivan's face like a halo as he dragged me into another of his intense kisses.

"No hogging the prize, Nicolescu."

With a grunt of protest, Ivan rolled off me. I whimpered with need of him, but Dorien's fingers were on my fly, unbuttoning my jeans and pulling them off my hips, and the kiss of the air against my skin and the prickle of their eyes on me sent a wild ache deep into my core. Ivan reached around and flicked off my bra, tossing it across the room. The boy who had been in my dreams since I was eight years old and the sapphire beauty who stole my breath stared down at my body covered only in a scrap of black fabric. I reveled in their gaze. Here, I was the one in power.

A wicked smirk crept over Dorien's face. He bent in front of me, nudging my legs open. His hand brushed over the fabric of my panties. I gripped the edges of the stool. "You're soaked," he whispered, his tone reverent.

Ivan bent down at the other end of the bench, beside me. I thought he'd lean in to kiss me, but instead, his lips closed over my nipple. The sensation of his hot tongue flicking over that sensitive nub sent molten lava flowing through my veins.

With one swipe, Dorien tore my panties off, tossing the ruined fabric aside. He bent over me, and as Ivan sucked my nipple into his mouth, Dorien's tongue circled my clit.

Holy fucktrumpets, that's amazinggggggggg...

Dorien's tongue worked in slow circles, taking his time, teasing out the heat inside me. Ivan moved to my neglected nipple and gave it the attention it deserved.

I writhed between them, knowing I was making a wet spot on the bench and not caring one bit. Dorien worked a finger inside me as he licked at my wetness, and I was gone gone gone.

Fire crashed over me in waves, like a tsunami of heat pulling me under, tossing my body on an ocean of ecstasy. I lost myself to the fire and the warmth and the pleasure, surfacing moments later to see the two Muses leaning back, their arms around each other as they stared down at me like I was some treasure they'd just uncovered.

Ivan's sapphire eyes twinkled with delight, and Dorien's smug expression begged to be slapped.

As the heady warmth in my veins subsided, I became aware of the tension hanging in the air again. We weren't finished yet.

Dorien turned to his friend, tugging on the edge of Ivan's shirt. "I'm not sure it's fair that Sprite's the only one naked."

Wordlessly, Ivan tugged off his shirt. My eyes widened as I took in the ethereal beauty of his alabaster skin and perfect form, and the disfigurement that marred it. I reached out to touch the lattice of scars covering his back. "What are these?"

Ice coated Ivan's eyes. He flinched away for a moment before turning to me again. He'd pulled up a facade, locking away his secret in a dark corner of his mind so I couldn't get to them. "They are not important, not when I am looking at a beautiful woman."

He means me. I'm the beautiful woman. No one had ever called me that before. Fatty, lardass, hippo – those were the names I was used to hearing yelled at me across campus by guys. Lecherous drunks drooling over the counter about how much they loved my curves and Creepy Cory following me after work was not the same thing as two members of Broken Muse looking at me like I was a goddess deserving of worship.

Dorien flung off his shirt and stepped out of his jeans. The candlelight flickered over his tattoos, illuminating the Latin script across his chest, the phrase *In Cauda Venenum*. I had to ask him about it, but not now.

Now I had other things on my mind.

Dorien gripped my hips and flipped me over like I weighed nothing. Honestly, that was the sexiest thing he'd done up until this point, which considering the shudders of pleasure still coursing through me from the orgasm, was saying something.

He trailed a finger over my ass cheeks. "Such a beautiful derriere," he murmured. "I'd love to turn it red with a whip one day."

Fuck. Why did that suggestion make my stomach pool with warmth?

Ivan's fingers knitted in mine, and he planted a gentle kiss on my forehead. I heard the tear of a condom wrapper, and then Dorien's hands were on my hips again. My whole body ached with a need I couldn't express. I tipped my hips back, inviting him, begging him, *commanding* him.

With a single motion, Dorien bent over and plunged into me, burying himself as deep as he could go. Balls to the wall, that was Dorien's style. I felt a sharp pain as his size stretched me, pushing me to the limit of what I could take. Once all of him was inside me, he held still, his forearms bracing against the piano bench, his body raised above mine as his ragged breath seared my skin.

"I never thought I'd get to be inside you," he whispered, his breath against my ear sending a shudder of delight through my already quivering body. While my body opened for him, warming to his presence, Dorien remained hard, tight, rigid, a coiled snake ready to strike.

His hand snaked around my throat, tugging my head up and back, attacking my mouth with his as he started to move. Slow at first, and then he was bucking against me, losing himself in the wildness of it, in the release of all the tension that had stretched between us for so long.

Ivan knelt down beside me, his fingers tangling in my hair as he tore my lips from Dorien's to devour me in his. I reached out and pulled Ivan toward me, dragging him up so my lips could close around his cock. He tasted amazing, hot and tart and uniquely Ivan, and his cock twitched against my lips as I took him in as deep as I could.

Two cocks inside me. Two broken muses all to myself.

I can't believe I'm doing this.

It feels so good.

So right.

Dorien's finger plunged between my legs, rubbing my clit as he slammed into me, pushing Ivan deeper. I moaned around Ivan's cock, and that might've been too much for him. He fisted a handful of my hair in his hand, his eyes never leaving my face as his jaw clenched. For the briefest moment, as he surrendered to his primal self, that tightly wound control slipped from his eyes, and I glimpsed the *real* Ivan. The proud and kind and scared guy who would do anything to protect the people he loved.

Ivan's body jerked. Hot, salty cum hit the back of my throat at the same time Dorien thrust deeper than ever and his finger slammed into my clit, and a second orgasm exploded through me.

My whole body came alive, my veins humming with the same magic I felt when I played music, only amplified times a million. The melody of our bodies meeting conjured a rush of sensory detail – the smell of my mother's home-cooked food, the taste of peanut-butter oreo doughnuts melting on my tongue, the ache in my shoulder after playing a difficult concerto, the swell in my chest whenever Mom told me she was proud of me. All of those bright moments and perfect details converged inside me in a single moment of rapture.

I saw stars and galaxies and the birth and death of the universe on the insides of my eyelids. I screamed as I came, my voice echoing through the cavernous room.

It was too much for Dorien. His body tensed, his muscles tightening. He fell over the edge with me, coming with a grunt before collapsing against me, skin on sweaty skin. His cock slid out.

Dorien pushed his hair out of his eyes. The gaze that met mine burned with something I'd never seen on him before – contentment. "Well, well, Sprite. You certainly played all the right notes."

I laughed as I sat up, tossing tangled hair over my shoulder, and reached for the whisky bottle and took a long swig. I sought Ivan's icicle eyes and gave him a flirty wink. "Drink up, boys. We've got all night."

FAYE

Why is my brain on fire?

I rolled over, arms flailing, trying to pat out the flames engulfing my skull. But there were none. The searing pain came from inside. I tried to open one shaky eye to gaze upon the world, but at the sight of the bright light streaming through my open window, my eye rebelled and slammed shut again.

I'm in a hell of my own making.

Shaky memories flickered through the pain. Me, grabbing a whisky bottle from Dorien, giddily ballroom dancing with Ivan while Dorien thumped out a waltz on the piano, breaking onto the second-floor balcony to howl at the moon, running naked across the overgrown lawn to jump into the freezing mountain stream at the bottom of the garden, sitting on Dorien's shoulders while we drunkenly tried to untangle my torn panties from the chandelier, more whisky... so much whisky...

Oh shit.

I bolted upright, gasping for breath as the memories solidified into a disturbing, terrifying, and *very* naked picture.

What have I done?

I slept with two guys. *Two guys.*

Two guys who had bullied me ever since I arrived at Manderley.

They fucked me on the bench. And then... and then Ivan on the chaise lounge, and Dorien bending me over the piano keys, and again beside the stream...

My cheeks burned.

I had... a threesome. Like I was a porn star or one of their groupies instead of the dowdy and not-at-all-sexually-deviant Faye de Winter.

I mean, wasn't there supposed to be a step between losing your virginity and group sex? The first and only time I had sex was with a guy named Henry at music camp in southern Maine. I may have been a geek with no friends at school, but music camp was where geeks like me went to get laid. Stick a hundred ostracized teenagers in dorms together with minimal supervision, and you've got one long sex party.

Henry Oxshott traveled to camp every year from his British boarding school, and we always hung out together. He wore wool sweaters and had an adorable accent and a face full of zits. We bonded over our shared love of Mexican food and absent fathers. Two summers ago, we decided it was time. Neither of us knew what to do, but Henry held me and whispered sweet things into my hair and it was nice, if not underwhelming. I came back from camp feeling older and wiser. I told my mom what had happened and that I didn't get what all the fuss was about.

Now I got it.

Sound the fucktrumpets. Dorien Valencourt gave me my first orgasm, and Ivan Nicolescu could make me come practically just by whispering evil things in my ear.

I wanted many, many more.

All the orgasms for me.

Only, not now. I moaned, clutching my head in some vain attempt to stop my brain leaking out my eyeballs. *Now I wanted to die.*

Fuck, why did I drink so much Scotch?

Beside the bed, my phone beeped, reminding me it was time to get up and start my chores. After a few blind tries, my fingers circled the phone. My whole body screamed as I dragged my arm back and tossed it at the wall. *CRASH. THUMP.* It clattered to the floor. That seemed to shut it up.

Beside me, something moaned.

Fucking ghost.

Wait, hold the poltergeist. My brain fog parted just long enough for a sliver of fear to slice through my skull. *Seriously, what is that noise?*

The ghost moaned again. I sat up, fumbling for the lamp, my heart hammering so fast it churned up the bile in my delicate stomach. As I struggled to open my eyes, something moved in the bed beside me.

"Morning, Sprite," the ghost murmured from beneath the sheets.

"Fuck!" I leaped from the bed, tugging the sheets over my breasts. The ghost rolled over as I revealed it to the light, and Dorien's sleepy face peered up at me with wry amusement. "What are you doing in my bed?"

"You mean she's already forgotten us?" Ivan sat up, his white-blond hair piled on one side of his head.

"Arrrrgh!" I yanked the rest of the sheet off and staggered back until I crashed into the wall. My hand flew to my churning stomach – my weakened disposition couldn't deal with two very hot and *very* naked Muses entangled together in my bed.

I died in my sleep. That's the only logical explanation. I've died and gone to some weird version of heaven. Or hell.

Definitely hell. Because the fact they both look that good after how much whisky we drank is downright sinful.

"I can't deal with this right now." I slumped against the wall, pressing my fingers to my temples. "Why are you here? You have much larger and less crowded beds downstairs."

"The company down there wasn't as good." Ivan yawned. "Besides, you were the one who dragged us up here."

"You wouldn't take no for an answer." That dangerous smirk played across Dorien's face. "You kept yelling that if the ghost of Manderley came for you in the night, you needed some big strong men to sacrifice while you escaped out the window."

"You were quite forceful," Ivan added. "It was hot as fuck."

I moaned again, my cheeks burning with heat. "I thought that was a dream."

"The best kind of dream." Dorien sat up, sliding his legs off the bed. His rumpled curls flopped over his face, and I went weak at the knees... from the hangover or his hotness, I couldn't say. "Hey, so we need to talk. About serious stuff."

"No serious before coffee." I bent down to pick up my jeans from where I'd thrown them on the floor. Big mistake. My stomach did not approve of bending.

Dorien's fingers circled my wrist, and he pulled me into his lap, brushing my hair from my face. His fingers against my skin were like a healing balm. "This thing that we're doing, Sprite, it's not a one-time thing – not if you don't want it to be. You're a Muse girl now. *Our* Muse girl."

I lifted an eyebrow. "Wouldn't Titus have to agree to that?"

"Oh, Titus agrees. He's going to be pissed he wasn't here. He's been wanting to ask you out since the start of the year."

What? "He has not."

"Mmmhmmm. He didn't make a move because he thought I laid claim to you."

I slapped his hand from my cheek. "This isn't the Dark Ages. I make my own decisions, and I'm not some object to fight over."

"I never doubted it." Dorien's hands skimmed my thighs, drawing circles on my back. Even through the haze of my hangover, it felt so good to be touched by him. "That's why we're not fighting. The three of us share everything, so why not share our girl? You don't seem to mind – for a straight-laced music geek, you turn into a lioness in the sack."

Ivan shuffled over, taking my hand and knitting his fingers in mine. "What Dorien is trying to say in his usual dicksome way is that we never wanted to hurt you. We did horrible things because we didn't believe we had a choice."

"You still did them." I pressed my hand to my temple, trying to stop the rush of bad memories from flooding my head, in case they made my brain leak out my ears.

"Yes. And we know we have a ton of groveling to do before you forgive us." Dorien rolled my nipple between his fingers, and I bit my lip to stop the moan from escaping my lips. "How does a morning orgasm sound?"

"Dorien." Ivan frowned, his voice thick with warning.

Reluctantly, Dorien pulled his hand away. The storm crept in the edges of his eyes. "Right. Serious stuff first. You're our Muse girl, Sprite, and we'll protect you. But we've got to keep this secret. We have to continue to bully you."

I stiffened. "Why?"

"Back in the library, I was trying to tell you Madame Usher wants you gone from Manderley. She came to me before you arrived, and said that Master Radcliffe had insisted you become his student, but she felt your background would be too much of a handicap. She mentioned her affair with your father, and how chins would wag in the music community. She said she couldn't go against Master Radcliffe, but made it very clear you needed to be driven away. Since then, I've heard her change the story."

"That's... either she lied to you then, or you're lying to me now." My chest tightened. "Madame told me she kept an eye on my career since I left her school. My invitation came from her, not Master Radcliffe."

"She lied to one of us. That doesn't surprise me. I just don't know what that means."

I squeezed my eyes shut. This was too much to deal with right now. I couldn't process this with hangover brain. "Why did you agree? It can't be because of your family—"

"She holds the sword of Damocles over my head," Dorien growled. "Over all our heads."

"People we care about are in danger if we don't do as she says," Ivan added.

Like Elena, I guessed. But that made no sense. What could Madame Usher possibly do to Elena with Ivan always in her shadow? And what power did she have over Dorien? It had to do with what Dorien told me about his family, but that didn't make sense – beautiful, wild Dorien who never gave a fuck what anyone thought. He wouldn't let Madame own him over that secret.

"Are you going to tell me what she has on you?"

Dorien shook his head. "Greedy girl. You already have our hearts, don't make us give you our secrets, too."

"For now, it's safer for you to live in ignorance." Ivan squeezed my fingers.

"I think – although I can't prove it – that she's behind all the weird things we can't explain. None of us smashed your violin or paid that homeless guy to hurt your mom. But I can't figure out how she did those things, either."

"And there's this, too." I fumbled on the nightstand for the *Grimm's Fairy Tales* book. As Dorien frowned at the inscription, I explained about the night I found it.

"Something is going on in this house. And my bet is it has something to do with that Carl Becker violin you picked up. We're going to figure this out. We will deal with Madame Usher," Dorien vowed. "She expects us to follow her like little lambs to the slaughterhouse. She has secrets of her own, and we'll bury her with them. But if we have any hope of figuring out what's going on at Manderley, then Madame Usher needs to believe things are normal. That means, we hate each other and we're trying to force you to quit. Plus, it might be the best way to contend with Heather."

"Heather?"

"Turns out I did my job a little too well." Dorien leaned forward and tasted my lips with his tongue. "She hates you with the fire of a thousand suns – the trailer trash who's captured Master Radcliffe's attention and my heart. Punching her nose didn't help, either. Heather's got some nasty plans for you."

"Plans she intended to carry out with her future fiancé, before he dumped her," Ivan added.

"I didn't dump her," Dorien shot back. "It's impossible to dump someone when you were only together in their imagination."

"Am I in danger?" I whispered.

"Heather will be the one in danger if she touches you." Dorien tipped my chin up with his finger. His ragged breath sent heat coursing through my veins. "What do you say, Sprite? Let us pretend to hate you in front of Usher, and we'll keep blowing your mind in private. You're stronger than anyone I know. You can handle a few harsh words and stupid pranks."

"Mmmm." His lips met mine, and I lost myself in the kiss. Ivan's hands crept over my naked skin, his mouth trailing featherlight kisses along my neck, raising the hairs on my skin. I sank back onto the bed as the two of them pressed themselves against me, lips and hands roaming freely, exploring every hidden place inside me.

Through the haze of hungover orgasm, my mind whirred with everything Dorien and Ivan told me. Was Madame Usher really going to such lengths to get rid of me?

And, most importantly, have I seriously just agreed to let the Muses continue to torture me?

 Faye

By the time the others returned, I'd managed to kick the guys out of my room, put on my black dress, and guzzle a million gallons of coffee. Dorien and Ivan (who both barely seemed to feel the effects of last night's whisky, the dickweasels) helped me clean the mess we made in the ballroom, then disappeared to get some practice in while I continued with my chores. I was struggling my way through polishing the banister on the grand staircase and trying not to think about Clare's body lying at the bottom when Elena, Heather, and Aroha burst through the door, all smiles and laughter. At the back of the group, Titus looked up at me, his dark eyes burning with questions.

Dorien's words echoed in my head. *He's been wanting to ask you out since the start of the year. He didn't make a move because he thought I laid claim to you.*

Titus' lips turned up in a smile that twinkled with promise. I dropped to my knees, pretending to polish between the railings when really my legs wouldn't support my weight anymore.

Madame Usher bustled in last, frowning as she saw me on the stairs. "Have you prepared lunch for us?"

"Not yet. I wasn't certain what time you'd return—"

She huffed. "Hurry and set it out."

I dashed back to the kitchen and nearly threw up in the sink. I managed to pull myself together and find a selection of cold cuts and leftovers to lay out. All through the meal, I kept sneaking glances at the Muses. True to their word, they continued to ignore me. Dorien even whispered 'wide load' under his breath as I took my seat, and Heather giggled. The comment stung until I caught the storm in his eyes – part regret, part promise of how he'd make things up to me when we were alone. I was surprised the electricity crackling between us didn't set the table linen on fire.

After lunch, I took my violin to the Red Room to practice. Just as I played the final movement of my version of "Confessions of an Opium Eater," Elena slipped into the room. She took a seat in the darkest corner, pulling her legs to her chest and hiding behind a curtain of hair. I was practicing the Paganini again, and I had to keep going over the same tricky passage to make my fingers bend in an impossible way. It had to be tedious to watch and yet, she stayed almost to the end, slipping out just before I'd finished.

Weird.

I climbed the stairs two at a time, my stomach wrapped up in knots, hoping to pass one of the guys on the landing and yet dreading the encounter. Already it felt as though last night had been a dream. Had Dorien and Ivan really said all those things to me, about protecting me? About me being a 'Muse girl'? Or was this just some elaborate ruse so they could keep playing games with me?

I didn't meet anyone on the stairs. I dropped my violin in my room and lay down on my bed for an hour, staring at the ceiling and trying to slip into sleep. My ruined mind and pounding temples refused to cooperate.

I glanced at my watch. Time to head back downstairs to start dinner. I popped a couple of ibuprofen, ran a brush through my tangled hair, and splashed cold water on my face. *Hangovers suck.* The last thing I wanted to do was face cooking right now.

As I trudged back down the servants' staircase, a familiar song wafted through the house – another Broken Muse favorite, called 'Graveyard Shift.' *The guys must be practicing in the Red Room.* I paused, resting my back against the wall, letting that dark, seductive music fill me.

No matter what happened next, I would always have my memories of last night. Nothing could take that away from me.

I hummed the melody under my breath as I went straight to the pantry. I opened the chest freezer to inspect my options. Maybe a fried chicken salad? Or I could use that New Zealand lamb leg and—

Hands wrapped around me, pinning my arms around my back. I cried out, trying to twist my head to see who it was. The cool steel of a knife pressed against my throat.

FAYE

I let out a yelp of surprise. The lamb leg I was holding dropped from my hands and thumped on the floor.

"Quiet, trash bitch," Heather rasped in my ear. "Make another sound and I'll cut you. Don't think I won't."

Shit. *Shit.* My blood froze. All the self-defense moves I learned in a YMCA class with Mom flew from my head. All I could focus on was the blade kissing my skin and Heather's hot breath in my ear. *She's holding a knife. Blow the asswhistle, this is bad.*

"Hold her tight," Heather barked. Someone grabbed my hands, twisting them backward at an angle arms aren't supposed to twist. I yelped as my body jerked forward in protest, pressing me against the knife. Panic rose inside me as I struggled against the grip, trying not to slit my own throat.

"I'm trying." Aroha's voice reached my ears, and my panic ratcheted up a notch. Two against one, and they had me cornered in the pantry, where no one would hear me even if I did cry out. *The guys are in the practice room.*

I was on my own.

"Move!" Heather shoved me toward the door. The knife bit into my skin. I hated the whimper that rose from my lips. My legs wobbled and the blood rushed in my ears, but I somehow managed to shuffle into the hallway.

Heather and Aroha shoved me across the kitchen, pressing my stomach against the edge of the stove. Warmth from the wood burner seeped through my clothing, stoking my rising panic. "You've been forgetting your place," Heather hissed as she leaned her weight into my body, jamming me in tight. "Swanning about the house like you're the mistress of the Manor, trying to take what isn't yours. It's time you remembered your place, *servant.* Aroha, get the gas."

Heather dropped the knife and grabbed my wrist, wrenching my arm out from behind me. I was so relieved to have the blade away from my throat that I didn't realize what she planned until it was too late. Aroha twisted the knobs until a ring of fire circled the burner. I tried to wrench my arm back, but I was at the wrong angle. Pain radiated along my arm as I fought for control, but Heather had the advantage – she snarled with triumph as she shoved my hand toward the flames.

"Let's see you impress Master Radcliffe with a burned hand," she rasped.

As the heat kissed my fingers, the bubbling panic exploded inside me. I swore and cursed and bucked and thrashed, but I was one and they were two, and Heather was used to getting her way.

"No, please."

No.

My whole world shrunk to those orange flames looming closer and closer—

Aroha wrapped her arms around my shoulder to pin me in place. I slammed my foot down, grinding the heel of my boot into a soft sneaker. Heather yelped, and I gained back a couple of inches before Aroha forced my shoulder down. Heather dug her nails into my wrist, biting deep. The flame licked the tip of my pinkie and I screamed.

No no no no no, not my hand, please, no—

"Take your punishment, trash whore," Heather rasped, her voice reaching through my panic. "He'll never want you after this—"

Her words broke off into a scream as something slammed into her from behind. I yanked my hand back just as Aroha lunged in a last-ditch effort to shove me into the stove.

I ducked under her blow and whirled around. Ivan locked Aroha against him, her arms pinned. Titus held Heather by her blonde ponytail.

"Touch her again and I'll burn you." Titus held Heather's head an inch from his face, and his features twisted with barely-concealed rage.

"Oh, will you?" she shot back in a singsong voice, even as she clawed at his hand in a frantic attempt to free herself. "It seems to me that the three of you have forgotten why you're at Manderley."

Aroha looked from Heather to Titus in confusion. "What's she talking about?"

"None of your business, junkie." Titus yanked Heather's hair, dangling her feet off the ground. Heather's smugness turned into screeches. I reached over with shaking hands and turned off the stove.

"Let me go!"

"As you wish." Titus opened his hand. Heather collapsed in a heap on the wooden floor, clutching her skull and howling with pain.

"It's not just Dorien's who's under the harpy's spell. It's all of you," Heather cackled, her eyes wide with agony as she dragged herself to the door. "You're all fucking her trash pussy. Madame Usher will love to hear this."

Ivan dropped Aroha and shoved her toward the door. She glanced back over her shoulder at me. "I didn't mean—"

"Get out," Titus growled, his deep voice like a rumble from the heavens. Aroha ran for it.

Titus was on me in a moment, sweeping me into those enormous arms of his. Being held by him was like hiding in the trunk of a tree, or getting a hug from a grizzly bear. I felt as though I had this force of nature larger than myself who was looking after me. Titus pressed my head into his shoulder, his giant fingers tangling in my hair. I breathed deep his luscious scent – musk and myrrh, with the slightest hint of English rose garden – and it was like coming home to somewhere I'd never been before but instantly felt at peace. The trembling in my limbs faded, although the fear of what they'd almost done bit into my skin.

Ivan took my hand, turning it over, running his fingers over mine. "They didn't burn you? Have they hurt you?"

I shook my head. The relief washed over me, and tears flooded my eyes, spilling down my cheeks. I collapsed against Titus again and Ivan wrapped his arms around us both, pressing his chest into my back until I was cocooned in their warmth.

"How did you—hic—know to find me?"

"Elena heard Heather and Aroha sneak off to the kitchen," Ivan said. "She barged into our practice to tell us, and we ran straight here."

"Dorien's waiting in the hall for them," Titus added. "He'll make sure they don't run to Madame Usher."

From the doorway, a worried face peeked in. *Elena.* I gave her a weak smile as I drew back from Titus. "Thank you."

Her eyes widened, and she darted off.

I collapsed against Titus' chest again, relishing the warmth of both their arms around me. "The two of you popped up like guardian ghosts." A panicked giggle bubbled up from my throat.

Like ghosts.

I never thought I'd be so grateful for the Muses haunting me.

"They will never touch you again," Titus whispered, holding my head against his chest. "We'll make sure of it."

I sagged into him, and I thought about the Titus I'd seen hiding his true self in a tiny, damp shack on the edge of the wilderness. If he couldn't protect his own heart, how would he protect me?

So many secrets crowded the halls of Manderley, stacked one atop the other like a house of cards. One wrong move, one anxious breath, and the entire house would fall. I'd seen the hated flare in Heather's eyes – what lengths would she go to get what she wanted? She was ready to burn this bitch down, and me with it.

 Faye

I clung to Titus and Ivan as long as I dared. Dorien appeared at the doorway, his eyes raging. "Madame Usher wants to see both of you. She won't wait."

"We're busy," Titus glared at his friend. "What's it about?"

Dorien shook his head. "We all have to keep our secrets, remember?"

Titus pulled away, staring down at me with those dark eyes. "You will be okay on your own?"

I nodded. As if I had a choice.

Reluctantly, Titus drew away from me. He raised one of his huge hands to ruffle Ivan's hair. "Let's go see what the witch wants now."

~

After a tense dinner where no one said a word and all three Muses deliberately avoided meeting my eyes, I retreated to the kitchen to stack the dishwasher. As I made up a batch of pancake batter to sit in the fridge for the morning, my neck prickled with the sensation of being watched.

I grabbed the knife I kept on the counter beside me and whirled to face the door. Ivan leaned against the frame, his icy eyes flicking to the weapon. "I didn't mean to frighten you."

"Then you probably shouldn't lurk in doorways and sneak up on people," I shot back.

"That is fair." Mmmm, that Romanian accent did things to my insides. Ivan stepped forward and held out his hand. "It's a lovely night. Madame Usher has retired for the evening, and the others are in the Blue Room playing cards and drinking. Will you walk with me?"

It was on the tip of my tongue to say no, but his crystal eyes begged. I couldn't resolve Ivan's cool facade with his possessive adoration of his sister, or the cocaine-addicted junkie the evidence of his room suggested. Curiosity got the better of me. I nodded.

I followed Ivan out into the kitchen garden. He held the gate open for me. I sucked in a breath as the frigid air pummeled my skin. I should have thought to bring a coat.

Ivan was already shrugging off his leather jacket and holding it out to me. "You want it?"

"Let me guess, it's filled with bugs?" I cocked my head to the side. "No, wait, I put it on and some sensor inside electrocutes me?"

"Suit yourself." Ivan started to tug the sleeve back on, but I snatched it from his hands and pulled it over my shoulders. If I had to be out here with a Muse, I wasn't going to freeze my tits off.

Ivan's lip curled back in what might have been the start of a smile. "Looks good on you."

"Damn right." I twisted around to admire it. "Don't expect to get it back."

We wandered past the gazebo. In the moonlight, it took on a sinister air. I dared to look back at the house – the gables pierced the cloudless sky, teeth of a demon taking a bite from Heaven. For some reason it made me think of my mother, all alone miles away in the hospital. My skin prickled from invisible eyes watching me. I shuddered and turned back to Ivan.

I'd been dying to get this guy alone, to peel back the layers of those icicle eyes, but now that it was just the two of us, I struggled to find something to say.

"Did you…" I tried again. "Is… I mean… sorry." I laughed, and then felt stupid. "I don't know what to say to my bully-turned-booty-call."

Ivan laughed. The sound was so rare, so unexpected, it caught me off guard. "Please, don't apologize. I thought you might want to talk about the cocaine."

The cocaine. That was right. I hadn't even stopped to consider the fact I was getting involved with someone who might not just be on drugs but dealing them.

"The drugs didn't belong to me. They're Aroha's. We all want to help her quit, and I was hiding them from her. It turns out to be pointless, as she's simply found another supplier." Ivan sighed. "I know you put that cocaine in my violin case. I wanted to say I understood why you did it."

"I did it because you went into my bedroom after I changed the lock. You've been trying to convince me there's a ghost."

"And if I told you I never set foot in your room until last night, would you believe me?"

I started at that. He sounded so earnest, but I knew how to math. That couldn't be true. "There's no one else it could have been, unless there's a secret passage between my room and some other place in the house, like the storage room."

"I have no key to the storage room. Madame Usher has never allowed any of us in there. She cites something called Health and Safety."

Mmmmm. Why did I never know I had a thing for Eastern European accents?

"But this is interesting." Ivan stared straight ahead. "A secret passage. We should all look for one."

"So if it wasn't you, who's been playing music through the wall and stomping around upstairs and turning my bedroom light on and off?"

Ivan raised an eyebrow in an expression that was far too much like Dorien. "Mice?"

I whacked him on the shoulder.

By now we had reached the poison garden. Whereas the path had been bright with forest noises – owls hooting, rodents skittering in the dirt, insects chirping – nothing stirred in this clearing at all. It was as if everything living knew to give the greenhouse a wide berth. Ivan stared straight ahead. "Did you know that Madame Usher is still my guardian?"

"That... doesn't make any sense." Why would he need a guardian? He was in his early twenties.

"I told you Elena and I did not grow up with money, but our house was filled with music. Our father played all kinds of instruments, mostly the fiddle – he would play Romanian folk songs for the tourists who visited our village every summer. We inherited our talents from him. I was always good, but Elena... she was touched by the gifts of the *zâne*."

"*Zâne?*"

"This is like a fairy godmother in Romanian stories. The *zâne* live in the woods and mountains, and they visit pregnant women to bestow their unborn children with the gifts of dancing, music, beauty, or luck. My mother believed she was visited by one of these sprites, and it is true that when Elena touches the keys, people sit up and listen. She conjures magic with her music."

"I know." I smiled, thinking of the first time I heard Elena play.

"My father never brought in much money, and what he did he spent on drink and cigarettes. That is why my mother worked several jobs and did laundry and scrimped and saved. She managed to purchase a house in our town with a spare room to rent to guests. Our government had announced plans to build a Dracula theme park near our home, and everyone was buying up property to cash in on the influx of tourists when the park opened."

"I remember reading about that theme park." I loved anything Dracula. It was the horror movie fan in me. Mom and I talked about going when it was finished. "Didn't it get canceled?"

Ivan nodded. "People complained. They said it was tacky and that it would be built on the ashes of an ancient oak forest. Historians noted that while our hero Vlad Tepes was born in my city, it had no link to the Dracula of fiction, and many Romanians do not like the confusion between the two. Prince Charles of Great Britain got involved, and the government decided it would not happen. But that left many of our people without hope for a brighter future from tourism, including my parents, who owed the bank a lot of money for this room they could not fill."

It was wonderful to hear Ivan talk. I nodded for him to continue.

"We had no choice – Elena and I had to work. My father pulled us from school and took us to Bucharest – more tourists equals more money. We stood on a corner by the Parliament Buildings and played for six hours a day. I noticed a woman who sat across the square, watching us. The same woman, day after day, wrapped in a fur even under the fierce sun. One day, my father came to collect us, and she approached him with her husband. She said she had a music school in the United States and that she would offer him a yearly payment if she could be allowed to take us with her and manage our career. She is like our manager. She pays my father the same paltry sum every year while she makes tens of thousands from our shows and recordings. We have toured Europe and Asia many times, yet we have not a dime to our names."

"I don't believe it."

"She says she has placed money in trust for us, but we cannot access it until we are twenty-five years old. That is two years away. Until then, she owns us. The only thing she cannot control is Broken Muse, and even then she exerts her influence in other ways. You may think you are the charity case at this school, but you are not the only one. I wanted you to know because... because it might be dangerous to be with me, and you should consider that before you choose to be with me."

Ivan shoved his hands deep in the pockets of his trousers, his face turned away from me, toward the moon. He looked kind of wiped out by speaking so much.

We stopped in front of the greenhouse. Ivan wrapped an arm around my shoulder and pulled me close. I stared up at the vines escaping from the broken glass, at the bulbous shapes that twisted in on themselves and bulged against the sides of the house. The moonlight hit a ball of plants and for a moment I saw a face – pale skin with violent eyes and a mouth that was a hole of darkness – but then I blinked, and it was gone. *Just a trick of the moonlight.*

A shiver ran through me as I thought again of my mother and the doctors working to rid her system of the poison.

"Why are we here?" I breathed.

In reply, Ivan turned to me. He reached up, his fingers brushing my cheek as he tucked a strand of my hair behind my ear. The world hung between us, suspended in a moment where everything was perfect.

"I wanted to be alone with you. I wanted to know that what I feel between us is more than just unfinished business between you and Dorien."

Those words ached with longing, with a desperate need that twisted in my heart. As Ivan's lips grazed mine, I let the bad thoughts go, releasing them into the crisp air. The mountains tore them from me as Ivan wrapped me in his warmth. Far from being ice, his kiss was sweet and light and breathtakingly beautiful.

A rustling in the trees startled me from my reverie. My eyes fluttered open. I caught movement behind Ivan's shoulder, and my breath hitched as I remembered that face I'd seen. I pulled back as Aroha stepped out of the shadows, a cigarette dangling from her lips.

"Just coming for a smoke," she sneered, patting her pockets for a lighter. I stiffened as she approached. I thought we were... not friends, exactly, but we had an understanding. That was before she tried to burn my hand.

Ivan narrowed his eyes. "Don't come near Faye again."

Aroha laughed, tossing her hair over her shoulder. She stepped into the shadow of the greenhouse and cupped her hand around her cigarette as she tried to light her smoke. "You think you have power here, Ivan?"

"I do not care what she does to me." Ivan's hands balled into fists, and he stepped toward Aroha. I grabbed his arm, and my touch seemed to steady him. Because I knew he spoke the truth – he didn't care about himself. But Madame Usher knew that – if he stepped out of line, she would go after Elena.

If she isn't already.

"Whatever." Aroha finally got her smoke to light. She took a long drag, tossing her head back. "It's nothing personal, Faye. I gotta survive here just like you, and sometimes that means aligning with a bitch like Heather. Little word of warning – I'd stay away from her. She's not done with you yet."

FAYE

"Students, we have a very special event to mark the end of the term."

My fork poised halfway to my mouth. I knew by now that Madame Usher saw her 'special events' as new ways to torment me. I didn't dare glance at any of the Muses – I was sure something in my face would give away the things we'd been doing together in secret.

"Is it another visit from one of your friends in Europe?" Heather asked, her voice high with excitement.

"It's even better." I watched through lowered lashes as Madame Usher passed a gold-lined envelope to Dorien. He flipped open the flap and drew out a fancy-looking invitation, his. "Harrison has left for the city to post a hundred of these invitations to my most influential friends in the business, including all your parents. We're to host a little party here at Manderley."

Dorien's fingers slipped, and the paper dropped into his soup. Madame Usher didn't seem to notice.

"I'm pleased with the progress you've made this year, and I want to show you all off. There will be many important people – conductors, producers, patrons, journalists – for you to impress. Master Radcliffe, perhaps you could make suggestions for the program."

"Certainly." The Master beamed at each of his students in turn, seemingly unaware of the tension crackling around the table. "Heather and Elena, you'll each perform sonatas. Elena and Ivan should tackle the Liszt piece they've been working on. Dorien and Faye, I'd like you to perform the composition Faye has written. Titus, Aroha, Faye, and Elena will delight with some Beethoven, and then we will finish with the world premiere of my newest concerto." His shoulders squared with pride. "I have the sheet music ready. You shall start learning it today."

Heather dominated the conversation about the party, gushing over the

Master's choices. Madame Usher offered Aroha a grant from her husband's endowment fund to pay for her parents' flights from New Zealand. I noticed no mention was made of doing the same for Elena and Ivan.

I escaped as fast as I could to the safety of the deserted Red Room. It wasn't safe for long. Elena let herself into my private practice, choosing the seat by the window again. There was no trace of the broken girl hiding in the shadows this time. She smiled as I played through my parts of Radcliffe's concerto until I was certain I had them perfect.

I set down my violin. "Why are you here? Did Madame Usher or Heather send you?"

Elena opened her mouth, as if to speak, then snapped her it shut. Instead, she shook her head.

I advanced, hands on hips, looming over her. "Then why?"

Elena's eyes widened with fright as she stared up at me. No, not at me. *Behind me.* I whirled around.

The door hung open. Elena must've forgotten to lock it after she came in. Ivan stood in the frame, his expression stony.

"Elena." He gestured to her and barked something in Romanian. She shook her head. He repeated the command.

"You are not the boss of me," she announced in a haughty voice, rising to her feet. She floated across the room to face him, and I was reminded of what he told me in the garden, about their mother being visited by the fairies.

Elena stuck her tongue out at her brother and slammed the door in his face.

"Please, play the concerto again," she said, folding her hands into her lap and settling back with a contented look on her pixieish face.

Elena wasn't the only one acting odd. Ever since Master Radcliffe told us we'd be playing together at the recital, Dorien made excuses not to practice with me. Finally, I cornered him. "I know you don't give a fuck what your parents think of you, but I need this to go well. If you're not willing to play with me, I will perform on my own."

I didn't have the power to make those decisions, and we both knew it, but Dorien's shoulders sagged. He flashed me a smile tinged with sadness at the edges, the kind of smile that could shatter a girl's heart from a million paces. "I'll behave, Sprite. I promise."

As we played through the piece, I could tell his head was a million miles away. His fingering lacked its usual aplomb, and the result was wooden, devoid of the emotion I desperately needed to convey in the piece.

I scratched the bow across the strings, creating an almighty screech that echoed through the room. Dorien jumped, his fingers tumbling over the keys.

"Fuck." He pounded the lid of the piano.

"That got your attention." I glared at him. "I told you not to fuck this up for me. Yet, here you are, fucking it up."

"I know." Dorien rested his head in his hands. "It's my parents. I've played for sold-out crowds in some of the greatest concert halls in Europe and Asia without breaking a sweat, but the thought of playing in front of them with *you*..."

"Just tell me what's got you twisted up so you can cry about it and get over it. They probably won't even recognize me from all those years ago."

Dorien shook his head. "They'll remember you. They remember everything. And they will want to know why I'm playing with you and not Heather. Fuck." He slammed his fist on the lid again. The tension in his shoulders could launch an arrow into space.

"Maybe they won't come?" I tried. "If they're as into this cult thing as you say, then maybe they're not allowed out to enjoy a recital?"

"They'll come. Madame Usher will make sure of that." Dorien's eyes glinted. "I can't hide you from them, and Heather won't let me *pretend* to be her girlfriend. She demands the real deal. They've painted us into a corner, and they know it."

"I wish you'd tell me instead of talking in riddles. I can help, you know. I'm quite clever."

"You are." Dorien lifted my fingers to his lips and laid a searing kiss on my knuckles. "But right now, the truth is dangerous to you. Unless I can find a way to convince them... *yes*." A spark of brightness shone through the storms in his eyes. "I think I have a way this could work out, for all of us."

FAYE

The whole house buzzed with excitement about the recital. Aroha danced around singing traditional Maori songs when she heard her parents would fly over. Heather seemed to have declared a truce with me and the Muses – or at least, she was too busy focused on improving her playing to put any effort into her torture attempts.

Elena slipped into my practice room again.

"You play beautifully," she whispered after I finished my as-yet-unnamed composition.

I snorted. "Sure. When people aren't hiding my instrument or ruining my performances."

Elena nodded but didn't offer up any kind of apology or explanation. People like her never had to do that.

"Do you want something?" I snapped the words, trying to show her that I wouldn't be intimidated by her beauty like others.

Elena winced. "I can accompany you. Would that be okay?"

The words 'Go to hell' danced on the end of my tongue. For a moment, I relished the satisfaction of denying Perfect Elena something, of seeing her face when she realized the whole world didn't automatically bend over backward to her whims.

But she was the one who warned the Muses about Heather's attack. I was so desperate for someone, *anyone,* to talk to. Not even a friend – just someone friend-adjacent. This was the first time since I'd bummed smokes from Aroha that someone at Manderley had reached out. Dorien and the Muses didn't count because I couldn't tell what was going on in their fucked-up heads.

I shrugged. "Yeah, sure."

Elena walked over to the piano and opened the lid, raising her hands to the keys with soft wrists, like a witch conjuring a spell. Without asking me what I wanted to play, she launched into Beethoven's *Violin Sonata No. 9* – a piece I loved for its raw beauty and that richness of musical color Beethoven gave to all his music.

She slowed the tempo from what I was used to, giving the opening an even more melancholy air. When she reached the lightning-fast *Presto,* her fingers danced along the keys with impossible lightness, like a butterfly flitting between flowers. I tried to match her deft, light style, but it was tough just keeping pace with her.

Halfway through, as the sweat pooled on my brow and my fingers nearly slipped from the strings during a particularly difficult bar, I realized this was a test. A kind of Manderley initiation. But something else occurred to me that made a smile play on my face.

I'm playing with Elena Nicolescu. The Elena Nicolescu, daughter of the Romanian fairies, who will one day become the greatest Classical musician of our age. Life goal, realized.

As we played, I snuck glances at her, admiring the way her graceful neck drew up as she threw her whole body into the performance, the placement of her fingers on the keys, every movement perfection. Elena *lived* the music in a way that awed and slightly terrified me.

We reached the final movement – a crushing A major chord on the piano, and then we soared together, ending on a jubilant flourish of contrast and light. I threw down my bow in triumph. Elena's hands slid from the keys. I beamed at her. A faint smile tugged at the corner of her lips, its momentum broken by the tears streaming down her face.

"Elena, are you okay?" I slid onto the end of the bench. There was something about her – that innocence, those pixie eyes, that made me instantly want to care for her.

She shook her head, dabbing at the corners of her eyes with her fingers. "I'm sorry. I don't know what came over me. I—"

"If you want to talk about something, I'm listening." I glanced toward the door, wondering about the significance of the lock. She always locked the door when she came to watch me. Was it to keep someone out? Her brother, perhaps?

I remembered their harsh conversation on the steps. *Is something going on between them?*

Elena sniffed. She must have sensed my inquiry, because she said, "Ivan likes you very much. I can see why."

"Is that why you've been coming to see me?"

She nodded. "He has never shown interest in another girl. Not ever. I wanted to make sure you were good enough for him. But now I'm wondering if he is good enough for you."

A knock sounded at the door. "Elena?" It was Master Radcliffe. "Are you in there? I wish you to go over the Brahms again."

Graceful as a cat, Elena rose. She wiped her face on the hem of her sundress, and when she lowered the cloth, her expression was blank, serene. I recognized it for what it was – a mask.

We all wore masks at Manderley. It seemed the only time we stripped ourselves bare was when we played. Elena didn't need to tell me what was wrong, because she'd just played her sorrow for me to hear.

"I must go," Elena whispered. She swept from the room as gracefully as she did everything else, but there was a fragility to her movement that betrayed her terror.

What is she so afraid of?

FAYE

After that, Elena started coming to more of my practices. We played together – Beethoven, Brahms, and a Romanian composer she loved named George Enescu. At mealtimes, she saved the seat next to her at the table, even going so far as to ask Heather to move over for me. Heather's face could have boiled an egg, but she moved. I found that interesting.

Elena rarely spoke to me, but each gesture spoke of a desire to break the silence Dorien had imposed. I wondered if he'd made some official lifting of his ban on interacting with me, or if everyone had sensed the shift in dynamics between us.

I knew better than to hope this was the start of a friendship, but I hoped anyway. Loneliness has a way of seeping into your bones.

Two days before the parental recital, Elena swept into our practice room (how quickly I'd started thinking of it as ours, even going so far as to write both our names down on the reservations board). Her cheeks flushed with happiness and she practically glided to the piano. I didn't think I'd ever seen her so happy.

"You must come with us next Saturday," she announced.

The weekend after the party, Dorien, Elena, and Ivan were booked to play a recital in New York City. They didn't want to drive back to Manderley in the dark, so they'd obtained special permission to stay over in a hotel. It sounded like an excuse to party to me, and I'd secretly been seething with jealousy about it, but I never imagined I'd be able to go.

I shook my head. "I have to clean the rehearsal rooms top to bottom. It's easier while you're all away as there will be fewer people using them. Besides, even if I wanted to, Madame Usher would never let me go."

"She will listen to me." Elena took my hand. I could practically feel her excitement sizzling through her veins. "I have already called ahead, requested you be added to the billing. We shall perform our Beethoven together. And I've booked us a suite. Please, say you'll come. I am tired of doing everything with Ivan. I want to have some girl time."

Aside from the fact that a night away from Manderley with my three Muses meant all kinds of delicious possibilities, no way could I say no to Elena. It would be like kicking a puppy.

Besides… I rubbed my bloodshot eyes. Another sleepless night listening to snatches of that music filtering from the room next door made me dream of a decent night's sleep in a non-haunted bed. If this was a horror film, Freddy Kreuger would have sucked me into the dream world by now.

Maybe I am *in a dream world – that would explain why three muses want to share me.*

The rest of the week sailed by in a blur. I was so excited for the recital that even cleaning the bathrooms and serving food to spoiled rich kids didn't seem so bad. Dr. Nelson called to say the preliminary tests on Mom had been extremely promising, and they were stepping up the treatment. I'd know in a few days if she'd be able to come off life support.

So what if Heather looked at me like I was a bug? So what if that obnoxious midnight concerto kept me awake? During my weekly hospital visit, I gushed about Elena to Mom (I decided to leave out all the naughty stuff about the guys. I wasn't sure she'd want to hear that). I even played her the second movement of our Beethoven. Dr. Nelson and some of the nurses came in to listen, and they clapped and cheered. I was too happy to tell them that people weren't supposed to applaud for classical music.

I crawled into bed the night before the party, my stomach churning with excitement. I knew from the square of bright light from the full moon and the buzzing in my veins that I'd struggle to sleep.

Sure enough, I wriggled down into the sheets and willed my mind to shut off. I counted Beethoven jumping over sheep. I pictured calm waves brushing against a white-sand beach. I touched myself and thought of the guys. But still, my mind reached toward the storage room, listening for signs of life.

After midnight, the footsteps paced across the floorboards. *Creak, creak, creaaaaak.* I had to hand it to Heather, even when she was pretending to be a specter, she moved with a certain musicality.

Then silence for a time. A long time, long enough for me to start to question myself again. *It's not footsteps – it's just the old house settling.*

I'd just started to drift off to sleep when the creaking started again. The footsteps moved across the storage room, then stopped. I strained to hear a sound, like the scraping of a piece of furniture. Then I didn't hear anything else for a long time except my heart hammering in my ears.

Then, the first mournful note sounded.

I peered at my phone. 3:02AM. Yet someone was playing again. That same haunting tune, over and over. Vaguely familiar, but impossible to place.

I threw the covers off, circling the room and pressing my ear to the walls, trying to figure out where it came from. I opened the door and stood on the landing, straining to listen. No, it wasn't someone practicing downstairs. It was definitely louder inside my room.

It doesn't make any sense. I circled my room again, straining to hear where the sound was loudest. Not in the bathroom. Definitely beside the bureau, and around the clothing rack...

My stomach tightened with fright. I held my ear to the wall. A tremble started in my legs and moved through my whole body.

The music was coming through the wall, from the other side.

From within the locked storage room.

FAYE

The music continued.

I banged on the wall. It didn't stop.

At 4AM, I tossed aside the sheets one final time and slid out of bed. If I wasn't going to sleep, I might as well get up and finish my chores.

As I padded downstairs, using my phone as a flashlight, I strained to hear the violin – but it was as if it stopped dead outside my room. The only time I'd heard it anywhere else in the house was when I stepped inside Madame Usher's private chambers. I didn't know what that meant except that she was probably to blame for it.

Down in the kitchen, I prepared spicy sausage, beans, and scrambled eggs for breakfast burritos. A treat to start our day. As I bent over the dishwasher, emptying last night's dinner dishes, the kitchen door banged open and Titus appeared.

"Nice view." He wiggled his eyebrows in a way that made me burst out laughing.

I straightened up, shoving the tray of burritos in the oven until I needed them. "Why are you up so early?"

"I wanted to get in a little morning practice." He nodded toward the wood-shed. "And I heard you on the stairs and I thought you might like some company."

My heart pattered, but this time it wasn't fear. I remembered what Dorien said about Titus wanting to ask me out.

"The others told me what happened when I was gone." His eyes darkened. "I wanted to... I guess I wanted to say that you've obviously got your hands full with the two of them, but if you wanted to add a third guy to your harem, I'm game."

"My... harem?"

"Mmmm." Titus leaned toward me. His fingers trailed along my arm, raising a line of fire that scorched through my veins. He loomed closer, his breath kissing my neck...

...as he grabbed an apple from the bowl behind me, bringing the fruit to his lips and taking a bite. Fuck, how did he make eating an apple look so hot? A shiver ran through my body that had nothing to do with the draft blowing through the window.

I backed away from Titus until my ass pressed against the dishwasher. "It may shock you to know I am not used to this kind of attention from guys. I'm not sure what to *do* with a harem."

"You can do whatever you like with me." Titus was on me in a moment, his bulk hemming me in, blocking any possible exit. I didn't mind. Not in the least. Now it was my turn to trail my fingers over the skin of his arm.

His expressive eyes begged for more. He wasn't going to make a move – he wanted me to be overt with my consent and control. This was his apology, his way of making things right for being in my room. He wanted to hand me back my power.

I took it, fisting my hands into his shirt and dragging him the final inch, until our lips met in a searing kiss.

He tasted fresh and tart from the apple. Beneath it, his distinct scent – the myrrh and musk, the roses dappled with early morning dew – swept me into the sheer force of his being. If Ivan was a dark elf, then Titus was some kind of ancient forest god – dark and chaotic and fiercely protective.

A floorboard creaked, and my eyes darted across the kitchen, nervous about who might walk in and see us. My eyes rested on the herbs on the windowsill above the table, their tendrils spilling over their pots and snaking down the wall. From between the leaves, a pair of vicious green eyes stared out at me from a pale face.

I pulled away, struggling for breath. *Fuck.*

I blinked, and the face was gone.

Titus frowned. "Is everything okay?"

I nodded, willing my heartrate to return to normal. I thought about telling Titus about the face, but it seemed pointless. It was just a trick of the light. Manderley had a way of crawling under my skin, making me believe impossible things. "I don't want us to stop, but if I don't get this baking done—"

Titus nodded, but he didn't release me from his arms.

"Have you ever heard violin music late at night?" I tried to reach around behind him to free myself. "I hear it in my room, but nowhere else in the house. It seems to come from the storage room, except that it's not loud enough to be someone playing in there, and when I go out onto the landing, I can't hear it through the door. Oh, once I heard it in Madame's chambers, too."

Titus' eyes darkened. "I've never heard this music. I have an explanation, but you're not going to like it. Consider who used to occupy your room."

"Who used to—" I folded my arms and glared up at him. "I'm too tired and stressed for riddles. Explain."

"Didn't Dorien tell you? Clare played the violin."

"Clare? You mean, the dead maid?"

Titus nodded. "She was talented. She worked for Madame for peanuts in exchange for free lessons. The only time she could practice was late at night, when we'd all gone to sleep. I know you don't believe in ghosts, but..."

...but why would I hear mysterious music in the dead of the night, music that could only be heard in my room?

It's impossible. It can't be.

Ghosts aren't real.

Are they?

DORIEN

I hummed a few bars of 'Confessions of an Opium Eater' under my breath as I buttoned one of my baroque dress shirts, debating whether to go the full Monty with my tailored frock coat. I never felt this cheery about seeing my parents, but for the first time in decades, my heart was light. I had a plan. I could fix it. I could make life better for all of us.

Faye was mine.

Yours and Titus' and Ivan's, I reminded myself. But I didn't mind sharing her for now. If anyone could handle the three of us, it was Faye de Winter. Besides, she would choose me in the end. Faye and I – we were written in the stars.

She'd walked back into my life by complete chance, and I wasn't going to let her go again.

There was a knock at the door. "Come in." I finished tying the knot in my cravat. "I've got—Heather?"

I'd expected to see Faye's gorgeous curves sashaying through the door. Instead, Heather stormed inside, her prissy nose high in the air. She shut the door behind her, threading the bolt into the lock.

"Dorien, we need to talk."

"I've said all I have to say to you." I turned back to the mirror and flicked my hand like I was flicking away an annoying bug, which Heather definitely was. A cockroach. Or a dung beetle.

Heather didn't like that one bit. The false smile dropped from her lips, replaced by a scowl that did nothing for her looks.

"I know your secret," she hissed. "I know all about what's going on at Valencourt Manor. Or should I call it, The Temple of Earthly Truths."

My blood froze in my veins. That was the first time I'd heard that name uttered outside the walls of my home.

There was no use pretending I didn't know what she was talking about. I fixed Heather's reflection with what I hoped was a terrifying look, even as my heart pounded against my chest. "How?"

Heather came up behind me, placing her hands on my shoulders. "It doesn't matter how. What matters is that I have the information. I'm still deciding what to do with it."

"What do you want, Heather?"

"Isn't it obvious? You don't need to be at Manderley, Dorien. You're too talented to be wasting away behind these walls. Master Radcliffe can't teach you anything new. You should be back in the spotlight where you belong. And you should have the right woman by your side."

Heather leaned forward to lick my earlobe. I couldn't stop the shudder that rocketed through my body at her touch. "It's what your parents wanted."

"I don't care. I won't do it."

"You'll do it," she whispered. "Or I'll be reporting your parents to the authorities. And where will that land your brother?"

Shit. Fuck. Shit.

She knows. How can she possibly *know?*

"Leave him alone," I hissed. "He has nothing to do with this."

"Tsk, tsk. All this is your fault. You shouldn't have lost your temper, Dorien. Aggravated assault. Someone with a serious felony conviction can't be appointed as a long-term guardian. Luckily, as a long-term friend to the family with an impeccable record, I'm happy to step up."

"Stay away from him," I growled.

"There's that temper again. Go on, Dorien. Hit me. Add another assault to your record. All you'll be doing is giving me more ammunition. I'll take your brother away from you, and what will you have? That trash whore *Faye* to warm your bed? I hope you've had your shots."

I sat on the windowsill, my head spinning. "You've made your point, Heather. Give me your terms."

"Faye is not playing with you on Saturday. My parents give a lot of money to this school, and they expect certain standards. They won't accept anyone else by your side, especially not a painted heifer. She will step down, and you and I will play together instead."

"You can't play Faye's composition."

"*Please.* Modesty doesn't suit you. There's no way that fat cow could write something like that. It has Dorien Valencourt stamped all over it." She stopped in front of my mirror, turning her body to admire herself. "I should say, Dorien Valencourt and Heather Danvers."

"Faye won't let you get away with this."

"She won't have a choice." Heather's smile could have chilled a penguin. "I intend to make it so that Faye de Winter never sets foot in Manderley again. And you're going to help me. Or *else you'll never see your brother again.*"

FAYE

When I went down to the kitchen to finish prep for the party, I noticed several sandwiches and meatballs missing from one of the platters.

Gah. I've got to remember to tell those boys not to steal food. If they're hungry I can give them something to devour—

Argh. I grinned stupidly at myself. *One night with Dorien and Ivan and even my internal monologue has become filthy.*

I shuffled the meatballs around, but now I had a big gap on the side of one of the platters. I racked my brain for something simple to fill it with. *I saw some crackers at the back of the pantry. If they're not stale, they'd be perfect.*

Humming Beethoven to myself, I went to the pantry and shifted the boxes aside, tossing anything that smelled funky. As I shoved aside a giant box of salt, I noticed something smeared on the wall near the back of the shelf, half-hidden in darkness. I took out my phone and shone the light on the wall.

What I'd thought was a smudge of ketchup or something was words scrawled in whiteboard marker in the same writing that had been on the noticeboard. *Clare's handwriting.*

The words chilled me to the bone.

THE WALLS ARE TALKING.

Faye

The walls are talking.

What the fuck did that even *mean*?

Clare wrote it there for a reason. She knew that the next maid would find it. No one else would have any reason to go into the back of the pantry.

It was a message for me.

I looked again at the words, and my stomach twisted. I'd been afraid enough times in my life that I could recognize fear. When Clare wrote these words, she felt afraid.

And then she fell down the stairs.

I believed Dorien's story, that he'd already been halfway down the staircase. I didn't believe he killed her. So who was Clare afraid of? Why did she say this?

Could someone else have pushed her?

I scrambled to my feet and snuck out the door under the stairs into the entrance hall. My boots padded on the thick carpet as I ascended to the first floor. From the top of the stairs, I looked both ways down the hall, and my heart sank. There was no vase or piece of ugly antique furniture large enough to hide behind, no conveniently-placed curtain. Madame Usher's apartments were right at the end of the hall. Dorien would have seen someone else standing in the hallway as he went past. There wasn't enough *time* for someone else to reach the top of the stairs and push Clare.

I couldn't see how someone could have pushed Clare, and yet... I felt certain her death wasn't an accident. *So what the hell happened?*

FAYE

I worked all day, scrubbing down the ballroom before the party and thinking about Clare's message. Madame Usher demanded everything be perfect, but obviously, she refused to hire extra help or ask the other students to lift a finger. Titus snuck into the kitchen while I was prepping food and trapped me in the pantry for half an hour, his enormous hands reducing my body to jelly as he kissed me until my lip bled. Ivan winked at me across the classroom and I felt like I was naked. Dorien passed me in the hall with a stack of clean towels for the guest bathrooms, and seeing no one else around, pinched my ass.

By the time I'd finished everything on my list, I could barely drag my feet up the stairs to change into my concert dress. I'd left the attic landing light on for myself, but the bastard ghost had turned it off. As I stepped toward my room, a rush of icy air engulfed me, driving the breath from my lungs.

Weird. It's never cold up here.

Unease prickled at the back of my neck. I hated being up here, knowing there was someone in the house trying to scare me. It was almost better when I thought the Muses were responsible for my haunting. Now...

Just ignore it. It's a draft from somewhere in the house.

I fumbled in my pocket for the key. As my hand closed around it, someone stepped out of the shadows in front of me, sending a fresh wave of ice curling around my body.

"Wha—" But I couldn't form words. My breath died in my throat.

The brown hair tied up in a bun. That button nose. Eyes that once sparkled with life but now burned with hatred.

Clare.

She stared at me, her head twisting to the side at an impossible angle, one eyebrow raising in a ghastly expression.

Through her skin, the wood grain of my door was visible.

Run. I commanded myself. *You have to run.*

But I remained frozen with terror.

Silence stretched between us. Clare opened her lips, but no sound came out – her mouth opened into a maw of terrifying darkness that swallowed all light and hope.

I staggered back, my chest exploding with panic. Shadows spewed from Clare's mouth and circled her body – reaching, grasping, *crawling* toward me. One grabbed my arm. Before I could tear myself from its grasp, something hot and hard closed around my mouth, pressing a sweet-scented cloth between my lips.

Then everything went black.

TO BE CONTINUED

❦

Find out who – or what – is after Faye in book 2 of Broken Muses of Manderley Academy, Haunted.

http://books2read.com/manderley2

❦

I should have kept my mouth shut.
I should have let them win.
Now the kings of the school are out for my blood,
... and they're not the only ones.

Need more dark, gothic, and delicious reverse harem bully romance in your life?

HP Lovecraft meets *Cruel Intentions* in the paranormal reverse harem bully romance readers are calling, "The greatest mindfuck of 2019". Warning: Not for the faint of heart – this story of three broken bad boys and the girl who stood her ground contains dark themes, crazed cultists, books bound in human skin, high-school drama, swoon-worthy sex, and potential triggers. Grab book 1, *Shunned*, in KU now.

http://books2read.com/shunned

VOLUME TWO

HAUNTED

"I know not how it was—but, with the first glimpse of the
building, a sense of insufferable gloom pervaded my spirit."

– Edgar Allan Poe, *The Fall of the House of Usher*

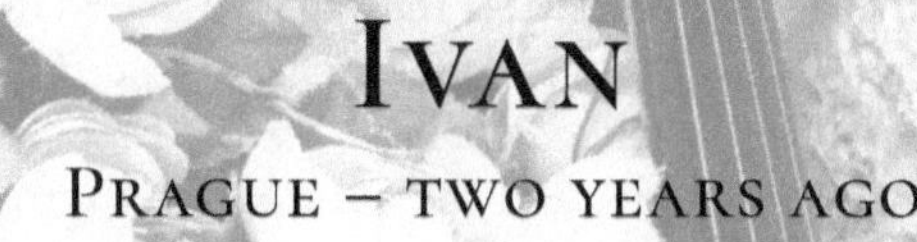

IVAN

PRAGUE – TWO YEARS AGO

"Where is he?" Elena's blue eyes scanned the crowd. "He said he would be here."

We huddled together for warmth. Elena tucked her gloved hands inside my sleeves. Outside, a storm battered the ancient city with bitter fury. Wind whipped rain and hail into the glass of the station building. A shiver twisted through Elena's body, but I didn't know if it was from the cold or because of what we were about to do.

My chest tightened. *He should be here by now. He said he had everything planned. If we can't—*

"There he is." Elena's face lit up as Dorien pushed through the crowds of tourists and commuters huddled around the ticket booths and bracing themselves for the dash to the exposed platforms. His black wool coat flapped around his long legs, and the end of his silk scarf trailed behind him like a ribbon of crimson blood. He darted a glance over his shoulder before pulling an envelope from the pocket of his coat and pressing it into my frozen fingers.

"I had to empty my account to get these, and promise him backstage tickets to future Broken Muse shows, but it was worth it," Dorien's grey eyes twinkled. "Who knew the finest document forger in the world is an angry Czech mobster ex-cellist Broken Muse fan?"

That twinkle unnerved me. I knew even given the seriousness of the situation, part of Dorien loved this – sneaking around the ancient city, making shady deals on the black market for fake passports. It was pure theatre, and Dorien's whole life was a performance.

But he was also my friend, and he'd taken a huge risk for us, for Elena. I took the proffered envelope and slid it into my coat pocket. "What about you?"

"For once, this isn't about me." Dorien reached into his coat pocket and withdrew a mobile phone, a couple of tickets, and a stack of Euros. "This will get you to St. Petersburg. You'll need to exchange the money somewhere. You've got visas in the passports, so you shouldn't be asked any questions. I don't care where you head after that – just make it somewhere far, far away from her. Stay on the move until I can sort things on this end. The phone is a burner and I'm the only one who has the number. Call me when you get there, let me know you're safe, then ditch the phone, too."

"Why Russia?" Elena's lip trembled. "I want to go home to Romania."

"You know that's the first place she'll look." Dorien folded my fingers over the tickets. "First, we get you away. Then Titus and I will expose her for the monster she is. Once we've got your money and she can no longer hurt you, you can go wherever you want."

I met his eyes. A hundred unspoken things passed between us. I'd been all over the world with this guy. I'd seen him at his absolute worst, and until today I'd never felt as if I knew him at all. He certainly hadn't known me. These tickets were more than just scraps of paper – they spoke of the depth of Dorien's friendship, of the way he took the pain of others and bore it on his own shoulders, weaving it into his music as if he hoped he could heal the world.

I swallowed. "I cannot thank you—"

"Don't." He cut me off. "Don't you dare fucking thank me."

I thought of everything Dorien was giving up by putting me on this train. We were only a week into our most successful tour yet – if we didn't perform in Bratislava tomorrow night, we'd be on the hook with our promoter for a ton of money. Not to mention our pissed-off fans. And Madame Usher... I shuddered to think about what punishment she'd dream up for him after she discovered he helped us flee.

Elena squared my hand, pulling me back to myself. As much as I loved Dorien in this moment, it paled in comparison to what I felt for her. Elena was my sunshine, my reason for breathing. The gifts of the Zână flowed from her, and it was my job to protect her. Now I knew Madame Usher's plans for her, I felt in my bones that we had to do this.

We'd been prisoners of Manderley since we were eight years old. The things we'd endured at the hands of that woman still made my skin crawl... and we'd survived it all in the name of a better life. But a respite from her torment would never come. I could live in the shadows – I'd been there all my life – but Elena was made of warmth and sunlight. Locking her away would see her wither and rot. It would break Elena, and watching her break would kill me.

We had no choice. We had to go.

Dorien must've sensed what I was thinking, because he smiled his sad, stormy smile. "I'm sorry, my friend. I thought things could be different for us."

I thought so, too. When Dorien blew into my life like a storm breaking against the shore, I dared to dream of something more for Elena. Now, he may be the only way to save her. I looked into that impish half-smile of his, and for the first time in my life, I felt what it meant to *trust* someone.

A whistle blew. The crowd of passengers surged toward the platform. Dorien gave me a nudge. I squeezed Elena's hand. With a last nod to Dorien, I dragged her into the fray.

Elena and I fought our way through the crowd to the waiting train. We stepped on board, ducking and weaving through people until we found our seats. I slid my violin case into the luggage rack, and Elena clutched a backpack with all our money and a few clothes hastily thrown inside. My heart hammered against my chest so loud I was sure the conductor would hear it and kick us off.

In front of us, a group of tourists from New Zealand in black t-shirts laughed and teased each other. They talked loudly about the bands they were going to see and the mead they'd drink at a heavy metal festival in Germany next week. I longed to be one of them – carefree, thinking only of fun things and friendship.

We were supposed to be playing at that festival. Titus could barely sit still, he was so excited about it. I was pleased I wasn't there to see Titus' face when he found out it wouldn't happen.

Elena huddled against me. As we pulled out of the station, her head drooped on my shoulder, her long eyelashes fluttering shut. I stared out the window, unable to sleep. I wouldn't sleep until we were far from Madame Usher's evil. Maybe not even then.

Prague sped by in a blur of narrow alleys, burgher houses, Soviet blocks, and towering spires. The city lights glittered off the Vltava River, and I wished we could be sitting on one of those open-topped tourist boats, enjoying a beer as though we didn't have the specter of Manderley bearing down on us. My mind cast back to the euphoria of last night – standing on stage with Titus and Dorien at our sold-out show in one of the most beautiful cities in the world. The audience in rapture, clapping and stomping for more, more, more of us. Our music heard and loved and *felt*. It should have been the high point of my career, and yet, here we were, sneaking away as ghosts in the night.

The train chugged on into the gloom. The city lights gave way to darkened fields and ugly villages of concrete brutalism. A cart offering reheated meals – stewed meat with potato dumplings – wheeled by, but the smell of the food made me feel ill. It reminded me of another home across the Carpathian mountains, a tiny walled city I'd once been so desperate to escape.

The roar of the crowd still coursed through my veins, mingled with the ever-present thunder of my racing heart.

The conductor turned out the lights, and the passengers reclined their chairs and pulled on sleeping masks. One by one even the metalheads fell asleep, hugging their enormous backpacks emblazoned with flags and ferns. I stared into the bleak night, knowing I should sleep but finding the idea of closing my eyes impossible. How could I sleep and leave Elena unguarded?

Even on the other side of the world, Manderley squeezed in on us, the walls of that house becoming our prison. Every year another fresh-faced group of music students entered its walls, but Manderley changed them. Hardened them.

Extracted their secrets and left them bound to it forever. Now that Victor was gone, Madame Usher had no one to temper her evil, and Master Radcliffe—

My body jerked as the train screeched to a halt. Elena's head whipped up. "Are we in Poland?" she asked sleepily.

"We are not." I peered out the window. Outside was pitch black – no lights from a platform, no glittering city sprawling across the horizon. We were stopped in the middle of nowhere, with rain driving into the train.

A commotion started at the front of the car. Doors swung open and two men barked at the conductor in loud voices. They spoke Czech, so I couldn't understand what they were saying. I didn't need to.

"Get up," I growled. I dragged my violin case from the compartment. Elena opened her mouth to argue, but she must've seen the fear in my eyes because she snapped it shut again. She picked up the backpack containing our worldly possessions and followed me toward the rear of the car.

I tugged Elena past the bathroom and through the next car, moving as quickly as we dared. The lights flickered on and passengers stared bleary-eyed into the gloom, trying to figure out why we stopped. I yanked open the compartment door, and we entered the gangway. A foul smell rose from the bathroom, and Elena pinched her nose in disgust.

I slammed my fist into the button. With a hiss, the external door released. A rush of frigid air tinged with diesel slammed into us. Elena coughed. I grabbed her hand and yanked her down the steps.

"Ivan, where are we going?" She hurried after me as I picked my way along the tracks, away from the lights of the train, away from the whistleblowing and men shouting. Wind battered against us. I slid into a ditch, dragging Elena behind me. My violin case banged against my knee, but I ignored the pain.

We have to run. We can't go back.

I tossed the violin case onto the other side of the ditch, wincing as it bounced against a rock. That violin was precious, and I hoped it wasn't damaged. I scrambled up the slippery slope and reached back to pull Elena up after me. My palms stung where they grazed the rocks, and the driving rain flayed at my skin. Behind me, Elena whimpered as her sneakers sank into the mud. But we didn't stop.

I plunged into the trees. Branches scraped my arms and attacked my violin case. Elena dropped my hand to hold the backpack over her head, trying to shelter her face from the onslaught.

My feet slammed into something hard. I pitched forward. My violin case flew from my hands. *Fuck.* I felt around in the gloom for what had stopped me. A fallen log. *A hiding place.* I tugged Elena down beside me, pressing our back against the log and using it to shelter us from view. She whimpered again as we sank into the mud, but I held my finger to my lips.

The wind howled around us, wild and angry. I pressed Elena into my body, wrapping my arms around her. She trembled – whether from cold or fear, I could not tell.

We needed a little of her *Zâne* magic now.

In the distance, the train blew its whistle. The tracks shuddered as the wheels turned and it took off. I squeezed Elena's hands, pressing them to my heart as we waited. Our breath puffed in clouds of steam. The tips of my fingers had gone worryingly numb.

I lost track of how long we waited, huddled together in the brutal cold. We could no longer hear the train or the people. I couldn't hear anything except the wild wind and the pounding of my heart. I helped Elena to her feet and bent to pick up my violin case.

"We'll follow the train tracks until we find a village. Hopefully, there will be a bus or—"

A hand fell upon my shoulder, snapping my body backward. My grip on Elena broke, and she screamed as another black-clad figure leaped from behind a tree and grabbed her hands, twisting them behind her back.

"You're coming with us," my captor hissed in my ear. "Madame Usher does not like it when her little birds fly the coop."

FAYE

FAYE

DORIEN

This is completely fucked.

FAYE

Ivan

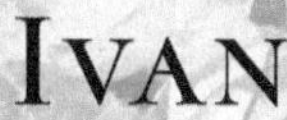

"Have you seen Faye?" I shoved open the door to the Yellow Room. Titus stood beneath the window, a silhouette against the golden glow of the setting sun. Blades of orange fire pierced the thick canopy of trees to torch the carpet around him. Titus preferred to stand when he played, his feet planted wide and his head bent over the strings of the cello, his braids swinging wild around his face as he practiced his performance piece for this evening. In a normal concert setting he was forced to sit, holding the posture of a 'proper' musician. But when we played Muse shows he stood like this, holding a place of power. Sometimes he'd swing his cello around the stage, stalking and slinking about with the instrument in his enormous hands as girls in the audience grabbed at his legs.

Seeing him standing like that – his statuesque features tight with concentration, his lower lip protruding as he fought with Sibelius for control – sent a rush of memories slamming into my head. Of the first time I met Titus in New Orleans during a choral competition, when he'd snuck me and Elena out from beneath Madame Usher's watchful gaze and took us to see an underground metal show. Of him surging into the mosh pit, dark hair flying, kind eyes glowing with abandon as he unleashed a beast that lurked inside him.

Of Broken Muse shows, of the look of utter rapture on Titus' face when he cast aside the mask he wore every day and lost himself in the music.

Of the tightness in his voice whenever he spoke to his parents – that desperate sense that he was trying to cram himself into a tiny box, but the seams were ready to burst and there was nothing he could do to stop it.

As I strode toward him, he set the bow down and jerked his head up, and I saw he had that desperation about him now. He wasn't comfortable. He didn't fit here, and he knew it. The only things at Manderley that truly made sense to him were Broken Muse, Faye, and that guitar under his bed. Like all of us, Titus was hiding from a truth that gnawed away at him, and tonight, with his parents in the audience, he'd have to be on guard, lest the seams finally broke and his darkness was unleashed.

"She went to her room to get ready." He kept his voice even, begging me to pretend I hadn't just seen what I'd seen. If I'd been Dorien, I might have tried to call him out on it, tried to convince him to come clean to his parents about what he really wanted. But I wasn't Dorien, and right now, we had more important things to worry about.

"She's not there." I cast my eyes around the room, feeling that familiar prickle of someone watching me, of the house itself betraying my secrets. "She's not in the kitchen or out fetching more wood. She's not polishing the silver or dusting the Fazioli. And I can't find Heather or Dorien anywhere, either."

Titus nearly dropped his cello. "Heather's missing?" His chest sank as he pushed out his breath. "We need to find them."

He replaced his cello into its stand, and the two of us barreled upstairs to the attic. Titus had to stoop beneath the low ceiling as he pushed open Faye's door. *Why didn't she lock her room?*

Titus swept through the small space, taking in the absence of her the same way I'd done a few minutes ago – the clothes thrown casually across the bed, the empty garment bag that had held her concert dress crumpled on the floor, the makeup case missing from the bathroom counter. The cold prickle on my skin told me something had happened to her.

Titus unlatched the window and pushed it open, inspecting the latches and windowsill. "This is locked, and I don't see any signs of a shoe scuffing or a struggle..."

His back froze rigid as he peered down at the edge of the sloping roof and the overgrown garden below. I knew he was thinking about Micah. His shoulders sagged in relief, and I knew he hadn't seen Faye's body crumpled and mangled beneath us. Titus pointed at a movement on the edge of the woods. "There's Dorien."

I crossed the room in three strides to stand beside him, peering out over the garden. Heather emerged from the path leading down to the gazebo, a chilling smirk playing across her lips. Dorien trailed behind her, his red shirt and trouser hems covered in dirt and dead leaves. Even more concerning, his shoulders were tight and his cruel mouth was set in a hard line. He stopped and turned to look over his shoulder. He turned back, and even from here I could see the bleak horror flicker in his eyes.

What has he done?

Titus met my eyes, and the unspoken message passed between us. We bolted for the door and crashed down the narrow stairs, meeting Dorien just as he slunk up the main staircase. Titus grabbed him by the scruff of his shirt and dragged him into his bedroom, slamming the door behind us.

"Ow, fuck." Dorien's face twisted as Titus slammed him into the wall. A

Broken Muse poster behind his head tore away, the colorful paper hanging in a jagged ribbon.

"Faye's missing." I'd never seen gentle Titus look so dangerous. He shook Dorien, tearing the ribbon of poster away so it floated to the ground. "You wouldn't know anything about that, would you?"

Dorien's gaze flicked toward the window. That one look told us everything. Titus dropped him. As soon as Dorien's feet hit the floor, he seemed to make a decision. The horror in his eyes glazed over and he cast his face into a mask of his usual arrogance. He reached into his closet and pulled out his suit, as if everything was normal. As if Faye wasn't in danger.

"Dorien, *fuck*." Titus' hands curled into fists.

"You must tell us." I picked up the ribbon of poster. It was the Broken Muse band logo, torn through the middle. I balled the paper in my hands and lobbed it at Dorien's head, wishing it was something harder, wishing I could knock some sense into my friend.

"Faye is fine." He removed his shirt. The words IN CAUDA VENENUM stretched and contracted across his pecs as he pulled a fresh white shirt from his closet and buttoned it over his chest.

"She's not here, and the concert starts in *two hours*. The guests will be here soon. Not to mention the fact it's dark outside, and the temperature will drop, and—"

"After everything we've been through, do you honestly believe I'd let anything happen to her?" Dorien slipped his muscled legs into his trousers and looped the belt at his narrow waist. "I'm taking care of Faye. Everything is under control."

I wanted to believe him. I wanted to find reassurance in the deft way he knotted his silk tie, in the casual ease with which he smoothed down his suit. But in his eyes I saw the same boy who'd handed me fake passports at a train station in Prague – the boy who wanted to save the world but was instead being immolated by it.

Dorien Valencourt was not the one in control here, and he was *terrified*.

And Faye – *our* Faye – was in trouble, and he refused to let us help her.

FAYE

I awoke in darkness. My head pounded like someone had stuck it inside a church organ and mashed down all the keys.

Once, I'd been invited to a prep-school party at some girl's fancy East Village penthouse. I met a group of stoners out on the fire-escape (what's the collective noun for a group of stoners? I'm going with a *bakery*), downed half a bottle of Southern Comfort, and woke up under a bush in Central Park wearing my panties on my head. The hangover had felt something like this.

Ow. Owie. Owwwwww...

I tried to grab my head to shove my brains back inside. The ground twisted out from beneath me, and my body lurched. I reached out a hand to steady myself, only instead of a wall or the brass head of my bed, my fingers slammed into some kind of slippery fabric.

Huh? Wha—

I lurched again, and though the fog in my brain I registered that I wasn't stationary. My ass jabbed against something hard, and my body jerked and jostled as I was shuffled by invisible hands. I threw out my arms, shoving against the fabric that held me, and my mind searched for a memory of what happened.

I'm not hungover. I've hit my head. And now I'm being moved—

"Fuck. She's woken up." A muffled voice reached my ears from the other side of the fabric barrier. "Dorien, you idiot. You didn't use enough of that stuff."

Heather.

Dorien.

With the hiss of those words, the memories came back to me. Climbing the stairs to my room and encountering that horrid vision – Clare's face staring at me from the gloom, her mouth open in a silent scream as shadows twisted from her body, reaching for me. Staggering back into the arms of an assailant. Fighting with two shadowy figures. The hand over my mouth. The sweet smell in my nostrils as whatever drug they gave me dragged me into oblivion.

And now...

I was trapped inside some sort of enormous bag – the kind of bag a romance reader would bring along to a book signing. And the bag was moving, being carried along by Heather and Dorien.

"It's tough to hold something over her mouth when she's just kicked you in the testicles." Dorien's voice cut through me like a knife. "If you had nuts, Heather, you'd understand."

"I've got more balls than you ever have." Heather laughed. "I'm willing to do whatever is necessary to succeed."

She wasn't lying. Nothing about Heather shocked me now, but...

Dorien.

Dorien the dickweasel.

Hot anger rose inside me. Dorien had convinced me he was on my side. I *trusted* him. He made me agree that he could continue to torment me for Madame Usher's benefit, but in private, he was supposed to be *mine.* He let me believe that we would play my composition together for the world to hear, for his *parents* to hear... but it was all a lie. Instead, he and Heather drugged me and kidnapped me, and were taking me fuck-knows where.

I gave him my heart, and he'd ripped it to pieces in front of me.

Sound the fucktrumpets, I'm so stupid.

My ass bounced on something hard, cracking my tailbone. I howled as pain rocketed up my spine.

"Shut her up!" Heather yelled.

"Don't be so dramatic. No one will hear her out here," Dorien said. "We've come far enough. Let's leave her and get back to the party."

The bag dropped on a hard surface, jolting my throbbing tailbone. Someone kicked the side of the bag, driving the wind from my lungs. I doubled over, gasping for air as fresh pain bloomed across my temples. Outside, Heather giggled. "Now that's what I call taking out the trash."

"You can't leave me here." I punched the side of the bag.

"We just did," Heather called back, her voice already distant. I imagined her flipping her perfect honey-blonde hair over her shoulder as she linked arms with Dorien. I imagined him staring down at me with a satisfied smirk playing across his too-perfect mouth. My hand curled into a fist, but it would only have the empty satisfaction of punching the bag.

"You can't do this," I yelled. "Dorien, let me out!"

I scratched my nails against the bag, but it was no good. The fabric was thick and made of some kind of extra-tough material – maybe leather? I felt for the zipper, trying to push it open, but they must've locked or tied it shut on the outside, because no matter how hard I pulled, it wouldn't budge.

Tears pooled in the corners of my ears. I swiped them away angrily. *Don't lose it now.* I thought of my mother, all alone in that hospital room two hours from

Manderley Academy. She should have been here tonight to see me play. But someone poisoned her. Someone attacked her.

I should never have come to Manderley. I should be with her.

But I am here. And I'm not letting Dorien fucking Valencourt win this round.

My jaw set with new determination, I felt around in my pockets and on the bottom of the bag, looking for something I might be able to use. Judging by the feel of the ground, I'd been set down on rock. I could hear an owl hooting and wind rustling through the trees. I was in the woods. But that didn't exactly narrow things down – Manderley was built on the edge of the mountain range, with a vast tract of managed forest and wild woodlands stretching down into the valley. I could be *anywhere*.

I swallowed down a lump of panic and forced myself to consider my circumstances rationally. I couldn't be too far from Manderley. My kidnappers would have left themselves time to get back for the party. *If I can just get out of this bag—*

I felt around for something I might be able to use, or a loose thread I could pull. My fingers brushed a long, thin object in my back pocket. I pulled it out, inspecting it with my hands. *It feels like a tiny flashlight.*

I flicked it on and inspected the inner walls of the bag. I wondered why I had the flashlight. I hadn't been walking around the house with a flashlight in my pocket. Why would Heather and Dorien drug me and drag me out here, then give me a flashlight? It didn't make any sense.

I aimed the light upward to examine the zipper in detail, and gasped. Along the seam of the bag were scrawled the words:

"I'M COMING BACK FOR YOU."

Fuck. Fuck. Fuck.

I sucked in stale air as I struggled to keep my panic in check. My mind flashed back to the message on the pantry wall in Clare's loopy handwriting, or the single word scrawled across my mother's forehead.

I'M COMING BACK FOR YOU. What did it mean? Was it a threat? They were coming back to finish me off? It was obviously from Heather and Dorien – they wanted me to wait in this bag in the cold and imagine all the horrible things they might do to me.

Or was it... something else? Clare's face flashed in my mind again, joining with all the other strange and unexplained things that had happened at Manderley Academy. Was the message from some entity or spirit from beyond the grave?

Don't be such a bitchbadger. Ghosts don't exist. All the weird things were just Dorien fucking with you, which he's gone and proved tonight. And even if there was a ghost, acknowledging that now is not going to get you back to Manderley. Find a way out of this bag and deal with the spectral maid later.

I swallowed once, twice, three times, forcing back my panic. I swung the beam of the flashlight all around me. All I could see were the rough inner surface of the bag, the slash of the zipper I couldn't budge, and my knees poking through holes in my torn jeans. And those words – those evil, malevolent words that swam in my vision and made bile rise in my throat.

"Help! Help me!" I yelled. Hikers used the trails on the mountain that snaked close to Manderley. If there was a chance someone was out there right now, I had to get their attention. I kept yelling as I scrambled around on my hands and knees, shuffling the bag across the ground. If I could rub the fabric over a sharp rock or thorned tree, then—

The zipper tore open. A shaft of moonlight punctured my gloom.

"If you hurry, you'll make it back in time," someone whispered in a voice so quiet I couldn't tell if it was male or female. I was positive I didn't recognize the voice, but something about it seemed familiar.

What the fuck?

"Dorien?"

Footsteps rushed away as I grabbed for the open zipper.

"Hello?" I popped my head outside. "Hey, where did you go?"

It took a moment for my eyes to adjust to the bright moonlight. Trees rustled behind me. I spun in the direction of the sound, but I lost my balance and tripped over the bag. I yelped as my knee cracked against the rocks.

My breath roared in my ears. I rolled out of the bag and scrambled for the flashlight. I clicked it on and trained it on the trees, searching for whoever freed me.

They'd disappeared into the mist.

FAYE

Even with the flashlight, the hike back to the academy would take some time. First, I had to climb to the top of the ridge to get my bearings. Luckily, Madame Usher had Manderley lit up like Fourth of July fireworks for the party tonight. Solar torches along the drive acted like a landing strip pointing toward the house, which glowed on the horizon – a beacon.

Not a beacon of hope, because hope had no place at Manderley.

I glanced around again, hoping for some shortcut to present itself, wishing for a knight in shining armor to appear from the trees, throw me over the back of his horse, and ride on to Manderley. I'd settle for a ride on Titus' shoulders or even to hold Ivan's hand for a single moment to steady my fractured nerves.

But Titus and Ivan weren't here. I didn't even know if they were involved in what Dorien did tonight. I remembered Titus throwing himself at Heather when she tried to burn my hand, how Ivan's cold eyes bore into Aroha as he twisted her arms behind her. How they swore to protect me. How they drew me into their world, into their hearts, knowing that they were footnotes against the history that weighed between Dorien and I. I couldn't believe they were involved, but then, I'd been foolish enough to trust Dorien, so what the fuck did I know?

Apart from an owl hooting, I was alone.

I had no choice. I started walking.

Branches tore at my skin as I pushed through the trees. My thighs ached, and every step jolted my stinging tailbone until tears itched the corners of my eyes. Hiking wasn't exactly an extracurricular activity offered at either of my previous schools. And even if it was, I'd never have opted for it. Nature wasn't my jam.

I stepped into a wide clearing. At first, I thought I must be near the poison garden because of the way the forest retreated from the center, as if afraid to accidentally brush against the fatal earth. But no. What stood in the clearing wasn't a Victorian greenhouse but a hexagonal building made of stone and covered so thoroughly with vines and weeds that it appeared to protrude from the mantle of the earth itself, as if thrust up from some deep subterranean city of cyclopean remnants. Curious, I stepped toward it.

As I rounded the building, a loud *CREAK* punctured the stillness. My heart stuttered before I noticed a gate swinging out from the structure, caught by the wind. No, not a gate as such. I stepped closer. It was a door made from a lattice of wrought-iron, elaborately cast to form a crest in the center. I pushed away some of the weeds to look at the crest. The word USHER was written in gothic script in a ribbon across the top, and beneath it, the words IN CAUDA VENENUM.

The same words written above the poison garden.

The same words tattooed across Dorien's chest.

I didn't understand the significance of the phrase. Latin hadn't been on the school curriculum, either. But I thought I knew what the stone structure contained.

This must be the Usher family mausoleum.

I stepped up to the grate, running my hands over the metal, tugging away the vines that held it until I uncovered a narrow doorway accessed by three stone steps. The doorway was flanked by two columns – their style echoing the columns holding up Manderley's crumbling front porch. A later, Victorian construction, then.

Inside, all was in gloom. I trained the beam of my flashlight into the depths. The hairs on my arms stood on end, and I felt a kind of twang in the air – a violin-string pulled too tight, ready to snap at any moment. Like the heroine in a horror film, I knew this was a bad idea, but I couldn't tear myself away. I had to see.

I stepped inside.

The temperature dropped as I descended three stone steps into a hexagonal room. I rubbed my hands on my prickling arms as I gazed around the space. Like so much of Manderley, the mausoleum was in great need of TLC, and I didn't mean the 90s hip hop group. The building was topped with an impressive cupola adorned with sculptures depicting the Stations of the Cross, but the stone had cracked in several places and many of the sculptures existed only as pieces of rubble littering the ground. Vines twisted through the cracks, hanging down into the space like a living chandelier. Spiderwebs glittered from the grated windows on either side of the hexagon, and my feet crunched as I moved through piles of dead leaves that had blown inside and piled up over the steps and the stone dais in the center.

There were three blocks of niches in the walls, some empty, others covered with capstones carved with names and dates. Between them were statues of weeping angels beneath the windows. The angels' eyes seemed to follow me as I moved toward the center of the room, where an above-ground stone tomb dominated the space. My eyes scanned the names and dates on the niches in the walls.

Most of the graves were from the 1800s, except for two closest to the door – Victor and Mary – who I presumed were Victor Usher's parents.

I stepped up onto the edge of the stone dais, my shoes crushing piles of dead leaves and fuckadoodle-knows what else. I scraped a hand through the detritus shrouding the stone – vines and weeds, and dried bunches of stalks tied with crimson ribbon, the remnants of floral bouquets and wreaths – pushing it away to reveal the stone sculpted into the figure of a sleeping man, holding a sword and a tablet upon which a name was carved – Victor Usher. Madame Usher's husband.

He died only last year, six months before Madame Usher invited me to Manderley. But this place looked like it hadn't been touched in centuries. Madame Usher didn't believe in keeping her husband's final resting place tidy. I remembered what she told me when we first met – that she planned to leave Victor Usher for my father before he disappeared. And even though that was over ten years ago, I wondered how much it had tainted their relationship since, as Madame Usher had tainted everything at Manderley.

I moved down the tomb, pushing away more leaves and vines. My fingers pressed into a crack running across the stone – the whole thing looked so heavy, but I wondered if this section would come away if I lifted it—

"Faye. Fayeee…"

What the fuck?

My name echoed across the stones. My heart thundered, and a fresh wave of agony pounded against my skull. I spun toward the sound, flicking the flashlight across the walls. *Sound the fucktrumpets, what now?*

"Hello? Who's there?"

"Fayeeeee…"

The hairs on my neck prickled.

It's just the wind whistling through the grated window. It's just—

A shadow thrust itself from one of the unoccupied niches, barreling toward me with malicious intent. I staggered back. The flashlight beam trembled as the shadows resolved themselves into the shape of a girl. A girl with frizzy brown hair pulled back into a bun, with the most adorable tiny nose, with green eyes that shone with pain, through which I could see the capstones on the wall behind her.

Clare.

"Fayeeeee…" The voice swirled around me, everywhere and nowhere.

My mouth moved, but I couldn't speak, couldn't scream. Wind lashed against me, and the fear tore away my voice. I stood, frozen, the flashlight shaking in my hands, as Clare moved across the tomb, gliding toward me without moving her legs.

Clare raised her hands. Shadows crawled from her skin and spilled from her mouth, swirling around her. She reached Victor's tomb, but instead of going around it, the figure went right through it like it wasn't there at all.

Like *she* wasn't there at all.

I forced my legs to move, staggering backward until my ankles clipped the edge of the step.

No. No no no no no. This can't be real—

"*Fayeeee,*" Clare's voice rasped against my skull, almost as if it came from inside my own head. "*Only you can save Manderley from the voice in the walls.*"

 FAYE

"*Fayeeeeee...*"

BANG.

The mausoleum gate slammed shut.

Clare's voice hissed at me, dry as the grave from which it had come. I swallowed back my fear and forced my legs to move again. I scrambled back up the stone steps, my chest heaving and heart racing. My head swam with a pulsing agony punctuated by the loathsome scratch of Clare's voice as I spun in a daze, pushing against the grate until it flew open.

I tripped on the step and sprawled into the dirt outside, driving the air from my lungs. I looked back as the grate swung in the wind, slamming shut with an ominous *CLANG*.

An owl hooted.

Dead leaves skittered across the damp ground.

My ears rang with a noise made of silence and fear.

I pressed my hand to my chest, against my galloping heart. I listened. I waited. Clare didn't appear, but I fancied I caught the whisper of her voice on the wind.

Fayeee...

I dragged myself to my feet and sprinted into the trees, gasping for air as I fought to keep moving through the cold. Some oppressive force bore down on me, driving me away from the mausoleum. I skidded over the damp ground, my fingers clawing at tree branches that attacked my face. I crashed forward into the gloom, letting the lights of Manderley guide me.

My chest heaving, I crested the steep slope where the stream trickled into the valley, and Manderley's glory came into view. I broke into a run. I'd never been so happy to see that oppressive building. Lights blazed from the downstairs rooms, and I could see from the figures moving in the windows the party was already in full swing.

The horror of what I'd seen in the mausoleum faded as I surged toward the very real reason I'd been stuck out in the forest to begin with. Dorien and Heather wanted me to fail. But I wasn't broken yet.

What time is it? Am I too late?

I raced through the dead forest surrounding the poison garden, my feet splashing in puddles left on the path by the retreating rain. I bolted across the overgrown kitchen garden and slammed into the back door. I twisted the handle – locked. I pounded my fists against the wood. "Help, help! Let me in."

Someone yanked the door back. Harrison's face appeared, haloed by the warm lights of the kitchen. "Miss de Winter? I was so worried about you. I wanted to call the police—"

"Harrison, was it you?" I gripped his collar. "Please, tell me if it was you who let me out of the bag."

"I don't know what you're talking about, love." He stared down at my filthy clothes. "But you'd best get yourself cleaned up before you join the party. All the guests have gathered in the ballroom for the performances."

Shit. Shit. Shit. I burst into the kitchen just as the first snatches of Elena's performance piece jarred in the air. My knee twinged with pain, and my head spun. I knew I was covered in dirt, my clothes soaked through, my hair a rat's nest.

How the hell am I going to get up to my room to change without anyone seeing me? I took a step toward the door—

—and stopped dead.

There, sitting on the corner of the kitchen table, was a stack of clothes. *My* clothes. The crimson gown I'd laid out to wear tonight sat neatly folded with some toiletries and a jewelry box on top of my violin case.

A note stuck to the box read, 'break a leg, Faye.'

FAYE

Cold dread settled in my chest as I stared at the pile of my belongings, here in the kitchen instead of behind the locked door to my bedroom. This was one too many creepy-ass things to happen today. "Harrison, where did these come from?"

He shook his head. "I've no idea, I'm sorry. When we couldn't find you, I came in to help with the food, and there they were. And a godsend, too, by the looks of it. Hurry, love, there's still time for you to make it."

He was right – I didn't have time to question who had broken into my locked room and placed this stuff for me to find. I grabbed the stack of clothes. Whoever had left them for me had even thought to add my makeup bag. Harrison left to carry out trays of food, giving me a wink as he shut the kitchen door behind him. I tossed my soiled clothes into a corner, scrubbed the dirt from my skin and hair over the kitchen sink, and pulled on my dress. I did the best job I could on my face with the tiny compact mirror and the horrendous lighting. All the while, the jewelry box stared at me from the top of the range, its presence unnerving.

I could have just left it there, unopened, unacknowledged. But I was far too curious. I flipped open the lid to reveal a beautiful set of jewels. A necklace glittering with droplets of red rubies, and earrings to match. They complimented my dress perfectly. I threaded the earrings through my ears, clasped the necklace to my throat, picked up my beautiful new violin, and raced through to the ballroom as the final bewitching notes of Elena's performance swirled around me.

I lingered at the doorway as Elena rose from the piano stool, her silver hair streaming down her back and a serene smile playing across her lips. She looked every bit a fae queen from some otherworldly realm, indulging her earthly subjects with a song that wove magic in the air.

Behind her, a semicircle of guests stood in rapt attention. Some clapped, others bowed their heads in silent acknowledgment of Elena's genius. Master Radcliffe rushed forward to present her with a bouquet of roses. In the low light, I could just make out Dorien and Heather standing behind him. Heather leaned over to whisper something to Dorien, but he didn't appear to have heard her. His face was hard, his mouth set, but his stormy grey eyes were drenched in misery. I glanced away, unable to face him. I couldn't let myself be drawn into his beguiling darkness again.

"Brava, brava, Elena." Madame Usher basked in the glow of Elena's glory. Tonight, she eschewed her usual funereal black gowns for a silk and taffeta number in a deep, royal purple. With her hair twisted back and a necklace of ruby droplets at her throat, I caught a flicker of what Victor Usher and my father might've seen in her. She had nothing on my mother, but there *was* a statuesque, powerful beauty about her – like a crash of a violent wave before it tossed a helpless boat against the rocks.

Madame Usher thrust her hands in the air as Master Radcliffe led Elena back into the crowd and Dorien shuffled forward to take his seat at the piano for our piece. "Thank you, Elena. That was perfection. Unfortunately, our next student, Faye de Winter, wasn't feeling well and couldn't join us tonight, so Dorien Valencourt will perform her piece accompanied by Heather Danvers—"

"Good news." I swept into the room. "I feel much better now, so I thought I'd join the party."

If looks could kill, I'd be dead and buried. Madame Usher's face froze in disbelief, her fingers dangling in midair. Heather swore. Titus started toward me, but Ivan held him back. I could tell from their faces they'd had no idea what happened to me, and the relief of that surged through my veins, driving my defiant spirit onward as I stepped into the light.

Dorien kept his head turned away from me. His shoulders stiffened. His back fused ramrod straight.

A collective gasp swept through the room as I glided across the floor in my crimson dress, my violin clutched in my hands. I kept my chin high, my eyes locked with Madame Usher, daring her to deny me.

Behind Madame Usher, Heather's cheeks burned with fire.

Titus broke free of Ivan's grasp. He crossed the room in three strides and took my hand in his, escorting me to my place in front of the piano. "Where have you been?" he whispered. "We were so worried about you."

I shook my head. I couldn't think about it now. I needed every ounce of strength within me to make it through this piece with Dorien.

Madame Usher composed herself. She clearly hadn't expected me to be here tonight, but whether that meant she had anything to do with my kidnapping I couldn't determine. "We're so pleased to hear it, Faye. If you'd like to join Dorien for your piece..." She turned to the people behind her. "Faye has made a study of Paganini this year, and she's inspired by his showy style. Her little finger can be quite weak, but she's managing."

I'll show you managing.

I rested my instrument against my chin. Dorien lifted his eyes to mine, and I reveled in the pain and regret swimming in those orbs. *Fuck you, Dorien.* With a smugness born of hiking through a fucking forest and twice seeing a ghostly visage I couldn't yet explain, I struck the first note.

The music soared through the ballroom, wild and vibrant and filled with my distinctive fire. Master Radcliffe's breath hitched as note after perfect note fell from my bow. At the piano, Dorien's fingers trailed along the keys – perfect as always, but this time fading away, becoming part of the background so I could shine.

I closed my eyes and poured all my pain and rage and hurt into the piece. I played better than I'd ever played before. Dorien and I soared together as the notes flew from my fingers, as the melody took the entire room on a journey with me, into the fires of hell and back. Even the near-impossible arpeggios felt like butter-flies fluttering against my skin. Sometimes playing music was about remembering the notes, and sometimes it was this – this magical, ethereal presence that takes over your body and makes you soar.

Smells circled around me – the scented memories I conjured whenever I played. This time, the air sang with polished wood flooring and Victor Usher's distinctive cigars – the smell of the old New York music school where Dorien and I first met, where we'd first started down the destructive path that led to this moment.

When I finished and took my bow, a deathly silence clung to the room. Master Radcliffe stood and applauded. "Brava." He kissed my cheeks. "I see our fears about your unconventional training were unjustified. You are a rare talent, Ms. de Winter. I see so much of your father in you."

BAM. Just like that, my good mood evaporated. No matter what I did, my father was always in the room with me, his legacy hanging over my head like my own personal sword of Damocles.

Dorien strode toward me, his eyes dark. He looked like he was going to be sick. "Sprite, I—"

Titus and Ivan were at my side in moments, pulling me back through the crowd. Dorien's eyes burned into my back, but I refused to turn and acknowledge him. Titus and Ivan pulled me right to the back of the room, into the small alcove formed at the base of one of the turrets. A table had been set up here, laden with the food I prepared and bottles of Champagne in silver buckets. The first tinkling notes of Heather's piece sounded in the vast room, muffled by the thick curtains – just as well, because she sounded as vapid and lifeless as ever.

"You were remarkable." Ivan pressed a Champagne flute into my fingers.

I lifted the glass to my lips and realized my hands were trembling. Titus' warm hands fell on my shoulders, and he moved me away from the table and into the alcove of the windows. I gripped the sill, my gaze flickering outside to where the trees bent toward the house, branches reaching like fingers beckoning, threatening to drag me back out into the cold forest. I remembered that creepy mausoleum and

Clare's horrific visage gliding toward me, and the words written inside the bag. A shiver cascaded down my spine.

"Where were you?" Titus demanded again. "And what did Dorien have to do with it? He's been acting fucking weird all evening, and then we couldn't find you anywhere."

Now that my piece was over, the full horror of what they did to me and what I'd seen tonight washed over me. I gripped Titus' arm as my knees buckled. "It was horrible. You swear you didn't know anything about what... what they did..."

"Hell no. We've been looking for you all afternoon." Titus wrapped his arms around me, holding me upright, steadying me against his bulk. "We were going to call the police, but someone stole our phones from our room and Madame Usher refused to let us use the house phone."

"We couldn't find Heather, either," Ivan said. "We thought that at least if Dorien went after you, you'd be safe."

"I'm never safe with Dorien Valencourt," I hissed. As Titus held me steady, I relayed everything that happened since I saw them last – going up to my room, being attacked and drugged, waking up in the bag, being let out by an unknown source, running back to Manderley, the mausoleum, then finding my clothes in the kitchen, waiting for me. As I spoke, the full horror of it weighed on me, and the headache bloomed across my temples once more. I couldn't believe it had all transpired in a few short hours. It felt like a lifetime had passed.

When I woke up this morning, Dorien Valencourt had my heart, along with his fellow Muses. Now, all he had was my hatred, and I'd make damn sure he suffered for what he did.

The only bits I left out were the words I found scrawled in the pantry and inside the bag, and seeing Clare's face. Now that I was back at Manderley and faced with the very real horror of what Dorien and Heather tried to do, I couldn't believe it was anything other than a trick of the drugs Dorien used on me. And in the mausoleum, it was the shadows and the wind playing a trick on me.

It *had* to be.

Because Clare's message makes no sense. There are no ghosts at Manderley – only evil, spiteful dickwizards who are going down.

I thought Dorien cared about me, and then he drugged me. All so he could play my song – *our* song – with Heather? As far as I was concerned, they deserved each other.

Titus and Ivan exchanged glances as I finished my tale in a breathless rush. "I'll kill him right now." Ivan's fists tightened at his sides. In his Romanian accent, the harsh words took on a sinister tone. In that moment, I truly believed my ice prince capable of murdering his so-called friend.

"We'll kill him together." Titus cracked his knuckles. His fingers were so large the sound was like approaching thunder. "But not tonight. His parents are here. That's torture enough for him for now."

Dorien's parents are here? I pulled the edge of the curtain back and peered into the room, searching the unfamiliar faces. Despite myself, I couldn't help being interested to see them. His mother was always a Grade A bitchbadger at Dorien's rehearsals and recitals. He said they were involved in that weird cult and hadn't been outside their compound for nearly a decade, so I hadn't expected them to show up, but I kind of wanted to see what cult membership did to a woman like her.

Also, I wanted to see Dorien *squirm*.

"You are just afraid to do anything in front of your own parents," Ivan shot back at Titus.

"Damn right." Titus made a face. "I don't like any of this. Dorien and Heather working together... something feels off. He wanted you so much he was willing to share you with us, Faye. He was genuine about his feelings. I don't understand what could have made him do this."

"I can." Ivan's gaze swiveled to the curtains. I leaped away just as a pale hand drew them back from the other side, revealing Madame Usher, her cheeks flushed with pride from the performances.

"Don't hide back here." She flapped her hands toward the ballroom. The cloying scent of her floral perfume wafted around her – she reminded me of the decaying blooms placed on her husband's tomb. She might have once been beautiful, but not even she could hide from the rot that devoured her from within. "Tonight, you are my stars. Your public awaits."

I opened my mouth, but her steel gaze stole my accusations from my lips before they could be spoken aloud. Ivan's nails dug into my arm. Madame Usher turned on her heel and glided back into the room, expecting us to follow her.

Titus sighed. "We should get out there."

"Don't leave our side." Ivan held me close.

"I wouldn't dream of it." I placed my hand on top of his. Titus filled wine glasses for all three of us. I knew I'd need the drink to get through the rest of this event with Dorien's eyes boring into me from across the room.

We stepped out from behind the curtain. Immediately, the tension in the room shifted. Conversations dimmed. Eyes roved over my body, and I heard the words 'Donovan de Winter' slip from several lips. I moved through the crowd, flanked by Ivan and Titus, and it was as if an invisible shield slammed down around me. The stares and whispers that might once have infected me rolled off my skin, leaving me unscathed. The unique intensity of Dorien's gaze touched my skin, but it was dimmed by the light of my two Muses.

I was Faye de Winter, and tonight, I was *untouchable*.

Ivan made a beeline for Elena, who stood with Master Radcliffe, making conversation with three of his friends from the New York Opera. All three men laughed at something Elena said, and Master Radcliffe stared at her with a look of utter enchantment.

Ivan's jaw set in a hard line, and he tugged my arm. But the crowd closed in on us before we could make it to them. "Faye, you were *sublime*." A woman drenched in sickly vanilla perfume and dripping with strings of pearls clasped my hands. "I must have you in my company. Get Gizella to call me. We'll talk about a summer tour—"

"Have you ever thought about joining the theatre, Faye?" A wiry man with horn-rimmed glasses thrust a card under my nose. "We're always in need of musicians, and with your stage presence, you'll be a star—"

"I cannot believe Gizella's had you locked up in this house for months and she didn't even tell us." A portly woman leaned in and pinched my cheek so hard it made tears pool in my eyes. "Wait until I tell my donors about this – the daughter of Donovan de Winter on stage at last. You are poised to be even greater than your father—"

Their voices swirled around me, and I drank in the praise that had never before been directed at me behind the walls of Manderley. I tried to ignore the comments and comparisons to my father, but his name made a burning rage coil down my spine.

Beside me, Titus beamed. He talked in his booming, sexy voice about my talents, while Ivan's fingers dug into my skin as he watched his sister over my shoulder. *What's his deal? Elena is perfectly safe in this room filled with people. She's the real star here, not me. And that's exactly as it should be.*

If I didn't know better, I'd say Ivan was jealous of the attention Elena got from Master Radcliffe and his guests. But I knew him better than that. Ivan lived for his sister – her life was more to him than his own. So what caused his spine to go rigid and his jaw to lock so? If it wasn't jealousy, what did he have to fear from this party?

As we moved across the room, I saw Madame Usher deep in conversation with a white-haired, square-jawed man standing military-straight. "Who's that?" I asked. Somehow, I couldn't picture that man as Madame Usher's type.

"That's the New York City police commissioner," Titus said. "His wife is a huge classical music buff. Madame gives him tickets to all the events, and they come for dinner several times a year."

I watched the two bend their heads together. They certainly appeared to be friendly. Which was odd, because I was certain Madame Usher didn't know how to have a normal human relationship.

Aroha stood at the edge of the room with a couple who bore a striking resemblance to her angular features and shimmering dark hair. They could only be her parents – her mother wore a deep blue evening gown, and over it, a short cape/cloak stitched with feathers. Her father's face was tattooed with similar swirls and lines to the ink Aroha had on her own skin. Aroha wore a similar cloak to her mother, although shorter. All three of them looked thoroughly uncomfortable, and I noticed no one else in the room was talking to them.

"Aroha, hi." I needed to know if she was involved. "I'm sorry I missed your performance. How did it go?"

Aroha touched her nose and winked at me. "Perfectly."

She was on drugs again. I guessed her parents couldn't tell.

"Kia ora, Faye." His father took my hand and leaned in. I thought he would kiss my cheeks – a greeting I was well used to after years of being around pretentious classical music types – but instead, he touched my nose with his. "Aroha has told us so much about you."

"She has?" I didn't believe Aroha wasted a single breath thinking or talking about me. She'd always made it clear she was here for the prize money and nothing else.

"Dad is *trying* not to be weird," Aroha rolled her eyes. "But he's failing miserably."

Her dad hugged Aroha to him, letting out a deep, kind laugh. "My daughter, she is the strong, silent type. Kiri and I, we beg her for news, for stories. We want her to tell us all about her exciting life in America. She says that you're the life of this school, you and your many boyfriends and your bold songs and your kindness. She says you're the one to beat for the Manderley Prize, and that she would not feel dishonored to lose to you. We worry about our daughter, coming all the way around the world to study on her own. It makes us so happy to see her with such accomplished friends."

Friends? I guess he doesn't know about the time Aroha tried to hold my hand over a stove element. I glanced at Ivan for support, but he was too busy glaring at Master Radcliffe as he handed Elena another glass of Champagne.

Aroha stared at me with wild eyes. "Dad, why don't you get us some kai? I want to talk to Faye for a sec."

"Excellent idea." Aroha's parents held hands as they made their way across the room toward the food table.

"Yeah, so... you can ignore all that stuff he said." Aroha stared at a spot on the wall behind me, her vision swimming. "Sometimes I have to tell them shit so they don't put me on the next plane back to New Zealand."

"It's okay," I said, without thinking. It wasn't really okay. I was still angry and afraid of this girl. I didn't trust her one bit. But I had enough shit to worry about tonight – I didn't have it in me to remain pissed off at Aroha, especially not when I'd just got a glimpse of what was going on with her. I already knew about the crippling stage fright she masked with drugs. I think she told her parents we were friends because she didn't have a friend here. She was lonely and out of place, in the same way I was lonely and out of place. So I decided to ignore it. For now.

"I know it's weird," she shrugged. "But you're all right, trash."

"What was the nose thing?" I asked.

"It's called *hongi*. It's the traditional greeting where the breath of life is exchanged. I figure if I have to spend all evening being wet-kissed on my cheeks from gross old white dudes, they can deal with a little nose-bumping from my fam."

"Agreed." I dared a smile, which she returned with a grin that was almost manic.

Two faces appeared at the back of the crowd behind Aroha, buried in shadows so I could not distinguish their features. Something about them made my heart hammer against my chest. I felt their eyes raking across my skin, lifting up the corners to peek underneath.

Aroha wandered off to find her parents. The crowd parted, splitting off into smaller groups, and I got a view of the unsettling faces. I gasped as I recognized them.

Dorien's parents bent their heads together, whispering harsh words and darting glances at me. Now that I was no longer the center of attention, I could take the opportunity to study them. And what I saw was... confusing.

While everyone else in the room strutted around in designer cocktail dresses and elegant suits, Mr. and Mrs. Valencourt wore floor-length robes made of rough grey cloth, belted at the waist with white cords. Their features were as aristocratic and imperious as I remembered, which made their attire stand out even further. It was as if the Valencourts *knew* beyond a shadow of a doubt that they were better than every other person in this room. Not despite their strangeness, but *because* of it.

I'd barely been able to believe it when Dorien said his parents were in a cult – I couldn't imagine his stern mother taking orders from anyone. And yet seeing them here, bold in their devotion, I understood exactly how they'd come under the spell of this 'Father Aaron.' Dorien's parents craved power – they always had. That was why they pushed Dorien so much, because in his talent they saw a world opening up to them, a world they so obviously *deserved*. Why limit their power to the earthly realm? The cult, whatever it was, would open up the heavens to them.

Another couple moved toward them – Heather's parents, I guessed, as they both bore the same honey-blonde hair and California good-looks – and they leaned in for the typical cheek kisses. I watched Dorien's mother's face as the honey-blonde woman turned toward her, the way her features pinched with surprise. I wished I could get closer to hear what was being said—

No. I don't care. Dorien Valencourt is dead to me.

"Are those Heather's parents?" I whispered to Ivan, jabbing my elbow at the new couple. Ivan was still watching Elena, who held Master Radcliffe's arm as he escorted her from group to group. I had to jab him again to get him to turn back to me, and when he did, his lips were drawn in a tight line. I'd yanked him out of some obsession.

What does he think will happen to Elena in this room, in front of all these people?

Or is it simply that after over a decade in this house, he knows tonight's display of convivial finery is only a mask to hide the real Manderley – the Manderley of ghosts and shadows...

Wow, I sound like Edgar Allan Poe after an absinthe bender. Must've been all the creepy things I've seen.

I forced down the images of Clare's face and that creepy writing inside the bag, and shook Ivan's arm again. He cursed under his breath, his icicle eyes swirling to meet mine. All I saw were glaciers – old and immovable. I repeated my question, and Ivan nodded. "Yes. Those are Heather's parents."

"There's something about them..." As I watched, Heather's mother turned to accept a glass of Champagne from her husband. The candlelight caught something glittering at her throat – a brooch she wore pinned to the nape of her neck. It was a strange cluster of fiery jewels set in a circle with a crescent moon on top and a cross beneath – it looked a little like an occult symbol or something, but completely blinged out.

Odd, I swear I've seen that before...

The memory rushed at me, transporting me back ten years to another city, another Faye, another room filled with musicians and fancy people we were supposed to impress. I *had* seen that piece of jewelry before. Back at Madame Usher's music school, at an end-of-year recital. Dorien gave an almost flawless performance. In the last bar, his finger slid on a note – it was a mistake, but barely perceptible. I could tell he was aware of it, for his shoulders tensed as he stood to give his bow, and he stormed off-stage without acknowledging me waiting for him in the wings.

Backstage, I wrapped my arms around him, whispering that he'd been incredible, that no one apart from his tutor Master Usher would have noticed the bum note. That he was special and everyone in the room could see and hear it. The corner of Dorien's lip had tugged upward, and I thought I'd almost managed to make him smile when we were interrupted.

"Dorien!" He stiffened at the sound of her voice – a shrill whistle that bounced off the floorboards. I resisted the urge to clamp my hands over my ears. I glared up at Dorien's mother as she loomed over us, her elegant arms crossed over a severe brown dress, her only adornment a black mesh veil and that *same glittering brooch* at her throat.

"Mom, I—"

She grabbed Dorien's ear, dragging him backward across the hardwood floor. Dorien's face twisted in pain as he scratched at her wrist. She let go, shoving him roughly and sending him sprawling. He cupped his ear, and blood trickled through his fingers.

"You *disgusting* boy. You are a failure and a disgrace. We indulge your every wanton desire, give in to your every whim. And this is how you repay us? You have spat in the face of our God. You cannot be saved."

You cannot be saved. At the time I thought it such a strange thing to say. But I never gave it a second thought. My heart was too busy breaking for Dorien.

The words hit Dorien as if they were a physical blow. He reeled, curling his body in on himself and wrapping his hands over his head, trying to protect himself from further attacks. His mother watched him, a satisfied smirk tugging at the corner of her mouth – the same expression I'd seen mirrored on Dorien's lips when he pulled some ridiculous prank. Only what Dorien craved was love and affection, and what she desired above all else was to cause pain. She took pleasure from the hurt she'd done to him.

My back pressed into the wall. I stood frozen, torn between the desire to run to comfort him and the vicious urge to step forward and kick her ankles out from under her, or to tug the brooch from her neck and stab her with the pin.

"Leave him alone." The words fell from my mouth before I could stop them. I was my mother's daughter, after all.

The woman turned to me. "You were supposed to make him great for us," she said. "It was all planned. But I see now he is beyond redemption."

With that weirdness said, she turned on her heel and left the room. I rushed to Dorien, but he shoved me away.

"Dorien?"

His eyes flashed with pain. He spun on his heel and fled out into the concert hall, where the parents gathered with the Ushers' prominent guests. I chased after him, but before I could reach him, warm arms reached around me and scooped me into the air.

"There's my Maestra." Dad's scent washed over me – that smoky aroma of cigarettes and expensive cologne, of his achievements and his vices colliding against my nostrils. He so rarely stepped back from his shining career to notice I existed, and this was the first time in years he'd actually been in the city to see me perform, that for a moment I forgot about Dorien and reveled in his attention, burying my head into his shoulder and kissing his neck.

"Darling, you were amazing." My mom swept me up into a hug. She wore her pride in her easy smile, and my heart stuttered as I wished more than anything that Dorien could have what I had, that his parents could see who he truly was. I held my mom tightly. Behind her, my father watched Dorien's retreating figure, a strange expression on his face, almost as if he—

"Faye?" Titus snapped his fingers in front of my face. "You disappeared somewhere inside that beautiful brain of yours."

"Do you have a concussion?" Ivan's eyes narrowed. "I will *kill* Dorien. I do not care who watches."

"I'm fine. Save the killing until after dessert. I made tres leches cakes and they are incredible. I don't want them covered in blood." I watched Heather's parents as they moved away from Dorien's family and surrounded their daughter. "I was just remembering something. It's probably nothing, but that brooch Heather's mother is wearing used to belong to Dorien's mother."

Titus rolled his eyes. "They probably brought it from the same designer store."

I nodded, but I wasn't convinced. "It looks more like a one-off piece or family heirloom."

"The Danvers and the Valencourts are prominent old-money families, and they definitely have business dealings," Titus said. "Dorien told me that his parents even have this written agreement that he and Heather will marry. Like an arranged marriage. From the way she carries on around him, she wants it to happen."

"I think they'd be perfect together." I was too busy watching the strange people of this party to say it with any real venom. No matter how much closer I got to understanding the secrets of Manderley, the old house revealed another layer. Why was Heather's mother wearing Dorien's mother's brooch? And did that have anything to do with Dorien's sudden desire to hurt me?

Dorien

Every moment of the party was agony. I couldn't keep my eyes off Faye as she circled the room with Ivan and Titus at her side. She greeted every guest with grace and mirth – no trace of what Heather and I had done penetrated her loveliness.

Meanwhile, I was a wreck. I couldn't eat, couldn't drink. During my second performance, I slipped on the keys. Heather glared at me over her violin as my clunky playing ruined her mediocre melody. Behind her head, I saw my parents exchange that familiar look of disdain and disappointment that had shadowed me my entire life. I was not living up to the standards they'd set – and it just wouldn't do.

Little did they know, I was just as bad as them. Father Aaron pulled their strings, and they danced for him. I let Madame Usher and Heather control me, and I lost one great love to save another.

I hated Heather for finding a way to manipulate me into hurting Faye. She'd been taking lessons from Madame Usher. But that hatred paled to what I felt for myself. I *loathed* my weakness.

I'd been conditioned to see myself as disgusting, useless, a pointless stain on existence. And I'd proven them right. Now it was like a tide pushing against the breakwater, and I could no longer bear the weight of holding it all back.

Having my parents here made everything worse. My heart was already raw and bruised, but they threw salt into the wound. Mother insisted Madame Usher send Harrison into the village to collect them. I knew they'd come in on the train but didn't want anyone to know. Father Aaron destroyed their car. He said fossil fuels were of the Devil. I was surprised he let them out to see me at all, but then, they were only here to remind me of my duty.

People stared at them in their strange outfits, and they stared at me as if I had a third head. Whispers followed me as I circled the room, staying as far from them as possible. I spoke with conductors and producers and classical musicians of renown. I swung my infamous Dorien charm like it was a weapon. I even had an awkward conversation with the commissioner – he asked if I was staying out of trouble, and the guests tittered as if it was a brilliant joke, but he and I both locked eyes because it was no joke. Madame Usher had brought him tonight for a reason – to remind me to toe the line, or she would send the whole house of cards falling down around me.

I tried not to stare at Faye, but it was impossible. Her light burned bright in the dull room, blotting over every nightmare that lurked in the dark places.

As the party wound down, my parents cornered me. They got my back against a wall (literally. I dug my nails into a gap between the paneling and felt a rush of air and wished like fuck it was a secret passage that would swing open and swallow me). Father beckoned me into the shadows of the Red Room.

"Dorien, you've been ignoring our letters." My mother leaned against the door so I couldn't escape.

"You could use the phone like normal people," I bit back. I sounded like a petulant child, but I couldn't bring myself to care.

"You know that mobile phones are not secure." My father stood by the window, his hands resting on the back of the chaise lounge. I noticed the callouses and cuts covering his fingers. My father once managed a vast real estate empire. For my entire life, his hands bore the smooth, soft touch of someone who barked orders and made deals on the golf course. He still bore that air of callous authority, but his hands betrayed what was happening behind the compound walls. What did Father Aaron have my father doing that had changed him so drastically?

"After all we've done for you, you repay us with this insolence?" Mother's voice dripped with poison. "You have forgotten all we taught you living in this house of privilege and frivolity. You've never done anything worthwhile."

Why, why, why, even when they're fucking looney-tunes, do they still have this power over me? I knew the answer to that question – because I knew what they were capable of. I lived through their hell and thought I finally escaped, but as long as they had Jacob, I was trapped and they knew it.

"If you've come all this way to hurl insults at me, you should have written a list and posted it to 69 Go Fuck Yourself Avenue." I moved to the port decanter on the sideboard and poured myself a glass, hoping like fuck they didn't notice my hand tremble as I sloshed the liquid. "You're not paying for my education. You cut me off because I wouldn't agree to be part of your barbaric religion. I'm legally an adult, so you don't have a say over my life any longer."

My life is controlled by someone else now. I have another puppet master pulling the strings.

"Son," my father warned. His face remained still and impassive as stone, but one hand balled into a fist beneath the bell sleeve of his robe. I noticed how thin his wrist appeared, the veins protruding through thin skin. Must've been that vegan diet.

"We came because we want to see our firstborn do what he was born to do – to move hearts and transform minds with music." My mother swung at my hand, flinging the glass at the wall. It smashed to pieces, leaving a stain of blood-red alcohol dripping down the molding. "Instead, we find a shallow brat who's pissed away his talent on sex, drugs, and rock'n'roll. It's not too late to return to your family. Give up this world of heathen debauchery and instead use your gift as God intended – to bring new disciples to his True Path."

"Not interested." I gestured to the door. "If that's all, I've got some heathen debauchery to get back to—"

"You didn't tell us you were seeing Faye de Winter," my father said.

I must be imagining that hopeful strain in his voice.

"I'm not *seeing* her. We just performed together. Why do you care?" I leaned back in the piano stool and fiddled with the lid, pretending I didn't give a shit that Faye's name was on his lips. "She has as much right to be here as any other student. Just because you don't want anything to do with such a 'volatile' family, doesn't mean I can't—"

"Madame Usher told us the two of you have become close, but that you were attempting poorly to hide it." My mother's lip curled. "She also told us this Faye was involved with those two other boys who play in your little band."

That fucking bitch. I let the corner of my mouth twist into a smirk. "I thought you cult types were all into free love?"

"Dorien, you can't allow those two to get in your way." My mother folded her arms. "Faye is your destiny. You must fight—"

SLAM.

I dropped the lid of the piano, narrowly missing jamming my fingers inside. "You can't be serious."

My parents exchanged a glance, and in their eyes, I read something that made horror tingle down my spine. I knew they weren't here to 'invite me back into the family.' I thought they'd come to make sure I was getting cozy with my future wife, Heather. But this, this was worse – now they had some plan involving Faye?

My mind flashed back to earlier today when Heather had come to my room to force me to do her bidding. She mentioned the Temple of Earthly Truths and my assault charges. I assumed Madame Usher had given her that information so Heather had leverage over me, and that was probably true. But there could also be something else going on here.

I knew one thing, I'd give my life to keep the Temple of Earthly Truths away from Faye.

I leaned back again, folding my hands in my lap and glaring up at them both. I hoped they couldn't hear my heart pounding in my chest. "Nothing's going on between Faye and I. I thought this would please you. I thought you wanted me to marry Heather. That's certainly what she wants—"

"You cannot marry Heather Danvers," my mother hissed.

"Son, this is important." Father came around the chaise lounge to stand over me. "You need to listen to us. We know what's best for you. And seeing your performance tonight has cinched it – Heather is not a good match for you. But Faye has her father's gift. She is an unorthodox choice, sure, but the Lord has placed her back in your path for a reason. He wants you and Faye to be together, to spread his message through your music. Did you hear how many conductors and producers in that room want you to tour with them?"

My hands balled into fists. I knew why they were here. They needed money. They always needed money. They were checking that their investment in me would be paying off.

"Why did you have to come?" I growled. "You should have just stayed at the compound."

"And miss seeing our baby play?" Mother cooed, her voice dripping with false sentiment. "Dorien, we need you at the Temple. With your talent and Faye at your side, you could spread our message across the world."

"What about Jacob?" I demanded. "What's his role in all this?"

"Your brother's star doesn't shine like yours. He is not made to be a Conduit of Truth, as you are. He is a disciple of the True Path, and he will serve the new world in his own way." Dad glanced out the window. "Father Aaron says the time of ascension is approaching, and we must be prepared."

"What does that even *mean?*"

"We can only reveal the truth to those who take the oath. Dorien, we want you to visit us at the compound. We're having an open day where we talk to our families and loved ones about the True Path."

"A recruitment drive, you mean."

Mother flashed me a self-satisfied smile. "Your brother misses you. He asks after you every day."

"That's your fault," I growled. "You won't allow him to speak to me, or see me when I visit."

"He's not ready to face the temptations of the outside world. Please, son, come home. The open day is next Saturday."

"I have a recital."

"Even better." She patted my shoulder. The contact made my skin crawl. "Come before your recital and pray with us, and the light of the Lord will shine on your performance."

The day of ascension. I didn't like the sound of that. My mind played over that famous recording from Jonestown – of prayers and words of faith, of women crying and children screaming, of gasps and thuds as hundreds of bodies dropped around them after they drank Flavor Aid poisoned with cyanide. The deathly silence that followed.

I suppressed a shudder. I knew what I had to do. I'd been putting it off because I thought I could save Jacob without making his life even harder than it had to be. Or maybe I'd just been trying to keep the ugly side of myself hidden from the world. Maybe my sacrifice was buried in selfishness and bullshit.

No more.

I'll come home, all right. I'll come and take my brother far, far away from your evil.

I forced a smile. "Sure, Mom. I wouldn't miss it."

"And you'll bring Faye?"

Faye will never speak to me again. She's sensible like that. "Sure. I'll try."

FAYE

I spent the rest of the evening sneaking looks at Dorien's parents and trying to steer myself close enough to overhear what they whispered to each other. But lucky for me, I was suddenly Miss Popularity. Everyone wanted to gush over my performance and hand me their business cards and talk about my father's mysterious disappearance, so I couldn't get any sleuthing in.

While a British musician with dreamy shale-grey eyes talked my ear off about his band, and his theory that my father had run away to join the circus, my mind wandered back to the cult that had Dorien's parents in its thrall. He hadn't told me much about it. I thought back to what I'd seen when Harrison dropped him off at his parents' estate – the barbed wire, the high stone wall, the pile of trash, and NO TRESPASSING signs. And that creepy guy Dorien called Father Aaron who'd watched us play that one time I visited Dorien as a kid – I guessed he was the cult leader.

"Gabriel, so good to see you." Titus came up behind me, slipping his hand through mine and clapping the other guy on the shoulder. "I can't wait to get back out on tour with Octavia's Ruin. Faye, can I tear you away? My parents want to meet you."

Titus' parents. Nerves twisted in my gut. I'd never had a boyfriend before, so I'd never had to meet anyone's parents. In fact, I still wasn't sure I was allowed to call Titus or Ivan my boyfriend, and Dorien... fuck Dorien. And Titus' parents weren't just anyone – Amos and Delphine Thibodeaux were famous in our world. I wanted them to think well of me. But also, I knew they were the reason Titus hid his electric guitar and played in a damp woodshed out the back of the school.

Before I could protest or beg for a moment to prepare myself, Titus swept me across the room, where his parents held court around the piano. Amos sat on the stool, his fingers tinkling the keys as Delphine leaned over the lid, her long fingers caressing the stem of a Champagne flute as she sang in a low, sultry voice. They may have been a classical duet, but they were born and raised in New Orleans – jazz was in their blood.

Titus' warm hand settled in mine as he drew me forward. Amos caught his eye and waved him over with a sweeping hand, keeping his other on the keys, playing through the scales. "Son, come join us for a song."

"Maybe later." Titus' jaw tightened, and I sensed a tension flicker between him and his father that hid behind their easy smiles and booming, kind voices. "I wanted you to meet my girlfriend, Faye de Winter."

My girlfriend. I started at the very words I wasn't sure I was allowed to utter falling so easily from Titus' sexy mouth. Behind me, Ivan stiffened. I wondered if this was Titus' attempt to stake a claim on me.

No, not him. Titus didn't believe in stirring trouble for the sake of it. That wasn't his style. He always wanted everyone around him to be happy and at ease. If he said the words, it was because he believed them.

My girlfriend.

A jolt of heat surged through me. I squeezed Titus' hand, my heart skipping as he turned to smile at me. *I like it.*

"The famous Faye de Winter." Amos rose from the piano stool and clasped his hands together. The sound was like thunder clapping before a ferocious storm. With his barrel chest and booming voice, Amos Thibodeaux had an imposing stage presence, but in person the sheer force of his personality filled the whole room. He took my hand in his and led me to sit beside him on the stool, where he tapped out a cheerful ditty on the keys. "It's a pleasure to meet you. We enjoyed your performance this evening. You are a vision."

"In the hands of a lesser musician, that piece might have sounded somber, but you inject a liveliness and vivacity into your playing that elevates you," Delphine said. "I understand you composed that piece yourself? Rarely are talented composers also exquisite performers, but it seems you are the exception."

"Thank you." I beamed at them both, wallowing in the joy of their praise. I could see why Titus wanted so badly to please his parents, even at the expense of losing himself. It felt amazing to have Amos' smile on me, his attention rapt, his fingers lacing in mine like I was some precious object he couldn't let go of in case I floated away. They did not mention my father, and I immediately liked them all the more for that.

"Son, your girlfriend's glass is empty." Delphine glittered from head-to-toe in a stunning designer dress as she leaned over to top up my glass with Champagne. "Never mind, it is easily remedied. Amos and I are trying to inject some life into this stuffy affair. Honestly, once you spend any time in New Orleans, you will find every other function dull and dreary."

"I do hope to visit one day," I said.

"We should arrange that. Amos and I will be on tour during Christmas, but perhaps in the new year? We would show you the sights, all the jazz bars and music venues, perhaps arrange a recital for some of our friends?" She stroked my arm. "I'd love to see you and my son play together."

I beamed up at Titus, thinking of the new composition I'd started working on – a bombastic piece of violin and cello. "I'd love that, too."

"Son," Amos' enormous hand landed on Titus' shoulder. "We must discuss your fingering. You got lazy toward the end, and I don't want to see it—"

He led Titus away, his voice rising into a boom as he went over every second of Titus' performance, critiquing and offering suggestions. To an outsider, it might have sounded like a friendly and helpful critique, but I knew better. As his father talked, Titus shrunk into himself, nodding and staring at his shoes. The Thibodeauxes were not like Dorien's parents, deliberately setting out to tear him down for their own twisted joy, so I knew there was a deeper issue that Titus couldn't – or wouldn't – face.

I didn't like to see him with his back up like that, cornered by his father's critique, when I knew he needed love and kindness. But I couldn't go after him. Delphine still held my arm, studying me intently with the heavy-lidded dark eyes of hers. She had her short, curly hair cut in a stylish afro that accentuated her sharp cheekbones, and diamond earrings glittered from her ears.

"It's an honor to meet you," I said. "I'm a huge fan of your music."

"Amos and I have fought hard for our careers." Her eyes penetrated mine. "You have Latina heritage, I see. Perhaps you know of what I speak. There are many in our world – in this room, even – who believe the music halls belong to those with a certain *pedigree*, and that perhaps we should stick to our own world."

"Music isn't owned," I said. "It's universal, bigger than any of us."

"I could not agree more," her eyes twinkled. "Titus' brother had a Plato quote written on the inside of his cello case. 'Music gives a soul to the universe, wings to the mind, flight to the imagination, and life to everything.'"

"That's beautiful."

"It is. And not attributable to Plato. Micah found it on a Facebook post and never thought to check if the famous philosopher ever spoke the words. Micah was no historian, but he loved anything beautiful."

"I didn't know Titus had a brother?"

A shadow of pain passed over her eyes. It was gone in an instant, but I knew I said the wrong thing. "Micah is with the Lord."

Shit. Titus' brother is dead? I felt awful, like that was something I should have known. "I'm so sorry for your loss."

"Yes. As we all are." She smiled then, an attempt to put me at ease. Her smile was so warm and kind, but that sadness flickered in her eyes again, and I knew she was well practiced at masking her pain. "Titus is a good boy, so talented, so full of spark. I always knew with the right partner by his side he would soar to the heavens. It's time for him to give up on his silly pop music and allow his real career begin, and I know you'll help him soar."

I couldn't believe she called Broken Muse 'silly pop music.' I thought of Titus hiding in that shed outside, his long, beautiful fingers shredding the strings of an electric guitar. How at peace he looked in that moment, how free.

But no one was ever free at Manderley.

As Delphine spoke, I could see the wheels turning in her head. She had visions of Titus and I playing concert halls together, building a glittering classical music career on the foundation she and Amos had laid for us – an entire life mapped out in front of him. A beautiful life. I knew heavy metal didn't factor at all into her plans.

In that moment, I understood Titus – I knew how hard it was to live in the shadow of a great artist. And *my* father had the good sense to disappear on me, so he would always be judged in stasis, whereas I would be able to grow and improve and one day, I hoped, surpass him. But Titus ran after a moving target, and his parents' success was a wolf chasing him down, snapping at his feet, ready to devour him unless he ran faster, worked harder, played better.

We were more alike than I'd ever guessed.

The room started to clear as guests moved to their suites upstairs or to their cars for the long drive back to civilization. Madame Usher frowned at me and nodded toward the door – her first acknowledgment of me since I waltzed into the party. Faye the musician had overstayed her welcome. Faye the servant was once more called to work.

I helped the guests find their coats and scarves. Dorien's parents stepped toward me. His mother looked me over, and she smiled. She actually fucking beamed. And all I could think of was that time she'd thrown her own son access the floor and told me he was beyond redemption.

"Thank you for a wonderful evening, Faye," she said, as if the weight of our history didn't bear down on us. "I hope you will come to visit us next weekend at the compound."

"Um…" I flicked my gaze to Dorien, who was helping his father into a scratchy woolen cloak.

"Bye, Mother." Dorien shoved them out the door. His eyes met mine over his shoulder, and he mouthed something to me that might've been an apology, but I didn't stick around to see. I looked away before I could consider what I saw in his eyes – the hurt, the fear, the regret. It wouldn't do to start feeling sorry for the dickweasel.

Amos clasped my hand in his. "It was lovely to meet you, Faye."

"And you too." I couldn't help but think there was something in the way he looked at me, like he didn't see a person, but the *idea* of a person. Even though his touch was warm, a shiver ran down my spine.

Ivan and Elena stood at the bottom of the steps while Master Radcliffe farewelled his guests. Ivan gripped her arm so hard I could see red welts on her skin, but she didn't cry out or brush him away. Instead, she leaned over and kissed his cheek, leaving a bow-shaped crimson streak across his skin that made me smile.

Heather kissed her parents on the cheeks, fingering the brooch at her mother's throat and flashing a broad smile. As soon as they disappeared into the night, she dragged Dorien upstairs. His eyes followed me as he climbed the staircase toward her room, and his face was a blank slate – utterly devoid of emotion. The storms in his eyes had faded into a mask. I tried to ignore the knife twisting in my gut as Heather's door shut behind them.

"What are you waiting for?" Madame Usher barked at me as soon as I shut the door behind the last of the guests. "I expect this house back to normal before you retire for the evening."

Of course she did. Hatred burned white in my veins as I ducked into the ball-room, staring at the mountains of dirty glasses and crockery, the napkins scattered over tables and stuffed between the sofa cushions, the crumbs that needed to be vacuumed away and the greasy fingerprints dotting the lid of the piano.

"We'll help." Titus' lips brushed my ear as he came up behind me. His hands slid around my waist, and I sank against him, drawing his red musk and myrrh scent deep inside me, taking strength from the sizzle of heat that passed between us.

And they did. Titus stacked glasses while Ivan wiped down the surfaces. Madame Usher watched from the top of the stairs as we removed the trash and dirty dishes to the kitchen, her mouth set in a frown. But she didn't say anything.

When the last of the dishes had been stacked in the dishwasher, Titus took my hand, his enormous fingers dwarfing mine. Ivan leaned against the doorframe, saying nothing, his icicle eyes boring into me.

"We will make Dorien regret ever hurting you." Titus' voice was rough. He wrapped his strong arms around me and pressed his lips to my forehead. The touch sparked a fire inside me – a flame that had burned bright ever since I held my violin to my chin and played my song of defiance. A flame that burned bright for two Broken Muses, even as the third tried to snuff it out with his callousness.

"I don't want to think about Dorien," I growled.

"Neither do I." Titus' lips found mine, his kiss hot, needy. He'd been dancing on a bed of nails since his parents arrived, and now all that emotion poured from his lips into me. I took it in greedily, demanding more of him, desperate to feed the flame and starve his pain of the oxygen it needed to fester.

Hands slid around my middle, and warm skin pressed against mine. Ivan dragged his teeth along the edge of my neck as Titus deepened his kiss. If you wanted a surefire cure for cockpoodles trying to ruin your life and a ghostly pres-ence haunting your ass, being the center of the world's hottest sandwich did the trick.

I felt Dorien's absence in every touch – and it felt *right*. Without the Prince of Darkness drawing all the life in the room into himself, Ivan and Titus could be truly themselves. I wanted to explore every ghost that lingered on the edge of their souls.

"Come upstairs with us," Titus whispered against my lips, his deep bass voice reverberating through my body, right down to my toes.

Mmmmm. Yes.

The three of us linked hands and left the kitchen, stepping out into the grand foyer. My eyes darted around the space, searching for any last speck of dust or a wayward glass Madame Usher could use as an excuse to punish me. My eyes fell on the gap on the wall – that dark square of bright wallpaper where a portrait once hung. Madame Usher said the portrait was with a restorer, but I'd been at Manderley nearly two months now and it hadn't been returned. I would've thought she'd want the foyer looking immaculate for her guests.

"Do you know whose portrait hung there?" I asked the boys.

Titus shook his head. "Some famous dead dude. I never paid much attention."

Instead of answering, Ivan lifted my hand, twirling me beneath his arm in a dance to the music that existed only in his head. As I came around again, he caught me around the waist, pressing me against the curved pillar of the balustrade. Wooden cherubs jabbed into my back, but I didn't care, not with Ivan's lips pressed on mine, his fingers tracing the line of my neck and sending delicious flames of fire through my veins.

As his tongue explored mine, Ivan became more sure of himself, more probing. He skimmed my arms, trailing fire across my bare skin with his fingers. He circled his thumbs on the insides of my wrists. He cupped my neck and tilted my head back until the room spun with color and light and the strength drained from my knees.

"I don't think you should sleep alone tonight," Ivan rasped into my throat, pulling me closer. I'd seen this possessive side of him before, with Elena, but he'd always held back around me, allowing Dorien to lead. Not anymore. Now he held me as if I were the one candlelight that held the darkness at bay, the only thing in a bleak and bitter world that could ever be truly *his*.

"I don't think so, either." I took Ivan's hand, and Titus in the other. "I know Elena is in your room, but what about—"

"Mine." Titus pulled me close, and I didn't know if he meant his room, or that I was his. I didn't care. I felt like I was his. His and Ivan's. And they were mine. Chains of fate bound us together in this prison. We turned to the staircase. Standing between the two of them, I felt as though I stepped into a piece of music, that the melody carried me along on a journey only it could see, and I was powerless to do anything but surrender.

I lifted my chin. I was Faye de Winter, and I *earned* this night.

I needed—

My eyes flicked to the top of the staircase, and the heat fled my veins.

No.

Fear tightened in my chest as a face watched me from the top of the stairs. Eyes made of shadow and secrets, a cute turned-up nose, and a black hole for a mouth.

It can't be.

But it was.

Clare.

IVAN

Faye staggered back, her face pale with fear.

"What is it?" I wrapped my arms around her waist, pulling her close. Her breath rasped against my cheek, and I could feel her heart pounding against her chest. She was *terrified*.

Of us? Of me and Titus? Did she think we would hurt her?

I will kill Dorien for breaking her trust, for making her doubt—

"I thought I saw..." Faye pointed a trembling finger to the top of the stairs. I realized she wasn't thinking about Dorien, and the relief of that disgusted me. Faye was in danger from more than just Dorien's callousness, of that I was certain. She needed us to stay alert, to keep her safe. "Can you see it? That face? *Clare's* face."

"No." All I saw was a table with a couple of lamps sitting under a mirror on the landing. "Maybe you just saw your reflection move in the mirror—"

"From down here?" Faye's eyes darkened. "Trust me, she wasn't in the mirror. She was in front of it, sort of between the railings."

Right where Clare would've been standing before she fell down the stairs...

"I bet it was Dorien playing some stupid trick." Titus stomped up the steps and peered at the railing. He shuffled the objects on the sideboard. "I can't see anything that looks like a face."

Faye rested her forehead against my shoulder, her whole body trembling. I wished I could protect her from all this *shit*. But I couldn't even protect Elena. The only thing I could do was—

"There's nothing here," Titus repeated. "Faye, come upstairs."

Something in the certainly of his voice spurned Faye. She nodded, her mouth set in a determined line. I gripped her hand as she took the stairs slowly, her eyes fixed on Titus as he waited at the top.

By the time Faye reached the landing, she seemed to have recovered a sense of herself. Titus wrapped his arms around her, and she collapsed into his embrace. She peered at a collection of objects arranged on the hall table, and a strange weariness passed over her face, so quick I might've imagined it. "I think... maybe the shadows and the railing made these look like her face. But I can see now it was just my eyes playing a trick."

"There's been more than enough tricks tonight." Titus drew Faye against him and tilted her head back for a smoldering kiss.

Yes.

I stepped up behind Titus, my hands circling Faye, running down her body as she sank back against me. I loved the way she melted into us like that. She was so strong that she refused to let what Dorien did break her spirit. She could be with us without his shadow haunting our embrace.

As my lips grazed her long neck, I felt eyes burning into my back. I broke away to peer over my shoulder. Dorien leaned against the doorframe in his room, his back rigid, his eyes fixed on mine. They burned with loathing.

I wanted to shrink from his gaze. I'd seen others burn under the heat of his ire, but Dorien had never looked at us like that before, like we were an enemy that needed to be crushed. It was always the three of us against the world. Until Faye. Until he turned against us.

Titus must've seen him, too. He did not break his kiss with Faye, but raised a long-fingered hand and threw Dorien the finger. Dorien watched for a few more moments, then slunk back into his room. The door locked with a *CLICK*.

Good. I hope he lays awake all night listening to us make Faye scream.

Titus unlocked the door to his bedroom, pushing Faye backward until her legs hit the edge of the bed. I walked around and slid in behind her so that when Faye sat back on the bed, she nestled between my legs. Her beautiful ass rubbed against my crotch, and it was all I could do to hold myself back from release right then.

Faye's lips swelled with passion. She licked her top lip as she looped her finger through Titus' belt and pulled him closer. Her fingers worked the buttons of his trousers, opening them and sliding them down his hips to reveal his cock, as rigid for her as mine, the tip already glistening with his need.

As I watched, Faye leaned forward. Her lips closed around Titus' shaft, a sigh of pleasure rolling from her throat as she took him deep into her mouth. Titus tossed his head back, delicious sounds pouring from his own lips as Faye stroked and licked and sucked.

I slid back to kick off my own trousers. Titus' fingers danced up Faye's legs, pushing the skirt of her dress higher, revealing her rich skin and luscious curves inch by perfect inch.

I took over from Titus, pulling the fabric over Faye's thighs, drawing it across her stomach, lifting it over her breasts so they spilled into my hands. Faye let Titus' cock slip from her mouth for a moment to lift her arms. I slid the dress over her shoulders, and Titus grabbed it and tossed it away. My breath hitched as I ran my fingers over her exposed skin. Everywhere I touched her felt like touching fire, like stoking some long-dead part of me until it flared to life.

I threw my shirt off. I wanted my skin against hers. I wanted to crawl inside her until we were one.

"Condoms," Titus growled, his voice tight. "In my top drawer."

Faye watched me with those wide eyes as I dug a foil square from the drawer and rolled the condom over myself. I inched closer to her, my cock brushing her soft skin. My insides coiled tighter, and it took everything I had not to unload on her right here.

Faye rose up on her thighs and sat back down, sighing as I slipped into her warmth. She closed around me and I was inside her, exactly where I wanted to be.

"Ivan…" Faye moaned. She gripped Titus' shoulders and pushed herself up, slamming back down on me, taking her pleasure, demanding it. Her body quaked and she tossed her head back so her dark hair streamed over my shoulder. I buried my face in her neck, breathing in the lavender and orange-blossom sweetness of her as she worked herself upon me. And all while Titus bent over her, his fingers flicking her clit as he sucked her nipple in his mouth.

With each stroke, Faye cracked me open. With each thrust, she tore apart the carefully-constructed walls that bound my fractured heart.

I never had anything in my life that belonged to me and me alone. That was the way I wanted it. I never wanted something if Elena couldn't have it, too. Titus and Dorien and I had many, many women together like this on tour. Groupies who wanted one of us, all of us, who demanded a night of being treated like a goddess by Broken Muse. We called them Muse Girls, and they even had a club of sorts – a group on Facebook where they compared us and formulated new plans to get close to us.

But not one of them compared to Faye de Winter.

I hadn't had a woman without Titus or Dorien. I didn't think I knew how. There had been girls I liked on tour, but when I'd get back to my hotel room some nameless fear would take over and I'd kick them out. As soon as one of the guys would leave the room and leave me alone with a Muse Girl, as soon as she looked up at me with pleading eyes and begged me to fix something broken inside her, I felt this fog descend on me, like if I stood alone with them long enough they'd see the truth I hid.

That I was the one who was broken.

That I didn't want to *possess,* as Dorien did. That I wanted to be part of something, part of a family.

Faye de Winter demanded more. So much more. She demanded worship. She commanded adoration. She *deserved* to possess and to be possessed, to have nothing less than everything I was.

Right now, my jagged edges cut into my skin, but instead of shrinking from the pain, I embraced it. Faye's skin slipped over mine. Her fingers slid in hot trails down my arms, and it felt like a claiming, like she branded me as her own. I wanted to be hers. I'd do anything to be hers, even as she broke me into pieces and put me together again.

My fingers tightened on Faye's thigh as she slammed down on me, her crimson lips forming an O as the scream of an orgasm tore from her lips. The sight of it threw me over the edge, and I came with the tremor of the earth shifting beneath me.

Titus drew back, his eyes meeting mine, the pupils thick and dark with lust. And I wondered what it might be like to kiss the taste of Faye from his lips, to feel truly as if I found my family.

As if I was whole.

As we tangled together in Titus' bed – all limbs and long hair and secret smiles, exploring fingers and desperate need – I watched Faye's face as she climbed off my cock to straddle Titus, and I tangled my fingers in her long hair and bent her head to kiss her. And I thought that maybe, with this girl, I could imagine being whole.

DORIEN

What have I done?

I laid on top of my bed, not bothering to remove my clothes or climb under the covers. I wouldn't sleep tonight. Not with Faye's muffled screams echoing from Titus' room. Not with the steady pounding of his iron bedstead hitting the wall.

I fisted my hands into my eye sockets, but I couldn't drive out the images of the two of them with her, *without me.* Of Faye reveling in their worship. Of *my girl* finding herself in Titus' kind hands or Ivan's glacier eyes.

Without me.

My whole body itched for action. I could've stuck in my headphones and driven out the sound of them fucking. I could have gone for a walk around the grounds, or even out to the poison garden or the mausoleum, where the secrets of Manderley hung thick and sweet in the air. I could have battered down Heather's door and tossed her out a window for what she made me do tonight.

But I stayed rooted in place, listening. Hating myself.

This is my punishment.

Every murmur.

Every gasp.

Every moan.

A knife through my heart. And it was exactly what I deserved.

With each excruciating sound, I turned over what my parents had said to me earlier. Their sudden fixation on Faye mixed in my mind with Heather's smug smile, and with her mother walking around with the Key of Truth pinned to her dress. Even as blinded as I was by Faye's appearance, I couldn't help but notice it.

Eustace Danvers *wanted* me to notice it. It was a performance for me and my parents. I thought of my empty bank account, and I wondered about this new urgency for me to visit the compound and date Faye. I put that together with their new mistrust of the Danvers even after they'd arranged for me and Heather to marry a decade ago, and this 'day of ascension' and Father Aaron's escalating anger. And I wondered if Father Aaron was all-too-aware he'd bled my parents dry, and was moving on to greener pastures—

"Titus... more..." Faye's breathy voice filled my head. I tossed my pillow at the wall and reached for my headphones. I jammed them on my ears and flicked it to a playlist Titus made me of the loudest, heaviest, darkest music he could come up with. The first haunting riffs of Blood Lust's 'Garden of Sorrow' filled my head, the thrashing guitars and deep bass blissfully blocking out any sound from the next room.

I can't take this any longer.

I may have lost Faye forever, but that didn't mean I gave up fighting for her.

All of this was connected. Faye's appearance at Manderley, her mother's poisoning, all the weird stuff she said happened we couldn't account for, Heather and her parents suddenly having intimate knowledge of the Temple and of my suppressed criminal record. I knew what the connection was – Madame Usher. She was the spider at the center of this web. What I didn't know was *why*.

I pulled over my laptop and opened my file. '*Concerning the Fall of the House of Usher.*' It sounded like an awesome song title. The ghost of a melody flickered between my ears – a song of battle lines drawn. My fingers itched to find Titus and Ivan and hash out a composition. But I doubted they'd ever speak to me again, not after I hurt Faye.

I didn't blame them, but still.

I read over the list I made – all the strange things that had happened since Faye de Winter arrived at Manderley. At the end of the list, I typed up everything that happened tonight – how Heather came to me with information she shouldn't have known. How she convinced me to use the chloroform from the old apothecary set to knock Faye out and carry her into the forest. Why Heather's mother wore the Key.

How had Faye managed to escape the bag? I'd run back out to the woods as soon as I could get away from Heather to free her, but she was gone. The zipper had been broken from the *outside*.

One thing was certain – as long as Faye remained at Manderley Academy, she was in danger. Having me and Titus and Ivan for protection wouldn't matter for shit in the end. We were no match for this kind of evil.

In Cauda Venenum. The poison is in the tail. Even if I cut off the head, the scorpion could still strike a deadly blow to the only people in the world I wanted to save.

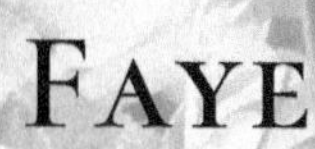

FAYE

That night, I dreamed of Manderley.

I dreamed of my mother dancing, swirling through the empty ballroom as candlelight cast fireflies against her skin. "*Mi cielo*, come dance with me." She held out her arms, her smile so bright it made my heart ache. I tried to move toward her, but my feet stuck to the floor.

"I can't." I tugged at my legs, clawing at my skin, jabbing my fingers at the soles of my shoes. But it was as if someone had superglued me in place.

"*Mi cielo*, come dance." My mother held out her hand, and I leaned forward and reached and reached and I was so close I could feel the breath of her fingers—

A shadow burst from the wall behind me and grabbed her hand, whipping her away in a frenzy of spinning hair and whirling limbs. My mother threw back her head and laughed as the shadow creature gyrated against her, their bodies moving as one even as its dark fingers wrapped around her throat...

"Mother!" I yelled, clawing at the floor. I knew that I had to save her from that shadow, that it was the ghost of Manderley, the dark spirit that dwelt in this house and turned everything to ashes and rot. I knew it would devour her beauty whole and snuff out her light forever, but I couldn't move. All I could do was watch helplessly as the shadow leaned in, closer, closer, its mouth of darkness pressing into my mother's neck as it laid a trail of deadly kisses—

"Faye, wake up, wake up..."

I moaned and rolled over. The hairs on my arms had raised up, and a sickly heat sprinkled my body. I rubbed my skin, drawing my mind back to reality. *It was just a nightmare. A creepy shadow didn't come out of the wall to take Mom away. You're with Titus and Ivan, and you're safe. It's just—*

"Faye, are you okay?"

That voice almost sounded like...

Dorien.

I bolted upright, yanking the covers over my naked body. Dorien leaned over the bed, his face inches from mine.

"Sprite." He stretched closer, his lips darting across mine, not quite touching, but threatening to touch. "Good morning. I hear you had quite a night. Do you—"

I drew back my hand and slapped him across the cheek.

Dorien's head snapped back. He let out a sound like an animal snarl as he tripped over Titus' desk, smacking his elbow into the wall. He scrambled to his feet, still holding his hand against the spot where I'd slapped him. When he spoke again, there was none of the arrogance in his voice. "I deserved that."

"It's the least you deserve." The horror of last night rushed back to me – being attacked in the attic, sucking in that sweet drug that sent me under (I suspected it was chloroform), waking up in that bag and not knowing where I was, and that terrifying text written inside the zipper. "I should call the police. I could have *died* out there."

Beside me, Ivan bolted upright, his hands curled into fists. "Come any closer and I'll hurt you."

"Faye's already taken care of it, trust me." Dorien winced as he rubbed his cheek. "I was going to come back and get you. As soon as the party started, I slipped out and ran back. That's why I left you that flashlight. Did you see my message?"

My stomach flipped. Of course. It was written on the inside of the bag, up near the zipper where he knew I'd see it. "You wrote 'I'M COMING BACK FOR YOU'? Do you have any idea how freaky that was?"

Dorien rubbed his cheek. "No, actually. In hindsight, I can see how that might've seemed a bit ghostly. How did you get out?"

"You don't get to ask the questions here," I shot back. His answer revealed he wasn't the one who let me out, which meant I didn't want him to play any part in figuring it out. "I guess it was also you who left my clothes in the kitchen, or who gave me the jewelry? If you think a few rubies can make up for drugging and kidnapping me, then you—"

Titus' arm snaked around my middle, and he stared up at me with wide eyes. "You didn't tell us about the jewelry."

I fingered the necklace, which was still around my neck. "I was a little distracted. Plus, I assumed it was one of you guys. Someone placed this on top of my clothing in the kitchen before the party."

Ivan shook his head. "This necklace... it looks very expensive."

Titus sat up. His fingers grazed my bare skin as he lifted the stones to inspect them. A shiver of pleasure coursed through my body from his touch, and my mind flashed back to last night, to all the things we did in this bed.

Dorien was in the next room. He must've heard *everything*.

Good.

"Someone who wasn't one of us helped you escape that bag and then left out your clothes and jewelry," Dorien said. "We need to figure out who it was."

Ivan glared at Dorien. "Why should we believe you had nothing to do with it? That this isn't another plan from you and Heather to terrify Faye into quitting?"

Dorien's shoulders sagged. "For fuck's sake, after everything we've been through together, you believe that I'd do this because I wanted to hurt Sprite?"

"Then *why?*" I meant to demand answers, but my voice trembled. After everything we'd been through, after all the promises he'd made to me, he was still trying to put me in my place, to prove he was better than me. "Why did you do it?"

"I didn't have a choice." Dorien squeezed his eyes shut. His face twisted into an expression of such exquisite pain that for a moment, a fucking *moment*, I wavered. I wanted so badly to believe that he hadn't really betrayed me, that this was all some mistake, some fresh plot.

But then I remembered the sweet stench of the chloroform, the foot kicking me in the side as he and Heather dumped the bag in the forest, the tortured expression on Clare's face as she flew toward me in the mausoleum – a trick of my mind, I was now convinced, trying to force me to accept that Dorien was rotten.

"You always have a choice." I fought to keep my voice even. Dorien's eyes fluttered open. Every moment he was here, pleading with me with his tortured eyes, was a knife twisting in my chest. He warped and mangled me until I no longer recognized my own misshapen heart.

Dorien sucked in a ragged breath. "All Heather cared about was that she would be the one to play with me for our parents. She had... she knows something about me, which meant I couldn't refuse her. But I tried to sabotage her. I didn't use enough chloroform. I slipped the flashlight into your pocket so when you woke up you could read my message. I honestly didn't mean for it to be scary – I just wanted to let you know I'd come back for you. As soon as Heather went to her room to change for the party I ran back to free you, only the zipper was broken open and you were nowhere to be seen. I thought you might be nearby, and I called and called but I couldn't find you, so I went back to the house."

That was the voice I heard calling my name when I was in the mausoleum, going on about the voices in the walls and saving Manderley. It was Dorien, not some ghostly figure. I was still feeling the effects of the drug, and being in that gloomy place, of course I'd imagine things...

This should have been a relief, but so many emotions bounced around in my head I couldn't even think about Clare's ghostly face right now.

Dorien knelt on the end of the bed. His knee brushed against my leg through the covers, and it was enough to send a sizzle of heat through my body. I wanted so badly to believe the words falling from his too-pretty lips, but how could I when trusting him brought so much pain?

"I know you don't believe me right now," Dorien's hand slid down my legs as he crawled across the bed toward me. "I would never hurt you, Sprite. I love you—"

The words hit me like a freight train.

I love you.

The cockweasel.

How fucking *dare* he?

There was a time in my life when I would have given anything to hear Dorien Valencourt utter those words to me. When I believed I was so worthless, so unloveable that my own father had run away because he didn't want to be with me. I clung to a broken friendship, wishing for what could never be.

And he throws that back in my face?

"No." I covered my ears. "No, no, no. You don't get to do that."

Dorien surged forward, but a dark hand thrust into his solar plexus, holding him back. Titus growled, "Get out of here. You're upsetting Faye."

"I know. I fucking wish I could take everything back. But I can't. I fucked up, and I love you, Sprite. Those two facts are not in dispute." Dorien slid off the end of the bed, leaning his back against the bureau. He looked defeated, drained of color and that indescribable essence that made him so entrancing. "I didn't come to convince you to take me back. I know that ship has sailed. I don't deserve you. I need you to know that you're not safe here. I've been looking into it and—"

"Damn right she's not safe. Not with you." Titus slid off the end of the bed, and Dorien shifted toward the door. "You're not going near Faye again."

"You don't understand." Dorien reared up so he was nose-to-nose with Titus. "It's all connected. Faye's mother, Madame Usher, Clare's death, my parents' stupid fucking cult. All of it."

What Dorien said echoed my own disjointed perceptions, but the words *I love you* floated inside my skull, blocking out any other thoughts.

I love you.

He can't mean that. He can't say it. He doesn't get to say it now, like this.

"Fuck *off*, Dorien." Titus grabbed him under the arms, dragging him across the floor and shoving him into the hall.

"You can't trust anyone at Manderley," Dorien yelled as Titus slammed the door in his face.

Titus turned the lock. Dorien pounded on the door, shouting my name. Ivan gathered me into his arms. I sank into his shoulder, breathing in his scent – the chilled apple and the salt-tang of the ocean, all the ice and lust that hardened his eyes soaked into me, steadying me.

"I will protect you," Ivan whispered into my hair.

"We won't let him near you again." The bed sank as Titus climbed up beside me, leaning his chest over my back, his arms lacing between Ivan's to cross over my chest. "Dorien Valencourt is dead to us."

DORIEN

The next day, I didn't leave my room. I lay on my bed and stared at the Broken Muse tour poster on my ceiling – the tour we were forced to cut short after Prague. Twenty-two cities over six weeks, playing larger clubs and festivals and opening for a symphonic metal band named Blood Lust who was charting big right now. The tour that would have made our careers, if I hadn't fucked it up trying to be the hero.

I should have known I was never the hero. I was the villain in this story.

The band had been the bright hope all three of us needed to keep on living and fighting – Ivan, who tasted freedom for the first time on our tours and dared to dream of a future out from beneath Madame's thumb. Titus, who was constantly tugged between two worlds, between the family he loved and the music that fed his soul. And me – Broken Muse was my baby, my vision. Titus and Ivan added their spark, but the songs were mine – my pain, my darkness. In those concert halls and dimly-lit clubs, I poured out all the things I'd never been able to say.

Back then, we'd felt invincible, as if embracing the darkness inside us through our music had become its own beautiful light. But Madame Usher took this light and turned it into our prison.

I turned over the horror show that was my life in my head, trying to see a solution where I got everything I wanted and Madame Usher was left with nothing. But I knew it was already too late.

I let Heather talk me into that evil thing.

I lost Faye. Forever.

And if Father Aaron was courting the Danvers, as I was starting to suspect, soon Jacob wouldn't even have the Valencourt name for safety.

I hurt Faye to keep Heather away from my brother. And I would do it again to keep Jacob safe, even if it meant destroying my own soul in the process.

But that was the problem. As long as Jacob remained at the Temple of Earthly Truths with my parents, I'd continue to be trapped too – a marionette dancing as Heather or Madame Usher or Father Aaron pulled the strings. That was no longer an option. I wouldn't play games with my brother's life any longer.

I had to get him out.

I had to make sure he never, ever got sent back.

I had to remove the leverage they had over me.

Even if that meant stepping back into the lion's den with a slab of meat strapped to my balls.

In the drawer of my bureau – shoved at the back behind my passport, multi-plugs for different parts of the world, old ticket stubs and festival lanyards, all the detritus of a career on the road – I found what I was looking for. The wireless mic I purchased in the early days of the band, when we were playing small clubs instead of concert halls and we needed the best gear. The mic could record as well as transmit.

I shoved aside the stack of music books on my desk, set down my laptop, and opened the recording software. Hours of tracks from Broken Muse practice sessions scrolled past the screen. We recorded everything in case one of us hit on a stroke of genius we wanted to remember later. My chest tightened as I looked at the list of recordings. The last date stood out at me – our last practice session before we hit the road for our European tour. Before Prague. Before I fucked everything up.

I jammed my headphones on my ears and checked the mic and software. I'd used this mic to storm all over different stages. I knew it had a decent range. I had to hope it would do the job when I needed it most.

As I packed up my things, I glanced out the window. My room looked out over the stable house where Master Radcliffe lived. I could see lights on in the window, and Elena sitting at the piano in his parlor, her fingers dancing over the keys as he stood behind her. He leaned in close, his hand touching hers, and a jolt of rage bubbled inside me. I lifted my gaze up, across the overgrown back garden, down to the edge of the path that led to the gazebo, and the poison garden and mausoleum beyond. The stream trickled down the mountain, swelling now from the rains and too freezing cold for the skinny-dipping we'd done with Faye when she finally gave in to the pull of our attraction. And beyond the stream, the towering trees descending the slope of the mountain, then ascending again, becoming a sweep of green as the mountains loomed over us all.

I would free Faye and my brother. I would bring Manderley Academy crashing to the ground.

FAYE

The week after the party was one of the most uncomfortable I spent at Manderley, and that was saying something. The house was a war zone – only instead of battles played out with guns and tanks, the weapons employed were intimidation and secrecy.

Heather, Dorien, and Madame Usher stood on one side, facing off against me, Ivan, and Titus. Aroha and Elena and Master Radcliffe stumbled into the crossfire. Our lessons had become tense standoffs, but no one wanted to admit defeat and not show up, so I endured each moment of Heather's smirk and Dorien's probing eyes with my chin high and my fingers dancing over the strings. I pretended I was my mother, raising her sword across the boardroom, accepting a duel with glee.

I pretended, but I didn't feel like a warrior inside. I felt *sick*. I didn't want to look over my shoulder all the time, or feel the prickling in my neck every time I walked the halls alone. When I closed my eyes, I saw Clare's face, her mouth open in that horrible scream as she loomed over me in the attic or came at me inside the mausoleum.

Had I really seen her?

Three times she appeared on the night of the party – in my room, in the mausoleum to deliver her creepy message, and on the stairs. Each time I could chalk the image up to a hallucination caused by distress, exhaustion, fear, or the drug Dorien used to knock me unconscious. But why would I hallucinate the face of a maid I'd never even met? I wondered if it was because of those strange words I found scrawled in the pantry – THE WALLS ARE TALKING.

I didn't believe in ghosts, but I also didn't believe in blindly ignoring what was right in front of my eyes. My mom did that – ignoring weeks of messages warning her to pay her insurance premiums or get cut off – and it destroyed our lives.

I needed answers. And I knew I could find some if I went to speak to Dorien, but I wouldn't give him the pleasure. That meant I had to do a bit of old-fashioned detective work myself.

As I stacked the dishwasher after another silent meal, Elena popped her head around the kitchen, her blue eyes twinkling. Even though she had the same ice-blue irises as Ivan, hers always caught the light in a certain way that made them sparkle. It was the same fae magic that seemed to swirl around her wherever she went.

"I *demand* to know what's going on with you and the Muses," she said.

"I thought your brother would've told you."

"He won't talk about it except to fume over how much he hates Dorien." Elena tipped her head toward me. "Ivan has worshipped at Dorien's feet ever since they formed that band. But now he wants to hang his testicles from a chandelier with rusty piano wire, and I wasn't sure if you wanted me to rescue Dorien's nuts before he goes through with it."

"Do you want to go for a walk?" I glanced through the narrow window above the sink. A bitter wind had been tearing through the valley most of the day, rattling the windows and sending several roof tiles crashing to the ground. But the wind had calmed now, leaving behind a crispness in the air that spoke of a landscape renewed – an old layer peeled away to reveal what hid underneath.

Elena pulled on her fur-lined coat and followed me across the garden. "You know there are plenty of places we can talk *inside*, beside a roaring fireplace, with a mug of your delicious spiced cocoa."

"Prying ears can't overhear us out here." I glanced up at the imposing facade of Manderley, my eyes darting across the windows that formed Madame's private wing. I noticed lights on in the room furthest away, a shape moving through the narrow gap in the drapes. *What is she doing right now? What fresh torture is she dreaming up?*

Elena and I linked arms and went side-by-side down the overgrown path toward the gazebo. When we were far enough from the house that I could not feel its specter looming through the trees, I told Elena everything that happened on the night of the party.

Once again, I left out the image of Clare – I felt certain now that I hadn't seen her at all, that she'd been a vision I'd invented in my mind to spurn me into action. I'd been swooning after Muses when I should have been focused on the crime or crimes that had taken place here, and why they'd drawn me to Manderley in the first place.

"I can't believe this happened right beneath my nose, and I didn't even know about it," she said as I recounted the story of Friday night. "Ivan never tells me these things. He thinks I should be sheltered from the darkness of this place. I don't want you to treat me like that."

"I get it. That's why I'm telling you now." I saw how Ivan doted on Elena, how he lurked in the corner of her private rehearsals as if he expected a horde of ninja assassins to leap out and attack her at any time. "When I got to the party, I just needed to play. I needed to bleed the horror of it through the music. After the performance, I don't know… there were so many people there and it all rushed at me at once, like a delayed trauma."

"My brother will protect you," she declared, the certainty in her voice borne of an entire life lived under Ivan's watchful gaze.

"I know. The way he protects you," I said. "Why is Ivan the way he is? Why does he sit in on all your tutoring? Why is he so against you going to Moscow with Master Solokov and Master Radcliffe over the summer?"

Elena sighed. "You'll have to ask him."

"I've tried, but—"

Elena flapped her hand to cut me off. "Ivan was born two minutes before me. He believes it is his job to watch over me always. I know he told you we are trapped here, that Madame Usher is our guardian, our jailer. Ivan feels he has failed me. To him, I'm still the innocent eight-year-old girl who needs protecting from the big bad world. But I am a woman now. I am not innocent, and I refuse to die locked away in this crumbling shithole because he won't do what needs to be done."

I gave her a friendly nudge with my elbow as we approached the gazebo, although I knew her answer was deliberately evasive. "You sound like you're contemplating murder and mayhem. Should I be worried?"

Elena smiled. "Not murder, but a little mayhem. Broken Muse tried to escape Madame before, and failed. Now they must let me try my own methods."

"Will you tell me? I'm down with a little mayhem."

Elena shook her head. "Maybe soon."

I stared up at the crumbling gazebo, with its rotting wood floor revealing jagged and gaping mouths into the darkness beneath, and the vines curling through the broken lattice and circling the roof, as if trying to drag the whole structure down beneath the void. A bitter breeze caressed my arms, and I shivered. "So many secrets here."

Elena took my hand in hers, squeezing my cold fingers between her warm gloves. "Manderley is built on secrets – they're like twisted roots growing deep underground. There's nothing that can untangle them."

"I say cockpoodle to that. I am going to bring them into the light," I said. "Starting with who poisoned my mother."

DORIEN

"You have failed me." Madame Usher spread her thick fingers over her desk. Stacked neatly on her left were thick books of musical scores. On the other, worn leather tomes I could only assume were spellbooks for summoning demons.

Madame Usher rose. I didn't bother to reply. She didn't expect one.

I stood in front of her desk, my hands clasped in an attempt to hold myself back from reaching over and wringing her pale, fleshy neck. Even though I had the height on her, I felt small. Her glare was enough to shrink me into the carpet.

Standing in her office always made me feel like this – perhaps because it reminded me so much of my father's study, of my mother marching me before him when I was little so he could recite a litany of my faults. Later, when it became Father Aaron's office, I spent hours with my nose pressed into the rug, forced into silent penance for my transgressions.

But perhaps it was because this office had always been Victor's domain. He died not long after I arrived at Manderley, and he'd always been a kind, but stern, teacher. My prevailing memory of Victor was of a man who spent his evenings reading on a bench in the garden while Harrison weeded the beds or tended the flowers. Victor would stare pensively to the heavens, wishing for a life he couldn't have. But he loved Manderley with a fierceness that bordered on obsession. It was only when he grew sick that Madame allowed it to devolve into its current state of ruin.

Or perhaps it was simply because Madame Usher's interior decor borrowed heavily from the school of "Dracula Chic." All this room was missing was the coffin where she slept at night to be a complete funhouse horror set.

She walked slowly around to my side of the desk, the hem of her black silk dress sliding along the floor. She reminded me of a snake inching toward her prey.

A clock ticked.

Madame smiled.

SMACK.

She struck me across the cheek – the same cheek where Faye slapped me only five days earlier. The sting of it pounded between my ears as my head snapped back. I didn't dare lift my hand to my cheek or show her any other reaction.

"You were supposed to get rid of her," she snapped. "Not fall in love with her. Your mother is right – you fail at everything you touch."

"I'm not in love with Faye."

The words had no strength. No venom. I knew it and she knew it.

"Don't lie to me," she hissed. "Heather saw you run back into the forest on Friday, and Faye mysteriously shows up at the house in time to perform? I admit you did an excellent acting job pretending to be surprised when she made her entrance. I almost believed you. But you were the only one who knew she was out there. You can't hide from me, Dorien. I always get my way in the end."

Clearly I wasn't the only one, because I didn't free Faye. I didn't say that, of course. Instead, I focused on the new nugget of information I learned. "So you *were* behind Heather sabotaging Faye's performance?"

"Of course." Madame leaned back, and her smile shriveled my balls back into my body. "I am the architect of everything that goes on at Manderley. Heather came to me with information she thought I might find useful. I'd always thought her a silly, dim-witted girl, but she's proving to have more of a penchant for deception than I expected."

"Why are you doing this?" I growled. "You told me that Master Radcliffe wanted Faye at Manderley, but you couldn't stand the daughter of Donovan de Winter under these walls, ruining your reputation with her father's curse, so you wanted me to get rid of her. But that's not true. Faye said you came to her yourself. She said you were Donovan's lover. So why invite her here if all you want to do is get rid of her?"

Madame's eyes flashed. "My business with Faye is my own. You're to do as I say and don't ask questions, or I will ruin you. Or have you forgotten what I hold over you, Dorien?"

My fingers curled into fists. "I haven't forgotten."

Madame glided across the room to pace in front of the hearth. Above the stone fireplace hung a painted frame containing a photograph of her and Victor Usher from their younger days. It wasn't a wedding portrait, for I knew they were married back in Prague, but Madame wore a virginal white dress with lace sleeves and a high collar. Her dark hair framed her face and she gazed up at Victor from in front of the Cupid fountain. Water filled the fountain, and the pristine marble gleamed in the dappled mountain light. Behind the couple, Manderley watched over them like a proud mother hen. Harrison stood on a ladder, painting the porch lattice, his face turned toward the couple with a pinched expression, as if they'd just spoiled Christmas dinner by shitting in the figgy pudding.

Gizella Usher clung to her handsome new husband with his aquiline nose and hawk-like eyes, her face turned slightly toward him, her breasts swelling from her dress. She might've even appeared beautiful and madly in love, if it wasn't for the gleam of triumph in her eyes. Even then, she had seen Manderley not as a home or a school, but a weapon to wield against the world.

Madame stopped her pacing, her eyes following mine. The portrait arrested her, and for a moment she seemed to retreat back into the body of that young girl, so possessed by passion. She was no longer the evil spider, but perfectly and beautifully human.

The emotion passed from her features in a moment, and she became Madame Usher once more.

"I brought three Broken Muses into my home. I made every concession, forgave every sin, and gave you the lives that would otherwise have been denied you. Yet still, the three of you betray me." She spat the harsh words at the blazing fire. "I have seen the way Titus and Ivan fawn all over her, hoping to be thrown the scraps of her affection. How the three of you could be turned simple by such a plain girl is beyond me. But it is over for you, Dorien. I will tell you what will happen now. You will stay away from Faye de Winter. I cannot trust you or either of your friends around her. Do this, or Commissioner Walpole will see no further reason to withhold certain information concerning Aaron Varney's assault. You know he holds sway over the county sheriff's office."

"I can't control Titus and Ivan, and I've already given her up," I said. The truth of it twisted in my heart – a wound I'd never heal.

She spun around, her eyes reflecting the orange flames. "I don't believe you."

"Fine. Do it." I nodded at her. "Have me arrested. I don't care anymore. But know that if you do, I have a few secrets of my own to reveal to the police."

Her eyebrow lifted. She tried to keep an expression of cool detachment, but I could tell she was interested. "Such as?"

Fuck.

All I had were suspicions and slim connections in my file. I had nothing concrete. Nothing the police would be interested in, especially not her precious Commissioner Walpole.

Nothing except...

"In Cauda Venenum," I said.

"Pardon me?"

I sucked in a breath, hardly daring to believe I heard a waver in her voice. "You heard me. In Cauda Venenum. I have that."

I knew what it meant, though not why it was important, but I saw the way Madame Usher rolled her eyes, as if I were some bothersome child who refused to be disciplined but must be indulged. And I knew I'd hit on some chink in her armor that could be exploited. "Very well, Dorien. For now, we have a truce. You will remain at Manderley, but if I find out you've revealed anything, you will feel the sting of my wrath."

~

Back in my room, I pulled on jeans and a black shirt and shoved the laptop and recording equipment into a bag. My cheek still stung from the force of Madame Usher's blow. I needed to get to my parents' place in time to see them before the recital today. I needed to move fast, because I'd be a fucking fool if I thought Madame Usher would accept a truce between us. She might decide at any moment to call my bluff. I had to ensure Jacob was safe first.

As I turned the lock in my door, my eyes fell on the narrow staircase that led to Faye's room in the attic.

The skin on the back of my neck prickled.

I'm being watched.

I hefted the backpack on my shoulder and stepped toward the staircase. "Faye?" I asked the empty air.

I didn't imagine she'd want to speak to me after everything that was said in Titus' room, but I wouldn't give up without trying. I squared my shoulders as I lifted my foot onto the staircase.

A loud creak echoed along the empty hall. In the distance, I could hear voices talking and laughing downstairs, and someone – Aroha, judging by the atonal dissonance and brutality of the piece – practiced in the Yellow Room. The prickling intensified, but when I looked around, I couldn't see anyone else in the hallway or on the stairs.

I placed my foot on the second step.

A face leaned out of the darkness into the square of light cast from the hallway chandelier. My heart skipped.

Clare.

I froze as she slid up beside me, her body formed of ash and air and sorrow. My heart hammered in my chest as she brushed against my skin, leaving a trail of goosebumps in her wake.

I tried to warn you, a voice rasped in my ear. Clare's voice – sweet and musical but tinged with moss and graveyard dirt. Invisible lips pressed against my earlobe, ice cold. *The walls are talking, Dorien.*

Fuck.

I staggered back, my heart leaping into my throat. Clare's face hovered above the stairs, her mouth open in a silent scream.

The walls are talking.

Somehow, through the haze of panic, I managed to tear down the grand staircase. I heard someone call my name, but like fuck was I stopping. I slammed Manderley's front door and leaped over the rotting porch.

I ran to my car, slamming the door behind me and tearing out of the drive. *Get me out of this hellhole.*

My fingers gripped the wheel so hard my knuckles burned white. I struggled to bring my shaking breath under control. My earlobe still tingled from Clare's icy kiss, while her words turned over and over in my mind.

It's not possible. It can't be her.

I glanced in the rearview mirror, back at Manderley Academy receding into the trees. Did I imagine the white-clad figure standing at the window in Faye's bedroom, staring down at me? Or was it my own guilty conscience?

Clare had been so strange those last few weeks of her life. She kept trying to talk to me about weird things going on around the house – food disappearing, odd sounds – but I wouldn't hear it. I didn't want to think about anything else apart from escaping Manderley and helping Jacob. The day she died, she'd been running after me, trying to get me to listen to her. "The walls are talking," she said. "You have to believe me, Dorien. I know Madame Usher's secret. I know about the man—"

And then she screamed. I turned back just in time to see her body fly down the stairs, to *feel* the snap of her neck as it broke – a twang in the air, like the buzz of a reverberating note at the end of a sonata.

I still heard that crunch in my dreams.

I always thought her ravings were a desperate attempt to hold on to me as I drew away from her, but Clare might've been the only one to discover the truth about Manderley, and now she was dead.

She's dead and I'm seeing her. I didn't listen to her then, but I need to listen now.

I'll do anything to save Jacob and Faye from the same fate.

The road snaked down the mountain. Every mile I put between myself and Manderley only quickened my resolve. By the time I turned onto the road leading to Valencourt Manor, my blood burned with righteous fire.

I'm coming for you, Jacob. I'm not going to let them hurt you any longer.

I knew they had someone watching the gate from the house – Father Aaron may have eschewed modern technology in the Temple itself, but his surveillance system was state-of-the-art. The gate swung open, and I drove inside. Past the mountains of trash and broken furniture discarded from the house. Past the piles of cars with their tires slashed – so those who showed up at the Temple could never leave. Aaron could have sold them for cash, but he preferred to use them as part of his indoctrination.

I was the only one who managed to escape the horror of this place, only to fall into the jaws of another sinister trap.

The concrete on the driveway had cracked in places, weeds twisting through the gaps to choke the bright flowers that once lined the path. Everywhere were piles of trash and old-fashioned farm equipment rusting where it had been dumped. From what I could gather from Jacob's sporadic texts, Father Aaron had plans to farm the land to sustain a larger population, but Valencourt Manor was built on the site of an old timber mill – little would grow in the nutrient-sapped soil.

The drive turned into the woods, climbing through the trees until it fanned in front of a sprawling mansion of wood and stone. There was a time when this house had been a haven to me – a place existing outside of the city where I could forget about being Dorien the perfect son, the musical visionary, the constant disappointment, and run around the woods like a real kid. But then Father Aaron moved in and things got weird. And then they got terrifying.

Now, when I gazed up at the manor, all I saw was a prison keeping my brother from me.

My mother glided down the cracked stone steps as I jerked the car to a stop. Her brown robe dragged across the dead leaves, and they clung in wet patches to the hem. "I'm so pleased you came, son."

I nodded mutely. She kissed my cheeks, but I couldn't bring myself to give her any affection in return.

"No Faye?"

I laughed hollowly. "If you want Faye to be your daughter-in-law, then you'll want to keep her far away from this freakshow."

"Of course. Very wise." She smiled, as if we were in on this scheme together, as if I hadn't just insulted the life she'd chosen. "We must ease her into our way of life. It's not easy to let go of earthly things and embrace the True Path. God knows how much you have struggled. Come with me."

As I followed Mother up the steps, I noticed three other cars in the lot – flashy cars like mine that oozed wealth and status. I thought again of Heather's mother wearing the Key of Truth, and the 'day of ascension' that was approaching. A sinking feeling weighed in my stomach as I tried to fit the pieces together.

Inside, the house bore little of its former grandeur. The high ceilings, marble floors and grand staircase still remained, although they were streaked with filth. All the furniture was gone – the finest pieces sold, others tossed into the piles or burned so Father Aaron could hammer home his teachings about casting aside earthly possessions. Bright squares of paint dotted around the walls indicated where lavish artworks once hung. Now, there were only strange phrases scrawled in loopy handwriting – the creed of the Temple of Earthly Truths.

A circle of children played beneath the stairs, tossing painted stones across the floorboards. They wore white versions of my mother's brown robes, the hems grubby from working in the gardens.

"You should all be at your tasks." Mother frowned at the tiny faces. They looked up, startled, recoiling from her stern expression. Genuine fear flickered in their eyes. She snapped her fingers. "Go. Do not let the Holy Father see you idle."

The children dropped the stones and scattered. My mother wiped her hands on her dress, as if she'd completed some great and satisfying work. She waited until I dropped my mobile phone into the tray in the hallway, then indicated toward the kitchen. "We will have tea."

The kitchen had once been a warm place where my parents' cook created piles of delicious food and my mother drank wine with her society lady friends in front of the double-height windows while I played Frisbee or croquet outside on the lawn. Now, it was as cold and neglected as the rest of the house – bare of furniture and mirth. Old-fashioned pots and enormous serving platters designed for many people were stacked in the corners, as were sacks of flour and grains that reeked of rot.

I stepped into the hexagonal breakfast room, where Aaron had forced me and Faye to play that one time she visited for my birthday. This was how I lost my family – over the breakfast room. Aaron started by suggesting Mother remove the table and have us all sit on the floor, to be closer to the earth. Then he removed the cushions, and the oak side table our staff used for serving. Then he got rid of the staff, and the meal of breakfast. Things spiraled from there until the whole house fell under his spell.

I peered out the windows, imagining I could still taste Faye's intoxicating scent perfuming the air. A group of figures wandered across the lawn – Father Aaron with his robe flapping around his reedy legs, leading a group of would-be acolytes around the grounds, pointing out the fountain fed from a freshwater spring and the fruit trees.

Trees my grandfather planted, so that future generations of Valencourts could enjoy this place. Instead of a pleasure palace, it's a prison of horror.

"Are you expecting more new recruits today?" I counted eight people in total listening to Aaron with rapt attention – two families with small children, and a couple of teenagers hanging back and smirking at it all. They thought the whole thing was a joke, that this tiny bald man in a brown robe couldn't do anything to uproot their comfortable lives. My fingers itched to grab them, shake them, make them see the danger.

Run away, now. Before it's too late.

"We shall have guests all day. Your dad has been hard at work spreading the word about our perfect life here. The Holy Lord will be pleased with him."

This was new. My parents never had to work to 'please' Aaron before. Signing over their estate, their savings, their family to him must not be enough any longer.

Footsteps clattered on the marble floor. I turned just as a boy hobbled into the kitchen, followed by two girls with braided blonde hair. They all wore the white robes of the children of the Temple of Earthly Truths.

"Dorien." Jacob rocked forward on his feet and threw his arms around me. He was fifteen years old – he should be as tall as me by now, but he barely came up to my armpits. I let him hold me as long as he wanted, feeling his love soak into my bones.

Why is he hobbling? Has he been injured? I longed to throw him over my shoulder and run out with him, but it would be pointless. My parents were his guardians, and Madame Usher and Heather would ensure I couldn't make a legal case against them. So I plastered a smile over my concern.

"Hey, bro." I ruffled his hair and he smiled, the smile of a boy trapped in a man's body. "Who are your girlfriends?"

Jacob rolled his eyes, like I'd said something really funny. "Girlfriends aren't allowed. We can't have impure thoughts ruin our good work. These are my sisters, Pearl and Emma Danvers. We're in charge of making bread. Do you want to help?"

I peered at the two girls over Jacob's shoulder. *Danvers.* They did have Heather's honey-blonde hair. It was impossible to know for sure, but I didn't remember the two of them from last time I'd been here. They were new recruits, which meant my suspicions were right – Father Aaron was courting the Danvers' family, and my parents were falling out of favor.

But I couldn't speak these things aloud. So I squeezed my brother's hand, grateful beyond belief to see him alive and smiling, even if every other facet of his appearance terrified me. "Sure. Just show me what to do."

Jacob hopped and scraped his feet as he made his way into the kitchen. At one point he had to grip the edge of the counter to remain upright. His face twisted with pain before Mother frowned at him, and he wiped it over with a forced smile. It looked like standing was excruciating for him.

My hands balled into fists. A deep, keening dread settled into my gut. *This is my little brother, and he can't walk. I have to help him.*

For once in my life, I'm doing the right thing.

The two girls pulled a large bowl from the windowsill and placed it on top of an old-fashioned scale. They started to measure out a mountain of flour while Jacob filled a jug with water.

"We need *this* much." He pointed a grubby finger at a mark on the side of the jug. "I make bread every day now. I'm good at it. I like it, too. It smells nice in here. Since my feet hurt I can't go back to the fields, so—"

"Jacob," Mom warned. "Dorien doesn't want to hear about that."

Dorien very much does want to hear about that. I shifted my weight, fighting the urge to touch the mic hidden under my shirt recording all this. She hadn't said enough. Even though my skin crawled with the thought of what Father Aaron had done to hurt Jacob's feet, I had only an uncomfortable conversation between mother and son on tape. No evidence of evil.

Jacob's face flushed with pain. He focused on the water. When the jug was filled, he carried it in two hands, hobbling and lurching across to the flour to dump it in. The older girl, Pearl, removed a large jar of something foul-smelling and dumped a quarter of the contents into the bowl, and then the three of them started to punch and stir and knead the mixture into a stretchy dough.

"Dorien, come help." Jacob's face lit up as he stretched and shaped the dough. "It feels so cold and funny."

I shuddered. "That's okay. I'll just watch."

Bread should come from an artisan bakery in New York. Bread was the crisp tortillas Faye rolled out and fried to perfection while she sashayed her gorgeous ass around the kitchen singing pop songs. Bread was warmth and happiness and sinful carbohydrates. It shouldn't be the product of a child labor camp to sate one man's desire for godhead.

When the loaves were finally kneaded and shaped and set out to do whatever bread was supposed to do, Jacob grabbed my hand again. "I'm going to show Dorien the chickens," he told Mother.

"I'll come with you." She stood up.

SMASH.

"Mother Valencourt, I'm so sorry!" Pearl stood on a stool above the oven, frozen in terror. Broken glass scattered over the counter and across the floor, and a cloud of brown dust coated everything in sight.

"You stupid girl. That was our coffee supply. Father Aaron will not allow us another for six months." Mother wrung her hands. "What are we going to serve our guests this evening? Clean this up, and take yourself to the penalty room for the rest of the afternoon."

The penalty room. That sounded *great*.

The two sides of my mother battled it out – the part of her that still believed in putting on appearances for guests, and the side that wanted desperately to be the perfect acolyte for Aaron. As she rushed to the kitchen to deal with the mess, Jacob tugged my hand, dragging me across the room and holding open the side door that led into the manor's courtyard.

My breath hitched as I followed him around the raised garden beds. He moved as fast as he could on his sore feet, gasping under his breath as he led me away from the house. What he was doing could get him into a lot of trouble. But the fact that he was doing it filled me with hope. Apart from the mobile phone I gave him, I don't think I'd ever seen Jacob defy Aaron's rules before.

We reached the other side of the courtyard. Here, the tall beds filled with vegetables obscured us from view of the kitchen. Up against the side of the house was a long run filled with a couple dozen birds. It smelled delightful. I pinched my nose as I followed Jacob around the back of a rotting wooden coop.

"Down here." Jacob dropped to his knees and pushed aside a board, revealing a crawlspace beneath the house. I thought of the nice shirt and freshly-pressed slacks I'd put on for today's recital. But Jacob's face begged me to follow, and I couldn't refuse him.

I sank to a squat and waddled into the gap. Jacob pulled the board over the hole, casting us into near darkness. Down here the smell was even worse – mingling the smell of the chicken shit with damp and rot.

I knew we didn't have much time. Jacob faced me, the pale outline of his face striped with the light that streamed between the wooden boards. He bit his lip, and I knew it had cost him dearly to get me here, but he didn't know what to do next.

"That girl in the kitchen, did she drop the bowl so we could talk?" I asked Jacob. He nodded.

"I haven't seen you in so long," he whispered. "Pearl says that our whole family is crazy and no one is supposed to live like this, that our house is supposed to be filled with furniture and we're *supposed* to have water coming from the taps. She said she'd help me talk to you, and maybe you could tell the police."

I couldn't help but smile. This Pearl was pretty smart. "She's right. You *are* supposed to have all those things. You're not supposed to feel scared all the time. And I'm going to help you, bud. I'm sorry I haven't done anything already, but that's going to change, all right?"

Jacob nodded. He hugged his legs to his chest. I noticed red welts striping across his wrists and around his ankles as the hem of his robe hitched up. Someone had tied up my little brother. *I'll wring Aaron's neck.*

I fought back the rage. I had to stay calm. I had my brother alone at last. I needed to use this time to get something I could use against Aaron. "How long has Pearl lived here?"

"She doesn't live here. She told me they live in a big house with real furniture and lots of money and she even has a pony. Father Aaron spends most of his time there now. He says he's preparing it for the day of ascension."

"What's the day of ascension?"

"It's when the world falls to ruin, crushed beneath God's wrath. It's when the oceans boil and burning rain falls from the sky, and the righteous are raised up to heaven while the sinners are tortured for all eternity. Father Aaron says if we please God, we will sit beside him in his kingdom."

Yup, that's not good. "And what date is this illustrious event?"

Jacob stared at me blankly. He didn't understand. He'd never been taught about numbers or reading a calendar. I tried another line of inquiry.

"Have you met Pearl's parents?"

"Mmmhmm. They came for our last feast day. Father Aaron let them sit with him at the top of the table. Their names are Fenston and Eustace."

Those were Heather's parents' names. I wished I could show Jacob a picture of them from the party and he could identify them properly, but I didn't have my phone with me.

"Tell me everything, buddy. I need to know what's going on in here."

"You always say that." Jacob put his thumb in his mouth. It was a habit he started when he was two. He had no other comfort in this place, so even though Aaron beat him when he did it, he couldn't stop. The sight of it broke my heart. Jacob should be chasing girls, breaking hearts, thinking about studying for college, not sucking his thumb, or limping, or hiding under the house because he feared *the penalty room*. "You say that and then nothing happens."

"That's because I fucked up. I let my anger get the better of me, and now we need a new plan." I lifted my shirt, showing him the microphone hidden on my belt. "This time is different, I promise. I'm getting you out before the day of ascension, which is bullshit, but the way. Don't believe a word Aaron says. If he says it's time for ascension and I haven't come for you yet, you need to get the mobile I gave you and call me *immediately*."

Jacob squeezed his eyes shut. He didn't like it when I swore, and he barely understood how to use the phone. He thought it was scary. "Father Aaron is so angry. He says we don't work hard enough. Mother and Father don't bring in enough new converts. The house is falling apart. Father Aaron says this was supposed to be paradise on earth, but God has abandoned us. The only thing that makes him happy now is visiting Pearl's family. Whenever he returns from their house he's in much better spirits. He says they've been touched by God's eternal light."

"Has he done anything to Mother and Father?"

"He made them sleep in a cage with the pigs for a week," Jacob said. "That used to only be a punishment for new converts, to help them to learn to return to the earth. But he thinks Mother and Father need help. He thinks he's been too soft on them, and now he has to undo the damage or they cannot ascend. And now if I do something wrong, he says it's their fault. I don't want to get them in trouble. I was working outside and I was so hungry. I'd been working since dawn and I wasn't allowed any food. There was a beautiful orange on the tree and I ate it. Father Aaron caught me – I thought he was going to yell at me, but he yelled at them instead. He made us cook a big, fancy meal for the Danvers' visit, but he wouldn't let us eat any of it. I didn't get food for three days."

This is torture. Pure and simple.

"It was my fault. I shouldn't have taken the orange," Jacob sniffed.

There was a cold, gaping hole where my heart should have been. "Jacob, can you show me your feet?"

I thought he hadn't heard me. He didn't move or react for the longest time, just kept staring at me with those eyes that were so much like mine, and yet nothing at all like mine. They were eyes that had seen nothing outside the walls of this shithole and yet had seen more than any teenage boy should ever have to see. They were the eyes of a boy with a rich imagination and a kindness toward all creatures that reminded me of what I loved about Faye.

I was just starting to worry when Jacob reached down and slid off one of his holey shoes. The inside of the sneaker had turned pink with blood. He wore no socks.

Bile rose in my throat as I stared at my little brother's foot. He winced as he turned his ankle toward me to show the torn, bloody sole. Someone had flayed off his skin in long ribbons. Burns around his ankle had blistered and wept into open sores, and dried blood crusted between his toes.

Red welts obscured my vision as hot, violent rage pulsed behind my eyes.

Someone did this to my brother.

Someone would *die*.

DORIEN

I tried to speak, but it took several deep breaths before I could form words again. "Jacob, how did this happen?"

Jacob shrugged, and that shrug hurt more than seeing what had been done to him. *He thinks this is normal, something he has to endure if he wants to be Aaron's special boy.* "I did a bad thing. Pearl and I were holding hands. I didn't know it was wrong. I didn't feel evil or sinful, but I was wrong. I promise I won't do it again."

"Don't say that." My knuckles cracked from the force of holding my hand in a fist. I needed to smash it into something. Preferably Aaron's smug little face.

"I had to go back to working in the field," Jacob said. "But then it hurt too much. I fainted, and Father Aaron said I could bake bread instead, even though men aren't supposed to bake bread."

"Men can bake whatever they want to bake," I growled. "The only thing men can't do is hurt people who can't fight back. Jacob, this is important. Are there weapons in the house? Guns and stuff?"

Jacob reached into his pocket and pressed something into my hands. "Pearl helped me make that. She's smart like you. She thought of all these things you might want to know—"

"Jacob, Dorien. Where are you?"

Jacob's face paled. He shoved the board aside and crawled out of the gap. I was surprised how fast he moved given the state of his feet, but he must've been forced to walk around on them for weeks now.

I hated to think of my brother being used to that pain.

Death isn't good enough for Aaron. Or my parents. How can they subject a child to this torture?

How could I?

Was I any better than them? I escaped Valencourt Manor to play music, and I'd left Jacob inside these walls, all alone, believing one day I'd come back for him. And then I fucked that up and I let myself fall into Madame Usher's trap. How long had this solution been open to me? How many nights had I tossed and turned in my comfortable bed, holding back for selfish reasons, pretending as if I had a choice, while Jacob slept in a pig pen and had his feet flayed?

I clambered out after him, trying to keep my clothes away from the dirt. Jacob winced as he tugged his sneaker back on. He rolled onto his feet, and for a moment he stood upright. Tears stung his eyes as his weight bore down on his ruined feet. I reached out to him, but he took off toward the sound of Mom's voice.

"I'm here." Jacob stopped in front of her, staring at his shoes. "I was showing Dorien my chickens."

"You shouldn't have run away like that." She looked to me, her face twisted with suspicion. "You know you're not allowed to be alone with Dorien. He cannot help that his head is filled with the sins of the world, but we can't have his wickedness poisoning you, not when you have worked so hard."

"We were just talking about chickens," I said, hoping like hell she didn't ask any follow-up questions. What I knew about chickens could fit into a demisemihemidemisemiquaver. That's the smallest musical note, for any philistines out there.

"Go inside and help Pearl serve cordial to our guests." My mother's cold eyes bore into mine as she placed her hand on Jacob's shoulder and pushed him in the direction of the house. "I want to speak with your brother alone."

Has she seen the mic? I thought I'd hid it carefully under my shirt, but I didn't dare look down to check. Maybe they had some kind of machine that sensed transmissions? I kept my face impassive. I wouldn't give anything away. I needed to make it out of here with Jacob's recording.

Mom looped her arm in mine, dragging me to the far corner of the courtyard, where a high hedge hid us from view of the fields below. I followed where she looked – another car had just pulled up, and Father Aaron raced over to help a woman from the front seat.

It was Heather's mother, Eustace Danvers. The Key of Truth sparkled in the late afternoon sun.

"What did Jacob tell you?" My mother's fingers dug into my arm.

"We talked about chickens. And baking bread. He has bruises around his wrists and ankles, Mother." My hands curled into fists. "How could you let Aaron hurt him?"

"Jacob acts out, especially now Pearl is here. Father Aaron has to discipline him." She turned to face me, her mouth set in a hard line. Out here in the sunlight, she appeared older, her face crisscrossed with wrinkles, her forehead sagging from stress. "Things will be better once Pearl learns to accept our ways. Dorien, we must talk about your marriage. Faye de Winter—"

"I'm not going near Faye," I said. It was the least I owed her. Ten years ago I destroyed our friendship to save her from the Temple. Life had come full fucking circle once more.

"You *must*." She snuck a glance back to the lawn, where Father Aaron had Mrs. Danvers on his arm and was gesturing to the orchard trees. "Or we will lose everything."

"You already lost everything when you joined this stupid cult."

"Just because you don't understand our ways does not mean they are not valuable. Jacob is growing up without the negative influence of money. He's eating wholesome food. He lives in a utopia without greed or lust or avarice—"

I snorted. "That's fucking rich."

But she wasn't listening. "—it's everything you should want for him, and for your own children. But if you don't marry Faye, it could all be taken away from us."

"Here's a shocking idea," I smirked. "Why don't you stop pretending we live in the Dark Ages and let me *choose* who I marry? Maybe Titus wants me to put a ring on it."

"This isn't funny, Dorien." Mother pursed her lips as she glared at Mrs. Danvers. "We need you to align with a powerful family, with someone Aaron respects and believes he can save, or this all goes away."

"I have no intention of marrying Heather. What are you talking about?"

"Ten years ago, things were so different. After you rejected Faye, I read the auguries and your union to Heather was preordained and God-blessed. The Danvers' influence and their wealth would enable the Temple to grow and blossom. It costs a lot of money to recruit the powerful people who are most in need of saving. Aaron has to infiltrate the right circles. We've given our entire fortune to the cause, but it hasn't been enough." Her face pinched. "Aaron no longer believes I'm his prophetess. He thinks he was mistaken before, that Eustace's energy was so powerful that he mistook it as coming from me. If we don't do something quickly, she will be his Blessed-Bride, and he'll punish me for deceiving him."

"Punish you, how?" Jacob's ruined foot burned itself into my brain.

"He wants to burn this place down. On the day of ascension, we will purify ourselves in a great conflagration, and be made anew. He'll move our community to the Danvers' California estate. I'll no longer be prophetess and Jacob will no longer be his God-son. He won't be safe from Aaron's wrath."

She meant that *she* won't be safe from his wrath. Below us, Aaron turned, leading Eustace back toward the house. Mother stiffened.

"He can't see us together like this. I'll contact you again soon. If you won't choose Faye, I will find another bride who will help restore me in his eyes." Her eyes flashed, and she darted back toward the kitchen.

What the fuck?

I followed her, climbing back over the crumbling steps just as Father Aaron stepped into the kitchen. His presence drained what little life remained in the room. The children stood back, hands behind their backs, faces turned to the floor. Eustace glared down at them as if she wished she could grind them into the dirt beneath her boot. Jacob's shoulder trembled, and Pearl's mouth set in a defiant line. I didn't need auguries to read the future from the tension tugging at the air. If Father Aaron moved the cult to California, my brother would be lost to me forever.

I couldn't stay in that house another minute. Now that Aaron was here, no one would dare say a word I could use, anyway. I fished my phone from the tray in the foyer. "I have to get to my recital."

"Yes. You must play for them, son." My mother thrust a stack of pamphlets into my hand. "Give one to anyone you meet who is searching for answers. We welcome all at the Temple."

She looked over her shoulder at Aaron, searching for his approval, but he was too distracted with his inspection of the rising bread to glance her way. He'd reduced my formidable mother to a pathetic mess, scrambling for scraps of affection. I felt no love for her, only revulsion. This was what she sacrificed our family and Jacob's future to obtain. She could drown in pig shit for all I cared.

But Jacob... he will be free.

"Goodbye, bud." I knew better than to give Jacob a hug in Aaron's presence. My brother nodded, his eyes never leaving the floor. I tore myself from the room and fled outside, feeling like a coward with every step I took away from my little brother.

My hands trembled as I gripped my Porsche's wheel. *I'm sorry, Jacob. I'm sorry I couldn't give you a normal life.*

At the end of the street, I parked the car. My chest felt so tight I struggled for breath. I took out my mobile phone and punched a number I memorized a long time ago. My finger hovered over the CALL button, but when I tried to press it, bile rose in my throat, burning at the back of my mouth.

I tossed the phone aside, flung open the door, and threw up into the grass.

When the heaving stopped, I sat back up, my head spinning.

I have to do this. It felt like a betrayal of my family. It was something I could never go back from. It might ensure I never saw Jacob again. It might send me to jail. But just like when I tried to help Ivan and Elena escape, it wasn't about me. Jacob deserved better than this. And he needed to be kept as far away from Heather's family as possible.

I picked up my phone and hit CALL before I could chicken out again. "Hello. This is Dorien Valencourt for Agent Rochester. Tell him I'm ready to talk about the Temple of Earthly Truths."

FAYE

All through breakfast, Elena was in her excited state, bouncing in her seat and talking with her mouth full. After I cleaned up the dishes, I made a quick phone call to the hospital to check on my mom (no change), collected my violin and overnight bag from my room, and climbed into the back-seat of the twins' Eldorado – the Cadillac old enough to be a beater. Originally, Dorien was going to be driving down with us, but after I told Elena what he did, she made him make his own way. His car was already gone, and I hadn't seen him at breakfast. But then, he'd made himself scarce most of the week.

I couldn't say I minded. I didn't want to be forced to remember the promises he'd broken.

Ivan got behind the wheel. Elena slid in back with me, leaning over to squeeze my leg.

"We're going to have the best time." She unzipped her purse to show me the clothes stuffed inside. "I have plans for after the recital."

I pulled out a tiny sequined dress. "Does it involve Ivan singing 'Like a Virgin' at a drag club? Because that's the only situation I can imagine where this dress would be appropriate."

Elena giggled. "It does not, but I like the way you are thinking. Brother, how about a little cabaret show tonight?"

"How about you two stop scheming and let me focus on the road."

"Did you know that Ivan wanted to be in musical theatre when he was a little kid?" Elena grinned.

I couldn't even picture it. In my head, Ivan had always been a serious, stone-faced icicle, even as a kid. I wanted more of this story. "Is that so?"

Ivan gripped the wheel. "Elena is telling fairy tales."

"It's true! Our mother used to do laundry for this old lady who lived next door, and Ivan would wrap himself in her winter coat and pretend to be Javert, or tie her black shawls and cackle like the witch Elphaba."

"You are making all this up so I look silly in front of Faye." Ivan yanked the wheel hard around. Elena screamed, but it was a shriek of delight.

All through the trip, the twins bickered. Elena came alive in the car, blossoming from the delicate flower into an excitable bunny. The further we got from Manderley, the more she bounced in her seat, the louder she laughed, the more she teased her brother. I loved watching Ivan with her. It felt like I saw beyond the mask he wore for the world.

Outside of Manderley, we were just normal people. How I longed to be normal for a few hours.

When we arrived at the museum where the recital would take place, Dorien's car wasn't in the lot. Odd, considering he left well before us. We'd been told to be there an hour early for set-up and tuning, and he never missed an opportunity to show he was the professional amongst us. It wasn't like him to be late.

I don't care. Dorien is not my problem.

We took our cases inside, and a woman named Karen introduced herself as the collections manager and showed us the space where we'd be performing – a beautiful octagonal foyer with a double-height ceiling and chandelier made from recycled Colonial farm implements. Wooden staircases swept off to either side. These had been roped off for VIPs and the museum staff. Visitors to the museum would gather around the grand piano and overflow into the adjacent galleries.

Ivan and I unpacked our violins and tuned while Elena sat at the piano and played through some scales. I kept glancing at the glass clock above our heads as the room filled with patrons. It was now only ten minutes to showtime, and he still hadn't arrived.

"Where's Dorien?" Karen wrung her hands nervously. "Many of our donors have come along today especially to see him."

"He will be here," Ivan said in his thick Romanian accent, but he glanced at Elena in alarm.

"I've tried his phone. He's not picking up." Elena raised it to her ear again. "He left before us, so why isn't he here? Do you think we should call the police?"

"I think we should get out there and play." Ivan glanced at his phone. "He's not coming. After that evil thing he did to Faye, I think he—"

Behind us, the crowd shuffled. Whispers circulated the room as a commotion started near the entrance. Dorien burst through the revolving door, nearly knocking down several patrons. He wore the same red shirt he'd been in this morning, the material creased and stained at the cuffs. His hair flopped over his face, and his eyes flashed with something that might've been horror.

"You are late," Elena snapped. Dorien didn't acknowledge her. Instead, he slid in beside her on the piano bench. She wrinkled her nose. "And you stink."

"It doesn't matter," Dorien barked, his fingers darting across a scale.

"Dorien, your sleeve," Ivan hissed.

I glanced down and noticed a dusting of white powder on the end of Dorien's sleeve. My whole body went rigid.

I thought of the baggie of white powder Aroha had the night of Boris Solokov's visit. I'd wondered then where she got it from. The cocaine I found in Ivan's drawer made me believe he was the one supplying her, but Ivan denied it. I also knew what Dorien was capable of when his back was against a wall. And I *definitely* knew he had no money to his name.

Is that where he's been? Out selling drugs for cash?

Ivan glanced up at Karen, who stepped back, her face horrified as she took in Dorien's rumpled appearance. From the staircase, I caught murmuring from the crowd. We weren't the only ones who noticed the powder.

Dorien frowned and started folding over his cuffs, rolling up his sleeves to hide the stain. Tattoos of ravens and bats circled his strong forearms, and it took everything I had not to lick my lips at the sight of him. *He's not yours any longer. He's proven he doesn't deserve you. So stop drooling over his forearms.*

If only I could get my hormones to listen to reason, but the damn things had a mind of their own. And they wanted Dorien Valencourt, on the piano, any time, anywhere.

Elena licked the tip of her finger and pressed it to the white stuff on Dorien's cuff, then touched to her tongue. "That's the worst coke I've ever had. It tastes like flour."

Dorien glared at her as he finished rolling his sleeves. "It *is* flour."

Flour? That was weirder than it being cocaine. Before I could stop myself I asked, "Why do you have flour on your sleeve? You don't even know how to boil an egg, let alone anything that requires baking."

"None of your business. Can we get this over with?" Dorien pushed the piano stool with so much force he tipped Elena off the end of it. She stumbled but managed to regain her composure. Dorien's rigid back and hard eyes said that was the end of the discussion.

Karen introduced us, and we played through our pieces. The adrenaline coursed in my veins as I drew from the crowd's nervous energy. As Dorien and I launched into my composition, a hush fell over the room. He had the power to do that, even when he was in a stormy mood.

Or perhaps *because* he was in such a stormy mood. *The Bad Boy of Baroque lives up to his title.*

This time, when we played, the music felt like a duel, a battle of wills. His fingers slammed into the keys, creating a grating harshness that I mirrored with my instrument. *Anything you can do, I can do better.*

As we reached the crescendo of the piece, the tension in the room swirled around me, drawing me into a dark tunnel where all I could see, all I could *feel*, was Dorien fucking Valencourt. His demonic music crawled inside my head, poisoning me, bleeding me out with his savage spell. *Not this time.* I pressed down so hard on the strings that one broke with a loud *PING*. The coiled tip leaped up to sting me across the cheek. It was the warning I needed to break the spell, to beat

Dorien at his own game. I finished with a screeching note – an improvisation that threw Dorien off and made me the focus. The defiant fairy facing off against the Prince of Darkness, and beating him soundly.

The applause that broke through the spell rippled over my skin, and for once I was grateful. This was why rockstars love performing so much. The adoration and the exchange of emotion with the audience punched me right in the heart. They didn't know what was going on between me and Dorien, but they felt my triumph and his defeat as I did, and that was all the revenge I needed.

High on the applause and the music in my veins, I circled the room in a daze. I only half-heard the praise heaped on me by the patrons. I waited for Elena to be done with a serious conversation she was having with two rich-looking men in dark suits, then we linked arms, the pair of us skipping to the car. "To the hotel, chauffeur," Elena commanded her brother. "We will change clothes and hit the town."

Ivan didn't say anything as he drove us to the hotel. "Do you want me to stay with you?" he asked Elena as he walked us to the door.

"Not even remotely." She slammed the door in his face and broke down in a giggling fit. "Poor Ivan. He worries about me so much. Just because he's forgotten what it's like to be alone, doesn't mean I don't enjoy it."

"Is that why he follows you around Manderley?" I said, thinking of the pair of them sharing a room when there were plenty to spare, and of Ivan searching her out whenever he hadn't seen her for a few minutes. "I noticed he goes to all your classes."

"Yes." She moved to the bed and rooted through her bag. I expected her to elaborate, but she didn't. The abrupt end to the conversation struck me as odd. Had I hit on something?

"What do you think was up with Dorien?" Instead of pushing it, I changed the subject. This friendship or whatever it was with Elena was still so new – a fragile trust tethered us, and I wasn't ready to test that yet.

"You mean, why would he kidnap you and leave you in a bag in the middle of the forest?"

"I know why," I said. "He didn't want me to be the center of attention. He wanted everyone focused on him."

"If you say so." Elena shrugged. "If you're referring to today, I can't imagine why he'd be covered in flour, but I'm just happy he turned up. You and he are so perfectly suited for your composition. The passion between you two today – it was like you were fucking the music. I could not have done it justice."

"Nonsense." Heat crept to my cheeks at her words. "Dorien may be the Bad Boy of Baroque, but you're Master Radcliffe's favorite for a reason."

Elena's face shifted into that doll-like mask of hers, and she returned to rummaging in the bag. Okay, there was definitely something going on. I opened my mouth to ask about it, but she thrust a black leather bodycon dress into my arms.

"Wear this. It'll look amazing."

I glanced down at my concert clothes – a floor-length black skirt and crimson turtleneck. I threw the scrap of fabric back at her. "You're like a size 0. Nothing you wear is going to fit me."

"Except that I brought that for you, and it's got these panels at the side that stretch." She held it up against me, her lips tugging into a satisfied smile. "Trust me. Where we're going tonight, you'll be overdressed."

"You're terrifying." I went into the bathroom and locked the door, peeling off my layers. There was something about undressing in front of a skinny bitch like Elena that made me suddenly self-conscious of the size of my thighs and stomach. I pulled the dress over my head, smoothing the leather.

Sound the fucktrumpets, she's right. The bodycon shape worked my figure to perfection. Thick halter straps gave me killer cleavage while keeping the girls contained – just as well, because no way would I be able to get away with a bra in this dress. It hugged my waist and thighs, accentuating my hourglass shape. I imagined Ivan's expression when he saw me in this dress – I wondered if I could break through that icy exterior of his.

What will Dorien think?

I bit my lip. Why did I care what he thought? Dorien was no longer part of my... harem, I guessed I could call it. I had Ivan and Titus, and the night of the party proved they were *more* than enough.

A tiny fist hammered on the door. "Are you coming out, or do I need to get Ivan to break down the door?"

I sighed. "I'm coming out."

I unlocked the door and sashayed into the room. Elena wore her own party dress – a scrap of dusky sequined fabric that looked more like Liberace's handkerchief than a dress. She squealed and embraced me, her stick-like arms wrapping around my bare shoulders.

On the bed, Ivan watched me with a wariness that set my teeth on edge. Elena must've let him in while I was changing. I couldn't tell what he thought beneath that icy stare. If Elena noticed it, she ignored it, shoving my purse into my hands and practically dragging me out the door.

Across the street from the hotel was an old-school diner. Elena marched me inside. With her waif figure and long legs, she looked like a runway model or a forest elf. When the guy behind the counter saw her striding toward him, he dropped a bottle of ketchup, sending red sauce splattering all down the wall and across the floor.

"C-c-can I help you?" His eyes bugged out of his head. He hadn't even noticed the sauce.

Elena ordered piles of food – chili fries and onion rings and deep-fried mac 'n cheese balls. All the stuff we never ate at Manderley. Ivan found a table near the back, and the three of us slid inside.

"Why so much food?" I asked. "How do you fit it all in?"

"This is a tradition we have for after a performance," Elena said. "Ivan and I come from this small medieval city called Sighisoara. There are a lot of tourists who come to see the medieval buildings. We would play together in the town square, and when we finished for the day, we were supposed to take our earnings home to our parents, but we would always go to this tiny restaurant on the corner of the square and gorge on fried food and meat and cakes, all the things we couldn't afford at home."

"Tell me about your city." I was looking at Ivan, but he glared at the salt shaker, determined not to look at me.

I remembered the words he said to me beside the poison garden before he kissed me. *I wanted to know that what I feel between us is more than just unfinished business between you and Dorien.* It was. Dorien and I had history, but Ivan and I had a future. I hoped he understood that after hearing Dorien and I play together today.

Elena answered my question.

"It's lovely. It's all cobbled streets and old medieval buildings. Tourists think it is marvelous." Elena reached across to squeeze Ivan's hand. "Of course, Ivan hated it. He thought it was too small for us. He didn't even like Bucharest when we played there. He always wanted to come to America. It is only a pity it was never as we dreamed it, but it still might be. One day."

The food arrived then – plate after plate of piping hot fried things that made my thighs grow two sizes just from smelling them. Elena dug into a stack of fried chicken while Ivan crunched down onion rings like he was hoarding them for winter. Clearly, both the twins were able to eat whatever they wanted without worrying about their weight, but they were both too wonderful to hate for that.

"Even with your voracious appetite, this is way too much food for three of us," I remarked, biting into an onion ring.

"I'll help."

Dorien slid into the booth next to me. He was dressed for a night out – dark jeans and a black tank that showed off those glorious inked shoulders and arms. He slung a leather jacket over the back of the seat. His thigh pressed against mine as he leaned across the table to grab a mac 'n cheese ball, and my throat closed.

"Nice dress." Dorien's eyes dropped from my face to my chest for a moment. Under his gaze, the scrap of fabric seemed to disappear. I felt like I was wearing nothing at all.

You do not get to have an opinion on my dress.

I glared at him and focused on the spread of artery-clogging goodness in front of me. If I had to sit next to Dorien, I'd eat until I fell into a carb-and-sugar-induced stupor and forgot how much I wanted him.

I had so many questions for him, about where he'd gone today, about the flour on his shirt from earlier, about what he'd said in Titus' bedroom. But I refused to break. I wouldn't give him the satisfaction of knowing I still thought about him, trying to unravel his mysteries.

Elena glared at Dorien, and her solidarity made my chest swell with love. The three of us continued talking – the kind of easy conversation that took place between longtime friends that I'd always been locked out of at school. We left no gap in our words for Dorien to fill with his overbearing presence, and he got the hint and stayed quiet. He didn't move, though, and I found it increasingly difficult to concentrate with his leg pressed against my bare thigh.

When we'd stuffed ourselves full to bursting, Elena linked arms with me. The pair of us strutted down the street like we owned the town. Tonight, I felt like maybe we did.

Ivan walked beside us, content to bask in the light of Elena's aura. Dorien walked a few feet behind, his eyes burning holes into my back.

"Where are we going?" I asked as we wandered away from the brightly lit streets filled with bars and restaurants toward an industrial block.

"You'll see." Elena turned down a dark alley. She counted doorways, pointing her pink nails at the roller doors. Beneath my feet, the ground vibrated from some nearby club, but there were no signs or crowds nearby – just rows of shitty-looking warehouses shuttered against the night.

She stopped in front of a nondescript roller door, the bottom corner decorated in orange graffiti. Elena flipped up a small box on the wall and punched a number into a keypad. The door rolled up, revealing a concrete and brick garage. She waved us through.

At the rear of the garage was another door that swung open on an automatic hinge, revealing a dark, damp hall. Inside, the floor vibrated harder, and I caught the faint, tugging beat of house music somewhere in the distance. We dug our phones from our pockets to see as we followed Elena to the end of the hall, where she pushed open a second door.

The music slammed into me – a wall of thudding, pulsing sound. We stood in some kind of old factory turned packed nightclub. Pipes and valves crossed the ceiling. In the center of the room was a giant steampunk art piece that doubled as a platform where a few brave souls danced high above the crowd. Beneath it, bartenders in old-fashioned clothing served colorful cocktails in test tubes and beakers.

Elena yelled something to me, but I couldn't hear her over the din. She dragged me through the crowd to the bar, where a bartender in a full steampunk outfit and top hat mixed drinks with flare. Elena leaned over the bar and moments later, a smoking test tube filled with pink liquid was placed in my hand.

"Drink up," a voice purred in my ear.

Dorien. His velvet voice dropped through my body, straight to my core. My veins buzzed with energy – the music touching something deep and primal and urgent. Everything about tonight felt like a web spun of his dark magic. Did he leave his leg there by accident, or because he knew he had this effect on me, or... or...

I dumped the drink over his head. Sticky pink liquid dripped down his face.

"Ivan, I need a drink." I leaned back and brought Ivan's lips to mine, tasting the sweetness of his longing. Ivan's fingers tangled in my hair, bringing my face closer as he set fire to my body with the heat of his tongue. Over his shoulder,

Dorien's mouth was a cruel slash across his sticky face, his eyes dark and fathomless.

"Isn't this place amazing?" Elena slid between us, breaking the spell. Her pink lips touched the end of a straw as she sipped on a rainbow concoction that smelled like a flower garden. She grabbed my hand. "Let's dance."

I glanced over my shoulder as Elena led me away. Dorien remained still, watching me – a dark face in the crowd of vibrant color. Even when I looked away, I felt his eyes on me. It was a little creepy, but outside of Manderley's walls, where I wasn't tripping over ghosts and secrets... I enjoyed knowing I had this effect on him, feeling the possessive need rolling off him in waves.

I felt powerful.

I felt like fucking with him.

Elena dipped and shimmied between throngs of people, leading me to a winding metal staircase with a velvet rope. She pushed the rope aside and bounded up the stairs. I followed her with less exuberance and significantly more trepidation, and Ivan came up behind me. A moment later, we stood inside a gilded cage, high above the crowd. Lights flashed on all sides of us as the dance-floor gyrated far below.

Elena drank in the lights and the music and the attention. She twisted and writhed against me until she swept me up in the spirit. Before I knew it, I was grinding against her, our bodies shimmying together in our skimpy clothes. I let the music fill me, moving my body, healing the scars Manderley left on my skin. Beside me, Elena and Ivan moved together, their bodies a perfect mirror of each other. Their twin magic enchanted the air around us.

Hands gripped my thighs, grinding me against something hard and needy. A salty, apple-laced scent hit my nostrils – ice-hardness that was sweet and luscious inside. Ivan's breath grazed my bare shoulder as he moved with me, letting his body say the things he couldn't articulate. The sweet kiss we shared in the poison garden lingered between us, the promise of something more than the torrid night we shared with Dorien. I wanted to crack the ice that trapped his heart – I just knew that underneath was a lost boy desperate for the love he didn't believe he deserved.

The music pounded in my ears, drilling down to my bones. I was no longer Faye, made of flesh and blood and bone. I became the music – the melody, the chords, the endless, relentless bass beat.

Ivan laced his fingers in mine, dragging me through the crowd. Elena waved and continued dancing, relishing the touch of two men who swooped in on her.

At the bar, Ivan got our drinks, and we wove our arms together to pour the bright test tubes down each other's throat. The zesty alcohol only made me bolder, more desperate to get Ivan alone. There was no privacy in this club, but I was so desperate for his pretty lips on mine that I nearly didn't care.

Behind the bar, a metal staircase wound up to a second story, blocked off with a velvet rope. Ivan nodded to a security guard, who pulled aside the rope and nodded to him. Ivan's fingers squeezed my hand as he dragged me up the stairs. I peered over the side, searching for Elena, wanting to give her a wave in case she wondered where I went.

She no longer danced in the cage. I scanned the surging bodies for her silver elfen hair. She wasn't on the dance floor, and I couldn't see her near the bar. I scanned the edges of the room and—

What the hell?

I paused, yanking Ivan's hand. He bent down to kiss my neck, but his body stiffened when he saw what I was staring at.

Elena leaned over a booth at the back of the room. It was surrounded by a low velvet curtain, so no one could see in, but from up here we had a view down on her. She reached into her bra, removed three bags of white powder, and dropped them on the table. A hand stretched out from the shadows and pressed a stack of cash into her hand, which she stuffed into her bra as she stood up, a satisfied grin creeping across her face.

Sound the fucktrumpets, did I just watch Elena Nicolescu do a drug deal?

IVAN

E*lena, what have you done?*

I watched my sister shimmy through the crowd, her calculating smile playing on her lips. I longed to go after her, but I knew it was pointless. I knew the same tired argument we had again and again would play out. Instead, I whipped my phone out and sent off a text to Dorien, asking him to watch Elena. I didn't want to speak to him, but Elena was more important than our feud. I had to hope he agreed.

A moment later, Dorien emerged from behind the bar and met her on the dance floor. His eyes flicked up to me and he nodded, once. So our friendship was not so severed that he wouldn't do this for me. I wanted to hate him for what he did to Faye, but I couldn't quite fall over the edge of animosity the way Titus had.

My feelings for Dorien were complicated. I hated him because I loved him. I needed him, because I could never possess him, or be possessed by him. I feared him, because he was a bottomless void within which I could lose myself. And if I lost myself, Elena would suffer.

Faye watched me as Dorien led Elena back to the bar. "Ivan, what's going on? What did I just see?"

I grabbed her hand again and dragged her up the staircase. Faye's eyes darted around as she took in the second floor of the warehouse. I don't know what she was expecting up here – some kind of private bar? – but it certainly wasn't the steampunk wonderland of metal gangways, moving chandeliers made of cogs and gears, and huge bulkhead doorways that opened with wheels. This place was called *The Engine Ward*, after some obscure steampunk novel. Elena was telling me the owners had a popular secret club in California named *The Grotto*, and they were trialing the concept on the East Coast.

I stopped in front of one of the riveted doors and punched a code into the keyboard before turning the wheel. The door opened with a hiss.

"Wow." Faye's eyes widened as smoke billowed from the room from a hidden dry ice machine. She stepped through the mist into a high-ceilinged room. Every available inch of wall was covered with pipes and gauges and cogs, and there were several large levers and buttons labeled 'PULL FOR BUBBLES' or 'PRESS TO HANG AROUND.' In the center of the room was an enormous four-poster bed, made of carved wood with metal vines twining around it. Hanging from the vines was an enormous spider, her metal legs reaching for us as she glared at us through a hundred beady eyes.

Faye grinned as she pointed to the spider. "I'm not sure I like the idea of Madame Usher frowning at us while we do filthy things on this bed."

I laughed, but the sound came out forced. The spider did have a certain resemblance to Madame, but I couldn't stop thinking about Elena tossing that cocaine on the table, and the filthy things Faye had planned.

Faye pushed a steamer trunk underneath the spider and climbed up to inspect its fixings. "I think I can turn this around so she's facing the wall. Are you okay?"

"No. I am not." I had Faye alone. This was supposed to be where I could say the things I wanted to say to her, let her see the person I hid from the world and show her what she meant to me. I could only do that away from Manderley and the shackles that tied me down. *But this is all wrong. Completely fucked up.* "Elena is..."

"I'm not mistaken, right? I *did* just see her hand that guy drugs in exchange for money?" Faye folded her arms.

"She does not know what she is doing."

"She looked pretty in-control to me. Like she'd done this before."

My legs trembled. I flung myself down on the bed, staring up at the spider's ass, trying to avoid Faye's penetrating gaze. "Elena thinks it's her turn to save us. I told you that Madame Usher owns us. She takes the money we earn from our performances. She says she adds it to our trust, but she will never show us the accounts. I know that she spends it, and I don't believe we have a trust at all. Our money pays Master Radcliffe's salary and for everything we eat at Manderley and for all those fancy tutors to visit. And I think it pays for other things – things I don't like to consider."

Faye perched on the bed beside me, her fingers tracing along my thigh, making me momentarily lose focus. "I thought the tutors and guests came because they were her friends, and they believe in the talent she picks and nurtures."

"Most of them would not make the trip to a falling-down house in the middle of nowhere even if Beethoven himself were performing, but she rewards them handsomely. In money, and in other things. In secrets."

Faye glanced up at the spider, and her shoulders straightened. "Yes. I guess she does. Ivan, I need the whole story here. No more giving me pieces of information or trying to 'protect' me by keeping me in the dark. It's bullshit and you know it.

It's more about protecting yourself. I don't want us to end up like Dorien and me. I don't want to hate you, but I will if I don't get answers."

I swallowed hard. Faye lay down beside me, propping herself up on her elbow so her dark hair cascaded over her shoulder and fanned over my chest. I folded my hand over hers and stared at them, noticing the callouses and dents from the strings – my same marks mirrored in Faye's fingers. "All our life, I thought our lives would begin when we escaped our parents. Even back then, I knew Elena was special – she was wasted playing on street corners to tourists. I never wanted to be famous, not like her. I just wanted to remain by her side, to bask in the glow of her love, to draw a little of her brightness into myself.

"When Madame Usher offered to take us to America, we never thought to protest. Our parents wouldn't have given us an option; they needed the money that badly. But it seemed like the perfect opportunity." I let out a bitter laugh. "If you'd known how badly I dreamed of escaping to America, you would laugh."

"I'd never laugh at you, Ivan." Faye's voice soothed over the turmoil of my memories.

"I thought America would mean freedom. I wanted Elena to be able to shine. Instead, we are prisoners here even more than we were in Romania. There, at least we were prisoners of poverty. Here, evil has us locked up and has thrown away the key."

"I can only imagine what it has been like for you both, trapped with that horrible woman for so many years." Faye danced her fingers along the inside of my thigh, and I struggled to keep hold of my rational mind. "I've lived at Manderley a few short months and I already want to throw myself over a balcony."

I gripped her hand. "You wouldn't think of it."

Faye laughed. "No. I won't let Madame Usher win. And I won't leave you or Titus or Elena." *Or Dorien*, I thought, but didn't say. As much as Faye hated him right now, her hatred was borne of love. If she didn't love him, she could not hate him so. I knew that dance all too well.

I shook my head. "You do not know the half of it. When she was fifteen, Master Radcliffe took Elena to Europe for the summer to introduce her to some of his contacts there. He believes that she should begin her career back in Europe. In this and only this, I support him. Elena is wasted behind Manderley's walls. Her talent should be on show for the world to see."

"I agree," Faye said. "I've never heard someone who plays like her before. Everyone at Manderley is talented, but Elena is one-of-a-kind."

"I knew you could see it. And although I hate him, Radcliffe sees it, too. But Madame Usher wants to keep us close so she can control us, and our money. Elena begged and pleaded Madame Usher to let her go on the trip, and I believe Radcliffe interceded for us, for she would not leave without me. And so we all went to Europe."

"And something happened on this trip?"

My hands balled into fists. "Elena played for sold-out crowds in Vienna, in Moscow, in Prague. It was incredible to sit in the audience and listen to her light up the world, to hear her talent spoken of in excited whispers. At the galas, she glittered on Radcliffe's arm – his darling, his *protégé*. And one summer's eve in Prague, while they walked over the Charles Bridge under the full moon, he asked her to marry him."

"He… what?" Faye looked completely lost, like I'd just told her I'd decided to play Tchaikovsky on a wet fish.

"Let me correct myself. He did not *ask* for her hand. For we are slaves at Manderley, and what we want does not matter. Master Radcliffe informed Elena that they would be wed as soon as she graduated from Manderley and received her trust, and they would return to Europe as a married couple to begin her glittering international career."

Faye wrinkled her face. "But he's, like, *sixty*."

"Sixty-four, and yet he lusts after my sister." My blood boiled at the thought of it. "But there is nothing I can do. Madame Usher will see Elena wed to Radcliffe, and our fortune will become his. And as he is indebted to her, we will remain Madame's to control. We will never be free."

Faye's mouth formed an O. "This is why you stay with her during her lessons, because of Radcliffe."

"Yes." I balled my hands into fists. "He is always pulling her aside for extra tuition or asking her back to his coach house, or trying to get her alone during our international travels. He looks at her as though he cannot wait to devour her. She says he has been a perfect gentleman, but she does not tell me everything, and I know she encourages him in her own way – if he's on her side, then we have more freedom. It's only because of Elena's charms that I was allowed to be part of Broken Muse. She knows that to reject him outright is to incur Madame's wrath, and that will come back on me."

"How do you mean?"

"Madame won't hurt Elena, because Master Radcliffe won't allow it." My body stiffened. I didn't want to talk about it – my shame. I should be able to fight back against a bitter old woman, but she had always been able to use my love for Elena against me.

Realization dawned on Faye's face. "Those marks on your back."

I nodded.

Faye's fingers traced beneath my shirt, lifting it up and off my head. I sat rigid while her fingers trailed along the scars. I forced back the tears that pricked in my eyes. I wished I was someone else – that I didn't have to be here with her in my broken, imperfect body.

"*She* did this to you." Faye's eyes fluttered shut, her dark lashes tangling together.

"These were after our trip to Prague, when she caught us trying to escape." I pointed to scars latticing the backs of my legs. "These are older, from childhood. I never let her touch Elena."

Faye's fingers against my skin felt like fire, like a thousand tiny needles boring into my soul. "Ivan, this is abuse. We should report her to the police."

I shook my head. "You saw her at the party with Commissioner Walpole. She has secrets on everyone who passes through Manderley's walls. We cannot trust the police."

"Tell me the rest of your story, then. Why does Elena have all those drugs? What does it have to do with Prague?"

"Elena never seemed serious about the engagement. She seemed to believe the marriage would never happen, or that when the time came she'd be able to charm her way out of it. A few days afterward, she returned from a party at the Rudolfinum in a state of excitement. She said she had a way to get us out of our mess. 'We need money, yes? I know how we can make money.' And she opened her purse and showed me the drugs inside."

Faye's hand flew to her lips. "I can't believe Elena would do that."

"Believe it. We were desperate. We still are. We stitched the drugs into the lining of my violin case and made it back to America without being caught. Then it was a matter of selling them on for a profit. Elena's contact in Prague had the names of prominent orchestra patrons who wanted what she had – a particularly pure cocaine that isn't usually sold on the street. Elena built up quite a discerning clientele, and we sold discreetly whenever and wherever we could, including in the audiences of Broken Muse shows. I didn't want Dorien or Titus to know, because I didn't want to jeopardize their careers. And because..." I hung my head. "I did not want them to know how bad things were for us."

Faye looked at me with those huge, dark eyes, and I wished more than anything I could be a man who was worthy of her whole heart. I took a deep breath and continued.

"The *Zână* gifted my sister not just with musical talent, but with the mind of a criminal genius. Elena made more money than we'd ever seen in our lives. Some she spent on clothes and makeup and trinkets, but the rest we kept hidden away for the day we would make our escape."

"Since you're still here, I'm assuming that didn't go so well," Faye said.

"It was the final Broken Muse tour, although we did not know it at the time. We had Elena with us as our opening act, on the condition Master Radcliffe accompanied us around Europe. When she wasn't on stage, he kept Elena under lock and key at the hotel. He was at her side at the parties, and she couldn't make the meeting with our dealer. I knew he suspected something, which meant that Madame Usher suspected something. We decided to run. Dorien helped us. He had fake passports made and organized our tickets so we didn't arouse suspicion. He said he would send our money once we were safe. Elena drugged Radcliffe with something she found in the attic at Manderley – some Victorian tonic for insomnia – and ran to meet me at the station, where Dorien saw us off on a train. We were going to head to Russia, wait until we turned twenty-five, and then it would not matter. We would be free of her.

"Madame Usher found us. We do not know how. We were on a train to St. Petersburg, and she had the authorities stop the train. They confiscated our passports and all the money we had left. They took us to a Czech jail. They held me there for days. Without food. Only filthy water to drink and a bucket to shit in. I was not allowed to see Elena, and for three days I thought of nothing but her, of what they might do to her, and that I was powerless to stop them. Finally, the police pulled me into a room. Madame Usher sat across the table, wearing her black lace gown and furs, glaring at me like I'm a piece of dirt beneath her shoe."

"What did she say?" Faye leaned forward, her nails digging into my thigh.

"That she expected more of us, that after all she'd done to give us a better life, we'd disappointed her. That she had done what she could to smooth things over with the Czech authorities, but we were facing serious charges." I shook my head. "To anyone observing, she might have sounded like a concerned guardian, but the truth sparkled in her eyes. She orchestrated the entire thing to bind not just me and Elena to Manderley, but Titus and Dorien as well. She left me in prison. Five days later, they released us to her care with no charges laid. I don't know what she did, but when we returned to Manderley we were met by two new students, Dorien and Titus. Our tour was canceled. Broken Muse was on hiatus. None of us have been free of this place since."

"I believe it." Faye's eyes flickered with malice. "I just don't understand it. What does she have on Dorien and Titus that make them stay? And *why* does she want Broken Muse so desperately? I understand controlling the two of you if she needs your money, but why does she need Dorien and Titus? What benefit does she draw from keeping you three at Manderley, apart from having Dorien available to torture me? All this happened long before Madame Usher found me in my mother's hospital room, so I can't be the reason. And none of this explains why Elena is downstairs selling drugs..."

"Because she still has hope. Because she still believes she can get us out of this. Because she knows I'm useless, and that as much as I wish I could save her, I can't—"

"Maybe you can't," Faye whispered. "But *we* can."

"It is of no use. Master Radcliffe will marry Elena at the end of the school year." I buried my face in my hands. "I'll lose my beautiful sister forever."

Faye crawled up beside me, curling her body around mine. She lifted my hands from my eyes. I stared into her face, saw her wide eyes set with determination. She was a lot like Dorien in so many ways – a force of nature, bending the world to her will. To hold her in my arms was like catching lightning – I felt like I'd been blessed with a remarkable gift, but that gift was made of fire and danger.

Her hellion eyes stared down at me, and her lightning forked across my body, setting my veins alight with panic. "We're going to be free. All of us."

 Faye

After Ivan told me his story, he cradled me against his body. His jaw sat heavy, and I knew the hot steampunk sex I was going to have with my ice prince was off the cards for tonight. Instead, I traced the lines of his scars, each one telling a story about what he endured for his sister, for love.

Ivan's breath hitched as I touched him, as I read his past on his body. For him, this was even more personal than sex. This was everything stripped away, pure and raw.

"If it bothers you so much, you could put your shirt back on," I teased him, trying to lighten the heaviness between us.

"I've never been... alone with a woman before." Ivan worked his jaw like he was trying to unclench it.

"What about all those hot Broken Muse groupies on tour?" I stroked his cheek. "Didn't they used to call you the Slavic Stallion?"

"I always shared with Titus or Dorien," Ivan said. "I know myself. I know that I cannot touch someone's body and then throw them away. Not the way they can. I would become attached. I would see love where there was only passion, and I would lose myself."

I wondered how he didn't end up falling for Titus or Dorien, but I realized he might be admitting exactly that.

"Elena would want you to be happy," I said.

"I cannot. Not until she is free."

His words cut into my skin.

"I wish you'd been able to meet my mom." A tear rolled down my cheek. "She was so incredible. She built her PR company from the ground up. In the early days, her office was our kitchen table. Once, this hip hop artist wanted to meet at her offices, so she rearranged our entire apartment to make it look like she rented it as an office. She draped a cloth over the kitchen table and dressed me up in a pencil skirt, and I served him coffee and pretended to be her secretary. It was so completely ridiculous but we pulled it off. That client booked her on the spot and paid us enough money she actually could move to an office.

"But even when she was hustling like mad, she never lost sight of why she was doing it. To give us both a better life. No matter how much work she had, she'd toss her laptop aside when I got home from school and drag me out for ice cream. Or we'd go skating in Central Park or to cause trouble at some fancy industry party." I sniffed as I thought of one of the last times I saw Mom looking normal – we went to a new rooftop restaurant, and the next table over was having a loud high school reunion. She told the waiter she wanted to be seated 'at the fun table' and we spent all night hanging out with this group of ex-theatre students, drinking cocktails and improvising filthy Shakespearean sonnets.

"The very next day, she doubled over in the office and was rushed to the hospital. But they couldn't figure out what was wrong. They didn't know she'd been… *poisoned*." My body shuddered. I still couldn't believe it. Everyone loved my mother.

Or so I thought.

Someone didn't love Marguerite de Winter. Someone hated her enough to poison her. And I needed to get to the bottom of it. I owed it to the remarkable woman who still lay in a coma in a hospital room I bought for the price of my soul.

"Hey." Ivan's fingers stroked my cheek, touching each tear as they rolled across my skin. "I will meet your mother, because she *will* wake up."

"I miss her so much."

"I understand," he whispered back. "I know what it is to love someone so much that their breath is your breath."

He stroked my cheek with his finger, drawing a line of fluttering butterflies across my skin. Those icicle eyes softened at the edges, melting into pools of endless blue. Our chests rose and fell as one, and our breath mingled into a warm flush as our lips hovered an inch apart, not quite touching but *wanting* to touch. Ivan stood on the edge of a great precipice, and he wanted to fly over the edge with me, but he didn't know if he was wearing a parachute or carrying the anvil that would send him hurtling to his doom.

Me? I was already flying, my wings made of phoenix feathers unfurled wide. I'd risen from the ashes of my father's lies, and I wanted to see Ivan Nicolescu soaring by my side. I wanted us to tumble through the air together, lost in each other. But he had to take the leap – I couldn't do that for him.

A knock sounded at the door. "Ivan?" Elena's voice called tentatively. "Faye? We should leave."

Ivan stared into my eyes, and I read there all the things he wished he could say. The ice slid over his gaze, hardening his body into the shell he wore to protect himself. He slid off the bed and pulled me to my feet. "Next time," he growled. "The only tears will be tears of ecstasy."

"I can't wait," I whispered back.

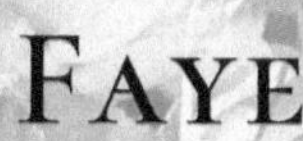

FAYE

Each day at Manderley was a little better than the last. Madame Usher still hated me. Heather seemed convinced that her little humiliations would supplant me, so she filled my bed with worms and put peanut butter inside my violin case. Dorien still stared daggers in my back, like he was convinced he could make me forgive him though sheer force of will.

But I had Titus and Ivan. And Elena's friendship, which became more precious to me every day.

They no longer practiced or performed with Dorien. Broken Muse was no more. I hated how sorry I was that I'd deprived the world of their music. And then I remembered being trapped in that leather bag, alone and terrified, and I didn't feel sorry anymore.

What concerned me is that I hadn't heard anything new about my mother's case. Dr. Nelson kept me updated with my mother's progress (slow, but definite progress). I called the police station every day about the investigation, but they kept giving me the run-around, passing me to different people who repeated the same information – they couldn't release any details at this time. Finally, I had a call from the investigating officer, Detective Carroll, and it wasn't good news.

"We've conducted a thorough inquiry, and we're closing the case and not investigating further."

"What? But the evidence clearly points to a malevolent act. Surely you've found a suspect who—"

"Unfortunately, the real world is rarely a neat little box the way it is on TV. Your mother ingested toxic amounts of a rare plant sometimes used in herbal reme- dies. We believe this was administered through a tea. We traced the brand of tea she drank back to a warehouse in Soho, but it's been abandoned. The company has long since skipped town. We have no leads. We've passed everything we have on to the FDA, who investigate cases like this, but these companies can disappear overseas in a flash, so these things are usually a dead end. If anything further shows up—"

"They *poisoned* my mother. How could you just let them get away with it? What if they start up again somewhere else? Surely this company has records, a board of directors, someone to take responsibility."

"I truly am sorry, Ms. de Winter."

"Sorry, my ass." I flung the phone across the room. It hit the wall and the face popped off. I picked it up and sighed. I'd cracked the glass, and I wouldn't be able to afford a replacement. Madame Usher gave me a small paycheck each week, but it was hardly anything, and I was trying to save as much of it as possible in case I had to leave in a hurry.

I flung myself on the bed. *This can't be happening. How can they say there are no leads? We had a lead – the herbal tea my mother was taking, and the fact that birthwort is still used in some herbal remedies even though it's poisonous.*

When Dad disappeared, they had task forces combing the entire country. But they can barely spare the time for Mom. I didn't want to believe it was a race thing, that my mother was so much more than her Latina heritage to them, but the grim reality of the world loved to bite me in the ass these days.

Mom wouldn't take this. If our positions were reversed, she wouldn't let this be the end of it. She'd knock on every door, bash heads together, find the clues the police missed.

This is ridiculous. I couldn't believe what I was contemplating. *I'm a violinist, not a sleuth.*

I swore that I would not let Manderley claim another victim. The whole reason I imagined Clare's ghost was because she never had justice. Dorien didn't push her down the stairs, but the police didn't look any deeper than that, and I couldn't help but wonder if that had anything to do with Madame Usher's friendship with the commissioner. No one investigated why she'd been acting strange, or talking about voices in the walls. Clare was all alone at Manderley, and no one listened to her until it was too late. But that would *not* happen to my mother.

I had to try.

I picked myself up and knocked on Titus' door. When he opened it, I didn't give him a chance to speak. "I need to go to New York City this weekend, possibly to do something illegal. Can you drive me?"

 ～

Our first stop on the way to the city was the hospital. Titus wanted to come in with me while I visited Mom, but I made him and Ivan wait outside. "She wouldn't want you to see her like this – silent and still in a hospital bed."

"I don't want you to have to go in there alone." His warm eyes bore into mine.

"I've been sitting in that room with her since she got sick. Besides, I'm not alone." I held up my violin. "I have music."

Titus backed away, nodding. I knew he understood. I knew that his music was the doorway into the lonely place where his heart and mind resided.

In the cold room filled with beeping machines, I played *Nigun* for my mother, as well as the composition piece I played at the party, since she hadn't been there to see it in person. Her machines beeped a steady rhythm of unrelenting sameness. No change. Why didn't she wake up?

I need you, Mom. Please come back to me.

Dr. Nelson dropped in to visit just as I was packing up. "Faye, I was hoping to see you. I wanted to give you an update on your mother's progress in person."

I frowned down at her still figure. "I think I can see for myself."

She beamed. "Actually, we've had positive progress. Your mother has responded extremely well to the antidote, and the damage to her organs is not as terrible as we feared. Her PET scan results showed an increased level of brain activity, which is a positive indicator for a patient waking up."

My heart stuttered. "You mean—"

"I mean, we expect her to wake up any day now. I need to warn you, it's not like in the movies. She won't suddenly sit up in bed and reveal the secrets of the universe. She may regain consciousness for only a few moments the first time, and then come back for longer periods. She may not be able to speak, and she may experience temporary or long-term memory loss."

"You mean she might not remember who I am?" The thought of that... I couldn't bear it.

"I don't want to alarm you," Dr. Nelson touched my arm in that kind way of hers. "I'm just trying to prepare you for what might happen. She might be perfectly normal, exactly as you remember her. From everything I know, your mom is a fighter, and she's raised her daughter to be the same."

I squeezed my eyes shut, trying to shove the tears back into my skull. "Thank you."

"I wanted to ask, since I know you'll want to come back more frequently to check on her, if you'd like to grace us with another performance? You were such a hit last time. I don't want to take your time as I know you must be busy with school, but I thought you might have a break for the holidays. Many of our patients will be in here over Christmas, and we do what we can, but I think they could use some brightening up."

"I'd love to play for you," I smiled back.

I packed up my violin with trembling fingers and met my muses downstairs. Titus must've seen the distress in my face, because he swept me into an embrace that threatened to crush the fear from my lungs.

"She might not remember me," I whispered the words into his warm skin, speaking aloud my greatest fear. My mother had been my whole world. What if I got her back but she had no idea who I was?

～

After the hospital, we headed to the police station, where I hounded the guy at the front desk until he handed over Mom's case file. Being flanked by Titus' bulk and stony glare definitely helped expedite the process. My giant teddy bear could look mean as fuck when he wanted to.

I slid back into the car and flipped the folder open. There wasn't much in the file – a few photographs and pages of written statements.

"What does it say?" Ivan peered over the seat.

"Not much." I flipped past the toxicology report – a photocopy of the one Dr. Nelson gave me. There were a few short transcripts of statements – from me, from Dr. Nelson and a couple of people at the hospital, of the homeless man who wrote 'LEAVE' on my mother's forehead. From employees of De Winter PR. Nothing I didn't already know, except...

Natalie. My mother's PA turned newly-minted CEO of her own PR company, with most of my mom's old clients on her books. Natalie's statement felt heavy in my hand, each word a stab of betrayal.

Natalie benefitted from my mother's hospitalization. And she was the one who ordered and prepared the tea. It was right there in her statement...

...along with something else. Something important. My eyes narrowed on the page as I read and reread the details, making sure I had it right.

"Here's the address of the company that sold Mom the tea." I held up the sheet in triumph. "Natalie gave it to the police."

Titus plugged it into his phone. "Let's go."

~

Titus jiggled the lock on the warehouse door. "This place is deserted."

I don't know what I expected to find – a cartoonish lair in a faux mountain with 'EVIL GENIUS THIS WAY' emblazoned over the door, perhaps? – but it wasn't this nondescript Soho warehouse in a row of industrial buildings. The only windows were seven-feet off the ground. I cupped my hands over the grimy glass panel in the door and tried to peer inside, but the filth was too thick and the interior too dark to see a thing.

"Stand back."

I jerked out of the way as Ivan picked up a broken roof tile from the debris and tossed it through the window. The glass shattered, spraying inside. Ivan picked up a second piece of tile and hefted it in his hand. His icicle eyes focused on that broken window with singular focus – the way he looked when he played a particularly difficult piece. Only, now he wasn't contemplating Beethoven's sonatas but breaking and entering.

"Help me up," he said. Titus knelt down. Ivan climbed on his shoulders, pressing one hand against the wall for balance. Titus stood up, propelling Ivan into the air. Ivan gripped the windowsill and used the piece of tile to knock out the glass around the window, creating a hole large enough for him to wiggle through.

Ivan counted down from three under his breath, then swung his leg up.

My hands flew to my mouth as Ivan missed, his body swaying dangerously as he struggled to maintain his balance. "That doesn't look safe."

"Don't worry," Titus grinned. "Once we were on tour in Paris and two groupies locked us out of their apartment, naked, in the snow, with all our clothes inside. I had Dorien sitting on my shoulders holding Ivan while he swung over a narrow third-floor balcony to sneak back in their window. Now *that* was dangerous."

"Don't tell her that story," Ivan growled. "If you'll recall, I slipped on the ice and nearly impaled my nuts on the iron railing, and the girl's father called the *gendarme* so you two hid in the bushes and left me to freeze my ass off in a cell for the night."

"Ivan's right. Don't tell me that story." I glared at Titus, hands on hips. "Just don't let him slip this time. I have plans that require all appendages intact."

Ivan swung his leg again. I gritted my teeth as he made it, pulling his body up and slipping through the narrow gap in the window like he was a professional cat burglar. I held my breath, half expecting an alarm to start blaring or a pack of ferocious hounds to descend upon us. A moment later, I heard a click. The front door didn't budge.

"Over here," Ivan called. A side door swung open, and he leaned out to wave us in, pulling the door closed behind us.

Inside, all was shrouded in darkness. The light from the row of windows along the front of the warehouse barely penetrated the gloom. I pulled out the tiny flashlight Dorien left in the bag for me (I had no intention of giving it back. I lived in the attic of a possibly-haunted gothic mansion – tiny flashlights came in handy) and shone it along rows of metal shelving. Titus moved to inspect a forklift in the corner coated in a layer of dust while Ivan aimed the beam of his mobile phone at some packing boxes.

I swept my flashlight along the shelves, taking in the empty boxes, the piles of rat droppings, the random piles of counterfeit clothing from brands that were trendy a decade ago, and oddly-shaped kitchenware that bore a completely different company's logo.

"It doesn't look like this place has been used for *years*," I said. "And none of the stuff here makes any sense. I thought this company sold herbal remedies. It's weird. My mom was drinking that tea right up until she collapsed. So that doesn't give this company a lot of time to disappear. I mean, how would they know they were under suspicion if we only just discovered the poison ourselves?"

"How did the cops get this address again?" Ivan asked.

"My mother's old PA, Natalie, gave it to them. She was the one ordering the tea. I wondered if she might be the one poisoning my mom so she could steal the company, but then what's going on here? I can't see a trace of a supplement or herbal remedy company ever having product in this place."

Ivan bent down and picked something from a nail protruding from the side of the shelves. "This is interesting. It's not as dusty as the other stuff."

He placed the thing in my hand. I trained my flashlight on the object, struggling to figure out what it was. It looked like a scrap of material – black, with floral lace along the edge. One side was a jagged edge where it had torn, and there was a hole in the lace where it snagged on the nail. It looked like it had come off someone's clothing.

Black lace.

I didn't want to think about the significance of that. Not until we had something more.

We reached the end of the shelves. A narrow door led off the warehouse into a small office. I peered inside and wrinkled my nose. Back here, the air smelled of rot and damp. Papers were strewn across the desk, too encrusted in rat feces to be legible. Titus tugged open drawers and peered into filing cabinets while I stared at the dusty portraits on the walls. They were all a lot older – one was from the 1960s – and related to import businesses, none of which were the herbal remedy company.

Titus straightened up, holding open a leather-bound ledger. His frown told me everything I needed to know. "I found something."

"What?" I rushed to peer over his shoulder.

"You're not going to like it. It's completely fucked up." Titus jabbed his finger at the page. "According to this, this warehouse was owned by an import company that went broke a decade ago. Afterward, it was leased by a company called Menabilly Holdings. The name of the contact at that company is Victor Usher."

TITUS

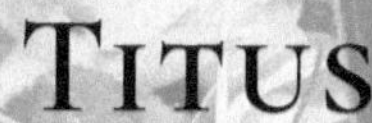

Victor Usher.

It couldn't be true. And yet, there was his name in faded black ink. Madame Usher's husband – the quiet man who first came to my parents in our New Orleans home after the canceled tour to offer me a place at Manderley, who'd convinced both them and me that it was an opportunity and not a curse – leased the building where the company that poisoned Faye's mother worked.

This is not a coincidence.

In that moment, I knew everything Dorien had been going on about was true. Somehow, it was all connected. Marguerite de Winter's illness was not some cruel twist of fate that brought Faye to Manderley. It had been *orchestrated* – a deliberate and malicious act to drive her into Madame Usher's arms.

But why?

And why, after going to such lengths to get Faye to the school, did Madame Usher wish us to drive her away again?

Faye tore the book from my hands. Her fingers remained steady as she held the faded pages under the light, carefully examining each word. The corner of her mouth twisted, and her jaw set in this look of grim determination that reminded me far too much of Dorien to be a good thing.

"How did the police miss this?" Faye breathed.

"I'll tell you how," I growled. "Madame Usher gave Commissioner Walpole VIP tickets to every show on the Vienna Philharmonic's touring season. He must owe her a pretty favor, and she called it in."

Faye sank to her knees, holding the paper up to the light as if it might reveal its secrets. "I know this is bad. But I don't understand what it means."

"It means your mother's herbal tea was purchased from the Ushers." Ivan knelt down beside her. "And from the looks of this warehouse, she might have been their only client."

"They set out to... to poison my mother. This was all planned to bring me to Manderley." Faye clutched the book to her chest as the full weight of it sank on her shoulders. She closed her eyes and swayed a little. Ivan placed his hand on her back, and it seemed to steady her. "What should we do?"

She asked the right question, but I didn't have an answer. Clearly, going to the police was out of the question. They could have found this information by doing a search with the secretary of state. They had to know the Ushers were tied up in this, and yet they closed the investigation. Who knew all it took to buy the police department was a few free concert tickets?

Ivan looked up at me. His eyes were two shards of ice – cold and determined. He would do anything necessary to protect what he loved, and I knew him well enough to know that he loved Faye with a passion he usually only reserved for Elena. But Ivan was a soldier – he wouldn't hesitate to spill the blood of his enemies, but he needed a leader. A general giving his marching order. He needed *me*.

Faye needed me.

My head spun with the weight of their need. Dorien was always the one who came up with schemes. Some of them were brilliant – pooling our musical talents to start Broken Muse. And some of them were borne of rage and desperation, like embracing Madame Usher's plot to destroy Faye in order to escape his feelings for her. But one thing I could say about Dorien – he picked a path and ran headlong toward it. I wasn't a leader any more than Ivan. I followed. I let things happen *to* me. I did what I was told.

All I had to show for my obedience was deception and misery.

I opened my mouth to offer banal words of empty solace. But Faye beat me to it. I should have known she didn't need me to take charge. She would find her path, and it was our job to protect her while she strode boldly into the unknown.

"I think..." Faye blew dust off the cover of the ledger book. "I think we need to talk to the person who purchased the tea."

The offices of Natalie Baker PR were located on a trendy street in the Financial District. Faye pointed out that it was only a block away from her mother's old office. We took the elevator to the thirty-first floor and got off in a slick space decorated in stark white with a motif of large red dots that made me feel stuck inside of a Yayoi Kusama exhibit.

"Can I help you?" the receptionist asked, her voice chipper. Faye shot her a filthy look and stormed past the front desk.

"Natalie Baker. It's Faye de Winter," Faye yelled into the glass walls and open-plan desks. "Come out, come out, wherever you are. We need to have a little chat."

Young women in pencil skirts darted out of the way and men with wingtip shoes threw themselves against the walls as Faye stormed through an open-plan office space. On the far wall was a suite of glass-walled offices, their doors decorated with red dots. Inside the central office, a perfectly-coiffed blonde woman with scarlet lips purred something into an earpiece as she typed on her computer.

"Wait, please. Natalie is a very busy lady." The receptionist hobbled after us on her stiletto heels. "You can't just walk in there without an appoint—"

Faye flung the office door open. A woman rose from her chair, her face a storm. She jabbed a pen at the door, but when she saw who it was she dropped the pen into her coffee, splattering dark liquid all over her perfect white blouse.

"Ow. Oh, shit. Sorry, Gary. I'll have to call you back." Natalie made no move to wipe away the coffee stain. She lifted the headphones from her ears and stared in wide-eyed surprise.

"Natalie," Faye hissed.

Natalie bit her lip. She was trying to keep it together, but I could see she was terrified. I couldn't say I blamed her. Faye busting in with her mane of wild hair streaming behind her and the fire for justice smoldering in her eyes – I was a little afraid of her myself.

Afraid. And madly, desperately fucking in love.

"Faye? Long time no see, girl." Natalie gripped the edge of her white desk. I noticed a row of glittering diamantes set in a row along the edge. "Wow, you look amazing. How's your mother? I heard about her slipping into a coma, I'm so sorry —hey, what are you doing?"

Faye turned and locked the door behind her. Outside, the receptionist banged on the window and mimed calling security. Faye yanked down a shade and pointed to Natalie's wing-back chair. "Sit down, Natalie. You and I need to have a chat about my mother."

Natalie gulped as she took in me and Ivan. I folded my arms, letting her get a full view of my muscles and the mean expression on my face. I was a huge, scary black dude, and today I wasn't ashamed of it. Not if it got answers for Faye.

Inside, my head spun. *What did Faye expect us to do here?*

It didn't matter. If Faye de Winter asked it, I would do it. I would do anything for this wild woman.

Natalie sat down, gripping the arms of her chair with crimson-tipped talons. She swallowed. "Faye, what's this about?"

Faye smiled, but there was no mirth in the expression. She curled a strand of dark hair around her finger. "My mother was poisoned deliberately."

"I know. The police told me. I gave them a statement. What a horrible—"

"The doctors call it acute poisoning – she was fed a tiny dose of a plant called birthwort over a period of months, and the poison built up in her system until it made her sick. She's been in a coma now for three months, but the good news is that now the doctors know what hurt her, they think that if she wakes up soon she may recover, albeit without the use of some of her organs."

Natalie gulped. "That... that is good news."

"Is it, Natalie?" Faye kept twisting her hair, pulling it around her fingers until it made red welts on her skin, then releasing it to spring free. "Or is it bad news for you, because if she wakes up and tells the world what you did, you'll lose everything."

"What do you think *I* did to her?" Natalie shot back. She was trying to look tough, but her eyes darted to mine, and I saw the terror there.

"You know this looks bad. You've always been ambitious. My mother gets sick and suddenly you're promoted in her company, and you're in the media talking about how she was *so* flighty and unreliable. *Then* De Winter PR goes bankrupt, and suddenly you've got a brand new company with half the same staff and all her high-profile clients."

"You're right. It does look bad." Natalie wrung her hands. "It looks like I steamrolled over her to get to the top. Of course it does – that's how I *wanted* it to look. That's how your mother and I decided it had to look."

SPRING. Faye dropped the curl and it bounced free. "I don't understand."

"When she first got sick, and it drew out over months and months, Marguerite knew there was a chance she might not recover. When she had her first episode and she realized she didn't have insurance to cover treatment, we held a war council. She'd been mentoring me on the side for years, showing me the ropes so I could run things if anything happened to her. After what happened to your father, she was so worried about protecting you and your future."

"If you were her successor, why didn't you fight harder for De Winter PR? Why did you swoop in and take over the moment she was out of the picture?" Faye gripped the back of the chair as she glared down at Natalie, but something had shifted in her demeanor. She believed this Natalie.

"If I quietly sat in the background like a demure fucking flower, everything Marguerite built would have been picked over by vultures. You wouldn't believe the nonsense the board came up with – the half-wits they tried to promote above me. I fought to keep this company going, and when it crashed and burned, I salvaged what I could. Did I take advantage of the situation? Of course. I'm a woman in a male-dominated, chauvinistic industry. If I don't stomp on toes to get here, I won't get my Louboutins through the door." She smiled. "Marguerite taught me that."

"But the tea…"

"That fucking tea." Natalie slammed her fist on the desk. "I hate myself so much for giving it to her. She started to get sick and nothing was working, and then a sample box showed up in the mail from some new supplement company. It said it treated her *exact* symptoms, and I thought it was just the universe shining on Marguerite de Winter like it always did. She loved that tea. She thought it was helping. She kept trying to get me to contact them to ask if they wanted some PR consulting, because she thought everyone in Manhattan would want this miracle fucking tea. But I could never get them on the phone."

"Why didn't you tell this to the police?"

"I *did* tell them. I explained all of it. I even dug out all the receipts and sent them over. It was a hell of a job, but I thought it might help find out who hurt Marguerite."

Faye dug around in her purse and pulled out the file. She lifted a page from it and handed it to Natalie. "That's your official statement from the police."

Natalie scanned the document, her eyes widening with every word. "This isn't what I said. I swear it. I told them everything. I even gave them a box of the tea so they could test it or whatever. Why would the police change my statement?"

Faye and I exchanged a glance. There was nothing about testing the tea box in the file, or that the tea had been sent anonymously. That confirmed our suspicion that the police had been bought off.

"We're trying to find out," Faye said. "That's why we stormed in here. I know it's a bit unconventional, and I hope your receptionist doesn't get us arrested, but I needed to hear you tell the truth."

"I still have a few boxes of that tea left." Natalie knelt down beside a white sideboard decorated with more diamantes. She pulled out a storage cube. "Here. Take the remaining boxes. Take it to a lab or whatever. Find the bastard who did this to Marguerite. If there's anything else I can do, I want to help. Your mother is the reason I am here today. She's a fucking inspiration."

"Thanks, Natalie. I really—" Faye's hands trembled as she stared at the box in her hands. I couldn't imagine what it must feel like to hold the poison that hurt the person you loved most, and to know that it also held the answers you desperately needed. To love an object and hate it in equal measure.

No. Scratch that. I knew *exactly* what that felt like. I knew because I felt it every time I picked up my guitar. Every time I played riffs that felt like molten lava in my soul, that tasted of power and freedom even as they closed around me like the walls of a cage.

Faye lifted up one of the boxes, holding it on the very tips of her fingers as if the cardboard packaging itself was laced with poison. Her perfect lips twisted, and I knew she'd noticed something new.

"What is it?" Ivan leaned over, his arm dropping around her shoulders.

"In Cauda Venenum," Faye read aloud. "That's the name of this tea. It's the same words above the poison garden at Manderley."

And on Dorien's tattoo, I thought, but didn't say. I could see from Faye's eyes she'd already put together that particular nugget of horror.

"What's going on?" Natalie leaned forward. "Did you find something? I told the police I thought it was someone who wanted her out of the PR business."

"That's what I thought too, but now I'm not so sure." Faye dug out her phone and flipped to the Manderley website. Her finger hovered over an image of Victor and Gizella Usher standing behind the piano in the opulent red room, inviting students to apply for their prestigious program. "One last question. Do you recognize either of these two people?"

Natalie squinted at the picture. "Yes. That woman. She's the one who dropped off the package of teas the first time. I think she's the woman I spoke on the phone with for orders, too, but I can't be sure. She had an odd way of dressing, like the villainess in some old storybook. Why, do you know her? Does she have something to do with this? She looks like such a harmless lady..."

"You're amazing," I said when we walked out of Natalie's office a half-hour later. After Natalie identified Madame Usher, Faye looked like she might be sick, but she recovered quickly. Instead, the two women found the common thread that united them, tugging and teasing out each frayed end until it bound them together. Faye unlocked the door, and Natalie had her receptionist bring in wine and a platter of deli meats, and by the time we left they were setting up a coffee date for next time we were in the city.

As we dropped into the car to return to Manderley, I reached over to squeeze Faye's hand. "That was amazing. When you strode in there, I expected you to explode on that woman's face. You were ready to *throttle* her. And yet, by the end of it not only had you'd got all the information you needed, but I think you made a friend."

"There was nothing amazing about it. I knew Natalie was ruthlessly ambitious, but I also knew she cared about Mom. No one is one hundred percent evil." Faye paused. "Except maybe Madame Usher."

FAYE

Fresh snow fell as we drove back to Manderley, kissing the towering trees and wrapping the mountains in a snug white blanket. I relished the quietness of the car, with the music turned up loud and Titus and Ivan in the front arguing over how best to tackle the treacherous forest road. I needed space to think.

My mind reeled from everything we learned. It was all so impossible, so completely ridiculous, like a twist in a gothic novel. But it was real.

The Ushers poisoned my mother.

Why?

Nothing about this made sense. It had to be about my father. Madame Usher claimed to love him, which meant her hatred of my mother was borne of jealousy, of possessiveness. But he was long gone. A moot point. A cul-de-sac on the map of history. She could not possess him. Poisoning my mother achieved nothing…

…except to give her something to hold over my head, to control me. The way she controlled everyone at Manderley.

Madame Usher used my mother's illness to draw me close. She knew I wouldn't give up, that leaving Manderley would rob me of the medical care I needed to save my mother. She brought me to her home, paid for the medical care that eventually revealed her plot, and then tried to drive me away.

I needed answers. Evidence. At least now I knew where I needed to start looking for it.

When at long last we pulled up in front of Manderley, Titus leaned over and clasped my hand. "I know it must feel impossible," he said. "But you can't let on to Madame that you know about this."

I nodded. "I'm going to strangle her."

"With your bare hands. I believe you. But not today. We know we can't go to the police with any of this. We need to figure out what to do next."

Cockpoodles, he's right. I nodded again.

"Where have you been?" Madame screeched as we traipsed into the house, tracking snow over the rug as we draped our coats on the carved stand. She circled around to loom over me, her eyes blazing. "I have a guest coming tonight and there's no dinner, the Red Room is a shambles, and you've left Harrison to light the fires himself with his bad back—"

"We went to see my mother. You never told me about a guest." I fought to keep my voice calm. *You poisoned her. You tried to kill her.*

"Titus, Ivan, you need to practice your Sibelius." Madame Usher turned to them as if I hadn't spoken. "I'd like you to perform for Commissioner Walpole and his wife tonight."

Neither of them moved.

"Go, now," Madame screamed.

Titus looked to me, and I nodded. I hadn't forgotten what we said in the car. I could handle Madame Usher. My muses slunk into the shadows, but I knew they hadn't gone far.

Madame leaned in close, her cloying perfume invading my nostrils. I longed to gasp for air, but I wouldn't give her the satisfaction of my discomfort. "You are on thin ice, *girl*. When you first came here, I informed you that if the house was not kept to my standards, you would not be allowed to continue here as a student. I'd hate to throw Donovan's daughter out on the streets, but I will do it. Do not chase after ghosts, Faye de Winter, or you won't be the only one who suffers."

She threw her fur stole over her shoulder and stormed off, leaving me shaking with rage, a sliver of fear burrowing into my spine.

As I chopped and sautéed and drizzled ingredients for a three-course dinner, my chest tightened as Madame Usher's threat weighed on it. She was trying to use my love for the guys and Elena to stop me. It was the same tactic she used to bring Elena and Ivan to heel, and probably Titus and Dorien as well, although I hadn't got close enough to their secrets to figure them out.

She wanted me to stop digging. That meant I was close. And as much as I couldn't bear the thought of her hurting anyone else, I knew for any of us to be truly safe, we needed to be free of her forever. We needed to bring her down.

It's time for Manderley's ghosts to come out and play.

After I served dinner to Madame and her guests in the dining hall, I grabbed Elena's hand. "Do you want to help me with something? It might be dangerous."

Her eyes sparkled with mischief. "Danger is my middle name."

We snuck outside through the kitchen door and hightailed it across the overgrown back garden before anyone could see us. As we dived into the shelter of the forest, I looked back at the looming stone facade of Manderley. Did I imagine it, or had it grown even more decrepit? Cracks snaked along the ancient stone – a lattice of ruin, as though the house itself felt the pain of those who suffered within its walls. A whole section of roof above Madame Usher's private wing had fallen away, leaving a section of the attic there open to the elements. Even though the flowers in the beds beneath the eaves refused to grow – no matter how lovingly Harrison tended them – the creeping flora of the wood slithered ever closer. Vines attacked the walls and choked the narrow windows of precious light. Master Radcliffe's coach house was now submerged beneath a blanket of weeds and creepers, as though it were being devoured by the earth itself.

The longer I stared up at Manderley, the more the house appeared to be alive, shifting in the wind, her bones creaking and groaning as she glared back at me. I shuddered and turned away.

"You lived here since you were a kid," I said to Elena as we made our way down the slippery path. "Has Manderley always been in such ruin?"

Elena shook her head. "It was Victor who loved this house. He was always outside tending the gardens or repairing the shingles, even in the deepest winter. He was fanatical about Manderley, about keeping it beautiful. He told me once that Manderley had a kind of magic – if she was respected and cherished, she would reward the world with beauty and light. But if she was neglected then all inside her would fall to ruin."

"I remember Victor from Madame's city school. He used to teach Dorien. I can't imagine him doing physical labor."

"Oh, yes. He and Harrison were always heading out to chop wood or repair shutters or tend the gardens. Sometimes they would go hunting and they would leave for days at a time. Madame never seemed to mind – I think she preferred to have the house to herself. In the final years of Victor's illness he was bedridden, unable to tend to the house in his usual way, and Harrison has never been able to nurse her back to her former glory. The flowers have not bloomed since Victor's death, but Madame does not seem to mind the weeds. What need does she have of beauty and light when she has her store of secrets?"

I nodded. Elena was right about that. "I'm surprised she doesn't hire someone to replace Harrison. He's not exactly young and spritely. Or even get him an assistant."

"Mmmm. She's not able to remove Harrison from his house – it's part of his contract. And she won't give up space in her private ring to house new help. Harrison can only do so much, and honestly, since Victor died he's been a bit strange himself."

"Strange, how?" Harrison had always been my ally here at Manderley. I wasn't sure I liked his character being called into question.

"I do not know." Elena frowned. "There's just... something different about him. He and Victor were always close. They grew up together. I know Harrison finds it hard to remain here under Madame Usher, but where else will he go? He's a remnant of a past era."

We emerged in front of the dilapidated gazebo. Elena sighed. "Ivan and I would spend every day in the summer down here after we finished our lessons. The other students in the house were always older than us, and Master and Madame Usher didn't much like to see children. They only seemed to care about us when there was a guest to impress."

"What did you two used to do down here?"

"We played games. I liked to pretend we'd been kidnapped by an evil witch and were trapped in her castle, but in her neglected garden we found this magical gazebo where fairies lived, and they'd take us on all sorts of adventures and invite us to wild fairy parties and defeat the witch so we could be free." She ran her fingers over the rotting balustrade. "Why did you bring me here?"

"Actually, this isn't what we came to see."

Elena lifted an eyebrow. "You're being secretive."

"No more than anyone else in this house of dickweasels." I wrung my hands. I needed Elena with me tonight – I didn't want to piss her off, but I had to get this off my chest. "Ivan told me about what you've been doing. Dealing drugs at recitals and such."

Elena pursed her lips, and her elegant neck seemed to grow an inch.

"Before you get mad at him, I saw you with that guy at the *Engine Ward*. I'd have used all my feminine wiles to wrestle the truth out of him. Here's the thing, I don't give a fuck that you sold drugs to a bunch of rich cockpoodles for a chance to escape this place. What I care about is that we had this secret hanging between us. Secrets are what has trapped us all here in the first place, and they're what she's using to divide us, to pit us against each other. She doesn't believe we can still love a person even when the darkest parts of their soul are laid bare, and she'll use that to destroy us. But I think differently – I think the darkness is beautiful, and *real*. So from now on, no more secrets, right? We're all in this together."

Elena cracked a smile, and it was as if a warm hand pressed against my chest. "Even Dorien?"

I screwed up my face. "Even Dorien. I hate his guts, but he's as much a victim of Manderley as the rest of us. I'm going to stop her, Elena, and I need your help."

I told her everything we'd discovered about my mother's poisoning, and how it had all been part of a plan to get me to Manderley. "We can't go to the police with this, but I need proof. I need something we might be able to use against her when the time comes."

Elena followed me down the overgrown path. Raindrops rolled off the leaves above us, splattering on our heads. I pulled my hood over my face and shoved my hands into my sleeves. The forest opened out around the Victorian greenhouse. In the moonlight it appeared grotesque – the squat building of wood and steel and grass being offered back up to nature, with the exotic fronds and deadly fingers spilling from every crack and pressing against the windows – a ruinous garden desperate to escape its cage.

Elena shivered. "I don't like to come here. It's scary."

"I think it's fascinating." I peered up at the structure. Strange fronds reached down at us from the broken roof. Dead purple flower petals stained the icy ground. A sweet smell lingered in the air that made me feel light-headed. "I'm also certain it's the source of the poison that sent my mother to the hospital. But I need to know that for a fact before I decide what to do next."

"Do you know what are you looking for?" Elena asked as we circled the building.

I dug my phone from my pocket and showed her the picture of birthwort I downloaded from the internet – the plant with the uterus-shaped leaves that had been erroneously used as a birthing aid for centuries. Elena pointed to a corner of the greenhouse. "That one?"

I knelt down and peered at the plant peeking through the cracked glass. It was tangled in another weed, but the leaves were unmistakable. "That's the one."

Elena leaned closer. "There are branches here that have been snipped off."

I looked where she pointed. Sure enough, empty stalks stuck up through the cracked glass. They looked as though they'd been snipped neatly with shears. Quite recently, too, and when I took a closer look at the plant I could see more evidence of regular pruning.

I pulled on the rubber gloves I used for cleaning and tugged the plant from its cracked pot. I slipped it into an empty yogurt container I'd cleaned out and punched with drainage holes, and packed some dirt in around the edges. "It's a long-shot, but I'll see if Dr. Nelson will do some tests on this. She might be able to identify if it's the same strain. Then at least I'll have some evidence to tie Madame Usher to the crime. I might be able to go over the police commissioner's head. For all I know she's invited him here tonight because she intends to poison him, too—"

"Or you can let me help you."

I bit back a retort as Dorien stepped out from the shadows. He looked like shit, with his hair a mess and his shirt splattered with rain and his eyes raging storms of despair. Dorien wore his pain as a noble tragedy. Even in despair he was beautiful, and it made me hate him and long for him at the same time.

"You've done enough helping," I snapped.

"No, I haven't." Dorien darted a look around, as if checking if the guys were nearby and if they'd pounce on him. Satisfied we were alone, he took a step toward me. I wasn't going to give him the satisfaction of backing away. "Sprite, I heard what you said about me at the gazebo. I—"

"You were spying on us?" Elena frowned at him.

"No... well, yes. But I only came out because I wanted to talk to Faye. Because I feel the same way you do, that our secrets are destroying us, and I want to—"

"You want to be honest with me, Dorien. You can start by telling me about the tattoo on your chest," I growled.

"What tattoo?" Elena asked.

In response, Dorien's fingers flew to the buttons. He tugged open his shirt, revealing the gothic letters inked across his alabaster skin. Elena's eyes widened as she read the strange phrase. She turned to me. "I do not understand."

I pointed to the sign dangling above the door. "It's written there, too. And today I discovered it's also the name used for the herbal tea that poisoned my mother."

"What?" Dorien's face paled.

"Don't play dumb. I've got the evidence in my hand. Madame Usher poisoned my mother, and *you* had something to do with it." Tears pricked in my eyes, but I forced them down. "Why? Why would you want to hurt her just to bring me here to torment me? Do you hate me *that* much?"

"I did not touch your mother. I would never do that to you, Sprite." Dorien's voice cracked. I wanted so badly to believe he spoke the truth. "I swear it upon all the gods who will listen."

"You don't believe in any god."

"Fine. Then I swear it on my love for you, a love that's burned bright ever since we were kids. A love that's inspired every song I've written and haunted my dreams every night. I had nothing to do with your mother's poisoning. If I'd known Madame Usher was doing that, I would have found a way to stop her, no matter the cost."

Fuck you, Dorien. Fuck you for speaking words that make my body sing with music. Fuck you for being the song that only my heart understands. How I wish I was indifferent to you, that I could toss away your storm-soaked words until you were nothing but dust and dry rot. Instead, I hate you as much as I love you, and the pain of it is tearing me apart.

Dorien slapped his hand to his chest, over his heart. His inked fingers obscured the gothic script of VENENUM. "I got this tattoo done after Prague. When Broken Muse was over and I fell under Madame Usher's control. I got it to remind me that I could never be naive enough to underestimate her again."

"What does it mean?" Elena asked. She threaded her fingers in mine, and she didn't even wince when I squeezed her so hard I heard her knuckle crack.

"It's Latin for 'the poison is in the tail.'" Dorien said. "It describes a scorpion – its pincers look evil, but it's the tail that will kill you. The Romans used it as a metaphor to remind them to be wary of their enemies – that the attack might come from where they least expect it."

"You got that right." I stared down at the plant in my hands. My fingers trembled.

"I know you don't want to speak to me again. I am trying to respect that. But I also can't live with myself knowing I could help but I didn't offer. You want to bring down Madam Usher? Believe it or not, so do I. And we need to act fast, or your mother won't be the only one in danger. We must—"

I shook my head. "You don't get to follow me out here and start barking orders. I meant what I said, Dorien. I've bled for you. I've cried enough tears over you. There can be no more secrets. If you want us to work together, you need to bleed your secrets for me."

His face twisted. Exquisite pain turned his eyes into storm clouds, and I knew that this man could never be dust to me, no matter how much I wished it. "You know how my parents are in a cult? It's called the Temple of Earthly Truths. The cult leader, Father Aaron, has taken over my parents' estate and turned it into an armored compound. My fifteen-year-old brother, Jacob, is trapped inside. They mistreat him, make him work all day, starve him, tie him up and cut his feet, and Satan knows what else."

Shit.

Dorien turned his eyes toward the heavens as he continued. "I believe Father Aaron has burned through my parents' money, and he's now trying to get money out of Heather's parents by making them new elders in the cult. I don't know what it means for my parents or for Jacob, but it's not good. He's scared, so scared, and I think something terrible is going to happen to him if I can't get him out. Madame Usher may have got to Commissioner Walpole, but I'm going above her head, to the FBI. There's an agent there who contacted me a couple of years ago, on their task force for dangerous organizations. He thinks he can help me get Jacob out, and if we tell him about the poison, he might be able to help us bring Usher down—"

Elena's fingers squeezed mine as I took in the litany of horrors he spoke. "I don't understand, if you knew someone in the FBI, why would you not have gone to them before now? You're in your twenties, you could have got custody of your brother if this cult is as bad as you say."

"Because..." Dorien squeezed his eyes shut. The storm inside him threatened to escape through his sockets. Now it clung to his alabaster skin, shrouding him in tragedy. "Fuck it. Because I did a stupid thing. I was going to get Jacob out. I planned to save all my money from the last Muse tour to sue my parents for custody. I even had the lawyer lined up. But then I tried to help Elena and Ivan, and Madame Usher cut the tour shut, and I had to go back to the States without the funds I needed. My parents had already drained most of my savings to give to the Temple. I didn't know what to do, so I thought I'd try to talk to them, convince them to let me leave with Jacob. I was prepared to do whatever they wanted, even marry Heather, if I could get him out of the cult. But I arrived at the house and Father Aaron, he... he wouldn't let me see Jacob. He said I was a bad influence. He threw tabloid articles about our tour in my face and said a court would never find in favor of a vile sinner like me. I was so angry at him and how he destroyed my family. And... fuck." He buried his face in his hands.

"And?" I prompted.

"I *broke*. I punched him. He didn't expect it. He went down and just held his broken nose and stared at me. And I kept hitting and hitting and hitting him. It was only when I heard Jacob screaming that I stopped. I couldn't even recognize him under all the blood. My mother called the police, and they arrested me. Dragged me off to make an example of. A rich dick like me? Walpole was going to come down hard and ruin my life. And then Madame Usher showed up. She said she'd make everything go away, but I had to enroll in Manderley Academy, and I had to do exactly what she asked me to do."

Dorien's shoulders shuddered. He scraped his nails down his cheeks, leaving scratches that filled with trails of tears. "That's my secret. That's what she has over me – I'm an evil person who beat a man within an inch of his life. If I didn't find a way to make you leave Manderley, then Walpole would arrest me for the crime and Jacob would be trapped in the cult. If I'm convicted, I can't be Jacob's guardian, even if my parents were deemed unworthy. Jacob will go into foster care, and I didn't want to do that to him. He's been raised under Father Aaron's crazy rules. He can barely read and write – he'll get eaten alive in there." Dorien gulped. "I thought if I could just do what she wanted, if I could hold on until the end of the year and win the Manderley Prize, I'd have the money to help Jacob. But I had to hurt you to do it. I sold my soul to the devil and now we'll never be free of her."

A savage battle raged within me – I wanted to wrap my arms around him, to hold him close and never let go, and I wanted to press my fingers into his throat and squeeze until he could no longer utter any words that would hurt me. Because it hurt too much loving Dorien Valencourt. Every word, every breath, every touch was a fresh and exquisite agony.

"Why didn't you just tell me?" I screamed. "If you'd come to me in the first week and explained all of this, I could have helped you. We could have worked together. Do you truly think so little of me that you assume I'd let an innocent kid be made a pawn on Madame Usher's chessboard of lies?"

"After I'd already hurt you so deeply, would you have listened? Would you have believed me?" Tears streamed down Dorien's cheeks. "I took the coward's way. I knew you were stronger than Madame Usher could comprehend. I knew you'd survive anything I tried to do to you, but *this?* I didn't know what seeing you again would do to me, how it would crack me open and let my sickness pour out, infecting everyone around me. I thought that if I pushed you away, if you thought I hated you, then you'd never see the *true* evil I was capable of. But it's better you do." Dorien turned away, his shoulders hunched, his face turned to the moonlight as he drank in the pale shadows. "I'm a monster. You're better off without me, Faye. But I will never stop loving you or fighting for you. Cast me out of your life if you have to, or use me to make her pay. Because the only way to fight a monster like Madame Usher is with one of your own."

FAYE

"It's settled." Elena bounced into the Blue Room.

"*Fuck.*" My hands fumbled with the vase I was dusting, and I nearly dropped it. I'd been thinking about everything Dorien said to me at the poison garden – as if it were possible to think about anything else since I'd run away from him that night. I couldn't reconcile the Dorien I knew with this brutal man possessed by violence. *I will never stop loving you or fighting for you.* All my life I'd wished for love like that – feral, haunting, beautiful. But could I give myself over to Dorien's bloodstained promises? And what about Titus and Ivan? Because I loved them too. I loved three Broken Muses, and I needed to have my head examined. I was such a tangle of wild thoughts I hadn't even heard Elena enter the room. "What's settled?"

"We will spend Christmas in Europe." Elena flopped down on the chaise, oblivious to the fact I was having a mild cardiac arrest. "Master Radcliffe is going to accompany us, but I'm sure we'll find ways to get up to mischief."

"How did you swing that? I thought we were all on Madame Usher's naughty list?"

"I just flitted my eyelashes at him, like this." She demonstrated some next-level eyelash flitting. "And he is putrid in my hands, as you say."

"Putty. It's putty in your hands."

Elena waved elegant fingers in the air. "I do not care. We are going – Ivan and I. We will visit our mother for the first time in five years. You will come, of course."

"I can't, Elena. My mom's in the hospital. They say she might wake up any day now. I can't just race off to Europe. I have to be here for her."

Elena's face fell. "But we're all going away for Christmas. Which means it will just be you and Madame alone in this house."

I swallowed. That sounded like my worst nightmare. "I'm sure I can manage."

Winter descended on Manderley Academy, hiding the untended gardens and cracked driveway beneath a thick layer of snow. Harrison's work became an arduous cycle of clearing the way for us to drive to Christmas recitals and chopping wood for the fires that roared throughout the house all day and night. I carried load after load of firewood upstairs to stack in the bedrooms and the basket in front of Madame's private door. By the end of the week, I could hardly lift my bow.

Heather had settled for ignoring me, turning her head away as I entered a room as if I carried a bad smell with me. I worried that her lack of interest in tormenting me was only because she had something dramatic planned. That worry compounded as I noticed her ducking into Madame Usher's office on several occasions for private meetings, and a smaller version of her mother's jeweled pin appearing at her throat.

I heard the footsteps in the attic only once more, and the soft violin music reached my ears just as I was slipping into my dreams. If Heather was behind it, she'd have to do better if she wanted to frighten me away.

Manderley's ghosts had declared a ceasefire. For now.

On the final Saturday before the Christmas break, Titus, Ivan, and Elena went into the city to perform a chamber concert by candlelight. I longed to go with them – we could have seen my mom on the way – but Madame Usher decided I needed to reorganize the linen closet, so I spent the evening refolding perfectly folded linens while she barked orders at me and I imagined how she'd look impaled on the sword that hung above the fireplace.

My chores done for the day, I served up mulled wine and spaghetti Bolognese for the other students and returned to the kitchen to eat in peace. While I slurped spaghetti, my phone rang, flashing the hospital's number.

Mom.

I snapped up the phone. "Hello?" I breathed.

"Faye, this is Dr. Nelson. Your mother is awake and talking. She'd like to—"

I didn't even listen to the rest of the sentence. The phone clattered from my hand as I leaped to my feet. She's awake. *Awake.*

I can see my mom again. I can hold her in my arms and—

Fuck. I had no car. The only friends I had in this place were playing a gig in the city two hours away. I could try to call a cab again, but that didn't work so well last time – if they didn't laugh in my face it would still take them hours to drive out here to pick me up.

I flew through the house to the Blue Room, which faced the sweeping drive. I pulled back the curtains and breathed a sigh of relief when I saw lights flickering through the trees from the gatehouse. Harrison was still awake.

I picked up my mobile to call his extension. It rang and rang and rang, but he didn't pick up.

His lights are on, and I can see his car in the drive. Maybe he's in the shower or something. I'll run down and bang on the door.

I sprinted upstairs to the attic to grab my purse, coat, and violin. On the way back downstairs I streaked past Dorien as he slunk along the hall toward the library. He opened his mouth to say something, but I wasn't sticking around to hear it. Madame Usher yelled something from the depths of the house, but I had my feet in my boots and was out the door and flying down the driveway before she could find some other inane task for me to do.

Tonight, I didn't give a fuck. Tonight, my mother was awake.

Maybe, just maybe, this was the first step toward this nightmare being over.

Outside, the mountain air bit at my skin as my feet sank into the fresh layer of snow. I shifted my violin case to my other hand as I tugged on my jacket one-handed. My violin case battered against my legs, and I abandoned my jacket to hug it against me so I wouldn't damage the precious instrument inside. I still didn't know who'd given it to me, but I guessed from the way he smiled whenever I raised it to my chin that Titus was involved. I ducked and dodged around the slippery patches of ice, sticking to the softer snow at the edge of the drive and barely noticing the branches scratching at my bare arms.

By the time I reached the gatehouse, my chest was heaving and I tasted blood in my mouth. I never ran that fast unless there were donuts at the end. I gripped the wall and sucked in several deep breaths. My cheeks stung from the cold, and because I hadn't stopped to put on my gloves, I couldn't feel my fingers.

Calm down. You can't see your mom if you give yourself a heart attack.

I stumbled up the steps and knocked on the door of the gatehouse. I couldn't believe Harrison was forced to live out here. Sure, Manderley was a bit of a relic, but this place was depressing. It was a squat stone building, barely large enough to be called a house. Vines encircled the building, obscuring most of the windows. Piles of gardening tools, old bricks, roof shingles, and car tires lined the broken path to the front door. I could see a tarp fluttering in the breeze, plugging a hole in the roof. Would Madame Usher's cruelty not allow her to have Harrison in the big house, or did he choose to live down here, away from her prying eyes?

"Harrison, it's me." The wind whipped my words away. I cupped my hand against the narrow, grubby window that pointed into his kitchen. Light flickered from somewhere deeper in the room – a candle, perhaps? A dark shape moved in front of it, momentarily obscuring the light from view. I pounded both fists on the door. "Harrison, it's Faye. Please open the door. I need your help."

I pounded on the door until my fists stung. I circled the house, jumping over the piles of detritus and flinging aside thick vines to peer in every window. Wet snow plastered my hair to my face and drenched my clothes. I was cold right down to my bones. Harrison didn't answer, and I couldn't see any light inside.

I slumped on the stoop, not caring that the ice soaked through my wool dress. Tears sprung in my eyes. *How will I get to the hospital now? Where's Harrison? I know he—*

"There you are, Sprite. What are you doing out here?"

I swung around. Dorien stood in the driveway, shining a flashlight on the path between us. He wore a red shirt that cast crimson shadows through his hair, and a dark wool coat that flapped around his frame.

"None of your business." The wind swallowed the words, making me sound high-pitched, desperate.

"It's your mom, isn't it?" He stepped toward me. "I can see it in your eyes."

I wanted to tell him he didn't have the right to see anything in me, but I was too full of emotions that were threatening to burst the floodgates any moment, so I nodded. "She's woken up, but Titus and Ivan have gone to the stupid recital and I need to get to the city and Harrison has decided today is the day to become a deaf hermit—"

"I'll drive you."

I shook my head.

"I know you hate me now, and that's a hundred percent fair. But you don't have any other options. I promise, if you get in the car with me, I won't try to convince you not to hate me. We'll drive to the hospital in complete silence. You'll see your mom. I'll call Titus and get him to collect you after the concert."

I stared up at him, trying to read his mind in his features.

Dorien stared right back at me, his slate-grey eyes remote, unreadable. "You can't sit out here all night. If you catch frostbite and your fingers fall off, you'll never be able to scratch Heather's eyes out."

I tried to laugh, but I was so cold and so distraught it came out as a hiccup. I stared at Dorien's outstretched hand, and against my better judgment, I took it.

As soon as my fingers touched his, that fire that flared whenever we were together danced along my veins. The magnetic pull of Dorien Valencourt called to me, and I had to summon every last ounce of strength to resist.

"Okay. Let's go."

Dorien kept my hand in his as we picked our way back up the drive. The wind howled through the trees, battering us. Dorien wrapped his arms around me and kind of shoved me forward. I wanted to not like the warmth of his body against mine, the protective feeling of his body trying to shield me against the wind. I wished the heat in my veins and the flutter in my heart could be real, that Dorien really was my dark prince and not the monster who would haunt my dreams.

I scrambled inside his Porsche, slamming the door against the snow squall. Dorien climbed in beside me and planted his foot to the floor before I'd even fastened my seatbelt. He took Manderley's winding driveway like it was a racetrack, even though it was impossible to see in the horrible weather. As we exited the high iron gates of the school and careened down the mountain road, he rested his phone in a cradle and tapped the screen. Loud, strange dark electronica pulsed from his expensive speakers.

"What the hell is this shit?"

"I figured you weren't going to talk to me," he said. "So it's either this or we sit in stony, uncomfortable silence."

"I never said I was going to stay silent." I grabbed his phone and switched it to a musical theatre playlist. I cranked the heat up as I belted out the lyrics to *Cats*.

My mother is awake. Awake.

My mind spun through everything that had happened since she collapsed and fell into that coma – everything I had to do to keep her alive. I worked all those crazy hours. I sold my soul to Madame Usher and climbed into bed with Dorien against my better judgment. But in this moment, it was completely and utterly worth it.

I tried to think of everything I wanted to tell her, and remind myself she might not be up to talking, or that I hadn't even waited to hear what Dr. Nelson might say about her condition. I wrung my hands around themselves in my lap and twisted my stomach in knots and tried to convince myself I wasn't sneaking glances at the beautiful boy who drove into the gloom.

By the time Dorien turned into the hospital parking lot, I was a wreck of nerves. I threw the door open before he even put on the brake, and darted out. He called after me, but like fuck I was waiting for him. There was a group of people huddled by the elevators, so I took the stairs two at a time. As I raced into my mom's ward, Dr. Nelson appeared like a magical fairy godmother. She wiped a hand across her face, tucking her lank hair behind her ear, and a tired smile played across her features.

I fell into her arms. "Thank you," I whispered.

"Just doing my job." She pulled away, giving me a slight push toward my mother's room. "You can see her now. She's been waiting for you."

She's been waiting for you.

That implied my mother was coherent. That she didn't have brain damage. That she remembered who I was.

I pulled open the door to Mom's room. Fear gripped me, rooted me in place as I stared at the figure in the bed – the tiny woman with the skinny arms staring at the ceiling. The tall, beeping machines that had kept her alive still hemmed in around her, beeping and clicking and chirping. *It's all a trick. She's not awake. It's another cruel joke by—*

Mom blinked.

She fucking *blinked*.

Her head swiveled toward me, and her eyes lit up with recognition. With love. Her dry lips curled back into a wobbly smile. "What are you waiting for?" she croaked out. "A written invitation? Get over here, *mi cielo*."

I rushed to her bedside, desperate to put my arms around her but not knowing if I'd hurt her. "Mami?"

"Faye de Winter, get the fuck over here right now."

I threw my arms around her. She felt so light, practically weightless. My heart soared. I thought it might fly out of my chest.

I don't know how long we held each other, her stroking my hair, me touching her dry, fragile skin. I know that at some point my tears spilled over and soaked her hospital gown.

When she pulled away, there were tears in the corners of her eyes. She stroked my face. "I'm so sorry to have scared you. I promise to never do that again."

"Don't make promises you can't keep." I laughed, and the sound was so foreign in this room that it startled me. "I know better than anyone that you run headlong into danger and trouble."

"And that's exactly why I came back to you. I couldn't have you becoming boring without me."

"What has Dr. Nelson told you about your condition?" Dr. Nelson warned me that when patients come out of a coma, it can feel completely disorienting. You didn't want to lay everything on them in the first ten minutes.

Mom leaned back and fluffed her pillows. "The doctor and I have had a nice chat. She wanted to save all the highlights of my little sojourn for when you got here, but I dragged it out of her. I've been MIA for a few months, and you've done a remarkable job coping on your own."

"Mom, I..." So much had changed since she first slipped into the coma. I didn't know where to begin. Instead, I held her tighter. "Don't ever go away like that again."

DORIEN

I waited in an uncomfortable chair for over an hour, staring at a poster advocating for prostate checkups until my balls shriveled up into my body. My mind spiraled to the darkest place it knew – a place where I dared to hope that Faye's mother might be okay, that she might be the missing piece we needed to nail Madame Usher for what she did. That Faye might forgive me.

Hope is a broken-winged bird that looks to the heavens and remembers what it is to fly. I had Faye's love once, and now I would be forever haunted by the ghost of her kiss. In my dreams I will see the sky through her eyes, and the hope that I might have her back will undo me utterly.

The doors swung inward, and Titus and Ivan raced toward me. "Where's Faye?" Ivan barked in his typical Romanian charm.

"Upstairs, with her mother." I stood up, shoving my phone into the pocket of my jeans.

"You're leaving?"

"She doesn't want me here. I'm trying to respect that."

Titus raised an eyebrow. I shot him a dark look. "Look after her, please. There's something I have to do."

"Dorien, wait—"

I didn't wait. Every muscle in my body screamed at me to turn around and go back to Faye, to hold her close and never let her go, but I summoned a strength I didn't know I possessed and pushed myself out the doors and into my car. Titus and Ivan would give her what she needed, and that was the important thing. If I had to lose Faye, I'm glad it was to them. They were better men than I could ever hope to be.

She got in the car with me. I clung to the dark hope unfurling its wings inside me. I needed something to cling to, especially with what I was about to do.

I parked on a side street a few blocks from the hospital. I peered out the windows as slushy snow drenched the glass, searching the street for someone who might be watching me. A raven hopped along the gutter of the house opposite – was it Huginn or Muninn, one of Madame Usher's spies? No, I was being fanciful. The snow came down harder now, thick sheets that obscured the buildings and cars from view. Dim headlights pierced the gloom.

Lavender and orange-blossom lingered in the car. I took a deep breath in, allowing Faye's scent to steel my nerves. I checked my watch. He should be here any minute—

Someone rapped on the window. I leaned across and shoved open the door.

The man who folded his sodden frame inside my car looked like an actor playing an FBI agent. He was a walking cliche with the All-American flat haircut, the college athlete thick neck and shoulders tugging at his impeccable suit, and those eyes that had seen too much. He slammed the door against the deluge and wrung out his tie.

"Dorien," he said, holding out his hand. "Agent Gavin Rochester. Thank you for contacting me."

His handshake was firm, reassuring. "Thank you for agreeing to meet on short notice."

Rochester nodded. "I understand it's difficult to get away in your current situation."

A dry laugh escaped me. "You don't know the half of it. There is so much I need to talk to you about."

"Why don't we start with the evidence you gathered on the Temple, and we'll go from there."

I held out the flash drive toward him. I thought he'd throw it into his briefcase, but he slid the flash drive into the jack on his phone and hit PLAY. I listened to the track on the drive back to Manderley, to make sure I'd captured everything Jacob said, and that had nearly killed me. Now, with Rochester in the car, hearing my boots crunch on the gravel and my mother's harsh voice greeting me made it all worse. *I should have done something sooner. I should never have let things get this bad.*

Jacob's voice came out, so small and quiet. He started talking about his feet. My chest closed up, and I struggled for breath. I wound down the window a fraction and let the freezing rain splatter my face. It didn't help the ache in my chest, but it did hide the tears.

When the track finished, Rochester remained still, his eyes darting across to me. He slipped the flash drive into his briefcase. "This is good," he said. "We can work with this. Combined with the other evidence we have, it's enough for a warrant."

My fingers played with the paper Jacob gave me. "Jacob and Pearl Danvers made you this map, too."

Rochester spread the map across his lap, taking in the floor plan of the house and grounds, with what had to be Pearl's neat handwriting in the key. He'd labeled Aaron's weapon stores with pictures of guns, the sleeping quarters of the five families that made up the Temple, and shown the security fences and the positions of the cameras. He may not have been able to write well, but Jacob's drawing skills were pretty incredible. He'd even included a scale in the top right corner, next to the key.

"That's a very clever brother you have," Rochester said.

"I know." *And it's time he got to shine in the real world.* "What happens now? I'm concerned about this 'day of ascension.'"

"You have reason to be. Our task force has seen an increase in activity amongst the Temple in recent weeks – not just their recruitment activities, but Varney has been moving money and goods around. These are often signs a cult is preparing for a major event. Not every cult ends up like Jonestown, but with Aaron Varney involved, we need to act fast."

"I don't know anything about him."

"He's an extremely dangerous individual. He used to homeschool for a young family in Maine. The father had made a fortune in the shipping industry, but it involved long hours and lots of travel, and he wanted a fresh start to see his kids grow up. So they purchased an old hotel in the mountains and started renovating it. One of their first guests was a teacher who'd recently lost his job – Aaron Varney. Aaron enchanted the whole family with his stories and games – especially the mother. Over time, Aaron convinced the couple to give up more control to him. First, he moved into their hotel as a full-time teacher, then he started to make changes to their schedules – 'suggestions' for healthier meals or activities for the children. Then he started to introduce religious teachings, which became more and more extreme. If any friend or family member expressed concern, Varney convinced the family they were trying to crush their fire, and they were cut off or driven from the property. Next, Varney started selling off the family's possessions and gained control of their finances to help fund his missionary work. He became increasingly agitated, speaking of armageddon and a battle of good and evil, of purging the earth with fire. The beautiful old hotel went up in flames and took the couple with it. Their two children – a son and a daughter – managed to escape by walking sixteen miles in a snowstorm to the nearest village. By the time an investigation was opened, Aaron Varney had disappeared." Rochester paused, looking me dead in the eyes. "That couple were my parents."

Fuck. A cold shiver trickled down my spine as I studied Gavin Rochester's face, seeing behind his All-American looks to the darkness within. I'd never met someone before who knew what it was like to lose your family to a religious nutcase with a God-complex, to see your supposedly-sane parents slip under a spell that allowed atrocities to be committed on their watch. Aaron had already destroyed one family; I couldn't let him rob the world of Jacob's light.

I balled my hands into fists and punched the steering wheel. *I hate this. I hate being so helpless.*

Rochester watched me pummel the wheel until my knuckles stung and I gasped for breath. He didn't admonish me or give any sign he found me disturbing. "We're going to do everything we can to stop Aaron destroying anyone else's life," he said. "I need to take the recording and the map back to my task force and get a warrant, and we'll plan our next move. I'll keep you informed every step of the way. If anyone from the Temple contacts you again, record the conversation if possible – if it's safe for you to do so – or at least write a transcript while it's fresh in your mind. Note the day and time. And get a hold of me immediately. Here." He handed me a crisp business card. "This is my personal line. Call any time. For any reason."

"Thank you." I pushed the edge of the card into my finger, slicing my skin so a single droplet of blood marred its pristine surface. "I have to tell you something else. I don't want it to impact the case. I'm... I'm ready to face the penalty for covering it up if it comes to that."

With my eyes screwed tight and Faye's scent lingering in my memory, I told Rochester *everything* – about assaulting Aaron, about trying to help Elena and Ivan in Prague, and how Madame Usher bribed me to cover it up. I itched to tell him about Faye's mother's poisoning, but I knew she needed to do that herself when she was ready.

Rochester recorded the conversation. "I'm not going to lie, the assault is probably going to come up if anything goes to trial. Aaron's lawyers will dig up any dirt they can find to discredit you. Things will get ugly. We'll do what we can to protect you, and it's likely a good lawyer could make a case for self-defense – you were defending your impaired brother. But you may have to answer for your crime. I'll warn you now, even if everything works out fine and we get the bastard, you might not get the happy family you're imagining. Most of the cases I've worked on like this where one family member gets out from an extremist cult, they remain estranged from the family even after deprogramming. Jacob may never forgive you for taking away the only family he's known."

I nodded. "I understand. All I want is what's best for Jacob. And it's not as if we were a happy family before Aaron came along."

"As for this Gizella Usher, I'll make some inquiries. If the commissioner is that deep in her pockets, that's something we need to keep an eye on. Are you safe at that house?"

I wasn't, but no way was I leaving Faye there alone to face Madame Usher's wrath. "Safe enough for now. Start by looking into Clare Fairbanks – she was a maid who died at Manderley earlier this year. She fell down the stairs; or at least, that's what the police decided."

"You're not so sure?"

I rubbed my eye sockets. "I don't know what to believe anymore. Clare was chasing after me when she fell. She wanted to tell me a secret she'd discovered about Madame Usher and the school. She was my girlfriend, and I treated her like shit. That's probably going to come out, too. I heard her scream, and I turned back immediately. I didn't see anyone else at the top of the stairs, but there is so much in that house that doesn't add up, and Walpole oversaw the investigation, and I think there might be something more there if you dig."

Rochester's shook his All-American head. "You get mixed up in a lot of weird shit, kid."

I laughed bitterly. "You have no idea."

FAYE

I stayed by Mom's bedside for hours. My eyes drooped with fatigue, but I couldn't bear the idea of falling asleep and risk not having her there when I woke up.

Instead, we talked. I knew I was supposed to let her rest and give her space, but Mom was desperate to have some kind of normalcy. She needed to grasp the new world she'd woken up in. So I told her everything that had happened since she fell into the coma – about losing the business, losing our apartment, about Madame Usher's offer, and all the weird stuff that happened at Manderley. Mom's face twisted in a painful way when I mentioned Madame Usher, and I knew she was thinking about Dad.

The nurses tried to make me leave, but Dr. Nelson gave them the hard word that I was allowed to stay.

Dr. Nelson poked her head in just as I was telling Mom about my violin getting smashed. "My shift is over, so I'm heading home for the night. Marguerite, I wanted to check on you. Is everything okay?"

"I have my Faye with me." Mom beamed. "The only thing that could make this day better is a pitcher of margaritas."

"I'm afraid I can't help with that." Dr. Nelson smiled. "Faye, there are some very beautiful men waiting downstairs for you. Should I let them up?"

Mom sat up, her eyes on fire. "These are your boyfriends?"

"I'm not sure it's a good idea—"

"Send them in. I *demand* to meet these boys who tormented you and then won your heart."

Dr. Nelson ducked out, and a few minutes later, I heard a commotion in the ward – deep voices talking, boots clomping on the tiled floor, beads clacking together. The door flung open, and in stepped Titus, Ivan… and Dorien.

What's he doing here?

Dorien hung back as Titus and Ivan swooped toward me. He leaned against the door as if it was the only thing holding him upright, and took in the hospital room and the wall of blinking machinery with those storm-dark eyes. A corner of his mouth twitched, and he had his hands shoved into his pockets.

Mom's eyes narrowed as she recognized him. "Dorien Valencourt, what an... interesting surprise."

I loved how uncomfortable Dorien looked. Marguerite de Winter could still make grown men tremble.

"Mom, this is Titus Thibodeaux and Ivan Nicolescu." I touched each of the Muses in turn, ignoring Dorien because I hadn't invited him here and I needed him to know that. "This is my mother, Marguerite de Winter."

"It's a pleasure." Titus leaned over and kissed her on the forehead, his braids falling over the sheets. She took his hand and squeezed it, then held Ivan's. Dorien stepped forward, but Mom shook her head at him.

"He insisted on coming with us," Ivan said. "If you do not wish him to be here, I'll deal with him."

"I drove her here, asshole," Dorien shot back. "You want me here, don't you, Sprite?"

"*Want* is too strong a word," I said.

My mother gave my hand a weak squeeze, as if to say, 'That's my girl.'

"Dorien took you to the hospital?" Ivan fixed Dorien with his icy stare. "You should have called us. Or asked Harrison."

"It would've taken too long for you to drive back and collect me," I said. "And I tried to find Harrison, but it was so strange. Lights were on in his house, but he didn't answer the door. Dorien offered, and I didn't have any choice."

Ivan folded his arms and shot Dorien another glare. Dorien stepped away, pressing his back against the wall. I noticed his shirt was soaked from the rain, whereas Titus and Ivan were dry – he'd been outside. I wondered what had drawn him out into the storm, and then I hated myself for wondering.

"How do you feel, Ms. de Winter?" Titus asked, changing the subject from Dorien. Titus was always the first to sense tension coiling in the air and try to find a way to dissipate it.

"Like I've been hit by a truck. Faye's told me everything that happened since I went under. It sounds as if you've all had quite the experience at that fancy school of yours."

"Everything?" Titus lifted an eyebrow to me.

"She left out the sex, but I've filled it in with my imagination." Mom grinned. "I'm *very* imaginative."

I shifted in my seat as Titus burst into his deep, beautiful laugh.

"I'm glad you boys are looking after my Faye." Mom said this with her eyes fixed on Dorien. "I don't like the idea of her being in that woman's house. I don't think it's safe for any of you."

"It's not, but we're going to fix that. Mom, do you remember after Dad disappeared, Madame Usher came to our apartment? She tried to give you an envelope, and you had an argument in the kitchen, then she left with the envelope."

"I'll never forget."

I bit my lip, then continued. "What was in the envelope?"

"It was money." Mom's jaw clenched. A shudder ran through her body. "She tried to pay me to send you to her school."

That... didn't make any sense. Tuition at Manderley cost tens of thousands of dollars. Why would Madame Usher want to *pay* my mother to send me there, especially when my father had only just disappeared?

Mom read my questions in my eyes before I could speak them. "Gizella is a formidable woman – it takes one to know one. That's why I refused her, because I can recognize the cunning in her eyes. I do not know why she had such an interest in you, but I did not like it. Not after she and Donovan..." Mom's eyelashes fluttered shut. "Perhaps she thought if she couldn't control him any longer, she could instead exert her power over you and in some sick way remain close to him. But I believe mostly she wanted to take you from me, the way she believes I took Donovan from her."

My stomach clenched. "I don't understand. How can she blame you for Dad's disappearance?"

Mom's eyes flickered shut. Panic rose inside me that she might be fading back into the coma. Dr. Nelson said it could happen. But no, those fierce green orbs fixed on me again, filled with the fire that mirrored my own. "Because Donovan did not disappear, *mi cielo*. After everything you've been through, you deserve the truth. Donovan de Winter is dead. I killed him."

FAYE

The world stopped.

My blood froze in my veins.

Sound the fucktrumpets.

What the fuck did she just say?

I killed him.

I stared down at the woman who had raised me, and for the first time in my entire life, I looked at a stranger. My knees wobbled. Titus rushed to grab me as I gripped the edge of the bed, fighting to keep hold of my lunch. He sank down into the chair and pulled me into his lap, wrapping his enormous arms around me. His braids fell over my face like a curtain, and I sank against him gratefully. I needed him to be my strength right now.

I killed him.

"I think you'd better explain, Marguerite," he said in his deep, kind voice. "Faye needs the truth, no matter how ugly."

I couldn't look at Mom. Part of me wanted to cover my ears to stop her tainting every memory of who I thought she was. But I needed to hear this. And she needed to say it. She took another sip of her water and began. "Gizella was the reason Donovan and I fought so much. I guessed about their affair long before she told me from the way he acted around her – as if she could do no wrong, as if she alone understood the great artistic yearning that rose up inside him. He hired her as his manager, and she demanded more of his time for practice and touring, more money for his trips abroad and his wardrobe, and his lessons that stretched long into the night. She wanted him to purchase an expensive instrument from a famed luthier that he could never hope to pay off. He told me that she was the only one who believed in his music, even after I worked three jobs to keep food on our table. Finally, I told him I would give no more. I would not see our daughter suffer because of his selfishness. He had a family, and he needed to live up to his obligations as a father. He did not want to hear it. He left for a tour with Gizella. He never even kissed you goodbye."

She paused to gasp for breath. I knew we shouldn't be taxing her like this, but she opened this wound. I dared a glance at her through Titus' hair. For a moment, I saw my mom as she was in those last years before Dad disappeared – tired, drawn thin like the cheap curtains that didn't quite fit the windows of our run-down apartment, her eyes rimmed in red as she stirred a saucepan of soup on the stove – our only meal for the day. I remembered her and Dad screaming at each other. Her calling him selfish, him saying she was a stealer of dreams. Doors slamming. Me hiding under my bed or climbing onto the roof with my violin, playing Bach until I drowned out their shouts.

She loved Dad in the beginning. She felt his music in her soul, the same way his recordings still captivate audiences a decade after he disappeared. But my father wasn't some immortal weaving magic betwixt his violin strings – he was a man, capable of great and terrible things in equal measure. He might play like an angel, but to her, he would always be the demon who accused her of stealing his dreams while he devoured hers.

I inherited so much from my mother – my thick, dark hair, my Mexican nose, my fiery nature, my penchant for the bad boys, the heartbreakers, the demons in disguise.

I would always love her. I would love her even if she was a murderer. I squeezed Titus' knee. "If this is too painful, you don't have to tell me—"

"Nonsense, *mi cielo*. Pain is part of life. I can't imagine what you've gone through, being a servant in that woman's house, knowing of her relationship with Donovan..." she coughed violently. "You must hear this – you must know the guilt I've carried with me all these years. You must understand why that woman is dangerous. The last night I saw your father, he came to the door in a panic. You were asleep upstairs and he... he was supposed to be performing in Canada, but here he was, on our doorstep, his hair a mess and his eyes filled with demons. He said he needed ten thousand dollars by sunrise or he would be killed. He had been borrowing money from an Eastern European crime organization to fund his expensive tours and lifestyle, and to buy the violin I refused to purchase. He'd fallen behind on his payments and they had finally called to collect. I told him he would not get another penny from me, that he had robbed his daughter of enough already. I slammed the door in his face. The very next day he did not show up for his recital. He was never seen again. Your father is dead, *mi cielo*, I tell you, because I killed him. I could have saved him, but I didn't."

Relief and love swept through me. I'd imagined my mother choking the life from Donovan with her bare hands, or plunging a knife into his chest. I pictured her taking his body to Central Park and digging him an unmarked grave, like the murderer on a TV mystery show. In her mind, refusing him that money was the same crime, but I couldn't see it that way. All I could see was the woman who'd always looked after me, and Madame Usher's poison seeping into our life, rotting the heart of our family.

I flung myself from Titus' arms to wrap myself around her. I pressed my cheek to hers, and our tears mingled together. "I love you, Mom." I closed my eyes. I didn't want to say this, but we couldn't have any secrets between us now. "We think Madame Usher might've tried to poison you. She owned the company that made the poisoned tea, and I found birthwort in the garden at Manderley with some of the branches snipped off."

Mom coughed. Titus handed her a water glass, and she took a sip. "I believe it. She blames me for his death. She told me so. What do the police say about it?"

"We can't go to the police. Madame Usher owns them – she's in bed with Commissioner Walpole."

Titus wrinkled his nose. "Hopefully only figuratively."

I glanced across the room at the dark prince hunched in the doorway. "Dorien thinks we should go to the FBI. He has a contact there, but I'm not sure about it. I'm not sure about him."

I will never stop loving you or fighting for you.

"You're not safe in that house." Mom's eyes narrowed. "You get out, you and your beautiful boys, before it's too late. I don't care about justice, only that you are safe. And when I can rise from this bed, *mi cielo*, I will go to that big house and strangle her with my own hands."

FAYE

I barely remember a moment of the final week of classes before Christmas break. The shadow of Madame Usher's crimes hung over all Manderley like a shroud. Weirdly, having closure over my father's death made dealing with Madame Usher bearable. All my life the Great Donovan de Winter loomed over me, but now I could see him for who he truly was – a small, selfish man who'd abandoned his family for the lure of fame and fortune. Madame Usher was welcome to his memory, because I didn't want it.

I hoped his ghost would be all that kept her warm in her frigid prison cell when we finally took her down.

Every day after I finished my private lessons with Master Radcliffe, I flew to my room to video chat with my mother. Sometimes Titus and Ivan joined me, but they seemed to sense that I needed this time alone with her. Instead, they puttered around in the kitchen, making the food and doing my chores so I could spend more time with her when we couldn't drive in to see her.

Our future was still so uncertain. Now that Mom was awake and I knew the truth about Madame Usher, all I wanted to do was drop out of Manderley. But Madame Usher, for all her (considerable) sins, was still footing Mom's medical bill, and I had no financial resources from which to draw if that dried up. Mom had spoken to Natalie, who had an old hotelier client from De Winter PR on her books that she sweet-talked into giving Mom a free room during her recovery, so at least she would have somewhere to live, but the rehabilitation process would be long, as Mom would be having surgeries over the next six weeks to deal with the damage to her organs.

"We've got the Christmas concert at the hospital on Thursday." I sat cross-legged on the bed, the laptop propped up on my pillows as I brushed my hair while I talked to her. "The boys will head home afterward and I'll stay with you. Elena wanted to come too, but she needs all the time she can get to pack her suitcase – her room is even messier than yours. I wish you could meet Elena; she's amazing, but she'll be in Europe with Ivan for Christmas."

"Why aren't you going with them?"

"Elena asked me, but I couldn't leave you." My brush hit a particularly snarly knot and stuck fast. I gave it a violent tug. "And now that you've woken up, I have plans. I downloaded a whole bunch of new horror films for us to watch together. Maybe Dr. Nelson will discharge you for a few hours and we could rent a fancy hotel room somewhere or go out for a fancy dinner."

Mom made a stern face.

"Okay, I don't mean a nice hotel room. I don't have that kind of money. But I'll settle for a cheap motel with clean sheets. Anything so that we can be together."

"Faye de Winter, stop being such a wet blanket. I'm not going to be the reason you avoid running off with your friends and getting up to mischief. You are nineteen years old and you never got the chance to be young and frivolous, and I won't stand for it."

"What are you talking about—"

"You are going to Europe, and I won't hear another word about it. You'll be away, what, ten days? That's nothing. You and I have the rest of our lives to watch horror films and develop our womanly figures with junk food."

"But—"

"Not another word."

Even I could not refuse Marguerite de Winter, no matter how much my heart stuttered at the thought of her being alone over Christmas. I couldn't help but feel a tinge of excitement as Elena screamed and jumped about and immediately called the airline to book me a seat next to her.

But just because I'd be gone over Christmas didn't mean that my mom would miss out. I got Harrison to trim a branch off one of the overhanging spruce trees, and I planted it in a large pot with tons of earth and stones. Titus, Ivan, and I loaded up his car with loads of decorations and Christmas treats, and on the day of the Christmas concert we drove it to the hospital and set up Mom's room. When we arrived in the pediatric ward where the concert would be held, we found the place decorated with bright streamers and balloons. Mom was in a wheelchair, tearing down the corridors and cackling with laughter, chased by a line of giggling children.

We set up in the corner of a large playroom. While we tuned, nurses wheeled in patients, and families crowded around the tables where festive food had been set out. We played through a selection of Christmas favorites. During the final number, Ivan slipped away, leaving me and Titus to perform a rendition of *Silent Night*.

I faced Titus, watching his fingers dance across the strings while he drew the bow with his usual gusto. My mind flashed back to that night I caught him in the woodshed playing electric guitar, his features wild with rapture as he flung his whole body into the music. He'd looked alive then in a different way than now –

he was going through the motions, playing the notes he'd been taught to play. But he didn't feel the music in his bones the way Dorien and I did. Not this music, anyway.

I didn't understand why Titus kept up the pretense he wanted to be a classical musician. Unlike Ivan and Dorien, he paid for his place at Manderley. He could leave any time and pursue the heavy metal he truly loved. His parents were so kind and lovely, just like him. I knew Titus desperately sought their approval, but I couldn't understand why they wouldn't approve of anything he did.

We finished with a few bars of Rudolph the Red-Nosed Reindeer, which turned into a few more bars when everyone started clapping and singing along. Titus beamed into the crowd as the kids in front got up to dance, and suddenly he was playing with zest and singing along. *This* was what he craved – knowing that his music moved people, that it made them *feel* something, and that he could live in the moment with them. He didn't get that from classical music.

After we finished with a flourish and a bow, Mom wheeled up to us. Tears streaked down her cheeks. "You were magnificent." She squeezed my hands.

"Let's take you back to your room." I grabbed the chair handles so she couldn't run off and cause chaos, and so I wouldn't think about the tears streaming down my own cheeks.

As we pushed Mom into her room, her face lit up as she took in our surprise. Ivan had done a great job, winding the tinsel around the rungs on her bed and across the windowsill, setting up the Christmas tree on the nightstand and stringing it with baubles, and laying out all our festive treats across the over-bed table.

"*Mi cielo*, you shouldn't have." Mom laughed as Titus plonked a pair of fuzzy reindeer antlers on her head. I laughed and hugged her, relishing her wriggling, laughing, and *living* in my arms.

Dr. Nelson stepped out of the bathroom with a bottle of fizzy grape juice, which she popped with much fanfare. As we passed around plastic cups, she said, "I need to get back to my rounds, but I couldn't miss this. Now, Marguerite, I'd like to point out that you shouldn't overexert yourself, and take it easy on the sugar."

"Good thing you're here to look out for my health, Doc." Mom held out a plate of Mexican chocolates for Dr. Nelson. "Please, remove these delicious temptations from my sight."

"If you insist." Dr. Nelson popped three in her mouth as she left. I shared around the presents I'd wrapped under the tree – homemade chocolates for Titus and Ivan and Dr. Nelson, and for Mom, a performance of *Nigun* right there at the foot of her bed where she'd be able to hear it.

"Ivan and I have a gift for you both." Titus unclipped his cello case, and Ivan raised his violin to his chin. They launched into one of Broken Muse's most famous songs – a hauntingly beautiful dirge of lost love and longing called 'Requiem for a Dying Swan.' A morbid choice for a hospital room, but without

Dorien's piano, they gave the piece a lightness and a faster tempo that made hope sing in my heart.

I didn't want to leave the hospital, but if we didn't go soon we'd be late for our flight. Mom pulled me to her chest and kissed my forehead.

"I want you to throw this sensible, grown-up Faye out the plane window," she scolded me. "You'll be in one of the most beautiful cities in the world. Have fun, do drugs, skinny dip in the hotel pool, shag that beautiful blue-eyed boy of yours. That's an order."

I laughed and stood back, staring down at her and trying to commit every curve and plane of her face to memory. It felt like I was leaving her for longer than ten days.

Titus squeezed my hand in his, reminding me of his promise that he'd watch over her while I was away. I didn't want Madame Usher trying to finish the job. "I won't let anything happen to her."

"Young man, if I were you I'd be more concerned about what might happen to *you*." She waggled her eyebrows at him. "Hasn't my daughter told you about me? I'm a menace. I hope you can salsa dance, because this ass is too damn fine to spend New Year's Eve sitting in a lumpy bed."

~

Ivan and I met Elena and Master Radcliffe at the airport. Now that I knew the truth about Radcliffe's intentions toward her, I couldn't believe I never noticed it before. The way he doted on her, always touching her arm and leading her places like she was a delicate Victorian flower. I thought he was just a kindly old man in awe of her talents, but now his behavior bore a sinister edge.

Ivan *definitely* noticed – his frosty eyes followed Radcliffe everywhere. I hoped he'd relax once we were on the plane. Elena knew exactly how to handle Radcliffe, giving him little jobs to do and treating him in a fatherly way. I trusted her when she said she was safe from his sexual advances until there was some kind of official engagement, and none of us would let that happen.

Ivan, Elena, and I had seats in a row together in economy, with Master Radcliffe sitting up the front of the plane in business class. Elena chose a movie she wanted to watch and made all three of us start it at the same time so we could enjoy it together. Ivan broke out a stash of Christmas chocolate he'd saved from the hospital, and I leaned my head against his shoulder as I fought to stay awake.

I was still worried about Mom, but it was hard not to get caught up in the excitement of our trip. The only time I'd ever been to Europe was a crazy trip Mom and I took to Istanbul a few years ago. We mostly spent our time there shopping and eating our body weight in *baklava*. This trip was the first time I'd be leaving America without her, and I'd be visiting Prague – a city with a long musical history I'd always wanted to visit – and Romania, Elena and Ivan's homeland.

We arrived in Prague mid-morning, and Elena made it clear we would not be allowed to sleep until evening, no matter how much my body protested. Snow blanketed the city's spires and bohemian buildings, making it even more magical. We settled into our apartment on the edge of the Old Town, and Master Radcliffe whisked Elena off to meet some old conductor friend of his. I made a quick call to my mom to let her know we arrived safely, then Ivan placed his gloved hand in mine and marched me across the city to the ancient Prague castle.

We joined a crowd of freezing tourists wandering the vast castle grounds. I'd expected a grey stone fortress filled with narrow staircases and turrets, but Prague Castle was more of a walled city, where Bohemian monarchs and Holy Roman emperors added, expanded, rebuilt and altered a whole complex of palaces, reception halls, gardens, fortifications, and churches.

As we entered the foreboding St. Vitus Cathedral beneath elaborately carved doors, I turned to Ivan. "Dorien thinks we should go to the FBI about Madame Usher poisoning my mother."

"I don't care what Dorien thinks. I care what *you* think." We stepped into the towering nave of the gothic cathedral, and for a moment I lost my train of thought as my gaze was pulled up and up and up by the elegant columns and arches fanning out across the vaulted nave like a forest of stone, and rainbow prisms of light filtering through intricate stained glass. A choir practiced Christmas hymns behind a wrought-iron screen beyond the transept. Their voices filled the space with a discordant resonance that made the old church feel alive. A delicious shiver ran down my spine. Even with all the problems facing us back home, I still couldn't believe I was in this magical city with Ivan.

I remembered Dorien's confession in the poison garden, how his whole body trembled as he forced out his darkest secrets. *I will never stop loving you or fighting for you.*

"I think... this is his way of reaching out and trying to mend what he broke. And maybe he's right – the only way to fight a monster like Madame Usher is by becoming monsters ourselves."

"It sounds as though you have made up your mind."

I shook my head. "Even if I trust Dorien – which I'm still not sure I do – can we trust this agent of his? What if Madame Usher owns him, too? Dorien said the guy approached him years ago. We know she plays a long game, so she could have set him up somehow. I can't risk exposing my mom to whatever's going on. I think we just need to wait and see, and find as much evidence as possible to build a case against her. If Dorien—"

"I do not want to spend another moment talking about Dorien Valencourt." Ivan's words rolled over my skin like liquid flame. Before I could speak, he yanked me into a dark corner of an ornate chapel and pressed his lips to mine.

His kiss shocked the protest out of me, and suddenly I wasn't thinking about Dorien anymore, either. How could I, when I was being held by a man whose body *trembled* with need of me? Ivan's hands entwined in my hair, the warm tips of his fingers brushing against my cheeks as he devoured me. His own cheeks were flushed from the cold – pools of blushed skin outlining his razor-sharp cheekbones.

Ivan's eyes locked on mine. Staring into those glaciers was like leaping off a cliff into ice water. The shock of the cold might kill you, but the thrill fills your body with such heat that you've never felt more alive. Ivan wore his sadness as a badge of honor, and all I wanted to do was kiss away the stories he told himself about who he was and what he deserved. Ivan tried not to be seen because he didn't believe he was worth the attention. But he was, and I saw him. How could anyone miss him? He was enchanting – not of this world, but some fae prince of a shadow realm.

He might not see it, but Ivan carried the magic of the *Zâne* within him. He wove beautiful, pain-drenched magic with his fingers, his apple-and-sea-salt scent tainting the air around him with ice and lust.

Tourists streamed past the door as Ivan dragged me behind a wooden screen decorated with the images of saints. He shoved my back against the wall, exploring my body with needy hands. My heart thudded in my chest. *We're going to get caught...*

I don't care.

I want him.

I crave him.

My body was on fire, and the only thing that would quench it was to dive into Ivan's glacier eyes. His hands snaked beneath my shirt, squeezing my nipples roughly until I moaned. Ivan's pressed harder against me to muffle my moan as he slipped a hand into the waistband of my jeans. Two fingers slipped inside my heat, his palm pressing against my throbbing clit.

I gasped against his lips as the heat inside me flowed through my skin. I clenched around his fingers. Touching me in this ancient building felt so filthy and sordid and so totally unlike Ivan that I wanted to tear his clothes off right then and—

BRRRRP.

A loud whistle blew right beside my ear. I jumped ten feet into the air. Ivan's hand slipped out of my waistband as he glared at the guards crossing the church toward us. The whistle hadn't been right by my ear, but the acoustics had made it seem as if the guards were closer than they were. But they definitely knew what we were up to, and they were determined to reach us and show us just how much God did not approve.

"Run." Ivan grabbed my hand. My wet shoes slipped on the floor as we bolted for the exit, escaping into the bracing cold. A crowd of American tourists wandered through the square, and we ducked into their midst just as the guard emerged and ran in the opposite direction, whistle blowing.

"That was crazy." Ivan laughed. A strand of his white-blonde hair had escaped from beneath his beanie and fluttered across his forehead. God, I loved to see him laugh, to lose himself in a moment. The blush in his porcelain cheeks deepened into a rosy glow, and the severity in his eyes softened to a blue shimmer.

"I can't believe we did that." I held my hand to my chest, trying to calm my racing heart. The wetness in my panties wasn't going away any time soon, not if I remained in close vicinity to Ivan Nicolescu.

Ivan took my hand and we wandered deeper into the castle, deliberately not speaking about what just happened. The ice around Ivan's heart had cracked, and I knew calling him out on it would make him freeze up again. Instead, I dragged him toward a cart selling hollow rolls of delicious-smelling warm pastry.

"What are these?" I pointed to the treats.

"Those are *trdelník* – a spit cake. You'll find these carts all over the city, even though the dessert itself is not a traditional Czech recipe but comes from Slovakia and Moravia. We have a similar dessert in Romania. Here in Prague, it is very popular with tourists, especially with ice cream." Ivan stepped up to the cart and returned a moment later with two of the towering cakes warm from the spit with their insides filled with ice cream.

I bit into the warm, sugary pastry. Cinnamon and cold ice cream struck my tongue. It was delicious. We finished our snacks while visiting the quaint shops along the castle's 'Golden Lane,' licking melted ice cream from our fingers.

"When we were here in summer they filled the trdelník with strawberries," Ivan said.

"I would love to come here in summer," I beamed up at him. "We could tour the concert halls and see the Mucha museum and walk through Petrin Park when it's not covered in snow."

Ivan turned away, but not before I caught a glimmer of sorrow in his eyes.

"Does this city make you sad?"

"Being with you could never make me sad," Ivan said. "But this city will never be only architecture and beer and *trdelník* to me. This is where Elena and I made our last stand against Usher, and we lost everything. I worry that she chose to come here to close the door on our plans to escape Manderley. She is swanning around on Radcliffe's arm – the girl who leaped onto a train with me last year is gone, and my sister is a stranger to me. You notice she does not push Radcliffe away? She practically encourages him. I worry that she thinks if she agrees to marry Radcliffe, he will be our key to freedom. I don't know how I can make her see that's a lie. She's too precious to sacrifice her life for me."

Always Elena's happiness was in his thoughts. I didn't want Elena to marry Radcliffe, either, but I hated that Ivan thought he wasn't worth sacrifice. "She won't have to do that," I said. "I promise, we will all escape her."

Ivan shook his head. The cold slid back into his eyes as he slunk deeper into his ice cave. "I cannot let you choose me."

"Who's choosing anything?"

Ivan blinked. "We can't all be with you, Faye. Dorien won't stomach being one of three, and Titus needs to be able to put you on a pedestal and worship you. I wanted to fight for you, but now I see that loving you means I have to give you up."

"Ivan, you're not making any sense." I reached for him. "I don't need a martyr, and neither does Elena. If you don't want to be with me, say that. Don't hide behind this absurd—"

"It's not absurd." He jerked away. "I am bound to Elena, and she will always come first. You deserve someone like Titus – or even like Dorien – who will place you above all others. It is that simple."

"You're being ridiculous." *Where is this coming from?* "I love you, Ivan. I can't choose—"

"We should get back to Elena," Ivan interrupted, taking off down the cobbled street, his coat flapping around his long legs as he widened the distance between us.

I just told a boy I loved him for the first time, and he ran away from me.

I raced after Ivan, my mind a tornado. The three Broken Muses sent my thoughts into a tailspin. The weight of my history with Dorien shrouded everything that passed between us, and I knew that as much as I hated him now, I'd never stop loving him. Then there was Titus, the impossibly kind boy who shed his skin around me and became completely and fully himself and encouraged me to do the same. And Ivan... Ivan of the glacier eyes, who wasn't made of ice at all, but who felt everything *too* keenly. Ivan who believed that he hadn't earned the right to love and be loved.

I didn't know how to show him that was bullshit. Especially not when he made a perfectly valid point. When Dorien told me that the three Muses wanted to share me, I'd accepted it readily because it was a fucking dream come true. This... harem I'd acquired was the least weird of all the things that had happened at Manderley, and all three of them lit up my body and my heart.

But it wasn't realistic. It was Manderley's dark magic corrupting us, making us believe in a future that couldn't be. I couldn't keep all three Muses. It would only end in all four of our hearts torn to shreds.

The time will come when I'll have to choose one of them. But who will it be?

Faye

Christmas in Prague was even more magical than I could have anticipated. Snow blanketed the city, and delicious smells of warming stews, trdelníks, and roasted nuts wafted from every corner. We went to a carol service in St. Nicholas Cathedral – the massive Baroque nave packed to bursting with people holding candles and singing carols. I didn't see our guard friend anywhere, thankfully. Afterward, Ivan and I got mulled wine (fruit lemonade for him) and warm trdelníks filled with ice cream and wandered back through St. Charles' Square to watch the astronomical clock chime the hour.

Ivan had been distant since his outburst, and I could see his grim thoughts weighing heavy on his mind. We continued our sightseeing around the city, keeping our conversations light and free of drama. He avoided touching me and stood two feet away from me at all times. We accidentally brushed together on a crowded tram, and a flame of heat engulfed my body. I wanted to finish what we'd started in the church, in the steampunk room above *Engine Ward*, but I didn't know how to bring Ivan back to me.

The constant presence of Master Radcliffe weighed on us both. I couldn't believe I'd ever respected him. He fawned over Elena, treating her like a spoiled princess. She lapped it up, but I could see it was a ploy to keep him at arms' length. As long as he believed her to be an innocent porcelain doll who couldn't read a city map, let alone walk around the corner to purchase her own toiletries, he would not touch her. But I knew their engagement loomed – Radcliffe had been patient with Elena and with Madame Usher, but soon he would demand his bride.

After Prague, we boarded a train to Romania. For the first leg of the journey, Master Radcliffe had booked a private compartment for himself and Elena. Ivan and I had seats in first class, facing each other across a table. I drank Czech beer and we played cards as the landscape rolled by. Sometimes, Ivan would stop, his eyes darting to the window, and his whole body would go rigid. Every time the train guard walked past, Ivan would drop his eyes to the table. I knew he was remembering the night of their failed escape. I wished he'd talk to me, but when I tried to bring it up, he shut down.

We changed trains in Vienna. The next train wasn't nearly as comfortable, and we all had to sit together around a narrow table – Ivan and I on one side, and Elena and Master Radcliffe on the other. Ivan stared daggers at Radcliffe for the whole trip – the master kept shifting in his seat, uncomfortable under Ivan's relentless gaze.

Good. He should feel awkward. Pervert.

We arrived at the station in Sighisoara in the early morning and alighted, making our way past an Orthodox cathedral and over a river. Ivan pointed to a towering church on top of the hill. "There is the Old Town, built by Transylvanian Saxon merchants as a commercial and strategic center."

The Saxon medieval heart of the city was so beautiful, it took my breath away. Snow dusted the sloping roofs and piled in the corners of steep cobbled streets. Everywhere were tiny shops crammed into alleyways and beneath stone arches selling t-shirts and mugs bearing the epically-mustached visage of Vlad Tepes. Restaurants lined a cobbled square where musicians and street performers added to the otherworldly atmosphere. Men in medieval garb and vampire capes walked between carts serving hot food and jugs of mead, ringing bells to advertise walking tours in a range of languages.

I couldn't help but think of Dorien, and how much he'd enjoy the campiness of the vampire schtick. In a souvenir shop, I fingered a garish t-shirt of a vampire bat grinning with a pair of googly eyes.

"Who's that for?" Ivan asked as the shopkeeper wrapped up my t-shirt.

"No one," I answered as I rang up the purchase. Buying Dorien a tacky souvenir didn't mean I'd forgiven him.

We made our way through the square, past a sign advertising 'Vlad Tepes' birthplace,' (Ivan informed me with a laugh that it was a complete farce). The twins' mother lived in a ramshackle house on the edge of the old town, consisting of three rooms and an attic for storage. Their father died not long after they were sent to America. Madame Usher's regular payments helped keep the house, and Elena and Ivan sent as much of their meager funds as they could spare back to help keep their mother afloat. It was another way Madame Usher kept them tied to Manderley, and I could see from the love shining in their eyes they would never leave her with nothing.

She was an older woman with arthritis in her hands, though tall and strong. She kissed my cheeks and insisted upon serving tea. She didn't speak a word of English, and Radcliffe and I sat mute while Elena talked a mile a minute and Ivan frowned into his cup.

After tea, we visited their father's grave. He was buried in the cemetery behind the church Ivan had pointed out on the top of the hill. Up close, the church's gothic shape seemed at odds with the serene Saxon cemetery spilling down the hill behind it.

"This is a beautiful place to rest," I said to Ivan's mother as I placed flowers on the modest gravestone. It really was – from here, their father had a view out across the city and to the formidable mountains beyond. She did not understand me, but she sensed the meaning of my words for she linked arms with me and chatted all the way.

We had a hotel overlooking the main square, where tents were being set up and a bonfire built for New Year's Eve festivities. Ivan and I watched them while I called Titus and updated him on our travels.

"How's Mom?"

Titus didn't answer right away. "Dangerous."

"How so?"

"She snuck us both out of the hospital last night," Titus said. "She found some underground salsa club where she insisted on dancing all night before jumping in with the band. I had to drag her away to get her back in her bed before Dr. Nelson started her rounds. I've never had a hangover this bad in my life. Your mother is something else."

"I know. She's wicked."

"And so are you. I miss you," Titus said, and I could hear the sincerity in his voice. "I wish you were here to rub my temples and cook me hangover food."

"Not likely. The men in my life cook their own hangover food. And I miss you, too." I thought of Ivan's harsh words the other night, and my stomach twisted at the thought that I might not be able to keep all three of my muses. How could I give up Titus? How could I give up any of them... even Dorien?

"I dread to think what your mother has in store for me for New Year's Eve," Titus moaned. "I'm not sure I'm cut out for a de Winter."

I hung up and pulled on a long-sleeved wool wrap dress that hugged my curves in the best possible way. It was crimson, of course. We invited Elena to come out with us, but she and Master Radcliffe had disappeared somewhere. She sent Ivan a text saying she'd meet up with us in the square after dinner.

Ivan and I toured the Dracula 'museum' – which was a dark room above a restaurant containing an old coffin and some dusty candelabras. As we moved around the coffin, a guy hiding inside leaped up and cried "blah!" and I nearly wet myself. I had to give him two euros to take a selfie with him. It was completely ridiculous, but it put Ivan in a great mood. We shared a platter of grilled meats and sausage and blood-themed cocktails at the bar downstairs, and Ivan couldn't stop mimicking my yelp after the guy jumped at me. He kept lunging at me, mimicking Count Dracula and collapsing into giggles. It was so completely adorable I almost forgave him for the relentless mocking.

Almost.

But as the night wore on, Ivan's agitation returned. He kept checking his watch and glancing toward our hotel. I knew he was thinking about Elena. The music in the square was in full swing when Elena appeared, alone, wearing a jersey dress over black leggings and an enormous fur-lined coat with sleeves that hung down past her fingers.

"Where have you been?" Ivan demanded.

Elena replied in Romanian. Ivan snapped at her, but she dismissed him with a laugh. She dragged us into the square as crowds of young people moved to join the dancing in front of a folk band.

She took my hands and the three of us spun giddily, stomping our feet and swaying our hips to the lively, hypnotic music. I dared to think that things might be mending between Ivan and Elena, that the wild abandon of the dance had shaken our secrets loose. Then Elena stopped, dragging us underneath an archway in a dark corner of the square.

"I have to tell you something," Elena said. Even though I gasped for breath after the dancing and my hair was plastered across my face in sticky clumps, the dancing had put a little color into her cheeks, making her even more radiant. "I need you to be happy for me. I cannot live if you are not happy."

Beside me, Ivan stiffened.

Elena held her head high. She slipped her hand from the pocket of her coat and held it up. The light glittered off a diamond engagement ring.

"Maxim asked me tonight, over a candlelit dinner. I have said yes. We will marry at the end of term," Elena spoke in a breathless whisper, her voice choked with emotion.

Ivan's fist pounded the wall. "No. You can't."

"You had to know this was inevitable. Why else would he pay for this trip? He wanted to ask Mother's permission and do everything right." Elena said. "It is a formality, of course. I have said yes to him, Ivan. I must say yes."

I tried to read Ivan's temper, but he'd retreated into his ice cave where I couldn't reach him. His body went stiff, and he stared at his sister as if he didn't know her at all.

"Do you want to marry him?" I asked. "Are you in love with him?"

"He is a good man," Elena said, but the way she pursed her lips and drew her eyes away, I knew the truth. She did not believe her own words. She was afraid.

"You have a choice," I said. "This isn't the fucking seventeenth century. Girls can make their own way in the world."

"What would you both have me do?" Elena threw up her hands. "If Madame Usher throws us out, we are penniless. The only thing Ivan and I can do is play music, and one word from her, and our names are mud in classical circles. For over a decade I've let Ivan protect me, watching him suffer to keep me safe and happy. It's time I did something for him. If marrying Maxim frees us both from our cage, then I will do it a thousand times over."

"But you're leaving one cage to enter another," I begged. Ivan stared at a spot behind my head. He'd gone a million miles away. "Do not shackle yourself to this man. Give us time, and we'll destroy Madame Usher."

Elena shook her head. "It is a foolish dream, Faye. You are just like Dorien, consumed by ancient ghosts and fiendish plots. You believe we are all characters in one of those horror films you love so much – that we'll triumph because we are good. But this is real life, and there's no good and evil. I'm not the pure virgin who needs saving, and I've already given too much of my life to that vicious woman. I *want* to play music. I *want* to travel the world and bathe under the brightest lights of the concert halls of Europe. I am fading away behind the walls of Manderley, and my brother is killing himself protecting me from every shadow." Her eyes swiveled to her brother. "Don't you see? If I marry Maxim, I don't need you any longer. You are released from your burden and you can have your own life."

"I don't have a life without you," Ivan's words rasped, harsh and cold with concealed pain.

"It is done," she said. Her hand fell on his shoulder, and she pulled her brother into her embrace. He did not return it, standing as stiff and still as a corpse. Elena's words turned over in my mind as I watched her try to call her brother back from his dark place, and I could see the situation as she did. How even a loveless marriage to an old goat could look tempting if it meant escaping Manderley's walls.

But what I couldn't shake was the look in Elena's eyes – that look of cold calculation. That look of dread. Elena Nicolescu had no intention of making an old man her husband, of that I was certain. What I didn't know was what she planned to do about it.

FAYE

I never thought I'd say it, but after Elena's announcement, I couldn't wait to return to Manderley. Ivan had been in a rotten mood, unable to hide his hostility toward Master Radcliffe or to deal with his feelings about me even a little. In Bucharest, we toured the Palace of Parliament and took in the Romanian National Opera, but the thrill of travel had lost its spark.

You want to know what's not fun? A fourteen-hour flight and two-hour car journey sitting between twins who aren't talking to each other. When I opened the car door at Manderley, I almost bent over and kissed the rotting porch.

Titus flew out the door and swept me into his arms, laying delicious kisses along my cheek. "Your mother wished she could be here, but she got me to leave a surprise in your room – Mexican chocolates and a recording from my phone of her jamming along onstage with a mariachi band."

"Thank you," I whispered into his cornrows. I couldn't wait to hear the tale behind that video.

Footsteps sounded in the hall behind him. Madame Usher appeared out of the corner of my eyes. A rush of emotion assailed me at the sight of her – mainly loathing, mixed with the tiniest hint of pity, the way a house cat might regard a spider before tearing its legs off. "Faye, I'll see you in the Blue Room."

She disappeared before I could reply. Titus squeezed my hand. "Do you want me to come with you?"

I shook my head. "I'll be fine. I won't drink anything she offers me, and there are no stairs nearby she can push me down. What else can she do to me?"

"That sounds like the words of someone tempting fate." Titus and Ivan followed me along the hall to the Blue Room. I pushed the door open and slipped inside. I did feel safer knowing they'd be in the hallway listening to every word, ready to swoop in if I needed them.

"Sit down."

Madame Usher sat in the wingback chair in front of the fire. She indicated the chair opposite her. Unable to bring myself to obey her command, I perched on the edge of an old piano stool under the window, as far from her as it was possible to get while still being in the same room.

"It's come to my attention that your mother has woken from her coma," Madame Usher said. "The terms of our agreement were simple. I would provide care for your mother in exchange for your services as our maid. Recently, you have been lax in your duties, and your absence over the holiday period is the final straw. Now that your mother no longer requires care, I see no reason for you to continue here at Manderley."

My stomach twisted. Of everything she could have done to me, I didn't expect this. She'd gone to such lengths to keep me here while using the Muses to torture me. She'd spun a deadly web around me. Why would she suddenly snip the cords and set me free? "My mother still has underlying health issues, and she'll require ongoing treatment..."

"This is not up for debate." Madame Usher stood, smoothing down her lace dress. "You are dismissed from the academy and my service. Pack your things and have them ready by the close of school on Friday. Harrison will drive you to meet your mother. Our business will be concluded."

I stood up. "This is ridiculous. Dorien refuses to do your dirty work any more, so you decide to drop me? At least drop the pretense that you wanted me here in the first place. You had to control the last piece of Donovan de Winter's legacy because you can't handle the fact that he's dead because of you—"

"Don't you speak his name in this house," Madame's eyes raged. "You have no right to claim his legacy. You are not fit to kiss his boots, let alone share his name. You are not his daughter. You cannot be – his light would shine through you like the sun. Instead, you are dulled by the stupidity and selfishness of that bitch wife of his."

"Selfish? My mother?" I wanted to laugh. And smash her face into the hearth. Either option could win at this point. "Donovan de Winter put his career before his family. He didn't think about us once when he was out living it up on tour with money he borrowed *from the mob*. He's wearing concrete shoes at the bottom of a lake somewhere, and I couldn't be happier."

"Get out." Madame Usher shot to her feet, tipping over the tea table in front of her chair. Cups and saucers shattered on the floor. She jabbed a finger at the door. She hadn't raised her voice, but her eyes were murderous.

"With pleasure." I stood and moved toward the door, taking my time about it, letting her know that I wasn't afraid of her. "I'll be glad to be rid of this place."

I slammed the door behind me, enjoying the way the antiques stacked in the hallway rattled. From somewhere in the wall behind me I heard a groan, like someone keening over a broken heart. But it was just the house re-settling.

I sucked in a deep breath, then another, trying to formulate a plan. A figure stepped out of the storage room, where I'd picked up the Becker violin that had got me into such trouble with Madame Usher.

Heather.

"Good riddance to bad trash," Heather twirled a strand of honey-blonde hair around her finger, making no secret of the fact she'd been listening in. "Count yourself lucky that you're walking out of here alive. I had different plans for you, but sounder voices prevailed."

"Stay classy, Heather." I grinned at her to show her I didn't care, but her words rattled me. *Did she just threaten my life? I don't want to leave the Muses alone with her.*

Heather stepped forward, and I noticed she held a violin in her hands. It wasn't her usual instrument, but the infamous Becker. Something about seeing it in her hands triggered a blip in my mind – a memory that I couldn't quite grasp. Heather lifted the Becker to her chin and played a funeral dirge. "You may be free of Manderley, trash, but I'd watch your back if I were you. The Temple will find you under whichever rock you crawl beneath. They don't appreciate having their plans interrupted. They'll make sure you pay."

Titus

"She can't do this," I growled to Ivan. We crouched around the corner near the Blue Room, with our backs pressed up against the wall. There was a crack in the paneling here where a draft sliced through, and it meant we could hear most of what was said inside. It also made the hairs on the back of my neck stand up, but whether that was from the cold air or Madame Usher's chilling words, I couldn't tell. "She can't send Faye away."

"Of course she can," Dorien muttered, from his own crouched position a little further down the wall. "We can't stop her."

I stood up, my fingers curling into fists. I'd never been a violent person, but at that moment, I wanted to knock Dorien's stupid, smug head off.

"Madame Usher is kicking Faye out of Manderley." I could barely get the words out through my rage. "She'll be gone by Friday."

"Isn't this what you wanted all along?" Ivan's eyes flashed as he swung around to confront Dorien. "Isn't this what the whole year has been about? You and Heather would convince Faye she's being haunted so she runs as far from Manderley as she can get."

Dorien squeezed his eyes shut. "I only went along with it because I thought she'd be safer far from Manderley."

"That's not what you said to us. You wanted to scare and intimidate her into leaving, instead of admitting to her the truth." Fuck, I hated him. "You might've been friends as kids, but if you thought that would work, you don't know Faye de Winter at all."

"Yeah, well, maybe I was fucking lying to myself," Dorien snapped. "But it was never about me. I never wanted any of this. You know what Madame Usher has over me."

"She has something over all of us," Ivan shot back. "We didn't use that as an excuse to drug Faye and dump her in the woods."

"You're right." Dorien turned his face away. "I should have talked to you both. I should have gone to the FBI earlier, when Rochester first contacted me. I shouldn't have pushed Ivan and Elena onto a train in Prague. I failed everyone, especially Faye and Jacob. Heather had me by the balls. She threatened to take guardianship of Jacob, and I... I get tunnel vision when it comes to him. I didn't see a way out."

"How would Heather even do that, though?" I demanded. "She's not related to Jacob."

"Simple. Usher gets her lapdog Walpole to put me away for assault. Heather swoops in as a 'concerned friend of the family,' and since my parents are bonkers and we don't have any other family who'd take him, she'll end up with custody. She knows I won't leave him, so I'm bound to her forever." Dorien laughed bitterly. "That's how this will go down as soon as they hear the FBI is involved, but believe it or not, I think it's the lesser of two evils. I think Father Aaron is gearing up for some Jonestown-level bullshit, and I want Jacob far away from him."

"Maybe it's for the best." I slumped against the wall, wishing I had some weed to take the edge off this blow. I *wanted* to hate Dorien, but we'd been friends for so long that I understood his fucked-up logic. I'd do anything for my brother, too. The real evil supervillain here was Madame Usher, and playing us off each other was part of her plot. "If Faye leaves Manderley, at least she's no longer in danger from Madame Usher. I've got money in the bank, I'll help her find a place, pay her mother's medical bills. My parents adore her – I bet they'd even let her stay with us—"

Dorien shook his head. "Faye's mother was poisoned outside of these walls, and someone broke into the hospital to write 'leave' on her face. I don't believe she's safe *anywhere*."

I buried my face in my hands.

Sound the fucktrumpets, as Faye would say.

"Faye needs us more than ever," Dorien said. "And she needs us united. I know I've been a fucking little shit, and you're both completely justified in punching me in the nuts and never speaking to me again, but will you do this with me? Will you help me bring down Manderley Academy?"

I slid my hands away and stared up at Dorien. He held out his hand to me, palm facing up. His mouth – which usually formed a self-satisfied smirk – turned up at one end into a nervous half-smile. Our history etched across his features. Broken Muse had been one of a kind. We'd tasted true power from the stage – we captured the stars in our music and played beautiful melodies that told of terrible things. We spoke a language that transcended speech – the literature of the heart. Together, we conjured the more enduring and elusive form of magic. Yet all along, one woman wielded an even greater power over us, and she was using that power to destroy the one thing we all loved.

Fuck that. I wouldn't let our ruined friendship with Dorien stand in the way of protecting Faye. Ivan looked to me for guidance – he'd do whatever I agreed, although I noticed he'd shifted his foot back, as if preparing to knee Dorien in the nuts. As tempting as that was...

I reached up and accepted Dorien's hand. "Count us in. Madame Usher will never hurt Faye again."

FAYE

Titus and Ivan wanted to spend the final night with me, but it felt wrong somehow. I'd come to Manderley alone, and I needed to spend my last night in that attic room – the same room Clare Fairbanks lived her final days – alone.

Only I wasn't completely alone. The mournful, haunting music wafted through the wall between my bedroom and the storage room. The tune had become such a fixture of my life here that I didn't find it threatening any longer, although I still wish I knew where it came from. I no longer believed it was Heather – she would have quit long ago when I failed to react to it. The music felt as though contained some vital clue meant for my ears only – a message that I hadn't figured out how to decode.

It bugged the hell out of me that I'd never got to the bottom of Manderley's secrets, but I wasn't done yet. I had my mother to care for now, and I'd have to get a job or seven to have a hope in hell of keeping her alive. But I still had the Muses. I would still dig into Manderley's secrets. I would solve this mystery.

I will get justice for my mom. I will save Broken Muse from the prison of their secrets.

I stayed in bed as long as I dared. Fuck going downstairs to make breakfast. I wouldn't find Titus in the kitchen, his delicious fingers moving over my hips while I bent to get something from the fridge. There would be no Ivan peering at me from across the table, those icicle eyes exposing my darkest urges. I would no longer pass Dorien in the halls and catch a whiff of his hypnotic scent – cinnamon and frankincense, dappled with sweet violets – that assaulted my senses with the weight of our history.

I showered for the last time in the tiny bathroom, pulling my hair back into a messy bun. I pulled on a pair of jeans and a red V-neck I knew made my tits look amazing. I wrapped my black trench coat around my shoulders, balled up Madame Usher's itchy wool dress, and tossed it into the trash, stomping it down.

I picked up a picture of Mom and me, the one I'd found in my old photo album and had framed. I debated throwing it out the window, watching the glass smash in all directions across the cobbles of the kitchen garden. But no, Madame Usher would only force Ivan or Elena out there to pick up the glass. No matter what I did, she still owned them.

But she no longer owned me.

I tucked the picture on top of the *Grimm's Fairy Tales* book – the only memory of my father I wanted to keep. I threw my duffel over my shoulder, picked up my violin case, and shuffled down the narrow attic steps.

Manderley stood silent – no sounds of utensils scraping and tinkling glasses from the dining room, no ghostly notes from behind the closed doors of the practice room. The grandfather clock in the entrance hall counted down to my expulsion.

My fingers gripped the balustrade as I descended the staircase. Slowly, they came into view. Everyone in the house had gathered to see me off. Nine pairs of eyes watched me – some glowed in triumph (Heather) while others glistened with tears (Elena) or drew heavy with resignation (Harrison). I couldn't bear to look at Titus or Ivan or Dorien – I wouldn't give Madame Usher the pleasure of seeing me burst into tears.

At the bottom of the stairs, Master Radcliffe greeted me with a kiss on both cheeks. "Goodbye, Faye. It has been a pleasure to teach you. I hope you will continue with your musical career."

I didn't say anything. I knew if I opened my mouth, I would call him all sorts of words I'd regret. I didn't want to hate him – he'd been kind to me, and I knew that he was trapped here like the rest of them, weighed down by some terrible secret Gizella Usher waved over his head – his own personal sword of Damocles. I knew that Elena was his ticket out from Madame Usher's thumb. But then Elena's engagement ring caught the light, and I remembered that look of dread on her face back in Romania. I recoiled from his touch.

Elena stepped forward now, pressing her face into my neck. "I love you," she whispered.

"I love you, too," I whispered back, burying my face in her hair.

Heather smirked at me. She hung off Dorien's arm, although he shrunk from her like she smelled bad. Over the last day as I packed up my things, I noticed him talking quietly with Ivan and Titus. I asked Titus if they were friends again, and he said, "as much as anyone can be friends with a selfish prick like Dorien." Which I guess meant yes. I hated how happy that made me feel. The three of them needed to look out for each other while I wasn't here.

Beside Heather, Aroha had her hands shoved in the pockets of a black hoodie. She stepped forward, touching her nose to mine as her father had done. "Kia Kaha, Faye. That means, 'stand strong.'"

I nodded again. I sensed that part of Aroha was trying to reach out. She saw in me something of herself. I'd forgiven worse things from Dorien. But now I'd never get the chance to connect with her.

Next, it was Titus and Ivan. They enveloped me into their arms, embracing me together, their cheeks pressed against mine, their fingers stroking my skin, reminding me that they would always fight for me. That we were a family. That I had their love to shine a light in the darkness.

"I'll find a way to save you," I whispered to Ivan.

"Maybe it will be us who save you," he whispered back.

Dorien flung off Heather's arm and surged toward me. "Sprite," he said.

That one word was enough. The tears I promised myself I wouldn't cry itched at the corners of my eyes. I swallowed hard and turned away from him. I heard the sharp intake of his breath and knew I'd hurt him, but I couldn't touch him or look at him right now. Dorien would undo me completely, as only he could.

"This farewell is needlessly drawn out." Madame sniffed. "Harrison, you should be going. I'd hate for you to be driving the treacherous roads in the dark."

Harrison reached down to pick up my bag. As he did, an antique vase sailed over the railing from the second floor and smacked into his skull.

He fell to his knees, clutching the side of his head and moaning. The vase bounced into the corner of the side table and exploded into a million pieces. Heather and Aroha leaped back as shards of pottery flew across their feet.

"Harrison!" I ran to his side, trying to inspect the wound. Blood spurted between his fingers, and he let out a low moan. "Someone call an ambulance."

"Don't be ridiculous. He's just—" But Madame's words cut off when a second vase hurtled through the air. She dived for cover just as the vase hit the wall behind her, where her head had been only a moment before.

What the fuck?

A picture came next. The corner of the gilt frame slammed into the floor, scratching a deep gash along the polished floorboards before it toppled over, sending more fragments of glass skittering across the floor. Heather screamed as a bust of Beethoven flew at her head. She dived away, sheltering under the stairs as torn scorebook pages fluttered down in a tsunami of confetti and destruction.

Objects, paintings, and a bronze horse figurine flew from the balcony above, raining down on us. Ivan grabbed my hand and dragged me under the stairs. The others crowded in around us, pressing hard against the wall. Still, the destruction continued as precious antiques smashed on top of each other, grinding their remains into the floorboards.

The fury of it stilled me – every time a new object dented the walls or smashed against the floor, Madame Usher shuddered a little, as though her body had been assaulted.

But who's doing it?

We were all here – all of us. Heather huddled beside me, her skin pale with fear. Aroha stood stoic at the back of the group, her hood pulled up around her dark hair. Dorien tried to creep closer to me, but Ivan and Titus placed themselves between us. Elena had her arms around a trembling Harrison while Master

Radcliffe tried to speak words of hollow comfort. Madame Usher's sickly floral perfume choked us all as she stared at the carnage with pursed lips.

Who's throwing this shit over the stairs? Who could—

It stopped.

The house fell silent and still, the only movement the swirl of plaster dust rising from the debris in the hall.

The grandfather clock ticked.

My heart roared in my ears.

"What the *fuck?*" Heather screeched.

Dorien was the first to step out into the open. He picked up the edge of a frame and held up the corner. It was the portrait of the Ushers from Madame's office. The glass had shattered and the frame bent, and a shard of wood from a serving tray pierced the canvas right over Victor's head.

"You have to call the police," Heather cried. "Harrison, get your gun. There's an intruder in the house. You have to—"

"That will not be necessary." Madame glared at the pile of broken antiques, her chest heaving. "Harrison, fetch the broom."

"But Madame, he needs a hospital—"

"Not another word from any of you." Madame turned her face to the ceiling, and there was something in her features I'd never seen before. Something that on any other human might've been read as fear. "The ghost of Manderley has spoken. Faye shall stay with us."

FAYE

"What in the fucktrumpets is going on?"

I paced across Ivan and Elena's floor, wringing my hands. My boot kicked a pile of Elena's makeup, sending tubes of lipstick skittering across the floor.

I waited for a response, but none came. Ivan's lips remained in a tight line, while Titus sat at the window, sucking on a joint like it would divine the answers. Elena sat at her dressing table, applying lipstick to her perfect lips. Her hand trembled so much she was starting to look like the world's hottest jittery fairy clown.

"That... was impossible." Ivan crossed the room and sat beside his sister, wrapping his arms around her shoulders. She rested her head on his shoulder.

"We were all under the stairs," Elena whimpered. "Who could have been throwing those things?"

Titus glared at Dorien. "Fess up. How did you do it?"

"I didn't." Dorien threw his hands in the air, his eyes fixing on mine. "I swear, Sprite. I had nothing to do—"

"So when you declared that Faye needs us and that we should bring down Manderley, that was just you waving your dick around?"

I glanced between the three Muses. "You guys are... friends again?"

"Not friends," Ivan muttered.

"We agreed that if we're going to stop Madame Usher from hurting anyone else, we're better off working together," Titus added, taking another long drag. "Which is why I'm surprised Dorien immediately went off and pulled this stunt without telling us—"

"I had nothing to do with it—"

"I believe you." I swallowed. "I'm going to tell you guys something, and you're going to think I'm crazy, but..."

Titus leaned forward, the joint dangling from his lips. "Go ahead."

"Right before Dorien and Heather drugged me, I saw Clare. She was standing in front of the door to my room. I could see right through her."

"Could it have been a trick of the light, like when you thought you saw her face on the stairs?" Titus sounded hopeful.

"See…" I wrung my hands. "I wonder if I actually *did* see her face there, too. I also saw her when I was walking back to Manderley and found the Usher mausoleum. I kept trying to convince myself it was a trick. That I was scared and cold. That I'd had too much of whatever Dorien used to knock me out. But today was no trick. And there have been other things – the music I hear at night, my father's book appearing in the Yellow Room. My violin being smashed. Dorien said he didn't do it and now… I think I believe him. And today…"

"Are you saying you think Clare's ghost is haunting Manderley, and she threw all that stuff to convince Madame to let you stay?"

"I don't know!" I threw up my hands. "I don't believe in ghosts. All I know is what I've seen and heard, and what we all saw today. Weird stuff has been happening ever since I came to Manderley, and it seems to be getting worse. It's as if… something has shifted. Madame Usher's power over this place is cracking, and through the cracks all this stuff is—what the hell are you doing?"

Dorien surged toward me, holding out his phone. "Read it."

Ivan's eyes narrowed at the screen. "What is it?"

Dorien jabbed his finger at the file's title. *Concerning the Fall of the House of Usher*. I had to crack a smile. Dorien could never resist a chance to be dramatic. He scrolled through lists and doodles and dates and images. "It's all my research on the strange things going on in this house, and on your mother's poisoning."

"What do you know about it?" I asked.

"When you told me about the tea, *In Cauda Venenum*, I started hunting around." Dorien zoomed in one of the photographs. "Clare and I found a case of old Victorian apothecary bottles in her room in the attic. That's where we got the syrup of ipecac I used to make you sick that first night. There was a notebook too, with observations about different drugs and their properties. There was a whole chapter on poisons, and another on birthing aids. The weird thing is, that book disappeared, along with several of the bottles. I thought Clare kept them, but now I'm not so sure. And I never put it together before you told me about the birth-wort, but what happened to your mother sounds *exactly* like Victor's symptoms leading up to his death."

"Holy fuck," Titus breathed. "You're right."

I narrowed my eyes. "What do you mean?"

Dorien scrolled down to a list he made. "Victor started to complain of stomach pains. He could hardly eat anything, and sometimes he'd double over during lessons. He was so weak that he couldn't climb the stairs to the private wing, so Madame Usher moved him to a suite of rooms on the ground floor. She brought herbalists from all over the world to the house. They gave him tinctures and teas to help him, and put him on strict diets Clare had to prepare. Every meal Madame

Usher would take the food from Clare and deliver it to Victor herself. We weren't allowed to see him, and she spent every moment she wasn't in lessons at his bedside, until one day, she emerged and told us he was dead."

"You think Madame Usher killed her husband?"

"There's only one way to find out. An autopsy was never performed, and no one suggested anything other than natural causes. But if your Dr. Nelson could test his tissues for traces of birthwort..." A smile tugged at the corner of Dorien's mouth. "What do you say, Sprite? Fancy a little grave-digging?"

Titus

After our meeting broke up, we all drifted our separate ways, too restless to commit ourselves to much. No one saw Madame Usher for the rest of the day, but we could hear shouting and objects smashing from within her private quarters. Twice, I stood in front of that locked door, debating the intelligence of breaking the door down under the pretense of seeing if she was okay, but both times I backed away.

"Do you think we should move you into one of our bedrooms?" I asked Faye. "Or one of us will sleep in the attic with you. I don't like the idea of you being alone at night if Clare's ghost is hanging around."

Faye shook her head. "If I really am being haunted by Clare, she's on my side. I feel safe with her. Besides, I kind of like it up there. It has personality, and it makes me feel like I'm the heroine in a gothic horror film. We all know the heroine is the only one who survives."

I couldn't argue with that logic.

Faye was right – something had shifted in Manderley. It was as if, with that display, the house had disgorged some kind of secret and it was now shrinking within itself. The high ceilings and gilded portraits that had always felt vaguely threatening to me now seemed smaller, almost homely. The shadows in the corners had dissipated. The grandness of the place had faded behind the cracked stone and peeling paint. It didn't hurt that many of the antiques were gone now, dashed to smithereens by our ghostly protector.

Perhaps because I grew up in New Orleans, where the living and the dead existed side-by-side, but I was more willing than anyone else to accept the idea that Clare was still with us. Dorien was having an emo moment about it, and Ivan was just... Ivan.

Faye pulled burgers and buns out of the freezer, and I made my mother's famous fried chicken and slaw. The five of us ate dinner around the kitchen table, warmed by the heat from the fire. Ivan brought in a couple of bottles of port from the Red Room cabinet and poured generous glasses for everyone but himself. No one stopped us.

I was admiring Faye wrapping her gorgeous lips around a huge piece of chicken when I sensed someone standing behind me. I turned to see Aroha leaning against the doorway. "Hey."

"Fuck off," Ivan growled.

Faye held up a hand before Ivan could say more. She swallowed her bite. "Would you like to join us?"

Aroha took a step forward, then seemed to think the better of it. "Don't you all hate me? I tried to burn your hand."

"Why don't you tell us why you did it, and then we'll decide if it's worthy of hate?" Faye said. "I'm interested."

Aroha shrugged. "It's the whole *place*, you know? You met my parents. They're so *desperate* for me to fit into this world, but I don't and I don't want to. None of you know what it feels like to walk into a room and be the only brown girl there. To know that your skin is seen, but you aren't. You all *fit* here. You make sense. I don't, and I thought I was okay with that. I'm proud of my history, my culture, but I also fucking miss home. I want to write and perform music, but I didn't realize how lonely that path would be."

"You want music on your terms," Faye said.

"Right." Aroha nodded. "And I know you're thinking, what did you expect, enrolling in a stuffy, upper-crust school like Manderley? Because I've come from a long line of warriors, but I'm fucking terrified of going on stage. I wanted to confront that. I thought if I could master Manderley, I could do *anything*. But I'm not mastering Manderley. I'm falling to pieces. And you know sometimes when you're falling into pieces, you want to drag others with you? That's me, guilty as charged. Faye looked like an easy target. I know you won't believe me, but right up until Ivan pulled me away, I didn't believe Heather was really going to burn your hand. I thought we were just giving you a fright. But then I saw her face when Titus stopped her, and I realized that bitch be crazy. I'd hitched my horse to the wrong cart."

Ivan met my eyes, unconvinced. I didn't want to trust Aroha either, but it wasn't up to me. Faye patted the seat beside her. "Try the chicken. It's delicious."

Aroha sat, gingerly, on the edge of the stool. "I tried to burn your hand."

"And I haven't fucking forgotten it," Faye said. "We're not friends. Yet. But everyone in this room has done fucked up shit they're not proud of, so you're allowed to sit with us. Titus, pour her a glass of port. We're celebrating. It's a new era of Manderley."

I watched Faye as she passed burgers around the room, her wild hair streaming down her back, her head tossed back as she laughed at something Aroha said. I saw again what she'd learned from her mother – to be big and bold and beautiful, but the biggest thing of all was her heart.

Across the room, my eyes met Dorien's, and I read his mind in those grey storms. If Faye could find it in herself to begin to forgive Aroha, then could she – *would* she – forgive him?

"You don't have to watch this," I grunted as I leaned my weight against the heavy stone lid, using the wall of the Usher mausoleum as leverage as I shoved the carved lid open a quarter of an inch.

I'd rarely visited the mausoleum. Dorien and I occasionally stumbled into the clearing when we took drunken walks in the forest, which wasn't often because that place was spooky. And filled with bugs. Honestly, we were indoor dudes. Ivan had explored more of the forest trails, but even he tended to steer clear of the mausoleum. We hadn't even come down here for Victor's internment. The place was creepy as fuck.

Faye twirled a lock of hair around her finger. "You assume because I'm a girl I can't stomach a little grave desecration? Step aside, Thibodeaux, I want a piece of the action."

I obeyed. Faye assumed my position, her back against the lid. She planted her feet on the edge of the step and pushed.

Absolutely nothing happened.

"Okay, fine." She slumped against the coffin, sweat glistening on her brow. "Maybe I'm more of a 'hold the flashlight while my boyfriends desecrate the grave' kind of girl."

Ivan handed her the flashlight. "Together?" I asked. He nodded. The two of us planted our hands against the lid and kicked off from the wall. A cloud of dust and dead leaves blew up around us as we scrambled for purchase. I strained, and Ivan growled, and we managed to shove the broken lid open a foot – wide enough for our purposes.

I bent down, knife and tweezers and baggies ready to collect tissue samples. Ivan grunted as he gave the lid a final shove. Faye leaned over and aimed the flashlight beam. A stale smell rushed out to meet me and—

"What the fuck?"

We peered into the tomb.

It was empty. Victor Usher was not inside.

FAYE

"Where the hell is his body?"

The four of us huddled together under the gazebo. Titus' arms fell around my shoulders, and from the way Dorien kept looking at him, I knew he was jealous as fuck. I wished that didn't affect me so much, but it did. I'd never had guys fight over me before, and it gave me a little thrill. At least, until Ivan's words echoed in my head. *We can't all be with you.* He'd been remote ever since we got back from Europe, never being in the same room alone with me. And it knew it was his way of trying to influence my choice. But I didn't want to choose. I wanted all three of them – even Dorien. I was a selfish bitch like that.

"Maybe Madame Usher had it removed precisely so that no one could gather evidence from it," Dorien suggested.

My face fell in my hands. "It doesn't matter. That was our shot at proving she poisoned both Victor and my mother, and it's gone."

"Not necessarily." Dorien dug out his phone. "I might be able to do something."

"What now?" I wasn't sure the world was ready for another of Dorien's cunning plans.

"My contact in the FBI is looking into Madame Usher for us. I know it's a risk because Madame bought off the police. That's why I didn't tell him about the poisoning."

"You should have talked to us before you told him *anything*," Ivan growled. "These are our lives you're messing with. What if he's on her payroll? What if he goes straight to her?"

"He hasn't done that yet, or we'd know about it. But you're right. I shouldn't have done it. I played all our cards because I trust this guy. I think he'll come through for us, but in case he doesn't, we've got Faye's creepy stalker friend – the one who so generously emptied my bank account for a worthy cause."

"Cory?" I hadn't expected his name to come up. "What could he do?"

"He could dig into Madame Usher's accounts, maybe cause a little chaos." Dorien's eyes were a storm of mischief. "It's your decision, Faye. If you want to do it, make the call. Otherwise, we'll keep digging around."

I remembered the horrible, crawling feeling of Creepy Cory's eyes on me as I moved around the bar where we used to work. The way he'd stand too close or deliberately brush up against my breasts as we moved around each other to pour drinks. He made me feel unsafe, and I was already in the crosshairs. Having him help me with Dorien's revenge invited him back into my life. He'd blown up my Facebook with messages and pictures before I blocked him again. I didn't particularly want to open that wound.

But then I remembered huddling under the stairs as vases and painting rained down from above. I remembered the strange message scrawled in the walls of the pantry. THE WALLS ARE TALKING. And I knew that something was going on in this house that neither the FBI nor Creepy Cory could help us with.

This was always about Clare, and we've been too distracted to see it. It's about getting justice for her. And that starts with figuring out how she died.

I nodded. "If Creepy Cory can cut off some of her resources, it might help us stay one step ahead of her. But that's not all we're going to do. We need to solve Clare Fairbanks' murder."

FAYE

As we trudged up the path back toward school, I felt the prickle in my neck of someone watching me. I raised my head to my room, certain now that face I'd seen in the glass all those weeks ago had been Clare. But she wasn't there.

Instead, Heather stood at the window of the Yellow Room. The light danced off her honey-blonde hair as she stared out at us.

A shiver ran down my spine. I knew that Clare's display today might have neutralized Madame Usher for a time, but Heather was still dangerous.

~

Madame Usher didn't emerge from her quarters for another week. The school term continued as though nothing had changed, although everything had.

Master Radcliffe assigned us essays on musical theory and continued our composition class and private lessons. Dorien and I worked on the piece I'd written, expanding it and building the tension, drawing out the third movement for a beautiful, haunting climax. I was starting to think that I could add instrument parts to it, that Titus and Ivan could have a place within the music, too.

Working with Dorien had me all twisted around. With every note he played and every smile he flashed, I drew a little closer to forgiving him. We reached for the same piece of scribbled score and his fingers brushed mine, sending a jolt of heat down my arm and setting the butterflies living in my stomach a-flutter.

Although we didn't speak aloud about what we'd seen and Madame Usher's decision to allow me to stay, everyone seemed to feel the ghostly attack marked the end of my servitude. Titus now helped me in the kitchen, while Ivan and Elena took charge of the cleaning duties, and we all pitched in carrying the wood for

Harrison and lighting the fires. Heather tossed a mountain of filthy laundry at me in the hallway, but when I refused to clean it and it remained in a stinking pile in the middle of the landing for three days, she relented and did it herself.

Manderley had entered a new normal, an uneasy truce. But we knew a reckoning was coming. We knew Madame Usher would find a way to reclaim the power she felt she'd lost. And from the way Heather stalked the halls, glaring at each and every one of us, we knew we had made another powerful enemy.

~

All seven students gathered around the Bösendorfer grand in the ballroom for Radcliffe's composition class. As I closed my eyes to focus on his use of *appoggiatura*, I was jerked from reverie by a series of heard thumps and bangs upstairs. My eyes flew open as everyone else turned their gaze to the ceiling. I figured it was Madame Usher raging in her quarters again, but when I heard furniture being pushed across the room above, I realized someone was up there.

"That's my room." Titus stood up, his eyes wide. "Someone's in my room."

Master Radcliffe glanced up from the piano. Something flickered across his eyes – a nervous energy. *He knows what's going on.* "I'm sure it's nothing to be concerned about. It's probably Harrison stacking wood for the fires. Let us turn to the study of *glissando*—"

Titus' eyes met mine, and when I saw the pain swimming there, it hit me. His guitar was in his room. If someone found it and told his parents, something bad would happen.

I didn't know why Titus had to hide his love for metal music, but I'd protect his right to do so with my life. I rose from my chair, setting down my violin. "I think we ought to see what's going on."

Titus wasn't waiting around. He flung aside his cello and rushed to the door, twisting the handle in both directions. "It's locked."

"I'm sure it's just stuck." Master Radcliffe looked pained. "Please, Mr. Thibodeaux, return to your seat and we'll sort it out at the end of the lesson—"

Titus pounded on the door with his fists. "Let us out!"

Wind howled outside, rattling the windowpanes. Tree branches scraped against the glass, their long fingers reaching toward us. Upstairs, more furniture scraped and objects thudded against the floor. A shiver ran down my spine as the wind whispered to me, *Fayeeee...*

Dorien and Ivan were on their feet in a flash. Heather remained in her seat, the hint of a smile playing across her lips. I didn't like that smile. Not at all.

Titus upended a chair, hefting it over his shoulders like it weighed nothing. He was just about to run at the door when it fell open.

Madame Usher stood in the doorway in all her glory – her dark hair pulled back into a stern bun, her black lace dress swirling around her ankles, her stick rapping against the wood floor. A terrifyingly satisfied smile tugged at the corners of her mouth.

"Greetings, students." She swept into the room, ignoring the raised chair in Titus' hands and the expressions of confusion and anger on our faces. "I'm pleased to see you continuing your lessons during my leave of absence. Unfortunately, it has come to my attention that certain rules of this fine school are being flouted, and that is unacceptable to me. My husband Victor left this house and his endowment in my trust to carry on his legacy and reputation, and I will not have that reputation laid to waste. Therefore, I have taken the opportunity to search your rooms, and my, my, what a horde I have uncovered."

"You can't go into our rooms without permission." Aroha surged toward Madame, fists raised. Titus held her back, although he glared at Madame Usher with such a murderous expression I barely recognized my gentle giant.

Ivan and Elena exchanged a glance, an entire conversation passing between their eyes. I knew Aroha was probably worried about her drugs, but I wondered if Elena still kept a supply here.

"This is *my* house, and I'm perfectly within my rights to go where I wish and seize property that brings the name of Manderley into disrepute." Madame Usher snapped her fingers.

Harrison stepped into the room, his shoulders sagging. He held a large case, which he dropped on the rug and unlatched, swinging open the lid to reveal a gleaming guitar.

Titus' flying V.

I stepped toward Titus, reaching out to touch his hand. He was gone to me. He dropped his grip on Aroha, his whole body sagging.

But Harrison wasn't done. On top of the case, he dropped an armload of other items. I recognized Elena's makeup cases – the bright lipsticks and eye shadows she loved spilling from the plastic boxes. Stacks of old books, their pages opening to reveal poetry and scores scribbled in Dorien's distinctive hand. Pill bottles and metal Altoids cases and baggies filled with white powder. "What are you doing with those?" Aroha surged forward. "They're my prescriptions. I *need* them."

Madame Usher thrust a bottle into her face. "This is *weakness*. In my day, a musician who couldn't go on stage would be a poor musician playing alone in a prison cell. You will learn to stand on your own two feet, or you don't deserve your place at this school."

As Harrison tipped more of Aroha's drugs and Elena's sexy clothing onto the pile, I noticed the corner of a leather-bound book sticking out, the words in gold lettering shooting a jolt of pain through me.

Grimm's Fairy Tales.

That's mine. I noticed other items that belonged to me, too – my crimson dress, the jewelry box given to me on the night of the party, the photograph of me and Mom. I reached for the spine of my book, but Harrison pushed my arm away.

"There's no point, my girl," he said, sadly.

"You don't understand. That's my father's book—"

SMACK.

One moment my fingers grazed the corner of the book. The next, I was on my back on the floor, my vision reeling. Dorien stood over me, offering me a hand. I reached up to accept it, and *then* the pain arced across my skull, and I fell back, pressing my fingers into my forehead in a vain attempt to stop my brain leaking out.

Madame had hit me with her stick.

Dorien advanced on her, fists raised. "You hurt Faye. You—"

"I'd rethink the path you're on, Dorien Valencourt," she whispered. "I'd hate to have to call my friend Commissioner Walpole and inform him that you hurt a defenceless old woman. In a room with all these witnesses, I doubt even your parents' money and influence would save you. Do your parents still have money, I wonder, or have they given it all to their vegetable cult?"

Dorien's skin reddened. I thought he would explode. But he stood, impotent, his hands clenching and unclenching. A slow smile spread across Madame Usher's face. She was enjoying her revenge.

"Your parents will be informed of these transgressions," Madame Usher said. "I'm well within my rights to remove you all from this school, but I will give you one final chance. I blame myself – I've allowed you to become too comfortable here, too complacent. I've let you believe that the privileges of this house are given freely, and not earned. That stops today."

"What do you mean?" Aroha demanded.

"I have supplied you with many pleasures and concessions to make your stay here comfortable. Harrison will be removing them all today – the Egyptian cotton sheets, the snacks and fancy foods, the designer clothing, free access to the internet and telephone. None of this is required to provide education. The greatest art is created under oppression, and you with your silk robes and iPhones can't conceive of the true sacrifices one must make for art. I am your teacher, and it is my job to help you on this path. I will do it by whatever means necessary."

Behind her, Heather beamed. I couldn't help but notice nothing on Harrison's pile belonged to her.

Madame Usher turned to leave. The wind howled my name. She turned, slowly, her face carved in stone, her eyes flicking to each one of us before fixing on me.

"You'd all better fall in line," she hissed. "Or I will see each and every one of you ruined. People who dig up secrets end up at the bottom of stairs."

FAYE

e watched from the window in the Yellow Room as Madame Usher ordered Harrison to stack Titus' guitar case and all the other confiscated items in the center of the snow-covered lawn. On top of this, he carried down all the luxury furniture and other items from the students' rooms. I recognized the inlaid desk from Ivan and Elena's room, sections of a wooden wardrobe that had been next to Aroha's window, Titus' hookah pipe, and stacks and stacks of crimson silk shirts and combat boots I knew belonged to Dorien. Harrison piled it high – a great edifice of power and indulgence. On Madame's orders, he struck a match and held it to the pile.

Beside me, Elena gasped and buried her face in Ivan's chest. I wanted to turn away, but I couldn't. The flames caught surprisingly quickly. Fingers of orange light wrapped around the legs of tea-tables and tore into billowing silk curtains. They curled the edges of Titus' music magazines and shot out sparks as Dorien's clothes went up in smoke.

Tears streamed down my face as the pages of my father's book curled into black ash, caught on the breeze to scatter across the snow-dusted lawn – a flutter of ash and bone and wasted dreams. The stories of my childhood – of fairy castles and violent witches – given back to the air and the forest by the wickedest witch of them all.

In the corner of the window, Ivan held Elena in his arms, the pair of them cheek-to-cheek as they watched what few possessions they owned go up in smoke. I turned to Titus, to offer him what comfort I could, but he wasn't there. The door to the Yellow Room swung with an ominous *creeeeeak*. Dorien turned at the sound, and realization passed across his stricken features. I took off toward the kitchen, Dorien at my heels.

As I flung open the backdoor, the heat slammed into me. A wall of orange flame plumed into the sky, licking dangerously close to the tree line. Smoke and ash rolled over the house, casting an apocalyptic haze over Manderley. I coughed into my sleeve as I surged forward, heading toward the Titus' shaped lump in the snow ahead of me.

Behind me, Dorien's breath stuttered.

Titus had fallen to his knees on the snow. His cornrows fanned around his face, the beads clicking together as the mountain breeze stirred through the flames. His eyes glowed as black coals – reflecting the firelight that stole his passion.

I fell to my knees beside him, wrapping my hands around his shoulders. The gesture felt so hollow, so pointless. Flames licked the edges of his guitar case, melting the plastic and rubber into dribbling, eldritch shapes. I wanted to tell Titus that he didn't have to watch, that it was only a guitar, that he would have another. But I did not believe any of it. There was something much deeper going on with him. The fire wasn't just burning his possessions – it consumed a part of his soul.

"It's over," he whispered.

"It's not over," I whispered back. "We have to be stronger than her."

Titus shook his head. He dug his mobile phone from his pocket and pushed play. I had to hold it right against my ear to hear the voicemail message over the roar of the fire.

"Titus," Delphine's voice came through, her usual sultry tone scarred with pain. "Madame Usher has just called to inform us what she found in your room. How could you hurt us like this? After everything we've done for you. Your father won't see you, not now, maybe not ever. And I... I don't know if I can, either."

Titus clicked off the phone. His mother's words hung in the air around us. I wanted to ask the questions that had nagged at me ever since I found Titus shredding that guitar out in the woodshed, but I couldn't find the strength to ask. Not when his heart was tearing apart in front of me.

It was Titus who decided to speak. "My older brother Micah died when I was five years old." His wide shoulders sagged, and he raised his chin to the sky as if the billowing smoke gathering over Manderley might offer salvation. "He was a lot like my dad – friendly, charming, the life and soul of any party. He'd walk into a room and instantly the whole place would feel lighter. He had that way with people, you know? Now that I've met your mother, I know you understand."

I nodded. Titus tipped his head back, his cornrows a dark waterfall streaming over his shoulders.

"Micah played the cello like an angel – like the instrument was an extension of his personality. He was twelve years older than me, and he used to look after me while my parents were on tours. I adored him, and from the time I could walk I followed him everywhere. I copied his style, his mannerisms, his way of dressing, even his love of the cello. I just wanted to be him when I grew up. Micah loved all music – classical, jazz, but most of all, he loved metal. He had this old turntable in his room, and when my parents were away he'd pull out all the records he'd collected that they derided as 'filthy noise.' 'Listen to this, Titus,' he'd say, and he'd play some Black Sabbath riff over and over. 'This is what freedom sounds like.'

"It happened on his eighteenth birthday. He'd just been accepted to Juilliard, and my parents threw him a big party at home with all their music friends. He left at 6PM to go to a metal concert with some of his friends. I remember sitting on his bed while he pulled off his suit and threw on a black t-shirt with a picture of Lucifer dancing on a pile of skulls, and he laughed and kissed me on my head and said one day we'd go to a concert together."

Titus sucked in a breath. He must've got a lungful of smoky air, because he broke down into a barking cough. My eyes stung and my throat itched from the fire, but no way would I leave his side. I rubbed his back as he pushed out the words, his face streaked with tears. "We don't know exactly what happened, but there was a fight in the mosh-pit at the concert. Micah got trampled. By the time people noticed and security pulled him out of there, it was too late. He stopped breathing."

Shit.

Even though the heat roared all around us, ice seeped into my veins as I held Titus. I knew nothing I could say would repair the wounds today had opened. I could not even imagine the horror Titus and his parents had gone through, losing Micah like that.

A single tear rolled down Titus' cheek – a symbol of the tears he'd already cried, the pain he'd already endured. "My parents left his room exactly the way it was. I used to sneak in there when they were out and play his records. Listening to the music he loved made me feel closer to him. I was so young when he died that I never really got to know him, but I felt like maybe he was listening to Metallica or Iron Maiden up in heaven. It was this thing we could share even though he was gone.

"His absence sucked all the life out of our house. In public, my parents were the happy, bubbly people you met at the party. But it's like they deflate as soon as they're alone – all the color drains from their faces and they're just these grey ghosts. I didn't want to be like them; I didn't want to be grey. I wanted to be full of life and passion, like Micah. When I was twelve, I asked for an electric guitar. I'd never seen Dad so angry. They forbid me from ever mentioning it. They burned all Micah's records and t-shirts and posters, locked his room and forbade me from going in there. I've hidden my music from them ever since."

It explained so much. The battle that raged inside Titus to be both the boy that held his family together and to express himself in the way that felt real and true to him. And Madame Usher had just ripped the heart right out of that boy's chest.

Another hand fell on my shoulder. Dorien leaned down, kneeling in the grass in his designer jeans. He wrapped his arms around both of us and pressed his cheek against Titus. "I swear to you, brother. You will be free."

I wanted to believe him. But as the fire raged in front of us, the heat boring into my skin, I felt so small.

I turned back to the house, picking out figures in the windows of Manderley through the haze of smoke. Ivan and Elena stood at the Yellow Room window, clinging to each other. Aroha leaned out her bedroom window, smoking a cigarette and watching us. Heather stood at *her* window – the only student room Madame Usher hadn't ransacked – with the smirk of a cat that got *all* the cream.

And in the private wing of the house, from a window high in one of the hexagonal turrets, Madame Usher watched us with cruel eyes, her lips frozen in a thin line.

I raised my hand from Dorien's shoulder, and I flipped her the bird.

Dorien laughed, holding me tighter. His laughter mingled with the fire's crackle, becoming the roar of our rebellion. I held two Broken Muses as the ashes of Titus' beloved guitar rained down on us, sticking to tear-stained skin and turning us grey with our sorrow.

No matter what Madame Usher did to us, she would never make us grey on the inside. Not where it counted.

∼

As the fire died down, I picked through the ashes, searching for a page from my book I could keep, or the the ruby necklace I'd been given by a ghostly admirer the night of the party. I found a charred piece of the jewelry box lid, but no necklace inside. The fire wouldn't be hot enough to destroy the necklace, and I felt certain Madame had taken it.

Dorien managed to convince Titus to return inside. Ivan and Elena met us in the kitchen. Ivan looped his arm under Titus' other shoulder and the two of them half-guided, half-dragged him up the stairs to their rooms.

I wanted to go to him, but Dorien said he and Ivan needed to speak to Titus alone first, so I stayed in the kitchen. The door swung open and Harrison appeared, his face ashen, a pile of wood in his arms.

"How could you do that?" I whispered, my hands balled into fists.

Harrison's face fell. I felt awful. I didn't want to hate him. He stacked the wood beside the stove with a stiff back. "I didn't have a choice," he said.

"There's always a choice, Harrison."

He shook his head. "Not when the Madame is concerned. You came to Manderley knowing her history with your father. You came because she found a way to remove your choice. That's what Manderley does – and before you know it, you're trapped forever."

"Harrison..." Tears itched the corners of my eyes. "What does she have on you—"

"She says I'm to tell you that lessons will commence tomorrow, but that she expects the ballroom and practice rooms to be pristine. She does not care who does the work, but the work must be done, or worse punishments will follow—"

"I'll help you."

Ivan's voice cut through Harrison's instructions. My ice prince stood in the doorway, those blue eyes watching Harrison with wariness. Wordlessly, I collected my mop and bucket and polishing cloths, and Ivan and I moved to the Blue Room, shutting and locking the door behind us.

"How is Titus?" I whispered.

"He is sad," was the reply.

"You and Elena don't seem so surprised about what happened today. Has she done this before?"

Ivan nodded. "When we were eleven years old, we started to ask questions about why we were kept here, why we couldn't see our parents or access the money we earned from our performances. She did not like that. She needed to remind us that we have nothing and we are nothing without her. She burned everything we brought with us from Romania – including the only photographs of our parents together."

"Ivan, I'm so sorry. I wish—"

"It does not matter. It is past." Ivan grabbed a silver candlestick from the side-board with such force, he left a scratch behind in the wood. "We should get to work. She will expect perfection."

I started to explain how to use the silver polish, but Ivan was already dabbing the liquid onto his cloth and rubbing the candlestick with the same deftness he used to play the violin. He looked away when he caught me staring. "Before Clare came to Manderley, Elena and I did most of the cleaning. Only when one of the students said something to their parents about 'child labor laws' did it occur to her to find a live-in maid."

I hated the way his shoulders slumped as he worked, how resigned he was to living out this wretched existence. I picked up a silver platter and started swiping at it vigorously, wishing it was Madame's cockpoodle head.

"What was Clare like? I want to hear about her from someone other than Dorien."

"We didn't speak to her much," Ivan said. "Madame Usher likes things to be a certain way, as you know. She wanted the help to remain the help. When Madame hired Clare, she made out as if it was this great gift for me and Elena because she loved us, because she wanted Elena to focus on her music. And so we did not question it, we never looked closer."

"Tell me what you do remember about her."

"She didn't say much, but every now and then I caught her pulling faces behind Madame Usher's back," Ivan said. "I think she was probably quite funny, like you. She was allowed to sit in on our lessons if she'd finished her daily duties, but Master Radcliffe didn't teach her privately. She would join me and Elena when we practiced sometimes – she played a passable Mozart, but her real talent was composition. When Dorien arrived at Manderley, Clare fell for him hard, and I remember her running around after him, practically falling at his feet. He lapped up her attention, because he's Dorien. He treated her the same as any of our groupies – when he was with her, she'd be the center of his world, but he didn't invite her to hang out with me and Titus. He doesn't let anyone into his heart...

not until you. But she wanted more. When their relationship soured in those final few months, Clare became a different person. She'd run out of the room when Madame entered, and she seemed to jump at every loud noise. She stopped coming to lessons, but sometimes I heard her playing in her bedroom late at night."

I was starting to build a picture of Clare in my head, and what I saw made my head spin. I saw a girl like me, trapped by her circumstances, caught up in a game with rules she didn't understand. The more I thought of it, the more I was certain Clare was the key to Manderley's secrets – that was why she appeared to me. She wanted to tell me something, and she trusted me of all the Manderley students to understand.

I needed more. I needed to give things a nudge. And Ivan had given me an idea.

After dinner, I declined to sit with the others, who were still reeling from the destruction of their possessions. I climbed up the stairs to my room, which I hadn't visited since the fire. I paused in the doorway to take in the carnage.

My drawers had been turned out, and all my clothes, bar my scratchy wool dress and a few spare pairs of underwear and stockings, had gone up in flames. My beautiful shimmering crimson recital dress was a pile of ash and broken memories. A lump rose in my throat as my eyes fell on the gap on my nightstand where the *Grimm's Fairy Tales* book sat only this morning, and the space on my bureau where the framed picture of Mom and me stood. But apart from that, I seemed to have got off lightly. Madame must've considered my meager possessions too modest to be concerned about.

Madame Usher thought she could silence us with intimidation. But her spider's web could not collect everything. The music in my heart and my fingertips belonged to me alone, and I could weave such magic with it. I could conjure ghosts and make beautiful men fall in love. I could even – if I played things right – bring her down.

I sat on the end of my bed and rested my violin to my chin. "Clare, I'm here if you want to talk."

I held my breath.

I listened.

Drip, drip, drip. The tap in my bathroom drummed a foolish beat.

This is ridiculous. My fingers twitched on the bow. *I don't believe in ghosts. And I certainly don't believe one will talk to me just because I—*

A lone, mournful note sang through the air.

I stared down at my violin, even though I knew I hadn't touched the strings. I remained frozen as the note ran out, swelling and building into a soft melody that echoed around my tiny room.

It was the same song I heard late at night. The song that I'd tried to blot from my memory, convinced it was one of the students torturing me.

Where's it coming from?

The answer was *everywhere.* The music rose around me, mournful and beautiful, sweeping and diving with a yearning trill. For the first time, I didn't just hear the notes, I heard the *voice* behind them – the story told without words, for music speaks in ways that letters never could.

Clare.

She's here.

The hairs on my neck and arms stood upright. My spine tingled, and the urge to flee the room itched in the soles of my feet. Instead, I raised my bow to the strings and played a simple harmony to accompany her.

My phrase reverberated through the small space, filling out the song to create a rounded *lacrimoso* as I entwined my story with Clare's. I paused, expecting the ghostly music to disappear, to be left feeling stupid for believing it was real.

Instead, the music continued, repeating the melody again, inviting me to continue. I stood, my neck bent beneath the low ceiling, and I closed my eyes as I played with Clare and *for* Clare. I did what she'd been asking all along – for someone to listen to her.

All we ever want is to be heard.

The ghost of Manderley and I played together. My fingers swept over the strings as I rose and fell, following where she led. And in our reverie, she gifted me with the one thing she had left in this world – her story, her truth. The one thing that could bring Madame Usher down.

 Faye

After I set down my violin somewhere around 2AM, I collapsed into bed and fell into a deep, restful sleep. No footsteps in the storage room nor phantom music disturbed me that night.

I woke with the alarm and went downstairs to prepare breakfast. Madame Usher held court from one end of the dining table while I set out stacks of pancakes, maple syrup, whipped cream, and other toppings. She stared at the food with disdain, but she could find no fault. I think she was hoping I'd serve stale cereal so she had an excuse for more carnage.

Heather kept up a steady stream of chatter with Madame and Master Radcliffe. No one else spoke. Even Master Radcliffe remained oddly silent, and he kept stealing glances across the table at Elena that made Ivan stab at his plate so hard he chipped the edge.

After breakfast, Ivan and Elena helped me clear the table, then we all joined Master Radcliffe and the others in the ballroom for composition. As soon as I entered the room, I became aware of a pair of beady eyes watching from the shadows of the velvet curtains. Madame Usher.

What's she doing here?

This can't be good.

Master Radcliffe stood behind the piano, clearing his throat repeatedly while throwing glances back at Madame. He looked like he didn't quite know what to say.

"Are we going to begin the lesson, Maestro?" Heather asked in her sickly sweet voice.

"Yes, well... um..." he scratched behind his ear. "Has anyone been working on a new piece? We can workshop it together."

An idea sparked. Heather beamed and moved to stand up, but I beat her to it.

"I've been playing with something." I held up my instrument, and Master Radcliffe nodded. I raised my bow.

I played the first phrase of Clare's song.

After all the nights of hearing it inside my room, inside my head, I knew the melody by heart. I played the story Clare couldn't speak, pouring all my fury and fire in building the haunting piece to its crashing, bittersweet conclusion.

It was as if I cast a spell in the room. Something living dropped out of the air. The temperature plummeted. A scent permeated the air – a fresh lilac smell, edged with the musty odor of a forgotten room and tainted with blood and betrayal. A memory, but not my own. *Clare's memory.*

I stood bone-still as I played, letting the music carry me, allowing me to view Madame Usher's face as I reached the final, pounding strike of the strings. I imagined this *staccatissimo* as the *thump thump thump* of Clare's body rolling down the stairs, followed by the stark silence as her flame was snuffed out.

I let the silence in the room hang, heavy as the drapes that shrouded the windows from the encroaching forest. I took my time to meet every pair of eyes in the room, to weigh their stunned reactions.

They all recognize this song.

In the corner, Madame Usher rose to her feet, her hands balled into fists. Her eyes bugged out of her head, the way they'd done the day I brought that Becker violin downstairs to play – the same violin Heather held tight in her hands.

Finally, my eyes fell on Dorien. I was so shocked by what I saw in him that my fingers slipped on the strings and a dull note rang out.

"Clare," Dorien choked out. But he wasn't looking at me. He was looking *past* me at an empty wall behind my head. I lowered my instrument and stepped toward him, but he spun on his heel and fled the room.

"How dare you claim that song belongs to you?" Madame Usher roared. She came at me, gliding across the floor as if she were forced by some unholy spirit. Her fingers raised to my throat, brushing my skin, digging into my flesh. "You don't have the talent, the *vision* to create music as beautiful as this."

Her fingers tightened, pressing the air from my lungs. I clawed at her, fighting for breath. Red welts appeared in my eyes, dancing over her face like warpaint. My chest heaved, and a burning radiated out from my lungs to consume my body.

I thrashed and bucked and lashed out at her, but nothing could move her steel hands from my throat.

The red welts swelled.

My ears screamed.

My stomach convulsed.

I am going to die.

Master Radcliffe cried out. The sound came from far away, as if I heard it underwater. Madame Usher's fingers loosened, and I stared through the pain with a kind of strange detachment as the curtains whipped against their rails. The heavy velvet billowed into the room, even though there was no breeze or draft in the air.

Ivan and Titus fell on Madame Usher, breaking her grip on me. I slammed into the floor, my skull roaring the pain, my chest heaving as I sucked in precious air.

Madame stumbled back, spinning, disoriented. Her foot hooked under the piano stool. Elena screamed as Madame went down. Her head smashed against the corner of the piano.

She flopped forward, her body limp.

A smudge of blood bloomed across the carpet beneath her temple.

She didn't move.

 FAYE

T he curtains dropped back in place, the invisible breeze no longer fluttering the material. The entire room felt eerily silent.

Silent as death.

"Madame." Heather rushed to her side. She glared up at me and Ivan. "If she's dead, you'll be next."

I grasped my throat, my fingers pressing at the scratches where Madame's nails dug into my skin. My head spun as I focused on that red stain on the carpet.

The song. This all happened because of Clare's song.

"She's not dead." Titus rolled her over. "She's still breathing. I think she's just knocked herself out. We need to move her to a couch and make her comfortable."

I bit my tongue at the idea of doing anything to make Madame Usher comfortable. "I need to go after Dorien."

Titus nodded. I darted from the room, checking in the practice rooms along the corridor. I bounded up the stairs two at a time, but he wasn't in his bedroom, or in my room. As I stood at the foot of my bed, chest heaving, trying to think where to search next, I caught the shape of a figure moving across the lawn below.

Dorien.

I raced back downstairs and out the kitchen door. "Dorien?" I called. No answer. I sprinted across the lawn, taking a wide berth around the burned circle in the center of the garden. He wasn't sitting beside the stream, or floating in it, and my heart lifted a little lighter when I saw the waters running clear. I continued down the path toward the gazebo, calling his name into the wilderness.

He was there, of course. He had his back to me, and he knelt on the rotting floor, his head bowed and a set of earbuds in his ears. He looked up at the trees, and the expression on his face was of such rapt torture that I couldn't bear it.

He didn't acknowledge me as I moved behind him. "Dorien." I planted both hands on his shoulders. "Talk to me. What happened back there?"

"Argh!" He whirled around. The anger on his face turned to despair when he saw me. I couldn't help but think back to when our roles were reversed. Dorien came to find me playing under the gazebo – a wild, angry song that I'd needed to purge the memory of him from my veins. Only that was impossible. A raw, primal hunger stretched between us – a cord of destiny that pulled taut, drawing us closer even as we threatened to destroy each other.

Judging by the look on Dorien's face, I'd most definitely won this round. I never believed Dorien Valencourt could be brought to his knees. But Clare's song had done it.

Dorien took a step toward me, trembling fingers raised. "Fuck, Sprite, what happened to your throat?"

"After you left, Madame attacked me." I touched one of the welts on my neck and felt a fresh flare of pain arc across my skull. "She tried to choke me, and Titus pushed her away, but she hit her head. She's alive, probably on account of that pact she made with the Devil, but she might have to go to the hospital."

Dorien stared through me. He made no movement or sound that he'd heard anything I said.

"I wanted to talk to you," I said. "About Clare."

Dorien tugged the earbuds from his ears, and before he clicked off his phone I caught a snatch of music. It was the same piece I'd just performed, the same haunting melody I'd played with the ghost in my room.

Dorien turned the screen of his phone toward me, showing me the title of the piece. "My Requiem – by Clare Fairbanks."

"Clare wrote that piece?"

Dorien nodded.

My stomach flipped. I couldn't think about Dorien like *that*. Not anymore. Too much darkness stood between us. Even though it seemed as if the universe was determined to throw us together, to make me let go of the anger that acted as a breakwater. He was a dark tide – alluring and dangerous – and I couldn't let down my defenses or I'd be swept away.

Dorien's eyes fluttered shut. His eyelashes tangled together. "I saw her."

"You saw Clare?"

"When you were playing. Her face appeared behind you. It looked... like she was smiling, but it was a cold smile."

I swallowed. "You saw Clare's ghost? Dorien, I need to—"

"She was there, and she's *dead*." Dorien buried his face in his hands. "She's come for me, because she knows I killed her."

DORIEN

As soon as the words fall from my mouth, I felt like a great weight had lifted from my shoulders – my spirit shrugging off its bonds.

Faye had been reaching out to me with those long, beautiful fingers. Her hand froze in midair, and those fierce eyes fixed on mine. Good. I'd sensed, ever since I gave her that ride to the hospital, something in Faye changing toward me. She was starting to think about forgiving me. I couldn't allow her to do that. And this would push her away once and for all.

I'd push her into the arms of my best friends – the two people who would love her as she deserved to be loved, as dark and hidden flowers are to be loved – with passion, with sacrifice, with a yearning that transcends the self. My love for Faye had consumed me utterly, and I couldn't allow it to consume her, too. I loved her enough to set her free of me.

"What do you mean, you killed her?" Faye's red lips pursed as she studied me carefully. "You said her death was an accident."

"No, no." I buried my face in my hands. "I drove her to do it. I made her crazy."

Faye folded her arms. "Dorien, I need you to stop being melodramatic and think very, *very* carefully about what you say next. Clare fell down the stairs. Did you push her?"

"I *killed* her."

"You were behind her. Your hands touched her skin. You *shoved* her."

"*No.*" The word slammed into me. I had done shitty things, so many awful things, so much that I was beyond redemption. But I never did that.

Faye sighed. She leaned against the rotting railing of the gazebo, gripping the pole with pale fingers. "You need to calm the fuck down and tell me *everything.*"

I sank onto the floor of the gazebo, my back against the rotting upright. Icy cold seeped through the seat of my trousers. If my ass got frostbite, it would be the least I deserved.

I buried my head in my hands. The weight of it all crushed me into the rotting wood. When my gaze dropped from Faye, Clare's dark eyes and grim smile haunted the inside of my eyelids.

I took a shuddering breath and began.

"Clare worked for Madame Usher for three years, since she was sixteen. She'd had a hard life – her mother died when she was young, and her father was a war vet who returned from Afghanistan with his head messed up. He drank, and he took drugs, and he became the evil that he'd gone to war to fight. Clare was put into foster care when she was ten. She lived with various families, each more awful than the last. Her last family pulled her out of school and sent her up here to work for Madame Usher, and Madame paid most of Clare's wages directly to them. Clare talked about running away a lot, especially at the end, but she had nothing of her own.

"Clare said that at first being at Manderley was a dream come true. She had a room to herself. There was no foster father sneaking into her bed at night. She cleaned and cooked and sat in on Radcliffe's lessons. When she turned eighteen, Madame Usher asked if she'd like to stay on at the house and keep her wages – she said that if Clare wanted, she would have Master Radcliffe teach her for a time in the afternoons. Clare was so happy to be able to steal a little bit of the joy of music we all took for granted."

"Was she talented?"

I closed my eyes as the memory of Clare's music rushed through my veins. "She was rough. Poorly trained. Perfectly mediocre. But she could compose. She wrote music that hummed in your veins long after the movement was over. In a lot of ways, you remind me of her."

"Tell me about when you met," Faye said. "Tell me everything. I need your secrets now, Dorien. Did you love her?"

The question shocked both of us. It hung in the air – a silent accusation. I lifted my head, and I fixed my eyes to Faye, and I hoped like hell Clare wasn't standing behind her, listening with ghostly ears. "She was a distraction, a warm body, a shoulder to rest my head on. Titus and Ivan were over listening to me wallow in my own bullshit, but to Clare, every word out of my mouth, every note I played, was genius. That's intoxicating. I cared for her. I enjoyed her company. But no, I didn't love her."

"Tell me about when she died."

"We'd been fighting. Clare was acting weird – one day she'd be happy and bubbly, the next day cross and angry. She'd be all over me, and then she wouldn't want me to touch her. She wasn't sleeping at night, said she kept hearing creaks and groans and weird footsteps. She said food kept disappearing from the kitchen, and objects would be moved around in her room, things not placed where she put them down. I thought it was just the other students playing tricks on her – no one much liked her, the weird maid who presumed to study alongside us. I tried to calm her at first, but then it got tiresome, and I started to ignore her. I'm not proud of myself, but you asked for the truth.

"And then, things got really weird. She was supposed to be a distraction from the hell that is my life. Clare wanted answers I couldn't give. She asked so many probing questions about my life, especially about my time studying with Madame Usher. She spoke to herself under her breath, asking questions and pausing as if she expected someone to answer. And sometimes I'd enter a room I thought was empty, only to have her leap out at me from some dark corner. I found her unsettling. So I broke things off with her. She wasn't happy about that. She cried, threw things. Madame Usher talked about sending her away, but Master Radcliffe stepped in and said she'd get over it."

"The day of her death, I opened the door to my room, and there she was, her hair wild, her eyes as wide as saucers. Her nightgown had been torn, and there was blood under her nails. She looked like she was on drugs, and she hissed all these strange things."

"Like what?" Faye leaned forward, her eyes wide.

"I don't remember, exactly. It just sounded like nonsense at the time. She kept saying, 'he touched me,' and I thought she was talking about me. I didn't want another fight, or to be blamed for something I didn't do. I shoved past her in the hall, but she kept coming after me. I reached the bottom of the stairs. I wasn't looking at her. She yelled, 'The ghost in the walls is real, and he's not happy. She's been lying to us all, and she'll burn for it, and you'll all burn with her.' Something like that. It sounded completely insane. Then she cut off into a scream, and there was this horrid *thump.* I turned around just as she slammed into the floor beside me. Her neck bent at this terrible angle. I felt for her pulse but—"

I turned away from Faye as the memory assailed me. Clare's body lying in my arms, her head bent a way no head should ever be bent, her glassy eyes staring up at me, her mouth open in a silent scream. I saw that face every time I closed my eyes, sometimes superimposed over my brother. I couldn't save Clare. I couldn't save Jacob. I was trapped in this cursed house because of my own selfishness, my own inability to control my passions.

Faye looked completely drained by everything I told her. She rested her cheek against the pole. "Her story is so sad. I wish you'd told me all of this earlier, that I'd known what happened in my room."

"But you don't know what happened in your room. All we have is Clare's crazy ramblings. How did you know that music?" I asked.

"I hear it at night," Faye said. "It's the song that's played over and over in my room. It's how I know Clare is haunting Manderley, haunting *me.*"

A chill ran down my spine as she spoke those words. I shook my head. "You're wrong. I'm the one she wants. You have to stay away from her. She'll use you to get to me, to punish me. Because of what I did to her. Because I wouldn't listen."

Faye fixed me with that intense stare. "We're listening now. We couldn't save Clare in this life, but she's giving us a clear message. Whatever she was afraid of, whatever she died over, it's still in this house. If what you said is true, it's not just Clare's ghost who's haunting this place."

Another shiver ran down my spine. "I can't believe we're out here talking about ghosts."

"Neither can I, but what did Sherlock Holmes say? When you've eliminated the impossible, whatever remains, however improbable, must be the truth. Clare can't be in the house because she's dead, and yet, you saw her and I saw her. And I knew her song."

I nodded. "And that's impossible because the only person she ever shared that piece with was me. Where does the music come from, *exactly?*"

Faye looked up toward Manderley. "I only hear it in my bedroom. It sort of... flows all around, but sometimes it seems to only come from the storage room, where you walked back and forth all night, keeping me awake."

"I swear, we never did that." I shook my head. All those things Faye thought we'd done to her in the beginning rushed at me. "I wonder how many of the weird things you experienced were actually Clare trying to hurt you?"

Faye shook her head. "I don't think she's malicious. I think she's been trying to warn me, to help me."

"But then why would she destroy your violin? Because I swear to you I didn't do that. I only moved it into the bathroom."

Faye touched her lips with the tip of her finger, and I could see the sparkle of an idea forming in her eyes. "I believe you. I just don't believe she had evil intentions toward me. I wish we could get into the storage room and see what's in there, but the only key to that room is on Madame's key loop. We could shimmy out my window and go in from the outside." Faye slapped her ass. "Well, probably not me, with this glorious rump. But maybe Ivan..."

"There's no need for any of us to risk falling to our deaths." I felt the corner of my mouth twist up at the possibility of answers. "I think it's time we beat Madame Usher at her own game."

FAYE

"Here it is." Dorien lifted an old case from beneath his bed.

Dorien and I stood under the gazebo for a long time after we decided what to do next. He held my hands in his to protect them from the cold, even though he was the one who'd run out wearing only his thin silk shirt. As he told Clare's story and confessed to the dark guilt that haunted him, it broke something open between us. I could feel the cords of our lives twining together again, even though the ends were all frayed and broken.

We talked over our plan, and we were all prepared to make it happen while Madame was at the hospital. But when we returned to the house we found her bandaged but awake, demanding we continue with the day's lessons. She glared at us all as she continued as if she'd never tried to strangle me, daring us to contradict her, to stand up to her. No one did.

So our plan had to wait for another day. Which was today.

"Wow, this is so cool." I lifted the lid on the trunk, admiring the rows of glass bottles and vials inside. There was even a tiny pair of tongs and some glass measuring cups and test tubes, all beautifully presented in the velvet-lined box. A Victorian apothecary set in perfect condition, saved from the fire because Dorien had hidden it in the back of the linen cupboard. Manderley might be full of secrets, but some of them were kind of cool. I pulled out one of the bottles and held it under the light to read the label. "What did you use to drug me the first day I was here?"

Dorien ran his finger along the row to find a small bottle. "This stuff called syrup of ipecac. Victorians used it to induce vomiting after a patient swallowed something poisonous. The chloroform is here."

I shook my head as he tried to hand me the bottle. I didn't want to be reminded of what he did on the night of the party. "How do you know how to use all this stuff?"

"Heather's mother is a professor of history. She wrote a book on medicine in the early nineteenth century." Dorien peered at the chloroform bottle in his hands. "Also, the internet."

"I don't think we want to use that one." I glared at the chloroform. "We need to hold that over her face, and I don't want her to suspect we did this. We just need something that will knock her out for a few hours."

"I have just the thing." Dorien held up a larger bottle. A black skull-and-cross-bones adorned the label. "Chloral. It was a common cure for insomnia during the Victorian period, until they discovered that prolonged use caused addiction and death. One dose of this and she'll be out like a light."

I stared down at the clearly marked skull-and-crossbones on the bottle. I thought of my mother, still in the hospital after poison had destroyed her body. Did I really want to be responsible for using a dangerous drug on someone else?

In Cauda Venenum. The poison is in the tail. My mother was in the hospital because of Madame Usher. She deserved a taste of her own medicine. I slipped the bottle into my purse. "Leave it to me."

~

Dorien no longer had access to Heather's book, and we no longer had our phones or the house internet, but we did have the Manderley library's many history books. I read everything I could about chloral and how it was often used to spike drinks for bars for nefarious purposes – a bartender at a Chicago saloon in the 1890s named Mickey Finn dropped the drug into drinks so he could rob his customers after they fell asleep, lending his name to both the practice and the drug.

Time to slip Madame Usher a little Mickey of our own.

Titus and I prepared the midday meal as usual, and I put Madame's on a tray to bring to her in her office, as she was still feeling weak and didn't want to walk to the dining room. I included a glass of her favorite port.

When I entered the room, I found her seated at a chair beside the fireplace, her eyes fixed on the space above the heath where her photograph used to hang. I set the tray down beside her and backed out of the room before she acknowledged me. I knew that if she saw my face she'd read my deception.

I paced in the hall, my heart racing as I counted down the minutes. When I checked on her again, she was sleeping deeply, her chest rising and falling in a steady rhythm. The port glass was empty. I leaned over her, waving my hands in front of her face, then poking her lightly in the belly. Nothing. She didn't stir.

Now or never. I slid my hand under her leather belt and unhooked the loop that held her ring of keys. It jangled as it fell into my hand.

I froze, my heart thundering.

Madame let out a gentle snore.

Phew. I palmed the keys and slipped from the room. Elena waited in the hallway, her hands at her throat. "I've locked the door to Heather's room."

"Good." I squeezed Elena's hand. "Stay here and keep an eye on Usher. Call out to us the moment she looks as though she's waking up."

Elena nodded. "Be careful."

I slipped my hand from hers and bolted for the stairs, Dorien and Titus only a few steps behind me. On the attic landing I fumbled for the ring of keys – it was nearly identical to the one she'd given me, so I knew that any keys that didn't match mine could work for the storage room.

I found a long, narrow key with a filigree decoration on the bow, but it didn't fit in the lock. Next was a much plainer key, which slotted in with a little jiggling. I held my breath as I turned the lock and the door pushed open.

Dorien leaned over me and shoved the door with his hand. "Let's see what's—"

"Not yet." An idea formed in my mind. "Back downstairs. Quickly. I think I know what this key unlocks."

The guys followed me along the hall past their bedrooms, to the door bearing the sign NO STUDENTS. The entrance to Madame Usher's private wing. I lifted the filigree key from the ring and tried it in the lock. It fell open, and the door swung inward.

My breath hitched as I saw the same drab reception room I'd seen last time, with the row of footsteps in the dust leading into the private chambers beyond. My feet itched to move forward, to explore the space, but I knew this wasn't the time. We couldn't risk Madame thinking anything was amiss when she came to, and I knew her well enough to know she'd notice if even a single speck of dust was out of place.

Titus held out his hand. "You stay here and search the storage room. I'll run to town and get a copy of the keys made."

I shook my head. "We should all go."

"Faye, Madame Usher is out cold. Even if we do get these copies made before she catches us, I don't know when you'll have another chance to use the keys. If I'm caught, my parents' renown might protect me from her wrath, but I can't say the same for anyone else." Titus slipped the ring into his pocket. "Go upstairs. Find your answers. You deserve that much."

I leaned forward to capture his lips in mine, using up a few of our precious moments to commit his kiss to memory, to sear the beauty of him into my soul. "Go like the wind," I whispered. Titus nodded before taking off for the stairs. A moment later, the front door slammed, and his car roared down the driveway.

"Hey." Heather banged on her door. "I'm trapped in here. Let me out."

I glanced at Dorien. I could see the cogs turning in his mind, the same way we used to read each other as kids. The connection that sparked between us flared to life, the end of our cords knotting and knitting together. Our wounds could never be repaired or stitched over as if like new, but we remake ourselves together.

I clambered up the attic stairs, my breath hitching at the sight of the storage room door still ajar. Darkness spilled from behind it. My chest tightened. That room had been the source of so much fear and anger and resentment. All those weeks I was certain the Muses were up there, using it as their personal playground to make me miserable. Now, finally, we had the chance to find answers.

Dorien extended his hand with a flourish. "Ladies first."

I stepped forward. My chest heaved as I drew a deep breath. The air stretched thin here, as if there wasn't enough to go around. As if something lurked in the darkness, devouring the oxygen.

My fingers grazed the rough wood.

I exhaled.

I pushed the door open.

It was stiff from the lack of use, and budged only an inch before it stuck in its frame – the wood swollen from the rising heat in the attic. I leaned into it with my shoulder and shoved hard.

The door scraped over the floor and banged open, revealing a narrow room shrouded in shadows. I reached for a light switch, but there wasn't one. They must have never installed electricity in this room, not intending it to be used as a bedroom. I dug my phone from my pocket and flicked on the flashlight app, casting the light across the floor in front of me.

My breath caught in my throat.

The entire floor was covered in a thick layer of dust, except for a narrow path across the floor, leading from a spot on the wall to the window. The edges of the path were ragged – this wasn't a piece of furniture being moved – but a trail of footprints. Someone walked this path so many times they'd kicked aside all the dust.

I hadn't imagined it. Someone had been in this room, walking around at night to scare me. But who? I believed now that it wasn't any of the Muses. And even though I believed in Clare's ghostly presence, I didn't think it was her, either. For one thing, she seemed to be mostly ethereal, and these footprints were evidence of a solid, corporeal being. For another, what she'd said to Dorien implied that she'd heard them, too. We were both victims of whoever was walking around in this room.

Dorien bent down in front of the window, moving aside boxes and broken chairs and tables, while I inspected the wall where the footprints stopped. It was lined with the same horizontal clapboard as my bedroom, with no adornment. I studied the wood, poking and prodding in search of a secret door. My fingers grazed over a knot in the wood, and I exclaimed in surprise as one of my fingers slipped through the center of the knot.

It was a hole. I pushed my finger through, feeling a rush of cool air from the space between the walls. I withdrew my finger and pressed my eye up to the hole, not expecting to see anything but darkness.

The hole looked straight through the wall into my bedroom.

"Fucking dickweasel," I growled. Dorien said something, but the blood boiled so loud in my ears I didn't hear him.

Ghosts don't fucking need peepholes.

I ran back around to my room, scanning the walls. My eyes caught on the painting above my dresser – a woman in a flowing white dress playing the harp in a moonlit garden – one of those slightly melancholy Victorian fancies. I leaned in close – the center of one of the flowers behind the woman had been drilled out, leaving a small hole. In the gloom, I never would have noticed it.

I peered through to the storage room, my stomach churning with sick thoughts. A shadow fell over the hole. My heart stuttered, then I realized it was Dorien's eye. He'd found the peephole, too. He blinked. "This is creepy."

"Yup." I fingered the edge of the painting. The hole had been carefully drilled out, the edges filed flat so it couldn't be seen unless you were looking for it. I'd turned my room upside down looking for a secret passage the Muses could have used to make that face at my window, and I'd never seen it. "Why does a ghost need a peephole?"

"An excellent question."

I walked back through to the storage room. Suddenly, I felt dizzy, lightheaded. I couldn't believe I'd been living in that bedroom for months while someone was in here, spying on me. I slumped down on top of one of the boxes, watching Dorien as he shifted furniture and searched the contents.

Was it Madame Usher? She was the only one who had a key to this room. But somehow I just couldn't picture her stomping around in this stuffy room, getting all dusty as she peered through the peephole to watch me sleep and change and... fuck Dorien and Ivan. Gross.

No, Madame Usher always got others to do her dirty work. That meant someone in this house was up here, night after night. My thoughts flew to Master Radcliffe, who had come to Manderley with the explicit purpose of marrying Elena. But the gross pervert had never shown any interest in me.

"There must be a secret passage that connects this room to downstairs," I said. "I can't see how anyone would be sneaking up here and unlocking this door without me hearing them."

"I thought so, too," Dorien said, flicking through a stack of old paintings leaning on the wall beneath the window. "I've been looking around here, where the trail of footsteps end, but I can't see anything..."

His voice trailed off. He frowned as he bent to look closer at something. I heard the sound of paper tearing.

"Don't damage anything. We need the room to look exactly the same as when we entered it—"

"Um, Faye. I think you should see this."

Dorien lifted something from behind the stack of boxes. It was a large, flat rectangle covered with brown paper. One section flapped free, revealing the gilded corner of a painting. Dorien's mouth set into a firm line as he tugged at the tape holding the corners of the paper.

"This is the portrait that hung in the hallway," Dorien said. "I never looked too closely at them before, but I'm sure of it."

"She said she sent that portrait away for repairs." I knelt down in front of it as Dorien tore the paper away. "So why is it up here—"

I gasped as the last of the paper fell away, revealing a man with a mane of wild, dark hair, piercing green eyes that seemed to stare straight out of the canvas at me. He wore an expression of serene contemplation.

My hand flew to my mouth.

Sound the fucktrumpets.

It's my father.

Madame Usher had a portrait of my father hanging in her hallway. And she hadn't wanted me to see it.

And that wasn't even the most terrifying thing.

My father held an instrument against his chest. Not the violin he played when he was alive – a secondhand Fiorini my mother worked herself ragged to afford. My mother sold it to a collector in Strausberg and used the money to start De Winter PR. This violin he cradled in his arms with all the love one might reserve for one's first-born daughter.

Not just any violin.

A Becker.

A very *familiar* Becker.

It was the same violin I'd picked up from the music room, the one that made Madame Usher freak out. But that didn't make any sense.

My father is dead.

So how does this portrait exist?

FAYE

I rubbed my eyes, thinking that I could rub away the impossibility of it. But the image of my father still grinned back at me, holding an instrument he couldn't possibly have held. I tore my eyes from it to glare at Dorien. "How did you not think to tell me the missing picture was of my father?"

"Because I'm a selfish bastard who never notices the world around him?" Dorien's mouth twisted up into that half-grin, the one that never failed to drive me wild. "The walls down there are filled with stodgy portraits of famous musicians. I never even noticed one was missing until you pointed it out."

"You mean this portrait has been missing since you started at Manderley?"

"I think so. I can't say for certain, but I think I would have noticed your dad. But that violin..."

I held my hand over my heart. I was having trouble breathing. "I don't want to think about what this means, but we have to. We have to consider the fact that this portrait might have been made after my father disappeared."

Dorien bit his lip. "She could have had this created from memory, from photographs and shit."

I shook my head. "No way. Look at the face. Look at the quality of the brushwork. This is not the kind of art you make from photographs. It's *living*. That's Donovan fucking de Winter. How did no one notice this?"

"Faye, this is crazy." Dorien glanced around the room. "We should get out of here. I don't know how long we'll have until she wakes up, and we need to make it look like we weren't here."

I glanced down at my feet. We'd both tried to remain on the trail, but when I'd seen the painting I'd stepped over the line, leaving fresh trails in the dust. Not to mention the boxes had been moved around, kicking up a cloud of dust that settled in the air, closing my lungs.

"I'll take care of it." Dorien wrapped the portrait up again and stashed it back behind the boxes. He spent a few minutes shuffling things back into place, closing lids and shutting drawers. Then he scooped a handful of dust into his fingers. "Back out of the room."

I did so, being careful to stick to the trail. Dorien followed me, stepping his feet where he stood before to avoid making any further prints. He tossed the dust into my footprints, erasing the steps.

"It's not perfect, but you say this person is up here at night, so it's probably too dark to notice." He coughed. "Plus, when this dust settles again, hopefully that should help."

I hoped like hell. If Madame Usher and whoever she had up here knew we were onto them, everything we worked on today would be in vain.

Dorien's fingers stroked mine as he turned the lock from the inside and slammed the door shut. My fingers tingled from the ghost of his touch.

I peered up at him. "Dorien, I—"

Dorien's fingers stroked along my arm. His lips parted ever so slightly. In a flash, he'd narrowed the distance between us.

We hovered there, lingering in the moment, not daring to let our lips touch, yet knowing the moment was inevitable. The cord that bound us pulled taut, smashing our bodies together, crashing us into each other like the waves upon a rocky shore.

The kiss tore pieces of me away and dashed them against him, crumbling my defenses to dust and tossing me all about until I didn't know which way was up or down. Dorien stole all the oxygen in the room, pressing against my lungs until all I tasted, all I breathed, was him. All the emotion I'd been stamping down since I saw that portrait of my father welled to the surface.

This is a bad idea.

This is the worst idea.

And yet, it felt like it was the only possible conclusion.

Dorien tore his lips from mine, staggering back until he pressed himself against the clapboard, bending his tall frame to the slope of the roof. His chest heaved.

I glared at him.

He shook his head. "Don't, Faye. Don't make the mistake of forgiving me. I'm the reason Clare is dead, and I won't be the reason you die, too."

"You can't blame yourself for Clare," I said, my lips tingling with want. "Lots of other shit, yes. But not that. It's this house. It does something to people."

"Yes, it makes you believe I'm somehow redeemable." Dorien tore his eyes from mine. He looked terrified as he half-ran, half-skidded down the steep steps.

I pressed my hand to my chest, willing my racing heart to calm again. Suddenly, I couldn't bear to remain in the attic, thinking about that peephole in my wall and Dorien's lips hot against mine. I shimmied down the stairs after him. Ivan met us on the first-floor landing.

"What happened up there?" he demanded. "You were gone a long time."

The heat of Dorien's kiss burned against my lips. Ivan's ice eyes bore into mine, and I knew he read the flush in my cheeks and the quickening of my pulse. He grunted and turned away, his shoulders hunching as he strode off down the hallway. I remembered what he'd said to me back in Prague. *I wanted to fight for you, but now I see that loving you means I have to give you up.*

I knew that was what he was doing, and it made me want to grab him by the scruff of his neck and kiss him until he agreed to be mine.

But I didn't have time to sort out my bullshit feelings. We raced back to Madame's office, past Heather's door rattling on its jamb. "I can hear you out there," she yelled. "I demand you open this door, right now."

Elena met us at the doorway, her perfect lips quivering with worry. "I was just about to call you. She stirred a few moments ago, but she seems to still be asleep."

I glanced at my watch. Titus had been gone for a little over an hour. He needed at least another hour. I glanced at the empty port glass. Had I given her enough? The books weren't exactly replete with detailed information about how to knock someone out with Victorian insomnia medicine.

I sat in the chair opposite Madame Usher, watching her face as her chest rose and fell. She seemed so serene – it was hard to believe she was such an evil spider. The ticking of the grandfather clock echoed through the house, punctuated by Heather's cries.

"We should have given Heather some of that stuff," Dorien mused.

"Next time," Elena promised.

Ivan wouldn't look at me.

I couldn't sit still any longer. I was desperate to search Madame's private chambers, but we couldn't get in there without the key, and I'd given that to Titus. We had to save that for another day. But there was one room where I did have access.

"Dorien, search her desk drawers," I said. "Look for any evidence we might be able to use against her."

"Don't disturb anything," Elena cried.

"Relax," Dorien opened a second drawer. "I know what I'm doing."

Not wanting to question why he'd claim to be an expert at snooping into people's private affairs, I removed my own keyring and went out into the hall. I opened the door to the storage room. The rows of dusty instruments watched me in silent vigil. There was always something about seeing musical instruments displayed in neat rows like terracotta warriors that gave me the creeps, as if they were waiting for the ghosts of their former owners to return.

My gaze fell to the Becker I'd picked up all those weeks ago. It was definitely the same one in my father's portrait. Heather must've returned it to this spot. My heart thudded in my chest as I picked it up. The temperature in the room dropped, and the air around me hummed with tension. I ran my hands down the body, searching for... what? I didn't know. For some sign my father had played this. For some occult symbol or portrait of his ghost.

I turned the violin over. An inscription stood out from the dark wood – I'd been in such a hurry last time that I hadn't noticed it. I held the violin beneath the one small window, focusing the light on the tiny words.

My heart flew to my throat.

A cold shiver ran down my spine.

"To my beloved Donovan. May we make beautiful music forevermore. Your Gizella."

Underneath was a date.

From nine years ago.

One year *after* my father disappeared.

Sound the fucktrumpets, this is my father's violin.

Given to him by Madame Usher.

But that's not possible. Because he's dead.

The instrument fell from my fingers as the room grew frigid. Out of the corner of my eye, I saw something move in the shadows. My racing heart pressed against my ribcage, desperate to escape.

What is this?

What's going on here?

"Wh-wh-who's there?" I choked out, my body frozen in fear.

"Faaaaye..."

My name hissed into the icy air. A cold breeze ruffled the sleeves of my shirt.

Creeeeeak.

Someone's here.

I swallowed and spun around to face whatever horror awaited me, just as the breeze stopped and the temperature returned to normal.

There was nothing. I expected to see Clare's creepy face with her gaping mouth, or something much, much worse. But there was just a rack of cellos covered in dust hung on a dark-paneled wall.

Get a grip, Faye. You're freaking yourself out.

I stared at the violin on the floor. I had every reason to be freaked out. But there had to be a logical explanation for why this violin and the portrait seemed to imply my father had been with Madame Usher after he disappeared.

What that explanation could be, I couldn't fathom. But it had to exist. Or... or... I was going mad.

I picked up the Becker and turned it over again. Thankfully, I hadn't scratched it when I dropped it. My hands trembled as I fixed it back into its stand. Wild thoughts swirled in my head.

Madame Usher bought that violin for him.

Madame Usher knows what happened to my father.

I returned to the office in a daze. Elena and Dorien tried to engage me in conversation, but I didn't hear a word. Ivan just watched me with those penetrating eyes, and I knew he read the truth – I'd seen something that had freaked me out. But I couldn't find the words to explain. Not right now. I needed to focus on getting the keys back to Madame Usher, or I'd go completely mad.

Just as I was starting to panic, Titus rushed in, pressing the ring of keys back into my hand. "I broke every traffic law that exists, but I got the copies. Now we have access to those rooms whenever we need it. Did you find anything of interest in the storage room?"

I nodded. I didn't trust myself to speak. Dorien swiped the copied keys Titus held out. "*Interesting* is not the right word. We'll explain later."

Titus' large hands circled my shoulders. "Faye, something's wrong. You look white as a sheet. Did—"

"Hurry," Elena called out. "I think she's waking up."

I tore my eyes from Titus and ran across the room. Madame Usher stirred, her hand falling across her face as she moaned. *Fuck.*

I leaned over her, trying to touch her as little as possible as I lifted the tab in her belt and slid the keys back onto the loop. They clanged together, the sound like a gunshot. Madame Usher groaned again. I jerked my hand away, my heart pounding.

She jerked awake, lunging at me and grabbing my arm. Her skin felt clammy, like a wet fish. "What do you think you're doing in my office?"

"I—I—I was worried about you." I organized my face into a look of concern. "There was a phone call for you, and we couldn't find you anywhere. Then Elena found you asleep in here. I was just checking your pulse. You know, you're not as young as you used to be, and you can never be too careful—"

Madame leaned forward, rubbing her temples. "I... fell asleep? In the middle of the day?"

Titus stepped forward. "You did. Do you want one of us to help you to your quarters?"

Madame shoved his hand away. "No. I'll do it myself." She gripped the side of her desk, holding herself steady as she turned to glare at us. "I'd better not find out any of you had something to do with this."

I knew if I so much as glanced at any of the others, it would give the game away. Instead, I turned my gaze to the floor, giving her that meekness I knew she so desperately sought. I could guess the others followed my lead, because Madame said nothing else. She shuffled into the hallway. A moment later, the door to her private wing slammed shut.

Dorien rushed toward me, and I was too freaked out to protest as he swept me into his arms. I breathed in the scent of him, but not even the fragrance of my childhood, of the boy who was forever entwined with my love of music, could staunch the cold horror creeping through my veins.

There's a peephole in my room, and a painting of my father after he died.

His violin is sitting in the storage room.

What does it mean?

Now that I knew about the peephole, I didn't want to set foot in my attic room ever again. But I also couldn't alert Madame Usher – because I was certain she was behind whatever was going on – that I knew about it. Instead, I took to changing clothes in the bathroom or downstairs in the boy's rooms. Whenever I stepped over the threshold, the hairs on the back of my neck prickled. I felt eyes following me everywhere – not just in the attic, but all over the house.

I remembered Clare's message in the pantry. 'THE WALLS ARE TALKING.' And I couldn't help but wonder if the peephole had been there when the room belonged to her. What might've been whispered through the wall by an unknown intruder to make her believe she was in danger?

FAYE

Madame Usher began to make plans for Elena's wedding. She set the date for the end of the semester and blew up the phone lines until she convinced some poor rental company to lug a pole tent all the way out to Manderley. She gave me and Elena the task of hand-lettering and stamping gold-rimmed invitations to mail out to a long list of contacts from all over the classical music world.

Elena's wedding party would double as the end-of-year function for Manderley, where we students could show off our repertoire to a room filled with potential employers and contacts. It would also be where the winner of the Manderley Prize would be announced.

I had a distinct feeling she didn't expect some of us to survive until then.

"We will find a way to stop this." I slammed Madame Usher's seal into a blob of wax. Globs of wax splattered across the antique table, and I knew I'd have to chip them off later, but I was too pissed off to care.

"Please, Faye, do not bother. Many people live in loveless marriages," Elena said. "It is not pretty, but it is life. Think of your own parents."

"Are you sure my parents are the shining example you want to use here?" I kept nudging Elena about it, but she would shut down the conversation to talk about floral arrangements or the dress she was having made by a Romanian designer.

Meanwhile, I'd tentatively allowed Dorien back into our circle. I still hadn't forgiven him, but I couldn't pretend I didn't still have feelings for him. After I'd endured all I could of Elena's wedding plans, he invited me to walk with him down to the gazebo.

Snowflakes dusted my nose as he slipped his hand in mine, and my heart skipped. The ghost of his kiss lingered on my lips, and an electric tension buzzed in the air around us as our feet crunched over the snow. The cord that bound us tugged at my chest, and I knew it was only a matter of time until I'd forgiven him completely.

It was too damn hard to resist those storm-darkened eyes and that cocky-ass grin, especially since I'd been dreaming of him since I was a kid.

As we approached the gazebo, I could see it was already occupied. Titus knelt on the rotting wood, his huge shoulders hunched, the tips of his braids dragging in the snow. He looked completely broken.

My heart shattered, all the promise of Dorien's lips on mine sucked from the air. Because no matter how much I worried about what the future would hold, I couldn't choose between the Muses. I loved three of them equally – I loved Dorien's passion, Ivan's protectiveness, and Titus' kindness. And right now, Titus needed me.

I dropped Dorien's hand and made to run to Titus, but Dorien held me back. "Don't, Sprite. He needs to be alone. If you go over there now he'll be so worried about how you feel that he won't be able to open up."

I sagged into Dorien's arms, my gaze never leaving Titus' slumped form. "You're right. But I can't do nothing. I'm guessing he still hasn't spoken to his parents?"

"No. And it's his birthday next weekend. Amos and Delphine were planning to spend a week in the city, stay over at school to watch him perform, and take him out to shows. They were going to take us, too." Dorien shook his head. "I'm guessing it won't be happening now."

How can they do this to him? Do they think they're the only ones who feel the loss of Micah? I knew how deeply their words cut Titus, who only ever tried to please them. Hell, he'd denied something primal about himself to try and fit in the box they wanted to throw him in.

My heart hurt not going to him, but I knew Dorien was right. Titus couldn't give his pain to me in this way – he needed to bleed it out through music. And only one kind of music would do the trick. I placed my hand over Dorien's. "I want to do something special for Titus." An idea formed in my head. "I don't want to worry Ivan about it – he's got Elena's wedding on his mind. I can see it twisting him around himself. Will you help me?"

"What do you have in mind?"

I grinned. "Something wild. Trust me, it has Dorien Valencourt written all over it."

~

On the morning of Titus' birthday, Dorien snuck out of Manderley early and drove away to make the final arrangements. I made Titus his favorite breakfast – blueberry pancakes with stacks of bacon and maple syrup – but he pushed the food around without eating it. I didn't like to see him so defeated. His smile was one of the only bright things that shone through the gloom of Manderley. To have it snuffed out because of Madame Usher's cruelty was more than I could take.

Titus retreated to his room after breakfast. Elena tried to speak to him through the door, but he blasted Wagner at top volume until she left in disgust. Luckily, I had keys to the student rooms, so I unlocked the door and barged in.

He sat on his windowsill, one leg dangling outside as he smoked a joint. "Go away," he growled.

I snapped my fingers. Dorien and Ivan emerged from the hallway behind me. Before Titus could react, they grabbed his arms and legs and tackled him out the door and down the stairs.

"What the fuck is going on?" Titus struggled as they dragged him to the twins' Eldorado.

"We have a surprise for you." Dorien opened the door and beckoned for Titus to have a seat. He slumped into the leather, his face a picture of misery.

"I don't like surprises," Titus growled. I knew he was thinking of his brother's death, and his guitar burned to ash.

"You'll like this one. But you can't know where we're going." I held up the blindfold they'd used on me. That got a grin out of Titus.

"Naughty Sprite." I loved that he'd started using Dorien's nickname for me. Titus allowed me to tie the blindfold. I climbed in the seat beside Dorien. We waved to Ivan and Elena, who decided to stay behind, and we took off.

Dorien drove the twins' car the way he drove his own – with a reckless disregard for traffic laws. I gripped the dashboard as we narrowly missed sideswiping a tree. Sibelius blasted from the stereo. Titus yelped as we hit a pothole and his head slammed into the roof.

Dorien pulled down a mountain track that was even more overgrown and treacherous than Manderley's driveway. After a time, the dense trees gave way to new plantings – forest blocks grown for timber. Dorien turned the car onto a dirt track. Titus gripped the handle as the car hurtled over the bumps.

His poor head must be one giant bruise by now. I hope our surprise makes up for it.

"Where the fuck are you taking me?" Titus sounded worried. In the front seat, Dorien and I grinned.

"Haven't you seen this horror film?" I asked. "The beautiful and talented musician lured into the woods by his supposed friends, only to be locked in the torture cabin and forced to saw off his own hand?"

"You're terrifying, Sprite."

I could see our destination up ahead, poking through the trees. Dorien pulled over on a patch of gravel, the wheel crunching over dead leaves. I helped Titus out of the car, positioned him facing the structure, and whipped off the blindfold.

"Um... so you weren't kidding about the torture shed?" Titus frowned at the crumbling brick and iron buildings in front of us. Piles of rusting machinery stood around it, and a tree snaked out a giant hole in the roof.

"It's a timber mill. Or rather, it *was* a timber mill. Now, it's a crumbling crapshack."

Titus looked confused. "Why have you brought me to a crumbling crapshack?"

I grinned wider. Dorien turned the key, and the trunk popped open. "Look inside and you'll have your answer."

Titus lifted the lid. "Holy shit." He staggered back, his eyes wide. "Holy fucking shit."

I loved his reaction as he took in the contents of the trunk. Nestled in a velvet-lined carrying case was a brand new electric guitar. Not just *any* electric guitar, but a St. Moritz SG replica 'Monkey' – the guitar Black Sabbath legend Toni Iommi used on *Paranoid, Master of Reality,* and *Vol. 4.*

"Why... why do you have this?" Titus cradled the neck of the instrument like it was a newborn baby.

"It's yours, man," Dorien said. "To replace the one that burned."

"How did you..."

"Creepy Cory did a little messing about in Madame Usher's accounts." I shoved my hands into the pocket of my hoodie to ward off the chill. "With all the payments going out for Elena's wedding, she won't even notice it's gone. Ivan said it was probably his and Elena's money anyway, and they wanted to get you an awesome present."

Titus' eyes glistened. "This is... it's incredible, but it's pointless. Madame Usher is searching my room regularly, and I can't go back to the woodshed again. She'll confiscate this the minute we return. You have to take it back."

"We're not taking it back, and you're not bringing this instrument anywhere near Manderley. There's an old root cellar out the back to service the miller who used to live on-site. It's waterproof, and we've added insulation. You can store it here. I've had the farmer set up a generator for you. Come on."

Dorien gestured for Titus to follow. I took his hand and squeezed it, staring into those depthless eyes. Titus' lips curled back, and the smile I'd been missing for weeks broke free of its cage. He had one of those smiles that took over his whole face. When Titus smiled, the whole world became brighter.

We picked our way through the fallen leaves and broken machinery and entered the main brick structure. Inside, the detritus of the old milling machines, conveyor belts, and railway lines stood as they'd been left. Dorien had come up here after classes yesterday and cleared away some of the debris, leaving a flat area large enough for Titus to run around in. Dorien jogged ahead of us and disappeared behind a hulking pile of machinery, emerging a moment later wheeling a Marshall amp stack.

"You need to hear yourself play, and so does the rest of the forest."

Titus dropped my hand and raced to Dorien, wrapping him in a crushing embrace. He looked giddy, like a kid on Christmas morning. In a few minutes, they had the guitar plugged in and amped up.

Titus stalked to the middle of the old mill. He strummed. A low purr reverberated from the amp. His grin could have lit the world.

He launched into a low, menacing riff. The music pounded through the space, reaching into every corner, punching deep into my chest. Titus used the riff as a theme, circling it back and playing with the shape of it, carving out meaning with each repetition. He angled the neck, bringing it close to his face as his fingers danced over the strings, tearing out a punishing solo.

Like Dorien, he loved to play fast, to build and build the tension of a piece until it exploded with sound. When he drew his bow across the cello, he could invoke an otherworldly dark power. But this was like nothing I'd ever heard before. The purr of the guitar pounded in my chest. I could *feel* the power of it coursing through my veins. My pulse quickened and hot need ached inside me – although that might've been the sight of my love descending into the chaos of the music, embracing the darkest depths of his heart.

Titus looked so completely natural with the guitar slung low and his tatted fingers curled around the strings, his long hair flying behind him as he banged his head along with the riff. All the tension that coiled inside him released in a wave of emotion. He *needed* this.

This is where he belongs.

I realized that what made Titus such a unique cellist was the tension of what he tried to force the instrument to do. He played cello like the lead guitarist in a metal band, all hair flying and unrelenting passion. He didn't fit in that world the way he fitted here.

He was wild, untamed, *demonic*. His music needed to be unleashed.

Watching Titus made my heart soar and the ache between my legs throb with desire. But after a time, my ears started to ring. I walked outside and sat on one of the old wooden wagons that brought logs to the mill from deeper in the forest. I swung my legs in the breeze and listened to the tendrils of sound blasting through the holes in the roof, and imagined Titus' tatted fingers caressing me the way he did that guitar—

Dorien flopped down beside me, interrupting my filthy thoughts. He pulled a pipe and bag of weed from his jacket and lit up. "I don't entirely understand the appeal of the music, but he's *good*."

I nodded. "He is. I just wish his parents would see it."

"They never will. To them, heavy metal – and even what we play in Broken Muse – will always be the evil music that stole Micah from them." Dorien sighed. "If I'd been their son, I wouldn't give a shit, but Titus cares too much about what they think. He wants to be their good little boy, but he's anything but good."

"I think he's *very* good." Despite myself, I licked my lip. I'd never been a big metal fan, but I had to admit, it was sexy as fuck. "What about you? You've gone a whole day without thinking about Dorien Valencourt. Does it feel good to do something nice for once?"

"I'll show you *nice*." Dorien leaned over me, planting his hands on either side of me. His lips hovered inches from mine, his body coiled with tension. My heart thudded against my chest. I knew he wanted to close that space between us, but after he'd lost control and given in to that kiss back at Manderley, he was waiting, holding back, allowing me to give permission.

And in that space he created, this *thing* danced between us. The cord of our destiny wound tighter and tighter, ready to snap. What I felt for Dorien made me reckless. But in this old forest with the lingering notes of Iron Maiden soaring out, I embraced that recklessness.

I rocked forward.

I pressed my lips to his.

The world exploded into flame. The touch of our lips sparked a fire that burned through my veins, turning my entire body into this molten puddle of desperate *wanting*. Dorien's lips drew mine open, and he plunged his tongue deep, tasting me like he'd been starved for weeks, which I guessed was true.

We were used to communicating without words. We poured our hearts into our compositions and spoke our deepest fears with the sweep of a tragic note. We spoke a language that transcended our egos, which was why we'd been drawn together after all these years to have a second chance at building something wicked and beautiful. I spoke to Dorien now, using the music of our bodies to tell him that I forgave him, that I was ready to open my heart to him. That I would give him everything, but I demanded everything in return.

Dorien's hands remained welded in place on either side of me. He groaned as he pushed himself against me, grinding his hard cock between my legs. His whole body shook with need as he walked the tightrope between what he wanted to do to me and what he thought I needed. *He still doesn't realize that all I need is him.* My feet came up of their own accord, hooking behind him, pulling him tighter against me.

"What if someone sees?" I whispered.

"Look around you." Dorien broke our kiss to flash me that shit-eating grin of his. "Who's going to see but those cows under the trees over there? They look like they could use a show."

Dorien's hands slid beneath my jacket, shoving up my shirt and bra to roll my nipples through his fingers. I gasped into his lips as my whole body shuddered with need. I couldn't wait. My fingers tugged at his fly. I would have him *now*.

"There are condoms in my bag," he growled.

"It's okay," I whispered. "I'm on the pill, and I had a clean test. So if you—"

"Oh, I've had my test results sitting in my drawer for weeks, waiting to show you." Dorien's eyes glinted. "Ever since that weekend when Ivan and I had you over the piano stool, also known as the happiest weekend of my life."

I leaned forward and kissed him, drawing out the truth of his words through his wanton mouth. We melted into each other, our twin flames burning together. Magic crackled in the frigid air. What we were doing here – it was more than sex. It felt like the start of something, the opening of a wound so the healing could begin.

"Faye de Winter, it's not my birthday." Dorien's hands trailed down my arms. He looked at me with none of that arrogance that had marked our relationship so far. Here was the boy I'd fallen in love with when I was just six years old – my dark prince, my destiny.

I was so lost in Dorien's eyes I didn't even notice when the music stopped. I leaned in to kiss him again. My lips brushed his before something large and hard forced its way between us. A curtain of dark braids cascaded over my face as Titus' immovable chest separated us.

"It's *my* birthday," Titus growled. The corner of his mouth twisted up, and I thought he was mad before I saw the twinkle in his eye. He planted his legs on either side of me, and I felt his cock press into my thigh. My body trembled, and I felt myself melt against his hard body. Like, I was no longer human, just a puddle of Faye goo.

A cool breeze whistled through the trees, carrying away all the bullshit we needed to discard. Out here, away from Manderley, we could be who we truly were. Titus was the heavy metal guitarist with the kind heart. Dorien was the broken bad boy who needed to forgive himself. And me? I was Faye de Winter, and I could take what I wanted. And I wanted *all* of Broken Muse – mind, body, and soul.

"That's right. It is." I sank to my knees in front of Titus, tugging open his fly. The leaves cushioned me on the hard ground as I pushed down his boxers and drew out his shaft, long and hard, the tip already wet for me. I reached out with my tongue to lick the tip, tasting the saltiness of him.

Titus sucked in a breath, his muscles knitting. Fuck, that was hot. I loved seeing him shed the misery that shrouded him at Manderley and surrender himself to me. Titus spent so much time caring about other people, I wanted him to feel kindness, attention, worship.

I sucked the tip of his cock into my mouth, circling my tongue around and pressing into the little dip. I curled my lips around my teeth and took him in, inch by glorious inch. He was so big I had no hope of fitting all of him in my mouth, so I gripped him with my hand, stroking in time with my mouth.

Titus' head rolled back, his cornrows flicking out like a halo. His whole body was a tight coil of tension, and had been since the day he lost his guitar. Playing metal again had started to loosen Madame Usher's strings, but I could do more. He *needed* this. He fisted my hair, pushing himself against my face, driving me deeper.

"Faye," Titus gasped out. My name sounded like honey on his lips.

I wanted to finish him, to taste him on my tongue, but Titus had other ideas. He lifted me to my feet and spun me around, pushing me against Dorien. Titus ran his hands down my sides, skimming over my curves, mapping my body with kisses and caresses while his stomach heaved with suppressed need. "I don't know what you think about this, Sprite, but Dorien and I could make you feel so good right now."

My heart skipped. The heat of their bodies burned away any inhibitions I had left "I think... I could like that. But I didn't exactly pack up supplies for..."

Dorien's grin widened as he reached into the picnic bag he packed and pulled out a package of lube. "I was never a boy scout, but I do believe in always being prepared."

I gave his chest a playful slap, which only made his devilish grin wider. "You're a cockweasel. All your sweet-talking, and you planned on getting lucky all along."

Titus swiped the lube from his hand. "It's my birthday."

"Of course." Dorien leaned back on the wagon, placing one hand lazily behind his head. The other beckoned me to climb up on him. "It's the birthday boy's choice. Come here, Sprite."

I shimmied out of my leggings and straddled him, rubbing myself against his cock. Dorien reached out and cupped my face, stroking my cheeks with his thumbs as he brought me closer for a kiss. He looked at me with such reverence. "You are so beautiful right now."

I *felt* beautiful, in a way I never had before. A power pulsed in my veins. Two guys wanted to put aside the bullshit that held them at arms' length from each other to make me feel good.

I'm a Muse Girl.

Even better – I'm the Muse Queen.

Dorien's cock jerked between my legs, reminding me that this moment wasn't made of sweetness, but of dark desire. I shimmied closer, straddling him and sinking down onto his cock. My body fluttered, like I was filled with butterflies with flame-tipped wings.

Dorien's grin widened as I ground my hips to drive him deeper. He felt so good, stretching me in all the right places. It felt different than last time, when I'd been so unsure of what we were to each other. Now, as I raised myself up on my knees and slammed down on him, the invisible cord that bound us wrapped tight against my skin. Dorien's grey eyes locked on mine, and I knew that I was his and he was mine, and nothing could break us.

Titus came up behind me, wrapping his huge, inked arm around my chest. His braids fell over my shoulder, and I felt the cord tugging at me, opening, relenting. I wasn't only bound to Dorien. I belonged to Titus, too, as he belonged to both of us.

"This will feel cold for a moment," Titus whispered. I heard the squirt, and then felt cold liquid running between my ass cheeks. Titus used his hand to spread the lube where he needed it. He pushed one finger inside my ass. It felt weird, but good weird. I had part of him inside me, part of Dorien inside me. I wanted this. I wanted *more*.

Titus used his finger to match Dorien's rhythm, and after a few strokes, it stopped feeling weird and started feeling really, *really* fucking good. I ground my pelvis against Dorien, rubbing my clit against him until my whole body hummed with need.

Titus pushed a second finger inside me, and I gasped against Dorien's lips.

"You're going to fucking love this, Sprite," he whispered. "But you have to surrender completely. Let Titus and I make you feel like the goddess you are."

I nodded. I was done fighting, done with pain and want and mistrust. I was ready to have Broken Muse, all of them, in every way imaginable. Titus wrapped his arms around me, and his strength coursed through my veins. I leaned forward to give him more room, pressing my chest against Dorien and feeling his heart thud against mine. Being between them like this, so close, so full of them, it felt like I had music in my *veins*.

Titus removed his fingers and pushed the head of his cock inside me. I gasped against the tightness of it. Dorien chuckled, his fingers digging into my hips. Titus' huge arm across my chest held me upright.

"Relax, Sprite. Let us take control."

I didn't have much choice. Between the two of them, I had no room to move, to force my will upon them. I had to surrender to them, to us. I gripped Dorien's shoulders and let my eyes flutter closed. Titus' breath rasped in my ear, and Dorien's heart thudded against my chest. I gave myself over to the new sensations assailing me as Titus pushed himself another inch inside me, his cock rubbing against Dorien's through the thin wall that separated them.

So full of them.

They started to move – a perfectly synchronized beat that had me lost. An orgasm slammed into me, and it didn't stop as they moved inside me, like one long cock threading its way through my body, undoing me completely. The cord no longer wrapped around us – now it was inside us.

My body tossed and shuddered on a swell of pleasure. I lost myself – my body became a pulsing ball of heat and light and peace as my Muses took care of me, giving me every dark deed and broken sin they'd held back. Stars danced in my eyes as their darkness became mine. And even though there was no music here – the only sound our breath, the birds, and the rustle of branches in the breeze, I fancied I could pluck notes from the air.

The song of us.

The scents that always accompany my music swirled around – Dorien's cinnamon and frankincense dappled with sweet violets, Titus' rose and myrrh and red musk, and other scented memories, too – the pine-fresh smell of the polished piano-stool in the ballroom where Dorien and Ivan first had me, the homely taste of delicious things baking in the house kitchen as Titus and I stood over the stove, the bitter smoke of the pyre that burned our possessions.

My eyes flew open just as Dorien came, his mouth twisting up in that adorable way it did, as if even in bliss he couldn't resist playing games. He sagged back against the wagon, remaining inside me as long as he could before he went completely limp.

Titus' hands closed around my thighs. He pushed up into me, and I saw the stars again as the two of us exploded together – a supernova of pain and hurt and healing.

"Happy birthday to me," Titus whispered as he sank back on the wagon. I pulled myself into the crook of his armpit, placing my head against his broad chest, listening to his heart thunder against his ribs. Like the rumble of the electric guitar, Titus' body purred with raw power and energy. No wonder he chose this music – it literally flowed in his veins.

Dorien fell into Titus' opposite arm, completely comfortable lying naked against his friend. He reached across to stroke my cheek, his breath kissing the air. "You belong to us, Sprite. We'll always love you. We'll always fight for you."

On the drive back, Titus couldn't sit still. After he pulled himself off me he'd headed back inside to shred for another two hours straight. I expected him to be sound asleep, but it was as though the music had ignited a flame inside him. His fingers drummed on the back of Dorien's seat until Dorien threatened to cut them off.

"Can we go back again?" he asked.

"Sure, man," Dorien turned into the mountain road that led to Manderley. "I'll drive you down next weekend when I take Faye to see her mother."

That's right. Mom was being discharged from the hospital next week, and she'd be moving into the hotel room in the city paid for by Natalie's company. Natalie said it was the least she could do, given everything Marguerite de Winter had done for her.

"We should bring Ivan next time," Dorien reached back to squeeze my knee. *I guess this means I'd forgiven him?* I wasn't sure. I think I'd forgiven him some time ago. Forgiveness wasn't a single act. It was a constant process of relearning how you felt about someone, and about yourself. And although I trusted Dorien again, I also trusted *myself* that if he betrayed me, I'd be able to survive it.

FAYE

Dorien swung the Eldorado beneath Manderley's high iron gates. He cursed as a figure dashed in front of the car, waving its arms.

"It's Harrison." I rolled down the window. "What's wrong?"

Harrison leaned in the window, his breath coming out in ragged gasps. "Get up to the house. Quickly now."

"What happened?"

Harrison shook his head. He slung the rifle over his shoulder and headed off into the woods.

Why the fuck does Harrison have his rifle?

Dorien, Titus, and I exchanged glances. What now? Madame Usher couldn't possibly know where we'd been all day. Was this about Ivan? Elena? Fuck, did Ivan finally give in to his brotherly instincts and do something to Master Radcliffe?

My heart leaped in my chest as we pulled up into the parking area. I could see other cars parked next to the fountain. I was out of the car and racing up the porch steps before Dorien even turned the engine off. Madame Usher met us in the hall. "Where have you been? I called the Dumfrees Institute and they said you had no recital today."

"Didn't we tell you that it got moved to next weekend?" Dorien lied as smooth as silk. "We thought we'd visit with Faye's mother since we were out."

"I know that's a lie. I called the hospital. You weren't there." Madame Usher grabbed my hair. Tears sprung in my eyes as she yanked my head so I was kneeling on the floor. My scalp screamed. "This is *your* doing. I know you're sticking your nose into your mother's investigation. You've been meddling in things you do not understand, digging up old ghosts. Well, you've gone too far this time."

"Let go of her." Dorien stepped forward. Titus was faster. He shoved Madame

Usher against the wall. She shrieked in fright as he held her head in his enormous hand, his muscles tight, his kind eyes murderous.

"You'll never touch Faye like that again," he growled. Madame Usher squirmed, trying to free herself. But Titus was the size of a freight train and angry as hell. "We're not playing your games any longer. I'll tell you what's going to happen now. We will—"

"Drop that woman right this minute, Mr. Thibodeaux, or you'll be in even more trouble."

I whirled around at the booming voice. Titus froze as Commissioner Walpole stepped out of the shadows, his arms folded. Behind him, the dim lighting revealed more figures – Dorien's and Heather's parents, and another robed figure with a bald head and eyes like an eagle – all-seeing, predatory. I remembered him from the one time I visited Dorien's house as a kid. Father Aaron, the cult leader.

My head spun. *What's going on here?*

The commissioner stepped toward Titus. "You heard me, young man. I can make a lot of trouble for you. And your parents."

Tension crackled in the air around us. Titus released his fist, his dark eyes unreadable. Madame Usher dropped to the floor, clutching her throat and coughing violently. Commissioner Walpole rushed to help her to her feet. I heard footsteps on the landing above, and Elena, Ivan, and Aroha poked their heads over the railing. Ivan's icicle eyes burned at the edges with questions. I shook my head, advising him to stay where he was.

"Really now, is this any way to begin a celebration?" When Eustace Danvers' smiled, the jeweled brooch at her throat bounced. She stepped toward Dorien and held her arms wide. "We came to offer our congratulations and welcome you into our family, son."

"What are you talking about?" Dorien demanded. He planted his feet wide, not backing away as she embraced him awkwardly, but standing his ground, as stiff and immovable as stone.

"Heather called us this morning to give us the good news." Mr. Danvers beamed, extending his hand. "I must say, we're extremely happy. We always believed you two would make a great match – the classical world is about to meet the new power couple."

I stared in shock as their words sank in. Heather told her parents Dorien proposed to her? But *why?* Dorien opened his mouth, but no sound came out. My dark prince looked completely floored.

Father Aaron stepped out from behind the Valencourts, his smile broad as he clapped Dorien on the shoulder. "Congratulations, Dorien. You've made a fine choice, as we knew you would. Your marriage will unite two powerful families and bring forth a new age of prosperity for the Temple."

Beside him, Dorien's mother stood, mute and remote. I glared at her, willing her to speak up, to protest this ridiculous marriage. First Elena marrying Radcliffe, and now Dorien had this marriage forced on him? What was this? We didn't live in Victorian England.

Dorien rallied, collecting the storms in his eyes and aiming all that fury at Father Aaron. He stepped forward, shaking his head. "I think Heather's made some mistake. I've been away from the house all day, so I couldn't possibly have—"

"But you did it this morning, silly boy," Madame Usher said, her voice syrupy sweet, like she was chiding Dorien for forgetting his lunchbox. The cloying floral scent of her perfume itched in my nose. "Under the gazebo, with the snow falling around you. It was quite the romantic proposal. Your social media is already blowing up with the news."

What? I yanked my phone from my pocket and scrolled to the Broken Muse Instagram page. The first photograph on the feed was a picture of a gazebo, looking hauntingly beautiful under a dusting of fresh snow. Heather stood beneath it wearing a black lace dress with flowing gothic sleeves, her honey hair perfectly styled and dappled with snowflakes, her face rapturous with love.

My heart stuttered as I peered closer. Dorien was wearing the same red shirt he'd worn when I'd followed him outside after I played Clare's piece. He hadn't taken one knee, but knelt on both knees, his head slightly bowed – the exact position he'd been in that day. Yes, and there was the corner of his phone sticking out of his pocket, and his suit looked a little odd across the breast, where someone had colored over the white cord of his earbuds.

Fuck. Someone took his picture when we were under the gazebo that day, and Photoshopped it into this of Heather. My finger hovered over the comments. The photograph already had twenty-three thousand likes. *This is out in the world now, even though it's not true.*

It's not true.

Footsteps clattered on the stairs as Ivan, Elena, and Aroha joined us. Ivan grabbed the phone from my hands. "This isn't what happened," he snarled. "You can't just fake an engagement and expect us to play along."

"Ivan, don't be so rude to our guests." Madame's voice was indulgent, like she was scolding a naughty puppy. That meant she still believed she had control of this situation, that this wasn't the end of the horrors we could expect.

Dorien looked from Madame Usher to Father Aaron. His shoulders hitched. I knew he was calculating his next move, weighing the cost. I saw the resolve in his eye, and I knew what he was going to say before he spoke. "Mr. and Mrs. Danvers, I'm so sorry, but I can't marry your daughter. There's something you need to know. Once, I viciously assaulted Aaron Varney. It was only because of Madame Usher's connections in the police that I wasn't charged. I should be in jail right now, and even if Commissioner Walpole doesn't take me in today, it won't be long before this comes out in the media. You don't want that stain on your family."

"I admire your sentimentality, Dorien," the commissioner said. "But you need to be truthful. There's no point covering up for Faye de Winter's crime."

Um, excuse me?

Father Aaron shook his head at Dorien as his eyes met mine. I felt like a field mouse caught in the talons of a hawk. "Yes, Dorien. You must never be afraid to raise your voice in truth. You are too young and talented to send yourself away for *her* crimes. Even though it's traumatic for me to remain in the room with that evil woman, I stand here as a member of your family to ensure you don't throw your life away."

"Dorien, listen to Father Aaron." It was the first time his mother spoke. Her voice sounded robotic, like she was speaking from a script. "This girl is dangerous. She's been stalking you ever since you rejected her, sneaking into our home, taking pictures of you. She hurt Father Aaron. She even got herself enrolled in this school because you were here. And now she wants you to go to jail for her? Don't let her manipulate you like this, not when you have a chance at a beautiful future with Heather."

I shook my head. "This is ridiculous. I've been nowhere near your house. I don't even know that man. This is complete horseshit—"

"We knew you'd double down on your lies; so delusional. So I kept these." Aaron held up a stack of photographs. Dorien ripped them from his hands and fanned them out for us all to see.

I gasped.

"These... these are fakes." But even as I saw them, I knew that my protests were pointless. The photographs were screenshots from a security camera feed, and they were expertly doctored – whoever had these made could pay for top-notch deep-fake. It really did look like my face twisted with rage as I slammed my fist into Aaron's face, straddling him to get a better angle as a pool of blood spread out beneath him.

"That's for a jury to decide." Commissioner Walpole held up a pair of hand-cuffs. "Which is where you'd be heading, if I had my way. Lucky for you, with such a large and important event to prepare for, Father Aaron is willing to overlook this attack."

Father Aaron inclined his head to Dorien. "As long as Dorien can continue with his wedding plan unmolested. I'd hate for *anyone* in the Valencourt family to experience the torture of separation from those they love."

The implication was clear. Dorien married Heather, or I went to prison, and something unspeakable happened to his brother, Jacob. Dorien's face twisted as understanding dawned on him. He made his decision in a split second, his jaw set with determination. I knew it was the wrong one. I surged forward, holding my hands out to Walpole so he could cuff me. "I'm confessing to a crime. You need to arrest me or—"

Ivan slapped my hands down just as Dorien said, "You're right. I've been a fool for not seeing things before. Of course my marriage to Heather will go ahead. Mr. and Mrs. Danvers, I'm excited to be part of your family."

"Oh, how wonderful." Mrs. Danvers clapped her hands together. "Dorien, Heather is waiting for you in your room. She's *so* looking forward to discussing your wedding plans."

FAYE

Dorien's features twisted with rage. His hands balled to fists at his sides, but as his gaze jumped from face to face, I saw the hopelessness settle into him.

If he refused to marry Heather, I would go to jail for his crime. And I knew that didn't even compare with what they could do to his brother. He was doing what he promised – protecting me. And in doing so he'd nailed shut his own coffin.

Dorien moved toward the staircase. I grabbed his arm, my nails digging into his flesh. "Call their bluff," I hissed. "Everything they have on me is fake, we both know that."

"Yes, and we know the commissioner is in her pocket," Dorien growled. He leaned down and brushed his lips across mine. "I'll be okay. Maybe I can get Heather to see reason."

Maybe pigs will fly. Maybe Mozart will rise from the grave to perform Phantom of the Opera. *Maybe Madame Usher will jump off a cliff.*

Dorien climbed the stairs as though he climbed the gallows. His shoulders squared, and a fierce determination settled on his features – his dark soul bent toward a singular purpose. That scared me more than the hopelessness. They'd trapped Dorien in this house and piece by piece eroded his freedoms until he had nothing left to lose, and like a caged lion, he was now at his most dangerous.

He disappeared over the landing. A moment later, I heard his door creak open and then click shut behind him.

The grandfather clock ticked.

"Come, let us discuss the wedding plans." Madame Usher herded the adults back toward the Blue Room. "We're hosting Elena's nuptials here at the end of the semester. If you wish, we could make it a double wedding..."

The five of us remained in the foyer, every face turned toward me. I couldn't hear raised voices from the floor above, and I didn't know if that was a good sign or not. The grandfather clock tick-tick-ticked in the gloom. The silence terrified me.

Titus gathered me in his arms. "It will be okay," he whispered. "Dorien's talking to his FBI agent, remember? He'll be able to see this evidence against you is fake. They'll get into the compound and arrest Aaron and save his brother, and all this will go away."

I nodded, but I wasn't so sure.

The secrets of Manderley ran deep – scar tissue that would never heal.

Ivan stood behind me, his body trembling with rage and indecision. He'd tried to stay away from me because of his own belief about what I wanted and what he deserved. But I saw in his icicle eyes the moment his love overcame him, and he collapsed against me, pressing his lips to my cheek and holding me close.

Elena slammed into me, joining our embrace. From the staircase, Aroha made a gagging face, but she flopped her arms around us. We remained still, wrapped together by the binding cords of Manderley, breathing as one, waiting, hoping.

Tick tock. Tick tock.

I couldn't take it any longer. I extricated myself from the group and slunk up the stairs, straining to hear a sound. The walls groaned, and I fancied I heard the creaking of footsteps darting across the room above my head, but I was so used to those sounds now they didn't even register.

I paused in front of Dorien's door. "Dorien?"

"Faye, don't come in. Don't—"

The fear in his voice spurred me on. I knew all this had been a set up. Heather had done this to him, and she wasn't finished yet. If she thought she could, then she had another thing coming.

I flung open his door.

What?

No.

Blood. So much blood.

 FAYE

D orien stood in the center of the room, his naked torso bathed in soft light. In his hands, he gripped a bloody knife. His eyes flicked to me, and the knife clattered to the floor, the blade leaving a long cut in the polished wood floor beside the body.

The body.

A slab of still flesh slumped on the rug. Jagged wounds cut into the back of a red gown. Blood dribbled from the wounds, pooling and staining the rug pink.

A pair of glittering red pumps poked out from beneath the hem of the dress.

Heather.

"Faye, this isn't what it looks like," Dorien's voice was sandpaper, scouring away the layers of my heart.

"Interesting." My own voice sounded far away, like I was trying to yell underwater. I could barely hear it over the roar of blood in my ears. "It *looks* like you brutally stabbed Heather to death. I'd love to hear an alternative explanation."

"I didn't do it," Dorien cried. "Faye, you have to believe me. I came in here and she was already dead. I picked up the knife because... because I wasn't thinking and she's fucking dead. But I didn't hurt her. I would *never*."

I searched his words for one shred of truth, one possible explanation I could latch onto that would prove to me he didn't do this.

I found none.

There was no other way into this room. The door had been locked – I heard him turn the key. The only other people who had keys were me and Madame Usher, and we were both downstairs. I scanned the windows. They were shut tight, and they looked out over the garden. No handy trees or drainpipes for an intruder to shimmy down. There was no other entrance to this room. No one had come, and all the other residents of Manderley were downstairs in the Blue Room with the guests.

My mind drew up another murder, another young girl brutally killed in this house. Clare lying at the bottom of the stairs, her neck snapped, and only Dorien's word that he'd been in front of her on the staircase.

I ran over his history of violence. That aggravated assault Madame Usher covered up. The secrets he held close like precious jewels. The lies – all the times he told me he had nothing to do with the bullying, when there was no other explanation apart from a ghost.

I trusted him.

The grim, determined look in his eyes, the straightening of his shoulders as he climbed the stairs. The tiger in the cage who sharpened his claws.

It can't be.

But it is.

There's no other explanation.

Dorien murdered Heather.

TO BE CONTINUED

~

Musician.
Heartbreaker.
Murderer.

http://books2read.com/manderley3

Dorien Valencourt is in deep shit.
His cheeky grin and stormy eyes won't help him this time.

But I will.
I've found love in the darkness.
Three broken muses possess me,
Mind, body, and soul.
I won't give them up for anything,
Especially not for a witch with a blackened heart.

In a school ruled by shadows and secrets,
I'll shine a light in the darkest places.
We'll expose a long-buried violation,
And force a villain to confront her sins.

If only our secrets don't devour us all.

With Titus and Ivan at my side,
we'll free Dorien from his cage.
We'll drag these skeletons into the daylight.

The ghost of Manderley will have her revenge.

A dark mystery unfolds around musician Faye de Winter in the final book of this gripping gothic college reverse harem bully romance by USA TODAY best-selling author Steffanie Holmes. Warning: Proceed with caution – this tale of three spoiled rich boys with unsettling secrets and the girl who refuses to put up with their shit contains dark themes, a creepy house, a smoldering second-chance romance, college angst, cruel bullies and swoon-worthy sex.

Read Manderley Academy 3, Spirited
http://books2read.com/manderley3

～

Get your free copy of *Cabinet of Curiosities*, a Steffanie Holmes compendium of short stories and bonus scenes. To get this collection, all you need to do is sign up for updates with the Steffanie Holmes newsletter.

http://www.steffanieholmes.com/newsletter

VOLUME THREE

SPIRITED

"I know not how it was—but, with the first glimpse of the
building, a sense of insufferable gloom pervaded my spirit."

– Edgar Allan Poe, *The Fall of the House of Usher*

PROLOGUE
TITUS

"You want to see something wild?" Dorien Valencourt peered at me over his absinthe glass, all pouting, rich-boy lips and self-satisfied smirk.

I tilted my coke toward him and returned his smile with one of my own. "You're going to vault over a piano again?"

"I learned my lesson. White pianists don't jump." Dorien winced. I could see he remembered the day at our summer music program when he bet me he could vault over the baby grand and land on his feet. Instead, he nearly impaled his testicles on a cymbal stand and destroyed the hopes and dreams of a generation of Dorien fangirls. He cut a long gash on his inner thigh and paid up from an infirmary bed – I still remembered his cavalier grin and the crisp notes he peeled off and tossed at me like confetti.

That was two years ago. We'd remained friends, causing chaos together whenever we met up at recitals and music camps. It was impossible not to like Dorien, not to be swept up by the whirlwind of his personality. We lived on opposite ends of the country and I hadn't expected to see him again until college auditions at the end of the summer, but a week ago he'd randomly shown up on my doorstep, touting a Louis Vuitton suitcase and declaring he was spending the summer with me. As if I couldn't possibly have had any other plans apart from hanging out with him.

He was half right – I didn't have plans. My parents made plans for me. I was to tour the South with them as part of their ensemble – a perfect opportunity to get my name on the lips of their influential friends. But Dorien intervened with his rich-boy smile and the promise of an influential friend of my own and somehow, they agreed to leave me behind to hang out with him.

"Don't you rich boys spend your summers in Martha's Vineyard or Majorca?"

I'd asked as he lugged his suitcase up to my second-floor bedroom. A shadow passed over his eyes, but it was gone before I could question it.

"You should be grateful I've decided to slum it with my pleb friend. I've saved you from a summer of dull recital rooms and cocktail sausages. Besides, I'm bored of my parents and their boring money. You'll take the fold-out, of course. I can't sleep on hard surfaces."

It was hard to stay annoyed at Hurricane Dorien bowling through my life, especially when he pointed out with an impish grin that spending the summer alone as two sixteen-year-olds in New Orleans would be infinitely better than tagging along after my parents.

He was true to his word. With Dorien at my side, my city came to life. It's funny how you can live in a place for sixteen years and not see it as special until you show it off to someone else. We spent our days walking along the banks of the Mississippi, keeping our eyes out for alligators, or buying cheap absinthe to guzzle beside the duck pond in Louis Armstrong Park (I didn't touch alcohol – my parents believed if Micah's friends hadn't been drinking, they might've saved him – but drunk Dorien was *hilarious*). We spent our nights sneaking into jazz clubs with the fake IDs Dorien purchased from a black market pancake shop on Bourbon Street (the shop was a hub for anything illegal in the city – guns, counterfeit money, secret poker games. The pancakes were also delicious).

We were in one of those jazz clubs now, enjoying our first drinks of the evening before the city rose from her slumber and breathed her first jasmine-scented greeting to the night. "Sure," I said. "Show me something wild."

Bob Dylan once said that everything in New Orleans was a good idea, but I wasn't sure even the Big Easy was ready for Dorien Valencourt.

Dorien pushed his chair back and stood up. I thought he was heading over to introduce himself to the group of girls at the bar who'd been eyeing us since they came in. They were college-aged – a good few years older than us – but with his arresting looks and my muscles, both Dorien and I could pass for twenty-year-olds. But he dodged around them and leaped onto the small stage in the corner. It was empty except for the polished piano in the center and some mic stands set up. A board behind the bar listed the three jazz ensembles that would play tonight – none of them were here yet. Live music in New Orleans didn't start until late. You had to give the city time to wake up and unfurl her wings.

The bartender waved an angry fist. "Hey, man. You're not allowed up there."

Ignoring him, Dorien mashed the piano with his fingers, launching into one of his wild, incomprehensible compositions.

And just like that, the bartender dropped his fist. And his jaw.

Dorien's music soared through the bar, reaching the ears of every patron and dragging their heads from their glasses to pay attention. Dorien played as only he could – dramatically, flamboyantly, with a passion and fervor that sucked the air from your lungs. Dorien bit his lip, his head bowed with focus as his fingers danced through the scales. The song soared and swooped, a breath of air that raised goosebumps along my arms.

Dorien had a gift.

I swallowed back the lump in my throat as I thought of another person with the gift. A person who could write music that could tear your soul to pieces and stitch it back together in three-and-a-half minutes. A person who should have been in this bar with us but was instead six feet under.

The girls crowded the stage, grinding against Dorien as he played on. One of them tipped his head back and poured her drink down his throat. Dorien dragged her into his lap and laid a trail of sticky alcohol kisses along her neck, all the while playing perfectly. Because he's Dorien.

A crowd of people wandered in from the street, drawn by the music conjured from Dorien's dark heart. They gathered around the stage – captured, enraptured, blessed by the melody of a music god.

My chest ached, groaning under the weight of memories.

At the end of the piano, I noticed a Les Paul nestled into a stand, a line of effects pedals lined up along the stage, waiting for the evening's booked performance to take the stage. My fingers itched to pick up the guitar and join Dorien. My mind pricked at the spaces in his composition I could fill. His eyes met mine across the bar. Those slate-grey orbs didn't beg me, they *commanded*.

I dug my nails into the sticky wooden table.

It took everything I had to remain in the chair.

The weight on my chest held me frozen.

If word got back to my parents that I was playing electric guitar in a dimly lit club...it would destroy them all over again. I pictured them the night our doorbell rang. I bounded down the stairs, thinking it was Micah home from the concert. But it was the police, to tell us he'd never be home again. I remembered my mother's face crumpling like tissue paper wadded into a ball. My father beating his chest, crying to God to bring back his son.

I couldn't do that to them.

So I downed the rest of my coke and watched Dorien's passion burn through his fingers as jealousy raged inside me. The bastard had everything – money, talent, brash confidence. I wished I could taste that kind of freedom, but Micah had taken it with him to the grave.

When he finished the song, Dorien stood and took a deep bow. The crowd erupted into applause. Even the grumpy bartender whistled and hooted.

All except me. No way was I going to applaud the cocky bastard.

Dorien slid back into our booth with two of the girls hanging off his arms and that arrogant grin perfectly arranged. His cheeks and neck were smudged with lipstick. He dropped three napkins on the table between us. Each one had a phone number scrawled in crimson lipstick. "You should have joined me up there."

I flexed my arm muscles. "That stage isn't big enough for my guns and your ego."

Dorien unbound himself from his two admirers and leaned forward, slapping his hands on the table. The mirth in his eyes vanished. "This should be our lives, Titus. Playing in bars like this, being on the road, writing music that speaks to us.

No rules, no obligations. Being in the real world, not trapped in stuffy concert halls and orchestra pits."

"You're being ridiculous."

"I'm not. I'm deadly serious. Let's do it, you and me. Let's make music on our own terms." Dorien's eyes flashed. I stared at him, for the first time seeing that the darkness behind them wasn't part of his act. Maybe Dorien wasn't here because he was bored and could do whatever the fuck he wanted.

Maybe the great Dorien Valencourt was running from something, too.

"You sound insane."

"You want to get out from under the thumb of your parents? This is how you do it. You need this just as much as I do."

"What exactly is the *this* you're proposing?"

"We form a band. We refine the songs I've been working on and show them to the world. We take classical music away from stuffy halls and elitist wankers and give it back to the people. We make it cool again."

I closed my eyes, trying to shut out the insanity. I had auditions this year at Juilliard, the Royal Academy of Music, Conservatoire de Paris. I couldn't just drop everything for one of Dorien's crazy schemes. But instead of shutting him down, my mind twisted around the melody he'd just played, seeing the gaps, hearing the harmonies and layers I could add. I could *feel* the music humming in my veins, and I hadn't felt music like that since Micah taught me the riff to Black Sabbath's 'War Pigs.'

I opened my eyes. Dorien leaned in close, his shit-eating grin devouring his whole face.

"I knew you'd say yes." With the certainty of someone who'd never been told no in his life, Dorien accepted another cocktail from the bartender – the aptly-named hurricane, on the house as thanks for his performance – and took a long sip. "Now, we need a third. A violinist, I think. I've someone in mind. Have you met Ivan Nicolescu?"

"Elena Nicolescu's brother?" I met Elena at a music camp last summer. She was a waif from Romania who barely said a word to anyone, but was the greatest pianist I'd ever heard. I remembered she had a twin brother, white-haired and silent, with those same ice-cold eyes that bore holes in your skin. He played the violin. He was nothing special compared to his sister, but he had a certain sledge-hammer style.

"That's the fellow. He *lives* at Manderley Academy, can you believe it?" Darkness passed through Dorien's eyes again, but it was gone before I could comment on it. "He must be a vampire. That's the only reason I can think someone would want to shut themselves away in that shithole."

"My parents made me apply." Both Dorien and I were attending auditions for the major college music programs at the end of the summer. Manderley was low on my list. Why would I want to go to a rundown old mansion in the mountains when I could study in Paris? Or London? *So* many metal bands played in London, and it was almost far enough away from my parents for me to be able to breathe.

Almost.

"If she offers you a place, don't take it." Dorien slurped his drink. "I studied at the Usher School in New York. Victor is a fine tutor, but Gizella Usher is a piece of work."

I could smell the syrupy licorice of Dorien's absinthe from across the table. My temples pounded. I didn't really want to go to any of the schools I was auditioning for. Four more years of playing cello sounded like hell on earth. But what choice did I have?

Dorien was offering that choice.

"My friend Gabriel has a band named Octavia's Ruin. They're heading out on tour in a month. The opening act just pulled out and they need someone to replace them. I played him some tapes I made and he said if I could find a band and put a set together in time, we can have the opening slot. If we want it. I know it's insane; that's what makes it fun. What do you say?"

I leaned back in my chair. It wasn't heavy metal. It wasn't the roaring guitars and pounding drums I craved, but it was *different*. It had heart and soul and feeling, and that was enough. Dorien left space in the music for me to make it my own. His song flowed through my head, and I *felt* rather than heard the rough edges where his genius met the hurricane of his soul. Instead of polishing all those edges off, we could create something raw and bold and beautiful.

I could make the cello heavy metal.

I could do my own thing, away from my parents, away from the pressure of replacing the perfect son they lost.

I slammed my fist down on the table. "I'm in."

Ivan flew down to New Orleans a week later. He was just as silent and terrifying as I remembered. But the moment he raised his bow and ripped through an improvisation that bowled me over with its quiet malevolence, I knew he was the violinist for us.

We recorded the album at Skulking Dog Studios, the same studio where my parents cut their first recording. The music flew from our fingers. Dorien joked that he sold his soul at a crossroads to give him the compositions, and I almost believed him. Every note, every motif, every phrase dripped with black magic.

Ivan spent every moment we weren't practicing or recording on his phone to his sister, talking to her in harsh, barked tones in his native Romanian.

One of the girls Dorien met at that bar turned out to be an amateur filmmaker. She took us to the Lafayette Cemetery one night and had us run around in black cloaks and pale face paint, then cut an arty video for our first song, 'A Graveside Story.' We released it online and Octavia's Ruin shared it with their fans and before we knew it, we were climbing the Spotify charts.

By the time my parents burst through the doors at the end of summer to take me to my auditions, Broken Muse amassed eighty thousand social media fans and we'd been booked on a ten-city European tour. I showed them the music video. Mom watched in stunned silence, tears streaking her cheeks.

Dad stormed from the room and slammed the door so hard it rattled the whole house.

I packed my cello and left with Dorien the next day. We blew off our auditions to play the nightclubs of Paris, Berlin, and London. We followed the Octavia's Ruin tour bus in a tiny van jammed with gear, partied every night until dawn, and slept on friends' couches, in roach-infested hostels, and in the van on the side of the road during a freak Polish thunderstorm.

Dorien was in his element – every night another crowd to enchant, in every city a new girl or guy to warm his bed. But sometimes, if I watched him carefully from across the stage, if the moonlight through the van window caught his face before he fell asleep, I saw that darkness creep into his eyes.

We never spoke about it, but I knew that Dorien wasn't just chasing fame and riches and hot groupies – he was running from something so rotten that even on the other side of the globe, he couldn't escape its hold on him.

Brutal Killing at Music School

A young woman's life has been tragically cut short at the elite Manderley Academy. Police recovered the body of twenty-two-year-old Heather Danvers from her fiancé's room at the music school. Her head had been brutally bashed against a steel bedpost, and she was stabbed seven times.

Heather's fiancé, musician Dorien Valencourt, has been arrested and charged with her murder. Dorien is the genius behind the neo-classical rock band, Broken Muse, who shot to fame six years ago when their first single, 'A Graveside Story,' went viral.

This is the second death to occur at the music academy in the last year. A young girl, Clare Fairbanks, worked at the school as a maid. She was found at the bottom of the stairs with her neck broken. Her death was ruled accidental, but given that Clare was reported to be dating Dorien Valencourt and he was in the vicinity at the time of her death, her case has been reopened.

Sources close to the school believe Valencourt may have influenced another student, Faye de Winter, to commit this crime. De Winter has a history of violence – she once violently assaulted a man named Aaron Varney – and resented the impending marriage between Danvers and Valencourt. At this time, de Winter has not been charged with any crime, although she is being investigated as an accomplice. She is the daughter of famed musician Donovan de Winter, who disappeared mysteriously ten years ago and has never been found.

Authorities face a tough challenge untangling this sordid saga. All this reporter knows is that Manderley Academy has more skeletons in its closets than a gothic novel.

FAYE

"The *genius* behind Broken Muse?" Titus made a face as he tossed the paper onto the grave. "How dare he?"

"*That's* what you take from the article?" Ivan growled.

"That even from prison, Dorien finds a way to take credit for *all* our work? Damn right that's the message I'm taking from the article." Titus' usually kind features twisted with anger. Angry looked good on Titus – but then, so did every other emotion. The guy was a walking clit closet. "The bastard even suggested Faye beat up this Aaron guy because she's *under Dorien's influence*. I wonder who told them that? Someone who still believes the sun shines out his own arsehole, that's who. When our girl goes nuclear, it's for her own reasons, not because the bloody Bad Boy of Baroque told her to."

"I'd like to point out for posterity that I didn't actually beat up Aaron." I drew my hands up to my shoulders in a vain attempt to rub warmth back into my arms.

We were splayed out inside the Usher mausoleum at Manderley. The hexagonal stone structure offered little shelter from the wet, gross rain dribbling down outside – bitter wind pushed the damp through the grated windows and into the cracks in the stone cupola. Our breaths came out in furious puffs, like steam locomotives building up momentum as they crested a hill. Elena sat next to me on Victor Usher's empty sarcophagus, swinging her legs lazily and nodding her head to a song none of us could hear. Titus leaned against a wall of niches, and Ivan paced beneath a weeping angel statue.

Just being in this stone tomb made my skin crawl. Evil itself seeped through the walls. I wanted nothing more than to walk away from Manderley and the Usher family forever.

But that was impossible.

Heather's death changed everything. Not even Commissioner Walpole could save Madame Usher from the media scrutiny of a second body to be uncovered at the school in the space of a year – both of them connected to Dorien Valencourt. The school was swarming with the press. At first, she tried to keep them out, barring the gates and forcing Harrison to stand out in the snow with his rifle to scare them off. But they'd flown out with helicopters and hiked in through the forest trails, and so she changed tactics and welcomed them inside, giving them the run of the place and filling their heads with her chosen narrative as she allowed them to paw through Heather's things. She even allowed a paranormal investigation team to film a segment on the staircase, calling for Clare to show herself and identify Dorien as her killer.

I was learning all of this now from Ivan and Elena because Madame Usher kicked me out. After her insane effort to bring me to the academy in the first place, my dismissal was somewhat perfunctory – she simply had Harrison deliver me a letter informing me our contract was terminated, and I was to be off the property by the end of the day or she'd have me arrested for trespassing. Heather's death had thrown a chink in her perfect plan, and now she couldn't risk keeping me around.

I longed to confront her about it, to throw my mother's poisoning back in her face, but I didn't want to play my hand too soon. Instead, Titus and Ivan helped me pack my meager possessions. Madame Usher didn't leave the east wing as I lugged my case downstairs, and a wicked idea occurred to me.

I marched into the storage room and took the Becker violin – my father's violin – and waltzed out of the school with it. It was my legacy, after all. As Harrison drove me away, I looked back at the house and couldn't see Madame Usher's face at the windows, but I could feel her gaze boring into me, promising that she hadn't finished with me yet.

My fingers closed around the neck of the violin. *Is my father alive? What has she done to him? Why does he haunt Manderley, taunting me with these clues?*

I wondered what Clare – the real ghost of Manderley – thought about it all. I came here today intending to ask her.

I moved into Mom's hotel room in New York City, paid for until the end of the year by Natalie's kindness. I found a job in a music shop and would hopefully be able to scrape together enough money to keep paying Mom's medical bills.

When the lurid headlines about Heather's murder hit, Amos and Delphine arrived to pull Titus out of Manderley. They were living in New York City too, while they applied to other programs so he could complete his schooling. They didn't let him see me in case it reflected badly on his chances at Juilliard. Titus wasn't talking about it much in the stolen conversations we had late at night, but I gathered living with his parents again wasn't exactly pleasant. They still hadn't forgiven him for having the guitar.

Aroha's parents tried to remove her as well, but I heard her on the phone as I was packing telling them that she would be graduating no matter what. I guess with fewer of us around, she figured her chances of winning the Manderley Prize just shot up.

Elena stayed with her fiancé, which meant Ivan remained behind at Manderley also.

Just like that, we were scattered. Madame Usher achieved her ends – she destroyed Broken Muse. If only Heather didn't have to die to make it happen. I hated that bitchbadger, but she didn't deserve *that*.

That was why we were gathered today. Titus and I snuck back while his parents were out. We hiked four miles through the forest to escape the reporters and approach Manderley from the rear, then peeled off the forest path to meet Ivan and Elena at the mausoleum. It was clear from its neglect that Madame Usher never visited, so it seemed a safe place to plot our next move.

We brought them mobile phones so we could communicate in secret, and exchanged news from inside and outside the school. Titus showed Ivan some of the newspaper articles and tweets about the band. It was clear that no matter what the police charged him with, Dorien had already been found guilty by the world, and I was his puppet, dancing to the tune of the powerful men in my life.

"What do we do now?" Elena asked.

It was a good question. One I'd desperately been trying to figure out ever since I walked into Dorien's room and saw him bent over Heather, the bloody knife in his hand.

"I suppose it depends if we believe Dorien is innocent," Titus said.

Three pairs of eyes bore into me.

I stared down at the bag of supplies at my feet, watching my cold breath swirl around the stones. I didn't know what to believe.

I believed the evidence of my eyes. Dorien had the knife. He was the only one in the room. We didn't see anyone else enter or leave the house. He was being forced into a marriage against his will, and I knew better than anyone that when Dorien Valencourt was cornered, he could lash out with unimaginable cruelty.

Dorien begged me to believe in his innocence. He sounded distraught and genuine as they shoved him into the police car, but I'd been through this with Dorien before. Every time I believed things were different or opened myself up to him, he betrayed me. I thought I trusted myself with him, but that knife glinting in the dim light, the blood on his hands, Heather's lifeless body staring up at me...

But *then* I came back to all the unexplained phenomena at Manderley – the objects flying over the staircase the first time Madame kicked me out, the face in the attic window, my dad's book appearing, food going missing from the kitchen, and those times I felt like I was being watched. I remembered Clare's words scrawled on the wall in the pantry. THE WALLS ARE TALKING. I'd seen the portrait of my father hidden in the attic, and we found Victor Usher's empty grave and discovered Madame Usher's plot to poison my mother. I knew we were on the cusp of unraveling Madame Usher's secrets, and now Heather was dead and Dorien was behind bars and it all seemed too...convenient. Especially considering the story Madame Usher was spinning for the press.

I raised my head. "What do you guys think? Did he do it?"

They exchanged glances. No one spoke. No one knew what to say.

I slid off the sarcophagus and paced across the floor, shoving my gloved hands into my armpits again in a vain attempt to prevent my fingers from falling off. "Okay, we have to agree on this before we go forward. So let's go through what we know. All of us were downstairs except for Aroha, and she met us at the doorway when I found Heather's body. She couldn't have snuck out of the room without Dorien seeing her, and if he'd seen her he wouldn't lie to save her ass. So that means all of us, Aroha, the Valencourts, the Danvers, Madame Usher, Father Aaron, and Walpole couldn't possibly have done it. That leaves only Dorien and Harrison. The only way Harrison could have made his way upstairs to kill her is if there was some kind of secret passage leading from outside to Dorien's bedroom, which we're not ruling out. But I don't believe Harrison's the murderer. His beef is with Usher, not Heather, and he had that gun with him, so why stab her? Why not shoot her?"

"That leaves only Dorien." Ivan's voice dripped with disdain.

"If we consider the living, yes. But what about Clare's words? What about that portrait of my father and his violin? What about Victor Usher's grave being empty?" I wrung my hands. "I've seen too many horror films to ignore the signs."

Titus stepped toward me, his huge hands wrapping around my shoulders. "Faye, are you trying to convince us, or are you trying to convince yourself?"

I sagged against him, letting his warmth envelop me. Being held by Titus was all-consuming – he wrapped his body around me like a shield, and inside his embrace I felt stronger, invincible. "I don't know what to believe. Is Manderley haunted by the living or the dead? Maybe Clare's ghost killed Heather. But why? Heather wasn't anywhere near the staircase when Clare died. And what about my father? Or Victor Usher? How are they connected to this? And it doesn't change the fact that Dorien was upset about the arranged marriage. He had every reason to lash out at Heather. I've given him seven million chances and each time he's broken my heart. I don't want to use a ghost to excuse him."

I looked up at the carved cupola. A rogue spiderweb brushed my face, its gossamer threads like fingertips reaching for me. I bit back a scream as the air sung with tension – the feeling that something monumental was about to happen. I remembered the sensation from the last time I'd been at the mausoleum, the night Dorien and Heather knocked me out with chloroform and trapped me in a leather bag. I remembered the cold in my veins as Clare rose from the shadows and closed in on me. Her hands reached for my throat as she rasped, *"Only you can save Manderley from the voice in the walls."*

My heart pounded. "Clare."

"What about her?" Titus murmured, burying his face into my shoulder.

"She broke all those antiques when Madame tried to kick you out," Elena said. "You think she killed Heather too?"

"She is dangerous." Ivan grabbed his sister's hand. "We shouldn't stay in the house with her."

"She's the key to all of this. I don't think she's trying to hurt us. I think she's trying to warn us, warn me. Maybe about Dorien, but I don't think so.

The walls are talking, she said. I don't think she's responsible. She's a victim, too. This is the second death at Manderley that's been blamed on Dorien, the second death that's been carefully constructed so he's the only possible suspect. He got away once, but someone has made sure he can't escape this time. We need the truth – we need to know what happened from someone who saw the whole thing. Heather can't tell us what she saw in his room, and the only people who know what happened on that staircase are Clare and Dorien. We all know his version, but we should get hers. Clare seems willing to talk to me. I came here today because I need to do what I should have done ages ago. I need to *listen*."

"How do you listen to a ghost?" Ivan said. "With a seance?"

"Exactly."

I expected Titus to laugh, but no one thought this ghost thing was funny anymore. Not after we'd all seen the portraits and vases flying over the staircase and smashing to pieces. Not after Heather had been carried out of Manderley in a body bag.

"When should we do this seance?" Ivan asked.

"No time like the present." I opened my bag to reveal a stack of candles and other supplies. Elena pulled her own from her tote bag. Ivan glared at her, then at me, but she poked her tongue out at him.

"Faye asked me to collect a few things," she said. "If we told you, you would have forbidden it."

He growled low in his throat. He knew we were right. "How do you know how to talk to the dead?"

I shrugged as I lit the last candle. "I don't. I based this off seances I've seen in horror films."

Ivan snorted. "Because they always end so well."

Elena set about placing the candles around the mausoleum and lighting them. On Victor's tomb, I laid out a serving tray from the kitchen, with a glass upturned on top. I tacked a piece of paper onto the tray. On a semi-circle around the glass, I'd written the alphabet and numbers 0-9, as well as the words YES and NO, just like a spirit board I found on the internet.

"The candles keep blowing out," Elena pouted as she tipped another match from the box.

"Don't worry about them." I hadn't needed a candle to see Clare in the mausoleum last time. "Come here. Everyone join hands."

We sat cross-legged on the dais holding Victor's stone tomb. The wind whistled through the trees, blowing out several of the candles. On my left, Elena giggled. Titus squeezed my right hand so hard I heard my knuckle crack.

"Clare Fairbanks," I said, trying to project my voice, to pluck the tension in the air and snap it into the corporeal world. "You've been trying to give me a message for some time. I'm ready to listen."

I narrowed my eyes at the glass, trying to see it and only it and not Elena's gleeful face, but also trying to see beyond it, into the shadow realm Clare inhabited. Goosebumps rose along my arms, but whether they were from the cold or from a looming presence I couldn't tell.

"Clare, please talk to us. We want to listen to you."

Faye. Fayyyyeeeeee...

My heart pounded against my ribs. The more I focused on that glass, the harder it was to believe the crackling voice was just wind in the trees, or that the mist encircling the tomb was just our freezing puffs of breath—

Wait a second...

The mists swirled and dipped, and I saw that the miasma didn't come from our mouths at all, but seemed to rise from Victor's empty tomb. It coalesced together, taking form and substance. Titus stiffened as he noticed it too, his fingers crushing my hand.

Elena cried out as a face emerged from the mist. On her other side, Ivan hissed.

Clare.

She met my eyes. Her turned-up nose pointed to the crumbling carvings of Jesus stumbling under the weight of his cross. Her lips opened a crack, my name hissing from her mouth like air leaking from a balloon.

She's here. I'm not imagining it. Clare's really with us.

"Hello, Clare." I kept my voice calm, even though I wanted to bolt from the mausoleum and never look back. "I'm sorry I've been ignoring your warnings. I won't do that again. We're here to talk to you, to get the story straight from you. Can you speak to us?"

Fayyeeeeeeee...

The gaping hole of her mouth opened, and what poured out wasn't words, not really. She issued forth a sound like no other, a sound like footsteps creaking on old floorboards and shadows moving in a quiet room. It was everything she already told me but spoken in a cold, creeping death that invaded my bones and squeezed at my organs. Dread pushed at the corners of my mind as I heard her, as I finally saw her for who she was. The girl wronged. The girl who must be avenged.

Elena whimpered. She heard it too.

An involuntary shudder rippled through my body. Clare snapped her mouth shut and shook her head. *Okay, so she can't talk to us without resorting to ghost speak, which I don't think I ever want to hear again. Let's try something else.*

"Can you move the glass? Spell out a message for us?"

Clare stared down at the glass and shook her head. The corners of her mouth turned down. She looked sad.

"You can't move the glass?"

She shook her head again.

"You can't pick up objects?"

Clare shook her head so furiously it sent a wave of nausea through my body. My chest squeezed, thinking of the violin music I played alongside her for so many nights, and the objects flying around the house the first time Madame Usher tried to kick me out, or the clothes left out for me before the party. Clare had to be responsible for them, which meant she'd been able to move objects. So why couldn't she now?

Or was she lying to us? But could ghosts lie? Maybe her ability to move things comes and goes.

I wish I knew more about ghosts than just which ones topped Fangoria's *best haunts list.*

Titus squeezed my fingers, reminding me I had more important questions.

"We want to make sure whoever hurt you sees justice, but we need your help. Did Dorien do this to you?" I demanded. "Did he kill you?"

I forced my eyes to remain open as my stomach tied itself in knots. I didn't want to see the answer, didn't want to shatter my hopes into shards of ice.

Clare shook her head so hard her hair whipped around her face. She was certain. It wasn't Dorien. My shoulders sagged with relief. I longed to fling myself at her and hug her, but I didn't want to feel her slip through my fingers. I held onto my calm and tried another question.

"Was it Madame Usher? Was it Heather?"

Shake. Shake.

Someone else, then. Answers started to form in my head, but I wasn't quite ready to test them aloud.

"Who else is there?" Ivan demanded. Clare whirled around to face him, spreading her arms out toward the door of the tomb, toward me. *She's pointing to me.*

She's saying I have the answers already.

I hated that Clare was right. I'd been flirting around the outside of this for so long, and I had to face the truth of my father's portrait and the Becker violin, of missing bones and murdered girls.

But first...

"Did you see who killed Heather?" I curled my fingers into Titus' palm.

A nod this time. My heart hammered against my chest.

"Was it Dorien?"

The question hung in the air between us. Clare's mouth hung open, her jaw slack, the dark void of her mouth yawning wide, threatening to swallow me whole.

She snapped her jaw shut and shook her head.

I let out a breath I didn't realize I was holding. The relief felt like dropping my bowing arm after a difficult concerto. Dorien didn't kill Heather. He was innocent. That meant he was being set up, and we had to help him.

"Who killed her?" Ivan demanded.

Elena screamed as Clare whirled around. She pointed to the house, and then down at Victor Usher's empty tomb.

I swallowed.

"Was it Madam Usher?" I whispered, although I already knew the answer.

Clare shook her head. She gestured wildly, pointing to me, then back at the house, then at the tomb again. She mimed playing the violin.

"He's been hiding in the walls," I whispered. "He was there when you were alive, whispering to you, like a ghost."

Titus' fingers tightened around mine. Elena let out a choked noise.

"Faye?" Ivan barked out, his voice dark with fear.

I couldn't tear my eyes from Clare. She nodded. I had my answer. The answer I'd been dreading but knew deep down inside all along.

Someone else has been at Manderley with us this whole time.

And that someone is a murderer.

FAYE

"Step this way."

The officer shoved open a steel door and led me down a urine-soaked hallway, past a double row of cell doors. Even though the inmates couldn't see out, they must've heard our footsteps, because they banged on the doors, rattled the hinges, and yelled and cried and shrieked. I squared my shoulders, wishing I could turn around and run from this nightmare.

The cop shoved his keys into the last cell in the row. The door swung open but it took a few tries for my leaden feet to shuffle forward. As I stepped inside, he caught my wrist in his hand, twisting it so I had no choice but to lean into him. His lip curled as he looked me over, nice and slow. His hot breath rasped against my cheek. "Fucking rich boy crims get all the good pussy."

I raised my hand to slap his stupid mouth, but he'd already slammed the cell door behind me. I sucked in a deep breath and looked around.

A concrete bench covered with a thin plastic mattress. A toilet and enamel basin hanging at a precarious angle from the wall. A stench of feces and desperation thick in the air, clinging to every pore. A narrow window high in the wall, covered with steel bars.

A beautiful, broken boy stood beneath it, his hands shoved deep in his pockets and a curtain of dark hair covering his face.

I sat down on the concrete bench.

Dorien leaned against the wall opposite, so fragile the gentlest breeze would blow him away. He leaned his head back, and his hair started to fall away from his face.

I stared at my hands. If I looked at him for another moment, I'd break.

"Hey, Sprite."

That voice. It fucking *undid* me. I dug my nails into my palm, but that only made me picture his fingers laced in mine as he and Ivan had me over the piano bench. I sucked in a shaking breath and diverted my gaze to the stained wall above his head. It was covered with scratched graffiti – nothing recognizable as words, just squiggles and cartoon dicks.

"Look at me, Sprite."

I shook my head.

"Please."

His voice cracked. I couldn't deny him. I'd always had trouble saying no to Dorien, especially when he was hurting. I shifted my chin, lowering my gaze to see him, to really *see* him.

Even in this hellish place he looked incredible – he hadn't been shaving, and the stubble on his chin and dangerous glint in his eyes made him appear worlds away from the polished performer who'd held my heart since I was a girl. Dim light from the window pierced the room, bathing his aristocratic face in dim light. The skin around his eye was bruised purple and swelling up. His normally cruel mouth twisted with misery.

"You're a sight for sore eyes." Dorien tried to flash that shit-eating grin of his, but the muscles wouldn't do the job. He leaned forward, his fingers grasping my knee. His presence stole all the air from the room, and I struggled for breath.

Sparks darted against my skin where he held me. It took all my restraint to shove his hand off me and jerk away. "We don't have much time. I can't do this if you touch me."

"I can't help it. I miss you so fucking much."

I sucked in a breath, anything to give me a moment to collect myself, find my strength. My mother's words spun on repeat inside my skull. "Give him hell, *mi cielo*."

"Sprite?"

"I'm still here." I gripped the edge of the concrete bench. "You don't have to keep saying my name."

"Sorry." He didn't sound sorry. "I just...I know what they're saying in the papers. When you didn't come, none of you, I thought...I thought she finally convinced you I'm evil."

He was right. We hadn't talked since the police dragged him away. He tried to call us, but Madame Usher refused to allow any calls through the house phone, and I told the concierge at the hotel not to allow his calls through to me. I'd had to go through his lawyer to arrange this visit.

"Dorien, what happened?"

"They're charging me with first-degree murder," he sighed. "My lawyer thinks that if I spill about Jacob's abuse, he'll be able to argue self-defense at a trial. But that will jeopardize Rochester's investigation. Rochester wants me to wait it out in here while he builds a case against Usher as well as Aaron, but I don't know if I can wait that long. I'm going insane, Sprite."

"Dorien, I can't—"

"I swear to you I didn't kill Heather."

"I'm not asking that." I stabbed my nail so deep I drew blood. "I'm asking you to tell me what happened that night. I need to know everything you saw."

"I waited in the hallway for a few moments before I went inside my room. I needed some time to figure out what I was going to say. Heather and I aren't so different. We both have siblings trapped in the Temple. I was going to ask her to help me. I thought I heard her talking or laughing inside, thumping my furniture around, but I might've imagined it. I was a bit of a mess." He laughed without mirth.

"I pushed open my bedroom door and...and Heather was lying on the floor with that knife sticking out of her chest." Dorien shuddered. "I'll never forget how she looked in all my life, her mouth hanging open like that. I see now it was stupid for me to touch the knife, but I thought...I was trying to save her. It wasn't supposed to be in her like that. I had to take it out, but then there was so much blood..."

His voice wavered, and he swallowed hard, his Adam's apple bobbing.

"The police say the knife was taken from the kitchen. My lawyer says it's my best defense – you were all at the bottom of the stairs, and you saw me head straight up to my room. No one saw me double back or stop to grab a knife. It's not much, probably not enough for reasonable doubt from a jury that will have already convicted me in the media. But it's something."

I let out a long breath. He was right. I definitely would have noticed. But there was a long period between Dorien heading upstairs and me racing up to see what happened, the time when he said he was outside his bedroom door. The police might argue it was time enough for him to have slipped out the window in Titus' room, shimmied down the tree, and come into the kitchen from the backdoor. Would it have been time enough for him to have grabbed a knife and got back upstairs without us hearing him?

Maybe. If he was fast.

"Please say you believe me." Dorien pressed his knuckles into his swelling eye. "I can't fucking survive in here if you don't believe me."

I think of Clare's adamance that Dorien had nothing to do with either death. I know what we decided in the mausoleum, but I hadn't been sure what I'd feel when I faced him again. Until now. I looked into those slate-grey eyes and saw the love and the hope shining there like a beacon in the darkness.

I dived into Dorien Valencourt, drowning myself in the depths of his anguish. I touched the edges of him, and I lifted off the weight of his betrayals that I'd been carrying for so long. He never smashed my violin. He wasn't keeping me awake with footsteps in the storage room, or trying to frighten me by stealing food from the kitchen. The thousand tiny cuts of his cruelty healed over with new, tougher skin. When I first came to Manderley, I thought Dorien was my bully. But he was one of the victims, and I had to save him.

I had my answer.

I nodded. "I believe you."

"Don't sound so sure."

"No, I do. I—" I closed my eyes. I needed a moment without his gaze on me, a moment to collect the maelstrom of emotions swirling inside me. "It's hard. We've been down this path before, you and me. You say things and then you do something else. And you might have noble intentions, but what I see is betrayal. When I saw you holding that knife, I slipped back into that same pattern. But when I search deep down, I do believe you. That leaves us with a terrifying truth – that someone else at Manderley killed Heather. Probably someone hiding in the walls."

"You think Clare did it?"

I shook my head, opening my eyes to meet those stony orbs once more. "I spoke to Clare. Well, not exactly. She can't speak and she can't pick up objects, but we had a seance and she informed me you were innocent."

Dorien smiled. "I'm glad my ex-girlfriend is still amenable to my charms."

I have never been able to resist Dorien's smile, and today is no different. How could the simple movement of muscle and skin and sinew sing such music in my veins? How could that flash of perfect teeth and the dimpling of his cheek vibrate in my memory long after we part? *Dorien.*

That smile had been my comfort and my torment in equal measure, but that was what it meant to be in love. The joy of our music was the tension that wove us together, the hard and the soft, the tremolo shuddering against an open string. Thunder approaching over a calm lake, stirring the waters to life. Without the torment, my heart couldn't beat for him.

My whole body ached to be his again, and I wasn't going to waste another moment. I threw myself at Dorien, catching him by surprise. He wobbled off-balance and the pair of us toppled onto the narrow mattress. Dorien caught me before I rolled off the edge and held me against him, pressing our chests together so I could feel his heart racing against his ribs.

"I won't let you go," he swore, his breath hot on my lips. His fingers tangled in my hair, drawing my head toward him.

I nuzzled his neck, a lump rising in my throat at the thought that soon I'd have to leave him in this gross room to meet a fate we couldn't predict. "I only have a little time."

"Every moment with you is a gift." Dorien's lips brushed mine, soft, searching. He kissed like a criminal stealing his way to safety, silent and stalking, slipping his tongue between my lips to search out answers. He tasted like Dorien – dark and wintery – but also nothing like Dorien at all. He tasted of shitty jail food and despair. His tongue stroked mine, and I fancied I could taste the coppery bite of blood.

I pulled back, tracing the lines of his face. I wishing I could sneak him out under my bra and carry him far away from this place. I'd probably suffocate him in my tits, but what a way to go. I hated how comfortable he was here, how resigned to his fate. Dorien had been in a prison his whole life. I would not let him die in one.

"I'll figure this out," I said. The words echoed in the concrete room.

"There's nothing to figure out. It was Usher," Dorien said. "Nothing in that house happens without her knowledge. All of this is her grand plan, and she's got the police in her pocket."

"Madame Usher has nine witnesses saying she was downstairs the whole time," I said. "Including me. We know she's ultimately behind this, but she didn't plunge the knife into Heather. She never gets her hands dirty. I know this sounds insane, but we think there might be someone else hiding at Manderley. Someone who's been sneaking around doing her bidding, making us crazy thinking a ghost is responsible. Someone who smashed up my violin, and who left my father's book and violin to torment me. Someone whose bones should be rotting in his grave."

"You think Victor Usher is still alive?" Dorien raised an eyebrow. Of course he was into this – it was like something out of a gothic novel.

I nodded. "I have no proof, but it makes perfect sense. At least, it makes more sense than the other option, which is that my father is still alive."

"Wait, hold on a second." Dorien's eyes crinkled at the edges. "What's this about your father?"

As quickly as I could, I went over everything I figured out about Manderley and the portrait of my father and his violin, before cycling back to Victor Usher. "There's someone else haunting Manderley besides Clare. That's what this is all about. That's Madame Usher's secret. It's either my dad or Victor, and I need to figure out which one it is. You said when Victor was sick, Madame Usher forbade any doctors to see him. We know she has knowledge of plants and poisons because of the birthwort she gave my mother. She probably fed him something from the poison garden to fake his death, and he's been hiding in her private wing all this time. It explains why his bones aren't in his tomb. I think he creeps around the house when we can't see him, and does things to frighten us, like smashing my violin. Clare says she didn't do that."

"But why?" Dorien asked. "Why fake his death? What does it achieve?"

I smiled sadly. "I was hoping you might have some idea."

"That's what she thought I knew," Dorien whistled through his teeth. "In Cauda Venenum."

"The words on the poison garden? What does that even mean?"

"It's Latin for the poison is in the tail—"

"I *know* what it means. But if I go to the police and say 'In Cauda Venenum,' they're going to lock me up in here beside you."

The corner of Dorien's mouth quirked up. "When she was threatening to have me arrested if I didn't stay away from you, I said those words to her and she relented. I was bluffing, but she didn't know that. She thought I knew that she faked Victor's death and I was going to go to the police."

I tapped his chin. "And that's why she's coming after you now. If she can put you away for Heather's murder, no one will believe if you tell an insane story about her keeping her dead husband locked up inside Manderley."

"Rochester is investigating her," Dorien squeezed my shoulders. "He's trying to connect her to the Temple and Father Aaron. So far he's got nothing, but if you tell him what you know, he might be able to help you. If you figure out what that means, you've got her. I know you can do that, Faye."

"Yeah." I kissed his lips. "It's all starting to make sense now."

Someone banged on the door. I started to pull away, but Dorien pressed his palm into my back, trapping me in place. He whispered against my lips. "What if it's not Victor? What if it's your dad?"

"Then I'll do what my mom should have done ten years ago and kill the bastard myself," I whispered back. The words trembled on my tongue. Dorien sighed against me as he pressed me into his chest. We both knew I was talking a big game. *If it's my dad...*

I couldn't face it.

If it's my dad, he let me believe he was dead. He let me cry a river of tears for him.

If it's my dad, he's spent ten years hiding with that witch instead of being here for me, for us.

If it's my dad, then he's part of her conspiracy to poison my mother.

If it's him, I will fall spectacularly apart, and I don't think even my broken muses could put me back together again.

BANG BANG BANG.

"Ms. de Winter, you need to come with us now," the officer barked.

Reluctantly, I slid out from beneath Dorien. He remained on the slab, his knees pulled to his chest, his arms still embracing the air as if he could still feel the ghost of my touch. As I slid out the door, my heart rattled like a marble in my chest, and the trailing notes of our song shattered into ash.

Faye

When I cracked the door to our hotel suite, delicious smells wafted from within, stunning my nostrils with their awesomeness. I threw the door open, my stomach growling.

Mom sat at the small table by the window, tearing the lids off takeout packages of Mexican food. My heroine. How did she always know exactly what I needed?

"How was Dorien?" she asked as I dropped down beside her and slid over a package of tamales. I peeled back the corn husk and shoved one in my mouth whole. The spicy beef burned my tongue as I chewed. But sound the fucktrumpets it tasted so good, and at least it took my mind off thinking about Victor and my father and Ivan and Elena still up at the house with a violent ghost in the walls.

I swallowed and reached for another. "About what you'd expect."

"Struggling without his silk shirts and Wagner recordings and an adoring audience hanging onto his every word?" She said it lightly, but there was a hint of motherly concern in her voice.

I picked up a shrimp taco, careful to keep my gaze steady as I met her eyes. I hadn't told her yet about my suspicions. I needed proof first, especially if it wasn't Victor in the walls. "He didn't kill Heather, Mom."

"If you believe that, then so do I. It doesn't mean I think that boy is good for you." Mom leaned forward to wipe a strand of hair from my eyes. "You've lived through too much heartache because of your father. I won't let you make the same mistakes I did."

Her voice wavered, her eyes pooling with tears. For the first time, I saw what she had endured as she watched me grow up without a father. It was always the two of us against the world, even when Dad was in the picture. To me, she was everything I needed, everything I ever wanted to be. But she thought she had failed me. And that sense of failure was what drove her to be her remarkable self.

I reached up to her hand, lacing her fingers in mine and bringing it back to the table. "Dad was the failure, not you. You're my strength. You're all I ever needed, so don't waste a minute wishing things could have been different. I never will. Besides, I'm the one who's supposed to be looking after you. So get your cute de Winter butt back in that bed and stop worrying about me."

"I'll never stop, *mi cielo*." Mom stabbed the last tamale with her fork and shoved it into her mouth as she moved with shuffling steps to the bed. She leaned back on her stack of pillows and chewed, a sheen of sweat on her forehead. The poison had done a number on her insides, and moving and laughing and living were painful for her now, but I had to hope Dr. Nelson could help her body once again reflect her spirit.

I polished off a pile of tacos with gusto and slid into bed beside her, touching the book splayed across her raised knees. "What are you reading?"

She flipped the cover so I could see it. "*Prose and Cons*, by Steffanie Holmes. It's this reverse harem murder mystery series, and one of the characters runs a death-faking business. It's fascinating. According to him, people fake their deaths for three main reasons – for financial gain, to be with a lover, and to escape violence or imprisonment. I already skipped ahead to the last chapter, so I know who the killer is, but it's a good read. Very steamy."

I laughed. That was just like Mom – even in her leisure activities like reading, she had to be the one in control. She didn't like surprises unless she was the one creating them for her clients.

I pulled out my phone and scrolled through my emails. Seven million messages from reporters, wanting to pay me for an exclusive interview to get the scoop on my sordid relationship with Dorien. I didn't have the stomach to see what the world was saying about me on social media, so I deleted the apps. Judging by the abusive emails from Broken Muse fans who found my private email address, it couldn't be anything good. Mom buried her face in her book. I gazed at the cover, thinking about what she said.

Why fake Victor Usher's death? It can't have been for love – the pair didn't have the greatest marriage if Madame Usher was screwing around with Dad. Elena said Victor would leave the house to hunt in the woods for days at a time and Madame Usher never seemed to mind. But what about financial reasons? Victor's family was rich – he probably had substantial life insurance.

Or what about to escape crime or violence? I could believe it. But I had no evidence, no way to prove it beyond random ideas and suppositions.

Or did I?

"I just need to make a phone call. I won't be long." I slid out of bed. Mom nodded, not looking up from her book as I crept into the hallway, pressing the phone to my ear as I dialed a number I wished I'd never have to dial again.

"Faye? I'm so happy to see your name pop up." Creepy Cory picked up on the second ring. I could hear chatter and music and glasses clinking in the background. He was at work. We were never supposed to answer our phones at work. I wondered if I should feel grateful he was risking his ass for me, but all it did was up the ick factor.

I can't wait until I don't need this guy anymore.

"Hi, Cory." I leaned against the wall, watching as the elevator doors slid open and shut on a businessman with a large briefcase. *Be strong. Remember that Ivan and Elena are still at Manderley. Every day that goes by puts them in danger.* "Remember last time we talked, you got me some money from Gizella Usher's accounts? I was wondering if you still have access to them?"

"Of course." I could hear the smugness in Cory's voice. "How much do you need?"

"No money. I just want you to have a look at the transactions – especially from twelve to twenty-four months ago. You're looking for big sums, like an insurance payout, or anything else unusual. Could you do that for me as a matter of urgency?"

"I'll get started tonight," he purred. "That is, unless you're coming over to show me how grateful you are."

"That's not happening."

"Come on, Faye. I've seen the papers. I know you're through with those boring musicians. You must be so upset with that girl being murdered. I can be your shoulder to cry on."

"I bet you're good at making girls cry." I couldn't help it.

My jab went right over Cory's head. I could practically hear him panting through the phone. "Are you still up at that school? Maybe I'll come and visit you—"

"Don't go near that school. It's dangerous." Cory was gross, but I didn't want him to become Madame Usher's next victim.

"Fine, fine. I know you're in New York City, anyway." My heart stuttered. *He shouldn't know that. There's no way he can know that.* Natalie has been careful to hide our location from the press. "You know we're meant to be together, Faye. That's why you keep calling me. And this time I'm not going to let your gorgeous ass get away from me."

He thought he sounded like a hot alpha male, but his words sent a chill down my spine.

"Call me when you have the information." I clicked off the phone and threw it across the hall, wishing I could wash his vile voice out of my ears. *Calling Cory was a mistake. I should have gone straight to Rochester.*

How does he know I'm in the city?

I glanced down the hallway to the elevators, my heart pounding as the bell dinged and the doors opened, revealing an empty car. *Stop it. You'll drive yourself crazy. You've already got enough to worry about. You can handle Creepy Cory.*

Sighing, I picked up my phone and headed back inside, crawling into bed with Mom as she surfed through channels until she found a horror movie. "You aren't hanging out with Titus tonight? I assume that's who you were talking to?"

I shook my head, not bothering to correct her. "He's got an audition first thing tomorrow. His parents won't let him out to play."

"He's a good man, *mi cielo*. He—" Mom broke down into a coughing fit, bringing me crashing back to reality. I wrapped my arms around her shoulders as her body convulsed.

"I'll call Dr. Nelson. We need to go to the hospital—"

Mom clasped her hand over mine, her eyes watering as she fought for control. "Don't do that. I'm fine. Dr. Nelson says this is normal. It's going to take time for me to heal, but I'll come out of this stronger than ever."

I hope so. I wrapped my arms around her, so beyond happy that she was awake and alive and with me again. *I could have lost her.*

I didn't want to think about what happened to her. If I dwelled on the poisoning too long, I felt my thin veneer of control slipping away and a violent rage bubbling up from the deepest, darkest parts of me. What Madame Usher did to her was *insidious*, and if my father was in any way involved, then...

Even if I found out the truth, I could never tell her. She would carry the guilt for his crime, and I wouldn't allow that to happen. She's spent her whole life taking care of me – now she needed me to protect her, to avenge her.

Mom hit PAUSE on the movie and turned to me with her big, brown eyes. "Will you play for me tonight?"

I'd had to leave my beautiful instrument Titus gave me at Manderley, because it was in the Red Room and Madame Usher barred the door with her body. I thought of the Becker hidden in my violin case under the bed, that vile inscription on the back. If Mom saw it, she would recognize it as his, and I'd have too much explaining to do.

I kissed her forehead. "I can't tonight. I'm too tired."

"Okay." She snuggled against my shoulder. A few minutes later, as the heroine was being chased through the forest by the serial killer, she let out an indelicate snore. I stared at the screen, my mind whirring and my father's instrument boring a hole through the bottom of the bed. I'd never kept secrets from my mother before, but how could I tell her it was possible that my father – the man who might've tried to kill her – was still alive?

IVAN

"I cannot believe it was really Clare," Elena whispered. She stretched out along the bench at the kitchen table while I chopped vegetables for *ghiveci*, a vegetable stew our mother used to cook for us. "You saw her, too. You weren't just pretending?"

Now that Faye was gone, Madame ordered Elena and me back into the kitchen. With only three students remaining at Manderley, plus Radcliffe and Usher, the meals weren't arduous. I did most of the work – I wouldn't risk Elena burning her hands.

I resisted the urge to spike Madame's meals with the bottles in Dorien's apothecary kit. She made it clear in her barbed comments to me that she knows that *I* know what she's hiding, but if I put a foot out of place she'd hurt Elena. We were at a stalemate until I got Elena out of this house, but that meant marrying her off to Radcliffe. Why did that have to be our only option?

"I saw Clare." Ever since the night of the seance, Clare's face haunted my dreams. In my mind, her see-through skin and that yawning, blackened hole where her mouth should be had become superimposed over Elena's face. I glanced at the wall behind the fridge. *Where is the man she has spying on us? Is he here now, listening to every word to report back to her?* I leaned in close and lowered my voice to a whisper. "We should leave this place tonight. It's not safe here. The man in the walls *murdered* Heather."

Elena reached for the open bottle of red wine and took a swig, licking the claret from her lips. "You can leave, brother. But my fiancé is here. He protects me."

I glowered at her. The knife slammed into the chopping board with enough force to score the wood. We weren't the only ones who had a stalemate with Madame Usher. I remembered the stories I'd heard about Radcliffe – how he abruptly left a glittering international career a decade ago to teach at Manderley. There were rumors of a scandal hushed up, and a breakdown that left him trembling after every performance. When he arrived at the house and took up his residence in the stables, he seemed a funny, harmless little man who started every time the doorbell rang and often ran out of his private lessons to throw up. It was Madame Usher who forced him to keep up his contacts in the industry, to bring his composers and patrons and collaborators to the school to lend her the airs of respectability. He did everything she asked, and his endorsement alongside Victor's fame and the school's exclusivity made Madame Usher a name to be feared and revered in Classical circles.

No one sees what I see, because he seems harmless with his round glasses and kind voice.

Even Faye told me that I have to let Elena make her own decisions. But none of them were here in the beginning.

I remembered the day he took an interest in Elena. We were nine years old and we'd been at Manderley a little over a year. We were cleaning the Red Room between Victor's classes. Well, I was scrubbing student footprints off the pristine floor while she teased me by sitting at the piano pretending to be Victor scolding me. I was so angry at her because I was doing all the work, as usual, but she kept laughing her infectious *zâne* laugh until I was laughing with her. And then I caught the eye of Radcliffe. He hovered in the doorway, sheet music scattered at his feet where he had dropped them in his rapture. His eyes were fixed on Elena with a lecherous hunger that even then made ice drip down my spine.

Radcliffe couldn't protect my sister. He was in Madame Usher's debt. She had delivered to him the prize he'd so desperately pursued all these years. And when the wedding bells tolled, he would finally sate his vile hunger for my sister.

"If you're not going to help, you should practice." I snarled the words with more venom than I intended. "You are still competing for the Manderley Prize."

Not that it was a competition. Faye and Dorien were the only ones at school who had any real shot at beating Elena, and they were gone now.

Elena fidgeted at the table. She seemed to reach a decision, and pulled a paper from her pocket and set it down in front of me. "I found that in Maxim's study last night. You should give it to Faye. If she wants answers about the man in the walls, she will know what to do."

"What is it?" I snatched the paper.

"Ivan, please don't overreact. It might not even be about him. That's why you must show Faye."

I scanned the paper. It was an article from a newspaper in some small American town I never heard of, dated four years ago.

LOCAL MUSICIAN WITHDRAWS COMPLAINTS AGAINST ACADEMY

Donelle McCoy, a talented young local musician, was thrilled to be given a place at the prestigious Manderley Academy in upstate New York. But her joy turned sour and she left the school less than a year into her studies. Donelle alleged depraved goings-on at the school, including drug use among the students and deviant sexual proclivities among the staff. She said she'd been afraid for her life and her chastity, but today was withdrawing her claims, stating, "I was angry because I couldn't keep up with the workload. I made up everything I said. Manderley Academy is not a den of sin, and Victor Usher is an upstanding man of high moral character and a brilliant musician."

Neither Donelle nor her family could be reached for further comment.

I remembered Donelle. She was a pianist. She wasn't very good, and she spent more time praying her rosary and lecturing Madame Usher about the evils of drinking alcohol than she did practicing. She left abruptly in the middle of the second term, but that wasn't uncommon – the Ushers were strict about the school's standards and often kicked out students rather than continue to teach those who were doomed to mediocrity.

I tucked the article into my pocket. Donelle could have been imprinting her own morals onto the school. We have lived at Manderley long enough to know that students had their own ways of surviving this place. Aroha wasn't the first musician who needed drugs to survive, and I've seen plenty of sordid acts that would have put a Broken Muse tour to shame.

But the article talked about a teacher, and it was in Radcliffe's possession. I tried to remember him with Donelle, but I never paid attention unless he was with Elena. I never wanted the two of them to be alone.

And I knew one beastly woman who had the power to make a righteous girl retract her accusations. What did Radcliffe trade her for covering up his crimes?

I shoved the article into my pocket and glared at my sister. Her face crumpled. "Ivan, don't—"

I grabbed her arm, shaking her, wishing I could shake sense into her. "You cannot marry him. Radcliffe is tied up in whatever is going on in this house. He won't protect you. We have to leave this place."

"You cannot change my mind, brother." Elena's touched the diamond on her finger. "Maxim has money. He has connections. He understands that I will not leave you behind. I marry him and I have the means to leave this place, and so do you. Can you not see? We will make a new life for ourselves with him as our patron."

I *could* see, and that was the problem. I could see that Elena was trading one type of servitude for another. The article burned a hole in my pocket.

Donelle called Manderley 'depraved.' The article didn't elaborate on the 'deviant sexual proclivities' she witnessed, but I could use my imagination.

What would Radcliffe do once he had Elena on his arm?

FAYE

"Relax, Faye. You're not in any trouble. We just want to ask you a few questions about Dorien Valencourt."

I shifted in the metal chair as Sheriff Laine Stanford set down a styrofoam coffee cup in front of me. She flashed me a smile that I *almost* believed could be friendly, but I knew her office was sharing information with Walpole and the NYPD. She couldn't be trusted. Beside her, a deputy rapped his pen on the table.

"Dorien didn't kill Heather," I said, ignoring the drink. "That's the only answer you need."

"You and Dorien were close, isn't that right?"

I gritted my teeth. I knew this interview was going to go to Valhalla in a wheelbarrow but I thought she'd at least butter me up first. "We were seeing each other, if that's what you mean."

She shuffled her papers. "According to other students and staff at the school, you were also dating Titus Thibodeaux and Ivan Nicolescu. Isn't that right?"

"If I was a guy, no one would bat an eyelid."

"Absolutely." She smiled at me then, trying to convince me that we were on the same side. Her deputy scoffed. "Can you tell me what happened the night of Heather's murder?"

I went over the story we all agreed on, that Dorien, Titus, and I had lied to Madame Usher about the recital so we could have a date, and we returned to find the Danvers, Valencourts, and Aaron Varney celebrating their engagement.

"You must've been upset when you saw Dorien proposed to Heather."

Mom and Natalie found me a lawyer, and I spoke to her and Rochester before I agreed to come to the station to answer Stanford's questions. We decided that I would go in alone, as having a lawyer present would give me a certain appearance.

But she told me to say as little as possible, especially about all the tricks Madame Usher pulled.

So I shrugged. "Dorien is free to propose to whoever he wants."

"And then he went upstairs to talk to Heather?" she shuffled some papers in front of her.

"He did. We all watched him go. There wasn't enough time for him to go to the kitchen and grab a knife." I didn't mention the secret passages in the school. I didn't want it to get back to Madame Usher how much I knew.

"I don't think you're telling me the whole truth, Ms. de Winter." She threw a stack of photographs on the table. "You will do anything for Dorien Valencourt, isn't that true? Including violently attack an innocent man of God?"

I knew what the photographs were. I'd seen them before, in Aaron Varney's hands. And now, splashed all over the tabloids thanks to Madame Usher. "These are photoshopped."

"I need the bathroom." Stanford patted her stomach. "That coffee went right through me. Rivers, can you grab me the Varney file from my office? Faye, what do you say we take a break?"

"Whatever."

"Tape paused at 4:45PM." Stanford clicked off the recording device. As soon as Deputy Rivers left the room, she leaned across the table and grabbed my hand. I cried out, and she tightened her grip, her eyes widening as if she couldn't believe what she was about to do.

"Listen, we don't have much time. I know these photographs are faked. I looked up Varney's original complaint at the NYPD, and it has your name, but the file was altered recently." She glanced at the door. "That schoolteacher of yours, Usher, she's tight with Walpole, but I don't answer to him, and just because he's corrupt as fuck doesn't mean I have to be. Tell me the truth and I'll do what I can to get you and your man out of this shitstorm."

I wanted so badly to believe the earnestness in her eyes, but I'd been in Madame Usher's web for too long to trust that easy. I shook my head.

"Shit, de Winter. Don't be an idiot. If you stay silent, they get away with this... whatever it is. Throw me a bone here."

"I can't help you," I whispered. "But this is bigger than you think. Talk to Agent Rochester at the FBI about Aaron Varney and his god. And dig into the Usher family. Find out if it was convenient timing for Victor Usher to be pushing up daisies."

I wouldn't give her anything she could use to hang Dorien, but maybe, just maybe, if she was telling me the truth, she could help stop Varney or Usher before they hurt anyone else.

FAYE

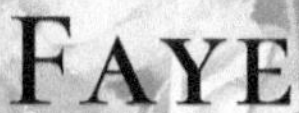

I stepped outside into the parking lot behind the music store, blinking against the vibrant sunset that streaked across the sky. The shop was on the first floor of an office building, and the owner, Gregor, blocked out the windows with black paper because he labored under the mistaken impression it deterred thieves. Emerging after an eight-hour shift was like waking up your body with a cold shower of natural light.

My feet ached. My throat was dry from talking about pianos all day. I couldn't wait to stand under the rain shower at the hotel. I turned to lock the door behind me, and a brown hand cupped itself over my mouth.

I cried out as my assailant dragged me backward. *Shit, shit.* I dropped my body-weight low, breaking their hold, and spun around and lunged out with my foot, hoping to trip them up so I could escape.

My foot connected with a shin, and my assailant went down. I sprung to my feet and grabbed for my bag and—

"Oof, what did you do that for?" a familiar voice snapped at me. My assailant rolled over, grasping at her leg, her dark eyes fixing me with an annoyed glare.

"Aroha?" I held out a hand and helped her up. "I thought you were a mugger."

"You see a dark skin in an alley and assume I'm a criminal? I expected better of a fellow brown girl, trash." Aroha fished around in her pocket and pulled out a packet of cigarettes. She tipped one into her hand and held the packet out to me. I accepted one gratefully and leaned up against the wall beside her. She lit our smokes and took a deep drag.

"I assume anyone's a mugger if they put their hand around my mouth in New York City," I shot back, but there was no bite.

"Fair enough."

I studied her face as I took a tentative puff. She looked terrible. Her black hair had spilled out of its tight bun, dancing wildly around her face. Her makeup was smudged, and her eyes glazed with the sheen of a chemical curtain. *She's high again.*

It didn't surprise me. Madame Usher had burned the anxiety medication she used to manage her moods. She needed something to help her through her performances. I just wished it didn't have to be this. Despite everything she'd done to me, I liked Aroha. She was prickly as fuck, but I respected the hell out of her and her vision for her career. In all the madness of the last few weeks, I hadn't given much thought to how she was a prisoner of Manderley, too.

I had a million questions to ask her, but I settled for an easy one. "How'd you escape Manderley?"

"I had a meeting with the philharmonic about doing a concerto in their Winter series, and I thought I'd see what you were up to now that you're no longer doing the old hag's bidding. Harrison's waiting down the block." She rolled her eyes. "He says we have to leave soon, or she'll get suspicious we came to see you."

I sucked in a deep drag. "I don't want you to get in trouble because of me."

"Too late, trash. Listen." She sounded serious. I turned toward her. "I told this to the police, but I'm telling you too because I don't trust that Walpole bastard. I saw Heather before she died. I was passing Dorien's room and I heard someone talking inside. Weird, because I knew he was out with you. So I pushed the door open a crack and saw Heather standing beside Dorien's bed, talking to the wall."

My tongue dried to the roof of my mouth. "Talking to a wall?"

She blinked, blowing out a row of perfect smoke rings. "Getting really pissy with it, stomping her foot and pouting and her whole act. She was still wearing that dress she used to take pictures down at the gazebo, too. I saw them all down there in the morning, and in the library editing it afterward. They really wanted to fuck Dorien over."

I winced at the memory of the photoshopped image of Dorien on his knees in the gazebo, proposing to Heather. It accompanied every lurid article about Heather's murder, and even though I knew it was fake, it made rage burn behind my eyes every time I saw it.

"What do you want me to do with this?" I asked her, curious about the answer.

Aroha rolled her eyes, sinking down to her knees. She giggled, and the giggle turned into a cackle that set my teeth on edge. "The bitch burned my medication. I was lucky Elena had some coke stashed behind the tank in the bathroom, or I'd have been a complete mess for this meeting today. Unlike you, I don't have my daddy's famous name to fall back on. I need that scholarship, or it's back to playing fucking church hymns for me. Raze Manderley to the ground if you have to, but at the end of it, let me walk away with a career, okay?"

Before I could say another word, Aroha stubbed out her cigarette on the ground and disappeared down the alley. I leaned my head back and drew the smoke deep into my lungs, letting the nicotine spin in my head, churning up this new dirt.

Heather had been talking to the wall.

Not just talking, by the sounds of it, but *scheming*.

An idea was forming in my mind.

I needed to get inside Manderley again. We needed the truth.

Titus didn't say a word as he drove the winding roads to Manderley. What was there to say? Everything was completely fucked up.

He'd been called in by Sheriff Laine Stanford to give his statement as well. She'd even shown up at the hotel to talk to my mother. But whatever they said to Stanford had no impact, or maybe she was in Walpole's pocket after all, because the authorities were officially charging Dorien with first-degree murder. And now Ivan messaged me from his burner phone, with a picture of an old newspaper article about some previous drama at Manderley. Ivan thought it was about Radcliffe, but I wondered if it might match up with the reason our secret Manderley ghost had to disappear. I would look into it, but not today.

Today we found out who was hiding in the walls of Manderley.

Titus drummed his fingers on the steering wheel in time with an Iron Maiden track. It was weird to see him like this, filled with pent-up aggression. He'd been incredible these last few weeks as more salacious news stories came out about me and Dorien, as I schemed and investigated and worried about Ivan and Elena and Aroha stuck at Manderley with this murderer inside the walls.

The press might call Dorien the genius behind Broken Muse, but Titus was our rock. He anchored us to each other and kept our wild emotions from making us do irrational things.

Which was probably why he'd gone weird and silent – what we were doing today was pretty irrational.

As we rounded the bend and climbed along a narrow road hugging the side of the mountain, a chill crept into my veins. Through the trees, I could make out the gabled roof and gothic windows of Manderley. The twin eyes of my old attic bedroom windows glared back at me in silent accusation.

I don't want to be here.

I wanted to be back in my cozy hotel room with my mom, watching horror movies and throwing hilarious shade at the terrible room service tacos. But the only way to clear Dorien's name was to enter the belly of the beast.

The road turned abruptly, leaving a wide gravel shoulder that served as the starting point of one of the hiking trails, as well as a lookout across the valley. Titus slammed his foot down and we jerked to a stop. I peered out the window over the rickety safety rail to the deep valley far below, the treetops shrouded with mist and the river winding through them like a snake. Manderley's twin eyes burned into me.

"You don't have to go back there." Titus reached across to squeeze my arm. "We could ask Ivan and Elena to do this for us. Or better yet, wait until his FBI agent is ready to move against Usher."

I shook my head. "I need to see. I need to know."

I need to know if my father is inside those walls.

I need to know if he left us for her.

Titus made a choking sound, as if he sensed what I was thinking. He trailed his fingers along my arm, raising goosebumps on my skin that had nothing to do with my trepidation about returning to Manderley. I looked over to him, and he cocked an eyebrow at me, his dark eyes hard with determination. I knew I wasn't the only one who was afraid of Manderley.

"Manderley took from you, too." I slid my hand across his cheek. Beneath my fingers, his stubble scratched my skin, reminding me that in this world of spirits and shadows, he was with me. He was real.

I moved my hand along his jaw, his neck. I flicked a stray braid from his face. His eyes watched me. Not my hand. Me. The intensity of his gaze halted my breath. All my life, when people looked at me, they saw only my name – de Winter. My father, the great virtuoso. They didn't hear my music, only the ghost of his notes. But Titus saw me, all of me, even the dark and ugly sides I tried to keep hidden. And he loved them unconditionally.

Neither of us belonged at Manderley. But here, in this car, we had everything. We had each other. We shared the same song, the same sad notes and haunting melody.

I bent my head, resting my forehead against his. "Please," I whispered as the first flakes of snow fell outside the window. "Make me feel invincible."

Titus' fingers closed around my neck. Strong, domineering. He tilted my head back and took my mouth with his. He didn't rush, even though we very definitely had somewhere to be. He kissed me slowly, beautifully, his lips like a butterfly unfurling its wings for the first time. I tried to fall into him but the gearstick was in the way, and when I swung my leg over to straddle him, I jammed it against the steering wheel.

Titus laughed his low, sexy laugh as he leaned our seats back. Between his massive bulk and my curves, we couldn't maneuver easily, and it was too fucking cold outside to open a door. I tried to straddle him, but he plonked me down on the passenger seat. I peered up at him, disappointed that we couldn't make this work, but he pushed me back down.

"Let me take care of you," he smiled.

The words sent a flicker of heat through my body. Titus kissed a trail over my neck as he folded down the waistband of my leggings. I tried to reach down to help, but he slapped my hand away, chuckling against my lips.

I captured his rumbling laugh in my mouth, and it tasted like summer, like happiness.

"You don't need me to feel powerful," he murmured as he pushed my panties to one side. "You're Faye fucking de Winter. I want you to say it for me."

"I'm Faye de Winter."

"Say it properly." He teased my entrance with his finger. I could feel how wet I was already, how much my body needed him.

I bucked my hips toward him, trying to make him give me what I wanted. "I'm Faye fucking de Winter."

"Damn right. You're a queen riding into war. And I, your humble servant, will always be by your side. Or between your legs."

Titus lowered his head, his tongue lapping at my swollen clit as he thrust a finger inside me. My fingers tangled in his hair, pushing his head down as he danced his tongue over me until the ache inside me became a scream pressing against my lips.

Sound the fucktrumpets, musicians are the best in bed. Seriously. The rhythm, the tempo, the natural sense of pageantry. Titus played my body like a guitar, his fingers conjuring magic from my skin.

Liquid heat coursed through my body as he curled his finger inside me, rubbing that spot that drove me wild. I gripped his shoulders, bending into him, driving him deeper. "Titus, don't stop. You feel so good. You're perfect."

You're perfect.

We don't tell people that enough, that they're perfect just the way they are. I don't think Titus had ever heard those words before, even though his whole life had been about striving for perfection. He groaned against my clit, lost in the intensity of the moment. With a shuddering breath, I lost myself, too.

The orgasm crested, and I rode it into the snow-dusted valley below us. I rode it as my body came to pieces, as bursts of bright magic sizzled beneath my skin.

Titus laid a trail of kisses up my chest as he leaned forward, supporting his weight on the back of the chair as he tugged down his pants with one hand. His cock sprung free, and he laughed again at my expression when I saw it. I still wasn't quite sure how something that majestic could fit inside me. Magic.

Titus shuffled back between my legs. He pressed my thighs wide and plunged his cock inside me.

I saw stars. A universe opened up on the roof of the car as he thrust inside me, filling me, making me his. Being his perfect, wonderful self.

My breasts crushed against his chest, my knees smashing against the dashboard, a handbrake jabbing where no handbrake should ever jab. I loved every moment of it because it was raw and real and true. Because my Titus, my broken muse, was inside me, and for a brief moment, I believed I was invincible, and everything would be all right.

Getting Madame Usher out of the house was easier than I thought. All it took was asking Dorien to request a meeting with her in jail. I bet she thought he was going to agree to anything she wanted if she'd call in a favor from Walpole to get him to drop the charges.

After our distraction in the car, we had to race down the trail and through the wood to Manderley. We watched through the trees as Harrison drove Madame Usher away. A sprinkle of snow fell. Wet flakes dotted my face as I turned to watch them pass through the iron gates. As soon as the car disappeared around the bend of the road, Titus and I scrambled out of the trees and around the edge of the house to the backdoor, where I let us in with my copied key.

The sound of Aroha practicing one of her atonal pieces echoed through the halls. Otherwise, the house remained completely silent. We crept upstairs, careful to stand on the edges where the boards were less likely to creak. Using the keys Titus copied, I unlocked Ivan and Elena's door. Madame Usher was keeping them locked in their rooms when they didn't have classes or chores.

Elena breezed past me, air-kissing both my cheeks.

"I'll be over at Master Radcliffe's, providing a 'distraction.'" She waved as she bounced off. Ivan frowned as he came to the doorway. She hadn't elaborated on what she meant by distraction, but Ivan's jaw clenched as he watched her glide down the staircase, so I didn't want to ask.

"I missed you." I wrapped my arms around his neck and pressed my lips to his. I could still taste Titus' scent on my tongue – the taste of an ancient forest god; myrrh and musk, and roses dappled with dew. But I needed to taste Ivan, too. I needed to reassure myself that he was here, alive and safe – at least while he was in my arms.

Ivan grunted in surprise as I nipped at his lower lip, but he returned the kiss, his eyes no longer focused on the staircase but boring into me with cold and beautiful clarity.

I missed you.

I've been so afraid for you.

I deepened the kiss, pressing against him and devouring him as bit by bit the tension in his body unwound. He sank into me, giving into the connection we shared. We didn't need words to say the things we'd been thinking all these nights we've been apart.

I knew that loving Ivan meant loving Elena, too. They were a package deal, and I was lucky they were such a wonderful package. I didn't want Ivan to ever feel like he had to dull his devotion to her – it might've made some girls jealous, but I had no room for that shit in my life. It made me love him more. I would always be safe with him because I saw how he'd kept her safe for so many years.

I just wish…

I wish he was free to be himself. To learn about who he is and what he wants from his life if he's not protecting her. I wish he saw the wonderful person I see in him.

"Faye," Titus warned.

"Right, yes." I pulled away from Ivan reluctantly. His ice-blue eyes raked over me, like he was trying to commit me to memory. "We should do this."

We made our way down the hall to Dorien's room, where I used my keys to unlock it. The forensic teams finished with the room weeks ago, leaving it smelling faintly of bleach. Manderley's antique furniture and paintings were still in situ, but Dorien's things were gone – Ivan told me the Valencourts showed up with Father Aaron to take them away. I'd found some of Dorien's more well-known stage outfits – including the shirt he wore in the video for 'A Graveside Story' – on eBay. The Temple was getting desperate for money, which couldn't be a good sign.

Titus peered under the empty bed frame. "No ghosts here."

"Aroha said Heather was talking to that wall." I cast my eye around the room. Dorien never went in for band posters and Suicide Girls. Instead, he decorated the walls with artwork from Manderley's extensive collection, as well as his own acquisitions. The paintings remained in place, spectral reminders of the complicated boy who used to call this room home. His smell clung to the air, hidden beneath the antiseptic scent of the crime scene cleaners.

Above his desk was a painting that referenced the Hell panel of Hieronymus Bosch's *Garden of Earthly Delights* in a heavy-looking gilded frame. A Manderley piece, but not one that could be displayed in polite company. *How very Dorien.*

Heather was talking to the wall.

I moved to stand in the doorway. From Aroha's position, she couldn't have seen the desk wall. Anything – or anyone – there would be obscured for her.

I stepped up onto the desk and peered at the edge of the painting. It looked solid. As my fingers grazed the surface, I felt cold air brush against them. I'd felt drafts before in other rooms of Manderley – air rushing through gaps and cracks in the walls. I thought it was just part of living in an old house, but now…

"Help me lift this painting down," I said.

I stepped off the desk and Titus leaped up. Ivan started climbing up to help, but Titus shooed him away. Ivan pulled me into his arms, pressing his lips to mine for another breathless kiss.

"I have missed you," he murmured against my lips, his fingers trailing down my spine.

"Ditto." I ran my hands over his shoulders, trying to memorize the shape of him. I couldn't bear the thought of having to leave him here again.

"Faye, you should see this."

Reluctantly, I broke the kiss and turned toward Titus. He jabbed his finger at the gilded frame. "I can't move this," he said.

"Stand aside," Ivan commanded. "I'll do it—"

"Trust me, your puny Romanian arms won't make a dent. If I can't budge it, then it's stuck to the wall with some kind of superhuman glue."

I climbed up beside Titus and stared at the frame again. In the corner – nestled amongst goat-demons feeding on human flash – was a man crucified on a harp, no doubt symbolizing the contrast between pleasure and pain.

Music.

I touched the harp, feeling the odd way the paint rose in ridges around it. Cold air nudged my fingers.

I pressed it.

The painting swung toward me. I flung myself off the desk, collapsing into Ivan's arms before the heavy bastard decapitated me. The painting hit the adjoining wall and stopped swinging, leaving a gaping hole in the wall behind it.

Sound the fucktrumpets.

Gotcha.

Titus held my hand as I clambered back on the desk and peered inside the hole. It was a crawl-space between the walls, wide enough only for a small person to walk through if they shuffled sideways. Titus wouldn't be able to fit. On the inside edge of the hole was a mechanism for operating the door. There was a bolt that could be slid in place, preventing the painting from being opened from the outside.

We got lucky. If that bolt had been shut today, we never would have found the secret door.

The crawl-space looked to stretch the entire length of the wall, but I could only see a few feet into the gloom – a yearning black hole threatening to swallow us. I patted my pocket for my phone, but then remembered I left it back in the car.

"I need a flashlight," I called over my shoulder.

Titus didn't have his phone on him, and Ivan's burner phone didn't have a flashlight app. We searched the drawers in Dorien's desk, but there was nothing. I ran downstairs to look in the kitchen. I found a packet of matches, which would do in a pinch, but I didn't want to risk burning the place down.

"I know where there will be a flashlight," I said. "Harrison's shed."

I didn't want to leave the house again, but we had at least two hours before Madame Usher could be back from her meeting with Dorien, and there was no way I was getting into that hole without a light. Ivan and I left Titus in Dorien's room, guarding the hole with the ax from the woodpile. We snuck back downstairs and headed for the collection of outbuildings behind the stables.

Steam puffed from our lips as we made our way past the old shed where Titus secretly played his music. I tried the door of Harrison's maintenance shed. The door was locked, but my copied keys dealt with that.

Ivan made to step inside. I grabbed him by the collar and yanked him out again, holding him against me as he tried to avoid looking at me.

"You're not okay," I said. It wasn't a question.

Ivan looked toward the stables. Lights shone through the windows, and if I strained I could hear the faint notes of piano music. Elena was working on her 'distraction.'

"I keep thinking what that woman said in the article," Ivan said. "Deviant sexual proclivities."

I stroked his cheek. "They're just playing the piano."

"And what will he do to her once they're married?" he growled, his hands balling into fists.

"We don't know Donelle was talking about Radcliffe."

"Who else could it be?" he said bitterly. "Madame Usher barely touched Victor."

An image of the portrait in the attic burned inside my mind. *Maybe Donelle saw something between Madame and my father.*

If the man in the walls was Victor, he's been living there since his supposed death eighteen months ago. But my father has been missing for ten years. He couldn't really have been living in the walls all that time, could he? Not with *Victor* in the house, in *her* bed. It seemed insane.

We're going to find out.

I grabbed two flashlights from a shelf of tools and supplies and clicked them on to make sure they worked. We headed back down the path, keeping low to avoid been seen through the stable windows. From inside, I heard the keys stutter. Elena shrieked.

I looked back at Ivan. He stiffened, his entire body rigid. I reached for him, trying to urge him on, but I knew it was hopeless. He dived into the overgrown flowerbed, his fingers gripping the edge of the sill and pulling his body up so he could see inside.

Fuck it. In for a penny.

I shuffled in beside him, straining my head to see inside the dimly lit room. Snow dotted my hair, flakes melting into freezing drips that rolled under my collar and down my back. I had to cup my hands against the glass to see inside.

Elena didn't look like she was in trouble. In fact, she had a smile on her face as she sat at the piano, her back perfectly straight, her delicate neck long like a swan. Radcliffe leaned over her, his fingers cupping hers as he corrected her positioning. She gazed up at him with perfect adoration. He leaned in closer to murmur something to her, and his lips grazed her neck.

Beside me, Ivan ground his teeth together.

"There's nothing to see here." I tugged his arm. He didn't move. "Ivan. *Ivan?*"

He glared at the window. A low, pained sound escaped his throat.

"You're seeing what you expect to see. They're playing the piano. He kissed her neck. They *are* engaged to be married." I knitted my fingers in his and tugged him gently. "Can I remind you that we were doing much more depraved things on a piano months ago, and you haven't put a ring on it?"

Ivan cracked a smile, but it was a long time before he tore his gaze from the scene inside. When he looked at me again, his ice eyes burned with frigid ire. I gripped his fingers. "Whether Radcliffe is a deviant or not, if we want to free her from this marriage, we need to discover the secrets of Manderley. Come on."

He nodded and let me drag him out of the weeds. We rushed back inside, careful not to slam the kitchen door against the freezing air and alert Aroha to our presence. In the kitchen, I grabbed two knives from the rack. Whoever was in the walls was armed, so we should be, too.

Titus set down the ax when we entered the room. Ivan tossed him a flashlight and he pointed it into the hole. "This definitely goes all the way back toward my bedroom, but I'm not going to be any use." He handed back the flashlight. "I won't fit inside."

"Too many protein shakes," Ivan scoffed. It took me a moment to realize he'd cracked a joke, and I had to stifle a laugh with my hand.

Titus pointed to Ivan's violin, which was resting on the bed. "I took that from your room. I figure I'll play a few bars of, say, Saint-Saëns' *Danse Macabre*, if you need to get back here, and some Shostakovich if you need to stay silent and hide?"

"Mmmm, clever as well as gorgeous." I climbed up on the desk beside Titus and slid the largest carving knife into my belt. "Help me in."

Titus made a cup with his hands. I stepped into it and he boosted me up. I grabbed the edge of the hole and swung myself over. I gasped as I slid down into the darkness. It went deeper than I thought, and I shrieked as the walls closed around me and I disappeared into the gloom before my feet slammed into a hard wooden surface.

I clicked on my light. Wedged in sideways like this, I had to twist my neck at an awkward angle to aim the flashlight into the crawl space. The stale air burned my lungs. *Whoever's been wandering around in here, they can't have been comfortable.*

My hand flew to the knife handle. My breathing steadied, knowing it was there.

The space stretched all the way between the walls in both directions. I couldn't believe we never noticed from the outside how the house's walls were so deep.

"There's a ladder here." I felt around the strips of wood nailed into the wall. "Someone wanted to make it easier to climb in and out of the painting."

A moment later, Ivan's legs swung over the edge. I grabbed his ankle and guided it onto the first rung of the ladder. He swung himself over and dropped down beside me, holding his light up to peer at the walls. His flashlight made his pale skin luminescent, the cold of his blue eyes searing in the gloom.

"Stay behind me," he ordered, trying to push past me.

"No way." I crossed my arms over my boobs. "I'm not going to let you walk headfirst into danger." *If anyone is going to confront my father, it should be me.* "Besides, there's not enough room for you to get around me in here unless you have secret contortionist abilities."

I held up my flashlight and shone it into the gloom as we shuffled forward. We didn't have to go far before we reached a junction. We could continue straight ahead to Titus' room, or turn off down the walls that divided their rooms.

I noticed a pinprick of light stabbing through the wall.

"That's a peephole," I whispered, angling my body down the junction to get to it. I was too short to see out of the hole, but Ivan peered through. His features hardened.

"What is it?" I whispered.

"This peephole looks straight into Titus' room," Ivan said. "Whoever was in these walls would've been able to see and hear everything."

"That's how Madame Usher seemed to know what was going on in the house. She had someone spying on us."

My stomach churned as the full meaning of this peephole dawned on me.

Someone was watching us.

Someone watched me and Titus and Ivan on that bed.

That's fucking gross.

This branch was a dead end, so we backtracked and continued along the wall of Titus' room. It was tough to move in the narrow space. My ass scraped across the rough wood as I shuffled sideways. My tits were smushed against my chest. Behind me, Ivan grunted as he wrestled with his shoulders.

"We must be nearly at Titus' doorway. This looks like a dead end—"

I screamed as my foot slid away into nothing and I toppled forward into a dark abyss.

Faye

Ivan grabbed me and yanked me backward, scraping my calf on rough wood as he hauled me to safety.

"Thanks." I nestled my head into his neck as I waited for my heart rate to return to normal. My leg stung, but I couldn't twist my body to look at it. I held it out for Ivan to inspect.

"You've scraped some skin off, and it's bleeding a little." He sounded concerned. "We should turn back."

"No way." I pointed my flashlight down into a dark hole that must lead to the ground floor. More wooden boards were nailed into the wall to create a ladder. I sucked in a few deep breaths of stale air. *I nearly fell down there. I could have broken my neck.*

Just like Clare.

"It goes up, as well." Ivan pointed with his flashlight. He didn't have to say what he was thinking. We both knew what that meant.

This tunnel leads into the storage room beside my bedroom.

Dorien and I had looked for a secret passage when we broke in there and couldn't find one. The button to operate the painting in his room was so well concealed I'm not surprised we didn't find a similar entrance in the attic. I leaned across the hole and grabbed a wooden board, testing my weight against it. It seemed sturdy. In fact, these boards looked as though they'd been hammered in recently, with modern nails. Ivan held my hips as I swung my legs across the hole and clambered up the ladder.

I moved through a small open hatch and stepped off the ladder into another narrow space. The ceiling of the tunnel was so low I had to stoop a little. Ivan looked ridiculous as he followed me, hunched over sideways in the tiny space. We crawled forward into the gloom. My heart hammered in my chest. Around every corner I expected to be pounced on by the tunnel's occupant.

Where is he?

Who is he?

If my father's face suddenly appeared like a ghoul in the darkness, what would I do?

The knife handle dug against my hip. As I dragged my legs forward, it felt like it weighed a million pounds. Or maybe that was my abandonment issues dragging behind me like dead weight.

Up ahead, two pinpricks of light pierced the gloom. I peered through one into my old bedroom – the peephole I found in the painting. This is where someone spied on me, and Clare before me.

The walls are talking.

But who was talking? Who?

The suspense of it weighed on my chest, so every step felt like moving through molasses. Ivan's presence behind me was the only thing stopping me from breaking down and yelling my accusations into the darkness.

A person could go insane hiding away in here. The walls tightened around me as I moved deeper. *How many horror films have I seen that start like this and end up with the heroine's guts splattered across the secret passage?*

I'm going to go insane if I don't get answers.

Where are you? Who are you?

From the corner of the storage room, we had to lie down and crawl through a low space, which I figured from the sloping wall and the map of the house I had in my head was the roof cavity beneath the attic windows. As I dragged myself forward on my elbows, I ran my fingers along the wall, crying out in triumph when my fingers brushed a mechanism – similar to the one we discovered behind the painting. I slid open the bolt, lifted the catch and a small hatch swung outward, into the storage room.

Dorien and I searched the whole room, but we never would have found this – it was too perfectly concealed in the paneling and it could only open from the inside.

I crawled out from the wall, shoving aside boxes and kicking up clouds of dust. I sucked in the hot air of the attic like it was the sweetest perfume. I clambered to my feet and swung my arms around. It felt so good to have *space*. I never thought I was claustrophobic or afraid of the dark, but my stomach cramped and my chest ached from being on edge.

Ivan climbed out after me. He winced as he rolled his shoulders and shone his light around the room, taking in the row of footsteps in the dust leading from the tunnel to the peephole and back again. His shoulders tensed. "This man will wish he's a ghost by the time I'm done with him."

"Get in line." My hands balled into fists.

All these months I lived up here, worried about my mom, hurting from the things the Muses did to me, someone was watching me, invading my privacy, finding fresh ways to torment me. And after I saw Clare I thought…I thought I was being visited by a ghostly friend. Someone who'd been just as much a victim of the house as I had.

But now I didn't know anymore.

The dead were still dead to me. But the living were determined to haunt my ass.

Ivan shone his light into the tunnel. "This passage keeps going."

"There's an entire network of tunnels," I breathed. I didn't want to go back into that narrow space, but we had to see where it led. *Who* it led to. I strained my ears to hear Titus – nothing, just a few stolen notes from Aroha's composition echoing and amplifying in the hollow walls. We were safe to keep going for now.

I kicked a box aside, no longer caring if they knew we discovered their secret. On my hands and knees, I turned my shoulders sideways and crawled back into the tunnel, aiming my flashlight into the unknown. My elbows scraped raw as I pulled myself along so Ivan could fit in after me. I heard a *CLICK* as he snapped the door shut behind us, snuffing out the thin beam of natural light.

My stifled breath came out in ragged gasps as I inched along the tunnel. My face felt hot, my lungs sticky, my temples pounding. I heard something squeak above me, and little feet *scritch-scritch-scritching* in the gloom. I shuffled faster, my elbows burning as the rough wood scraped off my skin.

At the end of the tunnel was another open trapdoor, another wooden ladder. As soon as we dropped down on the other side, the space around us widened out into a dark hallway, spacious enough for us to stand beside each other. The air still tasted stale and scratched the back of my throat, but at least I wasn't hemmed in on all sides.

Ivan clapped his hands over my shoulders, his breath coming out in ragged gasps. "That was horrible."

"No argument." I shone my flashlight down the corridor. "Look."

I noticed the tiny pinpricks of light dotting the hall. Little peepholes. I went up to one and looked out onto an ornate sitting room I'd never seen before. A Fazioli piano sat in the corner closest to us. I could only see the corner of it, beautifully polished despite the shabby condition of the other furniture. A violin rested on a stand beside it.

"I think…I think we're in Madame Usher's private wing."

"Look at this." Ivan tapped the opposite wall, showing me where a window had been boarded up from inside. I tried to map our location in my head. Many of the windows in Madame's private wing had the shades drawn constantly, so we couldn't see in from outside. *That's because she doesn't want anyone to know this corridor exists.*

Fear prickled in my chest, and the hairs on my arms and neck stood to attention. The air grew hotter, streaking my face with sweat. *He's here.* I *felt* him nearby, this creature of the gloom who had been haunting us. We were in his domain. He was watching us this very moment.

But where is he?

I tugged the knife from my belt and held it in front of me. Ivan did the same, holding his knife and taking my other hand in his.

Ivan squeezed my fingers as we made our way down the hallway, peeking through the peepholes into the different rooms of Madame's private wing – a master bedroom fit for a Russian Tsar, an opulent bathroom, all the furniture and fine objects coated in a thick layer of dust. Madame Usher certainly spared no expense on her own comfort, especially considering the rest of the house was in such a state of ruin.

The hallway stopped at a door. Ivan grabbed my wrist to stop me, but I shook him off.

I have to know.

The air sang with tension, pulled tight like a note ringing on an open string. I turned the handle, my breath catching. It was unlocked. I raised my knife and shoved the door open, and we stepped into the unknown.

My breath caught in my throat as I aimed the flashlight beam into the dim room.

I don't know what I expected to find. A pile of skulls, perhaps. Or a nuclear weapon with a comically large countdown timer. But I definitely didn't expect the sight that greeted us.

The room was furnished with simple furniture. It must've been on the end of the wing, because it contained one of the tall gothic arched windows that made Manderley such an arresting sight. The window was boarded up, but the decorative rosette at the top had been left bare. The ancient glass was cracked slightly, letting in a blast of cold air. *That could be the source of the drafts in the houses.* Beneath the window, a narrow, single bed was made up with fresh sheets, and there were books stacked on a chair beside it. Crime thrillers mostly, and a biography of Mozart. Ratty men's clothing hung from a rack in the corner, with shoes and slippers lined up underneath. A bookshelf on the opposite wall held more volumes, as well as a small MP3 player and headphones, an electric kettle, and a supply of coffee and candy bars.

"Someone's been living here," I whispered. When we were sure there was no one in the room, I stepped inside, fingering the threadbare mattress, peering at the titles of the books. I longed to flick through the MP3 player, but I didn't want to put anything out of place.

We knew someone was hiding in the walls, but this room... this was someone's *life.* I couldn't imagine being hidden away in here day after day after day, away from light and love and music. *It's so sad.*

Angry tears pricked at the corners of my eyes. *Did my dad give up his life with Mom, with me, for this?*

"Look at this." Ivan moved behind the clothing rack. "There's another room back here."

He pushed the narrow door open and lurched forward, his knife glinting as he raised it high. I crowded in beside him as he swept his flashlight beam around the second room. It looked like some kind of laboratory. A narrow counter with a sink stood against one wall, with glass jars and beakers lined up on shelves above. A mortar and pestle sat in the sink alongside metal tongs and other strange implements. Boxes and old file cases littered the floor. The room smelt of sulfur and disinfectant.

Opposite the sink was a desk with a battered laptop, a printer, and stacks of books. Unable to hold back my curiosity, I picked up the top one and thumbed through it – it was a Victorian plant manual. Beneath it was a book on famous perfumers, and others on chemical compounds and medicinal herbs.

As Ivan turned pages in a notebook beside the computer, I picked up a bottle from the shelf. It had been labeled 'Brugmansia: Angel's Trumpet' and contained dried leaves and white flower petals. *I think I've seen these flowers before, in the poison garden...*

"Faye."

Ivan jabbed his finger at the notebook. It contained what looked like recipes. After scanning a couple, I realized they were notes on experiments with various flowers and herbs, with measurements and notations about temperatures and chemical reactions.

"I recognize this handwriting," Ivan said. "It belongs to Victor Usher."

Victor Usher.

My breath whooshed in relief. I didn't realize how much I'd been hoping my dad wasn't secretly living in the walls of Manderley until Ivan's words registered. A dead Donovan de Winter was better than one who chose this squalid hellhole over his family.

Ivan's fingers squeezed mine. "You are okay?"

I sucked in another deep breath. "Yes. I'm okay." I gestured to the shelves, the lab, the boxes. "So then what is this place? Some kind of Frankenstein lab?"

Ivan pulled a leather-bound volume off the shelf and opened it. "These are ledger books for that company the Usher's owned, Menabilly Holdings. They detail a lot of money moving around."

What the fuck is going on?

I moved deeper into the room. There was a second door, even smaller and narrower, facing into what I assumed to be Madame Usher's master suite. A hidden door that granted her and her husband access to this little bolthole. As I bent down to inspect the door, my foot brushed a cardboard box with a shipping label addressed to Menabilly Holdings.

I trained my beam on it and peeled back the flap. The box was filled with square paper bags. They looked familiar. My heart raced as I picked one up and held it under the light. "It's the herbal tea my mom used to drink."

In Cauda Venenum.

I lifted the box aside and looked at the stack behind it, my heart racing. There were boxes and boxes of the stuff, hidden in this secret laboratory behind Madame's bedroom wall. In horror, I whirled to face Ivan, who held up a page in the notebook. The word 'birthwort' jumped off the page.

"This is the poison," he whispered.

We've found it. We've found the evidence we need to get the bitch. We need to—

The faint sound of a solo violin pierced my ears. Not Aroha's atonal playing, but a familiar tune that opened with the *diabolus in musica*, dripping with darkness and urgency.

Saint-Saëns' *La Danse Macabre*.

Shit.

Get out. We have to get out now.

IVAN

Faye's eyes widened as the familiar tune sung in the air. She hugged the tea box to her chest, clinging to the truth like she needed it to remain upright. I grabbed her wrist and tugged her to her feet.

She whispered. "We have to put everything back how we found it."

My heart raced as I kicked the boxes back into the corner. Faye bent over the counter, her hair tumbling down her shoulders as she flipped the notebooks shut, hiding away evidence of Victor's complicity. I wished we'd thought to bring a phone to take photographs for evidence, but Faye left hers in the car and my burner couldn't even text in lower caps, let alone take photos.

Titus' playing sped up now, the bow tearing across the strings. I winced as he bungled the contrapuntal. He wasn't a skilled violinist, but I read the urgency in his notes.

I grabbed Faye's wrist again and yanked her toward the door. "We must go."

Faye slid the notebook back into its position beside the laptop. She cast a final, forlorn look at the room that contained all the answers we longed for, and a million new questions that would keep us awake at night.

And then we fled.

Back through Victor Usher's sad little bedroom. Back into the corridor connecting Madame Usher's private apartments to the secret tunnels throughout the house. Titus' music screeched in my ears. I had only one thought – get Faye out.

Keep her safe.

Faye dragged her feet behind me. She yanked down on her arm and freed it from my grasp. I grabbed for her but she twisted away. "What are you doing?"

She copped her hands over one of the peepholes. "I want to see Madame Usher."

"We have to get out of here," I whispered. "What if Victor comes back?"

"*Exactly*. He's not in his rooms. Why wasn't he in his bedroom or that lab or the tunnels? Because he's out *there*, in her quarters. I want to see them together. Then we'll know everything."

"We already know everything." Panic crawled through my stomach. I tugged on her hand. "Faye, *please*."

She glared at me in defiance before turning back to the peephole. *Infuriating woman.* I paced across the corridor, wringing my hands in my hair before moving further down and choosing one of the other peepholes. Mine looked into the ornate reception room. I could clearly make out the door leading into the second-floor landing, where the student bedrooms and bathrooms led off.

Titus' music cut off abruptly. Faye and I exchanged a worried glance, but she refused to move. My stomach twisted in knots as I stared into that still room, waiting for something to happen. A few minutes later, the door banged open, shaking on its hinges. Madame Usher marched through the receiving room, her black skirts flying around her. Dust kicked up where she threw down her carpet-bag. She unwound her shawl from her shoulders and tossed it angrily in the direction of a coat rack.

"That infernal boy," she yelled into the gloom. "I'll be glad when he's locked away for good."

She passed into the next room. I hardly dared to breathe as I moved with her, creeping along the wall to find another peephole. Madame Usher stood in the middle of her sitting room, her nails digging into the edge of the piano as she breathed through her nose.

"I'd like to see that swaggering boy locked in a jail cell," a male voice said, the sound muffled by the wall between us. His voice rose with obvious delight. "What did he want?"

I started. *He's right there. He's been right here all this time.*
Did he hear us? Our footsteps? Our whispers? Does he know we're inside the walls? Why doesn't he tell her?

Even when we found the bedroom and lab, I didn't really believe it was possible until this very moment. But it's true.

It's him.

Victor Usher wasn't dead after all. He'd been living in the walls of Manderley, spying on us for his wife.

But why?

I couldn't see him from this angle, for he sat at the piano, his head to my left. I dared not move closer. I feared even my breathing could give us away.

Faye reached down the wall to me, hooking her pinkie finger in mine.

Madame Usher snorted. "He had the audacity to demand I intercede with the police, tell them he's innocent. He tried to threaten me with what he knows about the poison again, but this time he has no power over me. No one will believe a word from a trumped-up murdering shit. I don't need him any longer. Broken Muse will never play another show or make another record. That's for the best."

"What about our plan?" Victor's voice wheedled. "I needed Broken Muse."

"You destroyed the plan when you stabbed Heather," she snapped.

"I had to do it. If you heard the things she was saying... I had to protect—"

"I had it all planned. Every last detail was set in perfect motion. But as usual, you blundered in and made a mess of it." She flounced dramatically across the piano lid. "I never should have listened to you in the first place. If I hadn't done what you asked, none of this would have happened and you would have everything you deserve. Everything they took for granted could have been ours but you...you..."

"Shhhh." A hand reached out and tugged her onto the piano bench beside him. She was so close I could see the flyaway strands of dark hair that escaped her severe bun. He pulled her into him, so she rested her head on his shoulder. "My darling, please don't get worked up. We've worked too hard to give up now. You're right, of course. I messed up. But we can fix this. We will triumph. I know you have a brilliant new plan brewing in that beautiful head of yours."

She sniffed. "If Dorien goes away, Varney will get control over their estate. That will get him off our backs. Elena's wedding will secure Radcliffe's silence. All I have to do is keep the others from talking and we'll have the money we need to start over. It might not be what we imagined, but at least we'll no longer need to take in these wretched students."

"And Faye?" His voice was gentle, soothing. "What will you do with her?"

My stomach twisted as Madame Usher said, "You've become too soft. It's because of her our world is in disarray. I will take care of Faye, but you must trust me to do what's best for you."

"See? I knew you would think of everything." The floorboards creaked as the shadowed figure of Victor rose. I recognized the slope of his shoulders, the confident way he carried himself. "You have your lessons. I should get back to my lab. I will see you this evening."

Shit. *Shit.*

"Of course. Until tonight." She stood too, leaning over the piano. There was a wet, smacking sound as they kissed, and then she breezed from the room and Victor Usher started toward the bedroom and hidden door. I could see his back and his hair, long and tangled now, so different from Victor's usual tidy cut, and streaked with grey. He wore a perfectly-tailored suit streaked with dust. As he passed the violin, he tweaked the strings playfully.

As soon as he was out of sight in the bedroom, I let out the breath I'd been holding and grabbed Faye's hand. We'd taken two silent steps down the corridor when we heard a knocking on the wall.

"I know you're in there," Victor bellowed. "I heard you shuffling around, whispering to each other. Are you going to tell Faye? Because you should know the truth—"

At the sound of her name, Faye's face collapsed in fright. We bolted down the hallway, no longer caring how loud our footsteps were, how ragged our breathing. My elbow crashed against the wall as I slid my hands over her ass, helping her shimmy up the ladder. Behind us, the door to the bedroom crashed open.

"Go, go." I gave Faye one final push and she wiggled through the trapdoor, yelping as she hurt herself on something. Footsteps clattered behind me, but I didn't look back. I swung myself up and over just as the footsteps reached the ladder.

Victor cried, "Wait, please—"

Fuck no.

My elbows scraped raw as I scrambled after Faye. Her flashlight swung wildly as she tore along the narrow tunnel. Her skirt snagged on a nail, snapping her to a stop. She sobbed, but she couldn't turn around to free herself. I tore it away, straining to hear if he was coming behind us. At any moment I expected to feel Victor's long, bony fingers wrapped around my ankle.

But the fingers didn't come, and although I felt the itch of unseen eyes on me, when we turned the corner into the tunnel where we could stand upright and shuffled our way back to Dorien's bedroom, Victor didn't follow us.

"What happened?" Titus crawled out from under the bed as we pulled ourselves out of the painting. "I gave you the signal."

"It's my fault," Faye whimpered. "I wanted to see what Madame Usher did. And we found out...we found..."

Faye collapsed into his arms, her shoulders trembling with silent cries. Titus held her, rubbing circles on his back as he tore the answers from my eyes. I moved to hide behind the bureau, where I could watch both the painting and the doorway. I kept my knife poised to slice anyone who came for us.

We waited in tense silence until we heard Madame Usher enter the Red Room and berate Aroha for messing with the tempo. Titus reached inside the painting and ripped out the internal lock so we would always have a way into the secret passages. I pushed open the door and we crept down the hall, stepping over the places we knew had creaky floorboards. With every step my heart clattered so loudly against my ribs I felt certain I'd give us away. At any moment I expected Victor to burst from the walls and stab us, as he'd done to Heather.

We heard him confess. He did it, and they're deliberately framing Dorien for her murder. Does that mean they killed Clare, too?

So why isn't he coming after us now? Why didn't he keep chasing us or alert Madame Usher?

I didn't know, but I wasn't about to question it. At the top of the staircase, Faye paused, her hand lingering on mine. The look in her eyes said she didn't want to leave me.

I longed with every beat of my racing heart to follow her down that staircase, to escape into the bitter cold woods with them and be far, far away from this cursed place and the man in the walls who now knew we were onto him. I knew that sleep would never come to me at Manderley again.

But I couldn't leave Elena.

Especially not now.

Radcliffe wasn't the only danger to her.

And so we stood in silent parting. Faye's eyes pled with me, her fingers stroked my cheek, her lips quivered an unspoken promise. Titus tore her away, ripping my heart straight down the middle. I couldn't breathe. Something heavy squeezed my chest until stars blazed at the corners of my vision. The pain welled in my throat like tears until the warmth of her, the scent of her, was a ghost once more.

I stayed where I was at the top of the stairs for a long time, long after Faye and Titus disappeared into the hallway to the kitchen, long after Clare's face peered at me from around the corner of the balustrade. She was dressed in her maid's uniform, her wide mouth as black as the dress she wore as she waved a see-through duster over the carved banister.

Why is she shaking her head at me?

FAYE

Victor Usher is alive and living in the walls of Manderley.

I rested the Becker against my chin and drew my bow across the open strings, letting the sound ring in the empty hotel room as I decided what to play. I'd returned from another shift at the music shop to find Mom had gone to the hospital for another appointment. The quiet room assaulted me. The walls seemed to lean in, crushing my chest the way those narrow tunnels had done. I tasted the stale air on my tongue, and heard Madame Usher's chilling words pound against my skull. *I will take care of Faye.*

Despite myself, I found myself striking the strings to conjure a familiar, devilish tune. *Danse Macabre.* I closed my eyes as I lost myself in the furious fiddling – it was one of my favorite pieces to play, but today it felt ominous. I felt like Madame Usher was dangling us all from her fiddle, forcing us to dance in her fiendish revelry.

I left Ivan and Elena and Aroha in that house. I left them there knowing a murderer is hiding in the walls.

Ivan texted me every hour to let me know they were okay. He couldn't sleep and neither could I, so we stayed up theorizing over texts about why Victor was in the walls, what they meant by the things they said as they sat at the piano, and why they hadn't come after us yet.

Music had always been a friend to me. It comforted me after heartache, drove me to pursue my dreams, gave voice to my thoughts and fears and desires. And now – if I allowed myself to be consumed by it – it would give me answers.

I turned in agitated circles, focusing on my bowing as my mind conjured the scents of freshly dug grave dirt speckled with dew. This piece was written for orchestra, with an oboe representing a crow and a xylophone creating the sound of rattling bones. I closed my eyes and saw myself standing on the porch at Manderley as corpses rose from beneath the overgrown lawn to leap and gyrate.

Victor was alive. Madame Usher conjured him back from the dead and hid him from the world for eighteen months.

At least it's not Dad. At least the creep who's been spying on us through the walls isn't my own flesh and blood.

Everything that had happened at Manderley made a sick sense now. All the torments I blamed on my Muses, all the things Clare swore she hadn't done, it was Victor all along.

And he haunted Clare, too. *The walls are talking.* She left that message for the next maid. She knew he'd try the same tricks. And Donelle's accusations of deviancy...perhaps those peepholes had been in the walls long before Victor faked his death. But why us at all? Why risk exposing himself for the sake of frightening us?

Why bring me to Manderley at all? Why—

A knock sounded on the door, startling me from my thoughts. My bow screeched on the strings. *It must be Titus.* His parents had dragged him to another audition. He probably needed a good rant.

"You poor baby," I teased as I opened the door. "Tell me all about your evil parents wanting the best for you and making you audition for the London Academy of Music —"

I stopped dead.

Standing in the hall in a grease-stained shirt and an oversized grin was Creepy Cory.

How did he know I was here?

"Hey, Faye." Cory leaned against the frame, sliding his foot forward so I couldn't shut the door. I stepped back, my throat dry with fear. He still felt too close, like he sucked all the air from the room. I could see his greasy hair stuck to the skin behind his ears, and smell sugary alcohol on his breath.

"Cory, you...you...you didn't have to come here. I was going to call you." No one knew we were staying in this hotel except for Natalie and Broken Muse.

"I'd much rather see you in person, Faye. You're even more stunning than I remembered. I followed you from the hospital," he grinned, taking a step into the room as I shrunk from him. "Clever, right?"

No, not clever.

Seriously creepy.

"Um, sure. But it isn't safe for you to be here. These people I'm dealing with are dangerous." I leaned against the door, blocking his view of the room with my body. I didn't want him to see that I was alone. My hand slid into my pocket, and I wondered if I could unlock my phone one-handed and call one of the guys without Cory noticing. "It's not safe for you to be seen with me."

"If you're in danger, I can help you." Cory grabbed my wrist, his fingers squeezing so tight I cried out. I knew I made a mistake. He wasn't afraid of the

Ushers. He liked the idea of being my white knight, my savior. It fed into the fantasy he'd created about himself.

It took everything I had not to yank my hand from his grasp. I didn't want to risk making him angry. Not yet. I swiped my thumb across my screen again, waiting to hear the click that said I'd made a call. "Did you have something to tell me about the Ushers?"

"I do. Can I come in?"

I shook my head. "Sorry, Mom's just got out of the shower."

"No, she's not. She's at the hospital." Cory grinned wider, giving him a maniacal clown vibe. "I know you're alone, Faye."

I swallowed, my muscles tensing. I swiped my thumb again but no click, no way to know if I had even unlocked the screen. *Can I shove my way past him and run for the elevators? Or back into the kitchen and grab a knife?*

The seconds counted down in silence. Cory's grin froze in a terrifying leer. His fingers tightened around my wrist, and I couldn't hold back the whimper that escaped my throat. "I'm not inviting you inside," I said, trying to keep my voice firm. "Please say what you came to tell me and leave."

"You don't have to be like that." His fingers rubbed circles on the inside of my wrist, and it was all I could do not to gag. "We have something special, something those rich fucks you go to school with could never compete with."

My muses are ten times the men you could ever hope to be, Creepy Cory. But I know I can't say anything to antagonize him. I was walking a knife edge. *If I keep him talking about the Ushers, I'll be able to figure out how to get out of this.*

I kept my wrist loose, not giving him any resistance, but not moving from the door, either. I lifted my chin and looked Cory straight in the eye, trying to keep my features neutral, interested but not inviting. Inside, my stomach churned. "You're clever to get this information for me. So tell me what you found out."

"The Usher family made their money in the perfume industry," Cory said. "That's what that company is for. Menabilly Holdings traded raw materials for perfumes and cosmetics. Your teacher Victor had a chemistry degree as well as his music qualifications. He had been in Europe visiting artisanal brands the company was considering acquiring when he met his wife and gave up the family business for his music."

That explained some of the books we saw in the lab – Victor knew about perfumes and plants and mixing chemicals, which meant he had the skills to create poisons from the plants in the garden.

"And that's not all," Cory added. "The finances for the Usher School in New York City were more difficult to follow – a lot of money being funneled through accounts in the Cayman Islands – but it looks as if they were being paid huge sums of money."

"It was an expensive school." Mom worked three jobs to afford the tuition for me and my father to attend.

"Not this expensive. We're talking hundreds of thousands of dollars at a drop."

"Endowments from wealthy benefactors?" Dorien and I performed at various recitals and showcases in front of potential donors. Madame Usher would often wheel out my father as the final act to wow them into opening their wallets. It was one of the few times I was allowed to see him at the school, but even then I wasn't allowed to fawn over him in front of the guests.

"That's what I thought, and their accounts are set up to make it look like these were gifts from donors. But when I compared the Usher School to similar musical programs, it was given over thirty times as much money as Juilliard, and it's been gifted through shell companies that can be connected back to the Triumvirate – an alliance of three prominent West Coast crime families. This is illegal money."

Organized crime. My heart hammered in my chest, and not just because Cory was leaning closer, his tongue darting out to lick his lips. *My father was in debt to a crime family after purchasing the Becker. Is this related?*

"Does this money continue after the school shut down?" I asked.

"The opposite." Cory yanked on my wrist, pulling me against his chest. His free hand grabbed for my other hand, but I jerked it away. "They are paying out huge sums of money to these same accounts. It looks as though their finances have been on tenuous ground ever since they opened Manderley Academy."

Sound the fucktrumpets, this is insane.

"Thank you so much for this, Cory. That's exactly what I was hoping you'd find." I backed into the room, my skin crawling where he touched me. "I appreciate the time it took you to do this. I'll drop some money into your account, and that's probably the last we'll see of each other—"

"I don't want your money, Faye." Cory twisted my wrist. I cried out as he forced me to turn around. He wrapped his free hand across my chest, grabbing my tits and fondling them roughly as he ground his hardness against my ass. He licked my ear. "The way I see it, we should finish what we started at the bar. All those nights you flirted with me, asked for my help with closing up. I know what you really wanted all along."

To demonstrate, he grunted, jamming his crotch against me.

"Let go of me." I kept my voice firm, calm, even though panic clawed at my lungs. I dug my nails into his arm, but that only made him grip me tighter, pinning my arms to my body. I tried to wriggle out of his grasp, but my thrashing about only excited him now.

Please, no. Not this.

"You're so feisty," he murmured as he shoved me toward the bed. My mind raced with full-blown panic. *If he gets on top of me, I won't be able to stop him.* "Those boys don't have to know what we get up to. You're sleeping with all three of them, like a filthy little slut. You're absolutely gagging for it. You wanted me the day you walked into the bar. We're going to—"

"What do you think you're doing?"

I cried out as Cory's fingers bent my wrist, but then Cory was flung away from me. I collapsed against the bed, tears rolling down my cheeks. I whirled around to see Titus holding Cory against the wall. Dark fingers wrapped around Cory's throat. He looked like he was about to shit himself in terror.

Good. He should be terrified.

"Titus." Tears of relief splashed onto my shirt. Titus growled as he leaned in close to Cory's face, close enough Cory could see the muscles bulging in his temples, the curl of Titus' lip as he contemplated exactly what to do with the rapist scum.

"Hello, bro." Cory tilted his head up to stare at Titus. And up. And up. He had to crane his neck at an awkward angle to take in all of my gentle giant. Titus didn't look so gentle now as he slammed Cory's back against the wall. Plaster rained from the ceiling.

"Hey, hey, there's no need to get all possessive alpha on me," Cory choked out. "You and your friends have all had a piece of her. I was just taking my turn—"

His words cut off as Titus' grip tightened around his neck. Titus' face twisted with a dark rage I'd never seen before. I grabbed his arm before he could swing.

"He's a cockroach," I whispered. "He'll go running to the police and say you assaulted him."

The implication hung in the air, the words unsaid. The police would take one look at Titus' skin color and my name splashed all over the media, and make things a thousand times worse for us. I wanted to see Cory bleed, but not at the expense of Titus' freedom.

Titus breathed hard. I knew he was trying to push through his rage, to get to a place where he could let Cory walk out of here alive. His shoulders tensed, his fist tightened, then released. He looked over at me, and his eyes were no longer hooded with hate. He was my Muse again.

"You're leaving now." Titus dropped Cory's collar and pointed to the elevators. "Don't come near Faye again, or I'll harvest your toes and make cello strings from your intestines."

"I know you share her around with your friends." Cory reached for the pocket of his pants, apparently not knowing when to quit. "She's your chubby little whore. If it's a matter of money, I'll pay you to get in on the action—"

Titus' fist collided with Cory's face. I smiled at the satisfying smack as Cory's head hit the wall, spraying blood in the half-moon of an occult ritual and sending more plaster raining down. Cory slumped to the floor, his eyes flickering up to me, wide with pain and confusion, pleading for mercy.

Blood rushed in my ears.

Titus didn't hit him again.

When you step in front of a freight train, once is enough.

"You don't understand," he whimpered. "I'm in love with her. I can't live without her."

"Faye wouldn't be with a piece of shit like you. She only gave you the time of day because she's too nice and she felt sorry for you," Titus shot back. He shoved Cory's shoulder against the wall and withdrew his mobile phone from his pocket. Titus tossed the phone to me. "What am I going to find on here? Photographs? Maybe you've hacked her emails? Tell me the truth now, or I'll squeeze your brain out through your nostrils."

Cory nodded miserably.

"I thought so. This stops. *Now.* You will not see Faye. You will not follow her. You will not take photographs or video and you will leave her private things private. And if you even *think* about going to the police, I'll give them this phone and all the evidence on it. Stalking is so much worse than punching a dickweasel. Now get out of here, or I swear I will invert your ribcage and fill your eye sockets with urine."

Titus tore himself away from Cory, who didn't move, but slumped against the wall, his eyes reeling and blood streaming down his face. Titus leaned back and spat on Cory.

"I told you to leave." Titus cracked his knuckles.

Cory snapped out of his daze. He scrambled to his feet and lunged for the door, tripping over his own feet and face-planting in the hallway. His blood splattered the carpet as he got to his feet and ran for it.

"We won't be requiring your services again," I yelled after him.

When the elevator doors closed on Cory's stricken face, I collapsed into Titus' arms. "Thank you for being here, and for your oddly specific threats. I don't know what he would've done if you hadn't—"

"You'd have chopped his balls off, because you're amazing." Titus held me tight, crushing my body against his – my impenetrable fortress, behind which I was completely safe. "But I'm glad you didn't have to. That would have made an awful mess."

Wrapped in Titus' arms, the adrenaline faded and the sheer terror of what happened crept up on me. I started to shake, tears spilling down my cheeks. Titus pressed his lips to the top of my head. I sank into him, letting his strength hold me as I came to pieces.

"I'm sorry." Titus' huge hands cupped my cheeks, his forehead pressed against mine. "I'm sorry being a woman sucks so much. I'm sorry I didn't get here sooner."

"You have...nothing to be...sorry about." I struggled to get the words out between heaving sobs.

Titus stared over my shoulder at Cory's blood speckled across the wall. "I guess we can't use him to investigate the Usher's finances now."

I shook my head. "We won't get evidence from him, but he came here to tell me that Victor Usher had chemistry knowledge. The Ushers made their money in perfumes."

Titus rubbed his head. "That's true, although when Victor's parents went off to the retirement home, he stepped down from the business to focus on the music school. Sometimes he'd travel for board meetings, but he didn't seem to have much of a hand in the day-to-day running of the firm."

I nodded. "I think they only cared about the business as a front for other things." In a breathless stream, I told Titus everything Cory had found about the Menabilly Holdings and the Usher finances. "If we follow this trail, it will explain why they faked Victor's death. But it still doesn't explain what they planned to do to us. What did they mean when Victor said they needed Broken Muse? And how is my father connected? Finding out it's Victor in the walls instead of Donovan doesn't change the fact that Madame Usher has his portrait and his violin."

"You have the violin now." Titus' eyes fall on the instrument resting in its velvet-lined case.

"And I have no fucking idea what to do with it. Maybe it was a mistake taking it. Maybe it's stolen. Maybe it's cursed." I rested my head against his shoulder. "Maybe I'm cursed."

"Hey." Titus stroked a strand of my dark hair, curling it between his fingers. "We'll figure this out together."

"Everything we discover makes less and less sense. It's no secret Madame Usher maneuvered us all to that school. We know she wanted Elena and Ivan's money, but what about the others?" I stared at him. "What about you?"

Titus shrugged. "That's the thing. I had my choice of music programs across the country, especially with my parents' pedigree. I chose Manderley because that's where Dorien and Ivan were going. We wanted to stay together, see if we could keep that band alive."

Something niggled at me. "Your parents had no opinion about where you should study?" I found it hard to believe that Amos and Delphine didn't have their own ideas about Titus' schooling.

His face darkened. "Now that I think about it, yes. They did push me to choose Manderley. I...I...never realized it before."

I stroked his cheek, feeling his skin soften beneath me. "Are you okay?"

He kissed me, and there was such ferocity to the kiss that I knew the answer to my question was 'no.' And I knew the only thing I wanted to do was keep kissing him.

Manderley can wait. We're not under its spell anymore.

We flopped down on my bed. Titus kicked the door shut. He rested his elbows on either side of me, his cornrows flopping over to curtain our faces, creating this warm, soft, happy bubble for us. I lost myself in his smoky eyes – a cloudy grey so dark they were almost black, the edges ringed with deep, expressive midnight. Such beautiful, unique eyes – just like Titus himself.

He brushed his fingers over my cheek, and my heart did a little dance in my chest. He lifted an eyebrow in a cheeky way that was pure Dorien. He asked the question silently, not doing anything except stroking my skin until I gave him consent.

Tears threatened my eyes again. They weren't tears of fright, of anger. They were a deep welling of emotion at his thoughtfulness. Titus always saw what I needed before I did. He was just so impossibly *good* it broke my heart.

I leaned up and kissed him, letting my tongue linger on his for just a moment before pulling away. His mouth quirked up into a delighted smirk. He cupped my face in his huge hand and laid fluttery kisses on my nose, my eyelids, my forehead, before finally claiming my lips.

His lips started out all sweet and tender, light sweeps of his tongue on mine.

But I could feel my hunger for him growing in my chest, swelling in my heart and between my legs as he deepened the kiss until we were biting, panting, crashing against each other.

"You're everything," Titus whispered as he splayed his fingers around my neck, pulling me closer for a demanding kiss. I could taste his hunger for me, and it made me drunk on him, my mind a fog of heat and need.

He slid off the end of the bed, kneeling on the carpet as he trailed his hands possessively over my body. He shoved the shirt dress I wore over my hips and tugged down my panties, spreading my knees wide and pushing them back into the bed with the heels of his hands. I breathed hard as his fingers trailed fire along my thighs. He followed the blaze with his tongue, nibbling at my skin before touching his lips to the ache between my legs. My fingers curled around the sheets.

Titus circled my entrance with his tongue, darting the tip inside to taste me. I was already a mess, tilting my pelvis up to demand more, to chase away the terrifying memory of Cory holding me down with Titus' warm, soft, lips. He laughed as he clamped his huge hands over my legs to hold me down. I was ready to pout, but then he tongued my clit with such gentle reverence I nearly floated off the bed.

The world spun around me, and all that existed was was his mouth and his hands and the delicious warmth that swelled inside me. This was so different from his birthday when he and Dorien sandwiched me between them, or from the car before we snuck back into Manderley. That had been pure, animal bliss. And this, this was worship. Reverence. This was Titus kneeling at the altar of Faye, and let me tell you, I was here for it.

The sheets were a knot in my hands. My legs shook against his relentless grip as he moved his tongue in those slow, beautiful circles. All rational thought leaked from my ears, and I couldn't have remembered Creepy Cory even if I wanted to. All that existed was Titus' lips on me and the way he made me feel.

Precious.

Adored.

Exalted.

Titus pressed the flat of his tongue against my clit, and I was gone. I thrashed against his grip as my body rode the wave of pleasure coursing through me. Titus crawled up beside me, touching my cheeks and grinning down at me, all happy alpha male because he made me lose my mind.

I tried to pull him back on top of me, but my arms didn't work anymore. *Damn orgasms, so inconvenient.* Titus chuckled, stroking the bare skin of my thighs as he bent his head to—

"Mi cielo, I'm home," Mom's voice called up the hallway. "And I brought tamales."

Holy bitchbadgers, Mom!

I tugged down my dress and kicked my panties under the bed, while Titus leaped into the armchair, crossing his legs to hide his raging hard-on. I slid off the bed onto shaking legs just as Mom threw open the door, her arms loaded down with takeout bags.

"You look like you've just rolled out of bed." She smirked as she dropped her keys on the vanity. "Hello, Titus."

"Hi, Marguerite." Titus leaned forward to kiss her offered cheek. "I'd get up to hug you, but...you know."

My cheeks burned with heat, but Mom only laughed. She dropped the bags on the table, and the delicious scent wafted through the room. "What have you been up to? I mean besides all the carnal shenanigans? Did you find out anything more about Dorien's case—"

Mom stopped in front of the wall, tapping the spray of droplets. "I don't remember this being here before. Is it me, or does that look like a bloodstain?"

Titus and I cracked up laughing.

~

As awful as Creepy Cory was, he did give us vital information. We knew without a doubt that the Ushers conspired to fake Victor's death, and that it likely had something to do with the huge payments made to their bank account from organized crime families before they closed the Usher School. I looked up the Triumvirate and found out there were three families – August, Dio, and Lucian – who ran their empire out of Emerald Beach, California. What interested me was that the August family were well known as purveyors of exquisite black market antiques, including musical instruments.

What I didn't know was what to do with that information.

Titus helped us devour the enormous stack of tamales. He said nothing about driving back to see his parents, and I didn't want him to go. We needed to put our heads together, Scooby-Doo style, and come up with a plan.

I decided it was time to fill Mom in on what we knew (leaving out some of the details that would get me in trouble, like the fact I snuck back to Manderley and went snooping into the walls). I dialed Ivan and put the phone on speaker so we could all tell our parts.

Mom lay in bed, her hair piled on top of her head. Her face grew ever more grim as Titus, Ivan and I filled her in on what we found out in the last few weeks. She jabbed her finger at my violin. "You're telling me that's the instrument your bastard father brought with dirty money?"

I nodded.

"You can't keep it," she hissed. "You have to get rid of it. Those are dangerous people, and if they know you have it they will—"

Her face twisted as she broke down into a coughing fit. I crawled up beside her, rubbing her back as she coughed into her hands. When she drew back, there was a thin splatter of blood on her fingers. "Please, Mom, don't upset yourself. I have no intention of keeping it. It's another piece of evidence that will take Madame Usher down."

"You shouldn't have kept this from me." She glared from me to Titus, even giving the phone on the bed an angry scowl. "I don't want you playing detective anymore. You need to tell the authorities everything you just told me. Now. Tonight."

"The police and the sheriff's office are under Madame Usher's spell. Walpole is helping to frame Dorien—"

"Sheriff Stanford is on the level," Mom shot back.

"We don't know that."

"*I* know. And when have I ever been wrong?" She thrust her hands on her hips, and she looked so much like the old Marguerite de Winter, the scourge of boardrooms and PR pitches across New York City, that I wanted to hug her. "I liked her the moment I met her. She's putting everything together. You have to trust her, mi cielo."

I shook my head. "If I knew how to get ahold of Dorien's FBI agent, I would. But Dorien's given him my details and he hasn't called, and I can't exactly dial information and ask for an agent's private number—"

"I think I can help with that," said a voice from the door.

Dorien

"Dorien?" Faye's eyes widened with shock as I stepped into the room.

That's right, I'm back.

I strode into the middle of their circle, my eyes never leaving her face. As Rochester drove me to the hotel, I wondered if maybe I'd made a mistake by not telling Faye I'd been sprung.

But as I swept her into my arms and planted my lips to hers, I knew my surprise was worth it. She sank into the kiss, melting into me like the sweetest, darkest chocolate s'mores. She tasted the way she smelled – like lavender and orange blossom, like childhood memories and dark wintery nights – and I fancied a little nip of Titus dancing on her tongue.

It was good to know he'd been looking after her while I'd been away. I couldn't believe I ever wanted to compete for Faye's love with my two best friends. They gave her so much that I couldn't, especially when I'd been going crazy in a jail cell without her.

Her tongue wrote magic on my soul. I kissed and kissed and I didn't want to ever breathe again without her. I vowed I would never, ever leave her side.

Faye broke the kiss to nuzzle her face into my neck. It felt so right to hold her again. My lips tingled with fire as I cast my eyes around the room, taking in the rest of the scene. The other people I cared about who I hadn't seen for weeks.

Titus lay across the bed, watching me with an expression that conveyed his relief at my liberty. Marguerite de Winter leaned forward, her tangled hair falling over her eyes as she watched with a mother's apprehension. Ivan's voice barked from the phone on the bed, demanding in his usual Romanian charm to know what was going on.

Almost everyone I cared about.

Jacob was still trapped with Father Aaron, and I couldn't rest until he was free.

Faye pulled back to look at me, as if reassuring herself I was really there. "How did you...how can you be..."

"They dropped the charges." I nodded to Rochester, who stood in the door-way. "Apparently, I have friends in high places."

"Thanks to you, Faye." Rochester strode forward, his hand extended to her. "Gavin Rochester. You told Sheriff Stanford to look for me. I've been able to get Dorien out of trouble, and she's acting as an informant in an undercover inquiry into Walpole and his officers while their departments continue to work together. Thanks to you, a bunch of corrupt as fuck cops will get what's coming to them."

Faye shook his hand firmly, then turned back to me. "I'm so happy you're here." She pulled me close again, clinging to me like I was all that held her upright.

"Who are you?" Marguerite stared at Rochester, her bright smile pinched. She patted her hair self-consciously, and I realized with a selfish pang that I should have called first, given Marguerite a chance to put some clothes on, do her hair, feel like a proper human being.

"As I said, I'm Agent Gavin Rochester, FBI." Gavin stepped around the bed and extended a hand to Marguerite. She peered at him with amusement as they shook. "I don't want to keep any of you awake, but I think we need to talk."

Marguerite patted a space at the end of her bed. "Sit down, Agent. Once Faye has finished necking her boyfriend, I'm sure she'll fix you some tea. And we have plenty of food to go around."

"Is Dorien there?" Ivan barked down the phone. "What is going on?"

Faye poked her tongue out at her mother, then resumed devouring my lips, which I had zero problem with whatsoever. Rochester clicked the door shut and perched on the end of the bed. Marguerite sighed dramatically and flounced out of bed, heading to the kitchenette to put the kettle on and unwrap the takeout. Out of the corner of my eye, I saw Rochester cast a look at Marguerite's back that was both fleeting and filled with longing. I wasn't surprised that he'd been taken by her in just a few moments of meeting – even in her robe she was startling, all tumbling dark hair and wide eyes that burned with fire.

Faye may have inherited her father's musical talent, but she got her soul from her mother.

When Marguerite had supplied everyone with food and drinks, and Faye had stealthy slipped her panties from under the bed into her pocket (naughty girl) and settled on my lap in the armchair, Rochester cleared his throat.

"I'm sorry that I left Dorien hanging as long as I did. I've been busy with the Temple investigation, and I wouldn't usually be able to interfere with a non-Federal case like this. I can't undo the damage done by the media, but Dorien's free now, and will remain so unless Walpole comes up with new evidence." His steely gaze settled on me. I nodded back, unable to speak as I'd stuffed my mouth so full of tamales. Jail food was ghastly and I swear I'd lost ten pounds on the inside.

Rochester continued. "I have a specific reason for wanting Dorien free."

"This is about the Temple." Faye shifted in my lap as she licked her fingers. I growled against her ear that her wriggling was doing evil things to me, especially since I now knew she wasn't wearing panties.

Rochester nodded. "We know Heather's death and Dorien's arrest must have repercussions, but we don't have any information about what's going on inside the organization. All we know is that the Danvers' have retreated to their estate and refuse to speak to the press. I don't know if they're even still involved with the Temple. Aaron Varney hasn't kept any of his appointments with the rich families he hoped to recruit. We don't even know for certain where he is. Our agents have seen some signs of life at Valencourt Manor, but when an officer tried to open the main gate, someone shot at him, which has never happened in all the times we've sent teams out to monitor the cult. This change in behavior concerns my team, especially given what we knew about the arranged marriage and the day of ascension. We need to move against the Temple soon, and it would be better if we had someone on the inside."

He didn't have to elaborate. Faye buried her face in my shoulder. "You?" she whispered. I nodded.

Just thinking about Jacob made my stomach twist in knots and bile rise in my throat. All the time I'd been in jail, dread had been mounting in my gut. Heather's death ruined all the Temple's plans. What would Aaron do to him to punish me? Did they send him to the Penalty Room and subject him to unimaginable horrors?

"Not just Dorien. We want you to help him try to make contact with his parents," Rochester said.

I shook my head. "Not Faye. I'm not putting her in danger."

She squeezed my hand. "If it's for Jacob, I'll do it."

"I won't send you anywhere near that place." I glared at Rochester. How did he forget to mention this to me? From the way he avoided my eyes, I knew he intended to ask Faye all along.

"I never thought I'd say this, but I agree with Dorien." Marguerite kicked Rochester's thigh under the covers. "You're not sending my daughter into a cult stronghold to make nice with a madman."

"I wouldn't ask if there was any other way." Rochester touched his thigh where my mother kicked him. "We need intel of Varney before we can make a move. We need to cut off the head before we can hope to save the body. At this stage, we don't even know if they're still at Valencourt Manor. When a cult goes underground like this..." he shook his head, and my gut churned with hopelessness.

Faye shuddered. I squeezed her hand. "Why us?" she asked. "Surely you have agents who could—"

"It doesn't matter," Marguerite's eyes flashed with determination. "Because you're not doing it."

"Agreed," Titus added.

"Varney will sniff out our people at this late stage. It has to be someone they're willing to trust. We know they approved of your relationship with Dorien at one point. We think it's the best chance we have of getting inside."

"But they were prepared to frame Faye for assaulting Varney." I curled my hand into a fist, ready to slam it into Rochester's face. How could he even suggest this? I won't take Faye into that hellhole. "They hate her."

"Now that Heather Danvers is no longer in the picture, they may have changed their minds again."

"What if they try to hurt us?" Faye's lip trembled.

"We'll have a team covering you the entire time," Rochester assured. "We don't need you to get inside or record a conversation or anything like that. All we need is confirmation that the cult is still at Valencourt Manor with Aaron, and that Jacob is still alive."

I blanched at his words. *He has to still be alive.*

"I'll do it," Faye said.

"No," Marguerite and I shouted at the same time.

"Yes." Faye's eyes blazed. "I'm not going to stand on the sidelines when I can help an innocent kid. Mom, you'd do the exact same thing. You know you would."

Marguerite's eyes fluttered shut, and for a moment I saw her not as I remembered her – strong and wild and terrifying – but as she was now, her eyes sunken and lined with crows' feet, her skin sickly, her de Winter curves wasted away and her lips dry from the medication. She swallowed, and her eyes opened. She nodded at her daughter.

Faye glared down at me, daring me to try to speak for her again. "We'll get him back," she whispered, pressing her lips to my forehead. "I promise."

I pulled her face to mine, taking her mouth for a deep kiss. After everything I put her through this past year, after all those years of happiness the Temple robbed from us, she was willing to do this for me? "You're incredible, did you know that?"

"I've heard a rumor," Faye laughed as her tongue played against mine.

"Thank you, Faye." Rochester pulled a slim file from his briefcase. "If you don't mind me hanging around, I can go over some details of the operation with you and Dorien. We want to move quickly."

"That's fine, and I should probably tell you what we've uncovered," Faye said. "Madame Usher's husband is still alive."

"What?" I stared at her. "Victor? That's impossible. I saw his body."

"You sure about that?" Faye grinned.

Fuck. This is insane.

"If you're going to be staying, Gavin, you need to be properly attired." Marguerite tossed the other hotel bathrobe at Gavin's head. She lifted the receiver and dialed room service. "We'll need more food. And margaritas. *All* the margaritas. Every margarita in the universe."

"Mo-om, you're not supposed to drink alcohol."

"And you're not supposed to run headfirst into a cult stronghold with Dorien fucking Valencourt," she shot back, daring any of us to argue.

Faye went to the bathroom as Rochester pulled on his robe and Marguerite busied herself with the room service menu. I knew she was putting her panties back on – and I couldn't help feeling disappointed. I liked knowing she was bare with everyone in the room. When she returned, she told us how she and Ivan had snuck into the tunnels at Manderley and found Victor Usher's laboratory, as well as what Creepy Cory had told them about the Usher's finances.

By the time we finished off the food and my head swam from the sugar margaritas, Rochester was rubbing his eyes. He extricated himself from the duvet and shrugged off the bathrobe. "Thank you for a surprisingly lovely evening. They're too far between in my line of work. I'll leave you to your own devices for now but..." he looked over to Marguerite, who was frowning at her virgin margarita and, I thought, deliberately not meeting his eyes, "...I want you to know I've booked a room just down the hall. I'll have another agent staying with me. Her name is Amelia Velasquez. We'll take it in shifts to keep an eye out for you all. You're safe here."

"You'd better have a hundred agents when you send my daughter into that hellhole," Marguerite yelled at his departing figure. "And flame-throwers. And grenade launchers. And a fucking dinosaur cannon."

"What's a dinosaur cannon?" Faye snickered as Rochester pulled the door shut behind him.

"Armored vehicle pulled by a T-Rex, that launches baby T-Rexes over the wall to gobble up the enemy before you get there. I don't know. I made it up." She wagged her finger at Faye. "But if he doesn't have one, you tell me and I'll make him pay."

Faye and I exchanged a glance, the air heavy between us. I'd been nursing a hard-on for several hours, and if I didn't peel her clothes off and fuck her right now I was going to experience serious testicular damage. But I couldn't exactly throw Faye down on the bed with her mother here, but I also didn't want to drag her away to my own room when I knew that beneath her facade Marguerite was afraid for her.

Marguerite threw off the covers. "I'll be heading out."

"Mom, it's late." Faye slid off me and tried to lead her back to bed. I crossed my leg, wincing as my sore balls rubbed against the leg of my jeans. Marguerite shook her daughter off.

"Yes, but it's the crack of dawn in New Zealand, and I'm ready to shake off these margaritas. Titus is going to take me dancing." I glanced at Titus, who looked apprehensive. I remembered he spent New Year's Eve being dragged around New York City clubs by Marguerite, and I wasn't sure he was ready to relive the trauma of the experience.

Too bad. Right now, if it would get me alone with Faye, I'd fire my best friend from the dinosaur cannon.

I waited in agony while Marguerite chose a dress – an off-the-shoulder indigo number with a flared skirt that looked killer with her tousled dark hair and red lips – and fussed over Titus' hair before ushering him out the door with winks and promises that she'd keep him out all night.

"Help me," Titus whispered as the door shut behind him.

Sorry, friend.

As soon as the door slammed behind them, we crashed together, our bodies drawn by the pull of our need. Our teeth clashed, our lips burned against each other, raw and hungry and desperate.

"It's only been a few weeks," Faye teased, but her fingers tugged at the hem of my shirt with urgency.

"Every minute on the inside without you is agony." I swept her into my arms. I wanted to crawl inside this woman, build my life in her flesh.

She giggled. "On the inside, huh? So, my hardened criminal, did you learn any tricks in the prison showers?"

Her giggles turned to moans as I ground my cock against her thigh. "*Hardened* criminal is right. This is what you do to me, Sprite."

"Dorien…"

I shoved her down, so she was sitting on the edge of the bed, gazing up at me with those wide green eyes. I drowned in those eyes. "Take off your dress."

Faye's eyes glimmered at the authority in my voice, but she moved to obey. She slipped her shirt-dress over her head, revealing her breasts swelling from a pink bra and matching pink panties with lace around the edges. They clung to her pussy where she was already wet. For me.

My mouth went dry. *She's everything.*

"Have you been a good girl while I've been gone?" I loved seeing her squirm when I took on this tone with her.

She shook her head, leaning back on her palms, her tits thrusting out to give me an amazing view of cleavage that could crush a man. I undid my belt, fussed with my buttons, making her wait. My hands brushed over my throbbing cock and the pain tore a moan from my throat. Faye's lip parted. She liked seeing how much I wanted her.

"That's what I like to hear. Do you like a criminal telling you what to do?"

"Maybe." She said it cheekily, with demands of her own. "As long as he tells me to do things that make me feel good."

"Have you been thinking about me? Have you been touching yourself while you imagined what I'd do to you once I was free? What I'd do to you with Titus and Ivan in the same room?" I tugged down her panties. I pressed her knees wider, taking in the sight I'd been deprived of for too long.

She's swollen and wet and hot for me.

I breathed hard. I wanted this to be amazing for her, but I wouldn't last long faced with so much perfection.

"Yes." Faye's green eyes dared me to push her.

I cupped her breast in my hand, rubbing my fingers over her nipple through the fabric. Faye's lips fell wider, and she arched her back to give me more access. She demanded more, but I wasn't ready to give it to her just yet.

I knelt in front of her and pressed my lips to her inner thigh. She groaned with frustration. "I tasted Titus on your lips. Has he tasted you here, too? Has my friend licked your pussy already today?"

"Yes."

I used my fingers to spread her wide. She was so wet. I slid a finger inside her, feeling how swollen she was, how much she wanted me. I kissed her clit, my tongue fluttering over the bud. Just thinking that earlier today my best friend knelt in the same place, worshipping her, made her taste all the sweeter.

My cock throbbed painfully. *How the fuck am I going to last?* I could come right now just from the friction against my jeans and the way her thighs trembled and her mouth moaned little obscenities.

I pushed my tongue in beside my finger, then licked my way back to her clit, continuing with the fluttery circles.

"Dorien, fuck, please..." Faye's thighs rose off the bed. I had to hold her down with a firm hand. "Fuck, you cockpoodle. Harder. Don't play around. Fuck—"

But I wasn't ready for her to come yet. I was a man who'd been lost in the desert for so long. I'd finally reached water but I couldn't gulp it down or I'd drown myself. I wanted to savor her. I wanted this moment written across my memory forever. So I kept up the light kisses, the soft strokes that almost *but not quite* tipped her over the edge.

Faye grabbed my hair, grinding my face against her clit. I breathed in her sweet scent and gave her what she demanded. I thrust a second finger inside her, curling them to rub at her G-spot. My lips were slick with her need.

She breathed hard, her fingers digging into my skull. I slid a third finger inside, and with a cry, her hips clenched and her walls closed around me. Her whole body vibrated as the orgasm shot through her, and I almost lost it right then with her clamped around me.

My lungs felt full of water, full of her. It was hard to breathe. I crawled up her body, dropping my jeans to the floor. My cock brushed her thigh and I was so close...

I buried myself inside her. *So hot. So soft. So warm.* Faye brought her legs up to clamp around my back, angling her hips to drive me deeper. My thumb ground against her clit, dragging another climax from her as I thrust inside her like a man possessed.

I am possessed. Faye is everything, she's everywhere to me. She can haunt me any time she fucking likes.

She ground her pelvis against me as she came. It was glorious, feeling her walls contract around my cock, hearing her sweet cries as I fell over the edge and let my ghost capture me.

Faye de Winter was mine again. Madame Usher didn't control me anymore. And Aaron Varney wasn't going to know what hit him.

IVAN

Now that I knew about the way Victor was getting around the house, I felt his presence everywhere. Eyes pricked my back as I scrubbed the floors and dusted the pianos. They scratched at my back as I sat in the corner of Elena's private lessons, and watched over my shoulder as she crawled into my bed and burrowed into my shoulder at night.

I wondered if Victor had a passage to get out to the stables. If he was spying on Elena when she was with Radcliffe.

I wondered what he'd think if he found my sister bending over a piano for that vile man. The thought made me see stars. Elena said it hadn't happened yet, but it was only a matter of time. I could practically see Radcliffe licking his lips as he led her away from me for yet another date in his private rooms.

Unlike Victor, who skulked in the shadows, Clare grew bolder. She hung out with me in the kitchen, swinging her legs through the table as she watched me chop vegetables. She sat on our bed at night, helping Elena decide how to pin her hair. I couldn't find her frightening anymore – she was a friend, a victim of Manderley, just like us.

Life at Manderley without Faye and the others had reverted back to the days of our childhood, except that now we had a friendly ghost and a creepy man watching our every move. Madame Usher had me and Elena doing the chores, and with Elena preoccupied with her upcoming wedding and a steady stream of recitals and parties to attend with Radcliffe, I was doing it all. My classes were mostly a farce now. I couldn't hide my disdain for Radcliffe, and the idea of completing my degree seemed foreign – a pointless dream from another life. I was here to protect Elena. Nothing else mattered.

But being trapped at Manderley had its benefits, and I would not waste this opportunity. Instead of attending classes and practicing my repertoire, I pored through the library, searching for anything that would help us.

The Manderley library included one of the world's most impressive collections of texts on Baroque music, acquired by the Ushers on their various tours of Europe – or so the official story went. I had to wonder if the August crime family had their fingerprints on the more valuable texts. But buried on a dusty shelf in the corner where Madame Usher had obviously forgotten their existence was a collection of Victor's father's history books, including volumes written in Victor Senior's own hand about the history of his family and the house.

I set aside a history of the Usher perfume company and dug out the leather-bound volume on the house I started reading the other day. I couldn't spend too long in the library or Madame Usher would start to get suspicious. I turned the pages, scanning Victor's sloping handwriting for something we could use.

I learned that the house was built in the eighteenth century by the Usher family patriarch, confusingly *also* named Victor. At the time, the Ushers had acquired a great wealth importing perfumes from Europe for the burgeoning colonial upper class, but when the Seven Years War threatened their newfound prosperity, Victor the First became fearful of losing his wealth or his life, so when he built his family home, he added the tunnels to hide his family and gold from invading forces.

As I turned the page, a folded paper slid out of the book, yellowed with age. I unfolded it, resisting the urge to yell with triumph as it revealed a set of building floor plans. They were from the original house before it was expanded and renovated. The wing that now served as Madame Usher's private quarters was only half the size, the kitchens hadn't yet been enlarged, and some of the internal room configurations were slightly different. Drawn between the rooms were the narrow passages we discovered. Markings in Dorien's room, the attic, and what was now the Red Room showed where doorways opened into the tunnels.

It also showed a tunnel heading from the Red Room under the house, with an exit down beside the stream. An escape route, so the family could make their way down to the river and presumably get ahead of their enemies.

I glanced over my shoulder, peering at the library walls as my skin prickled with unease. Clare was off watching Elena's private tutorial. Was Victor watching? Would he see what I was about to do? The prickling on my neck intensified as I drew my secret phone from my pocket and quickly snapped a few pictures, which I forwarded to Faye. It would be helpful to know where the tunnels led, and where exactly in the house Victor could – or could not – go.

As soon as the photographs were sent, I shut off the phone, put away the books, and secreted my phone back into its hiding spot – taped to the tank in the bathroom, where Elena used to sometimes hide drugs for Aroha. The plans didn't show any hidden passages along our bathroom walls. I couldn't be certain they hadn't been added later, but I'd already inspected every inch of the bathroom before I started hiding my phone there, and I was certain there were no peepholes or secret doors.

I heard Madame Usher yelling for me, and headed back to finish my chores, feeling Victor's eyes on me the whole time.

Why doesn't he tell his wife he found us in the tunnels?

Madame's overheard words chilled me to the bone. "All I have to do is keep the others from talking and we'll have the money we need to start over."

Our money. The money from Broken Muse record sales and Elena's performances that Madame Usher held in trust for us. That had to be what she was referring to. We weren't able to access it until we reached our twenty-fifth birthday, unless we married first. If Elena married Radcliffe, Madame Usher wouldn't have access to our money any longer. *So what does she mean by this? Is she talking about some other funds, or...*

...or...she has a deal with Radcliffe – she keeps the money. He gets my sister. After all, she was the one who delivered Elena into his depraved arms.

Over my dead fucking body.

That night, I lifted Elena's arm from where she slung it across my chest and slipped from bed. Our bedroom door had been locked from the outside, but I didn't need to get out. I padded to the bathroom, untaped my mobile phone, and turned it on. Faye had sent me a string of text updates about the maps and helping Agent Rochester break out Jacob, and her mom dragging Titus to an underground swing club and forcing him to dance so hard he nearly broke his hip.

Faye. I missed her so much my chest burned with it. Every minute of the day I thought about what she was doing out there, the danger she was in. The danger she escaped. I didn't understand why Victor hadn't told Madame that he saw us in the tunnels.

I squeezed the phone in my hand and gritted my teeth against the frustrated scream building inside me.

Dorien was out. Which meant that Madame Usher's hold on the police wasn't as strong as she thought. And that made her position precarious. She was a tiger backed into a corner, made all the more dangerous because of her desperation.

And Elena was still here, in the heart of the tiger's den.

Faye's texts blurred together as I fought my frustration. I hated feeling helpless, stuck here while they were outside, trying to make a difference. Through the haze of rage, I noticed her final text message. My heart caught in my throat. I had to read it five times to make sure it said what I thought it said.

I tracked down Donelle from the articles. I'm going to call her in the morning and see if I can get her to talk about the things she experienced at Manderley. Sleep well, my Ice Prince. I love you.

She'd added Donelle's phone number and email address.

I clutched the phone in my fingers as my heart hammered against my chest. *Faye is going to call her. Faye should be the one to call her – she's good at making people do what she wants. I only have to wait until tomorrow to find out...*

I touched my chest, where Elena's arm had draped only a few minutes before. My sister's days were counting down.

I couldn't wait. This was too important.

I rolled up the towels and pressed them into the gap at the bottom of the door, hoping that would muffle the sound of my voice. I sat on the toilet lid and pulled up Donelle's number on the screen.

I hit 'CALL.'

The phone rang once, twice, three times. It was nearly midnight, too late to be polite. She had to pick up the phone. She just *had* to.

RING RING.

This is a mistake. Faye is right. I should have waited for her to make the call. I'm too cold. I'll frighten her. I'll—

"Hello?"

A woman's voice on the other end. She sounded groggy, her voice thick with sleep. I opened my mouth but all that came out was a dry croak.

"Who is this? Why are you calling so late?"

Just say it. Just tell her you're calling from Manderley and you're afraid. She's been here. She'll understand.

"Hello? If this is one of those overseas phone scams, then I'm hanging up now—"

"Help me," I managed to choke out. "You have to help me. Please?"

"Is that you, Robbie?" Her tone turned soft, kind. "I showed you where the church spare key is kept. If you need to get off the street, just go down to the youth group room and there are some pillows and blankets. I don't want you outside on a night like this—"

"No, I'm not Robbie. My name is Ivan Nicolescu. You might remember me. I'm calling from Manderley and—"

"Manderley?" Her voice turned sharp. "Is this some kind of sick joke?"

"No. I need your help. It's about an article in your local newspaper four years ago. I need to know if—"

"*She* sent you to harass me again, didn't she?" Donelle spat. "Well, you tell her I don't want another cent of her filthy blood money. I wrote her stupid retraction and gave all the money to my church, so we can fight against the forces of Satan here on Earth, including her and that husband of hers and that disgusting school of degenerates. I haven't opened my mouth about that horrid place and the ungodly things that went on there. God sees all, and he will strike her down for her sins."

"Yes, but what sins?" I wanted to reach through the phone and throttle her. "Could you elaborate—"

"I won't let another word about her sully my tongue or poison my soul. She can't come after me again. I haven't broken our agreement. I'm not an innocent girl anymore. I'll fight her. My church will fight her. If she comes after me, we will tell the world that Satan lives inside her!"

This woman sounds unhinged. "Please understand, I don't work for Madame Usher. I'm one of her students. My sister is in danger. I want—"

"Your sister?" Donelle laughed cruelly. "If she's at Manderley, buckle her chastity belt and pray. Pray for her immortal soul. Pray she makes it out alive. Call me again, and I go to the police."

She hung up, taking my only chance to find out the truth about Radcliffe's depravity with her.

DORIEN

"Remember, whatever you do, don't provoke Varney. If he doesn't let you see Jacob, don't ask to. Just get in, talk to whoever you can talk to, and get out again."

I nodded to Agent Velasquez, who was taping the wire to my chest over my IN CAUDA VENENUM ink with perhaps more enthusiasm than a female FBI agent should be showing. Faye watched me from across the back of the cramped van, where we were being prepped for our encounter with the Temple. Faye licked her lips, and I knew she didn't care that Velasquez was giving my pecs a good squeeze.

I guess she doesn't mind sharing, either.

I would have said something filthy to her if I wasn't so distracted with freaking the fuck out about going into my family home. I knew I wasn't supposed to try anything heroic, but if I saw Jacob I didn't know what I would do. *How can they expect me to just leave him there with Aaron Varney?*

I have to be strong. I have to do this their way. It's the best chance Jacob has.

Velasquez taped the last of the wire and patted my arm. "You're all set, Dorien." I pulled on my shirt and jacket, hoping like hell the Temple wouldn't think to search me. If they demanded it, we were under orders to turn around and leave. Loyalty was everything in my family. My parents would never in a million years believe I'd go to the Feds, but I couldn't predict Aaron.

All I knew was that I had to get Jacob away from him, no matter what.

Rochester threw open the rear doors of the van, and we climbed out and into my Porsche. Faye clasped my hand across the seat. Rochester patted my back. "Do you want to go over the plan one last time?"

I offered him a weak smile. Every muscle in my body was being squeezed in a vise. "I'm used to memorizing entire symphonies. The plan isn't the problem."

"I know." Darkness hooded Rochester's blue eyes. "Good luck, Dorien. We've got your back in there."

I watched him walk back the van, his shoulders hunched with tension. This was a big day for him, too. He lost his parents to the Temple. He had to help his sister walk off a mountain in a snowstorm to save her life. I felt the weight of his pain on my shoulders. He felt responsible for what happened to his parents. This was his day for redemption.

Satan knows I'd had so many of those – for all the evil it wrought, Manderley gave me the chance to start over with Faye, to undo the hurt I caused her. Despite fucking Ivan's and Titus' and Elena's life over completely, they still stood by me.

I wanted to give Rochester his redemption.

And more than anything, I wanted to feel Jacob's arms around me again. I wanted my brother to have the life I had, to have the chance to scrape his knees and travel the world and fall in love and make mistakes.

Faye squeezed my leg. "I'll be right by your side."

When Rochester first suggested she come with me into the mouth of hell, I wanted to throttle the bastard. But now, I couldn't imagine doing this without her. I placed my hand over hers and gunned the engine.

I'm coming to get you, Jacob. Just like I promised.

The van followed us at a safe distance. I kept an eye on them in the rearview mirror as we drove the winding country roads toward Valencourt Manor. My fingers tightened on the wheel until cramps seized my arms. I saw the stone wall topped with barbed wire, the rolling hills covered with trees that hid the mansion from view. Every fiber of my body told me to turn around and get away from this place. I spent my whole life fleeing my parents, and going back made me feel like a kid again – alone, terrified. But this wasn't about me any longer – it was about Jacob.

I should have pulled him out years ago.

Faye squeezed my knee. "Dorien, what's that?"

"Shit." I slammed my foot to the floor as I saw what Faye was pointing at. A pillar of smoke rose from the trees surrounding the house to pierce the frigid sky. My phone rang, the sound shrill and urgent. Faye picked it up. "It's Rochester," she said. "Hi. Yes, we see it. What is it—"

Her words cut off as I accelerated. The tires bit the road as I tore around the corner, passing a gap in the trees through which I could always catch a glimpse of the northeast turret of Valencourt Manor.

"Dorien, slow down."

I couldn't slow down. I had to see. I had to know.

The car hurtled past, and I glimpsed a flash of the turret and the black smoke billowing from its windows.

Smoke.

Fire.

The day of ascension.

"No." I pounded the wheel in frustration as the car kicked and bounced along the uneven road. The NO TRESPASSING signs flew by in a blur. Rochester yelled down the phone to Faye, but I didn't register his words. I saw the gates up ahead. They were closed and chained shut with a comically large padlock. Faye yelled as I planted my foot and drove straight at them. She braced her arms at her sides as we slammed into the gates.

Adrenaline surged through my body as we hit. It was like plunging over a rollercoaster – the moments before the impact hung in the air for a long time, long enough for me to realize what a fucking idiot I was for ramming a gate with my Porsche.

Then we hit.

It was like getting whacked in the head with a baseball bat after leaving one of Titus' heavy metal concerts with your ears buzzing and your brain filled with fog. Sound buzzed in my ears, a crunch, a scream, and then deafness that was louder than anything I'd ever heard before. I gasped for air as the airbags exploded. My neck ached. My whole body ached. I tried to swim through the airbag to get to Faye, but it felt like trying to push water aside – it kept filling in the gaps of air, choking me, drowning me. I tried to cry out but my mouth was full of blood.

Faye, are you okay? I'm an idiot. Why did I do that?

Faye, fuck, please be okay...

A warm hand clasped mine. Faye's face appeared in the corner of my vision. She yelled something at me, but I couldn't hear it. She broke down into a coughing fit as she shoved open her car door and tumbled out.

My door opened. Rough hands grabbed me, dragging me free of the airbags. Rochester dropped me on the ground, yelling something in my face that I couldn't hear. I was dimly aware of others circling me, of Faye stumbling toward me, but as I turned my neck painfully toward the sky, the black smoke curled across grey clouds, and I knew what I had to do.

I staggered to my feet, shoving Rochester aside. I had to get to the house. The van skidded on the cracked driveway in front of me, and Velasquez threw open the rear door, gesturing wildly for us to jump in.

Rochester helped me and Faye stagger inside. He didn't even have the doors shut before the van tore up the hill. Velasquez and Rochester yelled back and forth, their words dull thuds against my battered skull. Faye held me and I held the surveillance rig as the van's shitty suspension struggled up the broken driveway. The adrenaline from the crash was starting to cool, giving me full body shivers. Or maybe that was from watching the black smoke billow from the trees to surround the van. We rounded the final corner, the smoke now so thick I couldn't see a foot from the van.

The van was still moving when I slipped under Faye's arm and threw the doors open. Faye yelled something at me but I couldn't hear. "Don't follow me," I tried to yell back, but as soon as I opened my mouth, smoke poured in and my lungs collapsed. My feet hit the ground. My ankle crunched and I was dimly away that it hurt, but the adrenaline was back and I couldn't feel anything over the burning in my lungs. I broke into a run, coughing into my hand as my eyes streamed with tears. I couldn't see the house. I couldn't see anything. I crashed into a tree, picked myself up, kept running.

I stumbled on the broken concrete drive and toppled into a pile of scrap metal. Something sliced through my hand, which was going to hurt like a bitch later, but I didn't stop.

Jacob, I'm coming!

I fumbled my way across the parking area, around the dried-up fountain, and up the stone steps two at a time. A flash of memory assailed me – me standing with my father on those same steps as my mother returned from the hospital carrying the bundle of blankets that held my kid brother. She stooping down to show me Jacob's tiny screwed-up face, and I poked him until he woke up because I was a little shit and I promised the howling baby right then and there that I'd be the best big brother in the world.

In the distance, I could hear sirens.

"Dorien, wait." The words sounded muted, like they were being yelled underwater.

I didn't wait. My eyes stung so fucking bad. I kept them screwed shut as I slammed into the door, staggering inside.

A wall of heat and smoke burst from the depths of the house. It slammed into me, bowling me over. I slammed my tailbone into the stone as I skidded across the stone porch. Pain rocketed up my spine. I rolled over and dragged myself to my feet, my chest heaving as a fresh coughing fit bent me double.

"Jacob?" I cried, but my voice was lost, burned away. He couldn't hear me over the roar of the fire, the crash of ceiling beams falling and windows blowing out. I couldn't even hear myself.

I staggered through the entrance hall, bracing myself against the heat. I crashed into the kitchen, holding my sleeve against my mouth and nose to try to keep out the worst of the smoke. I couldn't see, so I stumbled in the direction of the court-yard door.

It's no use. I'm never going to find him.

My hip scraped along the kitchen island. Pots and pans toppled at my feet, the metal burning where it touched my skin. I kicked them aside and pushed onward. My shoulder hit the glass of the door, and it burst from the heat and the impact, spraying shards across the floor. They thudded against my skin, but I couldn't feel a thing in this heat, this demonic heat. I fumbled for the door handle. Too hot. Too hot. My fingers closed around it and they melted against the metal. I screamed and screamed as pain ate my fingers, swallowing them into a hellish black hole of terror.

Somehow, through a feat of inhuman strength I didn't know I possessed, I tore my hand from the door handle. The pain still rocketed through my body, and I didn't feel invincible anymore. Despite the heat, my body shuddered with the chill of certain death. With the fear that I wouldn't see my brother again. Red welts danced in front of my vision, and the roar and crackle of the fire tearing through the house penetrated through my deafness. I yanked my sleeve over my fingers and managed to turn the handle and shove the door open without blacking out from the pain. The rush of heat shoved me through the gap, sending me sprawling across the courtyard.

I lay on the cobbles, gasping for fresh air. I dragged myself forward, rubbing my eyes with my burned hand. "Jacob?" I coughed. "Are you out here?"

I bet he's hiding in his secret place.

I crawled across the cobbles. My knees scraped raw on the hard stone. My fingers touched something sticky. Water? In this inferno? I raised my fingers to my face. No, not water. It smelled awful. Poisoned. Like copper and dead animals and—

Whatever it was, it was dripping on my head. I felt the wet splotches sticking to my hair.

I looked up.

I wished I hadn't.

I wished for blindness, for madness – something that could wipe the horror of what I saw from my memory forever.

They were tied side by side to a makeshift scaffold, arms spread wide and legs tied together in a cruel mockery of their god's son. Metal nails had been driven through their hands and feet into the wood. From the dried blood caked to their skin and the wooden cross, I knew these wounds had bled profusely. The horror etched onto their broken faces told the story of their suffering.

Their chests were torn open with long slashes, so their guts spilled out, entrails decorating the ground around their feet. Bile choked my throat as I realized what dripped on me had come from their stomach cavities. The smoke and heat had dried their skin, so the edges pulled back and flaked off, scattered in the air like sadistic confetti.

They spent their final hours together in agony, with an overgrown garden their only witness.

My parents.

Crucified.

FAYE

"Dorien?" I clambered up the stone steps after him. But I'd twisted my ankle when they pulled me out of the car, so I could only hobble. Dorien seemed possessed of superhuman power. He crashed into the smoke like it didn't touch him, like his lungs weren't burning and his eyes weren't glued shut by the blinding pain.

My ankle screamed with pain as I dragged it up the steps. Something crashed above me, and I leaped back as a piece of the roof collapsed, caving in the entrance above the front door. Glass shattered as the French windows blew out. My heart leaped into my throat. *Dorien's inside.*

"Dorien?"

Hands wrapped around me, dragging me back from the house. "Don't you die in there, too," Rochester yelled. I tried to wriggle out of his grasp, but he held me firm.

Sirens wailed as fire engines and police vehicles swerved into the driveway. I watched with a detached horror as the firefighters unrolled hoses and Rochester thrust me at Velasquez. He moved amongst the officers on the scene, issuing orders like he rescued headstrong musicians from burning mansions every second Sunday. Velasquez had her arm around my shoulders – outwardly, it looked like an expression of empathy, but I could tell by her vise-like grip that she was preventing my escape.

"Dorien's in there," I struggled against her. "I have to find him."

"The firefighters will get to him faster if they're not looking for two of you," she yelled back.

Another crash shattered the forest. The section of the roof over the kitchen collapsed. Someone screamed.

It took me a moment to realize the person screaming was me.

Smoke stung my eyes, but I couldn't tear my gaze away from the horror in front of me as bit by bit the flames consumed the house. Firefighters trained their hoses on the worst of the blaze, running into the burning ruin and yelling instructions to each other over the roar of the conflagration.

From the haze of smoke, figures emerged. Rochester, wearing a firefighter's jacket. He had his arms around someone else, dragging him to safety.

Dorien.

Dorien. He's alive.

I didn't know it was possible to smile so much with smoke burning my lungs.

They hobbled toward the waiting ambulance. Paramedics swarmed, wrapping Dorien in blankets, thrusting oxygen into his face, checking his body for injuries. Velasquez lost her grip on me, and I elbowed my way through the crowd to get to him.

"Dorien, are you okay?" I bent down to smooth back his hair. A patch of it crumbled to dust in my hands. His eyebrows had burned away, and he smelled *delightful.*

He stared out at me, his eyes haunted. I'd never seen him like that before, like he'd stared into the face of evil itself. I wanted to slap him around the head and call him a cockpoodle for running into that fire, but he'd seen something inside. Something that had shaken him to his core.

"You idiot." Rochester ran up beside us, his own shoulders covered in a security blanket. A paramedic snapped at him to come back so he could finish his checkup, but he grabbed Dorien's shoulder and shook him. "What did you think you were doing, running into a burning building like that?"

Dorien tore off the oxygen mask, his face grave. "Jacob's not here."

Rochester patted his arm. "We're looking for him. But we had to spend precious minutes saving your ass. Don't ever do that again—"

"He's not here," Dorien said forcefully.

"I know. We'll do a thorough search of the property, of course. But this fire was deliberately set. I don't expect him to be here. I think Aaron has taken him—"

"He'll be at the Danvers'." Dorien leaped to his feet, shrugging off the rescue blanket. "We have to get there tonight."

"You're not going anywhere." Rochester shoved him back down. "You need to be treated by these good people or you'll do yourself permanent damage."

"My parents are in the courtyard. Aaron *crucified* them. If Jacob's with him then he's in real danger. We have to—" Dorien broke down into a coughing fit.

Crucified?

Holy cumpuddle, that's insane.

Dorien's eyes swam with pain. He looked like he was going to lose his shit any moment. I leaned in close and took him into my arms. "You'll be no good to him if you're all banged up. Please, let the paramedics do their jobs. I'll be right here."

His shoulders shuddered. I know he had a complicated relationship with his parents. He hated them, but like any kid who was made to feel unwelcome, he desperately wanted their approval, their love. But they'd chosen this nightmare over him, and now he'd never get the chance to prove himself.

"I couldn't save them," he whispered into my shoulder as the pain of it undid him. "Aaron got to them, and now he has Jacob."

~

Dorien was in the hospital for a couple of weeks. When he was given the all-clear, we took him back to the hotel and laid him out in the king-sized bed. Mom told Natalie what happened and she kindly upgraded us to a suite with three beds and an incredible view across the New York skyline.

My muse really was broken – half his beautiful hair had been burned away, not to mention his eyebrows. Without them, his face looked naked and permanently surprised. He had a twisted ankle and second-degree burns on his hand and lower legs. Looking at him tucked up in bed made my chest constrict, and when I opened my mouth to talk to him, I couldn't find words.

Because of the way he grabbed the door handle, only his pinkie finger was badly damaged. The doctors rebuilt it and put him on a rehabilitation schedule to regain movement, but he would never have the mobility to play piano at a professional level in the Classical world again.

Nothing I could say would be able to comfort him. Not after what he saw inside that house. Not knowing that Jacob was still in Aaron's hands, or that he had lost the music.

Mom brought Dorien a cup of tea and held a cold washcloth over his head. She dragged me over to the kitchenette and started opening cupboards. "I need you to go out for ingredients while I start making the tortillas."

This was what we did in my family. If someone was sick, you cooked for them, even if it meant making a mess of a tiny hotel kitchen.

By the time Dorien woke up, we laid out a feast of homemade food. I helped him to sit up in bed, and presented him with a plate of his favorites. His mouth twisted into an awful smile, a smile that felt like a betrayal of everything he witnessed.

"Someone's here to see you." I stepped aside, giving him a clear view of the armchair in the corner and the white-haired Romanian slumped in it, long legs dangling and icicle eyes watching us with a mixture of concern and loathing.

He'd been texting me less than usual, punishing himself for calling Donelle and losing the lead. So when he hadn't replied to my message about Dorien's discharge, I assumed he was ignoring me. Then he'd turned up in the hotel lobby as we wheeled a sedated Dorien upstairs. He must have broken several laws to get here from Manderley so fast.

"Well, I'll be damned." Dorien's voice croaked over the words. The doctors said it might be more than a month before he would sound normal again. Luckily, his hearing returned after a couple of days. I don't know what he would have done if he couldn't hear music again.

"Hello, Dorien," Ivan said. His gaze dipped to Dorien's bandaged finger before returning to his eyes. An unspoken message passed between them. I knew Dorien was asking about Elena and Ivan was telling him to mind his own fucking business.

But there was more to it. A palpable heat clung to the air. This *thing* that festered between them for so long engorged and fed and filled the room. My mother cleared her throat. Even she could sense it.

Ivan loved Dorien. It was obvious from the way his icicle eyes swept his body, cataloging every scar, every injury, every injustice. The thought that Dorien couldn't play again made his heart hurt, as it did mine. Ivan had spent his whole life living in the shadow of his sister's light. In Dorien, he'd found the one place where he could be his own man, and that man was adored.

And Dorien... I didn't know if he could ever love Ivan the way he wanted to be loved, because he blamed himself for Ivan's incarceration at Manderley. And now that his finger had been injured...he might not be able to love music the same way again, and Ivan and music were intrinsically linked. But as Dorien's eyes crinkled at the edges and his face broke out into that wicked smile, I could see he was trying.

I handed around plates just as Titus arrived, his arms loaded down with boxes of pizza and french fries. No one said much – it was enough to eat together, knowing how close we came to losing Dorien.

As we all dug in, someone rapped on the door. Mom started to get to her feet, but I held her back. Cory's assault flashed in my mind, and my body jerked with the memory of him pressing himself against me.

Titus went to the door and peeked into the hallway. "It's Rochester." He opened the door and the agent stepped in.

Dorien folded his arms. "Well? Do you have Aaron in custody yet?"

Rochester accepted a seat on the end of the bed and a heaping plate of food from my mother. He didn't have much choice in the matter. He looked haggard, the bags under his eyes ruining his All-American good looks.

"We've surrounded the Danvers' property in California. You were right, Dorien. The Temple has made it their new home. We've sighted five members patrolling the grounds with assault rifles. We don't know how many people are inside, but the information on your brother's map of Valencourt gives us a very good idea of how they set things up. He and Pearl also gave us a list of the cult members whose names they knew, and we've been able to track down some of their families for more information."

"When are you going in?"

Rochester spread his arms, his palms facing up in a pleading gesture. "Even if I knew, I couldn't tell you. We're waiting on orders from higher up. I *know* it's terrible waiting like this, but it's the way things work. Varney won't walk away from this."

Dorien's hand fisted the sheets. I could tell he wanted to bite back, but the truth was, the only person who knew the agony he was living through was Rochester.

"In the meantime, they can't leave the property without us knowing about it, and our people will move in at the slightest sign of something amiss. The best thing you can do right now is stay in that bed and heal, because Jacob is going to need you once he's free."

We finished up the meal in awkward silence. Rochester rose with a reluctant glance at my mother, and excused himself to sleep. Ivan rose, too. "I should return to Manderley. Madame Usher doesn't know I'm gone."

I grabbed his arm. "Stay. Please."

He stared down at me, his eyes twin storms that betrayed the demons inside him. He almost lost Dorien. He wanted to stay. He wanted to hold us both close and never let go. But Elena was at Manderley, and he couldn't bear the idea of something happening to her without him there to protect her.

Ivan's eyes flicked to the door.

I dropped his wrist. "Ivan, I'm sorry."

I shouldn't have asked him. I shouldn't have made him feel as though he had to choose. I had Titus and Dorien. Elena needed him.

Ivan's hand went around my neck, pulling my face to his. "I will stay," he promised, as his lips brushed mine. It felt like months since I tasted him last – the chilled apple and salt-tang of him, all that ice and lust wrapped into one delicious package. He struggled so much with moments like these, with letting his true feelings shine through. But he was making progress. His lips burst with love and wanting.

"I'm happy you're staying." I touched his cheek, drawing away because I knew my mother was watching. She was pretty awesome, but it was one thing to know your daughter was dating three guys and quite another to watch them at it.

I called the front desk and asked for a foldout bed, which they brought up for us. Titus and I made up the foldout while Ivan helped Mom with the dishes and Dorien directed proceedings from bed like an overzealous conductor.

"Your mom looks good," Titus said as he tucked the corners into perfect angles.

"She does." I smiled as she twirled in front of the windows, wearing one of her favorite cocktail dresses. "Dr. Nelson is a miracle worker. Once we knew the poison, they could give her the right drugs. She'll never heal perfectly, but she's able to be up and about now, and she's been enjoying life so much more."

"Don't I know it." Titus winced, rubbing the spot on his hip where he had a bruise from being kicked by an over-exuberant salsa dancer at Mom's favorite club.

There was a knock at the suite door.

"That's Natalie." Mom picked up her purse. "I'm off."

I leaped across the room and blocked the door with my body. "What are you doing?"

Mom glanced over her shoulder, nodding at my three Muses. "Mi cielo, this room isn't big enough for me and you and your harem of beautiful men. Natalie is taking me to a gallery opening downtown. They're supposed to have amazing cocktails. *Non-alcoholic* cocktails." She rolled her eyes at my expression. "I'll stay the night at her place. Please don't worry about me. I have to get my life back, too."

She blew kisses to us all as she left, leaving me alone with Broken Muse.

Dorien cracked a smile that was pure evil. He patted his lap. "Come here, Sprite."

It wasn't a command so much as a prayer. I crawled across the bed toward him, desperate to drive that hopelessness from his voice. *He might never play piano again.* Nothing I could do would repair his finger. But I could gift him tonight.

I straddled him, taking care not to rub against his bad ankle and his worst burns. Dorien's eyes fluttered shut, and he let out a sigh as he trailed his fingers along my arms before tangling them through my hair and bringing my face to meet his.

His kiss began soft, tender. His lips were soft and questioning. He was unsure now, of what was going to happen in this room, of what the future held for all of us. Seeing Ivan outside of Manderley's walls had thrown him off, made him consider what our lives could be like on the other side of this horror, if we could fight our way to that place.

I knew, because I had the same thoughts.

I returned his kiss with demanding certainty. I needed him to know that whatever happened in the future, I would be here for him, for all of them. Tonight belonged to us, and I wanted to taste every inch of Dorien Valencourt – the boy who was burned but not broken. My brave, stupid Muse.

The bed sagged as Titus lay down beside us, his fingers replacing Dorien's on my arm, trailing slow circles over my skin. Behind me, I heard Ivan draw a sharp breath. A moment later, he joined us on the other side, his hand resting with uncertain possession on the small of my back while I deepened the kiss with Dorien. Titus touched my cheek. "Faye." He whispered my name like an incantation.

I leaned over to kiss him, long and hard and deep. He kissed so differently than Dorien. He tasted different, too – dark and chaotic, but dappled with light, like early morning dew on an ancient forest. His fingers wrapped around my neck, and I felt so safe in his arms, so protected. I gasped a little as I ground myself down on Dorien's crotch and made him groan.

As I drew back, Titus' eyes devoured my body before flicking to Dorien and Ivan. I knew what they were discussing in those silent glances. They had shared other women together on tour, but those were groupies – throwaway faces and bodies to keep them warm, to make them forget their troubles for a few hours. I was so much more to them. And I'd been with two of them several times, but never all three.

I turned to Ivan, running my finger across his cheek. "If you want to go back to her, I won't stop you," I whispered. "It won't change anything between us. I'll still love you with my whole heart."

"There's nowhere else I'd rather be." Ivan's fingers closed over mine, and his cold eyes burned with determination as he kissed me. He gave me the kiss he was supposed to give me at the *Engine Ward* club, the kiss that burned all our doubts to ash.

As Ivan's lips blazed heat into my core, Dorien's fingers trailed over my skin. I didn't know how he and Titus got my clothes off. Everything became such a mess of kisses and caresses and the next thing I knew, my dress got tangled in the ceiling fan and Dorien's boxers were hanging over the lampshade, and the three of us were naked on top of the duvet, me sandwiched between them with my back against Dorien and my fingers tracing the line of Ivan's sharp jaw.

Titus lifted my knee, his breath coming out in ragged gasps as he touched his lips to my clit. I shuddered against Dorien, who held me tight as Titus ate me, savored me, fluttered his tongue against my clit like a goddamn butterfly. Ivan flashed Dorien a look of such longing that I would have bashed their heads together if my body wasn't currently building toward the best orgasm of my life. He tore his gaze away and bent to take my nipple in his mouth.

Their scents blended together in the air, and I didn't need music to conjure memories. As Dorien opened my legs wider and slid inside me, as each of my Muses touched me and stroked me and brought me to the edge, I saw in my mind everything we'd been through together, every moment of doubt and fear that we conquered, and every moment that might be ours in the future.

Music sung in my veins. This was how it was always supposed to be – the four of us, entwined together, for one night, for one moment, for eternity.

FAYE

I woke to warmth tingling down my legs.

I opened one sleepy eye and took in the scene. Sunlight streamed in through the windows. We hadn't bothered to close the curtains. Clothing was strewn everywhere, and I couldn't tell where my limbs stopped and the boys began, so tangled together were we, the sheets warm from the heat of our bodies, the air thick with our mingled scent.

Between my legs, someone gripped my thighs with calloused, musicians' fingers, their head firmly wedged in as they flicked their tongue over my clit and dipped it into my pussy, tasting the juices that already made me wet and wanting.

Mmmmm, this is the best way to wake up.

I reached down. My fingers tangled in short, fine hair. Ivan. As he realized I was awake, he curved his hands under my ass, lifting my hips to give better access to his punishing tongue. He swapped from flicks to small swirls, writing promises against my clit that had me writhing and cursing his name.

Heat pulsed inside me, building steadily to an ache that clawed along my spine. Ivan had my hips off the bed, twisting the bedspread into wild knots. Titus, who could sleep through a hurricane, remained a snoring rock, but Dorien stirred beside me. He threw a hand casually over my chest. His eyes widened as he saw what Ivan was doing.

Dorien quirked his lip into a cruel smile. He lifted the edge of the duvet and peered down at his friend. "What do we have here?"

Ivan lifted his eyes to look at Dorien as he pressed the flat of his tongue against me. The need in that look sent me over the edge. Dorien captured my mouth with his, swallowing my cry as the orgasm pulsed through me. Ivan stuck his tongue inside me again, tasting me as I soaked the sheets.

When my body quieted, Dorien pulled back and lifted the sheet again. The two of us peered down at Ivan, who planted a long, lingering kiss on my swollen clit before oh-so-casually reaching across to tug at Dorien's boxers.

Dorien was rock hard.

Dorien's cock jerked as Ivan's fingers brushed it through the silky fabric. His breath stuttered. The air fell still, expectant. Ivan lifted the hem and dragged the boxers down, down, down, over Dorien's thighs, freeing his cock.

Ivan looked to Dorien again, his eyes full of questions.

"I want you to suck it." Dorien's voice was husky but thick with power. Ivan closed his eyes, and a tremble rocked through his body. He bent down and brushed his lips reverently over the tip.

As I watched, Ivan's head bobbed down on Dorien's cock. Dorien couldn't take his eyes off his friend. He stroked Ivan's hair lovingly, like he was patting a beloved cat. All I could do was watch, grinding my pelvis into the bed as the ache between my legs burst anew.

It was so fucking hot.

To see Ivan getting exactly what he wanted, to hear Dorien's little grunts of pleasure as Ivan's mouth stroked him just the way he liked, to feel Dorien's fingers tugging at my hair, reminding me that none of this would be possible without the love and trust we shared.

Ivan's eyes never left Dorien's face as he sucked his cock in deep. I knew this was a thing that had been stirring between them for some time, and maybe this was the end of Ivan's worship of Dorien, or maybe it was the beginning of something more.

Huge hands wrapped around me. They threw off the covers and dragged me back, plonking me straight down on Titus' cock. "Oh," I cried out as he filled my pussy, his enormous shaft touching me in places only he could touch. I dragged my feet beneath me, so I knelt on him in reverse cowgirl, rocking against his cock as I watched Ivan suck Dorien off.

I ground down on Titus, driving him deeper, chasing the orgasm that teased at the tips of my toes. He was so big that it hurt a little, especially because I was still sore from last night, but it was the best kind of hurt.

Ivan's Adam's apple bobbed as he took Dorien in deep, his hand splayed under his thigh the way he did for me, thrusting Dorien's hips up to give him better access. I loved the expression on Dorien's face because I knew exactly what he was feeling. Ivan was very good at giving head.

Dorien threw his head back. His hands clamped on Ivan's shoulders as he came with a shudder that rocked the whole bed. Titus gripped my hips and ground me against him, filling me, stretching me.

"Come here," Dorien commanded. He grabbed Ivan under the arms and dragged him up the bed to lie beside him. "I want to taste myself on your tongue."

He took Ivan's lips with his own. Ivan's eyes widened like he couldn't quite believe this was happening. His body stiffened, but as Dorien deepened this kiss he relaxed, his body fitting against Dorien's like they were made for each other. Dorien tugged at Ivan's hair, nipped at his lip, scraped his teeth along his neck as he fisted Ivan's cock. His rough treatment made Ivan's eyes roll back in his head with pleasure.

This wasn't about giving me something to watch, even though seeing them made me grind down harder on Titus as my pleasure rose like a storm inside me. This was them taking the first steps into a dark, enchanted forest, slicing and cutting their way through the tangled vines of their emotions.

Ivan had spent his entire life living for his sister, trying to save her from the evil of the world. Dorien was the only person who'd ever put Ivan first, who thought *he* was worthy of saving. Dorien's fist worked Ivan's cock, and Ivan's back muscles tightened and his eyes grew wide with wonder and need, and he came in pale ribbons across Dorien's stomach.

Dorien looked down at him with such arrogant pleasure, like a spoiled king humoring a loyal subject. I half expected him to command Ivan to clean him with his mouth, but instead, he rolled over and pinched my nipple.

That little bite of pain was all I needed to send me tumbling over the edge. I ground myself down on Titus, feeling my walls clench around him as I rode the wave of pleasure unfurling inside me. His nails dug into my thighs as he thrust up to meet me, and he grunted as he too came, his cock twitching and jerking inside me.

Good thing this hotel had extra well-soundproofed walls, because we had no intention of leaving the bed for the rest of the day.

$\sim$

"What was that?" I grinned as I wrapped my arms around Ivan, pulling him back under the covers.

"I do not know." Ivan rested his head on my shoulder and smiled. His smile was so sweet and sad. "It was a dream, Faye."

We both glanced toward the bathroom. Steam curled from under the door as Dorien's booming voice sang 'Avant de quitter' from the opera *Faust*, which is the most Dorien shower-opera song ever.

We were both thinking the same thing – what happened today meant the world to Ivan, but what was it for Dorien? Was it another one of his games? Another way for him to wrestle back control when he was teetering so dangerously close to losing everything?

"I have to go back to Manderley," Ivan said.

I nodded. I knew nothing I could say would talk him out of returning. "You need to get her out of that house. She has to know she doesn't have to go through with this marriage now."

"She's determined to marry him," he said, his voice hopeful. "Maybe she truly loves him?"

Ivan had such a broken puppy dog face I wanted to rub him behind the ears until he wagged his tail again.

I shook my head, remembering walking with Elena by the gazebo, the determination in her voice as she spoke about her brother and what she would do to escape Manderley. *I am a woman now,* she'd said. *I am not innocent, and I refuse to die locked away in this crumbling shithole because he won't do what needs to be done.*

"I need you to talk to her," Ivan said. "She may listen to you."

I nodded. "I need to look after Dorien right now, but if you arrange it, I'll do everything I can."

Ivan rose reluctantly, picking his clothes from the mess on the floor. "Tell Dorien goodbye for me." He cast a forlorn glance to the bathroom as he picked up his backpack. "Tell him I—I'm sorry about his finger."

"Tell him yourself."

Ivan laughed hollowly. "If he steps out of that shower all haughty and glistening, I won't be able to leave."

I flashed him a grin. "I believe it."

We kissed goodbye. I wanted to drag him back into bed and use every trick in the book to make him stay, but that wasn't fair. Ivan needed to be with his sister, and I needed to stay with Dorien while Rochester and his team stormed the Danvers' mansion.

Last night and this morning we managed to make Dorien forget about his brother, Jacob. But now a knife of unease twisted in my gut. What would happen when the Feds broke inside the Temple? Would Dorien get his orphaned brother back? What would that mean for his future? For our future?

DORIEN

Jacob.

I gazed up at the Danvers' California estate through the trees, all garish Greco-Roman columns and gaudy carvings – a modern Barbie dreamhouse that seemed so at odds with the supposed values of the Temple of Earthly Truths. The skin on my injured finger pulled painfully, but I could barely feel it. Somewhere inside was my kid brother, and Aaron Varney had control of him.

I balled my hands into fists at my sides.

Faye and I had flown out to California two days ago to be on site when Rochester's team went in. They were in negotiations with Aaron Varney – they were hoping he would allow two of their team to enter the compound for a talk. This would enable the Feds to gather information about what was going on inside, maybe even allow Jacob and some of the other children to leave. Rochester wanted me nearby in case I would make a good bargaining chip – they wouldn't send me in blind now that they'd seen what Aaron did to my parents, but I was happy to be a chess piece they could move around the board if it meant I got Jacob back.

Rochester and Velasquez had been inside the house for four hours. They weren't on comms because that was one of Aaron's stipulations, and they hadn't checked in since they entered the double gilded doors, which wasn't good. Faye and I sat together in the back of the van, listening to the members of Rochester's team panic and bark orders at each other. Sometimes, the bushes would rustle a little – a sign of life from the officers closing in on the perimeter.

"I never knew FBI raids could be this boring." Faye rolled her eyes. I knew she was trying to distract me. "We should have brought snacks."

Baldwin, who was working the comms station, reached into an empty rifle case and drew out a bag of corn chips. "Rookie mistake. I've got food stashed all over this van. There are at least three packages of Oreos hidden under the front seat."

"You, sir, are a genius. I don't suppose you happen to have any salsa hidden in that server stack—"

Faye's words were cut off by a series of loud POPs from the house and a window shattering. I bolted to my feet. "What the fuck was that?"

But no one answered. Baldwin was barking into his comms, and I saw a flash of movement in the bushes as the officers closed in. My stomach flew to my throat. *Were those gunshots? Please let Jacob be okay—*

After the flurry of activity, the house fell silent – an oppressive silence that chilled my heart. Faye slipped her fingers into mine, squeezing my hand so tight she'd break bones if I had any left, but I was a quivering mess.

Hours seemed to pass as we watched that silent house. The gilded door squeaked and grated and swung open. Two figures stepped outside. They held hands, and their long brown robes swept around their feet. They each carried an assault rifle, not pointed at anyone but resting on their shoulder, indicating they could start shooting at any moment. As they moved toward the gate, the officers surged forward, guns trained, yelling at them to stop.

"Don't shoot," I yelled. "That's my brother."

It's him. It's Jacob.

My brother held up his hand and waved at me, his face breaking into a cheerful smile. My heart swelled in my chest and broke open, and I was laughing and crying and babbling. *Jacob is out. He's alive, and he's outside.*

Beside Jacob, Pearl folded her arms and glared at the officers advancing on them.

"You took your time getting here," she rebuked the nearest officer.

I surged forward, but Baldwin grabbed the scruff of my neck and yanked me back. "You can't go to him yet, son. It might be a trap. We've seen it before."

A trap...my mind reeled as I understood what he meant. Aaron might've put a bomb on Jacob.

Fuck, no, please.

Beside me, Faye whimpered. "Why haven't Rochester and Velasquez come out?"

She's right. The gilded doors yawned open, revealing a foyer dripping with crystal chandeliers. But no one appeared behind them, no triumphant Rochester or beaming Velasquez. Everything was too still, too quiet.

Something isn't right. It is a trap.

The officers circled Jacob and Pearl, ordering them to stop. Jacob set his gun on the ground, and he nodded at Pearl to do the same. "It's okay," he said to the officers. "You can go inside. Everyone is asleep. Even your friends are asleep, but they'll be okay."

"Jacob!" I yelled, shrugging out of Baldwin's grasp. Before I could reach him, he and Pearl were swarmed by officers. They closed around the children, barking orders as they took the guns and swept them for explosives and other weapons.

'All clear." They pushed the children toward the gate and the waiting medical unit. Toward me and Faye and freedom.

Jacob ran to me with a wide smile and fell into my arms. "You came for me. I was so scared that you were dead, too. But you came to get me, just like you said you would."

I rubbed Jacob's back, feeling his ribs poking through his skin like dinosaur spines. For a fifteen-year-old, he was so small and light – a twig that could snap at any moment. Tears streamed down my cheeks.

Don't thank me for this, brother. I should have pulled you out a long time ago. But I promise I will never, ever let anyone take your power from you again.

We held each other for a long time, until he wriggled with impatience, until I cried my body's volume in tears. I took his hand in mine and led him over to the van, where Faye was watching us with a broad grin on her face. "Jacob, I'd like you to meet my girlfriend, Faye. You're going to live with us now, if you want to."

"Hi, Jacob." Faye bent down, so she was at his height. "I'm so excited to meet you. Dorien has been telling me so much about you. I can't wait to hang out."

Jacob slunk behind me. A shadow passed over his eyes as he glared back at Faye. *It's nothing to worry about, he's nervous of strangers. He hasn't been outside the Temple in years.*

But as Faye stepped back and Jacob's frown deepened, I couldn't help but wonder if it was as simple as that. *What lies has Aaron been filling his head with? Jacob can't believe everything Aaron told him, otherwise he wouldn't be out here. But he doesn't know what's real and what's lies.*

Behind us, officers marched into the property. Minutes later, they were dragging bodies out on stretchers, covered in sheets with oxygen masks over their faces. I saw them lift Rochester into the medical unit, and my stomach tightened.

I looked down at my brother. A chill struck my veins. "What happened, Jacob? Did you do something to these people?"

"We didn't hurt them," he said, a little petulantly. "Pearl and I made the tea, and we put some stuff in it so they would fall asleep. Then we used the guns to shoot the padlock on the front door and came outside."

The gunshots we heard.

"It was all Pearl's idea." Jacob waved to his friend, who was standing in the medical van, refusing to sit down as she explained their daring escape in a dramatic voice.

Something about what Jacob said niggled at me. "What stuff did you put in the tea? Is it dangerous? You have to tell the medics so they can treat these people. That man over there helped me to save your life."

Jacob shrugged. "I don't know what it was called. Pearl's sister Heather gave her an old bottle. She said she took it from you at Manderley, and it made people sleepy."

It took me a few minutes to figure out what Jacob was referring to. The apothecary set Clare and I found in the attic. I showed it to Heather. The first day Faye showed up at Manderley, we used the syrup of ipecac to make her sick, and we got chloroform to knock Faye out before the party. Faye and I used a Victorian drug called chloral to knock out Madame Usher so we could copy her keys and explore the attic room. I hadn't looked at the apothecary set since then, but I was betting the bottle of chloral was missing.

I saw Heather's actions in a new light. She'd tried to fuck us all over and hurt Faye, and I'd never forgive her for that, and her brutal death didn't change the fact she was a 'class A bitchbadger,' as Faye would say. But her two younger sisters were trapped inside the cult. She must have seen what happened to my family and been determined not to let it happened to hers.

Thank you, Heather.

I pressed Jacob to me again, and I met Faye's eyes over his shoulder. She'd figured out the same thing I had, that Heather had been trying to save her sister. She'd been just as much a prisoner of Manderley as the rest of us.

Together, we turned to the gilded doors just as they brought out Aaron on a stretcher. He looked blissful in sleep, the edges of his mouth turned up into a contented smile. I *burned* to make him pay for destroying my family. He would wake up in a cell, and be put on trial for murder, and likely be locked up for life, but it wasn't enough. It would never be enough for the torment he caused for his god complex.

But he was only one part of this puzzle. Madame Usher was still the spider at the center of this web. And if I couldn't wrap my hands around Aaron's throat and squeeze until the life drained from his eyes, I could sure as hell bring her to her knees.

DORIEN

"He's doing great." Dr. Nelson peered at me over the chart. She wasn't even Jacob's doctor, but when she heard we were back in the hospital getting him assessed, she offered to help. "Apart from a few abrasions and the damage on his feet, he's healthier than I expected. He's severely malnourished, but he's receiving fluids, and he's making great progress. He'll need continued monitoring and care, and I'm making a recommendation for a child psychologist, who will determine his mental age and help with deprogramming. He became agitated when the doctors checked him over. I strongly advise you to take him to a dentist at your first opportunity, but he's a strong boy and with lots of love I think he'll thrive. You'll be able to take him home with you by the end of the week."

Home. What a joke. I didn't have a home. Valencourt Manor burned to the ground, and I couldn't live in a hotel room on Natalie's dime forever. I didn't even have a car anymore – crashing the Porsche into the gate completely wrote it off.

With my pinkie finger damaged, I'd likely never play the piano like I could before. The only thing in my life I was actually good at had been taken from me.

Jacob desperately needed stability and safety in his life, and I was anything but. I was a mess.

I'm already failing him.

Dr. Nelson must have sensed my apprehension because she patted my shoulder. "There's no easy fix here, Dorien. This is a long, hard road you're walking with Jacob. Children who come out of cults carry trauma they will struggle to understand. He'll be confused, angry, anxious, maybe even depressed. He may suffer PTSD from the terrible things he experienced in Aaron's care, but he's also been ripped from the only family he's known. He's been programmed to believe that everything outside the Temple is unsafe, evil, and corrupt, and that includes you.

It's going to be tough, but if you're gentle and patient, he'll come out the other side a strong, resilient young man, just like his older brother."

I blinked back tears. It wasn't fair. Jacob didn't deserve any of this. I took Dr. Nelson's papers in shaking hands. Psychologists. Group therapy. Dental work. Jacob needed all of this to get better, and Medicaid would pay for some of it, but where the fuck would I get the money to look after my brother?

"Can we see him?" Faye asked Dr. Nelson, her hand never leaving mine. She'd been by my side ever since Jacob walked out of the Danvers' estate – I would have collapsed with grief by now if it weren't for her steadiness.

Dr. Nelson stepped aside, and Faye held open the door for me. I swallowed down my tears. Jacob needed my strength now. Looking at him reminded me of my own guilt, my failure, but I couldn't put that on him. He'd already endured so much.

My feet dragged as I walked through the door. He sat up in bed when he saw me. He was so impossibly tiny, like a little kid. "Hey, buddy."

Jacob smiled at me, and that smile broke my heart. "Dorien. They gave me jelly beans. Look."

He pushed his fingers through a rainbow of colorful candies on his tray, his eyes wide with wonder.

"That's great." I swallowed back the lump welling in my throat. "You seem better today. It was so brave what you did, putting everyone to sleep and walking outside like that."

"It was Pearl's idea. She's been telling me about jelly beans! And school and go-karts and wrestling and baseball and Pop-Tarts!" He smiled again, but the smile was a little manic.

"Well, the good news is soon I'm going to take you out of here and we'll go and try all those things. Anything you want to do, you can do it."

But Jacob was frowning. "Where's Pearl?"

"She's in a hospital just like this, but in California," Faye said.

"I didn't ask you," Jacob snapped at her. I started at his tone – I'd never heard my gentle brother speak to someone like that before, his voice dripping with disdain. Faye looked unperturbed, but I felt my heart sinking. I remembered those fleeting visits I've had with him over the years, how meek and kind and anxious he was. But this Jacob...I didn't know how to deal with him.

I wonder if that's how Father Aaron talks to the women in the Temple.

"Faye's telling the truth." I try to keep my voice gentle. "Pearl's cousins are looking after her while her parents get better—"

"You're lying." Jacob's face fell, and when he peered up at me, his slate-grey eyes were dark with rage. "God punished her, didn't he? God punished her and now she's dead because I didn't save her."

"No, that's not true. She's in California. I can set up a video call with her if you want—"

"No no no." Jacob's face screwed up, his tiny fists beating at my chest. Every blow felt like the sword of Damocles slicing off my head. "Father Aaron said she was wicked and sinful. He said it was my job to make her godly and good, but instead, I helped her and now she's burning to hell." Jacob shoved the tray so hard it rolled across the room. The jelly beans rolled over the edge and scattered on the floor. "You're going to hell too."

I know.

"I'm not going to hell. I'm going to be right here with you, buddy." I reached out to touch his hair. "Father Aaron has told you lots of things that aren't true, but I'm going to help you—"

"No!" he yelled, pummeling my chest again. "I don't want you. I don't want your whore. I want Mommy. Where are Mommy and Daddy?"

"Dorien, I think you should come outside now," Dr. Nelson called out from the doorway.

I can't. I can't leave him like this.

Jacob's fists pummeled my back, my chest, my arms. Faye had to pull him off me. When she touched his arm, he hissed at her, like a cat cornered by an overexcited puppy.

Even when I drew away I could still feel his blows raining down on me. "I hate you, I hate you," he screamed as Dr. Nelson hurried in, the door swinging shut behind her.

The news of the federal raid on the Temple of Earthly Truths and Father Aaron's arrest made headlines. The hospital did a great job keeping the press away from Jacob, but once they figured out the connection between me and the cult (with a little help from Madame Usher, according to Ivan), they hounded us relentlessly. They banged on the car windows as we pulled into the hospital parking lot, chased us into the lobby of the hotel, and stalked us as we met with Rochester to give our statements about Aaron's treatment of my family. Marguerite and Natalie were working as our unpaid PR team, fielding media calls and releasing statements, and Broken Muse topped the Classical Music charts for the first time since our last album released three years ago. It was a river of lies flowing beneath a mountain of shit, and we could do nothing but ride the current and hope we didn't get pulled under.

The press weren't even the worst thing hounding me. Nightmares kept me awake – the twisted faces of my parents leering down at me from their cross, reminding me that I was a failure. I assumed Jacob had seen them too, for he was haunted by his own nightmares – visions that sent him screaming and flinging himself from his hospital bed. But that could have been from any one of the horrors Aaron visited on him over the years.

At least Aaron was behind bars now, and from the looks of the case Rochester and his team put together, he'd be staying there for a long time. The thirty-five adults and seven children who drank the poisoned tea were being released from the hospital back to their families, and some were starting to speak about what went on within the cult. I tried to read their stories, but my eyes blurred with rage and regret and I couldn't see the words anymore.

My ruined finger mocked me, a fitting punishment for my crime. *I'll never be able to forgive myself for going to Europe with Broken Muse instead of doing everything I could to get Jacob out.*

I couldn't change my mistakes, but I had my chance for redemption. Jacob would be coming home with me in a matter of days. I went to visit him in the hospital every day. He was brighter and happier when Faye wasn't in the room, but his emotions wavered all over the place, from relief to anxiety to excitement to anger.

I can't help him. I don't have the emotional maturity to deal with my own shit, let alone his trauma.

But it didn't matter how useless I was as a brother. I was all Jacob had left now. What a great prize I was.

Back in the hotel suite after a tiring day with Jacob, Faye and I made plans. As much as I didn't want to deal with the fallout of my parents' murder, I had a meeting with their lawyer to prepare for. Social services needed to talk to me about Jacob's guardianship, and we couldn't keep staying in the hotel with the media circus, but every apartment in the city cost seven million dollars in rent.

"You're going to love this." Faye made a face as she tossed the newspaper down in front of me. "As if we didn't have enough problems to deal with."

I picked it up and scanned the headlines. It was an exclusive interview with Madame Usher, who styled herself as my artistic mentor and a close family friend. She spoke with astonishing conviction about how much she cared about me, and how the cult might have influenced my actions in the house. She implied Clare and Heather had been afraid of me, and that the cult had given me the skills to manipulate them.

"This doesn't seem like her." I slid the paper back across the table and reached for one of the little bottles of minibar Scotch Faye lined up down the center of the table. "It reeks of desperation."

"I know." Faye sipped her coffee. "She's lashing out because she knows we know her secrets. She's discrediting us before we speak up about Victor."

"Why haven't we spoken up about Victor?" If she wanted to fight this battle in the court of public opinion, she could be my guest. I'd been making headlines since Broken Muse first released our debut single, 'A Graveside Story.' She shouldn't pick her battles in her enemy's front garden.

"Because Ivan and Elena are still inside that house, and I don't want to give her any reason to hurt them." Faye popped the cork on her own bottle and took a long slug. "We need more than just this wild story of a fake death and a creepy old man hiding in the walls. We need the story, the reasons. We need to follow that money."

~

"This is where we're going to live for a while."

Jacob's eyes widened as he took in the apartment. Even though she hadn't lived there long, Marguerite had done an amazing job making it ready for us all. There were two bedrooms, one for her and one for Jacob, and a large kitchen and living room (at least, large by NYC standards) where Faye and I could sleep on a foldout sofa. She painted his room with a soft green that reminded me of the rolling lawns of Manderley, and filled it with everything a boy needed – toys and video games and new clothing and toiletries.

When Marguerite saw Madame Usher's article, she declared war. Madame Usher might've been a venomous spider, but she couldn't play the media like Marguerite de Winter. Faye's mom sold her own story of poison and stolen husbands to a rival paper, and used the check to lease a three months' apartment for all of us.

Now, she leaned against the doorframe, watching Jacob with a shy smile as he circled the room, touching all the new things she placed there for him.

"This is Marguerite. She's going to be living with us, and she'll look after you when I'm not here." *Because I have to get a job.*

I'd never had a job before that wasn't 'rockstar' – but with my finger unlikely to regain its previous mobility, Madame Usher determined to sully my name, Ivan trapped at Manderley and Titus on track for Juilliard, the band was over.

Faye's mother bent down, so she was at his level, even though I could see it caused her pain. "Hello, Jacob. It's so nice to meet you. I heard you know my daughter, Faye. I got you these things so you feel at home here. I hope you like them."

Jacob sat on the edge of the bed, his eyes wide as he took in all the stuff. He wouldn't even remember owning toys or clothes he didn't have to sew himself from old towels. From Rochester's damning reports of the Danvers' residence, Jacob might not even have had a bed. There was evidence the children slept on piles of old blankets on the floor.

Both Jacob and I still woke several times a night, screaming from the nightmarish visions of our parents hanging from a cross.

Jacob didn't say anything. He picked up a stack of perfectly folded t-shirts and tossed them on the floor.

"These things are evil. They make me unclean. We shouldn't have them here."

"Hey, buddy, hey." I sat down beside him and clasped his hand in mine. "I know that's what Aaron told you, but look. I wear all sorts of clothes. So does everyone else who you've met, remember? It's okay to wear these clothes and feel comfortable. You can even choose your own, in whatever colors you want."

The therapist we started seeing (yet another reason I needed an income source other than paltry Spotify royalty checks, stat) said that I should challenge the logic of Aaron's teachings. If Jacob sees Aaron's rules being broken without consequence, he'll start to understand the rules themselves were false. *Hopefully.* The therapist was always quick to warn that every child was different and some couldn't break the patterns of manipulation from a cult. But that wasn't going to be my brother. Not while I was here to help him.

"I want to go home." He stomped his foot. "You said I could go home."

I clasped my hand over his before he could wreck more of Marguerite's hard work. "This is what I meant, buddy. This is our home for now. And Pearl is going to visit soon. You wanted to see Pearl again."

I was nervous about Jacob seeing Pearl. I thought seeing someone from the Temple might trigger Jacob. The therapist who charged more per hour than we used to make in t-shirt sales from an entire *tour* believed that because Jacob trusts Pearl, and she didn't grow up in the Temple and knew about the outside world, she could be a good influence on him, help him to adjust. So I arranged with her cousins to have her visit in a month, just before she started at school.

"I don't like this place. I want to go back to our house. I want Mommy." Angry tears clouded his face.

"Jacob, you remember what happened to Mommy." I had to tread carefully here. The therapist said we couldn't indulge delusions, but we had to do it in a way that wouldn't trigger the trauma of Jacob's memories. I don't know how much he saw of what Aaron did to our parents. Forensics said they died several hours before the fire took hold. Knowing Aaron's ways, he would have made an example of them in front of his followers. "Father Aaron did that, and so that means I have to keep you here so you're safe from him—"

"You said you'd keep me safe, but you let them die. They just wanted you to come home so we could be a real family. Aaron's right. You're evil." He kicked the bedside table.

I wrapped my arms around him, holding him still as a tsunami of emotion welled inside him. He kicked and screamed and railed against the world. His tiny fists pummeled my chest and every blow twisted inside me like a knife slicing me to pieces.

He wasn't wrong. I am evil. I left him in Aaron's clutches and now he's broken. Just like me.

Jacob raged until his anger spent. He collapsed in a pile of his ruined things, his eyes closed. Marguerite helped me to my feet and led me outside, closing the door behind us. "Give him time, Dorien. He's been through hell." She touched my arm. "You both have."

"I don't—" I fought for words between the sob rising from my chest. "I don't know what to do to help him."

"You're doing everything you need to by being there." She gave me a warm hug, the first she'd given me since I walked back into Faye's life. "Follow me, I'll make you some cocoa. Everything is better after a pot of my cocoa, mostly because of the large amount of whisky I put in it. But don't tell my daughter."

As I followed Marguerite to the kitchen, I wondered. What if Jacob never got better? What if he could never learn to trust me, or Marguerite, or Ivan and Titus, or Faye? If Jacob didn't improve, I couldn't keep him here where every day he was greeted by the life I built without him. That wasn't fair to him.

Would saving my brother mean giving up everything I won, including Faye's heart?

Faye

I traipsed up the stairs to the apartment, cursing the cockpoodle who decided elevators in NYC apartment buildings were a bourgeois luxury. My back hurt. My feet hurt. I smelled like furniture wax and old cabbage (piano shops always smelled like old cabbage, don't ask me why. I don't make the rules). All I wanted was a glass of wine and maybe for Dorien to fuck a smile onto my face. As I inserted the key into the lock, I could hear Jacob screaming.

Poor kid. No matter how much my life sucked at the moment, Jacob had it worse. Some days he was all smiles and kindness with Dorien, but his mood would turn on a violin string. He didn't like me. He spoke to me in this haughty, condescending tone that reminded me far too much of his older brother during my early days at Manderley.

Jacob had the same slate-grey eyes as Dorien, and the same crooked smile that melted your heart. But while Dorien's grin flirted with devils, Jacob's smile – when he allowed us to see it – was pure kindness and innocence.

I wanted to help him so much, but what he was going through was more than any of us could ever comprehend. We had to be there for him through every awful mood and every cutting remark. And that meant when I turned the key in the door I plastered a smile on my face.

Mom greeted me, throwing her coat over her shoulders and tossing her keys into her purse. She had to yell to be heard over the screaming. "There you are. I'm running late for my appointment with Dr. Nelson. Jacob's hasn't eaten a bite all day, but he'd been happily watching cartoons for hours until one of the characters set another on fire." She blew a kiss. "I'll be home in a couple of hours. Maybe longer."

"You can't leave me here." I stared over her shoulder at the boy on the sofa, lying on his back kicking his feet while he tore his lungs out. Panic crawled through my chest.

"I'm sorry, mi cielo. I'm getting test results back and Dr. Nelson wants to introduce me to another specialist. But you'll be fine with Jacob for a little bit."

Doubtful. "Where's Dorien? Why can't he watch Jacob?"

"Dorien has the meeting with his lawyer." Mom glanced at her watch. "He was supposed to be done an hour ago, but they must have had a lot to talk about. I have to go. You'll be fine. Just...um...you'll be fine. Byeeeeee." She air-kissed my cheeks as she dashed into the corridor. Was it my imagination, or did she breathe a sigh of relief as she darted toward the stairwell?

Great.

I set down my bag, noticing my violin case hidden behind the potted plant. I hadn't practiced in a while – thinking about music depressed me. The only reason I was able to attend Manderley was because of Madame Usher. I couldn't afford another music program and no school would offer me a scholarship with my name splashed across lurid headlines. But right then, there was nothing I wanted to do more than draw my bow across the strings and transport myself somewhere far away.

I unclipped the case, pulling out the Becker and setting it against my chin. Jacob watched me from the sofa as I drew the bow across the strings, twisting the pegs to get the proper tuning. He kept screaming, but without enthusiasm.

"Don't come any closer." Jacob's face clouded with rage. He looked so like the Dorien I remembered from Madame Usher's school it made my chest ache. I wanted to wrap Jacob in my arms and make him laugh and teach him about horror films and Mexican food and buy him so much ice cream he got sick, but that wasn't my role. I had to give him the space to learn to trust me. Maybe he never would. Maybe Aaron had already corrupted his relationships with women beyond repair.

"I promise I'll stay over here. I won't touch you or talk to you." I struck the strings to emphasize my promise. "I'm just going to play for a little bit. You don't even have to listen. You can go right on screaming."

Jacob frowned at me as I raised the violin and started to play. I chose Sarasate's *Zigeunerweisen Op. 20* – a piece composed for piano and orchestra that Dorien arranged for violin and piano for one of our duets at the Usher School. I tried hard not to look at Jacob as I played, but it was impossible – those dark eyes that were so much like Dorien's bore into me as I dove deeper into my memories.

Dorien's enchanting scent wove around me, that dark heart of cinnamon and frankincense dappled with sweet violets dragging me under its spell. This wasn't simply the lingering residue of Dorien's recent presence in the room – it was a memory from long ago conjured by the music. It was me and Dorien practicing this piece in an echoey room, accompanied by the slightly boiled pork odor that wafted from the school's old furnace vents.

It was a time when all I thought about was classes and violin and making my dad see me and Dorien's perfect grey eyes.

During the melancholic third section, which is played muted, Jacob stopped screaming. He curled his feet beneath him and sat watching me as the piece swelled and dipped. The Spanish composer Sarasate drew inspiration from Hungarian folk music, although he thought they were Romani gypsy tunes. The fourth and final section called for frenzied playing of long spiccato runs, double stops, and left-hand pizzicato. His eyes widened as he watched my fingers, his body moving in a jerky dance as if the music controlled his limbs. When I finished with a breathless flourish, I lowered my bow and met his eyes. Tears glistened in the corners.

"I think..." he screwed up his face. "I remember that song."

I tried to hide my surprise. "I used to play with your brother at a music school in New York City. I'm surprised you remember it at all; you must've been barely five years old."

He shook his head. "I don't know if I do remember. I don't remember the school. I don't remember you. But I remember the music. It makes me want to dance."

I dared a smile. "Me too. But it's hard to dance and play at the same time. Dorien can do it, and he plays the piano. He makes every song into a performance, and not many people can do that."

"My mother said Dorien has a gift."

"She's right. Your brother is exceptionally gifted. Has he played you any of his music?"

Jacob shook his head. I didn't blame Dorien for not showing him Broken Muse. The songs were quite dark, and the band's existence was tied to Dorien's guilt for leaving his brother inside the Temple.

"I could play one for you." I picked up the remote and navigated through my favorite playlist, selecting one of their lighter songs and pumping the volume up until the music swelled from the speakers. Jacob's eyes widened again as Ivan's violin added a melancholic air, while Titus' deep cello dueled for supremacy with Dorien's florid playing. When it was over, he begged for another.

I paused. I didn't want to overstep, and Dorien was so nervous about Jacob feeling betrayed by his absence. But Jacob didn't look betrayed. He looked like a little kid in awe of his big brother. So I put on another song and navigated to a folder I kept of images from their tours and fan pages (If Dorien finds out I kept tabs on him all these years, I'd never hear the end of it), and brought them up on the screen.

"Here's Dorien performing at the Wiener Musikverein in Vienna, and this is from their show at the Royal Albert Hall in London." I flipped past a photograph of Dorien crowd surfing in the famous venue. "Here is Dorien with Titus and Ivan on a photoshoot in Prague. They've been all over the world playing for their fans."

"Wow." Jacob pointed to a photograph. "Who's that with him?"

I peered at the photograph. It was of Dorien and Titus at a music award event in London, dressed in their stage costumes and surrounded by men and women in black tie. They smiled at the camera with their arms around an older couple, but the smile didn't reach their eyes.

"Her name is Madame Usher, and that was her husband, Victor Usher. He died nearly two years ago. She runs the music school Dorien and I have been attending. She's not a nice person."

"She came to the Temple once. I remember her. She met with my parents and Father Aaron in the kitchen. We baked a special loaf of bread for her visit."

What? A cold fist clenched around my heart. "When was this?"

Jacob counted on his fingers. "I think…five summers ago. I remember because we had an amazing orange crop that year, so we made an orange seed cake to go with the bread."

"Was she alone, or did she have anyone else with her?"

Jacob shook his head. "She was all by herself. Father Aaron must not have wanted her to feel lonely, because he invited her to sleep over in his bedroom."

Did he now…

I leaned toward him, heart pounding. I didn't want to push Jacob, but this was important. "Did you happen to overhear what she and Aaron talked about?"

Jacob frowned. "Eavesdropping is a sin."

"You're right. I'm sorry. I just meant…what did you all talk about when you were together?"

"She talked about Dorien lots, and how he was in Europe with his band, and he had this great power to spread the Temple's message all over the world but he was wasting it with sinful music. She and Aaron and Mother agreed on that a lot. She had one of those glittery keys pinned to her neck, like my mom used to wear. When she left, she gave Father Aaron a big brown envelope." His eyes flicked to the ground. "I asked him if it was a present and he said it was none of my business. He wouldn't even let me have any orange seed cake."

I wanted to keep pressing him, but I had an idea. A way to connect to Jacob. A way to help him draw a line between the things that made him happy about Temple and the big, wide, scary world he lived in now.

"I bet that orange cake was amazing, too. I heard you're an excellent baker." I felt my lips curling into a smile. "Hey, do you want to learn how to make tortillas? That's flat bread from Mexico, where my mother comes from. You roll them up and fill them with meat and vegetables and spices, and they're delicious."

Jacob scrambled off the couch. "Flat bread? That's totally crazy."

As I tied an apron around Jake's narrow waist, my mind whirred a mile a minute. Madame Usher was visiting Father Aaron. That was before Dorien tried to help Ivan and Elena escape, before she trapped all three Broken Muses at Manderley. So what was she doing with Father Aaron? Why did I have a terrible feeling we'd only scratched the surface of what was going on?

Dorien

When I came home from the appointment with my lawyers, Jacob and Faye were in the kitchen. He was rolling out the dough for tortillas while Faye chopped and mixed fillings. She'd put a playlist of Broken Muse songs on quiet in the background, and was sashaying her gorgeous hips as she moved around the kitchen. When Jacob looked up at me, he actually *smiled*.

After what I just learned, the scene made my throat tighten. I slid into a chair and breathed in the delicious scent of fresh tortillas. "I'm sorry I'm later than I planned. It looks like you two are having fun."

"Faye taught me to make tortillas," Jacob held up a lopsided circle of dough proudly. "Look."

"That's amazing."

"We've got to fry it first, silly." Faye had a frilly apron tied backward around her middle, so it covered her butt, with the strings dangling down between her legs. The front of her shirt was dusted with flour, which might have given me ghost Clare flashbacks if I wasn't so distracted by Jacob's broad smile. He wore a newspaper chef's hat and was just as coated in flour.

The pair of them bustled around, preparing food for me. Jacob presented a plate of fish tacos with a flourish. I exchanged a glance with Faye as I dug in. *You're a genius,* I mouthed. She found a way to connect with him through baking – an activity that felt familiar to him. It was perfect.

After we'd all eaten our fill of tacos, Jacob went to his room to play with his toys. I grabbed Faye around the waist and twirled her, planting kisses along her jaw until she pushed me away.

"I have to tell you something," she said. "You're not going to like it."

"No. Me first." Faye sounded grave, but I had a feeling once she heard my news, hers wouldn't seem as bad. "I've been dying to tell you how the meeting with the lawyer went."

"Okay, fine. You first."

"As I suspected, both Jacob's and my trust fund had been cleared out by Father Aaron, as have most of their investments."

"I'm sorry, Dorien." Faye laid her head on my shoulder.

"It's actually a blessing, in a way. They changed their will several years ago to give everything to The Temple, which means that we'd spend the rest of our lives fighting the cult in court for that money, and now we don't have to, because it's all gone...except the house."

"What?"

"Mom and Dad left Valencourt Manor – the house, the grounds, the whole property – to me and Jacob, to be shared equally between us. I don't know if they simply overlooked it or if somewhere in the back of their warped brains they knew Aaron was taking them for a ride. But the house is ours. Even with the fire and the piles of trash and the decades of neglect, the estate is prime land. It's worth a few million, at least."

Faye pressed her hand to her mouth. "I can't believe it."

"I can't, either." I spun her around until she squealed. "The lawyers are working through the tangled web that is my parents' finances now, and then we could put the place up for sale. And then we'll have money – real money we can spend on giving Jacob the best possible future, the life they stole from him."

"Dorien, that's amazing." Faye held my cheeks. "You can't call it our money, though. This is your money, not mine. Yours and Jacob's. Please, don't spend a cent of it on me."

"I can give Jacob a great life and still buy my girl a new frying pan." I lift the thrift-store pan to show her the cracks running across the handle. Faye grabbed it and tried to swat me with it, but I ducked out of her grasp.

"Seriously, I have to tell you about my thing now." She set down the frying pan. "I want you to promise you won't grill Jacob about it. We made real progress today and I don't want to frighten him."

That cold lump in my throat returned. "You're scaring me. Spit it out, Sprite."

She took a deep breath. "Jacob said Madame Usher visited your parents and Father Aaron at their house, about five years ago. They made a special cake for her and she spoke about you, and she *stayed the night*. In Aaron's room. Apparently, when she left, Father Aaron was in a good mood."

She didn't have to elaborate on what this meant.

Father Aaron was another one of Madame Usher's pawns.

Over the next couple of weeks, I spent every waking moment with Jacob. We went for slow, meandering walks around the nearby park, stopping to purchase chestnuts from a peddler and to feed the ducks in the pond. We returned only when

Jacob's ruined feet made it impossible for him to walk, and I'd carry him back on my shoulders like he was a kid.

I bought him picture books to help with his reading, and sports equipment and action figures and enough junk food to put the meat back on his bones. He smiled more and more.

His smiles made me angry. Mostly at myself. He was fifteen years old. He wasn't supposed to be struggling his way through picture books and feeding ducks at the pond. At the park, we passed a group of boys his age having a snowball fight, and Jacob hid behind me.

He'd had his whole life taken from him. I should have got him out years ago, Madame Usher be damned. I'd been selfish, so happy to escape the sinking ship that was my family that I went on tour with Broken Muse. I'd like to say I at least thought about Jacob all the time, that I was planning and plotting to free him. But that would be a lie. And I paid for that lie with my finger and any chance at continuing my career as a musician. I was too angry at myself to be sad about it.

I was determined that from now on I'd make sure he had everything to make up for the shitty brother he'd been given.

And that started with selling off Valencourt Manor as soon as possible so I could get my hands on that money. I was scrolling through my laptop, looking for the name of a local company that could clean up the property, when Faye waved at me over the screen. She had her phone in her hand.

"That was Titus. His parents are dragging him back to New Orleans. They invited me down as well. I think his mother believes I'll talk some sense into him about choosing a new school." She frowned. "I'd love to go, but that would leave you here on your own with Jacob and Mom, and with everything going on and Ivan still at Manderley—"

"Go." I waved my hand at her. "There's nothing much more we can do about Manderley and Madame Usher. It's in Rochester's hands now. I want you to enjoy yourself."

"Are you sure?"

I thought of my time in New Orleans during the early days of Broken Muse – trawling the jazz clubs with Titus, puking into the Mardi Gras Fountain after a night on the absinthe, hooking my veins directly into the lifeblood of music and culture and magic. Faye would have an amazing time. "I'm sure. It'll give me a chance to spend some time alone with Jacob. We've got a lot to talk about, and soon, hopefully a lot of money to spend."

She kissed my forehead. "You're doing great with him, you know that?"

"It doesn't feel like it," I growled, the anger bubbling to the surface again.

She smiled at me. "You have to be patient, which I know you suck at."

"I can be patient."

"Says the boy who would throw his sheet music across the room if he couldn't master a piece first time through."

"I'm not—" A laugh caught in my throat. "Okay, yeah. That's me. I just...I waited too long to get Jacob out of there, and he's lost so much. I want him to start his life now."

"He's already started," Faye said. "Every time you see him smile, remember that's a smile you gave him. He may not ever be like other kids, and that's okay. We weren't like other kids, either. And we turned out all right. If you'll excuse me, I need to start packing. We leave in a few days."

Faye sashayed her hips as she left the room. I stared at the spot she occupied long after she'd gone. It was true what I said – we'd reached a stalemate with Madame Usher. Despite what Faye and Ivan overheard, she hadn't made any move against us beyond that article trying to paint her as a concerned teacher. According to Ivan, she hadn't stepped up her torture at Manderley. In fact, she seemed to have lost interest in him and Broken Muse.

I knew better than to assume Madame Usher had forgotten us completely. She and Victor were planning something diabolical. But she had already taken so much from us, and while we knew what she hid at Manderley, we had more over her than she had on us. We had the power. So it was safe for Faye to leave for a bit.

Wasn't it?

FAYE

I was packing my bags for New Orleans when Ivan stormed through the door. Jacob dropped the wooden blocks he was playing with and dived behind the sofa. Dorien gathered his brother in his arms and glared at Ivan, but our Romanian didn't notice.

He stood in front of me, his shoulders shaking, a square of white card clutched in his hands. He looked like he was going to explode.

"What's wrong?" I shot to my feet and wrapped my arms around him. He remained stiff and irresponsible – an Ivan made of stone instead of flesh.

It took Ivan a couple of tries to form words.

"I am to give you this." He thrust the card into my hands.

I held it up. It was an invitation printed on cream card stock with a gold border, asking me to attend the wedding ceremony for Elena Nicolescu and Maxim Radcliffe, at Manderley, a week from today.

"I don't understand..." I frowned at the card. "Their wedding wasn't supposed to happen until June. I addressed the envelopes myself. What about all those important musicians and directors and patrons Madame Usher invited?"

"Elena decided she didn't want to wait." Ivan's face twisted with rage. He gripped my wrist. "You have to come with me. You have to talk to her."

He dragged me downstairs. Harrison waited outside in the limo. He smiled as Ivan bundled me into the back while horns sounded around us. The moment gave me a flashback to my very first day at Manderley, where Harrison showed up at my Bushwick apartment in the limo. Only this time, I was stepping back into the spider's lair to save Elena instead of my mother.

"Miss Faye, it's lovely to see you again."

"Hi, Harrison." I buckled my seatbelt. Ivan climbed up beside me and reached for the vodka in the bar. "How are things at Manderley?"

"Quiet without all you students around." Harrison frowned. "So much trouble, I don't like it. It's not good for my nerves."

I wanted to tell Harrison about Victor living in the walls, but he looked so much older and more frail than I remembered him. I didn't want to give him a fright, especially since it seemed Madame Usher left him alone. Instead, I tried a different tack. "I was wondering, could you tell me more about Madame Usher and Victor? What were they like as a couple?"

Harrison's lip curled back, showing me without a single word what he thought. "In the early days, Victor was besotted. It was as if she bewitched him. He thought the sun shone out her asshole, pardon my language. But over the years, there was a distance between them, especially after they closed up the city school and started teaching at Manderley. Victor loved having his house filled with music and bright students and international musicians, but she...well, you know what she's like."

"A spider," I said before I could stop myself.

"That's right. A spider. Victor told me once that she wanted—" Harrison swallowed. I expected him to continue the thought, but he stopped himself. "Do not misunderstand me, they had many loving moments between them. I got the feeling there were financial troubles, which can be a strain on any relationship, but it's no business of mine. I just cut the roses."

As we made the long drive out to Manderley and Harrison distracted himself singing along with his music, Ivan filled me in on everything that had been going on at the house. How Elena had been frantic with wedding preparations. How Madame Usher seemed to have given up all pretenses of running a school or of holding them prisoner. How Aroha had become increasingly erratic – Ivan often found her walking the halls at night, or banging her head repeatedly against a window.

He didn't talk about Victor, but I read his concern in his icy gaze.

The high iron gates of Manderley loomed over us as the limo bumped along the overgrown drive. We pulled into a parking space beneath the trees, next to the twins' truck, which hadn't been used in a long time, judging by the thick layer of dead leaves obscuring it. Ivan told me Madame Usher confiscated the keys.

I pushed the door open, my face tilted up just as the first icy drops of a snowstorm hit my skin. Harrison wrapped a long, dark coat around me, and the pair of them bundled me around the back of the house to the stables. Elena opened the door and ushered us inside.

I'd never been inside Master Radcliffe's living quarters before. It looked exactly as I imagined the home of an older bachelor to look – a dark oak desk and floor-to-ceiling bookshelves lined the living area, with a couple of threadbare armchairs and a Turkish ottoman. There was no TV. In the center of the room, a beautiful polished Fazioli grand piano dominated the space, the carpet around it strewn with sheet music and scribbled notes.

Elena flopped down on the piano stool and patted the cushion beside her.

"Play with me," she said.

"Elena, I wanted to—"

"I know Ivan brought you here to talk me out of marrying Maxim. I want to play with my best friend."

"I didn't bring my bow."

She snapped her fingers at an instrument in the corner. I noticed a beautiful violin nestled on a stand, as if it had been reluctantly set down while its owner did some unfortunate chore. Master Radcliffe's instrument. I rarely saw him play the violin – he taught mainly composition, which he said came more naturally to him on the piano. Even so, I didn't want to touch it – there was something sacred about a musician's instrument, and I shouldn't play without permission – but I couldn't refuse Elena.

I picked up the violin.

Elena opened with Beethoven's *Violin Sonata No. 9*. I played the raw, emotionally-charged piece with her, my fingers flying over the familiar notes. I watched as she played, her eyelashes fluttering closed and a look of complete and utter contentment on her lips. She truly was magic. Being able to conjure music with her was one of my life's greatest joys.

And I knew in that moment that I would never change her mind. Because Elena didn't comprehend love the way I did. She didn't seek wild yearning the way I did with Ivan and Titus and Dorien, because she'd already found that love in her music. She loved the music in a way none of us fully understood. She was doing this because Radcliffe could give her something Ivan couldn't, something no other man could – access to the world's stage, where she could weave her magic for an adoring audience until the day she died.

As the final notes died away, Elena lifted her shapely fingers from the keys and peered up at me. "I know my brother has brought you here to convince me not to go through with this marriage," she said.

"He did. But I'm not going to do that." I placed my hand over hers. "I only ask one thing – make sure you get access to your trust fund. It should be in your name, not Radcliffe's."

Elena played a few bars. "Maxim has taken care of all that boring stuff."

"I know you're not that naive."

"Faye, I'm fine. Everything is wonderful between me and Maxim. We're to be husband and wife, and we will go off to Europe and leave this damp, disgusting house behind us. Maxim has already booked me on a ten-city tour over the summer. I am happy, and if Ivan cannot see that, I have nothing to say to either of you." She rose. "Harrison will drive you home."

"Elena, I—"

She turned away, waving her hand at me. "I will not discuss it anymore. I will see you at the wedding."

~

Too soon, I was in the back of the limo on the way to Manderley once more. Titus gripped my leg as we turned the narrow corners of the mountain road, the wheels skating over deep puddles as rain pelted down in sheets. Beside me, Dorien braced himself against the side of the car and poured his second Scotch of the day.

"I don't know what I'll do when I see Usher again," he murmured, curling his lips around the glass.

"You won't do anything," I said. "You will smile and you will shake hands and you won't do a single thing to ruin Elena's day. Because there is life for all of us after Madame Usher, and you need to remember that."

As I said the words, I curled my fingers around Titus' body. He looked at me nervously. We would leave for New Orleans tomorrow, and neither of us knew what to expect from his parents when we got there. He'd been accepted into both the Royal Academy of Music in London and the Sibelius Academy in Finland, and I had a feeling they were going to put the pressure on him to choose soon. Honestly, I thought both programs sounded amazing. I'd kill for that opportunity. Even if Dorien could get enough movement back in his finger to play at the same level, his notoriety had probably killed any chance he had at being taken seriously by the classical scene. But Titus could still build a traditional career. Plus, being in a country far from his parents would give him a chance to shine in his own light.

But I knew that wasn't what Titus wanted. And I wasn't going to push him toward a future that made him miserable.

We turned into Manderley and my stomach sank to my knees. Despite the fucking abysmal weather and the fact the wedding had been moved up several months, the parking lot was jammed with cars. I shouldn't have been surprised. The musical world loved to gossip, and anyone who was anyone wanted an excuse to set foot inside the walls of Manderley, crawl over Heather's corpse, and see the magical Elena Nicolescu in the flesh.

Ivan met us in the foyer. I didn't even have my coat off when he grabbed my hand and dragged me toward the stairs. "Elena wants you in her room."

We wove our way through guests standing on the staircase as they sipped Champagne and admired the remaining gilded portraits. I noticed Madame had ordered some modern artworks and large floral arrangements to cover the bare spaces after Clare (or Victor) destroyed the antiques to manipulate Madame Usher to let me stay.

Why did he do that? Why did he do any of it – kill Heather, and probably Clare, too?

I debated knocking on the hollow wall and asking him, but we didn't have time.

I pushed open the twins' door. No locks – there's no point. Elena sat in front of her mirror, applying makeup. A snow-white dress swirled around her ankles, the sweetheart neckline perfectly accentuating her narrow shoulders and nipped-in waist, while giving her the barest hint of cleavage. (A pox on all flat-chested women. I have to strap my girls in like they're competing in Daytona). She shooed Ivan out and closed the door behind us.

"Help me with my hair."

She settled back into her chair, and I swept her white-blonde hair into my hands and began to twist and pin it. It felt like spun silk in my fingers, so impossibly soft and smooth. She had clips with little glittering diamonds on them, and I used these to secure it in place. It looked like her hair was held together with glittering snowflakes. She was a winter princess, a *zâne* blessing us with her magic.

She preened in the mirror, turning her shoulders to admire herself from every angle. "If you wish to tell me that I still have time to pull out of this marriage—"

"I'm here for one reason only," I swiveled her chair around so I could tuck in a loose strand at the front. "To make you the most beautiful bride Manderley has ever seen."

"And tonight, we will party." She grinned salaciously. *There's that wicked Elena I know and love.*

"I wish we had more time to be students together," I said, feeling a wistful sadness wash over me. Instead of attending wild parties and kissing boys, I spent my last year of high school working multiple jobs and worrying my mother wouldn't wake up from a coma. Music school was supposed to be my chance to let loose a little – I could work hard, but have fun, too. But Madame Usher took that away from me. Both Elena and I have had to grow up too fast. I wished we could have been young and reckless together.

"You are so silly sometimes! Married women still get to party, especially when they can finally lay hands on their own money. We will stay here at Manderley until the end of the semester," she said. "It is between me and Aroha for the Manderley Prize, so I don't think I shall have any problems, even if I take a few days to come and see you in the city."

"I'd like that," I smiled. "My mom knows all the good clubs."

"You'll look after my brother." Elena clasped my hands to her breast. She tilted her face to mine and her eyes...something flashed in them that filled me with dread. "We don't all of us get to choose for love, and if I can give him that, he might one day forgive me."

I closed my eyes, willing away the lump of emotion that swelled inside me. "You deserve more than this, Elena."

"I won't hear another word about it. Now," she dropped my hand. The dreadful thing in her eyes evaporated, leaving behind my calm, beautiful friend. She held the jeweled comb up to her hair. "I think you should fasten this just so."

A knock sounded at the door. I rose to see who it was, but the door flung open, hitting the wall behind with such force the picture frames twitched on their strings. Madame Usher stood in the hallway, her black gown gathered at the waist with a jeweled clasp. At her throat dripped a necklace of blood-red rubies. A very familiar necklace.

My necklace.

She must have rescued it before she burned all my belongings. And now she dared wear it like it was hers?

Madame Usher stared daggers at me as she tapped her finger on her wrist. "Elena, it is time to go."

Elena stood and wafted to the door, turning her nose high as she breezed past Madame. The pair exchanged a look that was as perplexing as it was loaded with meaning. Madame looked every bit the triumphant spider, but Elena...she looked at Madame as if she were a bug she was about to squash.

A shiver ran down my spine.

Whatever Madame Usher had traded for Elena's hand in marriage, Elena didn't intend to be anyone's prize. I just wish she'd confide in me what she was thinking.

I rose to follow Elena. I tried to slide past Madame Usher without touching her, without acknowledging her. She caught my wrist, twisting it back so I had no choice but to turn and gaze into those cold eyes. Her cloying perfume invaded my nostrils – the sickly sweet flowers that clung to her like a funeral wreath. Behind her head, a sad face appeared, floating against the flocked wallpaper.

Clare.

"This is not the end," Madame Usher hissed. "You may have got Dorien out of prison, but I can reach you wherever you hide, Faye de Winter. I know their secrets. I will destroy them all just to watch you suffer."

My neck prickled with the weight of her threat. It took everything I had not to turn toward the wall, where I knew her husband was sitting, peering at us through one of his peepholes.

Instead, I flung up my hand, clasped the necklace, and tore it from her neck. She winced as the chain bit into her pale skin before the clasp snapped, and it came away in my hand.

Mine, bitch.

Behind her head, Clare's ghost smiled.

"You want to be careful about threatening me. Don't think that just because you're still walking around being a hateful witch that I've forgotten you poisoned my mother. *In Cauda Venenum*, Gizella. I'm not the only one with secrets that can destroy." I yanked my wrist down, snapping her hold on me but not the spell of her harrowing gaze. I shoved my way past her and stomped down the stairs, the prickling feeling following me like Clare's ghost.

FAYE

As dusk fell, Radcliffe and Elena spoke their vows in front of the crumbling gazebo. Aroha and I had wrapped fairy lights and sprigs of dried herbs around the gazebo, giving the scene a fae-like quality. Elena's white dress billowed around her, and she wrapped her fur-lined cloak close to her throat to ward off the chill. She looked like an elven queen.

The ceremony was beautiful. Enchanting. And yet, as she spoke her vows in that breathy, wooden voice, I couldn't help but wish she said them to someone of her choosing, someone other than a man at least forty years her senior.

She made this choice with eyes wide open.

I thought of that superior tilt of her chin and the cold, calculating look in her eyes as she breezed past Madame Usher earlier, and a chill ran down my spine that had nothing to do with the wintery mountain air.

Afterward, we gathered in the ballroom for drinks and canapés. The crowd spilled out into the hallway, the Red Room, and the Yellow Room, talking and laughing in tight circles as they sipped on Victor's finest port. Madame had brought in caterers. The food was not as good as mine.

Elena lit up the room as she moved between the groups, bending her graceful neck to speak to every person. At her side, Master Radcliffe beamed as he showed her off to his friends and colleagues. His jewel. His prize.

We gathered in the corner, beneath the heavy drapes. Titus had twisted a safety pin through the broken clasp of my necklace so I could wear the rubies, which glittered at my throat like a warning of blood to be spilled. Hardly anyone spoke to us, but they all whispered about us. Aroha came over, her plate loaded down with mediocre food, and chatted to us.

I noticed she swayed as she stood. Her eyes were glazed over. I thought she might be on drugs again, but before I could ask her anything more, Elena and Radcliffe joined our group.

The conversation died. I watched Ivan as he worked his jaw, trying to find the words to say something to his sister. The silence stretched between them. Elena's shoulders' sagged as she realized she wouldn't get what she wanted most from him. She turned to me, and I hugged her.

"I'm happy for you," I said. I meant it.

I think I meant it.

Aroha fell against her. "You're going to be amazing," she said in a stage whisper. "Did you leave anything in the bathroom for me?"

So Elena had given Aroha cocaine. I wasn't surprised, but it made me sad. Aroha had so much talent. If she could just get over her stage fright, she'd be a star. She'd been doing so well before Madame Usher threw away her medication. I didn't blame her for falling back into her coke habit. In our world, you had to do what you could to survive. But I wished Elena hadn't indulged her.

Titus and Dorien embraced Elena next, then shook Radcliffe's hand. Judging by the way Radcliffe's chin wobbled, I suspected Titus crushed his fingers.

Ivan leaned forward and kissed Elena's cheeks, pausing long enough to whisper something in her ear in Romanian. He gripped her waist with trembling hands, and I didn't think he'd let go, but he finally tore himself away.

Radcliffe extended a hand. Ivan stared at it for a long time before he shoved his own hand forward to shake it.

The moment their hands touched, it was as though a spark ignited. Darkness closed over Ivan's blue eyes.

He drew back his free hand and slammed it into Radcliffe's face.

IVAN

"I can't believe you did that." Dorien slapped me on the shoulder as we piled into the car.

I flexed my knuckles, enjoyed the sting across them from where they connected with Radcliffe's smug fucking face. Over and over I replayed the moment when my fist connected. Bone crunched. Blood spurted from his nose. His rheumy eyes froze with shock before the pain hit and his face crumpled into his hands. He staggered backward, knocking over a table piled high with food, sending petit fours and salmon puffs cascading to the floor. The guests scattered in chaos, and Elena screamed at me as she ran to his side.

"Get out of here," Madame Usher barked in my face. "You are released from my care. I do not want to see you ever again."

And just like that, I was banished from Manderley. I was free. Homeless and penniless and now, sisterless. But free.

It was probably for the best that I now watched through the back window as the dark towers of Manderley were swallowed by the mountains. If I had to hear the sounds of Elena's wedding night through the walls, I couldn't be held responsible for what I might do.

Their wedding night.

I couldn't reply to Dorien. If I opened my mouth, all that would come out was a scream.

After all these years of fighting, all these years of sacrifice, Elena had chained herself to that man and his deviant sexual proclivities. I knew on the surface it looked like she was getting everything she wanted, but no one knew her like I did.

"You know that she had to do this." Faye ran her fingers over my bruised knuckles.

"No," I rasped.

"You saw her tonight. She loves the music. And Master Radcliffe loves her. He will give her everything she's ever wanted. And I think, for her, that's perfect." Her fingers laced in mine, and she squeezed hard enough to crack the bones. Hard enough to draw me from my dark thoughts.

Harrison wound down the window between the two cars. "I promise you that I will look after Elena for as long as she's at Manderley."

The rest of the journey passed in wrathful silence. Harrison swore at the drivers as we hit New York City's impossible traffic. We finally reached Faye and Dorien's apartment, and each of us hugged Harrison for the last time. Faye held him close, and he patted her back and whispered to her, and I wondered if he saw her in some ways as the daughter he never had. He'd been the same with Clare, I remembered.

"Don't go upstairs," Dorien's eyes twinkled as he clasped Faye's wrist. "I have a surprise for you all."

"We're going to New Orleans tomorrow," Faye pointed out. "Titus and I should get an early night."

"Sleep is for the old," Dorien said. "Besides, I can see Ivan needs something more from tonight."

Dorien was right. I wouldn't sleep, not with this rage burning inside me, not with the sting of Radcliffe's blood on my knuckles.

"Should we change?" Faye touched the necklace of rubies. "I would hate for the safety pin to snap while we were at a club."

I exchanged glances with the others. The necklace was one of the many mysteries we still hadn't solved. The night of the recital, when Dorien and Heather trapped Faye in a bag far from Manderley, someone set her free and left her clothes downstairs for her, along with that necklace.

It had to be Victor, but why? He didn't tell Madame Usher he saw us in the walls. For some reason, Victor wanted to help Faye. But we didn't yet understand why.

"Don't change," Dorien kissed her neck, his teeth tugging lightly at the chain. "I want you just the way you are tonight."

"Okay, but this can't be an all-night thing. Seriously, Dorien. We leave..." Faye glanced at the screen on her phone, "in twenty-six hours."

"That's right," Dorien grinned that wild grin of his as he hailed a taxi. "We have all the time in the world."

The taxi driver let Dorien put on his playlist, and Beethoven's *5th* boomed through his speakers. I didn't think he'd want to listen to music again with his injured finger, but it was almost like he didn't care.

Instead of drawing me out of the darkness, the music pulled me deeper. If I wanted to wallow down here in blood and hate, Faye and Dorien and Titus would be right here with me.

Faye rested against my shoulder, and I wrapped my arm around her waist, holding her close. Her eyes hooded with sleep and in a few moments, she was nodding off.

I was nearly asleep myself, lost in the music and my memories, when the taxi pulled over. I looked up, expecting to see the glittering lights of a club. Instead, we were parked in front of a decrepit building with high ionic columns. It looked like a bank or government building. It also looked completely abandoned, with graffiti strewn across the stone and dead leaves gathered in the portico.

"Where are we?" Titus asked.

"I can't believe it." Faye punched Dorien in the arm. "What have you brought us here?"

I thought I understood, but Dorien didn't confirm. Instead, he threw a brick at the window. I cringed as the glass shattered, piercing the night. But no one came running, no wailing siren alerted us to an alarm. This was New York City. No one wanted to get involved with the ghosts.

Titus boosted Dorien up and he clambered in the window. A few moments later, the large carved doors swung outward, and Dorien welcomed us inside.

The building had once been grand. Plush carpet, now damp and musty, squelched under my feet. Trash stacked along the walls, and one of the crystal chandeliers in the grand entranceway had come down, breaking the marble tiles and scattering shards of glass everywhere. The other chandelier was thick with spiderwebs. The air stank of piss and rotting food, and I saw a sleeping bag and trash bags covered with rat droppings. Someone had been squatting in here.

We followed Dorien along another grand corridor, kicking up clouds of dust. He stopped in front of a door, breathing hard. Faye's fingers dug into my arm. Dorien shoved the door open and ushered us into the darkness.

"Let there be light." Dorien clicked on his phone's flashlight and shone it into the gloom.

We stood in a studio. It was all clean lines, polished floors, and acoustic battling – the kind of modern space I loved, so far removed from the stuffy antiques of Manderley. Our feet made a rich resonant sound as we walked through the space, even though the floor was coated in a thick layer of dust and the soundproof foam had been torn to shreds. A white sheet at one end of the room covered the unmistakable shape of a piano. At the other end were piles of beanbags.

I turned to Dorien. Bathed in the light of his phone, he appeared otherworldly – a demon summoned by the *diabolus in musica*. He walked over to the piano and threw aside the ghostly sheet.

"This is the Usher School." Dorien's fingers trailed along the piano. Dust swirled around him as he left claw marks against the wood. A tug at the corner of his mouth was the only clue that he couldn't move his pinkie finger the way he wanted. "This is where I first saw Faye de Winter play."

I couldn't speak. My lungs felt full of blood.

Dorien blew the dust from the keys. His face screwed up as he perched on the edge of the filthy stool. He bent down beside the piano and swept something into his hands. A violin case, battered from years of being carried around by music students. He cradled the case like it was a child. "I decided to look it up the other day. I assumed they sold the building – it must be worth a fortune – but they've left it here to rot."

I exchanged a glance with Faye. Titus moved to the end of the room and tossed some of the beanbags aside. "The ones underneath aren't dusty and gross."

Dorien beckoned me and Faye forward with a curled finger. When I was beside him, he held out the case to me.

"Play," he commanded.

If Dorien ordered it, I would obey. I lifted the violin from its velvet lining, gripped the bow in my fingers, and played. I played snatches of songs, pieces from the old Romanian folk songs Elena and I performed on street corners for coins, movements from my favorite classical pieces, bits of Paganini I heard Faye play in her intense theatrical style that I would never be able to master. I played the Broken Muse songs that I wrote with Dorien when I realized I was fucking in love with him – songs of hope and longing.

I played the shattered pieces of my soul.

I played my story.

At some point, I became aware that I no longer played alone. The instruments inside my head had become living, breathing music. Titus and Faye had found another violin and a cello somewhere. The cello was missing a string, but Titus made it work. Dorien sat at the piano, conjuring dark magic with his fingers, expertly improvising to avoid stretching his pinkie beyond its limited range of motion.

He hadn't sat at a piano since the fire. We'd been walking on eggshells around the question – could he play again? Would he? But tonight, he dashed those fears to dust. Dorien Valencourt might have a more limited range now, but that only made his music more powerful.

Into the night we played, bodies and instruments swirling around each other. No one spoke about needing to sleep, about Titus and Faye leaving tomorrow, or about Elena tucked into Radcliffe's bed. The room felt charged with electricity. We didn't dare stop for fear of breaking the spell.

As the sun peeked over the city, Dorien's fingers slid off the keys, and he grabbed me by the collar and dragged me over to the beanbags. Titus had piled the clean ones up together to create a kind of nest.

Dorien removed his black wool coat and laid it over the beanbags. He tugged my collar to him, forcing me against his body. His fingers wiped a trail beneath my eyes. I didn't even realize I'd been crying until I felt the wet tears touch his skin.

"You have a family," he whispered. "The best kind of family, one who doesn't mind doing depraved things to you."

Before I could reply, Dorien claimed my mouth with his just as delicate fingers yanked down my fly. Faye's hand reached inside and tugged out my dick. Her hot mouth circled the tip as Dorien's tongue dipped into my mouth. I breathed him in until he was my blood, my body, bonded to me.

Dorien took the kiss with arrogance. He knew how much I wanted it, craved it. I'd lived in cramped hotel rooms on tour with this guy. I'd seen him at his absolute worst and it never was enough. I'd never have my fill of rich asshole Dorien Valencourt. I'd never get tired of him biting my lip, staking his claim.

My fingers curled in Faye's hair as she sucked me in deep. It was because of her that Dorien was kissing me right now. She saw this thing that haunted me, and she made it real. She made all my dreams come true. I would never stop loving her and this gift she has given me, the gift she gave me every day she looked at me with eyes warm with love instead of cold with jealousy.

Titus lay back on Dorien's coat, stroking himself as he watched the three of us. His eyes met mine, and I felt our connection, too. Nothing that needing fucking out of us, but something deeper, better, that branded itself into my skin.

My brother.

My family.

Everyone I ever needed to be whole.

"I want to try something." Dorien bent toward Faye and whispered in her ear. Even in the dim light of the rising sun, I could see the heat flare in her cheeks. *It must be filthy.* But she nodded.

"Lie back, Titus," Dorien declared. This was always his role, to command, to take control. On those nights in hotel rooms with groupies he barked orders and they scrambled to obey. But we'd never done anything like this before – not with someone we loved. Not when our hearts were raw and open and bleeding.

Titus did as he was told, tossing off his clothes and leaning back on the coat with his hands folded behind his head. His skin was almost invisible against the fabric, his cock standing proud. Cornrows swept across the planes of his chest. Dorien whispered to Faye, who slid up between Titus' legs so that her back was pressed against his chest. Dorien tapped me on the shoulder.

"You're next."

Faye spread her legs wide, and I could see her cunt glistening in the low light. *She wants this. She loves us. She trusts us.* Titus crept a hand around her middle, pressing a finger to her clit and circling, slowly, slowly, as we three watched her wriggle and squirm. Titus clenched his teeth as she ground her ass against him.

"Ivan, get down here now before she makes me come early," Titus gritted out.

Dorien's fingers circled my wrist, his grip tight, holding me in place. A whimper of excitement escaped my throat.

"Will you let this be mine tonight?" Dorien palmed my ass. His words bit against my earlobe. My stomach soared as the force of his words hit me.

"I was always yours," I answered.

It was the truth.

I belonged to Dorien Valencourt the day he tried to save me and Elena. And I'd belonged to Faye since the day she saved me from Dorien. I needed them both like I needed the air I breathed.

Dorien removed my clothes, his fingers unbuttoning my shirt. He chuckled as my stomach jerked against his touch. He slid my feet free from my shoes, leaving my socks on as he rolled my pants over my hips, trailing fire with his evil fingers until I was so hard from being denied him I wanted to burst.

I knelt down in front of Faye. She stared up at me with heavy-lidded eyes, her raven hair spilling over her shoulders. "You're so beautiful," she whispered, touching my cheek, so soft, too soft for what Dorien wanted us to do.

I touched her skin, danced my fingers over her, committing her curves and dips and perfect rounded breasts to memory. I placed my hands on either side of her, touching Titus' warm skin.

"Fuck her," Dorien whispered roughly. "I want to watch your beautiful cock move inside her."

I must obey.

I slid up inside Faye, gasping at the wet heat of her. *So warm and soft and slick.* Faye tilted her chin up at me, her wide eyes filling me with love. I drew back, giving myself a moment to catch my breath, to collect myself. I couldn't come now. That would ruin Dorien's plan, and I very much did not want to do that.

Dorien's fingers grabbed the skin of my ass. He shoved against me, using his momentum to manage my speed, my strokes. It was as if we were only fucking because he commanded it, he controlled it, and I never thought I'd get off on that, but I was struggling to breathe and my balls were tightening up into my body.

"Now, Titus..." Dorien's voice was right beside my ear, hot and rasping as he leaned over me. The silk of his shirt brushed my skin. "You fit yourself inside her too."

He handed Titus a bottle of lube. While I thrust slowly into Faye, lifting her hips high for him, he got himself into position. I felt the pressure of his finger inside her ass through the thin wall of her, and I had to stop thrusting for a moment because it felt too good. When Titus pushed his cock inside Faye, inch by inch, her eyes rolled back in her head.

"It's..." Her eyelids fluttered closed. "It's intense."

Titus met my eyes over Faye's shoulder, and I could tell he was struggling with the intensity of it, too. I know I was with the two of us inside her like this. I drew out, long and slow, as he thrust in deeper. It took us a few strokes, but we fell into an easy rhythm. We were musicians, after all.

Faye leaned back against Titus as we continued to thrust together. Her nails dug into my arms and her pretty, perfect lips fell open as she reveled in the sensation of it. I kissed her neck, nibbled at her lower lip until I smudged red lipstick across her skin.

Dorien's lips found my neck, biting down until I sucked in a breath through my teeth. Warm fingers trailed along the bare skin of my back, and a moment later Dorien's hot breath kissed my ear. "Are you ready for me?"

I swallowed, my body rigid.

"I want you to say it, Ivan." Dorien curled his fingers around my neck, not squeezing, not hurting, just promising that he *could*, if he wanted to. He could make me hurt so fucking good.

"Yes."

"Good." Dorien chuckled. I heard the squirt of the lube, and then Dorien had me in his grip, one hand bracing my shoulder as I thrust into Faye, the other stroking over my skin, pressing at my hole. His slippery fingers opening me for him.

I can't this is too much I need to catch my breath I need to fucking stop I need...

"Just a second—" I started to say, but he pushed a finger inside me and there were no more seconds left. I was here and Dorien had his finger in me and Faye scraped her teeth along my jaw and I thought I might break apart from the joy of it.

Dorien kissed Faye over my shoulder, his tongue darting between her waiting lips. "Hey, Sprite." He grinned. "How does it feel to have all three Broken Muses at your mercy?"

In my wrecked mind, it seemed like an odd thing to say, because she was sandwiched between us. But it was also the truest thing Dorien had ever said. Everything we had in this moment that was good and perfect came to us because of Faye. Dorien might be making commands, but she was in total control.

"Like coming home," she whispered, and it was true. It was so true. This, tonight, is what it felt like to have a home.

I'm exactly where I belong.

Dorien pushed a second finger in beside the first, pumping them inside me until I no longer gritted my teeth, until I arched my back against him and begged for more.

He removed his fingers and I cried out to be bereft of him. But for only a moment. Then the head of his cock was against my entrance and my toes curled and he angled my hips back and thrust inside.

At first, it was like a kiss, but then the kiss grew into painful pressure as he glided deeper, pushing his crown past the tight rim. And then the pressure became a wild piercing – an invasion so deep and intense and satisfying that I forgot to breathe. I couldn't think.

Dorien drew back his hips, giving me a moment of respite as my cock jerked inside Faye, a moment to breathe, to sense, to be. He bit down on my neck.

"Don't you worry," he whispered against my ear. "I will never forget you."

He thrust inside me, hard and fast and needy, and I saw stars. The sunrise collapsed in on itself, and the darkness crept in from the edges, punctured by bright pinpricks of violent light.

I'm lost.

Dorien wasn't gentle. He didn't give me another moment to catch my breath. Inside me, he was a man possessed. He shoved me forward so my chest pressed against Faye, so his body bore down on all three of us, controlling every stroke, just the way he liked it.

He grunted, moving against me with animal cruelty, lost completely to his possession. With each thrust, he pushed me into Faye, who sank deeper onto Titus, and so it was as if we were no longer four bodies but one writhing mess of humanity sating our need with each other.

It felt like a line of fire stretching directly from her through to him – a chain of bloody hearts and broken promises that bound us together.

"I love you," Dorien whispered. "You're mine now, all of you. And I love you."

It was like a hot poke slicing through my chest. Dorien's teeth dug into my neck. My balls squeezed up inside my body. And then...I let go. I released with short, violent strokes into Faye as her walls clenched around me. And it was like a rolling wave that kept crashing, an ocean of pleasure that would never end.

And I didn't want it to, because who wouldn't want to have a family like this?

DORIEN

I extracted my arm from beneath Faye and stood up. For a while I sat at the piano, tinkering with the keys, feeling the tug in my burned finger where the muscles wouldn't quite do what they used to. The ghost of a melody plagued me, something beautiful to capture the emotion of tonight. But I didn't want to play it imperfectly into the world and wake them all up. I needed to let the sound linger, to allow the new song to take shape.

The way Ivan looked at me sometimes, I knew he thinks I plan these things. That I have some devious scheme always in my head he longed to be let in on. But I didn't know this would happen tonight. I didn't know I'd wake up the happiest spoiled rich prince that ever lived.

Me and Ivan; that'd been on the cards for years. I would've jumped that tight ass of his sooner if only he'd given the slightest indication that was what he wanted. But he was too good at hiding and I was too skilled at only seeing what I wanted to see.

Before, the two of us together would have complicated everything. It might've been the end of Broken Muse. But here, in the rubble of our lowest point, when our future looked so dark and uncertain, it felt like the beginning of something beautiful.

I left the three of them curled in a pile on the beanbags. I clicked on my flashlight app and set about exploring the derelict building.

It occurred to me that it was odd the Ushers never sold the school. I think of the illegal money entering their accounts while the school was open, and how it reversed then they closed the school. If all this was about money, then surely Madame Usher could have sold the school and got on with her life. She wouldn't have needed Broken Muse or Faye for whatever insane thing she had planned.

I knew there had to be something inside this building she couldn't let anyone find out.

Which was why I took everyone here. Well, that and I wanted to fuck in this place where Faye and I began our story. But mostly it was for the mystery.

I moved down the hallway, peering into the old studios and practice rooms with their ghostly furniture covered in sheets, the costume wing and the administration office with its shelves of dusty files. I kicked an old scorebook, watching as the pages scattered across the floor.

My feet dragged me to the staircase. Upstairs were more practice rooms and a larger hall we used for recitals. Downstairs was a basement. I hesitated on the first step before my feet dragged me downward, my shoulders pushed forward as though some invisible hand shoved me from behind.

In the basement was a giant old furnace that heated the building. When it was on in winter it made the whole school smell like boiled pork. All us kids were too afraid to go down there because this beast of a thing looked like it ate children. Madame Usher encouraged our stories, barking at students who flubbed their notes that they were so useless at music that she could throw them in the furnace, and then at least they'd be good at keeping the rest of us warm.

The old fear clawed at my stomach as I made my way down the narrow steps into the furnace room. But after everything I saw at my parents' house, a creepy basement in an abandoned music school couldn't keep me away.

I shone my flashlight around the basement. It was filled with weird-ass stuff – broken chairs and instruments, file boxes, weird shapeless lumps I couldn't identify. I felt that prickling in my neck I felt at Manderley – the sense of being watched.

Something's down here. I'm close. I know it.

I knew behind the furnace was a second room with a dirt floor, where coal bags were stored. I went to move around the furnace, but my hand was compelled to grab the rusted handle. I felt like I was being directed by some external force to open the door and shine my flashlight inside.

What's that?

I picked up the object nestled in the ashes, bringing it into the beam of my flashlight. From its blackened color, I knew someone had tried to burn it. It was round and convex, uneven, with a jagged edge where it had been broken—

No.

I cried out as I realized what I was holding.

It was the top of a human skull.

DORIEN

"Fuck."

I dropped the skull back in the furnace. My instinct was to run as far away as fucking possible, but I was here because we needed answers. And a skull in the fucking furnace was a good start.

I swallowed back the bile and shone my flashlight into the furnace, using an old wrench to push around the thick layer of ash and coal dust crusted to the bottom. There were other shapes that looked like bone fragments and...yup, those were teeth.

As Sprite would say, sound the fucktrumpets.

I steadied myself against the belly of the beast as I hauled myself to my feet. My legs trembled as I walked around the other side of it, locating the wooden door to the second room. The door was padlocked, but the wood was so rotten that a couple of swift kicks knocked the lock from the frame. The door swung inward, and I swung my phone in front of me to peer inside.

What I saw made blood rush to my head.

The dirt floor had been disturbed – it was no longer flat and compacted but rucked up into random piles and littered with debris. As I scraped my boot through the dirt, I kicked up an object. A leather shoe with elaborate broguing around the toes. A men's shoe.

With the bone of a foot sticking out.

I had to hold my hand over my mouth to hold back my gagging as I swept the room with my flashlight. I recognized more shapes poking from the dirt – bones, skulls, a neat row of teeth. A few metal scraps of cufflinks and belt buckles. The bits of bodies that wouldn't completely burn away.

Bodies.

The entire room had been filled with bodies.

Yup. That's not good.

It looked like some attempt had initially been made to bury them in the dirt, but then they were just shoved into the room. There were dark patches in the dirt around a pile in the corner, but I would not go any further because I could hear the scritching of rats and I wasn't fucking stupid.

My foot caught on something. I jerked it away, kicking an object out of the loose dirt. It glinted in the light. That same eerie presence that shoved me down the stairs buzzed around me, urging me to pick it up.

I bent down. It turned out what I kicked was a skeletal hand, still held together in places with the frayed fabric of a shirt and... other stuff I didn't want to consider. I had the wrench in my hand and I used it to knock the shiny object free. It toppled into my hand, and I rubbed off the dirt to reveal its shape.

It was a silver cufflink. It depicted a treble clef wrapped around a violin, with the bow crossed over to make it look like a coat of arms.

I remembered Faye working with a fancy jewelry designer in Soho on this design. I remembered her showing me the sketches while we practiced sonatas together for our recital. She and Marguerite had the cufflinks made as a surprise gift for Donovan after he won the prestigious Vienna Award. Faye wanted to give him something unique, something he couldn't find in any store so he would remember her when he was overseas. According to the papers, Donovan wore them to every performance.

He'd been wearing them the day he disappeared.

Holy shit. This belonged to Donovan de Winter.

DORIEN

*F*aye's father is buried here.

I staggered out of the corpse room, slamming the door behind me as I fought to keep my stomach contents inside my body.

Donovan de Winter has been here all along.

This is why the Ushers never sold this building. They couldn't risk another owner discovering what they'd been up to down in the basement. But who are these other bodies they burned down there? How long has this been going on?

Were these people dying down here while we learned scales in the school above?

I remembered Madame's lips curling back as she threatened a student with being burned in the furnace. Was the music school heated with burning flesh?

I couldn't stomach any more of it. My skin burned where it touched the cufflink. I didn't want to deliver this news to Faye, but I had to. I pounded up the stairs. *I need to get the others. We have to leave. If Madame Usher figures out we found this, she'll—*

I slammed into something warm and hard.

Ivan cried out as he lost his balance and crashed to the floor. He bit his lip as he looked up at me. It was so delicious I almost fell on him there and then. But I couldn't be distracted by hot little Romanians. Instead, I reached down and hauled him to his feet.

"What were you running from?" Ivan tried to peer around me into the gloomy corridor.

"You won't believe it. There are a bunch of bodies in the basement. Burned bodies and bits of bodies. Someone was using the building's furnace to dispose of people."

Ivan frowned. "Be serious."

"I *said* you wouldn't believe it. And it gets worse." I opened my hand to show him the cufflink. "This belonged to Faye's father. It's a one-of-a-kind piece. Donovan de Winter's body is down there."

Ivan studied my face, his teeth biting into his lip again. This time I couldn't bear it. I leaned forward and kissed him. He yelped in surprise, but responded by opening his lips to grant me access. I

"You really did see bodies?"

I nodded. "We found the reason the Ushers never sold this building. It probably explains why Victor had to disappear, too. We know the Ushers were taking money from organized crime. Perhaps this is why. They were using the furnace to dispose of anyone the gangs needed to get rid of. My guess is Donovan found out, and..." I couldn't finish the sentence.

"What will we tell Faye?" He glanced back toward the studio, where I could hear Faye and Titus talking together.

"The truth. She deserves to know after all this time. I just hope she doesn't cancel her trip with Titus. Donovan and Madame Usher have already taken enough from her. Speaking of which." I clamped a hand on his shoulder, dragging him close so his nose touched mine. "Elena leaves with Radcliffe for Europe in a couple of weeks. She now has access to your money. All of us are free of Manderley now. Whatever Madame Usher and her creepy stalker husband tried to pull off, she failed." I stepped closer, kicking my boots against his to push his feet wide so I could slide right up against his body. So I could feel how hard he was for me again. I tugged his lip between my teeth. "You're free, Ivan."

"I have nowhere to go," he choked out.

I shrugged. "Come and stay with me and Jacob."

"You just got your brother back. I can't intrude—"

"You're my brother, too." There was no mistaking the command in my voice. Ivan's eyes fluttered shut, his chest heaving as he let the words sink in. "Stay with me. I'll look after you while Faye and Titus are in the Big Easy. We'll make this work. We'll figure out your future together, okay?"

He flinched as I thrust out my hand toward him. *I've gone too far. It's too much. I've frightened him away.* But then he surprised me by surging forward and clasping my fingers in his. "I would love to."

"Good. Now," I tugged him away from the basement. "Let's call Rochester and get these skeletons dug up. I want to know what secrets the Ushers have been hiding down there."

FAYE

It was hard to say goodbye to Dorien and Ivan with everything going on. But they needed some space from us too, to figure out what the thing between them meant. So as a sleepy-eyed Dorien led Rochester and a forensics team into the Usher School basement, I climbed into a taxi with Titus and sped to the airport.

All through our flight, I clasped that tiny silver cufflink. I kept my earbuds in my ears and hoped Titus didn't notice I played my father's music over and over, as if I might find some answers in his intricate compositions.

My dad is dead.

All these years...I always knew it was a possibility. Mom certainly believed he'd fallen foul of the crime family he'd been in debt to. It was strange how calm I felt, how much I realized that knowing the truth about him didn't make any difference. He still left us. His death was his final betrayal.

I begged Mom to get these cufflinks made for his Vienna Award ceremony. She spent money we couldn't spare so I could work with a jeweler to create the unique design. I knew Dad liked everything in his life to be unique, special, glittery. He beamed when I presented them to him, counting the diamonds inlaid in the tiny violin. He wore those cufflinks at every performance and proudly told reporters that his daughter had them made for him, and they gave him good luck.

He loved those cufflinks more than he loved me.

I refused to cry for him. I'd already cried so much.

Delphine traveled with us. Amos had already gone south a couple of weeks ago to prepare for their winter tour. As we wheeled her heavy suitcases through the airport, she kept up a steady stream of friendly conversation about musicians and touring and some of the cities they would visit. Not once did a word about Manderley Academy or the electric guitar leave her lips.

Titus' parents lived in a modest house in the Garden District, but they gave us the keys to a little place they owned in the French Quarter. Titus referred to it as the 'shotgun' house. It was long and narrow – the front door opened directly into the living room. Behind that was a bedroom and ensuite, and a kitchen right down the back. Titus said they called this style shotgun houses because every room left off another, so if you shot a bullet through the front door it would pass through every doorway and out the back without damaging anything.

It was past 11PM when we got in, so Delphine went back to her place, and Titus and I went straight to bed. It felt weird to be so far from New York and everything going on there. So far from my dad's body and the case mounting against Madame Usher. The sounds of the city were so different here.

Titus fell into a deep sleep, but I tossed and turned and struggled to quiet my whirring brain. Dorien had texted to say Rochester had confirmed DNA matches for some of the remains recovered from the Usher School – three notorious crime lords who disappeared after falling foul of the Triumvirate. It was looking more and more like the Ushers were paid by the gangs to dispose of their dead. Nothing on my father yet, but Donovan de Winter didn't have a criminal record so he wasn't in their database, and I wasn't in a hurry to get back and give them a sample. I had the cufflink. I knew what I needed to know.

My father was dead.

They had a team of forensic accountants working on the Menabilly Holdings accounts, trying to get the dirt they needed to build a case. I was positive if they followed the money they'd be able to connect Madame Usher not just to the Triumvirate, but also to the Temple of Earthly Truths. I hoped we'd get justice for everyone who'd been wronged by the Ushers.

All those people buried under the music school. Who were they? What had they done to die in such a brutal way? I shuddered to think how close we came to joining them.

Eventually, I fell into a restless sleep. When I woke, sunlight streamed through the windows, and even though my clock said it was barely 7AM, the city already teamed with life. Down the street, someone was playing the saxophone. I rubbed my eyes. *It's no good. Sleep won't happen. New Orleans is already working her spell on me.*

I extricated myself from Titus' slumbering embrace and took my violin out onto the front porch, which was done up with bright, gingerbread trim. The saxophonist was across the street and a few doors down. I raised my bow to my chin and answered him with a jaunty reel. We dueled back and forth for a bit, pulling funny faces at each other, until—

"Hello, Faye."

I jumped out of my skin, nearly dropping my bow. "Delphine?" I whirled around to see Faye's mother sitting on the steps watching me. "I didn't know you were there."

"You were lost in the music." She smiled. "I understand. Would you like some breakfast?"

I nodded and followed her inside. Too late I realized we had to walk through our bedroom to get to the kitchen. My face burned as I took in my clothing strewn everywhere and our rumpled bed with Titus snoring away, but Delphine didn't say a word about it. She headed straight to the stove and started the coffee machine.

"I brought beignets." She pointed to the bakery bag she'd placed on the table, which emitted a delicious scent. "A New Orleans special."

I pulled out one of the delicious squares of dough. Sugar dusted my chin as I took a big bite. Delphine set a steaming cup of coffee in front of me and grabbed her own beignet from the stack, and we chewed happily.

"These were Titus' favorites growing up." She finished the beignet without leaving a single granule of sugar on her skin.

How does she do that? I look like I'd been dipped in sugar.

"I can see why. These are amazing."

She gazed out the window. "Tell me about your life, Faye. Titus says you grew up with your mother."

Luckily for Delphine, one of my favorite topics was Marguerite de Winter. I told her about my mother growing up as an immigrant in New York City, meeting Donovan, and building her PR firm from the ground up. I told her about how my mother made our life fun, our house full of great food and loud music, and how she hadn't let her current medical setbacks stop her from living her life on her own terms. Delphine nodded and seemed genuinely interested. I thought they would get along like old friends if they ever met.

As Delphine made us second cups of coffee, I found myself talking about Dad. The corner of the cufflink jabbed my thigh through my pocket. I told her how I did everything I could to make him *see* me. I wanted to please him so badly. On the surface he made all the right noises – he told every reporter who interviewed him about his brilliant daughter. When we saw his performances, he'd invite me on stage at the end to present him with flowers. He encouraged me in my lessons and insisted I had only the best tutors, even though we couldn't afford them.

But he only saw me as an extension of himself. When he was on tour, he would forget to call us. He never played a game with me or asked me how I was. He used me to charm influential people and score points in a game with rules I never understood. He rarely came to my recitals, and if he did, he'd bring along a horde of reporters to write about what a great father he was. "He was so different than you and Amos," I said. "My father was a narcissist. He charmed people into loving him, then killed that love with neglect. Titus is lucky to have parents who care so much about him."

"I met your father many times," she said, skillfully avoiding any talk about Titus. "We moved in the same circles. I remember how charming he could be. I understand if you don't want to talk about him. I know how grief can make us all mute. But if you ever have questions, if you want to know him as his peers knew him, I will answer them for you."

And suddenly, I did want to know very much. I reached into my pocket and fingered the cufflink. "Tell me about him. Please."

"He was a magnet. The moment he walked into a room, heads swirled." She sighed. "But there was always something that didn't add up. He lived a flashy life, the life of a rockstar – not a classical violinist. He never revealed where he got the money to fund his lifestyle, but people speculated, of course. There were wild stories about a mystery inheritance, an affair with a wealthy patron, a link to organized crime. Donovan encouraged the gossip to fuel his image in the press, a little like your friend Dorien does now. He drove up to events in fancy cars, he wore designer suits, and his instruments... the last time I saw him play, he had a Becker. That instrument alone cost more than Amos and I make in a year."

My fingers closed around the handle of my violin case. She must not have seen the instrument I played. I knew the Becker was valuable, but Delphine reminded me that it was probably paid for with dirty money. The violin in my hands probably sent my dad's body into that basement.

"I wondered if I could ask you something," I said. "It's about Manderley Academy. Titus said you encouraged him to choose that school. I guess I wondered why? Surely it's not as prestigious as some of his other options."

"If I'd known that place was so...haunted, I never would have let him go," she sighed. "It was very strange. We were so excited when he got into the Royal Academy of Music. But then Madame Usher and Master Radcliffe showed up at our door. Radcliffe's friends in Vienna wanted us to headline their next season, but as Manderley was sponsoring, it could only happen if we were connected to the school. I didn't want to influence Titus' decision. It felt too much like accepting a bribe. But Amos said we had to take every diamond offered to us, because the world would give us only scraps. And Titus wanted to be where his friends were, so we thought it was a win for everyone. Titus thinks his father doesn't see him, and he might be right. But not because Amos sees Micah. I think he sees his own failing—oh, son, you're awake?"

I turned to see Titus in the doorway. I wondered how much he'd overheard. He frowned at the empty bag on the table. "Did you eat all the beignets?"

I pretended to hide the last two beignets behind my coffee cup. "Sorry, big boy. You snooze, you lose."

He poked his tongue out at me as he swiped the donut on his way across the room to kiss his mother on the forehead and make his own coffee.

Delphine rose, leaning in to kiss Titus on the cheek. "I'll leave the two of you to explore the city. Don't forget the party tonight, darling."

Titus pulled back, so she kissed the air instead. His body went rigid. "How could I forget?"

The screen door banged as Delphine left.

"Party?" I asked.

Titus frowned as he stuffed the beignet into his mouth. "Ifffduffmmmmmmeretsssssshoooooffff."

"Pardon?"

He swallowed. "It's just my parents trying to show us off. All their friends are going to be there. Everyone will take turns around the piano."

"It sounds like fun."

He slammed his coffee cup down with such force he broke the handle off. "They want me to play. Well, they want *us* to play."

"Nice of you to tell me," I said lightly. I knew this wasn't about me.

"This is Amos putting his foot down. He's worried about the media attention around you and Dorien and Manderley. He doesn't want our family associated with any of that *unpleasantness*. So he wants us to show up and be polite and civil and charming, and play polite, civil, charming music so everyone will congratulate him on having one almost perfect son left."

"Do you think that's fair?"

"It's the truth," he growled.

I took his hand and wrapped it around my waist. With my free hand, I reached for the last beignet and held it against his lips. "Your parents made their names by defying what the world expected of them. I know they're afraid because of what they've lost, but I think if they experienced your music for themselves, and the effect it has on people, they won't stand in your way."

Titus swallowed. "That's your mother, Faye. Not mine. They just want me to do what they say and not rock the boat for them."

"I think we should give them a chance." I twirled one of his cornrows between my fingers. "What do you say? Let's bring them a real party."

FAYE

We spent the day exploring the city. I loved New Orleans. I especially loved being there with Titus. It reminded me of touring Prague and Romania with Ivan – it was one thing to travel and be new to a place, but to see it through the eyes of someone who had lived there, loved there, grown and changed there made it completely magical. It gave every encounter hidden meaning and depth. On every corner, Titus battled against memories – some happy, some upsetting. All of them part of who he was.

We went shopping in the French Quarter, and I purchased a fuchsia evening dress with layers of tulle and a plunging neckline. It turns out, the woman at the boutique had a matching fuchsia shirt that fit Titus perfectly. Never in a million years would I have expected to love Titus in a pink shirt, but he looked so fucking hot with his narrow waist and braids spilling over his broad shoulders that it made my knees weak. I think it made him feel bold, and he needed every ounce of boldness tonight.

By the time we arrived at the Thibodeaux' house, the party was already in full swing. Lively jazz music bled out into the street as couples gathered on the narrow balcony, laughing and toasting. Someone howled at the rising moon. It was that kind of night.

Delphine greeted us the moment we stepped inside and thrust glasses into our hands. I lifted mine to my lips and sniffed the strong cocktail. "Sazerac," Delphine explained. "Rye whiskey, bitters, sugar, and a dash of absinthe. The official drink of New Orleans. Drink up. Son, I've made you a non-alcoholic punch."

"Careful," Titus whispered as I took a generous mouthful. "I need you with a clear head and perfect form for our performance."

"One thing you should know about me by now is that I can play perfectly anywhere, with any kind of alcohol in my stomach." I grinned, but he wasn't wrong. The Sazerac had a mighty kick.

Titus gripped my hand so hard I had to grit my teeth against the pain. Our instrument cases banged against our legs as we entered a beautiful open-plan living space decorated with Delphine's lush modern style. There was hardly space to move. The place was wall-to-wall people dressed in glittering evening wear and tables laden with amazing-smelling food, but we squeezed through the crowd.

Amos sat at the piano, his fingers flying over the keys as a gorgeous woman with dark ringlets and the voice of an angel sung Nina Simone's 'Sinnerman' with such throaty sexiness that I swear Nina herself was in the room with us. Amos pounded the keys with aplomb, enjoying the attention of his fans.

When he finished, his gaze fell on us. He regarded his son as if he was wary, as if Titus was a wild animal sent to Amos for taming, and the maestro didn't quite know what to do with him.

"Titus, Faye, come meet our friends." He took my hand and sat me on the bench beside him, introducing me to a sea of people whose names I had no hope of remembering. Not-Nina leaned forward as Amos repeated my name.

"Donovan de Winter's daughter?" asked Not-Nina.

"She is a maestra in her own right," Amos declared. And even though I was angry at him for the way he treated Titus, I warmed to him a hell of a lot in that moment for not letting them lump me in with my father. "Perhaps we can twist her arm to play something for us? I've heard she's a particular fan of Paganini."

"Consider my arm twisted." I set down my case and drew out the instrument. Delphine's eyes widened as she noticed the Becker, and I knew she recognized it as the instrument my father played at the end of his life. But she didn't say anything, and I was grateful for that. Amos' eyes trained on me as I tuned. I launched into one of Paganini's tricky caprices.

Performing Paganini was a chance for a violinist to show off their skills, provided you could nail the sometimes-impossible fingering. Paganini was famous for his demonic performances, and I played into that, letting my body move a little as I performed, screwing up my features and pointing my bow to tell a story.

When I finished, there was a beat of silence in the room. Then Amos erupted with applause and his friends followed suit. Their clapping rumbled like thunder in my chest. There's a tradition in Classical spaces of not clapping until the very end of the evening's performances so as not to interrupt the enjoyment of the music for others, and I had to admit sometimes I thought it was dumb. Feedback from the audience was addictive. No wonder Titus loved heavy metal – how cool would it be to have fans screaming your name?

Speaking of Titus...I fixed my eyes on Amos. "Titus and I would like to play something for you."

"Of course." He waved his arms, pushing his friends back to make enough space for Titus to bring in his cello case. I nodded to Titus. He looked over at his parents, and for a moment he wavered. His shoulders slumped, and I felt sure he was going to back out.

I stepped forward and touched his arm. That seemed to be enough. He squared his shoulders and unclipped the case.

Nestled inside was his St. Moritz SG.

Tony Iommi's guitar, with its evil black finish and body curling into spikes like devil horns.

Amos' cheeks puffed out. Delphine let out an audible gasp. Now the room fell truly silent. Titus lifted out the instrument and plugged it into the portable amp the jazz musicians were using. Amos' breath rasped, his chest heaving. I expected him to yell, to rage, but he remained frozen in place.

Titus wouldn't look at his parents as he tuned and tested the effects pedals. But I watched them. I watched Amos' jaw working with anger and Delphine hiding her face in her husband's shoulder. The rest of the room buzzed with nervous energy. The guests leaned forward, drinks clutching in whitened knuckles, waiting to see what we came out with.

I raised my bow and nodded to Titus. He bent over his guitar, letting his braids fall over his face. A curtain to protect himself from his parents' ire. And he struck the first sinister riff.

After four bars I came in with the melody. It was a cover of Black Sabbath's 'War Pigs' we arranged for guitar and violin. We chose this song deliberately because there was no mistaking what it was. I knew many in the room would recognize it. I knew Amos and Delphine recognized it, because it had been one of Micah's favorites.

Titus' fingers tore at the strings, his whole body swinging with the riff as he found his groove in the music. We traded riffs, dueling each other for supremacy within the music. His braids flew wild around his head, and that guitar *purred* in his hands.

By the time we finished the song with a pulsing, pounding riff, we were sweaty and smiling. Whatever happened now, we had a blast, and Titus had never played better.

Titus raised his chin, his gaze to heaven as sweat dripped from his brow. Tears pooled in the corners of his eyes, and I knew he felt his brother in every riff. As the final note rang through the amp, the silence in the room was more deafening than ever.

Titus slowly lowered his face. He stepped toward me. His hand shook as he cupped my cheek, but the lips that brushed mine burned with fire. *We did it. We—*

SLAM.

We both jumped as Amos dropped the lid on the piano. Titus bit my lip, and I sucked the blood that spurted from the cut. He turned to his parents.

Tears rolled down Delphine's cheeks, speckling the front of her silk gown. She didn't hide her face but wept silently and openly, her grief terrifying in its rawness. I longed to pull her into my arms, but I didn't know what she'd do if I touched her right now.

Amos' grief had turned him hard as granite, though the blood the burned in his veins was so hot with rage that it cracked the stone of his skin, seeping out of every pore. He leered at his son, his face monstrous. Women whimpered and shied away.

Amos took a step toward his son, his hands raised. I stepped in front of Titus, certain Amos was about to slide his hands around his throat. Instead, he let out an inhuman howl, spun on his heel, and shoved his way through the crowd. A moment later, a door slammed deep within the house.

Not-Nina began to shoo the guests from the room. "Go. This party is over. Get out of here."

Titus' chest heaved. Delphine leaned over the piano, seeking its strength to hold her upright. Her tears splashed on the keys.

Only when the room was empty, when the only sound was the chime of a clock and the slam of car doors and scandalized voices on the street outside, did Delphine rise up to her full height. She smoothed down her dress and glided toward her son. Titus shrunk from her as she raised a trembling hand, fearing the physical and emotional blow that would surely follow.

Delphine lowered her hand, placing it on his shoulder. Her fingers curled around him, and she pulled him close. Their arms went around each other in the same moment, and they collapsed like they'd come home at last. Titus buried his face in her shoulder.

"His spirit lives in you, son," she sobbed.

Titus' shoulders shook as he held her, as together they did what they should have done years ago and honored Micah with their tears, their togetherness, their music.

Delphine leaned back, her lips tugging into a wobbly smile as she stroked his cheeks. "I'm sorry, my beautiful boy. I'm so so sorry I didn't see you through my grief."

I reached up to touch my own cheek, and found it wet with tears. Titus needed this moment. As much as he tried to do his own thing and not care what anyone thought of him, I knew that he would never be happy unless they were happy, too. That was part of what I loved about him – that he wanted to honor the legacy they built for him.

"What about Dad?" Titus sniffed.

Delphine's shoulders tightened. "I won't do him the disservice of speaking for him. Your father loves you, Titus. You know he does. But this isn't the life he sees for you."

"But shouldn't he be happy Titus has chosen his own path?" I asked. "That's what you both did."

My voice cut through the poison air, breaking her gaze with her son. Delphine's eyes fluttered shut. She'd fallen into a memory that gouged out her heart. "We wanted Titus to have what we didn't have. That was the gift we wished to give both our sons – the gift of a world where they didn't have to work twice as hard just to get a seat at the table."

He kissed her forehead. "I know, Mom."

"I don't think you do, son. We know we've failed you in so many ways. You cannot imagine the grief of a parent who outlives their child. I've learned to harden my skin and resist my tears, but when something joyful happens, no matter how small – the roses in the garden bloom after a long winter, I hear a song that makes my heart – it's as if the levees open and it all comes crashing down again. And you, my beautiful, bright son, you are my greatest joy." She caressed his cheek, and I thought my heart might burst from my chest for how much Titus needed to hear her words. "We never meant to force you into Micah's shadow. So much that was good in him lives in you, and I'd be heartsick to think I snuffed that out because I was afraid and ashamed. We're never guaranteed a happy ending in this life, but a happy beginning and a happy middle – those are in my power to give you. Please, son, play your music if it makes your heart light and free. Micah would be so, so proud of you."

"Thanks, Mom. I—" Titus' words caught in his throat. He stared at the door through which Amos had disappeared. "Tell Dad...tell him I'm sorry we ruined his party. Tell him that if he wants to talk to me, he knows where to find me. I won't be going back to school to study the cello. I hope one day he'll understand."

With that, Titus released his mother's embrace. He slipped my hand into his arm, and with his ax slung over his shoulder, we stepped over the empty cello case and strode from the house, out into the night.

Titus

"Here." Faye slapped an amber drink in front of me, along with a basket of po boys. "I'll drink it if you change your mind."

I wrapped my fingers around the glass. It was 10AM the day after my parents' party. I'd barely slept thinking about my father's face as he stormed out and my mother's heartfelt apology. Faye finally got sick of me moping and thinking, and dragged me to this diner, where I'd surprised myself by ordering a Sazerac.

I didn't drink because I knew alcohol played a part in Micah's accident. I wanted my mind and wits about me so I could save the people I loved from their own drunken stupidity. And my sobriety had definitely come in handy on the road, especially with Dorien being...well, *Dorien*. But I realized that, like so many things I did, I chose not to drink because I thought it would please my parents. But after last night, I felt as though that weight had come off my shoulders. My mother loved me for who I was, and my father...well, I would never please him, no matter what I did. It was time to stop living for them and start figuring out who I was.

I raised the Sazerac to my lips with a trembling hand. My lips still burned from my mother's kiss. Her tears left pricks of fire against my skin. I felt strange all over as I sipped – fuzzy and heavy with grief, but light at the same time.

Micah.

I *felt* him with me when I played last night – his breath on my shoulders, his infectious energy making my fingers dance along the fretboard. His smile bright in every riff. I could never have my brother back, but I could keep his memory alive through music. And now my mother could see that.

I just wish Dad could understand...

"I smelled something," Faye leaned back in her chair, dangling her own glass from her fingers. "When we played that song, I could smell coffee and sweet cherries, very rich and dark. I thought it might be someone's perfume, but it seemed to be everywhere, all around us."

My back stiffened. Faye had told me about this strange ability of hers, about the scents she smelt when she played sometimes – scents that were intrinsically linked to her own memories, but this... "That's Micah's aftershave."

His old girlfriend gave Micah that scent – she loved him drenched in the stuff, so she brought him a lifetime supply. Everything he owned smelled like it. I had some old concert t-shirts of his I stole from his drawer before my parents got rid of his things, and I wore them for months without washing them because they were soaked in coffee and cherries.

Faye picked up one of the po boys and took a huge bite. Juices dribbled down her chin. "I hope you're not regretting what we did. This is progress, Titus."

I slid across the booth and wrapped my arms around her, pulling her close. This was why I loved her, because she was a perfect mirror of me. She made me brave and bold, like her.

"Did you know this was the very bar where Dorien first came up with the idea for Broken Muse?"

Faye sat forward, her lip curling with excitement. "It was?"

I told her the story about Dorien leaping on stage and attracting all those girls. "Broken Muse played one of our first ever gigs right there." I pointed to the stage in the corner. "There were only twenty people in the place. Some of my brother's old friends mostly, and a couple of dudes we knew from summer music camp. It was wild. Dorien poured whiskey all over the piano and some girl licked it off."

"Typical Dorien." Faye laughed. "I wish I could have been there."

"I miss them." It felt good to say it. "Ever since we had to cancel the tour and go to Manderley, nothing's been the same. I feel anxious and on edge all the time. I miss playing music with my friends. We've been so caught up in our shit that we forgot why we started the band in the first place, and now it's done."

"Is it done?" Faye asked. "You're free of Madame Usher now. Broken Muse can play again if you want to."

I shook my head. "The songs were a moment in time, and the moment is over. It doesn't matter what really happened at Manderley; the image the world has when they think of us is Dorien pulling a knife out of Heather's back. We can't change that."

"Do you have to change it?" Faye asked. "Ozzy Osbourne bit the head off a bat. Paganini sold his soul to the devil so he could sell out concert halls. Varg Vikernes stabbed his bandmate, and he's got a successful YouTube channel. Okay, Varg's a terrible example, but what I'm saying is that Madame Usher was counting on all this bad press to destroy the band, but we know that controversy sells records. Broken Muse has never had more press, and if you were to go out on tour or release a new song now..."

"I just can't see it," I sighed. "Maybe we'll play together again one day. But I think we all have to do our own things for a while, try not to fuck everything up this time, especially with Dorien's finger—"

"Well, sound the fucktrumpets, that makes things a bit awkward."

"What does?"

Faye held up her phone. "I maaaaay have already invited Dorien and Ivan down here to have a little fun with us, just like you used to on tour. Dorien said they're heading to the airport now – they'll be here in a couple of hours."

What?

She did what?

I stared at the tiny stage where my story with Dorien Valencourt had began, where we set in motion a series of events that would bring Faye into my life and intrinsically link me to my bandmates forever.

"Perfect." I grinned. "Let's get wild."

~

As day turned into evening and evening became a deep, rich night, Faye and I danced from bar to bar, stuffing our faces with po boys and gumbo and sampling the finest Sazeracs until my head spun and I felt a tap on my shoulder. I turned around to see Dorien's evil grin. Behind him, Ivan stood like an ice king surveying his kingdom.

"You made it!" Faye threw her arms around Ivan. He melted in her arms, wrapping her in his embrace and swinging her off the ground so her legs knocked over several barstools and the waitress shot us a filthy look.

Dorien leaned across the bar, his hair falling in his face. Something was different about him, and it took me a few moments to put my finger on what it was. *Ivan.*

Decent cock will give a man a glow.

I watched Ivan burn with jealousy every night Dorien walked up to his hotel room with some random guy or girl. The three of us had shared enough girls that I'd seen the longing behind Ivan's icy glare.

Faye brought them together. She gave them the gift of each other. She didn't believe she had to be enough for either of them, just as each of us on our own weren't enough for her. That made me love her even more.

"Where's Jacob?" I asked Dorien.

"Marguerite has him for the weekend." Dorien's eyes danced at the mention of his brother. "She's taking him to the zoo. He's excited."

"I want to hear all about it."

And I did. I truly did. We went back to the bar where Dorien and I sat all those years ago and dreamed up the concept of Broken Muse. The stage still stood in the corner, although it was smaller now with crimson curtains as a backdrop and no grand piano in sight. We ordered another round of Sazeracs and fried shrimp po boys, and Dorien regaled us with stories of Jacob's recovery. Ivan and Dorien took him to an ice skating rink, and he had an absolute blast until they had to clear the ice because a hockey league had their practice. They'd stayed to watch, and when Jacob realized the enormous guys bashing each other around out there were his age, he went quiet. He didn't talk for days. Sadness tinged Dorien's words as he grappled with the reality that his younger brother might always experience the world differently and live on the outside of his peers.

"I've been taking him to church," Dorien told me. "I don't like it. I *hate* it, actually. I don't want religious shit messing up his head. But it's familiar to Jacob and the pastor seems like a good guy. Jacob joined the youth group and…it's too early to hope, but he might even be making friends."

It felt so strange, so wild, to be sitting together in a bar in New Orleans, *the* bar where Broken Muse started, with Madame Usher a distant memory. She wasn't gone from our lives completely, but right now we were free of her. And it felt amazing. Judging by Faye's giddy laugh and Dorien's aristocratic smile, I wasn't the only one who thought so.

Only Ivan couldn't give himself over one hundred percent to the moment, and I understood why. He would never be free of Manderley until Elena was, and we all knew that wouldn't happen while she was chained to Radcliffe.

We didn't have all our answers, but it was out of our hands now. We needed to trust Rochester and his team to do their jobs. Answers would come.

As the band on stage wound down their set and packed out their gear, the waitress came over with more baskets of po boys and curly fries. As she set them on the table, her eyes narrowed at each of us before settling on Dorien. "You're from Broken Muse? I remember you – the arrogant little shit who took over my stage without so much as a 'please and thank you, ma'am.'"

"Broken Muse doesn't exist anymore." Ivan tipped back his drink.

"I remember you, Laverne." Dorien turned his thousand-megawatt smile to her. "Did we finally turn you into a fan?"

"Can't be a fan of a band that doesn't exist," Laverne smirked, but I could see Dorien's charm wearing away her sharp edges. "I heard y'all broke up. I heard there was some big scandal. Your fiancee dead with a knife in her back, and her blood on your hands."

"I was never charged with anything," Dorien held up his hands, turning them over so she could see they were clean. "I'm innocent."

"Too bad." The waitress rolled her eyes. "Innocent is so much less rock'n'roll."

"I told you," Faye mouthed as she nudged my hand.

"See that guy?" The waitress pointed to the saxophonist as he hobbled off the stage. "He spent twenty-two years in prison for a crime he didn't commit. He still comes in here every week and plays the roof off."

Ivan started to say something, but Laverne whirled around and jabbed her finger at a woman nursing a lavish cocktail. "She was a rising jazz singer until she had a love-child with her manager. He promised her the world. When she got pregnant, he tossed her out to chase after the next floozy. She's on stage in an hour and she'll pack this place out."

"What's your point?" Dorien growled.

"My point is that no one gives a fuck what's on your rap sheet if you can play a groove we can lose ourselves in. The music comes first, and the music isn't about you, it's about your audience." She narrowed her eyes at each of us in turn. "At least, it's supposed to. I'll give you an hour."

"What?"

"Your set. I'll bump my final act. You have an hour on stage. Now get your asses up there." She tapped her wrist. "Times' a ticking."

I shook my head, but Dorien leaned across the table. "You serious, Laverne?"

"I don't joke about music." She dropped a po boy in Dorien's lap and flounced away.

I stared down at my food. The last thing I wanted to do was get up there and play. It had been so long since we played those songs. Did we even remember what to do?

But of course, Dorien couldn't resist. "We have to do this. Ivan's got his violin in our rental car, and we can send a cab to grab Titus' ax."

"You mean my cello," I said, thinking of the instrument resting on its stand at the shotgun house, where Faye left it after she fitted my guitar into the cello case for the party.

"I meant what I fucking said," Dorien's blue-blooded smirk stoked a fire in my veins. "You should play our songs the way you want to play them. I know you can do it."

"What about you?" Faye asked him. Dorien's instrument wasn't exactly portable.

"I'm not worried." Dorien waved Laverne back. "You still have a piano somewhere? I'll even take a keyboard in a pinch."

"Son, this is New Orleans." Laverne gestured for us to follow her onto the stage. She yanked back the curtains, revealing a deeper stage area. She threw off a dusty sheet, revealing an polished Fazioli baby grand. Dorien sucked in his breath. He wasn't in control of his hands as they reached out and stroked the keys. His whole body swayed. It was a beautiful instrument, but I knew that wasn't what had arrested him.

I felt it too – the tingle in my fingers, the pulse in my veins. The desire to *play*, to be Broken Muse once more. I was still supping on the thrill of playing in front of my parents, of finally standing up to Dad and admitting who I was. I *could* play our songs the way they deserved to be played, the way I always imagined them.

I looked straight up into Faye's eyes. She burned bright in the dim bar, her halo of dark hair sparkling under the red-soaked lights.

I wrapped my arms around Dorien and Ivan. "Fuck it, let's do it."

～

No less than ten minutes later, I was backstage with my guitar in my hands. Dorien sat at the piano, practicing finger exercises and scales to warm up his muscles. Ivan paced the length of the stage, his violin rested on his chin. He looked like he was going to be sick.

Memories rushed at me – of other nights, other clubs, other nervous preconcert rituals and post-concert debauchery. Of the fire and flames I walked through to make music with these two, my brothers. It was the same fire burning inside us now and it...it was completely different.

The weight of my ax around my neck steadied me. *I am Titus Thibodeaux, and I know who I am.*

Laverne, who turned out to be the bar's owner, stepped on stage and addressed the room. "Ladies and gentlemen, we have a surprise for you tonight. You might've heard of a band named Broken Muse. The press dubbed them The Bad Boys of Baroque for their fiery reinterpretations of classical music and their hedonistic antics. They've been in hiding for a long time now but tonight, Broken Muse is back in town and they want you to party like it's 1799. Are you ready?"

We stormed on stage as the lights went up. And even though we'd only decided to play twenty minutes ago when the bar was practically empty, it was now packed with people. Laverne worked fast. She'd sent runners to some of the nearby clubs to tell them what was going down, and word of our impromptu set had spread like wildfire over social media, attracting our local fans like the call of the sirens.

The roar of the crowd washed over me, cleansing me of my sins and making me anew. At the piano, Dorien grinned like a blue-blooded Cheshire Cat. Even Ivan cracked a smile.

We started to play.

The moment my fingers touched the strings, I *remembered*. Every song, every note, came to me with perfect clarity. I remembered what I loved about this music, *our* music, how it told our stories in a way that opened veins and bled our lives across the stage. Our pain and our hopes and our fears on display so that our audience could find themselves in the music.

And now I got to tell my story in my own words.

I missed this. Fuck how I missed this.

I missed playing the music I loved for people like me. I missed looking out into a sea of faces, rapt as I brought them to their knees.

I was used to giving the stage over to Dorien. Even an instrumental band like ours needed a frontman, and Dorien filled that role with aplomb. But tonight, he let Ivan and I share the spotlight – this wasn't just his moment, it was for all of us. Tonight, I leaped across the stage, swinging that guitar on my hips, kicking out my legs and letting my hair fly wild around my face. I could have been in Iron Maiden or Metallica instead of a weird gothy classical trio. It was perfect.

It was *me*.

I gazed out into the sea of rapt faces. I saw only one. Faye was in the front row, throwing her hair around, jumping and screaming and yelling. Our Faye. Our muse. She brought us together again. She brought us all home.

Back to where we belonged. With each other.

With our music.

And as the crowd screamed my name, as they roared for their hometown boy, their Jesus risen from the dead, as they stamped their feet and cried for more, I felt a peace sweep over my body. It didn't matter what Madame Usher tried to do. It didn't even matter if my father never spoke to me again.

Somewhere above, Micah's light shone down on me.

FAYE

"That was incredible," I breathed as Broken Muse climbed off stage, each of them falling into my arms for a sweaty, stinky hug. Titus' ax brushed against my hips and my dress snapped on Ivan's bow, but I didn't care.

They were *perfection*. I'd never seen a live show like it. I've seen plenty of live bands – not just in concert halls, but in bars and stadiums, too. No one had a presence like Broken Muse. Maybe I was biased because I loved them with a fierceness that clawed at my chest, but they were the best. The fucking *best*.

We pulled apart to see Laverne standing there, holding out four Sazeracs with a wicked smile on her face. "Next time you're back in town, you play here." She thrust the drinks into our hands and stormed off to serve the crowd at the bar.

"To the best night of my life." Dorien raised his glass.

"I thought the night you and Ivan had me over the piano stool was the best night?" I teased him, but I clinked glasses. I knew what he meant. I leaned in and kissed Dorien, long and hard, giving him a promise of what he could expect later. He was snatched away from me by a trio of adoring fans.

He wasn't the only one. Ivan had been cornered by an intense-looking goth girl who was grilling him about Count Dracula, while Titus laughed as he tried to stop a tiny girl with cute black pigtails from climbing on his shoulders.

Maybe other girls would feel jealous and protective of the attention they were getting, but I reveled in it. These were my Muses and they were beautiful and perfect and fucking hot and they deserved to have every person in this room fall at their feet. I threw my arms around fans and snapped pictures for them with their favorite Muse boys and listened to a girl gush for twenty-two minutes about Ivan's eyebrows and I loved every sordid moment of it.

"What are you going to do now?" I asked when I was able to catch a breath again.

It was 2AM. We made our way across town with a horde of Broken Muse groupies in tow, ending up at a smoky jazz club off Bourbon Street nursing potent Sazeracs because we were in New Orleans and that's what you did. Dorien had lipstick smeared across his face, but I knew from his heavy-lidded eyes when he looked at me that he had only eyes for me.

"More absinthe." Titus slammed down a tray of green shots.

"I think we've drunk all the absinthe in the city." Ivan collapsed on the table, one finger rubbing his temple. "It certainly feels like it."

"I meant, what are you doing about Broken Muse?" I said. "Is this the last ever show?"

The three of them exchanged a glance.

"I fucking miss the band," Dorien said. "I miss being on stage with you both."

Ivan nodded, then winced as he realized how much he didn't want to move his head. Titus tossed his braids over his shoulder, and the smile that stretched from ear to ear was all the answer he needed to give.

"I say we keep going," Dorien said. "I know my finger is an issue, but I think if we adjust the compositions for Titus' guitar, we can re-allocate some of my trickier parts. Madame Usher can rail against us in the press all she wants. Anything she says is only going to help us sell out a tour. The Bad Boys of Baroque are back, and we're more dangerous than ever. But we do things differently this time. We don't let anyone dictate what we do, where we play, or what we can do with the money we make. It's the three of us, no management, no label, no Usher in the background pulling the strings. What do you say?"

Titus wrapped his arms around me and Dorien and Ivan, crushing us in a hug. Ivan managed to choke out a quiet. "I agree."

And just like that, Broken Muse was back.

As the sun rose, they regaled me with more wild stories from the road. I reveled in their past, for the first time feeling as though I was part of their story.

Titus dragged us down the street to a twenty-four-hour burger place. Ivan glanced down at his phone. The carefree twist fell from his face, replaced by a frown.

"What is it?" I asked.

"It's from Elena," he said. "She says we have to come back to Manderley."

"What? Why?"

"She doesn't say." Ivan held the phone to his ear, his eyes swimming as his fear slammed against his encroaching hangover. I heard Elena's chirpy voice on the other end. "It's going straight to voicemail."

Titus whipped out his phone and was frantically tapping the screen. "Shit, all the planes to New York are grounded."

"What?" Ivan looked murderous.

"There's a wicked Nor'easter rolling down the coast, heading straight for Manderley. They're predicting five feet of snow by tomorrow evening."

Ivan drew back his hand, preparing to shatter his glass against the wall. Dorien caught his wrist, pulling Ivan against him so Ivan could rail against his body instead of the innocent establishment. "We will get to her, I promise."

Titus slid his phone back into his pocket and tossed some bills on the table to pay for our burgers. "I've got us a flight to Baltimore – that's as close as we can get. We'll rent a car at the airport. If we want to make it at all, we have to go *now*."

FAYE

Ivan was a mess the whole flight. He spilled water all over his lap, barked at the flight attendants, and crushed my fingers in his iron grip. But we touched down in Baltimore just as they announced all flights were grounded. At least we were closer.

Elena, please be all right.

Titus and Dorien took turns driving. I sat in the back with Ivan, white-knuckling it the whole way as the pair broke every road rule and speed limit. Ivan called Elena every ten minutes until his phone ran out of battery, and then he bugged Dorien for his spare battery cord until Dorien tossed it out the window.

We crossed into New York just as the snow started to fall harder. Fifty miles later it was so thick we could barely see the next car in front of us. I gripped the edge of the seat as Titus flung the car around the bends. We made it to the foot of the mountains and started climbing. Ivan gritted his teeth in frustration as we crawled along, watching out for patches of ice. We didn't pass a single car on the road.

"What could have happened to her?" Ivan snapped. "Why won't she answer her phone?"

Dorien tapped the screen of his own phone. "I think the lines are down. There's no signal."

Ivan leaned forward, his eyes glued on the window, his fingers laced in mine. Wind battered the car from all sides, and the snow fell so thick and hard I had no idea how Titus kept us on the road.

It seemed to take days to crawl through the storm to the gates of Manderley. Lights were on in Harrison's cottage, but we didn't stop to say hello. As Titus jerked the car to a stop in front of the busted fountain, Dorien reached into the glove compartment and pulled out a pistol.

"What the fuck?"

"I bought it at the airport, can you believe it?" Dorien grinned. "God bless America."

"Put that away." I snapped. "We're not going into that house shooting, and that's final."

Dorien looked like he wanted to argue, but Titus wrestled the weapon from his fingers and shoved it back into the glove box, and that was the end of it. The moment I opened the door, the wind blasted me with an icy chill. We staggered up the front steps and inched our way around the edge of the porch, where the wood was sturdiest. I had to grip the railing as my feet slipped and slid on the icy porch. A foot of snow had blown against the door, with more piled up around the pillars. I turned back to the car, seeing it was already nearly obscured by the rapid snowfall.

We were trapped at Manderley until the storm passed.

Ivan hammered his fists on the door. "Elena, open up." He jiggled the handle, but the door was locked. I didn't have my Manderley keys with me – it seemed pointless to bring them to New Orleans, so I'd left them with Dorien, and he left them at the apartment when he'd rushed down to meet us.

No one answered. Snow blasted us sideways. I was cold right through, cold in my bones and my heart.

"We should try the stables," I yelled. The wind whipped away my words, but Ivan was already running back down the steps and around the side of the school. Dorien powered after him, his crimson scarf whipping in the wind. Titus helped me down the steps, steadying me so I didn't slip on the ice.

By the time we trudged through the snow to the stables, Ivan and Dorien had broken down the front door. It hung open, banging against the wall as the wind howled inside. Titus dragged me in and slammed the door shut behind us.

"Elena?" Ivan yelled from deeper in the house. Dorien stood in the middle of the room, staring at the mess strewn on the floor. The whole house was a disaster zone – Elena's clothing and makeup scattered everywhere, plates smashed on the kitchen floor, torn sheet music blowing about like confetti. It looked as though a tornado had ripped through the place. I rubbed my freezing hands together as I picked my way through the house, toward the bathroom. I wished instead of a gun, Dorien had bought some gloves at the airport.

The bathroom light was on. I turned in the dim circle, taking in the bloody handprints on the edge of the basin, the smashed mirror, and the bottles and lotions strewn across the tiles with a sinking feeling in my stomach. My feet scuffed more clothing and torn pages, dusted with snow blown in from outside.

What happened here? Who made all this mess, and where is Elena? Did someone break in and attack her? Is that why she called Ivan so frantically, and then her phone went dead—

I screamed as a dark shape lunged from the shadows of the linen cupboard and grabbed me around the neck.

 Ivan

Faye's scream curled through my body. I raced from the bedroom to find her in the door of the bathroom, struggling with an intruder hidden in shadow.

Victor Usher.

Anger surged through me as I took in the man's fingers wrapped around her neck. *We never should have left Elena here, knowing Victor lived in the walls. Now he's got Faye.*

I lunged at them, all the rage and fear coalescing inside me. *I will kill this bastard.*

I grabbed Victor's wrist and twisted it behind him before he could hurt her. Victor whimpered, and I noticed how thin his wrist was, how soft his skin, and that I could break it one quick motion if I so desired—

"Ivan? Please stop. You're *hurting* me."

My blood froze in my veins. *Not Victor.*

"Elena?"

My beautiful sister staggered from the shadows. She didn't look so beautiful now. Her eyes were wide with terror, her skirt was torn, and her pale skin was marred with bruises and dried blood.

"Ivan, help me."

Her voice trembled with terror. I dropped her wrist and she fell into my arms, her cheeks wet with tears, her shoulders heaving. I held her as she sobbed, and the story told by the broken furniture, the torn music sheets and the bruises clawed at my insides, turning my anger into a rage that boiled in my veins.

Deviant sexual proclivities.

Radcliffe did this to her.

I'll kill the bastard. When I find him I'll string his balls from the ceiling with piano wire and—

My heart stopped as I looked over my sister's shoulder at the piano and realized someone already had.

Radcliffe lay on the floor beside the piano stool, his pants pulled down around his ankles and his hairy, knobbly legs twisted underneath him. His face turned toward me, a pair of glassy eyes staring right through me, the mouth open in slack-jawed surprise. A dark halo of dried blood circled his head – a stain on the Persian rug no amount of scrubbing would ever be able to lift.

Dorien loomed over Radcliffe, the tip of his Barker Blacks scuffing the blood-stain. "There's a wound on the side of his head, and blood on the corner of the piano. I think someone hit him, and he fell and hit his head, and that's what killed him."

I looked down at my sister trembling in my arms. At the broken jug handle she clutched in her hands, the corners stained with blood. At the shattered pieces of the jug lying around Radcliffe's body. I held her at arm's length and watched her face crumple as I asked, "Elena, what did you do?"

 FAYE

Elena's lip trembled under the intensity of Ivan's gaze. She dropped the object she'd been holding, which I could see now was the handle and part of the side of a broken jug. It rolled across the rug, coming to rest against Radcliffe's thigh. Dark blood stained the rim. It looked exactly like the broken shards that were scattered around the body.

Radcliffe's body.

He's dead. He's not a person any longer, just a corpse.

"I...I needed you," Elena whispered, so that only Ivan and I could hear. The words punched Ivan in the gut. His face crumpled and he jammed his sister's face into his shoulder, as if he could squash the demons out of her. I knew he was hating himself for leaving her, even though she told him to go.

I stepped around the twins and bent down beside Master Radcliffe, careful not to touch his clothes or the dried blood. We couldn't risk getting our fingerprints on anything. I pulled a tissue from my pocket and used that to cover my fingers as I touched his wrist. No pulse. I didn't expect there to be.

"He's dead," I said.

"Thank you, Sprite the Obvious," Dorien said, a hint of dark sarcasm in his voice. He looked rattled, and I knew he was remembering the last dead bodies he saw – his parents. Elena buried her head in Ivan's shoulder.

I leaned over and peered at Radcliffe's face, at the sheen on his skin and the glassy, surprised look in his eyes. He felt cold and stiff – I knew from the number of horror films and true crime I watched that rigor mortis was normally over after thirty-six hours, but the freezing temperature had probably helped to prolong it. He'd been dead a couple of days, definitely before Elena called Ivan.

What the fuck?

"Elena, you have to tell us what happened." I tried to take her hand in mine, but she clung to Ivan and shook her head.

"*Elena*," Dorien said with more force than kindness. "We nearly killed ourselves getting here to help you. Whatever went down, we are on your side. You know this. But we need to *know* what we're dealing with here so we can figure out what to do. And I'm assuming Madame Usher doesn't know about this—" he indicated Radcliffe's body "—but if she sees our car in the snow, she could be over here any moment. So talk quickly, please."

Ivan glared at Dorien, but Elena bit her lip and nodded.

Titus found the only remaining chair that wasn't broken and dragged it over. Elena collapsed into it, her long limbs flapping out the sides like a frightened bird. Ivan stood behind her, his hands on her shoulders, playing with her bedraggled hair. I knelt on the carpet and took her hands in mine.

She sniffed. "He...he was a different person after we said our vows. If he had been the Radcliffe of before – the kindly, chivalrous old man – I could have lived with it. He looked after me. He wanted me to be famous, to have a career that overshadowed his. But as soon as the ring was on my fingers, he turned beastly. If he'd shown his true nature earlier, I would have run a mile, but he acted the perfect gentleman. Waiting until our wedding night to reveal himself was part of the game to him. He had what he wanted, and so did *she*." Elena turned her gaze to the window, where Manderley's east wing loomed. I could almost *sense* Madame Usher's eyes fixed on us – like the eye of Sauron, lidless and ever-watching.

"Was this about your money?" Dorien asked, gently this time.

Elena shook her head. "I don't think Madame Usher has even given him access to our trust. I don't think she ever intended to. They had an agreement – I heard them speak of it late at night when they thought I was asleep. She enticed him to come to Manderley by dangling me in front of him. She played him recordings of me, and he came here to seduce me. It was a game to him, and we played right into her trap. She always intended for me to marry him, a sacrificial lamb to his peculiar tastes in exchange for something she wanted."

"What?" Dorien's eyes blazed. He looked like he was ready to shake it out of her.

"I do not know," Elena sobbed. "It was something to do with his nervous breakdown, why he retreated from performances. And there is something else about him you do not know. I must show you. But it doesn't explain why she gave me to him – his little toy."

"Did he hurt you?" I gripped her hands. My mind went to a dark place, where Creepy Cory held me beneath him and I couldn't move and all I could taste was his deep-fried stickiness as his hands—

Elena nodded slowly. "He has visited more injustice upon my body than a human being can endure. I tried to fight him off, but you see what happened." She gestured at the destruction around us. "When he touched me, it was like a snake slithering under my skin. And even then I thought I must endure it for what he could give me, for in a few days we would go to Europe for our tour and I would play in all those beautiful concert halls and at least I would know some happiness. But when he came at me that night he told me he would put a child in my belly. He chose me because of my talents – so I would breed with him to create his true legacy, his next maestro. The glittering career he promised me was not to be mine – that belonged to our child. But I will not be caged again. I will not bring a child into this world to be raised by him, not knowing what he's capable of. We fought. He lunged at me and I..." she glared at the jug and shuddered. Ivan pulled her to his chest. "I hit him and he fell. I didn't mean for it to happen. I knew Ivan could help me."

She sobbed into Ivan's shoulder. I looked down at Radcliffe's body, at his white legs and speckled ass. My stomach turned. I resisted the urge to kick him. He hurt Elena. I couldn't feel sorry for him. I wanted to bring him back to life so that I could kill him again myself.

I noticed bruises on his arms. *That must've been where she fought back. That's my girl.*

"What was the other thing you found out about him?" Dorien asked. He peered around the room with a puzzled expression on his face.

"Look at those papers." Elena pointed to a stack on top of the piano.

I peered over Dorien's shoulder as he read them. My stomach churned as I saw the splatters of blood across the page. Dorien frowned as he looked at the names on the documents.

"This is..." he said. "I don't understand."

"Aaron Varney is Master Radcliffe's son," Elena said. "That is the legacy of the man I married."

FAYE

Wait...what the fuck?

How is that possible? How did everyone miss that? Rochester has been chasing Varney for years. Surely he would have figured out his connection to Radcliffe, to Manderley?

Dorien's hands trembled as he flipped the papers over, scanning each line.

"Aaron uses his mother's name," Elena explained. "I confronted Maxim about it and he said she was a flautist he met on tour with the National Youth Orchestra. She was a member of a radical religious sect that believed God and demons could speak through music. Maxim didn't even know he had a son until Aaron found him a decade ago."

Around the time Radcliffe stepped away from performing because of a scandal.

My mind whirred. I could imagine it – Aaron Varney, would-be religious leader and desperate for quick and easy cash, discovered his father is a world-famous classical musician. Elena hadn't said it out loud, but I was certain Aaron's mother was underage when Radcliffe slept with her. So Aaron found Radcliffe and...what? Tried to convince him to join his burgeoning Temple? But if Radcliffe refused...we knew that Aaron would use every tool at his disposal to further his cause. He probably threatened Radcliffe to go to the papers, maybe even have his mother press charges. Radcliffe would be ruined, his career in tatters.

And that was where Madame Usher came in, with her connections in law enforcement. She offered Radcliffe a job at Manderley, and in exchange, perhaps she would keep Aaron's cult and the truth about his paternity out of the public eye. Radcliffe owed her his freedom, his reputation, as long as she kept Aaron off his back by any means necessary.

But he could also give her what she needed – his contacts in the music world, a means to place Manderley on the global stage as a fine institution. He lent her the legitimacy of a real music school while in the background she schemed and maneuvered to...what? We still didn't have the final piece of the puzzle – Madame Usher's real motivations.

I didn't know if that was the full story, but I felt certain I'd hit on the crux of it. It explained Madame Usher's link to the Temple, and Radcliffe's need to hide behind her. Judging by the murderous look on Dorien's face, he came to the same conclusion.

This is completely fucked up.

"What do we do now?" Titus said.

An excellent question. We still had a dead body on our hands.

"We call the police," Dorien said. "We tell them exactly what happened. Radcliffe was a brute with a fetish for young women and Elena defended herself. This is self-defense – anyone can see that."

"And you think they will believe me?" Elena shot back. "I am a foreigner, and he's a respected musician and my husband. With everything going on in the house and Walpole in Madame Usher's pocket, they will send me to prison for his murder. They will say I did it to take his money. Now everything that is his belongs to me."

I glanced at Dorien, and I could see him thinking the same as me. Elena was right. Madame Usher had the police commissioner in her pocket. She was the one who sold Elena to Radcliffe for his awful scheme. She'd already nearly successfully framed Dorien once before, so she had no qualms about planting evidence and lying to get the result she wanted. If Elena's case had a fair trial, I didn't think a jury would convict her, but I couldn't be sure.

"We could go to Rochester," Dorien said. "He knows Walpole is crooked, and he's closing his net around Madame Usher. Knowing Aaron is Radcliffe's son is the final piece of the puzzle."

"I don't trust him." Elena folded her arms. But Ivan nodded to Dorien. He looked so small. This was too big for us.

Dorien tapped his phone, then frowned. "Fuck, I forgot we didn't have signal."

"The storm knocked it out," Elena sniffed, tucking a lank strand of hair behind her ear. "That's why I couldn't call you again. I've been waiting in here with him for *days*, hoping you'd come to rescue me. But instead, you want to turn me in to the police!"

Her voice rose with distress, and she threw herself into Ivan's arms. He shot Dorien a reproachful look.

"We could try to make it back down the road," Dorien said hopefully. "If we go slow in the car, I'm sure we'll be fine."

I glanced out the window at the snow pelting down. At this rate, we'd have to dig the car out. Even as Dorien said the words, his face betrayed him. He knew it was pointless.

We're not going anywhere.

"What do you propose, Elena?" Ivan's tone was harsher than I'd ever heard him use with her before.

Her chin trembled as she glanced down at her husband. "I don't want to go to jail."

"You won't." Ivan's fingers laced around her neck. He held her fiercely, his eyes boring into mine over her shoulder. "We won't let that happen."

I read his intention in that icy glare.

"We can't do that." I shook my head.

"It is our only choice," Ivan said sadly, stroking Elena's hair.

It wasn't. Of course it wasn't. We were panicked, stressed, driven to the end of our rope by the terror of Radcliffe's body and Madame Usher's final betrayal. It was obvious we weren't thinking clearly.

But we had to do *something*. We couldn't just leave him there. And we were all alone out here, with no one but Harrison, Aroha, and Mad Madame Usher and her crazy husband living in the walls. Who knew what they'd do to us if they found out what happened?

I leaned against the bathroom door, trying to think.

"We wait out the storm," I said. "The phone tower will be repaired and we'll be able to get through to Rochester."

"And Elena goes to jail," Ivan snapped.

"We don't know that for a fact." I looked down at Radcliffe, and I knew that as much as I had liked the man while he was alive, I wouldn't let Elena be blamed for his death. He was Aaron's father. His DNA was part of the man who broke Dorien's family and tormented Jacob and deprived him of a normal life. And look what he did to Elena. All this time we thought Madame Usher was the enemy, but Radcliffe was a *beast*. The monster hiding in plain sight.

People go missing in storms all the time. Perhaps Radcliffe was walking in the woods and got caught in the snow. If we take him far away and bury him deep, no one will ever find his body. He'll be just another of Manderley's secrets.

It became impossible to breathe. I rushed into the bathroom and cracked the window, gasping at the frigid blast of air.

Dorien appeared in the doorway. "Sprite?"

"We can't bury him in this storm," I said, thinking fast. "It's too dangerous. But we can't leave him here, either. Madame Usher or Harrison or Aroha could walk in at any moment and we lose our chance. We have to hide the body until the weather clears, and we need to clean this place up and agree on a story."

"Okay," said Dorien. "Okay." He looked haunted. His jaw worked, like he wanted to say something but thought better of it. Instead, he opened his arms and I fell into them. I didn't realize how much I needed a soft place to fall until my head rested on his shoulder and hot tears burned down my cheeks.

∼

We pulled down the shower curtain and rolled Radcliffe into it, careful not to touch anything in his exposed crotch area. *Too fucking gross.* His limbs were still a little stiff, making him ungainly to lift, but at least he wasn't a large man. Elena and I cleaned up the broken objects and stuffed the pieces into trash bags. Ivan got to work cleaning down the piano, removing every last trace of blood from the wood.

"What do we do about the bloodstain?" I pointed to the rug.

Titus grunted as he lifted the piano, while Dorien rolled up the rug and set it on top of our trash pile. There was now a large bright square under the piano where the wood around the rug had faded.

"Ivan, wipe the floor carefully with bleach. We can't take any chances. We'll take the rug with us when we leave," Dorien said. "We can dump the trash in the pit at the old timber mill. No one will look there. I think there's an old rug in that storage room in the attic at the house. We can bring that in here and lay it under the piano and no one will ever notice a change."

We worked in panicked silence, filling five garbage bags with broken objects. Titus screwed the legs back on chairs and used glue to repair some of the more expensive pieces. Elena and I wiped down the kitchen counters and cupboards. If we were going with the story that Radcliffe went out for firewood and never came back, then we needed this place to be spotless.

Through our cleaning, the body of Radcliffe lay in the doorway. Even through the shower curtain, his glassy eyes seemed to follow me as I moved around the room.

"Where are we going to hide him?"

"Not in here," Dorien said. "We don't want any more DNA or other material to end up in the stables, because if we report him as a missing person, the police *will* look here first."

"It's snowing worse than ever." Elena shuddered against Ivan as the wind rattled the shingles. "We cannot hope to dig a grave in this."

I couldn't help but notice how quickly she'd resigned herself to covering up the crime. Something about her story niggled at me, but I couldn't put my finger on it.

"We won't be able to get him to the mausoleum." I thought about hiding him in Victor's empty grave, but we'd kill ourselves trying to drag him all the way there and back in this weather.

"It's simple," Dorien said. "We hide him behind the painting in my old room."

I glared at him. "Be serious."

"I am. It's perfect. Even if the police search the house, they'll never think of looking *inside* the walls."

"What about Madam Usher?" I hissed. "She's going to notice when he doesn't show up for classes, and she'll see all of us sneaking around. Or Victor will find the body in the tunnels and tell her, and it's over for us."

"Sure. Victor could go to the police and say, what? I've been living in the walls creeping on young girls at my wife's school, and I saw them dump a body in here? Madame Usher won't report it because it'll expose the tunnels," Dorien shot back.

"They have too much to lose. And speaking of Madame Usher, we should lock her in her rooms."

"Well, at least you have a solid plan," I said sarcastically.

"She might know we're at the house, but she can't know what we're up to. Ivan has the map showing the other exits for Victor's tunnels. We block them all, and when we leave, there's no evidence we were ever here."

"This is insane. We could be stuck here for days while this storm clears. He's going to start to smell."

"The cold air blowing through the walls will help keep him cool," Ivan said. "I am with Dorien. I think it is our best option."

Dorien nodded. He glanced at Elena again, and that strange, haunted look passed over his eyes again. I wanted to ask what he was thinking, but I was too grossed out by our plan to dig into it. "We don't have our keys with us. Elena, you've got that spare key I cut for you? I need you to go back to the house and lock Usher and Aroha in their rooms."

She nodded, and leaned forward to kiss Dorien's cheek. He held her arm and whispered something in her ear that made her body go stiff. I knew he was telling her what he suspected, asking for her to confirm or deny. Instead, she pulled away, her eyes downcast. "I will return."

I don't know how long she was gone, but it felt like forever. Ivan paced the room, wringing his hands and occasionally stopping to give Radcliffe's corpse a violent kick. Dorien sat at the piano, his hands in his lap and his head hanging. Titus held me tight, and I squeezed him as waves of nausea and fear rocked my body. *What the fuck are we doing? Not even ten hours ago we were in New Orleans, celebrating the return of Broken Muse. And now we're trying to dispose of a dead body.*

The door slammed open, startling us out of our skins. Elena rushed in and sank against it to hold back the storm. Her pale cheeks were flushed with color.

"I did it," she whispered, hugging herself. "They are locked inside their rooms."

"Okay." Dorien stood, dusting off his hands on his pants. "Let's do this, then."

The four of us each picked up one corner of the curtain. Elena held the door open for us as we struggled out into the snow. Bitter wind pelted us, nearly ripping Radcliffe from my hands. Somehow, with lots of staggering and swearing and falling over, we managed to make it across the back garden.

Elena held the kitchen door for us, and we shuffled inside. As quietly as we could, we huffed and struggled upstairs and into Dorien's old room. I dropped my leg on the rug and rubbed my screaming arms while Dorien jumped on the desk to open the painting. Luckily, we'd thought to dismantle the internal lock last time, so we could get inside.

Dorien peered into the wall cavity. "Victor? Are you in there?"

"Stop fucking around and give me space," Titus grunted as he lifted the body onto his shoulders. "This bastard is heavy."

Ivan and I moved in beside Titus to help lift the body while Dorien maneuvered it into the hole. Elena leaned against the wall, watching us. As I turned to help push, I caught a glimpse of her. She was smiling – a sweet, eerily-calm Elena smile.

The smile of someone who got exactly what she wanted.

As we strained under Radcliffe's deadweight, Dorien met my eyes. He saw her smile, too.

In his gaze, I read the same duplicitous thought that had entered my head. Elena had been close to Radcliffe for months and never shown any fear of him. We'd all taken classes with him and he seemed to be a perfect gentleman. It was her word against his about what happened in that room, and now he was dead. We believed it because we read Donelle's article about the 'deviant sexual proclivities,' but she never mentioned Radcliffe by name. She could have been talking about Victor or Madame Usher or even one of the visiting teachers.

And the scene in the stables...that's what was bothering me. All that broken furniture and smashed crockery – it seemed too erratic, too spread out. It was odd, wasn't it, to have such chaos in every room of the house, not concentrated in the living room where Radcliffe fell? If I didn't know better, I'd say it wasn't caused by a vicious fight, but someone deliberately and maliciously turning the place over.

It seemed perfectly designed for maximum impact – to agitate Ivan to the point where he'd do anything to secure Elena's safety.

As if...as if it had been staged.

Wait, what am I thinking?

Elena was my friend, and too many women had been silenced by the threat of not being believed. I had a feminist duty to stand by her.

She looked so upset when we found her in the stables, so lost and broken. And Ivan said he noticed Radcliffe lusting after her from a young age.

And yet...Radcliffe's pants around his ankles...the shards of pottery on top of his body, as if they'd been smashed after he died...the surprised look on his face...

It was *too* perfect.

I remembered something else, too. I remembered Elena's words back in Sighisoara, when she first told us she was engaged. "This is real life, and there's no good and evil. I'm not the pure virgin who needs saving."

I remembered looking into her cold icicle eyes – so much like Ivan's, and yet infinitely more impassable – and feeling *certain* she had no intention of going through with her marriage to Radcliffe.

Is Elena really the victim of a violent, depraved man?

Or did she lure him into the marriage and then hit him over the head? Did she plan this? Was this always her endgame – to get rid of Radcliffe and have Ivan cover it up for her so she could take Radcliffe's money and fame and run?

FAYE

"There." Dorien fell against the painting, his forehead coated with sweat. "It's done."

I got the bucket and mop and cleaned the floor in his bedroom. Then, we went to Aroha's room. If we were going to wait out the storm at Manderley, we were doing it together. There was no noise from inside. "Aroha?" I knocked gently. "It's Faye. Can we come in?"

No answer. I took the key from Elena and shoved it into the lock. Dorien pushed open the door. Aroha lay on her bed, her face pointed at the ceiling, her arms crossed over her stomach. She didn't move.

"Aroha?" My heart raced as I knelt beside her. Dorien shook her, but she didn't wake up. Her limbs flopped about uselessly, and her lips fell open.

"She's alive," Dorien pressed his fingers into her wrist. "But her pulse is erratic. Her breathing is slow. And look at her eyes. She's overdosed on something."

Ivan held up a bottle. "This? It looks like it's from your apothecary set."

Dorien snatched the bottle from Ivan's hand. "This is chloral. But I don't understand. Heather gave the bottle from the set to Pearl, so why..."

His eyes met mine as the answer occurred to us at the same time. *Victor.* He had a ton of these old apothecary bottles in his little laboratory. He must have given the bottle to Aroha. He clearly couldn't stop himself from talking with students – we know he'd chatted with Heather before he killed her, but he'd also tried to scare me, and he'd obviously been talking to Clare as well. *Did he intend for Aroha to be his next victim...*

I tried to remember what I'd read about chloral when we were planning to use it on Madame Usher. The Victorians had used it as a cure for insomnia, but also to treat melancholy. It was highly addictive and poisonous in large doses, and could also cause hallucinations, nausea, and a range of other non-fun symptoms, including death.

Shit. Aroha, no.

"What do we do?" Elena leaned over her, concern written over her features. I felt awful for suspecting her of murdering Radcliffe. I *knew* Elena – she was kind and good and truthful. She couldn't possibly have planned such a fiendish thing.

"I don't think there's much we can do except wait with her and hope she pulls through." I rearranged Aroha's pillows and rolled her onto her side into the recovery position, so she wouldn't choke if she threw up. We couldn't call an ambulance – not even the rescue helicopter would make it up the mountain in this weather. We couldn't even use the internet to see if it had any clever (or not so clever) suggestions.

So we waited. Elena and I parked ourselves on Aroha's bed. I stroked her hair and Elena sang Romanian folk songs in her sweet, breathy voice. The Muses went from room to room in the house, checking doors and windows and blocking off all the exits of Victor's tunnels.

I don't know how many hours passed. Aroha's breathing grew stronger. She started to murmur and thrash, clutching at her stomach. I had to hope that meant she was improving.

At some point, Madame Usher realized she was locked in and started banging and cursing at the door. Weirdly, the sound of her anger soothed me. She was in there and we were out here. Manderley belonged to us now.

Thankfully, despite the storm raging outside, the lights remained on. We were able to keep Aroha's room warm and bright during our long night-time vigil at her side.

Sometime later, as the sun once again threatened the horizon, Aroha opened her eyes. "What are you doing here, trash?" She gripped my arm so hard she pinched my skin.

"Elena called us. Radcliffe disappeared in the storm, and Madame Usher..." I racked my brain for some lie to explain why we locked her in, then decided not to bother. Aroha winced, doubling over with pain. "Are you okay?"

"I think I need to shit...or puke..." Aroha gasped. "Or both...yup, definitely both."

Ivan brought food and fresh water. Aroha spent the day moving back and forth between the bathroom and her bed. We changed her sheets three times, tossing the sweaty, soiled ones into Heather's old room. Madame Usher had abandoned her assault on the door and was now playing Mozart at top volume from her record player. The walls of Manderley shook from the assault of the music.

When Aroha declared she was well enough to brave the stairs, we all gathered in the Red Room. I tried the house phone, but the line was still dead, so I couldn't let Harrison know we were here. Titus helped me bring in a load of wood and we lit a roaring fire. We passed around port glasses and I heated up some chili I stored in the freezer.

"What happened?" I asked Aroha.

She winced, pushing her chili bowl aside as she clutched her stomach. "What does it look like? I have been going fucking mad, is what happened. The competition is coming up, but it's like no one gives a shit. It's as if the school is just a facade for something else, and the cloak is slipping and all the spiders are crawling out. There's no one here except Dopey and Mopey over there," she gestured her elbow at Elena and Ivan, "and Radcliffe who is so lovesick he doesn't come to my lessons half the time, and *her*. And she's fucking mad. Good thing you've got her locked away upstairs, because I think she'd kill us all. But maybe that's just me going mental. I'm all alone with my thoughts all the time and this house...this fucking *house*..." she rolled her eyes at the ceiling. "I snorted all Elena's coke. Usher refused to let me get the drugs I *actually* need, so fuck her. But he said this would help and I was fucking desperate. I wasn't trying to off myself, just to get the voices to stop."

"Who said the chloral would help you?" I already knew the answer, but I needed to hear it from her.

"The man in the walls. The one Clare and Heather talked to, obviously." Aroha rolled her eyes. "I thought you knew all about him. He never stops going on about you. Faye this, Faye that, isn't she amazing? He's such a wanker."

"Where is the man in the walls now?" Dorien stared at the spot behind my head, and I know what he's thinking – is Victor about to burst through the walls with an ax and murder us all? It had definitely crossed my mind.

Dorien touched his hand to his pocket. I knew he'd gone back to the car and retrieved the gun. I didn't like it, but I didn't say anything.

"Probably back in his hole. He says he has a room where Madame keeps him. She locks the door so he can't see us without her permission. He's afraid of her, it's fucking pathetic—"

Aroha's words broke off into a coughing fit that racked her whole body.

When she withdrew her hands from her mouth, they were covered with blood.

Shit. This isn't good. We need to get her to a hospital.

But the snow and wind and hail battered the house all day and into the night, determined to keep us trapped in Manderley's belly.

The power went out in the night, plunging the house into a darkness so complete I knew it was what death must feel like. Luckily, we had planned in advance and had boxes of candles placed next to the fireplace in the Red Room. We all slept in there together, huddled on the opulent sofas with blankets drawn up to our chins.

I warmed soup over the fire for breakfast, and we spent the day reading ghost stories to each other and playing music together. Aroha was still sick – just a mouthful of soup made her double over with pain. But she managed to drink some water and warm tea, so that was something. She hadn't coughed up any more blood, but I noticed her hobbling off to the bathroom every few minutes.

"We have a problem." Dorien grabbed my hand and yanked me out of the room. He glanced over his shoulder as he slammed the door, and I knew he didn't want the others to hear us.

"Elena?" I wondered if he was going to address the fears we hadn't voiced.

But Dorien shook his head. He turned his head to the staircase and inhaled deeply. "Sniff."

I followed his example, surprised to get a lungful of sickly sweet air, with the faintest undercurrent of putrid rot.

Dorien pinched his nose. "I think our friend upstairs is succumbing."

"The heat from the fires must be traveling through the wall cavities," I said. "It's going to speed up the decay. We have to live with it. We'll freeze in here if we don't keep the fires going—"

A noise from the second floor startled us. Madame Usher was banging on her door again. She screamed and howled, more wild and desperate than angry. *She must smell him, too.*

Maybe Victor has discovered him.

Maybe they're both up there wondering if they'll be next.

Good.

"I want to talk to her," I told Dorien. "We should probably bring her some food."

"You think that's a good idea?" He raised an eyebrow.

"No. But we're doing it. This stalemate of ours ends now."

Dorien poked his head into the room and beckoned Titus to join us – we needed his muscle. We went to the kitchen, and Titus held a candle for me while I made up a tray of simple food – an apple that was only a little mushy, a couple of candy bars, a handful of almonds. A small glass of slightly rancid-smelling milk. I was being a petty bitch but I didn't care.

We took the tray upstairs. With every step into the darkened hallway, I expected Clare's ghost to waft out of the walls and warn us away. But she didn't, which probably meant she was watching somewhere and smiling.

Titus and Dorien flanked the door. I held the tray with both hands, trying to calm my racing heart. Dorien slipped the key into the lock and flung the door open. It hit Madame Usher in the face. She staggered backward, howling and clutching her forehead. Blood seeped through her fingers where the door had torn her skin.

Her eyes widened when she saw me holding the tray. For the first time, she appeared genuinely surprised. Victor was either trapped in the wing with her, or he decided not to tell her we were in the house. I thought about what Aroha said, about him being obsessed with me, and wondered again why he seemed to be on my side even as he tormented me.

"We know what you did," I snapped at her before she could talk. "We know about the bodies under the Usher School and the Triumvirate's money and Radcliffe's connection to the Temple. We know you've been hiding Victor in the walls of Manderley. We got all the evidence we need to put you away for a long time, and your friend Walpole won't be able to stop us. Maybe we'll go to the police, or maybe we'll keep you here and torture you, the way you tortured us. I haven't decided yet. Either way, we're trapped in this house together until the storm passes, so I suggest you do what we say, because I might feel calm now but I can't say how I'll feel in a few hours. You're not leaving this room. Someone will guard this door at all times. We've blocked Victor's exits, and if we find him in the walls, we'll kill him. Do you understand?"

Madame Usher tossed back her head and laughed. Although using the word 'laugh' couldn't convey the sheer terror of her banshee howl. Titus and I exchanged a glance. I didn't know what to say to that.

She didn't give me a chance to respond. She grabbed the tray from my hands and kicked the door with her foot. It slammed shut in my face.

"Get in there," I nudged Dorien. "We're not letting her out of our sight. Show her your gun if you need her to cooperate. If Victor wants to save her, he can show his face."

Dorien made a face at me, but followed her inside. I heard him bark at her to sit down and shut up, but as Titus and I descended the staircase, her unhinged laughter boomed off the walls around us, filling the silent house with dread.

～

By the third night, the smell became unbearable. At dinner, everyone pushed their food around their plates. No one would eat a bite because my improvised fireplace stew tasted like decay, like death.

The smell clung to our clothes, our hair. It burned into our skin and burrowed into our eye sockets. We couldn't distract ourselves with parlor games or ghost stories any longer. A man was decomposing in the walls and we were forced to bear witness.

But still the storm refused to relent. I stuffed my feet into rain boots to stand outside on the porch every few hours just for a respite from the stench, but I could only handle a minute before I had to rush back into the warmth. We had no window with which to steal away into the forest to dig him a grave. Dorien and Ivan decided to head out on their own to try and make a start, but returned twenty minutes later after they'd nearly lost each other in the tree line.

At least Aroha was feeling stronger. We filled her in on the whole sordid story – everything we knew so far. She was still groggy and drugged, saying strange things that didn't make sense. But then she sang to us in the language of her people, and she was clear and bright, her words barbed and powerful. Her song gave me the strength to endure what I had to do next.

"It's my turn." I set down the book I'd been staring at for the last hour without reading a word, and went upstairs. I knocked on the door to Madame Usher's wing. "Titus?"

He'd been sitting with Usher for the last four hours. Ivan, Dorien, Elena, they'd all had their turn. They all said the same thing – that as much as they tried to ignore her, they couldn't block out the cruel words she spat at them, the secrets she dangled like carrots if only they would grant her freedom. Aroha was too weak to be of use now. That left one person who hadn't sat with her – me.

I didn't want to be alone in a room with Madame Usher and a gun. I didn't trust myself not to use it.

Titus still hadn't come to the door. I called him again. Nothing. I listened for footsteps on the other side, but all I heard was the wind howling against the house and the ticking of that infernal grandfather clock. My chest tightened. I fumbled in my dress for the other set of keys we found and shoved it into the slot.

I stepped into the room. My breath hitched as I crossed the receiving room, noticing Titus' huge footprints in the dust. He had crossed this room, but he never returned.

With a racing heart, I entered the sitting room. I'd only ever seen this room from the peepholes in Victor's tunnels. From this angle, I could see the holes had been cunningly hidden in gilded portraits of Usher family ancestors. A portrait of Victor hung over the piano, a crystal perfume bottle in his hands.

"Titus?"

He wasn't in this room, and neither was Madame Usher. Panic surged inside me. I grabbed a fire poker from the stand – noticing as I did the small ax for chopping kindling was also gone – and rushed into the bedroom.

"Titus?"

He was slumped in a chair beside the bed, his chin to his chest, his huge feet jutting out at odd angles. I dropped the poker and grabbed his face, tipping his head up. Glassy eyes stared back at me. A sheen of sweat made his skin cold and clammy. He was breathing, slow and shallow, but when I slapped his cheeks, he didn't stir.

Titus, no, no.

"What's she done to you?" I picked up a broken teacup from the floor and sniffed. It smelled faintly of pears. "You gullible bastard. You should've known not to accept anything from her. Fuck."

I searched his lap, but of course Dorien's gun was gone. I picked up the poker and made a search of the bedroom, but Madame Usher wasn't anywhere in her apartments. I rushed to the door and yelled downstairs.

"Dorien, Ivan, help me."

They were by my side a moment later. Dorien set down the silver candelabra he brought up and picked up Titus' wrist, watching it flop limply across his lap. "What happened?"

"Exactly what it looks like – Usher drugged him and took his gun." I glanced at the spot on the wall where the secret door was concealed in the paneling. "She's gone into the tunnels with Victor. She knew we closed the entrances, so they either have an escape route we don't know about, or they're hoping to hide and wait out the storm. We can't let them leave this house."

"We need weapons," Dorien said. Ivan nodded and darted away. He returned a few moments later carrying two curved rapier swords he'd torn from one of the antique displays. Ivan tossed one to Dorien. My hands tightened around my poker.

Dorien located a spring in the panel. The door didn't open – I assumed they locked it behind them – but Dorien sawed through the paneling with his sword, making a hole large enough to reach through with his hand and release the lock. His eyes met mine, their edges laced with danger. "Take Titus downstairs. Give him the same treatment as Aroha. Luckily, it looks like he hasn't had enough to hurt him, just to put him to sleep. I'll call you if I find anything—"

"I'm coming with you." I shoved past Ivan and lunged for the door. Dorien threw out his body to block me.

"Sprite, you can't—"

I shoved him into the hidden room. "You don't have time to argue with me."

"Fine." Dorien looked miserable, but he knew I was right. "Ivan, take Titus back to the Red Room and keep everyone there. Bar the door as best you can."

Ivan nodded, his sword swinging at his side like some kind of elfin prince as he lifted Titus' arm across his back and managed to drag him away. Dorien turned to me and shoved the candelabra into my hands. "It's just you and me now, Sprite."

He went first, sweeping the weapon around the room while I held out the candelabra to give us some light. I noticed some of the bottles on the shelves had been disturbed. *How much goddamn chloral does he have in here? I guess with his chemistry degree he can make as much as they need.*

We passed into the next room. The bed was unmade. Seeing a different book on the nightstand made my stomach turn. To think that the Ushers were somewhere in the walls of this house, trying to make their escape, while Titus was out cold and they'd nearly killed Aroha... After everything they'd done, they deserved to *burn*.

I won't let you get away with this.

"Careful, Sprite."

I surged ahead of Dorien in the long corridor. We had to find them. If they got away they'd take the truth with them. Dorien elbowed me out of the way to hoist himself up the ladder first. My veins itched with fire as I held up the candelabra to give him enough light. I needed to find them. I needed answers.

"We could really use Clare's help finding them," Dorien mused. "She chose a fine time to ghost us."

"Ha ha. Keep going up," I whispered. "To the attic." I didn't know why, but something told me they would go to the storage room and try to come down the attic stairs. We nailed a board across the door, but if they had the ax, they could just chop their way to freedom.

Dorien disappeared into the shaft. I handed him the candelabra and he held it from me as I pulled myself up after him. We crawled our way into the roof space, pulling ourselves along on our elbows. The candles flickered wildly as warm air rushed through the space, bringing with it the sickly, cloying scent of decay. I coughed, desperate to clear it from my lungs, and blew out one of the candles.

Dorien's boots twitched. "They broke through the door. They're in the house." He shuffled forward and kicked off the rest of the door, thrusting his weapon into the room while I tried to give him enough light.

"I can't see them. And the door is open." Dorien slid out, feet first, then reached back to help me. As I dragged myself to my feet and lifted the candelabra, my eyes caught the light glittering from two orbs in the corner of the room.

A pair of eyes glaring at us from the gloom.

My heart stopped beating.

She's here.

"This ends here, Usher." Dorien kept the tip of his sword trained on the figure as he inched forward. He displayed more confidence than I felt. The Ushers had the gun, which meant at least one of us was taking a bullet tonight. And I wasn't going to let it be Dorien.

I don't want to die.

"You want to fight in the shadows like a coward?" Dorien took another step. "I'm fine with that."

The shadow stepped into the square of light.

Dorien cursed.

I gasped as his features stood out against the pale moon. Those high, proud cheekbones. That strong jaw. And the eyes of clear crystal green.

My eyes.

"My love." Donovan de Winter staggered toward me, hand outstretched, fingers brushing my cheek. "My beautiful daughter. You're mine at last."

FAYE

It can't be him.
It's impossible.
It's a trick. He's a ghost.

But his hand on my cheek was warm. It had form, substance. His green eyes bore into mine as his features twisted in ecstasy – a distorted mirror of my own horror. His breath made a circle of mist in the chilly attic. His dark curls fell wild around his face.

If Donovan de Winter was a ghost, he was doing a fucking great job of pretending to be living.

"Stay back," Dorien rasped, jabbing the sword at my father's head. "I'm warning you."

"You don't know how long I've waited for this day." Tears rolled down Dad's cheeks. "Look at you, Faye. I've seen you from afar, but up close, you're even more beautiful than I expected."

I tried to speak, but words wouldn't come. There was no word in any language to describe what I felt as I let my father run his fingers across my cheek.

"I said, get away from her." Dorien grabbed Dad by his collar and slammed him against the wall. The wood creaked in protest as Dorien slammed the blade against his throat. "You don't deserve her. You don't deserve to breathe the same air as her."

"Daddy." The word escaped my throat before I could stop it. It rose up from a deep memory I'd locked away inside me, a desperate longing for him to wrap me in his arms and tell me I was good enough, talented enough, clever enough, beautiful enough, to deserve his love.

Dorien winced as though I physically slapped him with the word. Tears welled in my eyes and broke through my defenses. *It's him. It's my daddy.*

I wanted to hate him. I wanted to curl my hands around his throat and choke the life from him for what he did to us. But the little girl inside me who desperately wanted to be worthy of him, she cried and wept and keened because her daddy had come back to her at long last.

It was too much.

"Faye, my love, don't cry. Please don't cry. I'm here now. Daddy's here."

"You don't get to say that to her. You weren't there when she needed you. You weren't there when she cried herself to sleep in my arms because her daddy never loved her." Dorien's eyes flicked to me. "Remember, Faye? Remember what he did to you. What he's doing to you right now."

I swallowed hard, swallowed back the little girl who wanted to fall into his arms and have him kiss away her pain. Dorien was right. I had him, and Titus, and Ivan. I didn't need my scumbag of a father.

"Start talking," Dorien shoved the blade against his skin. Dad swallowed, and a thin line of blood bloomed on his skin. "Where are the Ushers?"

His eyes closed. "We heard you coming and Gizella ran downstairs, but I wanted to see you."

"And Victor?"

Dad looked confused. "Victor Usher is dead."

Victor Usher is dead.

And just like that, the pieces slotted into place.

We thought Victor was the one hiding in the walls, spying on us for his wife. Ivan said he recognized his voice through the wall, and the books in the lab were in his handwriting. But it was my dad. He was the one who left the fairy tale book for me to find. He smashed my violin so that I'd find his Becker, and he played the haunting music in the storage room night after night, keeping me awake so he could duet with me.

Even now, I was still just an extension of Donovan de Winter's own narcissism. He made me dance for his amusement while he hid in the walls with his lover. *But for what?*

"You're lying," Dorien snarled. "We opened Victor's grave. We know it's empty."

"He's not lying, Dorien." I stepped in close, so close I could smell the rot and dust that clung to my father's worn clothing. Beneath it, the sage and bergamot scent that belonged to my memories assaulted my nostrils. I closed my eyes, letting the box of memories inside me fall open and the pieces of my childhood tumble free.

Or rather, all the pieces that didn't include him. All the times he missed my birthday parties or recitals because he was off doing his own music. All the times he looked right through me like I was the ghost. All those nights my mom came home from her third job with bags under her eyes and horrors heaped on her shoulders, while he came home smelling of Madame Usher's sickly floral perfume.

I remembered my mother waking up at 6AM after a grueling night shift to hide Easter eggs around our apartment. I remembered her beaming at me from the front row of every recital, and taking me and Dorien out for ice cream when his parents forgot to pick him up. I remembered building blanket forts and shrieking at horror films and stuffing my face with tamales and churros until I threw up. I remembered love that burst from my veins like spring flowers. And none of that love belonged to him.

Mom gave me everything so I would never need him. And now, I needed every ounce of strength she'd given me to face this monster.

"My baby girl," he whimpered.

"How could you do this to me?" The memories churned inside me, becoming a storm of rage and power. "You *chose* to live in these walls as a ghost, didn't you? You chose her over me. I'm *not* your baby girl."

"No, no, no. You don't understand!" he cried. "I had to leave. I had to leave to save you. I lost *everything*. You don't know what it's like, the big tours, the stardom, the glitter and glamor. I got swept away by it. I didn't see the finances. I thought my good fortune would just go on and on forever, I'd live for the moment and pay them back with the next record, the next check, the next big award. Gizella encouraged me – she wanted me to have everything I deserved, everything I earned. She introduced me to her friends who had money they were willing to lend to artists like me. But every dollar I spent was soaked in blood, and I didn't understand that until it was too late. I borrowed from the wrong people, and they were coming after you. You and Marguerite. They would hurt you if I didn't pay. Gizella agreed to help me pay back my loans, but only if I walked away from you forever. I thought it was for the best. I was such a fuck-up that I'd put your lives at risk. You were better off without me."

Tears spilled down his cheeks. Beside me, Dorien breathed deep and jagged. I touched my hands to his shoulders. I needed his strength, his fire. I needed his strong body to hold me upright because I was in danger of floating away.

"And look at you. I was right all along. You were better off without me. You've become so beautiful, so accomplished. Marguerite must be so proud." He reached up to touch my face again. "I never should have brought you here. But I missed you so much."

What?

I jerked away, as if he slapped me with his words.

"What do you mean, you brought Faye here?" Dorien's eyes blazed. His sword arm twitched. He was on the edge of losing control, and I didn't think I could stop him even if I wanted to, and I wasn't sure I wanted to.

"Of course I did. I was tormented being away from you, my darling, missing out on seeing you growing up. This was just supposed to be a temporary arrangement. Gizella had a plan for my comeback. We had to pay my debt in full, she had to divorce Victor, and we had to fix things with the Triumvirate so no one could come after me in the future. But then everything took so much longer than we thought. Months turned into years and I was still a ghost in the walls and then finally, *finally*, Victor got sick and I could at least live most of my time in her private wing."

"You...you lived in the walls of Manderley for *ten years?*" I couldn't believe it. I'd been in those claustrophobic spaces. No wonder his eyes looked wild, and his speech was so erratic and poorly constructed – not the immaculately tailored charmer I remembered.

"It took Gizella that long to pay off my debts. Don't blame her, blame the greedy thugs who kept asking for more, more, more, even after all she and Victor had done for them in the past. And then Victor died and I was ready to make my return to the world, but she had a plan. She had the perfect project for me, but we needed to wait until all the pieces were in place." His Adam's apple bobbed. "Everything she's done has been for me, for the music. She's so different from Marguerite, who never understood us, Faye. A good woman, but she never understood us. We need more than good people. We need fire. We need blood. Your man here understands that."

"Don't talk about my mother like that," I growled. "She has fire enough to burn the world."

"But her fire was for earthly things. Not for the heavens. Not for music. She didn't understand me like Gizella did." His eyes flicked away from mine, staring into the shadows, and I wondered if he was deliberately speaking in the past tense. He sucked in a quick breath, and continued.

"But the years without sunlight, without people, without stimulation...I was going mad. I could only play music when Victor was away on tour or outside in the woods with Harrison. I had to sit in the walls and listen to clumsy students flub their notes and have awkward sex. Gizella kept saying things would change, but they never did. And then Clare moved into the attic. I was lonely, and so was she." His eyes flicked toward the bedroom Clare had before me, and the hole he made in the wall so he could watch her. "The peephole wasn't for perverted reasons. I just wanted to see when she was up there so I could talk to her. That's all we did, just talk. Oh, we wrote a song together. You've been playing it with me."

Bile stung my throat. All these years I'd mourned him, cried for him, raged against his mysterious disappearance, and he was here comforting another girl, being the friend he'd never been to me.

"You told Clare you were a ghost," I whispered.

"It was easier than explaining. I couldn't very well have her run off and tell someone and spoil Gizella's plan. But Clare was clever – she figured out who I was. She compared the composition we made to some of my recordings. She saw my portrait in the hall and asked about me and found out about Gizella's affair. She was going to tell you, Dorien. She was going to tell everyone. And all these years I lived in the walls would have been for nothing."

"So you pushed her down the stairs." Dorien's jaw locked. His sword arm trembled with rage.

"I didn't mean for her to die! I wanted to talk to her in person, show her who I really was. I wanted to tell the truth. I lost the chance with my real daughter, but maybe with Clare, I could love someone the way they deserved to be loved." His shoulders trembled. "I'm so so sorry. I wanted to show her that she wasn't alone, but when I stepped out of the wall I frightened her, and she fell backward and I—I —I—didn't mean for her to die!"

His body shuddered with silent sobs. Dorien worked his jaw. A bead of my father's blood rolled off the tip of the sword.

"Keep talking," I said. "We need to hear everything. We need to understand."

Dad sniffed. "After Clare's death, I didn't want this life anymore. But Gizella told me she worked too hard for me to back out now. I knew I wouldn't survive another year without someone else to love. I told Gizella I could not live another day in these walls, listening to inferior musicians get the opportunities my daughter and Clare should have had. I packed my things. I told her I was leaving, and then she said that if I stayed, she'd make sure you came to Manderley, that I'd see you again. She said she would bring you to me, but it would be your choice if you stayed. She really did try to bring us together, my darling. I think if things had worked out the way they were supposed to, in time you could have loved Gizella like a mother."

He's mad. He's mad if he thinks for a second I could have loved a woman who took my father from me, forced him to live in the walls, and then dangled me in front of him only to torment me into leaving. Does he not realize what she was trying to do? She didn't want me here, but she couldn't kick me out because she would lose him. It had to be my choice to leave. That's why she enlisted Broken Muse to torture me – she was trying to drive me away.

Dorien watched my face, his eyes darkening as he realized what he'd been part of. Every move of Madame Usher's was a carefully designed gambit to keep my father in line.

"She poisoned Mom to bring me here," I gasped out. "Did you know that? Did you help her? I saw that lab back there…"

"The lab belonged to Victor, and his father before him, for designing their perfumes – although he hardly used it. I would never hurt Marguerite. You needed her." Tears rolled down his cheeks. "I did everything I could to make your stay at Manderley happy, even when I figured out what Gizella was doing. I played music for you and with you. I gave you gifts. I watched every performance, all those performances I missed. I was a better father as a ghost than I ever was in real life."

I gulped back a sob. He was right. And it hurt so so much that he was right. It felt like Dorien's blade slicing through my chest over and over again.

I told Dorien once that I loved him and hated him in equal measure, and it was true then, because of how much he hurt me. But hate is part of love – you can only hate someone if you first loved them with your whole heart. And I *hated* my father. I hated him with a white-hot rage that burned my eyes to embers.

And I loathed myself for my hatred, because it was my weakness. Because beneath it, my love still festered like rot that couldn't be cut out. My weakness made me stand here and listen to a man utterly incapable of love try to justify a lifetime of hurt and neglect. It made me lock eyes with Dorien Valencourt, a boy who only *ever* loved me, who done stupid and reckless and dangerous things because he loved me, and wish and wish and wish for my daddy, as if my father's love could somehow make whole the wounds his neglect inflicted.

Everything made sense now.

It was my father all this time.

Nothing would ever make sense again.

"Daddy?"

The word choked on my tongue – a desperate little girl wishing to be more than an afterthought.

Dorien sighed. He tore his blade from Dad's throat and stepped back, his hand searching for mine in the dark. Blood dribbled down Dad's stained blazer as he staggered toward me, arms outstretched. He wanted to hold me.

I *ached* to be held. I hated that I ached.

I *wished*.

Daddy.

"My Faye." Tears mingled with the blood streaming from his wound. "All those years I thought I loved Gizella, but I was wrong. So wrong. Clare taught me that I never loved you the way you deserved. I want to be a good dad to you once again—"

His voice cut off abruptly.

"Daddy?"

His face contorted in silent agony. He tried to speak, but all that came out was a ruptured gurgle.

He crumpled to the floor.

I screamed as my flickering candles illuminated a dark pool of blood spreading around his still body, and the small kindling ax buried in his back.

A shadowed figure loomed in the doorway. Madame Usher leaned into the light, a sadistic smile on her face.

Dorien

"You killed him," I said. I tried to sound matter-of-fact about it, as if we were chatting about the weather. I needed to keep this shit calm so I could get Faye away from Madame Usher.

It was just as well I was doing the talking, because Faye looked as though if she opened her mouth, she would scream. I tried not to think about the body of her father at my feet, or about my own parents hanging from the cross with nails through their hands and their stomachs sliced open. *We* were alive, and I needed to keep it that way.

"He was weak." Madame Usher fixed her eyes on the tip of my sword, which I kept pointed at her throat. A lifetime of exclusive boarding schools had turned me into a mediocre fencer, but it didn't take much skill to drive a sharp blade through flesh. And I'd do it – I saw in her eyes she knew I'd do it to save Faye.

Sprite, I'm so sorry.

Faye leaned against me, her whole body trembling, her eyes burning with tears she didn't want to cry for the man who fucked her up and fucked her over. I wished I could take away the pain tearing her apart and make it my own. I wish I could feel everything she felt right now so she didn't have to. I already knew that pain so well. Sprite and I were too much alike. We both spent our whole lives looking for the approval of people who didn't love us, didn't deserve us, and now they were dead and we didn't even get the comfort of anger. They were dead and we still wanted them to love us.

Faye screamed as Madame Usher kicked her father. Madame Usher whipped her hand to the pocket of her dress to retrieve my pistol, which she aimed at Faye's head. "After all I did for him, he comes crawling back to you, begging for love as if he had been bereft of it? What about *my* love? What about everything I sacrificed?"

"You took him from his family, locked him up to wither away as a ghost in the walls, and tried to destroy his daughter in front of his eyes," I shot back. My hand twitched. I was holding the sword with my injured hand, and my pinkie finger wasn't up to the task. I had to hope Madame Usher didn't notice. I used my other hand to shove Faye behind me, placing my body between her and the barrel of the gun, between her and the rapidly-spreading pool of her father's blood. "You're evil. How can anyone love a monster like you?"

Behind me, Faye whimpered.

Madame Usher's face reddened with rage. She kept her body turned toward me, but her poisoned words – and her aim – were for Faye.

"You think you're so amazing, just because you carry his blood," she hissed, stomping her boot in the crimson pool at her feet. "You see now how easily blood can be spilled, spoiled, destroyed. You may wear his name like a fashion accessory, but you'll never have his talent. You and that ungrateful mother of yours tried to drain the life from him, always so clingy, so demanding of his attention. I had to get him away from you both, don't you see? He was becoming distracted by your petty concerns. He had greater things to do, to be."

"It's you who doesn't understand," I cried back. "By depriving him of his family, you prevented him from becoming the great musician he could have been. It wasn't Marguerite and Faye who made him crave the finer things, the fame, the trappings of success. You blinded him with baubles and made him into a shallow, uninspired shell of greatness. The best art is about truth – it's the mundane made beautiful, the human experiences that are uniquely ours and yet also shared by everyone. Frida Kahlo painted flowers so they wouldn't die. But what truth could Donovan de Winter breathe to life in his art if he lived a shallow, heartless lie? You killed his talent, not them."

"Is that what you think?" she spat back. "Then you are even more arrogant and oblivious than I imagined. You with your pampered life and your songs of teenage angst. You're nothing but a foolish child. Everything you ever wanted has been handed to you on a silver platter. You've never known pain or hardship. I gave those gifts to you, and you squandered them, as you squandered every opportunity you've had in life. You've never had to make a tough choice or make a sacrifice for your art, and that's why you will never surpass him. Great art comes from hardship, from loss, from *longing*. Donovan de Winter needed to lose everything before he could be *magnificent*."

"But he never became magnificent, did he?" I didn't dare break her gaze to look down at Donovan, but I could feel his blood oozing beneath the soles of my shoes. "He withered away inside Manderley's wall. You never gave him the chance to be reborn."

"He was going to make his return," she said. "I had it all planned out, a way for him to make his mark on the musical world. You'd done so much of my work for me, you beautiful, simple boy. But first, you needed to prove you were worthy of him. I needed you to be absolutely loyal to me, to the house of Usher. I took care of Marguerite, and I gave you one simple assignment – drive Faye away from him, get rid of his last distraction."

"That's what this is about?" I snorted as her words sank in. "You did all this because you wanted Donovan to join Broken Muse?"

Did she think we would just let Faye's once-dead father into the band, a band made famous from songs I wrote about longing for Faye? But then, Madame Usher didn't have to convince us. She had manipulated everything behind the scenes so expertly that we would have had no choice but to agree. Donovan would be in Broken Muse, or we would be utterly ruined.

She's insane. She's an absolute fucking psychopath.

"He would have made you legendary." Madame frowned at me. "You would have gone on to fame and fortune the likes of which even you could only dream of. And I would have been behind you, managing it all. It was perfect. But you had to mess everything up by falling in love with *her*."

She spat at Faye, who shuddered against me.

Madame Usher smiled, and it was almost a sad smile, but I was certain she had no capacity for true emotion. Her eyes were black pinpricks, without light or warmth. She pulled back the safety and pointed the gun square at my head. "But never mind that now. It is time to put everything right."

She squeezed the trigger.

DORIEN

My eyes slammed shut. I couldn't look down the barrel to the triumphant grin of Madame Usher as she took my life.

I love you Faye. I love you, Jacob. I'm so sorry—

But the shot didn't come. There was no loud bang, no searing pain, no final moment of clarity before I rushed toward the light. There was a faint clicking nose, and a frustrated grunt.

I opened my eyes.

Madame Usher squeezed the trigger again. *Click, click, click.* Nothing happened.

"Dorien," Faye's voice cracked. "Did you by change purchase a gun, but no ammunition?"

"I thought they came pre-loaded?" I cocked an eyebrow at Madame Usher. "I guess you've been foiled by my stupidity."

Madame Usher *snarled.* She bent down and jerked the ax from Donovan's back. Faye screamed as blood spurted from the wound, splattering us. An arc of crimson decorated the front of Usher's dress, a few speckles dotting the pale skin of her neck.

I lunged at her, but she dodged around my sword and swung down with her ax. I shoved Faye back. The ax hooked on my shirt, ripping the fabric and whispering against my skin.

Faye screamed again as her back pressed into the wall. Madame Usher's grin was wild, triumphant. I thrust at her face, but the angle was wrong, weak. She whacked the sword with her ax and knocked it out of my hands.

Fuck. Fuck.

I cast around for something else to use as a weapon. She roared as she came at us, ax raised. I picked up the first thing I laid hands on – the portrait of Donovan – and swung it at her just as the ax came down, right toward my skull—

The ax splintered the wooden frame and tore through the canvas. Madame Usher's body toppled forward, thrown off-balance by the momentum. I lunged for my sword. Usher roared and slammed down on top of me, her bony elbow crushing my neck.

"Sprite—" I gasped, my fingers reaching, reaching, brushing the sword's hilt but not close enough to grab it. Madame ground her elbow into me, pushing the air from my lungs. Red welts danced in front of my eyes. Blood rushed in my ears. *Any second now I'll pass out and—*

"When I think how many times I longed to slip a little poison into your food," Madame purred in my ear, wrapping her other arm around my neck and bending my head back. The gun was still in her fingers, so close but completely out of reach. My chest burned like I'd swallowed hot coals. Pain rushed my temples as I fought for air, but I could already feel the tips of my fingers, my legs, going numb. Her voice sounded far away, and I wasn't sure if I heard her words or just imagined them as the dark at the edge of my vision closed in. "My husband kept impeccable diaries – the one helpful thing he did in his whole useless life. It was too easy to follow his instructions and use plants from the garden to poison Marguerite. But if you hadn't used the chloral on me, I never would have thought to make a supply for my own purposes. Do you think that oaf Titus will ever wake up? It's a pity he's not here to save you..."

Her voice trailed off as red blossomed over my eyes. I thought I must have finally run out of air. My chest no longer burned and an ethereal white light burst in the center of the red and rushed toward me. *All I have to do is head toward the light...*

But I could hear someone screaming. And no one should be screaming in heaven, unless...

Madame Usher was no longer on top of me. My chest heaved, my lips burned as I gasped and sucked and gorged myself on air. Every breath burned, but I was breathing, I was alive and the light...

The light was Clare.

She glowed with a pale light that had no source. She floated across the room, moving toward us with deliberate, menacing slowness, her green eyes filled with malicious delight, her mouth open in a ghastly cry of defiance.

Madame Usher was screaming.

I coughed, my lungs on fire. My fingers closed around the hilt of the sword.

Madame didn't try to stop me. She was frozen, glaring at the ghost as though she could stop Clare with the force of her hatred. "You ungrateful wretch. I took you in when no one else would. I gave you a home, a job. I even let that dolt Radcliffe give you lessons. And you had to go and turn him against me. You were lucky you fell down the stairs, because you didn't succumb to the arsenic I'd been rubbing on your violin strings."

Clare stretched out her fingers toward Madame Usher's neck, her blackened mouth opening, yawning. The temperature dropped to freezing, and even though we knew Clare couldn't move objects, that all the ghostly things were really Donovan's doing, I believed this time may be an exception.

Madame Usher staggered backward, just out of reach. "That's right, every time you and Donovan betrayed me, you killed yourself. So I know you can't hurt me."

Clare's fingers brushed her neck, and Madame's eyes bugged out. She flinched away. She *felt* Clare's icy grasp.

You killed me, the air whispered. *You killed me and now you will pay.*

"Get away from me!" Madame Usher grabbed the candelabra from Faye's frozen fingers and threw it at Clare. It sailed right through her, hitting the rolled-up rug in the corner of the room, which burst into flames.

"Shit." I leaped to my feet and tried to tip the carpet on its side to smother the flames, but all I succeeded in doing was spreading the fire to the boxes stacked behind it. Behind me, Madame Usher screamed. Faye stood behind her, still staring blankly at her father's broken body. She didn't seem to have even registered Clare's presence at all.

"Faye." I held out my hand to her. "I need you to come here."

"Daddy." She pulled on his boot. "We can't leave him here. We have to save him."

Fuck. Shit. Fuck.

My strong, beautiful, fearsome Sprite. In the last ten minutes, she'd learned enough truths to undo her utterly, and now I needed to pull her away from the body of the one man she'd spent the last ten years hoping to see alive.

"Faye." I choked on her name as the room started to fill with smoke. I stumbled over Donovan's body and grabbed her shoulders, giving her a gentle shake. "I wish I had the time to give you the mental breakdown you so desperately deserve. But we have to leave. *Now.*"

I wrapped my arm around her shoulders and dragged her toward the door, turning her away from Clare just as Madame Usher let out a bloodcurdling scream. I wanted so badly to turn around and witness Clare's revenge, because it would be beautiful and so, so deserved. I wished I could jerk the pistol from her fingers, because I didn't like turning my back on a woman with a gun. But I had to get Faye out.

As I staggered out of the storage room, a dark shape appeared in the narrow stairwell. Faye screamed as Titus grabbed her around the waist and threw her over his shoulder. He shot me a look fraught with pain before stumbling back toward the stairs. He gripped the banister with both hands and half slid, half shuffled, down. *He must've woken up, then.*

At the bottom, Ivan tried to take Faye from him, but he growled incoherently and continued his shuffle toward the main staircase. By now, I could smell the smoke curling through the air, and the orange flames leaped so high they provided up a square of flickering light. Madame Usher's screams became one long, agonized wail – a sound I knew I'd hear in my nightmares for the rest of my days.

"What's going on?" Elena cried out, taking the stairs two at a time to meet us as we shuffled down. "I smell smoke."

"No time to explain. The house is on fire." I shoved her toward the front door. "We have to go. Ivan, get Aroha."

"What about Madame Usher?" Elena's eyes bore into mine, and I knew what she was really asking.

"We leave her."

Ivan returned with Aroha under his arm. She bent double, her body racked with a coughing fit. I pressed the sleeve of my shirt to my mouth and nose as the acrid smoke began to sting. Titus held a squabbling Faye over his shoulder as he threw open the door. "It's no use," he said groggily, surveying the solid wall of snow piled the full height of the door. He punched it a couple of times. "There's too much snow. We'll be dead before I can dig through this."

Not to mention the fact that you barely have use of your arms and legs, I thought but didn't say.

"The kitchen." I raced ahead, ducking into the kitchen and turning the handle on the back door. It pushed open with ease. I yelled in triumph for the others to follow, but as I did, a giant clump of snow fell loose from the eaves above and dropped in the doorway. I staggered back as an avalanche of snow slid into the kitchen, splattering my legs with wet ice and completely blocking our exit.

"What now?" Elena cried. "The smoke is getting thicker."

Upstairs, something crashed. I could no longer hear Madame screaming. I whirled around, staring at the faces of my stricken friends. Faye was usually the one who had clever ideas, but her father's death had destroyed her, and I needed to step the fuck up. *Think, Dorien. We could try smashing a window, maybe even going back upstairs and sliding off the porch roof onto the snow—*

"The tunnels," Faye whispered.

Okay, so maybe she was still our beautiful, clever Faye.

"Yeah, nah. I'm not getting into some rank-ass tunnel while the house is burning," Aroha shot back. "We don't know if there's an outdoor exit. We'll get stuck and burn."

"No, we can get outside," Faye argued. "The night of the parents' recital, Daddy came from the house and followed Dorien through the woods. Then he had to get back into the house to leave those items for me in the kitchen without Harrison or any of the other party guests seeing. There's an outside exit, I'm sure of it—"

"It was on the map," Ivan said. "I remember it clearly. It goes from the Red Room to down beside the stream."

I raced into the Red Room and tore the boards we nailed over the hidden entrance. I drew back my leg and kicked the paneled wall with everything I had. It didn't even make a dent. Titus shoved me out of the way and threw his body at the wall. With a crack, the wood splintered. Titus tossed the pieces away, revealing a dark hole leading along the wall.

"Quickly." Titus grabbed Faye's arm, pulling her close to him and caging her in his arms. She seemed to be free of her father's spell, and with him behind her she wouldn't be able to run back for her father's body. Faye accepted another silver candlestick from Aroha and stepped into the gloom. As she disappeared, Titus turned sideways to squeeze his broard shoulders inside. He gasped as he had to wriggle to fit in the narrow gap. Ivan helped Elena inside next. That left me to help Aroha.

The room was dense with smoke now. I could barely see Aroha's body as I grabbed her arm. She shook her head. "I'm staying."

"No, you're not."

"This is the only place I ever did something worthwhile," she muttered. "My insides are on fire. I'd rather die here than in a bloody mess in a hospital bed."

"Don't be stupid." I yanked her close. "This house has taken too many victims."

She struggled against me, but I picked her up and plonked her in the hole, climbing in after her so she could only move forward. I knew Aroha could kick my ass if she needed to. She didn't want to stay behind. She wanted someone to save her. Didn't we all?

I shoved her into the tunnel, kicking at her heels to make her run faster. Inside the walls, the rotting smell was unbearable. It mingled with the smoke to create a poison that made my whole body burn. Every step was agony as my lungs and stomach cramped and disgorged, and my eyes had clamped shut with protest so I couldn't see a thing. I kept moving into the darkness, not knowing if we were even going in the right direction, but trusting Faye.

"I see a doorway," Faye called from somewhere above. I picked up the pace, urging Aroha onward as more crashes sounded behind us. Light punched the air around Aroha's shoulders, and I found my breath came a little easier, the burn a little duller.

Frigid cold air enveloped me, but it was blissfully fresh and free of burning. The world opened up around me and my Barker Blacks scuffed in fluffy snow.

We collapsed into a heap in the snow, holding each other as we emptied our lungs and stomachs of the foulness of Manderley. I gasped in mouthfuls of frigid mountain air. Behind us, the fire blazed, an unholy conflagration that consumed the house from the inside out.

Manderley was burning.

In all my nightmares, I'd never imagined such a sight. We huddled in a tight circle to warm ourselves as we watched. The fire spread through the rooms on the first floor, tearing at the ancient drapes and blowing out the windows with a sound like gunshots. Flames licked like orange tongues as they eviscerated the ancient house of Usher. Stone walls broke apart as the heavy wooden ceiling beams collapsed upon them, and the beautiful carved wooden gables dashed themselves against the ground.

Madame Usher is inside.

So is my father.

I've always thought of fire as a destructive force, wild in its hunger and undiscerning in its tastes. But as Manderley burned beneath a raging sky, I saw something else. I saw that fire *cleansed* – it burned away the rot, the evil, the bad seeds, leaving behind a clean slate.

What we saw tonight was the exorcism of Manderley.

As we stared up at the burning building, I thought I caught the faint snatch of music on the wind. The same song I'd played in my room at night, the song my father wrote with Clare, the notes twining in the breeze – their funeral dirge.

We made our way to the broken fountain just as the porch collapsed, sending up a cloud of black smoke that burned my lungs. The flames tore through the building, gutting the second floor, moving like dancers – a living fire to brighten this dark night, transforming the house into an altar where all the ghosts of Madame's deeds sacrificed for absolution.

The sound of it was incredible – the roar rumbling through the valley, the howl of the wind tearing through the skeleton, the crackle like drums beating, and the crash and shatter of beautiful objects consigned to ashes. And above it all, the sickening melody of a horrible, inhuman scream.

"I see her." Ivan pointed to a window in the east wing. It took me a moment to recognize her face staring out of the orange flames.

Madame Usher.

The moment froze in time, like a movie paused in my memory to provide one final horror – Madame Usher's body wreathed in flames, her black skirts ablaze, her hands black and her mouth open in a scream of bitter terror. She met my eyes and for a moment, she recognized me. She saw that she had lost.

Then she fell.

The crunch as she hit the ground would haunt my dreams for the rest of my life.

She didn't move.

We rushed to her. Ivan rolled her over, beating out the flames with his foot. There was no saving her. Her neck bent at an impossible angle, and her eyes peered up at me, glassy and unseeing.

She was gone.

Numbness settled in my veins. I should have been happy. She was evil, and now she could never hurt another human soul. But I felt nothing for her, only an ache in my heart.

She did all of it for love. For the love of my father. But that love corrupted her, turning her heart into coal. And I felt certain my heart would become coal, too.

I turned my gaze to the window where she'd fallen, startled to see another face peering down. The figure held out both hands, as if she had just shoved something heavy out the window. Piercing green eyes, a cute turned-up nose, and a blackened mouth outlined in orange flames.

Clare.

The flames crackled and moved, and a second figure joined her. My father put his arm around Clare's shoulders, pulling her head into him, the way he never did with me.

She smiled. And it was the most beautiful smile I'd ever seen.

Fire blazed around them, and they disappeared.

"We should get to Harrison," I said, balling my fists into my eye sockets in a vain attempt to hold the tears inside. "He has a satellite phone."

Because while cleansing fire is a good thing when it comes to creepy houses and their malevolent mistresses, I do not want to see this thing burn through the pristine, beautiful forest.

Dorien held me as we trudged through the snow, stepping into the ruts Titus made with his body as he shoved his way ahead of us. Wind blasted the skin from our faces, and for every step forward we seemed to be blown three steps back. We had to circle around to the front of the house, taking a wide berth as the wall of heat shoved us away from Manderley, and then make our way down the drive. Our candles had blown out long ago, and we followed each other blindly until Titus called out with triumph and I could just make out the glow of light from Harrison's windows, so very faint and far away.

The wall of heat rose up behind us, and fear clawed at my chest. If the forest caught fire, we'd be in big trouble. We had to get word to the authorities. Aroha still needed medical attention.

Maybe there's a chance they could put out the fire before it spreads.

I couldn't think about it. I had to focus on putting one foot in front of the other.

Finally, *finally*, we reached Harrison's gatehouse. Snow piled into my boots as I swung myself up the steps.

"Harrison." I slammed into the door, pounding with my fists. Nothing moved inside, but the fire flickered brightly from the hearth. "It's Faye. Open up. Manderley is on fire!"

Nothing moved or stirred inside. Manderley's destruction reflected in the window, but when I cupped my hands against the glass I thought I could see the fire crackling in his hearth. "Harrison?" I stepped down and banged on the high window of his living room. "It's Faye. Please, help us."

"He might've fallen asleep. Watch out." Titus wrapped his scarf around his fist and punched out the glass pane in the kitchen window. He reached through and unlocked the door. We piled inside, drawn toward the roaring fire. Two chairs were pulled close to the blaze, facing the flames. Harrison leaped up from one, his face a storm.

"How dare you break in here?" he boomed, his face beet red. "Get out!"

I never knew our kindly groundskeeper had such demons in him. Dorien rounded Harrison's chair, his eyes wide. Harrison stormed toward him, arms outstretched, roaring with defiance, and I honestly thought he was going to flatten us all.

"We're sorry for barging in, but you have to help us. Madame Usher is dead, Manderley is on fire, and my father...his body...We need to use your satellite phone to call—" I stopped short as Harrison shoved Dorien from the room. Dorien was fighting him, trying to force his shoulder into Harrison's gut to get around him.

"You ungrateful, wretched boy. You've ruined *everything*."

"Faye, look in the chair," Dorien cried out as Harrison pushed him out the door and down into the snow. "Look in the other chair."

"Don't!" Harrison barked. I jerked my head around, but all I could see was the wingback with the top of someone's head reclined there, and a thin, skeletal hand on the rest, the fingers curled around an empty whiskey glass. Harrison had a guest, but why hadn't he moved—

Wait a second...

I took a step closer. Bile rose in my chest as I moved into the light of the fire, as I saw the terrifying sight that Dorien warned me about.

A human skeleton had been arranged perfectly in the chair, its feet in fluffy slippers, the fingers of its other hand clutching a fat cigar. The bones had been lovingly cleaned and dressed in pressed trousers and a plaid shirt. In some places, bits of leathery skin and gristle still clung to them, and I could see wires and wooden pegs propping the body in position.

The skull of Victor Usher grinned up at me, his eye sockets black as night.

FAYE

"Harrison," I choked out. "What's going on?"

He stood in the doorway and plucked his rifle from its rack. He hung his head with sadness as he loaded two bullets into the chamber. "You shouldn't have barged in here like this, Miss Faye. A man's business is his own."

"That's Victor Usher, isn't it?" Dorien cried from outside. "You dug up Victor Usher's corpse. But why?"

"Why? Because he never should have died!" Harrison roared. "That witch never loved him, but she strung him along in a loveless marriage because if she lost him, she'd lose this house. After Victor's parents died, we thought we would finally have a chance to be together. All those years waiting, pretending, wishing for a world that would accept us. And when Victor's parents finally bit the dust, we thought we would be able to live out our days together in the solitude of Manderley. But she wouldn't dream of it. She refused to divorce him, to accept the generous settlement he offered to be rid of her tyranny. She used his secret against him, binding him to her in a marriage of misery while she finally took him from me."

He's in love with Victor Usher.

Of course he was. I couldn't believe I hadn't realized it earlier. The way he talked about Victor and the Usher family, about growing up in this house and walking the grounds and hunting together. I remembered the photograph hanging in Madame Usher's office – the wedding portrait with Harrison on a ladder behind them, glaring at the newlyweds with untamed hatred. *He was glaring at Madame Usher because she took his love from him.*

"Manderley died with Victor," Harrison sobbed. "The flowers haven't bloomed since he drew his last breath. I tried everything to make this place blossom again, but she prefers it to be rot and weeds."

Tears rolled down Harrison's cheeks as he snapped the barrel closed and stepped toward the door. "I just wanted the time that had been stolen from us. I was going to put him back in the mausoleum, but I couldn't bear to part with him."

He sighed, his shoulders shaking, as he raised the gun and pointed it at Dorien.

"Faye, I'm so so sorry," Harrison said. "I've tried to protect you all from her evil, but if you tell them about me, they'll take me away from Manderley. I'll lose him, and I can't bear to be apart from him. So you see what I have to do."

He lifted the gun and aimed it at Dorien's chest.

FAYE

"Wait. You don't have to do this," I cried. "We all understand what it's like to have to love in secret. We all know what it's like to lose someone. We won't tell a soul what we saw tonight, will we?"

Dorien, Titus, Ivan, Elena, and Aroha all shook their heads.

"Please, Harrison, don't do this. It's not you. You're not a murderer. You—"

Harrison sighed. "I'm sorry, Miss Faye. it's too late. I promise I'll make it quick. Not like Madame Usher. She would have you suffer out of spite." He glanced out the window. "The fire will hide the evidence."

He raised the rifle again. Dorien blew me a kiss, his eyes wide and dark and impossibly sad.

I screamed as a shot rang out.

Titus

Ow.

Fuck.

Ow.

FAYE

Everything happened so fast.

I surged forward as Titus leaped in front of Dorien, his hands wrapped around the barrel of the rifle. My gentle giant collapsed, clutching his abdomen. The snow around him turned pink with blood. Harrison froze, stunned by the scene, and Ivan took the chance to tackle him, knocking him into the snow.

"Titus, no."

I fell at his side, pulling his braids away from his face. He peered up at me, his eyes swimming with pain. *No. This can't be how it ends.*

He's not dying tonight. He's not. I forbid it.

"Faye..." the word gurgled in Titus' throat. Blood dribbled from the wound. He pawed at the snow, trying to grab the rifle that had fallen beside him. But his body was slipping into shock and he couldn't make his hand work properly. The pink snow grew around him.

I grabbed his hand and held it to my chest, pressing it against my heart. "Titus, stop. Please, listen to me. You have to—"

My words died as blood spurted from the corner of his mouth, splattering the front of his shirt.

That's not good. That can't be good.

Titus closed his eyes as he battled with his demons. He jerked his hand from mine and fell on the gun, trying to pick it up, but someone knocked him out of the way. Before I could scream, Ivan tore the rifle from Titus, flung his body around, and fired.

BANG.

The shot rang out across the valley, echoing through the mountains. Harrison's body slumped into the snow. He didn't move.

"No," Titus murmured. "I was supposed to carry that guilt. I was..."

His eyes fluttered closed, and his body slumped in the snow.

"No, Titus." I held his head up and slapped his cheek, pulled on his eyelids, kissed his freezing lips. "Wake up. You have to wake up, you beautiful, impossible man."

Tears froze on my cheeks. I knew what he'd tried to do. In his dying moments Titus had decided to kill Harrison to save us all, because he didn't want any of us to have to live with the guilt of pulling the trigger. He never once in his whole life put himself before others. And he wouldn't do that even at the edge of death.

You can't die. Not now. You're not allowed. We were supposed to have our whole lives ahead of us. We were supposed to make music together and have a beautiful family and travel the world and you can't die you can't you can't—

"Fuck." Dorien crawled forward, lifting Titus' drooping head. "Man, you have to stay awake, okay? Please, stay awake for Faye. Stay awake for me. Can you do that?"

Dorien knew Titus wouldn't fight for himself. But he'd fight for *us*. Titus' lips parted, and a quiet moan escaped, or maybe it was my big stupid heart imagining it.

"Please, Titus. Keep fighting. I need you. We all need you."

Ivan staggered over, dropping the gun as he knelt beside me. His shirt was splattered with blood and his cold eyes haunted with what he'd done.

"Ivan," Elena rushed to her brother's side, planting kisses on his cheeks. "You saved us all. You are my hero."

"There is no time for that," he barked, pushing her off. "Titus is shot."

"And we can't drive anywhere because of the bloody snow." Dorien rose shakily to his feet. "We need a rescue helicopter. Wait with Titus, I'll find Harrison's satellite phone."

"Elena, I need your help." I shrugged off my jacket and balled it up, pressing it against Titus' gunshot wound. "Hold this here. Try to staunch the bleeding. You can pack a bit of snow behind it, too."

I cradled Titus' head into my lap, and looked up at the burning house in the background. I sucked in a breath as I caught sight of two figures walking through the snow, their bodies translucent and circled in light. A smell shifted in the air – it was like nothing I'd ever smelled before, a cacophony of scents that stirred a surge of memories inside me. Some of them belonged to me – my father kissing my mom after a concert, and smiling shyly as he handed me my first ever violin. But others were not mine – Dorien snuggled in the attic bedroom with Clare, Ivan bringing Dorien's hand to his lips and kissing his ruined finger, Titus headbanging with Micah as they jumped on his bed.

The beautiful dead – the memories that Manderley couldn't take from us.

I turned up my hand and waved at my father and Clare.

"Faye." Elena squinted at the house. "What are you waving at?"

I blinked, and they were gone.

"Nothing." I drew my gaze back to Titus' face. The music swelled in my ears, driving out the roar of the fire. "Nothing at all."

Elena rested her cheek against mine as she pressed against the wound. Ivan held us both close, his body sheltering us from the icy snow. I did not look back at Manderley as the final snatches of my father's song faded into the cold night.

Epilogue: Faye

"Are you ready for this?" Dorien knitted his fingers in mine. He leaned in close, the dark smudges of eyeliner making his face appear demonic, but in the best possible way. Demons were all about possession, and this man was welcome to my eternal soul if he kept looking at me like *that*.

"I was born ready." I squeezed his fingers, wishing I could squeeze away the butterflies in my stomach.

I was lying.

I am not ready.

This is insane.

Sound the fucktrumpets. Why did I think I could do this?

Dorien planted his lips on mine, the rush of heat coursing through my body, tugging at my nerves and making the edges fray even worse than before. He pulled away and flashed me that wicked grin of pure aristocratic confidence. "You're going to slay tonight."

I glanced over his shoulder, picking out Titus and Ivan standing behind me in the dim light. Ivan nodded, and Titus flashed me the devil horns.

That's right. That's why I'm doing this.

For them. For us. For our future.

The light dimmed on stage. *That's our cue. Too late to back out now.*

Fog swirled around my ankles as I dragged my leaden feet to my designated spot. Dorien flashed me his megawatt grin as he settled himself behind the piano, then gave a signal to the crew.

The lights went up, and Titus strummed his guitar. A haunting, somber note rang through the club, and six hundred Broken Muse fans erupted into raucous applause.

Their reaction nearly knocked me off my feet. I'd never heard a sound like it – a physical force that grabbed my heart, tugged it right out of my chest, and tossed it into an electrical socket. My body buzzed with sizzling energy – the same wild abandon that came over me whenever I kissed my Muses, only amplified and returned to me a hundredfold.

Dorien punched the keys, and a few bars later Ivan came in with a scorching melody. Spotlights flickered between them, highlighting Ivan's sharp cheekbones and Dorien's devious grin and Titus' wild and beautiful smile.

A smile that I almost lost eight months ago.

Miraculously, Harrison's shot missed Titus' vital organs. He'd spent weeks in the hospital and months hobbling around with a cane, and he couldn't quite leap around stage yet like he wanted to, but he was gloriously alive and that was what mattered. He was living proof Manderley could grant life as well as take it away.

His father hadn't left his side during his recovery. Amos and Delphine Thibodeaux were in the audience tonight. They were still filled with pain over Micah's death, but they were working hard to rebuild their relationship with their living son.

They weren't the only special guests here tonight. My mom, Agent Rochester and Natalie were in a private box with Jacob. Mom and Natalie had joined forces again to build a PR consultancy. Mom was also looking after Jacob while Dorien was on tour, and the pair of them had bonded. I loved seeing her share her energy with another kid, and Jacob thrived under her care. He'd stopped asking about Father Aaron (who had died in a prison brawl – and I can't say anyone would mourn him). He moved up a year in school, and was taking dance classes with her and Rochester.

That's right – Mom and Rochester were an item now. It was weird at first, but she looked so happy and he looked so completely smitten with her that I sensed the flutter of true love in the air.

I raised my violin to my chin, and I struck the strings. The spotlight bathed me in brilliant light as we launched into *The Fall of the House of Usher* – the composition Dorien and I wrote together.

A new song for a new era of Broken Muse.

I twirled around my Muses, dancing with Titus as his fingers assaulted the strings, dueling with Ivan as we played the complex *spiccato*. I lay across the piano and kissed Dorien's head as his fingers fluttered over scales. He beamed up at me like I was a goddess, never once betraying the pain in his hand from his old injury. There were still some pieces he'd never be able to play again, but he was happy to be behind the piano with his family, and he was getting more into composition now, where it didn't matter how many working fingers he had.

We finished the song to rapturous applause. Dorien leaned forward to speak into his microphone. "Thank you so much for being here tonight. You're the first to meet the new and very much improved Broken Muse. Faye de Winter joins us on violin, and you'll be seeing a lot of her since she's now a permanent member of the band. We think you'll love her just as much as we do."

Judging by the wild whistles and applause that greet my name, he's right. My cheeks flushed with color as I took a deep bow, then returned my violin to my chin to begin the next song.

We tore through the rest of our set, a mix of classic Broken Muse songs, some fun covers, and another new piece Dorien had written especially for us, called *Manderley Burns*.

As I ground up against Ivan during our violin duel in 'Manderley Burns,' I realized that Madame Usher was right about one thing – Broken Muse was better as a foursome. But it wasn't Donovan de Winter who would accompany them to stardom, it was me.

Something wonderful sparked on stage that night – a bit of Elena's *zâne* magic scented the air. I felt as though I'd stepped into my future, and it looked bright and full of adventures and music and love.

We emerged from stage after the show, sweaty and beaming. Elena bounced in the wings, rushing forward to shower us with kisses. She had been lucky to catch this show – her solo tour just happened to be in New York City this same weekend. "You are all amazing." I was grinning so hard I could barely feel her kisses touch my cheeks.

"You didn't make me violently ill, trash." Aroha wrapped her arms around me. She was back in America after a stint in a rehab center back in New Zealand. She and Titus were recording this weird album of atonal music inspired by addiction and mental health, with all the proceeds going to support mental health services for her Iwi (tribe) back home. She signed with a label and the press were calling her the Maori Chelsea Wolfe, a comparison she wore with pride.

In the green room, Dorien flopped onto the sofa, kicking off his boots and massaging his sore finger. Titus sat down opposite him, resting the guitar on his knee and playing a Black Sabbath riff, his braids falling over his face. Ivan hovered at the table, where the venue had laid out a rider of all our favorites. He poured a glass of port for each of us – a tradition we kept from our time at Manderley.

I waved the glass away. "Not for me tonight."

He lifted an eyebrow. It was the third night in a row I hadn't imbibed. I'd been waiting until after we got through this first show to tell them, but from the excited glint in Ivan's icicle eyes, I think he figured it out.

"You're…" He couldn't even get the words out, he was so excited. I nodded.

Ivan broke into a wild grin. It was this crack in this armor that alerted the other two.

Titus' head snapped up. "You're not drinking again?"

I shrugged, barely able to keep the grin off my own face. "Maybe I just don't feel like it."

"Or could there be another reason, Sprite?" The corner of Dorien's mouth quirked up.

"Sound the fucktrumpets, you're *pregnant?*" Titus' eyes bugged out of his head. He picked me up, crushing me to his chest and spinning me around so my legs flew out at crazy angles.

"Careful, you'll spin the little peanut right out of me," I laughed.

Titus sat me down and the three of them crowded around me, kissing me and peppering me with questions about the baby. *Our baby*. I still couldn't believe it myself.

The timing wasn't great – we planned to tour for a year – but as I touched my stomach and felt a surge of intense love for the peanut growing there, I knew it would be okay. Better than okay. It would be amazing. We would be amazing.

Our child wouldn't have a normal life. Not with a mom and three dads and an uncle who survived a cult and a grandmother who loved to go dancing and a godmother who was a famous classical violinist and another godmother who was a ghost. But who cared about normal? We had our family, and we had the music flowing in our veins, and that was all we needed.

Not one of them asked whose baby it was. They didn't need to. It was all of ours. A new Broken Muse. A new life we would love and cherish and who would fill our lives with a different type of music – the kind of music that sings in the heart.

~

"We don't have to do this," Titus reached across and squeezed my knee. "We can turn around and go home if you want to."

"Don't drive so wildly," Ivan snapped, reaching across to steady Dorien's hand. "This isn't the Monaco GP. In fact, don't drive at all. Pull over, I'm taking the wheel."

"I love it when you order me around like that," Dorien shot back. "It's *adorable*."

While the two of them bickered in the front seat and Titus rubbed reassuring circles on my leg, I trained my eyes out the window, looking for the turrets of Manderley poking through the trees. Even though objectively I knew they weren't there any longer, that nothing at the house could ever hurt me again, I couldn't help the fear twisting in my gut as we neared the tall iron gates.

Beside me, our daughter, Claire, made a gurgling noise in her sleep. Her long eyelashes fluttered as she stirred, but didn't wake. I touched my finger to her tiny hand, the love in my chest swelling as I reveled in how soft and small and perfect she was. She had light brown skin like mine and a mop of glorious dark hair.

When she'd first been born, I thought she had Titus' dark eyes – they were so impossibly deep and she wore such a serious expression that she always appeared to be considering the problems of the universe, rather than contemplating her next poop. But at three months old, it was clear to me that Dorien was the father – her cheeky grin was all him.

It didn't matter who contributed her DNA. She was ours, and we were hers. Completely and utterly. My muses were the most amazing fathers. Dorien spent hours playing peekaboo with her and zooming her around the room like an airplane while she giggled with delight. Ivan took her for long walks every day, and Titus loved to fuss over her – sourcing the best baby food and changing her diapers and carefully folding her tiny baby clothes.

The Broken Muse tour was so successful we were able to take six months off to spend time together as a family while Dorien wrote new music. We were going to make our base in Prague for the summer, but before we left America there was one thing we had to do.

I held my breath as we drove through the gates, half expecting some bolt of lightning to shoot from the sky and fry us. Harrison's old gatehouse loomed beside us, empty now and being consumed by the forest. Vines twisted across the walls and crawled through the broken window and open door. We had Harrison buried in the Usher crypt, in the tomb beside Victor that had been reserved for Madame Usher. It felt right, even after what he tried to do to us.

We pulled into the parking spot underneath the trees. Elena was already there, leaning against the hood of her shiny new Bentley, a cigarette dangling from her jaws. Behind her, Manderley sprawled across my vision – no longer the grand and imposing house that dwarfed the ancient trees surrounding it, but a blackened scar on the landscape.

Just a pile of ashes and bones.

"I want to meet my goddaughter." Elena rapped on the window before Dorien had even turned off the engine. Grinning, I unclipped Claire's carseat, flipped the handle, and brought her out to show her off.

"She's sleeping," Ivan said, throwing her arm around his sister's shoulders and kissing her forehead. They hadn't seen each other since the first show of our tour. Elena had a six-month residency in Vienna, and we'd been doing shows every second night across Europe and Asia. We even went down to Australia and New Zealand. Aroha and her family showed us around the country, and it was so beautiful, I wanted to live there. Maybe one day.

We had so many wonderful days ahead of us.

"Well, wake her up." Elena stubbed out her cigarette with her. "We need to be properly introduced."

I laughed at Elena, who didn't understand a thing about babies. She declared that she would never have one – a trauma she carried from her short marriage to Radcliffe. She said she wanted to focus on her career, but I think it was more than that. Between her father, who effectively sold her, and the Ushers, she didn't exactly have great role models. I understood – I'd been so worried that I would turn out to be like my father, but that curse died with him because I loved my daughter more than life itself. And Ivan had proven he was an amazing dad, which I never doubted.

Claire opened her eyes then, and we let Elena have cuddles and spent some time catching up before we decided to make our move toward the ruins. My boots crunched on the gravel, kicking aside dead leaves and bits of charred debris. The winter weather and the encroaching forest hadn't been kind to Manderley – the eastern end wall had been standing when we were helicoptered to safety, but now it lay in pieces atop the rest of the structure. Vines and weeds tangled amongst the charred remains of the house that had become a tomb. An eerie silence pervaded, as if trees didn't dare rustle and birds were forbidden to sing. Madame Usher had silenced the music of Manderley forever.

The police were able to analyze Victor's remains and determined he'd been poisoned. It was exactly as Harrison said – Madame Usher got rid of Victor so she could control the house, the finances, and my father. *In Cauda Venenum* – that's the secret she thought Dorien had figured out.

As for Madame Usher, her body was never recovered. The fire department said that there was no way she could have survived the fall, but even though they scoured the whole area where we said we saw her, they hadn't been able to locate her body. They believed she might have been dragged off by wolves.

Thinking about it gave me an uneasy feeling. My gaze flicked to the trees at the edge of the overgrown gardens. Had her burned, broken body been sacrificed to the mountains, scattered across the landscape by animals, forever separated from the house she cursed with her malice and never allowed to rest in peace? Or did we just imagine seeing her body with its broken neck? Was that the final horror Manderley visited upon us? Was she still out there, alive after dragging herself free of the fire? Was she licking her wounds and lying in wait to spring another trap for us?

Neither option felt right, or just. But you don't always get closure in life. So much about Madame Usher would be forever a mystery to me.

The firefighters did manage to pull my father's remains from the house. Mom refused to give him a funeral, and we buried him in a small, cheap grave in the Bushwick cemetery, close to the crappy apartment I rented after Mom became ill. I hadn't visited him, and I never would.

As for the third body consumed by Manderley, the body of Maxim Radcliffe hidden in the walls, that had also been recovered. He was too badly damaged for the police to conclude anything from forensics. His death was ruled a sad accident.

"Here it is." Titus set down the object he'd taken from the trunk of the car, unwrapping the blanket to reveal a round, smooth lump of granite. We'd had it engraved with a simple message.

For Clare and Donovan. Who brought about the fall of the House of Usher.

Titus dragged over a bag of quick-dry cement and a spade, and the boys dug a shallow hole where the front door had stood and set the stone inside. There was a gap at the side of our marker, where Titus had dug the hole extra-wide. I removed an object from my pocket and dropped it into the earth.

My father's cufflink.

Rochester had the furnace room and all its remains carefully studied. They found the remains of at least twenty-six people. He concluded that the Ushers were being paid by the Triumvirate to get rid of bodies. "Crime families always leave a trail of collateral damage in their wake," he told us. He believed when Madame Usher decided to make my father disappear, she had his clothes burned in the furnace with the last of the bodies.

I'd thought about returning my father's violin to Manderley. It seemed right, symbolically, but I couldn't quite stomach burying a Becker in the dirt, especially knowing where it came from. Instead, we wrapped it carefully and had it delivered anonymously to Nero Lucian, a casino owner in Emerald Beach who Rochester was able to connect to the Triumvirate. Hopefully now, all debts were repaid.

I stepped back, admiring the marker as the guys cemented the stone inside. Now anyone who set foot at Manderley would know its legacy. Hopefully, the ghosts would finally be able to rest in peace.

I half expected to see Clare's ghost staring back at us, but I knew she was gone. We'd given her the justice she needed to be free of Manderley. I liked to think that Dad and Clare were together in the afterlife. Dad brought me to Manderley in search of his own redemption, but I didn't need a parent. Clare did. I hoped that wherever they were now, they were together, and happy. Even if I did want to punch his stupid ghost in its stupid face.

"I wonder what's going to happen to this place now," I said, kicking one of the charred beams that once held up the ceiling of the Red Room. Beneath it, sunlight twinkled off shards of crystal that had once been Madame's antique port decanter.

"You do not need to wonder," Elena piped up. "I own it."

"What?"

"Madame Usher willed it to me in the event of her death," Elena said, reaching into her pocket to tip out another cigarette. "Apparently, she wrote that I was the one woman capable of following in her footsteps. But I do not think it should be a school any longer. We should let sleeping ghosts lie. Instead, I think a wildlife sanctuary. We will give the land back to the wolves and the trees. I've already set up a trust, and I found an expert named Eli Hart down in Emerald Beach who's putting a team together to manage it."

She flashed that beautiful, enigmatic smile as she gazed out across her husband's funeral pyre. And I wondered again, as I had wondered so many times since that awful night, if Elena was a victim or a cold, calculating murderess. Did she accidentally kill Radcliffe trying to defend herself from his vicious advances, or did she catch him by surprise with a blow to the head and then staged the scene by pulling down his pants and smashing up the house? Was Donelle talking about Radcliffe when she wrote about the 'deviant sexual proclivities' she witnessed, or was she an ordinary old homophobe who couldn't stomach seeing Victor and Harrison together?

Just another mystery that would be buried with Manderley.

I threw my arms around my friend and kissed her cheek. Dorien came up beside us and wrapped his arms around us both. Ivan and Titus joined us, Titus jiggling our daughter on his hip. I rested my face on Ivan's shoulder and thanked the ghosts of Manderley. This place had taken so much for all of us, but it hadn't taken our love. The music that beat in our hearts for each other still thrummed in our veins.

Hand in hand, we turned our backs on the charred remains of Manderley Academy, and stepped forward into our future.

THE END

Want to meet the dark and dangerous men of the Triumvirate and the girl who holds their heart? Check out this new dark reverse harem series by Steffanie Holmes:

Psst. I have a secret.

Are you ready?

I'm Mackenzie Malloy, and everyone thinks they know who I am.

Five years ago, I disappeared.

No one has seen me or my family outside the walls of Malloy Manor since.
But now I'm coming to reclaim my throne:
The Ice Queen of Stonehurst Prep is back.

Standing between me and my everything?
Three things can bring me down:
The sweet guy who wants answers from his former friend.
The rock god who wants to f*ck me.
The king who'll crush me before giving up his crown.

They think they can ruin me, wreck it all, but I won't let them.
I'm not the Mackenzie Eli used to know.
Hot boys and rock gods like Gabriel won't win me over.
And just like Noah, I'll kill to keep my crown.

I'm just a poor little rich girl with the stolen life.
I'm here to tear down three princes,
before they destroy me.

Read now:
http://books2read.com/mystolenlife

Get your free copy of *Cabinet of Curiosities*, a Steffanie Holmes compendium of short stories and bonus scenes. To get this collection, all you need to do is sign up for updates with the Steffanie Holmes newsletter.

http://www.steffanieholmes.com/newsletter

BONUS EPILOGUE: FAYE

TEN YEARS LATER

"What an incredible show." Titus sank into the soft hotel bed, pulling me down beside him to smother me in kisses. He was high from the performance, his skin slick with sweat, his plaits draping over my shoulder as his lips grazed mine. Even after all this time together, being kissed by Titus made me weak at the knees.

Especially after I'd been jumping around on stage for two hours. One thing's for sure – I'm not twenty-one anymore. Life on tour is *tiring*. I curled around my beautiful muse and let Titus' expert fingers knead away the knots on my shoulders.

Tiring, but fun. So much fun. Especially when we can go back to our hotel suite after a sold-out show and I can be kissed by three Broken Muses until I'm wet and panting. I wouldn't trade our life of music and adventure for anything.

"They loved the new songs." Darien slid in the chair opposite the super-king bed, kicking off his heavy New Rock boots and massaging his tired calves. His dark eyes gleamed with the rapture of the music – I swear when that man gets on stage it's like he's a demon unleashed from hell.

Come to think of it, he's a little like that between the sheets, too.

"Yeah, yeah, don't get a big head about it," Titus shot back as his fingers worked a particularly tight knot in my bowing arm. "We know your songwriting has improved since you started working with Gabriel."

Gabriel Fallen – the singer we added to Broken Muse a few years ago – was still at the club, partying with his girl, Claws, and her two other boyfriends, Noah and Eli. They didn't usually join us on tour because Claws had a criminal empire to run and a kid to raise, but this was a special occasion. It was the first time our band toured Australia and New Zealand, and everyone in the Broken Muse extended family wanted a couple of weeks to explore a new part of the world. We timed things perfectly so that our last show – tonight's show – landed us in Auckland. Now we had a full week to ourselves for a family vacation.

"Aroha should get credit for tonight's success," I murmured as I rolled over to give Titus better access to my shoulder. "I swear the crowd was there to see her, not us." Our sort-of friend from Manderley Academy – Aroha Rawhiri – had agreed to come on stage to perform two songs with us. She's pretty well-known locally and the fans went absolutely wild for her. She was going to be showing us some sights around the country this week. "That duet she did with Ivan gave me *chills.*"

Ivan said nothing, which wasn't unusual. While the rest of us needed to shout and fuck and dance to burn off the post-show adrenaline, Ivan preferred to retreat into himself. He stood at the window, gazing out across the city. The lights of Auckland spread out like a map of the stars – so similar to New York, San Francisco, Prague, and all the other cities we've played and yet, so utterly different. Every city we visited has its own spirit, the very air alive with personal ghosts.

They drive on the left side of the road here, and call French Fries 'chips.' Weirdos.

"What are you thinking about, Romanian Rocket?" Dorien teased as he strode toward Ivan, his long, dark hair streaming behind him. "I bet you're dreaming about visiting Hobbiton tomorrow, all those second breakfasts will give you a pot belly if you're not careful, and then what will your groupies do?"

Ivan turned to scowl at him, but Dorien stifled his protests with his lips. Ivan's hands reached up and tangled in Dorien's hair, drawing him closer. I watched through tangled eyelashes as Dorien slotted his fingers into Ivan's belt and jerked him closer, so their chests pressed together and their mouths met in a clash of hot need.

It had been ten years since the two of them deepened their relationship and declared their feelings for each other, and Ivan still looked awed whenever Dorien or I kissed him, like he couldn't quite believe he deserved us. Which was so far from the truth it's not funny. If anything, we're the one's lucky to have *him.*

Dorien rocked back on his heels, staring down at Ivan with eyes hooded with lust. "Not thinking about hobbits now, are we?" he grinned.

"I was thinking about Elena," Ivan said. "She would love it here."

Ivan missed his sister the most when we were on tour. Elena had her own impressive solo career and a string of lovers who kept her busy in Europe. Ivan grew increasingly morose during the long stretches of time when the two of them weren't in the same room together, their fae magic carving enchantments in the air. But Dorien was also right when he said that Ivan was more himself when Elena wasn't around. Without her light overpowering everything, his own shone all the brighter.

Dorien tipped Ivan's head back, laying a trail of kisses across his neck. Titus copied him, laying sweet, lingering kisses on my skin, stoking a fire inside me that had burned for the three of them all these years.

"We should go up there," Dorien said, breaking the spell of the moment.

"Where?" I murmured against Titus' lips.

"That tower thing."

Reluctantly, I rolled over and looked up. Dorien pulled on Ivan's hand, jerking him back toward the window with the view of the Sky Tower – the antennae-shaped protrusion that rose from a nearby casino and defined the Auckland skyline.

"We're going. Right now. Faye, get Claire and Maxim. It's our first night in Auckland and we're having an adventure."

Titus looked momentarily annoyed at our sexytimes being interrupted, but Dorien's enthusiasm infected us all. Of course we should climb a mysterious tower in a strange city at 1AM. Sound the fucktrumpets, that's exactly the thing to do.

I moved into the adjoining room of our suite, picking my way through toys and broken bits of board games. On a couch in the corner, my mother lay on her side, hands clasped beneath her cheek, one leg thrown out from under the duvet in utter exhaustion. I stepped around her, not willing to wake her after the tiring day she must've had. I moved around the king-sized bed, and there they were.

Star-fished in the middle of the bed, their heads bent together like two little cherubs and not the unholy terrors they were during waking hours – Claire and Maxim. My children. *Our* children.

They're so beautiful I cannot stand it. Claire's arm curled around her younger brother's shoulders, and Maxim's cheeks puffed out as he slept. I sat on the edge of the bed, not daring to touch them, just enjoying this moment.

Claire stirred, muttering something in her sleep. Maxim opened one sleepy eye and grinned up at me. It was a grin of pure Titus. He is his father's son.

"Hi, Mommy."

My heart bloomed, the way it always did whenever he looked at me with those soulful eyes – the kind of eyes that seemed older than his five years. "Hey, you."

"Mom?" Claire's eyes were open, too. She sat up, running a hand through her dark, knotted hair.

"I'm sorry for waking you. But I wanted to tell you that we got back from the show. And your dads and I are going on a little adventure in the city. Want to come?"

"Yes." Maxim threw the covers off, revealing a plushie sloth and several action figures he'd snuggled in the blankets with them. He bounced across the room, yelling 'Adventure! Adventure!" at the top of his lungs as he hunted for an appropriate adventuring outfit.

"You don't have to get dressed, Maxim, honey." If he had to pick out clothes, we'd be stuck here all night. "Put your coat and socks and boots on, okay."

"Okay." He bent down to pull on clean socks, and let me help him lace up his tiny New Rock boots. He wanted a pair just like Daddy Titus. Claire pulled my favorite red leather jacket over her threadbare Snoopy pajamas. Unlike Maxim, she didn't care much about fashion. I noticed she slipped her gaming console into her pocket.

I left a note for Mom in case she woke up, then urged the kids into the main suite, where their Dads were dressed and waiting. Dorien bent down and opened his arms, and Claire and Maxim ran into them.

"Adventure!" Maxim yelled as he reached up to draw Ivan into the hug.

We never did any tests, but it was obvious when Claire was born that she had Dorien's eyes. And Maxim was *all* Titus. I worried sometimes that Ivan would feel left out, not having a biological child, but when he bent down to kiss Maxim's head with tenderness, the love in his eyes was that of a true father, the father he was born to be.

We all know, better than most, that family is so much more than DNA.

Ivan checked the kids were bundled up against the cold, and Dorien swung Maxim onto his shoulders and led the way out of the hotel. We passed party-goers and couples walking home after romantic dinners. On the next street over, I could hear a group of people drunkenly singing one of our songs.

"Faster, Daddy!"

Dorien and Maxim raced toward the base of the tower. Claire took my left hand and Ivan's right as we entered the large concrete structure. Dorien and Maxim were already leaning over a desk, putting on their very best alluring smiles for the grim-faced attendant.

"I'm sorry, sir. The tower is closed." She tapped a sign that indicated the last guests were admitted over three hours ago.

"But I still see lights on up there," Titus said.

"Our revolving bar is open for a couple of VIP guests, who will be leaving shortly."

"We should be VIPs," Claire piped up with all the precociousness of her father. "My parents are *famous*. They're in a band called Broken Muse."

The attendant didn't look convinced. "As I said, the tower is closed, so—"

"Give me two minutes of your time. I bet I can change your mind." Dorien flashed his devilish grin, and Claire and Maxim followed suit. I could see the attendant wavering. Dorien took her aside, and I saw bills exchanging hands before they both returned, all smiles, and told us that we'd be allowed to travel up the tower.

We crowded into a large elevator, with the attendant explaining to Claire – who was interested in such things – how the tower was built. Glass doors clicked shut behind us. It wasn't until we started to rise that I realized the exterior wall was cut with glass windows so that we could look out over the twinkling lights of the dwindling city.

"Cool." Claire squatted down to peer into a glass window cut into the floor of the elevator, cut so we could view the mechanisms of the shaft as we rose up up up to impossible heights.

"Daddy Daddy look." Maxim jumped on the glass panel, dancing over the empty space beneath.

"That's great, little man." Titus gripped the handrail and glared at the wall. I'd forgotten he was a little afraid of heights. All this glass probably didn't help.

"Here's your stop." The attendant grinned, used to unsuspecting tourists stepping into the elevator to the heavens. I suspected she chose the glass-bottomed one on purpose.

We stepped out into a plush bar area. Armchairs and tables were arranged in cozy circles around the floor-to-ceiling windows that made it appear as though we were hoving in a flying saucer over an unsuspecting city. The kids immediately claimed a large sofa in the window, right next to the only other customer in the place – a woman in funky red-tinted glasses reading a book and sipping a cosmopolitan.

"Don't mind us. We'll get out of your hair." I tried to shuffle the kids off to another seat. Claire ducked under my arm and raced to the window, pressing her nose against the glass.

"Nonsense." The woman with the red glasses closed her book and patted the chair beside her. "I enjoy the company. Sit here, little man, and tell me why your parents dragged you out of bed in the middle of the night."

"We're having an adventure," Maxim announced pompously, tugging on the collar of his favorite jacket. Excited to have a captive audience, he started to tell her his entire life story before becoming waylaid by listing his favorite dinosaurs. The women with the red glasses listened with rapt attention. She even knew the difference between a Brontosaurus and a Brachiosaurus.

Ivan leaned across the seat and whispered. "Maxim has made a new friend for life."

"Mom, you can see *everything*." Claire cried. "All the cars are so tiny. And there's a giant volcano."

"Now you're telling stories," Ivan said with a laugh in his voice as he went to join her at the window. "There's no volcano in the middle of a big city."

"There is. I read about it." Claire smudged her finger against the glass. "That hill over there is a volcano, and that one too. Mom, I can even see the theater where you played. It's not very big."

Dorien and Titus returned from the bar with drinks for all of us, including another cosmopolitan to our new friend. The kids got fancy ice chocolates which they sucked on happily, giving us approximately seventeen seconds of blissful silence where I could ask our friend about herself."

"My name is Steffanie. I'm an author. I write books about relationships like yours."

"Like mine?"

Steffanie winked in the direction of my three husbands. "One very lucky heroine falls in love with three handsome men, and she doesn't have to choose between them. In the publishing industry, we call them reverse harem, and they are very popular. You wouldn't believe how many readers wish they could have exactly what you have right now. I sometimes wish it myself. But the next best thing is writing about it."

She sipped her drink, meeting my eyes with a steely, penetrating gaze of an author trying to parse my most secret thoughts.

"It wasn't always this way," I leaned back in the chair, remembering the first disastrous day I arrived at Manderley Academy. "In the beginning, they hated my guts."

"We did not," Dorien piped up. "The moment I saw you I wanted to shag you on a piano stool."

"Ew, gross," cried Claire.

"We were trapped by the evil headmistress of our school, Madame Usher," Titus tried to explain to Steffanie. "She traded in secrets and lies. She convinced us that the only way to keep our own secrets safe was to hurt Faye. I didn't even know Faye before she came to Manderley, but the more I saw of her, the more I realized I could never go through with our plans."

"I never would have let them bully me out of my dreams," I laughed. "But they gave it a good try. They sabotaged my performances. They played mind games. They smashed my violin—"

"Not all of it was us," Titus pointed out. "Some of it was your father, who was secretly living in the walls of the school under the spell of the evil headmistress."

"And don't forget the ghost of Claire, Madame Usher's previous maid," added Ivan. "Who was having an affair with Faye's father, until he accidentally pushed her down the stairs."

Steffanie leaned forward in her chair, her eyes sparkling. "Ghosts? A father living in the walls? Three redeemed bullies finding true love? This sounds like the plot of one of my books."

Titus lifted an eyebrow at me from his place near the bar, as far from the large windows as it was possible to be. "And we haven't even told her about the cult or the Victorian poison garden yet."

"What if I brought you all another round of drinks, and you told me the whole story from beginning to end?" Steffanie whipped out a purse and produced a beautiful silver pen and a notebook. "That is, if you don't mind it appearing in a book one day."

"We wouldn't mind at all," I said. "As long as you label the story as fiction. I don't think anyone will believe it really happened."

"Probably not," she agreed. "And that's half the fun. "

I tucked my feet beneath me and reached across to squeeze Ivan's hand. "It began in a hospital room, where my mother was fighting for her life from a mysterious illness, and I'd brought my violin along to try and reach her—"

"No, no, no." Dorien set down his glass and folded one leg over the other. He steepled his fingers and leaned forward, looking every bit the narrator of a lush gothic tale. "If you're going to tell this story, you need to start from the *real* beginning. At a New York City music school where a raven-hair vixen first enraptured me with his haunting music..."

THE END

FROM THE AUTHOR

When Faye popped into my head, fully formed and stomping her foot for her story, I pushed her aside.

Not because she isn't badass – she is. Not because she didn't deserve a chance to live and fight and love – she does. Definitely not because 'fucktrumpets' as a swear word should never see the light of day – that shit should be shouted from great heights.

But because I was afraid.

Faye needed to be a classical musician. She needed to live and breathe and love the music, and I... I am a classical *philistine*.

I was raised on a diet of heavy fucking metal. I'm more at home in the mosh pit than in the concert hall. I've always seen classical music as something for the rich and snooty, where everyone pretends they're having fun because it's *culture*. I didn't think I was the right person to do Faye justice.

But Faye's a stubborn bitch. She wouldn't go away.

She led me to a book called *Rock Me Amadeus*, by Seb Hunter – the story of an ageing rocker (Seb wrote this hilarious history of heavy metal called *Hell Bent for Leather* I highly recommend) trying to uncover what there was to like about classical music. Sadly, the book is out of print now – I tracked down a second-hand copy.

In it, Seb explores the history of classical music in chronological order, including many bizarre road trips across Europe, strange encounters, and a Wagner drinking game. Through this book I discover that (d'uh) musicians like Bach, Beethoven and Liszt were the rockstars of their day – wallowing in the excesses of drugs, drink, and women. Paganini sold his soul to the devil for his musical talent. And the music... phew. Where have you been all my life?

All music fans can recount their 'Come to Jesus' moment – the exact point when they went from not knowing a musical thing existed to loving the thing with their whole heart. I remember exactly the day I first heard Metallica's 'Enter Sandman' and realised music could be deeper and richer and more powerful than I ever imagined. And I remember when I first cranked Beethoven on my speakers at Seb's suggestion and fell in love with classical music.

Meanwhile, Faye's flashing me a satisfied smirk.

Told you so.

The interesting thing about being a writer is that when you work on a story, you give a piece of yourself to the world, to your readers. But it's not a one-way thing – the story gives something back. You can never predict what that 'something' will be. Sometimes it's a sense of peace, or closure on trauma that's haunted you. Sometimes it's righteous anger, or a sense of purpose, or a desire for action. Sometimes it's confidence, or chaos, or acceptance.

Sound the fucktrumpets – Faye gave me music that lifts my soul.

I've created a playlist for the Manderley Academy series. You'll find it on Spotify here. I've tried to include every song I mention in the text, as well as some I love that I feel Faye and the Broken Muse boys would adore. I've included some more modern music, too – a bit of goth, a smidge of metal (for many metal musicians, like Titus, are classically-trained and heavily inspired by classical roots). Maybe it will spark your own 'Come to Dories' moment, or you'll find some cool new tunes to jam along.

Writing Manderley Academy has been a joy and a pleasure, but as always, it takes a village to bring a book to life. I'd like to thank my cantankerous drummer husband, for reading this manuscript and giving me so many ideas to make it better. And for being my lighthouse. And for putting up with me blasting Bach at full volume.

To Kit, Bri, Elaina, Katya, Emma, Jamie, Kim, Mila, and Jenna, for all the writerly encouragement and advice. To Meg and Eveis for the epically helpful editing job, and to Amanda/Aria/Lori for the stunning covers. To Sam and Iris, for the daily Facebook shenanigans that help keep me sane while I spend my days stuck at home covered in cats.

To you, the reader, for going on this journey with me, even though it's led to some dark places. If you're enjoying *Manderley Academy* and want to read more from me, check out my dark reverse harem bully romance series, *Kings of Miskatonic Prep*. HP Lovecraft meets *Cruel Intentions* in this dark paranormal reverse harem bully romance that's definitely not for the faint of heart. Hazel is the most badass FMC I've ever written, and I think you'll love meeting her. Read here: http://books2read.com/shunned.

Every week I send out a newsletter to fans – it features a spooky story about a real-life haunting or strange criminal case that has inspired one of my books, as well as news about upcoming releases and a free book of bonus scenes called *Cabinet of Curiosities*. To get on the mailing list all you gotta do is head to my website: http://www.steffanieholmes.com/newsletter

I'm so happy you enjoyed this story! I'd love it if you wanted to leave a review on Amazon or Goodreads. It will help other readers to find their next read.

Thank you, thank you! I love you heaps! Until next time.

Steff

A Note on Manderley Academy's inspiration

In writing Manderley Academy, I drew on numerous novels, poison manuals, and true hauntings for inspiration. If you're a fan of gothic literature, you may notice some of the illusions and names in homage to my literary heroes and heroines. At the centre of it all is Manderley – named in honour of the grand house at the centre of Daphne du Maurier's *Rebecca*, one of my favourite books of all time. If you haven't read it, I encourage you to do so, although you may not be able to turn the lights out until you reach the last page.

I've waited to the very end to tell you about the true story that inspired these books. I didn't want to give you any spoilers. I'd like to tell you now.

Walburga Oesterreich was a housewife in the early 20th century, married to Fred – the owner of a Milwaukee apron factory. Fred's business was successful and he gave Dolly (everyone called her Dolly because you would, with a name like Walburga, wouldn't you?) everything she wanted – a nice house, lovely clothes, lots of antiques and objects and things, a good life. He was also away from home a lot, and when he was home he drank. And got mean. Fred and Dolly had huge screaming rows that caught the attention of neighbours in their upper-class street. Those neighbours often gossiped about Dolly's 'wandering eye' and flirtations with men who weren't her husband.

One day in 1913, Dolly's sewing machine stopped working. She called up Fred in a tizzy and he sent over 'a boy' from the factory to fix it. That boy was 17-year-old Otto Sanhuber.

Dolly and Otto began their affair that day. At first, they met at a hotel, but soon Dolly was inviting Otto over to her home when Fred was away. But those nosy neighbours started to notice Otto's comings and goings. Dolly tried to cover up the affair by telling people Otto was her 'vagabond half-brother' but no one was buying it.

Word got back to Fred, and he told his wife to choose – her lover or her lavish lifestyle. She chose the house and the money and the fancy clothes and Fred. And Otto disappeared from their lives.

But all was not well. Fred was drinking more than ever, and he'd become convinced their house was haunted. He'd find items moved from where he left them, noises in the house when he and Dolly were in a room together, food missing from the kitchen, and the sensation of being watched. It was starting to freak him out.

The couple moved to Los Angeles for a new start and to expand Fred's business, but the ghost followed them to their new home. Dolly was preoccupied setting up their lavish new pad with all her beloved things, so she might not have noticed that Fred's drinking was worse. Or that he would never be alone in the house – if she was out, he would invite a friend around. She never saw his paranoia – Fred was convinced this nameless phantom intended to do him harm.

Dolly and Fred went out to a friend's house. They came home around midnight and got into a screaming fight. Neighbours heard the argument, and then they heard gunshots. They kicked in the front door and found Fred's dead body on the floor, shot three times, and thumping and knocking coming from upstairs. They followed the sound and found Dolly crying, locked in a closet. They found no trace of the intruder, but Fred's cash, gold watch, and other valuables had been taken. However, no one had seen an intruder entering or leaving the neighbourhood. For a long time, the crime went unsolved.

A year later, Dolly was in a relationship with Roy Clum, a film producer. One day, she handed him a pistol and asked him to dispose of it in the Le Brea Tar Pits. Roy agreed to do it, but a few months afterward their relationship went sour, and Roy realised the gun was the exact one used to kill Fred. He went to the police with his story, and Dolly was arrested.

Dolly's attorney, Herman Shapiro, was quick to point out at her trial that she couldn't be the murderer, since she was locked in the closet. Herman – who was Dolly's new lover – wore a watch that looked suspiciously identical to the one taken from Fred's body.

One day during the trial, Dolly came to Herman and gave him some strange instructions. Herman was intrigued, but he did what Dolly said. He went home and prepared a meal, placed it on a tray, and took it upstairs to Dolly's room. He set the food down in the closet and whistled. A moment later, a panel slid open in the closet wall and a man's face appeared.

The man in the wall told Herman everything. He *was* Otto Sanhuber. He had been living in the walls and attic of Dolly's homes for over a decade, ever since Fred forced her to break off their affair. He had been the one making the noises that had so terrified Fred. And he had heard their screaming fight on the night of the party.

Otto was concerned Fred would hurt Dolly, so he took Fred's gun and went downstairs. Fred attacked Otto, and the gun went off twice into his chest. Fred fell to the ground, and Otto shot him again to make sure he was gone.

Herman told Otto to run away. He knew that Dolly wouldn't be convicted of murder because she'd been locked in the closet. If he took Otto to the police, Herman's reputation would be ruined. So Otto went to Canada and in 1925, Dolly got off scot free.

(There's even more to this story, as Otto returns to LA in 1930 and gets arrested, but I've already rambled enough).

I heard this story on a podcast called *Lore*, which explores true stories of our dark past. I think you'd probably enjoy it.

EXCERPT: KINGS OF MISKATONIC PREP, BOOK 1

READ THE FIRST CHAPTER OF SHUNNED

Enjoy this short teaser from book 1 of Kings of Miskatonic Prep, Shunned. http:// books2read.com/shunned

Who the hell builds a school on top of an inaccessible cliff?

Whoever built Derleth Academy, my new school. I answered my own question as the car's wheel skidded over the rough gravel on the way up the steep peninsula. A scream escaped my lips as the car lurched toward the edge of the cliff, one wheel spinning completely free.

Muttering under his breath, the driver for the school slammed the car into reverse and backed us onto the road before slamming on the gas again. We continued our wary climb along the narrow gravel path.

Surely the Academy can't be completely *cut-off.* The school had to bring up food and supplies. Parents must visit on the weekends. My driver was certainly giving it his all, tearing around the corners like he was on a Formula 1 racetrack and not a goat path hugging the side of a mountain. I gritted my teeth and gripped the back of the seat as rocks rolled from beneath the wheels and clattered over the sheer drop into the raging waters below. One wrong move, and we'd tumble down a two-hundred-foot cliff and be dashed against the cliffs so hard and fast that boats would mistake our remains for rock paintings.

Not the way I ever imagined I'd go.

We passed into thick vegetation, the cliff and ocean on one side giving way to looming trees that blocked out the grey sky. I let out the breath I'd been holding. Branches scraped the sides of the car, and my phone beeped with protest as we moved out of cell range. *No contact with the outside world,* the school brochure read. *At Derleth Academy, we foster a competitive academic program requiring the full attention of our students. Distracting technology or personal items will not be tolerated.*

In other words, I couldn't call for help. It was the opening sequence to every horror film, ever.

Not that I had anyone to call. Not anymore.

"Almost there," the driver said, swinging the car around a hairpin corner and launching my stomach into my throat. It was the most words he'd spoken to me the entire trip. "You can see the school through the trees."

I squinted into the forest, trying to make out some kind of building that might pass as a school. But I couldn't see a thing. We rounded another corner and—

Well, that's terrifying.

We rolled between two towering stone pillars obscured by creeping vines, past an ornate sign that read DERLETH ACADEMY. A wide, pristine concrete drive flanked by an avenue of towering trees and wide, manicured lawns led up to an imposing stone building, stretching in all directions with narrow arched windows, spiky towers, and a row of leering gargoyles along the roof.

What is this place? It looked more like Dracula's castle than a prestigious preparatory school.

I couldn't believe the wealthiest people in the country sent their children up that winding road to get educated. *Who's the headmistress, Morticia Addams?* But according to the brochure, that was exactly what they did. In droves. Derleth Academy had a waiting list a mile long, and you couldn't even pay to get in. You had to be *invited*.

Somehow, I, Hazel Waite – an overachieving orphan from the wrong side of Philly – ended up on their radar.

I flashed back to the day two weeks ago, when a banging on the door of my dingy apartment dragged me from a deep slumber. A woman with coiffed hair and a designer suit that cost more than a car staggered backward in surprise when I glared at her through the chain wearing only my pajamas and what must have been a terrifying scowl. Well, *she* wasn't the one being dragged from a pleasant Jason Momoa sex dream during the four-hour reprieve between night shift at the diner and cleaning rooms at a retirement home.

"Are you Hazel Waite?" she asked, her brown eyes wide and curious.

"No. Piss off." I glowered, slamming the door in her face. She was probably from CPS, trying to force me into foster care. Fuck that. I only had seven more months to survive before I turned eighteen. No way was I going to spend it in the hell that had killed Dante.

The woman didn't go away. She sat out on the road in her sports car and waited me out. I had to leave for work or I'd lose my job, and it wasn't easy to find work when you were underage and using an obviously fake ID. As soon as I left the house, she ambushed me.

"I'm not here to hand you over to the authorities," she said hurriedly, shoving a thick envelope into your hands. "I'm a scholarship administrator from Derleth Academy in Arkham, Massachusetts. Your current school put you forward for one of our four senior scholarship positions – a fully funded year at a first-class prep school, where our students go on to attend the top colleges in the world. I know the first quarter has already started, but it's taken me this long to track you down. You've only missed a week so far."

I stared at the envelope in my hands, at the red, black and gold school crest – a crooked five-pointed star inside a shield with some kind of Latin phrase beneath it. *This has got to be a joke.*

"I know what you're thinking," the woman said. "It's not a joke or a trick. I promise you that it's not. If you come to Derleth, we will assume guardianship duties until you turn eighteen. You'll be housed, clothed, and have all your schoolbooks and other needs met, as well as receiving a first-class education. You're a promising student, Hazel, and I know you've been dealt a cruel lot in life. This could be where you turn everything around. Don't answer me now. Read over the paperwork, and I'll return tomorrow for your decision."

And now, just ten days after I signed my soul over to this school in exchange for paid tuition, room, and board, I stared up at the imposing facade and wondered if I'd made a terrible mistake.

Sure, my life was miserable. I was drowning in grief, and even working two jobs I could barely pull in enough money to survive. College was out of the question, because I couldn't finish high school without going into foster care. But at least all that was familiar territory. That was the world I'd grown up in – the world of pain and struggle and loss. Derleth Academy was the exact opposite. Every element of this building screamed wealth and privilege and *you don't belong here.*

The driver pulled to a stop on the wide circular drive beside a towering stone fountain. A black woman in a drab grey smock darted out of the shadows of the porch and approached the car. I held my hand out to her. "Hello, I'm Hazel Waite—"

The woman ducked her head, avoiding me. She popped open the trunk, hauled out my heavy suitcase and bookbag, and hurried off to the house with them before I could offer to help.

Weird much? I swiped a dreadlock off my face. My friend Dante's foster sister had done them for me last year, back when things were perfect and the most I had to worry about was whether my mom would ground me for getting dreadlocks.

An awful feeling twisted in my gut. I wished Mom was here, hating my loss, right now. But she was gone, gone, gone, and so was Dante, and it was just me and this terrifying school and no other options.

Three figures descended the grand stone steps toward me: A woman with translucent skin and a flowing black dress, flanked on either side by two students wearing the Derleth uniform. Fallen leaves skittered away from the woman's hem, and she moved with such poise that she appeared to float over the steps. With her severe features and a gauzy black ribbon pinned in her hair, she looked more like she was attending a funeral. Behind her, the two students – a guy and a girl – glared at me, distrust emanating from their every pore.

The woman stopped on the second-to-last step, peering down her nose at me as if I were a bug that wasn't even worth squashing. "You'll have to do something about that hair. We enforce a strict dress code in my school, Ms. Waite. I'll not have you flouting it on your very first day."

This must be the principal, Hermia West. My Morticia Addams guess wasn't far off. This woman looked like she drank the blood of students to sustain her beauty. The way her grey eyes stabbed right through me sent a cold shiver through my body.

There was nothing in the student handbook about dreadlocks. Although, of course, I'd only skim-read the thing on the bus from Philly. The handbook was boring. And *long.* "I'm sorry, Ms. West. I didn't know—"

"Ignorance is no excuse. That's 3 demerit points for you. And you're to refer to me as Headmistress."

Beside her, the boy sniggered. I turned my gaze to look at him, and my heart nearly stopped. *Wow, he's beautiful.* I had no idea boys that hot existed outside of magazines and Hollywood movies. He stood practically the same height as Ms. West, his broad shoulders accentuated by the tailored cut of his red-trimmed blazer. Prefect and merit badges decorated both lapels. Dark brown curls caught the grey light filtering through the clouds, throwing back beautiful shades of russet and silver. His clean-shaven face and high, majestic cheekbones appeared angelic, but his ice-blue eyes were cold and cruel.

The girl moved closer to him, touching his arm and shooting me a possessive glare, like a cat in heat. She had the appearance of a cat, too – slanted green eyes accentuated with heavy makeup, pointed chin, and the lithe body and long legs of a panther. Beautiful but deadly.

"This is Trey Bloomberg and Courtney Haynes," Headmistress West said. "I've appointed them as your student guides. They will show you the dorm, library, and dining hall, go over your schedule and classrooms, and ensure you understand *all* our rules. You will dine with the student body in two hours' time, and tomorrow you begin classes. I've had a copy of your schedule and the school handbook placed in your room. Memorize them, for failure to comply will result in further demerits. Here's your dorm room key."

In my pocket, my phone gave another defiant chirp. *Great.* I'd practically worn down the battery looking for a signal on the death road.

Headmistress West descended the last step to drop an ancient-looking metal key into my hand. Her pointy black boots lined up with my scuffed Docs. She loomed over me, her disapproval seeping into my bones. "You have a phone in your pocket." It wasn't a question.

"Yes."

Behind her, the boy smirked. I felt naked, exposed. My legs itched to make a run for the woods. Headmistress West held out her hand, unfurling long fingers topped with red-painted nails, the tips pointed like talons. "Hand it over. We don't allow outside technology on campus."

Instinctively, my hand flew to my pocket. "I won't use it to call or text. It doesn't work here, anyway, so what's the—"

"Ms. Waite, failure to obey a teacher's command is an automatic loss of 10 points. You seem most anxious to find out what punishments await the students at the bottom of the class list."

A lump rose in my throat. My phone contained photographs – snaps of my mom smiling demurely or brushing her hair in the mirror before she went out to work at the strip club. Of Dante and I hanging out around the neighborhood, smoking on the rusted playground beside his house, tagging the concrete wall behind the boxing gym on the corner. Every other one of my possessions had been destroyed in the fire. Those photographs were practically all I had left of them.

Trey and Courtney covered their mouths with their hands, barely disguising their laughter. Courtney leaned over and whispered something to Trey. They both cracked up. Despite myself, my cheeks flushed. *Better get used to this.*

Headmistress West, of course, ignored them. She wasn't backing down on this phone thing. My fingers closed around it, the comfortable weight of it in my hand reminding me that it was one of the last connections to my old life.

What does it matter? They're gone. Looking at their photos won't bring them back. But this school could be the only chance I have at a real future.

My hand trembling, I dropped my phone into her talons. As soon as it left my hand, I itched to get it back. Headmistress West slipped the phone into a fold of her dress, where it disappeared from sight.

"Follow me." The headmistress swirled on her heel and floated up the stairs. Numb, I fell in step behind her. Trey came up beside me. His arm brushed mine, and a jolt of warmth rocketed through my body. I dared a look up at his face. As we moved into the shadow of the porch, the colors in his hair changed, becoming a deep brown and blood red. A curl flopped over his eye, and I noticed flecks of silver on the edges of those arresting blue irises. My fingers itched to reach up and swipe that curl off his face, to touch his smooth skin, feel his cheek move beneath my fingers, to cut myself on his cheekbones. A familiar longing pooled in my stomach, an ache that I'd never been able to sate before, and now never would.

I'd never seen a boy that *perfect*.

Trey's fingers brushed me again. My breath froze in my mouth as his hand lingered on my elbow. To anyone looking at us from a distance, it would appear as though he was helping me, steadying me up the steep steps. The touch on my skin was white-hot, lighting up parts of my body that hadn't felt anything since Dante... since before the fire. *How can this boy with such cruel eyes have this effect on me?*

When he caught me looking, Trey's perfect lips curled back into a sneer. His fingers tightened on my arm, squeezing my skin. Tighter, tighter, until he was cutting off circulation. I yelped in protest.

"You don't belong here," he murmured, his perfect lips forming hateful words. "You should leave now."

He said it so casually, like he was chatting about the weather, and that self-satisfied smirk never left his face. My stomach twisted, the air driving from my lungs as though he'd punched me.

"No thanks," I said brightly, pretending that I misunderstood him. "I'm good."

"We don't want you, and we're used to getting what we want. We're going to eat you alive, new meat." Trey flashed me a smile that was all teeth and violence. The venom in his eyes frightened me. *This is not a guy to mess with.*

Too bad he seemed to already have it out for me, and I hadn't even got inside the school yet. My plan to keep my head down and stay invisible fizzled before my eyes. Already I could see how the school year was going to play out. *We don't want you here.* Trey spoke for the entire student body. He was a King in this school. It was written in his smile, dripping from the menace in his words.

I'd pissed him off. Just by existing. Just by setting foot on the hallowed grounds of his kingdom. *Well, fuck you, Trey Bloomberg.* I could handle a year of insults and loneliness if I got my diploma at the end of it. My life was already hell on earth – if Trey Bloomberg thought he could break me, he'd have to try a lot harder.

I wrenched my arm away from us. "Don't touch me." Behind us, Courtney giggled.

"Yeah, Trey. You should know not to handle garbage. She's a gutter-trash whore who's probably fucked so many guys that your dick wouldn't even touch the sides."

The comment stung. I thought of my sweet mother, all candy smiles and sticky skin as she stripped off her sweat-soaked lace g-string and six-inch heels after her shift and pulled on the cloud-pink pajamas I found for her in a thrift store. A hard lump rose in my throat. I shoved the image aside. *Not now.*

Wait until you get to your room, until you're alone, then you can break down.

"I guess we're not going to be braiding each other's hair," I muttered to Courtney.

"I wouldn't touch that rat's nest on your head if someone hid a *Faberge* egg inside," Courtney sneered. "I bet it's got real eggs in it, though. Insect eggs, laid by the gross things crawling around in there."

Instinctively, my hand flew up to my face, to touch the dreadlock that always fell over my eye, to tuck it behind my ear – a gesture that Dante would so often do when he noticed my loss in my eyes, which was all the time because I liked them unruly. Ever since the fire, I'd been touching my own hair more and more, seeking the comfort of the familiar weight of a hand moving the dreadlocks. But it wasn't the same. It would never be the same.

Courtney wrinkled her face in disgust, while Trey continued to smirk at me. The force of his loathing sank my stomach to my knees. He didn't even know me, but it didn't matter.

At the top of the stairs, the headmistress turned and frowned at me. "Don't dawdle," she snapped. "The school doesn't bite."

"She's wrong," Trey whispered. "Are you ready to find out just how bad we bite?"

The lump of hard, bitterness burned at the back of my throat. They were right.

I didn't belong here. I was the poor gutter-trash girl from the wrong side of the tracks, and they were *royalty*. They were the monarchs. *They're going to make my life miserable, and there's nothing I can do.*

Read Shunned now
http://books2read.com/shunned

About the Author

Steffanie Holmes is the *USA Today* bestselling author of the paranormal, gothic, dark, and fantastical. Her books feature clever, witty heroines, secret societies, creepy old mansions and alpha males who *always* get what they want.

Legally-blind since birth, Steffanie received the 2017 Attitude Award for Artistic Achievement. She was also a finalist for a 2018 Women of Influence award.

Steff is the creator of *Rage Against the Manuscript* – a resource of free content, books, and courses to help writers tell their story, find their readers, and build a badass writing career.

Steffanie lives in New Zealand with her husband, a horde of cantankerous cats, and their medieval sword collection.

Steffanie Holmes newsletter

Grab a free copy *Cabinet of Curiosities* – a Steffanie Holmes compendium of short stories and bonus scenes – when you sign up for updates with the Steffanie Holmes newsletter.

http://www.steffanieholmes.com/newsletter

Come hang with Steffanie
www.steffanieholmes.com
hello@steffanieholmes.com

www.ingramcontent.com/pod-product-compliance
Lightning Source LLC
Chambersburg PA
CBHW020344220726
48290CB00014B/1008